THE BEST
SAILING
STORIES
EVER TOLD

THE BEST
SAILING
STORIES
EVER TOLD

Edited by
Stephen Brennan

Skyhorse Publishing

Skyhorse Publishing books may be purchased in bulk at special discounts for sales promotion, corporate gifts, fund-raising, or educational purposes. Special editions can also be created to specifications. For details, contact the Special Sales Department, Skyhorse Publishing, 307 West 36th Street, 11th Floor, New York, NY 10018 or info@skyhorse-publishing.com.

Skyhorse® and Skyhorse Publishing® are registered trademarks of Skyhorse Publishing, Inc.®, a Delaware corporation.

www.skyhorsepublishing.com

10 9 8 7 6 5 4 3 2 1

Library of Congress Cataloging-in-Publication Data

The best sailing stories ever told / edited by Stephen Brennan.
     p. cm.
  ISBN 978-1-61608-219-2 (alk. paper)
  1. Sailing. I. Brennan, Steve, 1952-
  GV811.B425 2011
  797.124--dc22

                    2010054571

Printed in the United States of America

CONTENTS

A CHRONICLE OF THE VOYAGES OF SAINT BRENDAN

STEPHEN BRENNAN

Remember Brendan, not as a graven saint, he was a man and suffered so; in no ways proud, he sought the will of the Lord God full meekly and contrite of heart. And I have seen his eyes start from his head at some marvel, and I have seen the cold gray oceans break over him for days, and I have seen him spit salt seas and tremble with the cold. But no thing overmanned him, because in every tempest he saw the hand of God, and in every trial he sought the will of God, and trusted so, and was not afraid, and thereby gave us heart and courage. And we brethren took example from him, and thereby saved our souls.

Remember Brendan, later called *Saint*, born in the land of Munster, hard by the loch Lein. A holy man of fierce abstinence, known for his great works and the father of almost three thousand monks, he lived at Clonfert then, where we knew him at the first and last.

Recall the night, just past compline it was, when the holy abbot Barrind, later called *Saint*, came out of the darkness into our circle to visit Brendan. And each of them was joyful of the other. And when Brendan began to tell Barrind of the many wonders he had seen voyaging in the sea and visiting in diverse lands, Barrind at once began to sigh and anon he threw himslf prostrate upon the ground and prayed hard and then began to weep. Now Brendan comforted him the best he could, and lifting him up said: *"Brother Abbot, have you not come to be joyful with us, to speak the word of God and to give us heart? Therefore for God's love, do not be afraid, but tell us what marvels you have seen in the great ocean, that encompasses all the world."*

So Barrind began to tell Brendan and all the gathered monks of a great wonder. These were his words:

"I have a son, his name is Meroc, who had a great desire to seek about by ship in diverse countries to find a solitary place wherein he might dwell secretly out of the business of the world, in order to better serve God quietly in devotion. I counseled him to sail to an island in the sea, nearby the mountain of stones, which everybody knows. So he made ready and sailed there with his monks. And when he came there, he liked the place full well, and there settled where he and his monks served our Lord devoutly. And then I saw in a vision that this monk Meroc was sailed right far westward into the sea more than three days sailing, and suddenly to those voyagers there came a dark cloud of fog that overcovered them, so that for a great part of the day they saw no light; then as our Lord willed, the fog passed away, and they saw a fair island, and thereward they drew. In that island was joy and mirth enough and all the earth of that island shone as brightly as the sun, and there were the fairest trees and herbs that ever any man saw, and here were many precious stones shining bright, and every herb was ripe, and every tree full of fruit; so that it was a glorious sight and a heavenly joy to abide there. Then there came to them a fair young man, and courteously he welcomed them all, and called every monk by his name, and said they were much bound to praise the name of our Lord Jesu, who would out of his grace show them that glorious place, where it is always day and never night, and that this place is called the garden of paradise. But by this island is another island whereon no man may come. And the fair young man said to them, 'You have been here half a year without meat or drink or sleep.' They supposed they had been there only half a day, so merry and joyful they were. The young man told them that this was the place where Adam and Eve lived first, and ever would have lived, if they had not broken the commandment of God. Then the fair young man brought them to their ship again and said they might no longer abide there, and when they were all shipped,

suddenly the young man vanished away out of their sight. And then within a short time after, by the purveyance of the Lord Jesu, Meroc and the brothers returned to their own island where I and the other brothers received them goodly, and demanded where they had been so long. And they said that they had been in the Land of the Blest, before the Gates of Paradise. And they asked of us, 'Cannot you you tell from the sweetness of our clothes that we have been in Paradise?' And I and the other brothers said, 'We do believe you have been in God's Paradise, but we don't know where this Paradise is.'"

At hearing this we all lay prostrate and said, *"The Lord God is just in all his works and merciful and loving to his servants, once again he has nourished our wonder with his holy spirit."*

On the day following Barrind's visit, Brendan gathered twelve of the brothers and closed us up in the oratory saying, *"If it is God's will, I will seek that holy land of which the brother Abbott spoke. Does this appeal to you? What do you say?"*

We answered Brendan thus, *"Not our will, but God's. To know God's will, we leave our families, give away what we possess, put away the lives we led and follow you, if it is the will of God."*

To better know the will of God we fasted forty days, tho not oftener than for three days running as is the rule. And during this time we sought the blessing of the holy father Edna, later called *Saint*, in his western island. We stayed there three days and three nights only.

Old Edna's blessing got, we took ourselves to a lonely inlet place we called Brendan's Butt, for he had known this spot as a boy and there sat many hours, looking away out over the ocean to the west, his seat upon a butt of stone. Here we built a vessel sufficient for a voyage of seven years. With iron tools we ribbed and framed it of ash and oak, the stepping for the mast was oak, and covered it in ox hides, well tanned, stitched together and greased with lard. Therein we put provisions for a forty days journey and many spares of ox hide, and then we got ourselves aboard and here lived devoutly twelve days, afloat but well in sight of land.

On the day set for our departure we received the sacrament and got ourselves aboard, when just as Brendan blessed us all, there came another two of his monks who prayed him that they might come with us. And he said, *"You may sail with us, but one of you shall die and go to hell ere we return."* Even so, they would go with us.

And then Brendan bade the brethren raise the sail, and forth we voyaged in God's name, so that on the morrow we were out of sight of any land. For eleven days and nights we sailed plain, and then we saw an island afar from us. We sailed thitherward as fast as we could, and soon a great reach of stone appeared afar off above the waves, and for three days we worked our way around the island before we found an inlet fit for a landing. At last we found a little haven and there we beached our leather boat.

Suddenly, bounding up to us, there came a fair hound who laid down at Brendan's feet cheering him. So Brendan said to us, *"Be of good heart, for the Lord has sent his messenger to lead us into some good place."* And the hound brought us to a fair hall, where we found tables spread with good meat and drink. Then Brendan spoke the grace and then we brethren sat down and ate and drank. And there were beds made ready for us that we might sleep after our long labor. But Brendan did not sleep, but prayed the night away upon his knees.

On the morrow we returned again to our skin boat, pushed off and sailed a long time in the sea before we found any land. At last, by the purveyance of God, we saw a full fair island of green pasture, whereon were the whitest sheep that we had ever seen. And every sheep was as big as any ox. Just after dragging our ship ashore, we were welcomed by a goodly old man who said, *"This is the Isle of Sheep. Here it is never cold but ever summer. This is why the sheep are so huge, they feed all year on the best grasses and herbs anywhere."* When the old man took his leave he told us, *"Voyage on, and by God's grace, you soon will come upon a place like paradise, whereon you ought to spend your Eastertide."*

We sailed forth and soon came upon another island, but because of shallows and broken stone and the fury of the seas, we bore off and beached our skin ship instead upon a rock, where nothing grew, a small desolate island. Or so we thought, for when we lit the fire so that we might bake our grain and dress our meat, the island began to move under us. And all a panic then, amazed and full of fear, we threw ourselves into the boat, and pulled and twisted at the oars, swatting and thumping one another in our haste to be away. And lo, the island seemed to dip and we floated free and soon were well away. And all that night we spied the beacon of our fire leaping and dancing in the cold, dark ocean. Brendan must have smelled the terror on us, for he said, *"Do not be afraid. It is only a great fish, the biggest in the sea. He labors night and day to swallow his own tail, but he cannot because of his great size. He is called Jasconius."*

And then anon we oared three days and nights before we sighted any land and the weariness was heavy on us. But soon after, as God would, we saw a fair island, full of flowers, herbs, and trees, whereof we thanked God of his good grace, and then anon we found a little stream and followed it, walking our hide boat well in land. And then anon we found a full fair well, and thereby grew a mighty tree, full of boughs, and on every bough sat a white bird, and they so thick upon the tree, their number being so great, and their song being so merry that it was a heavenly noise to hear. Then Brendan fell to his knees and wept for joy, and made his prayers devoutly unto our Lord God that he might understand the meaning of the bird song. And then at once a white bird flew from the tree to Brendan. She flapped and fluttered, she hooked and danced and called, and made a merry noise full like a flute. It seemed to us no holy hymn ever was so joyful. And Brendan said, *"If you are the messengers of God, tell me why you sit so thick upon the tree and why you sing so merrily?"*

And the bird said, *"Once upon a time, we were angels in heaven, but when our master Lucifer fell down into hell for his high pride, we fell with him for our offenses, some higher, some lower, depending on the quality of their trespass; and because our trespass was but little, our Lord has sent us here, out of all pain to live in great joy and mirth, here to serve him on this tree in the best manner that we can. Today is Sunday, can you not guess why we are all white as snow?"*

And when we all remembered, we fell upon our knees and hymned praise to our good Lord Jesu Christ. And the white bird sang to Brendan, *"It is twelve month past that you departed from your abbey. In the seventh year you shall come unto the place of your desire. For each of those years you shall spend the Eastertide here with us, as you do today."*

Then all the birds began to sing evensong so merrily that it was truly a heavenly noise to hear. And after supper Brendan and all of us went to bed, and slept well, and on the morrow we rose early, to hear the birds sing matins, and later prime and all such services of the holy rule.

We all abided there with Brendan eight full weeks, til after Trinity Sunday when we again sailed for the Isle of Sheep, and there we victualed well and were blessed again by the goodly old man, and returned again to our leather boat, and waited for the wind to blow fair. And ere we put out, the bird of the tree came again to us, and danced upon our prow and flapped and fluttered and sang, *"I am come to tell you that you shall sail from here to an island whereon there is an abbey of twenty-four monks, and there you shall hold your Christmas, but Eastertide, do not forget, you spend with us."*

And then the bird flew off.

The wind with us now, we sailed forth into the ocean, but soon fell a great tempest on us, which we were greatly troubled by for a long time and sorely belabored. And we saw, by the purveyance of God, a little island afar off, and full meekly we prayed to our Lord to send us thither in safety. It took eleven days, and in this time we monks were so weary of the long pull and the mountain gray oceans that we set little price upon our lives, and cried continually to our Lord to show us mercy and bring us to that little island in safety. And by the purveyance of God we came at last into a little haven, but so narrow that only one ship might come in. And after we had come to anchor, the brethren went ashore, and when we had long walked about, at last we found two fair wells; one was of fair clear water, and the other was somewhat troubly and thick. At this we thanked our Lord full humbly that had brought us here, and made to drink the water, but Brendan charged us thus, "Take no water without license. If we abstain us a while longer, our Lord will purvey for us in the best wise."

And soon after came to us a good old hoar-haired man, who welcomed us full meekly and kissed Brendan, but did not speak, and by this we understood that he observed a rule of silence. And he led us past many a fair well til we came to an abbey, where we were received with much honor and solemn procession. And then the abbott welcomed Brendan and all our fellowship, and kissed him full meekly, but did not speak. And he drew Brendan by the hand, and led us into a fair hall, and sat us down in a row on benches; and the abbott of that place, in observance of the new commandment, washed all our feet with fair clear water. And afterward, in silence still, led us into the refractory, there to seat ourselves amoung the brothers of the abbey. And anon came one who served us well of meat and drink. For every monk had set before him a fair white loaf and white roots and herbs, which we found right delicious, tho none of us could name; and we drank of the water of the fair clear well that we had seen before when first we came ashore, that Brendan had forbade us. And then the abbott came, and breaking silence, prayed us eat and drink, *"For every day the Lord sends a good old man that covers this table with meat and drink for us. But we know not how it comes, for we do nothing to procure it, and yet our Lord feeds us. And we are twenty-four monks in number, yet every day of the week he sends us twelve loaves, and every Sunday and feast day, twenty-four loaves, and the bread we leave at dinner we eat at supper. And now at your coming our Lord has sent us forty-eight loaves, that all of us may be merry together as brethren. And we have lived twenty-nine years here in this abbey: tho we did first come out of the abbey of Saint Patrick in Ireland eighty years ago. And here in this land it is ever fair weather, and none of us is ever sick since we came here."*

And then Brendan and the abbott and all the company went into the church, and we said evensong together, and devoutly. And when we looked upward at the crucifix, we saw our Lord hanging on a cross made of fine crystal and curiously wrought; and in the choir were twenty-four seats for twenty-four monks, and seven unlit tapers, and the abbott's seat was made close upon the altar in the middle of the choir. And then Brendan asked the abbott, *"How long have you kept silence one with another?"*

And the abbott answered Brendan, *"For this twenty-nine years, no one has spoken to another."*

And Brendan wept for joy at this, and desired of the abbott, *"That we might all dwell here with you."*

And the abbott answered Brendan, *"That will not do, for our Lord has showed to you in what manner you will be guided til the seventh year is done, and after that term you will return with your monks to Ireland in safety; except that one of the two monks that came last to you will dwell in the island of anchorites, and the other will burn in hell."*

And as we knelt with Brendan in the church, we saw a bright shining angel fly in at the window that lighted all the tapers in the church and flew out again and then to heaven. And Brendan marveled greatly how fair the light burned but wasted not. And the abbott said to us that it is written how Moses saw a bush afire, yet it burned not, *"and therefore marvel not, for the might of our Lord is now as great as ever it was."*

And when we had dwelled there even til Christmas was gone twelve days and eight days more, we took leave of this holy abbott and his convent, and returned again to our skinned-ship. And then we sailed from thence toward the island of the abbey of Saint Hillary, but aching cold and furious tempests troubled us til just before the start of Lent, when we bespied an island, not far off; and then we pulled for it but weakly, our strength all spent, our stomachs empty, our bodies raw with thirst. And when at last we gained the island, and dragged our battered boat upon the beach, we found a well of clear water, and diverse roots that grew about it, and multitudes of sweet fleshed fish that swarmed in the river that flowed to the sea. And Brendan said, *"Let us gather up this bounty which the Lord makes a gift to us, and then let us renew our bodies with meat and drink, and our spirits in hymns devoutly sung."*

And we obeyed Brendan, and we dug many roots and put them in the fire to bake, likewise we netted many fish and cleaned and baked them also. But when we made to drink, our holy father Brendan said, *"Of this clear water drink only what is meet for your good health, lest this gift of God do you some harm."*

And after grace was said, we fell to meat and drink, and then when we had eaten and drunk, we began to sing the holy office and promptly, one by one, each man fell to sleep. Tho Brendan did not sleep, but prayed three days and nights upon his knees, and full devoutly for our awakening. And so at length we did awaken, and those of us who had drank three cups of that clear water slept three days and nights, and those who drank two cups slept two, and one cup only one day and night. And Brendan gathered us about the fire and said, *"Brothers, we see here how a gift of God may do us harm. As Lent is nigh, let us now get ourselves to sea; take only meat and drink for one meal every three days, as is the rule, enough to last this holy season out."*

And then again we pulled our hide boat upon God's ocean, and for three full days the wind blew foul, and then a sudden all grew still. The wind blew not and the sea calmned and flattened and seemed to set into a thing solid. And Brendan said, *"Brothers, lay off your oars, let us drift; and in this show true submission to the will of God."*

And then we drifted twenty days. And this was a time of meditation and prayer, and of perfect observance of the rule, and of good fellowship amoung the brethren. Then at last by the purveyance of the Lord, the wind arose and blew fresh til Palm Sunday.

And then at last we came again unto the Isle of Sheep, and were received again by the goodly old man, who brought us again into the fair hall, and served us. And after soup on Holy Thursday, he washed our feet, and gave us each the kiss of peace, alike our Lord had done with his disciples. And on the Friday of the passion of our Lord we sacrificed the lamb of innocence, and on the Saturday we did all holy rite and prayed together full devoutly, that we might find ourselves prepared for the miracle of of the resurrection of our Lord Jesu. And at eventide we toiled our skin vessel into the sea, and as Brendan bid us, pulled our ashen oars against the seas that blow shorewards at eventide. And Brendan made his seat upon the oaken tiller and captained us unto a place in the sea that he did chose. And on that Easter vigil, just at the hour of lauds, when all the world is blue with first light, he bid us lay upon our oars, and Brendan asked unto us, *"Do you not know where it is you are?"*

And we did not know, but Brendan did know; and lo, we seemed to rise up heavenward, and the seas fell away from our frail craft, and we beheld ourselves again upon Jasconius' back. And we beheld the smear of char where twelve months past we laid a fire to bake our meat, and we were amazed, and Brendan seeing this said, *"Do not be afraid."*

And one by one we stepped out upon this living isle. And Brendan said, *"How splendid is the will of our good Lord, that even savage monsters do his bidding and make this place upon a fish's back to keep the holy service of the resurrection."*

And after Mass was said, and Brendan sacrificed the spotless lamb of innocence, we got ourselves again aboard our skin vessel, and lo Jasconius dove beneath the sea, and we sailed free. And on that same morning we gained the island where the tree of the birds was, and that same bird welcomed Brendan and sang full merrily. And there we dwelled from Easter til Trinity Sunday, as we had done the year before, in full great joy and mirth; and daily we heard the merry service of the birds sitting in the tree. And then the one bird told Brendan that he should return again at Christmas to the abbey of the monks, *"and Easterday, do not forget, you spend with us. But every other day of your journey, you labor in the full great peril of the ocean, from year to year til the seventh year has been accomplished when you shall find the Land of the Blest, before the gates of Paradise, and dwell there forty days in full great joy and mirth; and after you shall return home in safety to your own abbey and there end your life and be admitted to blessed heaven, which our Lord bought for you with his most precious blood."*

And then an angel of our Lord ordained all things needful to our voyage, in vitals and all other things necessary. And then we thanked our Lord for the great goodness that he had often shown us in our great need. And then we sailed forth in the great sea ocean, abiding in the mercy of our Lord through great troubles and tempests.

THE LADY OF THE BARGE

W. W. JACOBS

The master of the barge *Arabella* sat in the stern of his craft with his right arm leaning on the tiller. A desultory conversation with the mate of a schooner, who was hanging over the side of his craft a few yards off, had come to a conclusion owing to a difference of opinion on the subject of religion. The skipper had argued so warmly that he almost fancied he must have inherited the tenets of the Seventh-day Baptists from his mother while the mate had surprised himself by the warmth of his advocacy of a form of Wesleyanism which would have made the members of that sect open their eyes with horror. He had, moreover, confirmed the skipper in the error of his ways by calling him a bargee, the ranks of the Baptists receiving a defender if not a recruit from that hour.

With the influence of the religious argument still upon him, the skipper, as the long summer's day gave place to night, fell to wondering where his own mate, who was also his brother-in-law, had got to. Lights which had been struggling with the twilight now burnt bright and strong, and the skipper, moving from the shadow to where a band of light fell across the deck, took out a worn silver watch and saw that it was ten o'clock.

Almost at the same moment a dark figure appeared on the jetty above and began to descend the ladder, and a strongly built young man of twenty-two sprang nimbly to the deck.

"Ten o'clock, Ted," said the skipper, slowly.

"It'll be eleven in an hour's time," said the mate, calmly.

"That'll do," said the skipper, in a somewhat loud voice, as he noticed that his late adversary still occupied his favourite strained position, and a fortuitous expression of his mother's occurred to him: "Don't talk to me; I've been arguing with a son of Belial for the last half-hour."

"Bargee," said the son of Belial, in a dispassionate voice.

"Don't take no notice of him, Ted," said the skipper, pityingly.

"He wasn't talking to me," said Ted. "But never mind about him; I want to speak to you in private."

"Fire away, my lad," said the other, in a patronising voice.

"Speak up," said the voice from the schooner, encouragingly. "I'm listening."

There was no reply from the bargee. The master led the way to the cabin, and lighting a lamp, which appealed to more senses than one, took a seat on a locker, and again requested the other to fire away.

"Well, you see, it's this way," began the mate, with a preliminary wriggle: "there's a certain young woman——"

"A certain young what?" shouted the master of the *Arabella*.

"Woman," repeated the mate, snappishly; "you've heard of a woman afore, haven't you? Well, there's a certain young woman I'm walking out with I——"

"Walking out?" gasped the skipper. "Why, I never 'eard o' such a thing."

"You would ha' done if you'd been better looking, p'raps," retorted the other. "Well, I've offered this young woman to come for a trip with us."

"Oh, you have, 'ave you!" said the skipper, sharply. "And what do you think Louisa will say to it?"

"That's your look out," said Louisa's brother, cheerfully. "I'll make her up a bed for'ard, and we'll all be as happy as you please."

He started suddenly. The mate of the schooner was indulging in a series of whistles of the most amatory description.

"There she is," he said. "I told her to wait outside."

He ran upon deck, and his perturbed brother-in-law, following at his leisure, was just in time to see him descending the ladder with a young woman and a small handbag.

"This is my brother-in-law, Cap'n Gibbs," said Ted, introducing the new arrival; "smartest man at a barge on the river."

The girl extended a neatly gloved hand, shook the skipper's affably, and looked wonderingly about her.

"It's, very close to the water, Ted," she said, dubiously.

The skipper coughed. "We don't take passengers as a rule," he said, awkwardly; "we 'ain't got much convenience for them."

"Never mind," said the girl, kindly; "I sha'nt expect too much."

She turned away, and following the mate down to the cabin, went into ecstasies over the space-saving contrivances she found there. The drawers fitted in the skipper's bunk were a source of particular interest, and the owner watched with strong disapprobation through the skylight her efforts to make him an apple-pie bed with the limited means at her disposal. He went down below at once as a wet blanket.

"I was just shaking your bed up a bit," said Miss Harris, reddening.

"I see you was," said the skipper, briefly.

He tried to pluck up courage to tell her that he couldn't take her, but only succeeded in giving vent to an inhospitable cough.

"I'll get the supper," said the mate, suddenly; "you sit down, old man, and talk to Lucy."

In honour of the visitor he spread a small cloth, and then proceeded to produce cold beef, pickles, and accessories in a manner which reminded Miss Harris of white rabbits from a conjurer's hat. Captain Gibbs, accepting the inevitable, ate his supper in silence and left them to their glances.

"We must make you up a bed, for'ard, Lucy," said the mate, when they had finished.

Miss Harris started. "Where's that?" she inquired.

"Other end o' the boat," replied the mate, gathering up some bedding under his arm. "You might bring a lantern, John."

The skipper, who was feeling more sociable after a couple of glasses of beer, complied, and accompanied the couple to the tiny forecastle. A smell compounded of bilge, tar, paint, and other healthy disinfectants emerged as the scuttle was pushed back. The skipper dangled the lantern down and almost smiled.

"I can't sleep there," said the girl, with decision. "I shall die o' fright."

"You'll get used to it," said Ted, encouragingly, as he helped her down; "it's quite dry and comfortable."

He put his arm round her waist and squeezed her hand, and aided by this moral support, Miss Harris not only consented to remain, but found various advantages in the forecastle over the cabin, which had escaped the notice of previous voyagers.

"I'll leave you the lantern," said the mate, making it fast, "and we shall be on deck most o' the night. We get under way at two."

He quitted the forecastle, followed by the skipper, after a polite but futile attempt to give him precedence, and made his way to the cabin for two or three hours' sleep.

"There'll be a row at the other end, Ted," said the skipper, nervously, as he got into his bunk. "Louisa's sure to blame me for letting you keep company with a gal like this. We was talking about you only the other day, and she said if you was married five years from now, it 'ud be quite soon enough."

"Let Loo mind her own business," said the mate, sharply; "she's not going to nag me. She's not *my* wife, thank goodness!"

He turned over and fell fast asleep, waking up fresh and bright three hours later, to commence what he fondly thought would be the pleasantest voyage of his life.

The *Arabella* dropped slowly down with the tide, the wind being so light that she was becalmed by every tall warehouse on the way. Off Greenwich, however, the breeze freshened somewhat, and a little later Miss Harris, looking somewhat pale as to complexion and untidy as to hair, came slowly on deck.

"Where's the looking-glass?" she asked, as Ted hastened to greet her. "How does my hair look?"

"All wavy," said the infatuated young man; "all little curls and squiggles. Come down in the cabin; there's a glass there."

Miss Harris, with a light nod to the skipper as he sat at the tiller, followed the mate below, and giving vent to a little cry of indignation as she saw herself in the glass, waved the amorous Ted on deck, and started work on her disarranged hair.

At breakfast-time a little friction was caused by what the mate bitterly termed the narrow-minded, old-fashioned ways of the skipper. He had arranged that the skipper should steer while he and Miss Harris breakfasted, but the coffee was no sooner on the table than the skipper called him, and relinquishing the helm in his favour, went below to do the honours. The mate protested.

"It's not proper," said the skipper. "Me and 'er will 'ave our meals together, and then you must have yours. She's under my care."

Miss Harris assented blithely, and talk and laughter greeted the ears of the indignant mate as he steered. He went down at last to cold coffee and lukewarm herrings, returning to the deck after a hurried meal to find the skipper narrating some of his choicest experiences to an audience which hung on his lightest word.

The disregard they showed for his feelings was maddening, and for the first time in his life he became a prey to jealousy in its worst form. It was quite clear to him that the girl had become desperately enamoured of the skipper, and he racked his brain in a wild effort to discover the reason.

With an idea of reminding his brother-in-law of his position, he alluded two or three times in a casual fashion to his wife. The skipper hardly listened to him, and patting Miss Harris's cheek in a fatherly manner, regaled her with an anecdote of the mate's boyhood which the latter had spent a goodly portion of his life in denying. He denied it again, hotly, and Miss Harris, conquering for a time her laughter, reprimanded him severely for contradicting.

By the time dinner was ready he was in a state of sullen apathy, and when the meal was over and the couple came on deck again, so far forgot himself as to compliment Miss Harris upon her appetite.

"I'm ashamed of you, Ted," said the skipper, with severity.

"I'm glad you know what shame is," retorted the mate.

"If you can't be'ave yourself, you'd better keep a bit for'ard till you get in a better temper," continued the skipper.

"I'll be pleased to," said the smarting mate. "I wish the barge was longer."

"It couldn't be too long for me," said Miss Harris, tossing her head.

"Be'aving like a schoolboy," murmured the skipper.

"I know how to behave *my*self," said the mate, as he disappeared below. His head suddenly appeared again over the companion. "If some people don't," he added, and disappeared again.

He was pleased to notice as he ate his dinner that the giddy prattle above had ceased, and with his back turned towards the couple when he appeared on deck again, he lounged slowly forward until the skipper called him back again.

"Wot was them words you said just now, Ted?" he inquired.

The mate repeated them with gusto.

"Very good," said the skipper, sharply; "very good."

"Don't you ever speak to me again," said Miss Harris, with a stately air, "because I won't answer you if you do."

The mate displayed more of his schoolboy nature. "Wait till you're spoken to," he said, rudely. "This is your gratefulness, I suppose?"

"Gratefulness?" said Miss Harris, with her chin in the air. "What for?"

"For bringing you for a trip," replied the mate, sternly.

"*You* bringing me for a trip!" said Miss Harris, scornfully.

"Captain Gibbs is the master here, I suppose. He is giving me the trip. You're only the mate."

"Just so," said the mate, with a grin at his brother-in-law, which made that worthy shift uneasily. "I wonder what Loo will say when she sees you with a lady aboard?"

"She came to please you," said Captain Gibbs, with haste.

"Ho! she did, did she?" jeered the mate. "Prove it; only don't look to me to back you, that's all."

The other eyed him in consternation, and his manner changed.

"Don't play the fool, Ted," he said, not unkindly; "you know what Loo is."

"Well, I'm reckoning on that," said the mate, deliberately. "I'm going for'ard; don't let me interrupt you two. So long."

He went slowly forward, and lighting his pipe, sprawled carelessly on the deck, and renounced the entire sex forthwith. At tea-time the skipper attempted to reverse the procedure at the other meals; but as Miss Harris steadfastly declined to sit at the same table as the mate, his good intentions came to naught.

He made an appeal to what he termed the mate's better nature, after Miss Harris had retired to the seclusion of her bed-chamber, but in vain.

"She's nothing to do with me," declared the mate, majestically. I wash my hands of her. She's a flirt. I'm like Louisa, I can't bear flirts."

The skipper said no more, but his face was so worn that Miss Harris, when she came on deck in the early morning and found the barge gliding gently between the grassy banks of a river, attributed it to the difficulty of navigating so large a craft on so small and winding a stream.

"We shall be alongside in 'arf an hour," said the skipper, eyeing her.

Miss Harris expressed her gratification.

"P'raps you wouldn't mind going down the fo'c'sle and staying there till we've made fast," said the other. I'd take it as a favour. My owners don't like me to carry passengers."

Miss Harris, who understood perfectly, said, "Certainly," and with a cold stare at the mate, who was at no pains to conceal his amusement, went below at once, thoughtfully closing the scuttle after her.

"There's no call to make mischief, Ted," said the skipper, somewhat anxiously, as they swept round the last bend and came into view of Coalsham.

The mate said nothing, but stood by to take in sail as they ran swiftly towards the little quay. The pace slackened, and the *Arabella*, as though conscious of the contraband in her forecastle, crept slowly to where a stout, middle-aged woman, who bore a strong likeness to the mate, stood upon the quay.

"There's poor Loo," said the mate, with a sigh.

The skipper made no reply to this infernal insinuation. The barge ran alongside the quay and made fast.

"I thought you'd be up," said Mrs. Gibbs to her husband. "Now come along to breakfast; Ted'll follow on."

Captain Gibbs dived down below for his coat, and slipping ashore, thankfully prepared to move off with his wife.

"Come on as soon as you can, Ted," said the latter. "Why, what on earth is he making that face for?"

She turned in amazement as her brother, making a pretence of catching her husband's eye, screwed his face up into a note of interrogation and gave a slight jerk with his thumb.

"Come along," said Captain Gibbs, taking her arm with much affection.

"But what's Ted looking like that for?" demanded his wife, as she easily intercepted another choice fatal expression of the mate's.

"Oh, it's his fun," replied her husband, walking on.

"*Fun*?" repeated Mrs. Gibbs, sharply. "What's the matter, Ted?"

"Nothing," replied the mate.

"Touch o' toothache," said the skipper. "Come along, Loo; I can just do with one o' your breakfasts."

Mrs. Gibbs suffered herself to be led on, and had got at least five yards on the way home, when she turned and looked back. The mate had still got the toothache, and was at that moment in all the agonies of a phenomenal twinge.

"There's something wrong here," said Mrs. Gibbs as she retraced her steps. "Ted, what are you making that face for?"

"It's my own face," said the mate, evasively.

Mrs. Gibbs conceded the point, and added bitterly that it couldn't be helped. All the same she wanted to know what he meant by it.

"Ask John," said the vindictive mate.

Mrs. Gibbs asked. Her husband said he didn't know, and added that Ted had been like it before, but he had not told her for fear of frightening her. Then he tried to induce her to go with him to the chemist's to get something for it.

Mrs. Gibbs shook her head firmly, and boarding the barge, took a seat on the hatch and proceeded to catechise her brother as to his symptoms.

He denied that there was anything the matter with him, while his eyes openly sought those of Captain Gibbs as though asking for instruction.

"You come home, Ted," she said at length.

"I can't," said the mate. "I can't leave the ship."

"Why not?" demanded his sister.

"Ask John," said the mate again.

At this Mrs. Gibb's temper, which had been rising, gave way altogether, and she stamped fiercely upon the deck. A stamp of the foot has been for all time a rough-and-ready means of signalling; the fore-scuttle was drawn back, and the face of a pretty girl appeared framed in the opening. The mate raised his eyebrows with a helpless gesture, and as for the unfortunate skipper, any jury would have found him guilty without leaving the box. The wife of his bosom, with a flaming visage, turned and regarded him.

"You villain!" she said, in a choking voice.

Captain Gibbs caught his breath and looked appealingly at the mate.

"It's a little surprise for you, my dear," he faltered; "it's Ted's young lady."

"Nothing of the kind," said the mate, sharply.

"It's not? How dare you say such a thing?" demanded Miss Harris, stepping on to the deck.

"Well, you brought her aboard, Ted, you know you did," pleaded the unhappy skipper.

The mate did not deny it, but his face was so full of grief and surprise that the other's heart sank within him.

"All right," said the mate at last; "have it your own way."

"Hold your tongue, Ted," shouted Mrs. Gibbs; "you're trying to shield him."

"I tell you Ted brought her aboard, and they had a lover's quarrel," said her unhappy spouse. "It's nothing to do with me at all."

"And that's why you told me Ted had got the toothache, and tried to get me off to the chemist's, I s'pose," retorted his wife, with virulence. "Do you think I'm a fool? How dare you ask a young woman on this barge? How dare you?"

"I didn't ask her," said her husband.

"I s'pose she came without being asked," sneered his wife, turning her regards to the passenger; "she looks the sort that might. You brazen-faced girl!"

"Here, go easy, Loo," interrupted the mate, flushing as he saw the girl's pale face.

"Mind your own business," said his sister, violently.

"It is my business," said the repentant mate. "I brought her aboard, and then we quarrelled."

"I've no doubt," said his sister, bitterly; "it's very pretty, but it won't do."

"I swear it's the truth," said the mate.

"Why did John keep it so quiet and hide her for, then?" demanded his sister.

"I came down for the trip," said Miss Harris; "that is all about it. There is nothing to make a fuss about. How much is it, Captain Gibbs?"

She produced a little purse from her pocket, but before the embarrassed skipper could reply, his infuriated wife struck it out of her hand. The mate sprang instinctively forward, but too late, and the purse fell with a splash into the water. The girl gave a faint cry and clasped her hands.

"How am I to get back?" she gasped.

"I'll see to that, Lucy," said the mate. "I'm very sorry—I've been a brute."

"*You?*" said the indignant girl. "I would sooner drown myself than be beholden to you."

"I'm very sorry," repeated the mate, humbly.

"There's enough of this play-acting," interposed Mrs. Gibbs. "Get off this barge."

"You stay where you are," said the mate, authoritatively.

"Send that girl off this barge," screamed Mrs. Gibbs to her husband.

Captain Gibbs smiled in a silly fashion and scratched his head. "Where is she to go?" he asked feebly.

"What does it matter to you where she goes?" cried his wife, fiercely. "Send her off."

The girl eyed her haughtily, and repulsing the mate as he strove to detain her, stepped to the side. Then she paused as he suddenly threw off his coat, and sitting down on the hatch, hastily removed his boots. The skipper, divining his intentions, seized him by the arm.

"Don't be a fool, Ted," he gasped; "you'll get under the barge."

The mate shook him off, and went in with a splash which half-drowned his adviser. Miss Harris, clasping her hands, ran to the side and gazed fearfully at the spot where he had disappeared, while his sister in a terrible voice seized the opportunity to point out to her husband the probably fatal results of his ill-doing. There was an anxious interval, and then the mate's head appeared above the water and after a breathing space disappeared again. The skipper, watching uneasily, stood by with a lifebelt.

"Come out, Ted," screamed his sister as he came up for breath again.

The mate disappeared once more, but coming up for the third time, hung on to the side of the barge to recover a bit. A clothed man in the water savours of disaster and looks alarming. Miss Harris began to cry.

"You'll be drowned," she whimpered.

"Come out," said Mrs. Gibbs, in a raspy voice. She knelt on the deck and twined her fingers in his hair. The mate addressed her in terms rendered brotherly by pain.

"Never mind about the purse," sobbed Miss Harris; "it doesn't matter."

"Will you make it up if I come out, then," demanded the diver.

"No; I'll never speak to you again as long as I live," said the girl, passionately.

The mate disappeared again. This time he was out of sight longer than usual, and when he came up merely tossed his arms weakly and went down again. There was a scream from the women, and a mighty splash as the skipper went overboard with a lifebelt. The mate's head, black and shining, showed for a moment; the skipper grabbed him by the hair and towed him to the barge's side, and in the midst of a considerable hubbub both men were drawn from the water.

The skipper shook himself like a dog, but the mate lay on the deck inert in a puddle of water. Mrs. Gibbs frantically slapped his hands; and Miss Harris, bending over him, rendered first aid by kissing him wildly.

Captain Gibbs pushed her away. "He won't come round while you're a-kissing of him," he cried, roughly.

To his indignant surprise the drowned man opened one eye and winked acquiescence. The skipper dropped his arms by his side and stared at him stupidly.

"I saw his eyelid twitch," cried Mrs. Gibbs, joyfully.

"He's all right." said her indignant husband; " 'e ain't born to be drowned, 'e ain't. I've spoilt a good suit of clothes for nothing."

To his wife's amazement, he actually walked away from the insensible man, and with a boat-hook reached for his hat, which was floating by. Mrs. Gibbs, still gazing in blank astonishment, caught a seraphic smile on the face of her brother as Miss Harris continued her ministrations, and in a pardonable fit of temper the overwrought woman gave him a box on the ear, which brought him round at once.

"Where am I?" he inquired, artlessly.

Mrs. Gibbs told him. She also told him her opinion of him, and without plagiarising her husband's words, came to the same conclusion as to his ultimate fate.

"You come along home with me," she said, turning in a friendly fashion to the bewildered girl. "They deserve what they've got—both of 'em. I only hope that they'll both get such awful colds that they won't find their voices for a twelvemonth."

She took the girl by the arm and helped her ashore. They turned their heads once in the direction of the barge, and saw the justly incensed skipper keeping the mate's explanations and apologies at bay with a boat-hook. Then they went in to breakfast.

DEAD RECKONING

RALPH STOCK

I have killed a man because he disagreed with me. Anything more futile it is hard to imagine in cold blood, for by killing him I have proved nothing. He still holds his view. I know it because I have spoken to him *since*, and he still laughs at me, though softly, compassionately, not as he laughed on that night when the absurdity happened.

Perhaps I am mad, but you shall judge. In any case, that is of no great importance, for by the time you read this, my confession—if, indeed, it is ever read—I shall have ceased to encumber the earth.

He was young and strong, and filled with that terrible self-assurance of youth that sets an older man's teeth on edge. During his short term of tuition in the schools of the South there was nothing that he had not learned to do better (in theory) than a man of fifty years' experience; and obstinate—But I must not let myself go. It is my duty to set down here precisely what happened, without prejudice, without feeling even, if that were possible. Yet as I write, my pulse quickens—I will wait a little. It is unfair to him to continue at present.

Here on this reef off the Queensland coast there are unbelievable quantities of fish. Even I have never seen so many, nor of such brilliant colouring. It is possible to wade into the tepid water and catch them with the hand. I have caught hundreds to-day, for lack of something better to do—and set them free; for I will have no more blood on my hands, even that of a fish. Besides, what is the use? There is no drinking water here, nothing but blinding sunlight, a ridge of discoloured coral cleaving the blue mirror of the sea like a razor edge, and myself—a criminal perched upon it as upon a premature scaffold.

But I have overlooked the pickle bottle. It came to me floating, not quite empty, and corked against the flies, just as he and I had left it after the last meal. When the wreck sank, it must have risen from the fo'c'sle table and up through the hatch—it is curious that nothing else should rise—and it occurred to me that by its aid, and that of the little notebook with pencil attached which I always carry, it would be possible to set my case before the world. I must continue, or there may not be time to say all.

I am what they call an old man on Thursday Island, for none but blacks live to any age in the neighbourhood of this sun-baked tile on the roof of Australia. But I come of Old Country stock, and blood will tell.

I have mixed little with others, preferring the society of my only child, a daughter, to the prattlers and drinkers of a small equatorial community. Perhaps I have been too circumscribed, too isolated, from my fellow-creatures. I only know that until *he* came I was content. My small weather-board house ashore, the ketch in which I brought sandalwood from the mainland coast, were my twin worlds. In each all things were conducted according to my wishes—according, rather, to the methods I had evolved from long experience, and that their merits were borne out by results none could deny.

The house, with its small, well-tended garden, was the best on Thursday Island. My daughter, dutiful and intelligent, managed it according to my wishes, so that it ran like a well-oiled mechanism. And the ketch— that was my inviolable domain. Above and below decks, although only a twenty-ton cargo-carrier, she would have put many a yacht to shame. There was nothing superfluous, nothing lacking. Everything aboard had its place and uses; that is how I contrived to work her single-handed for nearly ten years.

They called me a curmudgeon and a skinflint, but I could afford to smile. My cargoes were not so large as theirs, and took longer to gather, but while they were eating into their profits by paying wages and shares to lazy crews, mine came solely to myself, and never in all those years did I have a mishap. Trust an owner to look after his craft, say I, and trust none other.

Then, as I have said, *he* came. How he gained entrance I have never known, but he had a way with him, that boy, and when one evening I returned from a trip, he was sitting on the verandah with Doris. She was evidently embarrassed.

"This is Mr. Thorpe, father," she said, and went in to prepare supper, which was late for the first time that I could remember.

"Indeed?" said I, and remained standing, a fact that Thorpe appeared to overlook, for he reseated himself with all the assurance in life.

"Yes," he said in a manner that I believe is called "breezy," "that is my name, Captain Brent, and I'm pleased to make your acquaintance. Have you had a good trip?"

"Passable," said I. "And now, if you'll excuse me, I must go in and change."

"Oh, don't mind me," returned Thorpe, spreading himself in the cane chair and lighting a cigarette; "I'm quite comfortable."

For a moment I stood speechless, then went into the house.

Doris was preparing the meal, but turned as I entered. Never before had I seen the look that I saw in her face at that moment—fear battling with resolve.

"Who is that boy?" I asked her.

"I have already told you, father," she answered; "he is a young man named Thorpe—Edward Thorpe."

"Ah," said I, momentarily at a loss, "a young man—named Thorpe. And why does he come here?"

"To see me," returned Doris in her quiet, even voice, but I saw that she trembled.

I took her by the arm.

"Girl," said I, "tell me all."

"We love one another," she told me, looking full into my eyes with no hint of timidity; "we are engaged to be married."

I could not speak. I could not even protest when, at no invitation of mine, this youth had the effrontery to come in to supper. The world—my twin worlds—rocked under my feet.

It was a terrible meal. I, speechless, at one end of the table, my daughter, pale, but courteous, at the other, and this clown sat between us, regaling us, as he no doubt thought, with anecdotes of life down South.

And this was not enough, but he must come into the kitchen afterwards and help to wash up. He said it made him feel more at home. Now, it has been my custom, ever since leaving a civilisation that I abhor and finding comfort in this far corner of the earth, to help wash up when I am at home. The thing is part of the routine of life, and as such demands proper management. A nice adjustment of the water's temperature is necessary, for if too hot it may crack glass and china and ruin knife-handles; and if too cold, in spite of a certain amount of soda, it fails to remove grease. Then, too, it is my invariable habit at the end to turn the washbowl upside down to drain, and spread the dishcloth upon it to dry. It occurs to me that these may appear small matters to some, but is not life composed of such, and do they not often turn out to be the greater? And our uninvited guest disorganised the entire routine by pathetic efforts at buffoonery such as tying one of Doris's aprons about his waist, making a napkin-ring climb his finger by a circular motion of the hand, and laughing openly at what he evidently regarded as our fads.

The spreading of the dishcloth on the wash-bowl appeared to amuse him most of all.

"I suppose you always do that," he said.

"It is the custom in this house," said I.

"And when you come to think of it, why not?" he reflected, with his handsome head at an angle.

"There are many things one has to come to think of before one knows anything," said I.

And at that he laughed good-naturedly. He always laughed.

At length he went. From my easy-chair in the living-room I heard the last "Good-night" and his assured footfall on the verandah steps. Doris came straight to me. I knew she would. Perching herself on the arm of my chair, as she used to when a child, she encircled my shoulder with her arm.

"Do you hate him, father?" she asked me.

I answered her question with another.

"Do you fear me, Doris?" For the look in her face that evening had shocked me.

"I used to sometimes," she said, "but not now."

"And what has worked the transformation?"

She leaned over and whispered in my ear.

I held her from me and studied her as though for the first time. She was young, beautiful, fragile, yet she was stronger than I. I am no fool. I knew that nothing I could do or say would have one particle of weight with her now. She loved, and was loved. So it is with women; and such is this miracle of a day, an hour, a fraction of time, that shatters lifelong fealty like glass.

"Then I have nothing to say," said I.

"Nothing?" she questioned me, and again presently, "nothing?"

And at last I heard myself muttering the absurd formula of wishes for their happiness.

It was bound to come some time. It had come, that was all, and I made the best of it. Of an evening that boy would sit with us and make suggestions for the betterment of the business—my business. He pointed out that new blood was needed—his blood. By heavens, how he talked! And there is an insidious power in words. Utter them often enough, with youthful enthusiasm behind them, and they resolve themselves into deeds.

I cannot explain even to myself how it came about, but this was the plan—to take my ketch to Sydney, where she would apparently realise an enormous sum as a converted yacht, and buy another, installing an auxiliary motor-engine with some of the profits. With an engine, and this new blood, it seemed, we were to make a fortune out of sandalwood in three years.

I wanted neither engine, new blood, nor fortune, yet in the end I gave way.

So it was that, rather late in the season, we let go moorings, he and I, and set sail for the South. For the first time in my life I had a crew. My inviolable domain was invaded. What with the thought of this, and the unworthy mission we were engaged upon, it was all I could do to look my ketch in the face. Those with the love of ships in their bones will understand.

More than once I caught Thorpe smiling at one or another of my own small inventions for the easier handling of the boat, or the saving of labour or space below; but he said nothing beyond called them "gadgets," a word that was new to me.

"Not a bad little packet," he said, after the first hour of his trick at the tiller.

"I am glad to hear you say so," said I, with an irony entirely lost on one of his calibre.

"But she ought to sail nearer the wind than this," he added, staring up at the quivering top-sail. "Six points won't do. Under-canvased, that's what she is. By the way, when we get through the reef pass, what's the course?"

"Sou'-sou'-east," said I.

"And where's your deviation card?"

"Never had to bother with one," I told him.

He seemed thunderstruck.

"Of course, she's wooden," he began; "but surely—"

"The course is sou'-sou'-east," I repeated, and went below.

From then onwards he took to reeling me off parrot-like dissertations on devioscopes, new pattern compasses, and whatnot, until the sound of his voice sickened me. Amongst his other accomplishments, he had sat for a yachting master's ticket, and passed, though every one knew, it appeared, how much stiffer were the examinations nowadays than in the past, when half the men called ship's masters had no right to the title, nor even knew the uses of a chronometer.

"Yet they managed to circumnavigate the globe," I pointed out.

"By running down their latitude!" he scoffed.

"Perhaps," said I, whereat he burst into a gale of laughter, and expressed the devout hope that I would never expect him to employ such methods.

"I expect you to do nothing but what you are told," said I, exasperated beyond endurance. "At the present moment you are not getting the best out of her. Give her another point, and make a note of time and distance in the scrap log hanging on yonder rail."

"Dead reckoning," he muttered contemptuously.

"Just that," said I, and left him.

Why did I "leave him"? Why did I "go below"? At all costs I must be fair. I did both these things because I knew that he could argue me off my feet if I remained, that he knew more about deep-sea navigation than I, that I was one of those he had mentioned who are called ship's masters and have no right to the title, nor even knew the uses of a chronometer.

Such a confession is like drawing a tooth to me, but it is made. And as vindication I would point to my record—ten years, single-handed and by dead reckoning without mishap. Can an extra master show better?

As day succeeded day, the tension grew. Often I would sit on a locker gazing on my familiar and beloved surroundings and ask myself how long I could suffer them to be sneered at and despised. Trust small craft for discovering one man to another. Before three days and three nights had passed, we stood before each other, he and I, stripped to our souls. His every movement was an aggravation to me, especially when he played with the bespangled sextant and toy chronometer he had brought, and when each day, on plotting out my position on the chart according to dead reckoning, I found his, by observation, already there. I rubbed it out. I prayed that there would come such a fog as would obscure the sun and stars for ever.

And it was as though my prayer were answered, for that night we ran into a gale that necessitated heaving to. Luckily it was off the shore, and for forty-eight hours we rode it out in comparative comfort, until it died as suddenly as it had been born, and was succeeded by a driving mist that stilled the sea as though with a giant white hand.

"You see," said Thorpe, "dead reckoning is all right up to a point, as a check, but how do you know where you are now?"

"Can you tell me?" said I.

"Not until the mist clears," he admitted.

"Well, then—" said I.

He flung away from me with an impatient movement.

"These are the methods of Methuselah," he muttered.

"Nevertheless," I returned, the blood throbbing at my temples, "I know our position at this moment better than any upstart yachtsman."

He turned and looked at me strangely, then of a sudden his mouth relaxed into a smile. At that moment I could have struck him.

"There is no call for us to quarrel," he said gently, "but how—how can you possibly know where we have drifted to in the last forty-eight hours?"

"I have my senses," said I, "and to prove them we will carry on."

"In this mist?"

"In this mist," I thundered. "The wind is fair, the course is now south-half-east, and you'll oblige me by taking the tiller."

He seemed about to speak, but evidently changed his mind, and turned abruptly on his heel.

In silence we shook out the reef and got under way. In silence we remained until the end of his watch, when the mist was dispersed by a brazen sun. Thorpe at once took a sight, and again at noon, and when I had plotted our position on the chart, he was still poring over volumes of nautical tables.

Towards dusk he came to me at the tiller.

"Are you holding this course after dark?" he asked.

"That is as may be," said I.

"Because if you are," he went on, as though I had not spoken, "you'll be on the Barrier Reef inside of five hours."

"I thank you for the information," said I, and he went below.

He knew ship's discipline; I'll say that for him. He might consider myself and my methods archaic, but he recognised my authority and carried out instructions. I am aware that up to the present my case appears a poor one, but I can convey no idea of the pitch to which I was brought by these eternal bickerings, by the innovation of another will than my own, and the constant knowledge that he was laughing at me up his sleeve.

But it was a little thing that brought matters to a climax. It is always the little things.

With a fair wind, and in these unfrequented waters, it has always been my habit to lash the tiller and eat in comfort. We were washing up after supper, or, rather, he was washing and I was drying, for the dryer puts away the utensils, and I knew better the proper place for each. At the end he tossed the dishcloth in a sodden mass upon the table and turned to go.

"The dishcloth, if you remember," said I, "is spread on the washbowl to dry."

He turned and looked at me, and in his eyes I saw a sudden, unaccustomed flame leap to life.

"It'll do it good to have a change," he said.

"I do not think so," said I.

"Naturally," he returned; "but I do."

"And who is the master of this ship?" I asked him.

"As for that, you are," he admitted, "but a dishcloth is another matter." Suddenly he dropped on to a locker and laughed, though there was a nervous catch in it. "Heavens!" he giggled, "we're arguing over a dishcloth now!"

"And why not," said I, "if you don't know how to use one? Will you be so good as to put it in its proper place?"

He did not answer, but sat looking down at his naked feet.

"This is impossible," he muttered.

"As you will," said I.

"It can't go on; I can't stand it."

"Do you imagine it is any pleasanter for me?" I asked him.

"And who's fault is it?"

"That is a matter of opinion," said I; "but in the meantime things are to be done as I wish. Kindly put the dishcloth in its proper place."

Again he did not answer, but when he looked up it was with compressed lips.

"You are a frightful old man," he said. Those were his words. I remember every one, and they came from him in deliberate, staccato sentences.

"You are that, though no one has dared to tell you so until this minute. You have lived in a rut of your own making so deep and so long that you don't know you're in it. That is your affair, but when you drag others in with you, it is time to speak. I rescued Doris—bless her!—just in time. Why, man, can't you see? There's no light down there; you can never take a look at yourself and laugh. You have no more sense of humour than a fish. If you had, this absurd quibble could never have come to a head. We should have been sitting here laughing instead. Think of it—a dishcloth! You are my senior; I ought not to be talking like this to you, but I am; it's just been dragged out of me, and you can take it or leave it. Why not open up a bit—do something different just because it is different, admit there may be something others know that you don't, fling the dishcloth in a corner . . ."

Those were some of the things he said to me, and I stood there listening to them from a—from my future son-in-law on my own ship. It seemed incredible to me now, but I was dazed with the unexpectedness of this attack. All that remained clearly before me was the issue of the dishcloth. In the midst of his endless discourse I repeated my command, whereat he burst into another of his inane fits of laughter.

"You find it amusing," said I in a voice I scarce recognised as my own.

"Amusing!" he chuckled. "Think—try and think—a dishcloth!"

"And one that you will put in its proper place," I told him.

"What makes you think that?" he said, sobering a little.

"Because I say so."

"And if I refuse?" His face was quite grave now. He leant forward, as though interested in my reply. Somehow the sight of it—this handsome, impertinent face of his—caused a red mist to swim before my eyes.

"You will be made to," I said.

"Ah!" was all he answered at the moment, and resumed the study of his feet. If he had remained so, all might have been well. I cannot tell. I only know that at that moment one word stood for him between life and death, and he chose to utter it.

"How?"

I tried to show him, that was all. I swear that was my sole intention. But he was obstinate, that boy. I had not thought it possible for a man to be as obstinate as he.

My weight carried him to the floor; besides, I am strong, and the accumulated fury of days and nights were behind me. He was like a doll in my hands, yet a doll that refused to squeak when pressed. There is a sail-rack

I rushed on deck to be caught by a roller.

in the fo'c's'le, and we were under it, my back against it, my knee at his chest; and I asked him, lying there laughing up at me, if he intended to do as I had ordered. He rolled his head in a negative. It was all he could do, and the pressure was increased. I must have asked him many times, and the answer was invariably the same. At the last something gave beneath my knee, and his jaw dropped, and no movement came from him, even from the heart.

The ripple of water past the ketch's sides brought me back to the present. I rose and stood looking down on him. As I live, it seemed that there was a smile still upon his face!

Of the rest I have no clear recollection. At one moment I was standing there trying—trying to realise what I had done; the next I was flung against the bulkhead as the ketch struck and rose—I can describe it in no other way—struck and rose. Even as I rushed on deck to be caught by a roller and hurled headlong, it seemed to me that a mocking voice called after me: "Dead Reckoning!"

It was the Barrier Reef.

And for me it is the Barrier Reef to the end, which is not far off. When I came to, the ketch had sunk, and I tried again to think. I have been trying ever since, and I can get no further than that I have killed him—for a dish-cloth; that if by some miracle I am rescued, such is the message I shall have for Doris.... Is it comedy or tragedy? I am not so sure now. *He* seemed to find it amusing to the very end, and he was right in some things. Perhaps he is right in this.

I never laugh? Did I not catch myself laughing aloud just now? Perhaps I am developing, somewhat late in life, to be sure, the "sense of humour" he tells me I lack.... I have finished. It is for you to read and judge.

The foregoing, with such editing as was necessary to render it intelligible, is the message I found in a pickle bottle firmly wedged amongst the mangrove roots of a creek in the Gulf of Carpentaria. It must have been there for years.

I was duck-shooting at the time, but somehow, after happening on to this quaint document besmeared with pickle juice, my interest in the sport flagged. I wanted to know more, and there is only one way to do that on Thursday Island—ask Evans. Consequently, that evening found me, not for the first time, on his wide verandah, discussing whisky and soda, and the impossible state of the shell market.

"By the way," I ventured presently, "did you ever know a Captain Brent?"

"Still know him, for the matter of that," said Evans. "Why?"

"Then he—I mean he still lives on T.I.," I stammered like a fool.

"Certainly. I used to buy his sandalwood. Buy his son-in-law's now."

"His son-in-law's?"

Evans rolled over in his chair and grinned at me.

"What's the game?" he questioned good-naturedly. "I never saw such a fellow." He rolled back again. "But, come to think of it, there might be something in him for you. The old man's ketch is the first thing I ever heard of to jump the Barrier Reef. I thought that'd make you sit up. But it's the truth. Ask Thorpe—he was aboard when she did it. He and the old man were going South for something—I forget what—and they took the Great Barrier bow on at night. It's been done before, you know, but never quite like that. Must have struck it in a narrow place or something. Anyway, Thorpe says that ketch jumped like a two-year-old, slithered through rotten coral for a bit, and plumped into deep water beyond, carried by the surf, I expect, and nothing more to show for it than a scored bilge—oh, and a couple of broken ribs—Thorpe's not the ketch's. He was beaten up pretty considerably when we took him ashore. Is there anything else I can serve you with to-day, sir?"

Evans is a good fellow, but provokingly incomplete.

"Yes," said I. "What happened to the old man?"

"Oh, he rushed on deck at the first shock, it seems, and was promptly bowled over the side by a breaker. But there's no killing him. He just sat on the reef, thinking his ketch sunk and Thorpe dead, until some one came and took him off. Shook him up, though. He's never been quite the same since. Which is all to the good, most of us think."

The next evening I took occasion to wander down T.I.'s grass-grown main street, through its herds of cavorting goats, and up the galvanised hillside to where a neat little weather-board house stood well back from the road.

In the garden, enjoying the cool of the evening, were four people—a white-bearded man seated in a cane-chair, a bronzed giant, prone and smoking, on the grass, and a woman beside him, sitting as only a woman can. Curiously enough, their eyes were all turned in the same direction— to where, in short, the fourth member of the party was engaged in the solemn procession of learning to "walk alone." His progress towards his mother's outstretched arms was as erratic as such things usually are—a few ungainly steps, a tottering pause, and an abrupt but apparently painless collapse.

"Seven!" exclaimed the white-bearded man, with an air of personal accomplishment.

"I made it five," grinned the giant.

"I said seven," boomed the other, and I left them at it.

They were Captain Brent and his son-in-law, and somehow I wanted to preserve that picture of them intact.

That, too, was partly why at the summit of the hill I tore my quaint, pickle-stained document into minute fragments and scattered them to the four winds of Torres Straits.

HOLLIS'S DEBT

LOUIS BECKE

One day a small Sydney-owned brigantine named the *Maid of Judah*, loaded with coconut oil and sandalwood and bound for China, appeared off the little island of Pingelap, in the Caroline Group. In those wild days—from 1820 to the end of the "fifties"—the sandalwood trade was carried on by ships whose crews were assemblages of the most utter ruffians in the Pacific Ocean, and the hands that manned this brigantine were no exception. There may have been grades of villainy among them; perhaps if any one of them was more blood-stained and criminal than the others, it was her captain.

There being no anchorage at Pingelap, the captain sailed in as close as he dared, and then hove-to under the lee of the land, waiting for the natives to come aboard with some turtle. Presently a canoe put off from the long curve of yellow beach. She was manned by some eight or ten natives. As she pulled up alongside, the captain glanced at the white man who was steering and his face paled. He turned quickly away and went below.

The mate of the sandalwooder shook hands with the white man and looked curiously at him. Only by his speech could he be recognised as an Englishman. His hair, long, rough and dull brown, fell on his naked shoulders like that of a native. A broad-brimmed hat, made from the plaited leaf of the pandanus palm, was his only article of European clothing; round his loins was a native girdle of beaten coconut leaves. And his skin was as dark as that of his savage native crew; he looked, and was, a true Micronesian beachcomber.

"You're under mighty short canvas, my friend," said the mate of the vessel by way of pleasantry.

The man with the brown skin turned on him savagely.

"What the hell is that to you? I don't dress to please a pack of convicts and cut-throats! Do you want to buy any turtle? that's the question. And where's the captain?"

"Captain Matson has gone below sick, sir," said the steward, coming up and speaking to the mate. "He says not to wait for the turtle but to fill away again."

"Can't," said the mate sharply. "Tell him there isn't enough wind. Didn't he see that for himself ten minutes ago? What's the matter with him?"

"Don't know, sir. Only said he was took bad sudden."

With an oath expressive of disgust the mate turned to the beachcomber. "You've had your trouble for nothing, you see. The old man don't want any turtle it seems—Why, what the hell is wrong with *you*?"

The bearded, savage-looking beachcomber was leaning against a backstay, his hands tightly clenched, and his eyes fixed in a wild, insane stare.

He straightened himself up and spoke with an effort.

"Nothing: I'm all right now. 'Tis a fearful hot day, and the sun has giddied me a bit. I dare say your skipper has got a touch of the same thing. But gettin' the turtle won't delay you. I want tobacco badly. You can have as many turtle as you want for a couple of pounds o' tobacco."

"Right," said the mate—"that's dirt-cheap. Get 'em aboard as quick as you can. Let's have twenty."

The beachcomber laughed. "You don't know much about Pingelap turtle if you think a canoe would hold more than two together. We've got 'em here five hundredweight. You'll have to send a boat if you want that many. They're too heavy to bring off in canoes. But I'll go on ahead and tell the people to get 'em ready for you."

He got over the side into the canoe, and was paddled quickly ashore.

The mate went below to tell the skipper. He found him sitting at the cabin table with white face and shaking limbs, drinking Sydney rum.

"That beachcombing cove has gone ashore; but he says if you send a boat he'll give us twenty turtle for some tobacco. We want some fresh meat badly. Shall I lower the boat?"

An instantaneous change came over the skipper's features, and he sighed as if a heavy load was off his mind.

"Has he gone, Willis? . . . Oh, yes, we must have the turtle. Put a small twelve-pound case of tobacco in the whaleboat, and send half a dozen Sandwich Island natives with the second mate. Tell Barton to hurry back. We're in too close, and I must tow out a bit when the boat comes back—and I say, Willis, keep that beachcombing fellow on the main-deck if he comes aboard again. I don't like his looks, and don't want him down in the cabin on any account."

The second mate and his crew followed the white man and a crowd of natives to the pond where the turtle were kept. It was merely a huge pool in the reef, with a rough wall of coral slabs built round it to prevent the turtle escaping when the tides rose higher than usual.

"A real good idea—" began the second mate, when there was a lightning rush of the brown-skinned men upon him and his crew. At knocking a man down and tying him up securely your Caroline

Islander is unmatched, he does it so artistically. I know this from experience.

"This is rather sudden, isn't it, Barton?" The beachcomber was speaking to him, looking into his eyes as he lay upon the ground. "You don't remember my face, do you? Perhaps my back would improve your memory. Ah, you brute, I can pay both you and that murderous dog of a Matson back now. I knew I should meet you both again some day."

Across the sullen features of the seaman there flashed a quick light—the gleam of a memory. But his time was brief. The beachcomber whispered to a native. A heavy stone was lashed to the second mate's chest. Then they dropped him over the wall into the pond. The native sailors they left where they lay.

And now ensued a hurried, whispered colloquy. The story of that day's work is not yet forgotten among the old hands of Ponape and Yap. Suffice it to say that by a cunningly contrived device the captain was led to believe that the second mate and his men had deserted, and sent the chief mate and six more of his crew to aid the natives in recapturing them. The presence of numbers of women and children walking unconcernedly about the beach made him assured that no treachery was intended. The mate and his men were captured in one of the houses, where they had been taken by the beachcomber for a drink. They were seized from behind and at once bound, but without any unnecessary rough usage.

"What's all this for?" said the mate unconcernedly to the white man. He was an old hand, and thought it meant a heavy ransom—or death.

The beachcomber was standing outside in the blazing sun, looking at the ship. There were a number of natives on board selling fish and young coconuts. The women and children still sauntered to and fro on the beach. He entered the house and answered the query.

"It means this; no harm to you and these six men here if you lie quiet and wait till I send for you to come aboard again. The other six Sandwich Islanders are alive but tied up. Barton is dead, I have settled my score with *him*."

"Ah," said the mate, after a brief outburst of blasphemy, "I see, you mean to cut off the ship."

"No, I don't. But I have an old debt to settle with the skipper. Keep quiet, or you'll follow Mr. Barton. And I don't want to kill you. I've got nothing against *you*."

Then the beachcomber, with some twenty natives, went to where the first six men were lying, and carried them down into the mate's boat.

"Here's the second mate's chaps, sir," said the carpenter to Matson; "the natives has 'em tied hand and foot, like pigs. But I don't see Barton among 'em."

"No," said the captain, "they wouldn't tie up a white man. He'll come off with Willis and the turtle. I never thought Barton would bolt."

The *ruse* succeeded admirably. The boatload of natives had hardly been ten seconds on deck ere the brigantine was captured. Matson, lashed in a sitting position to the quarter railing, saw the last man of the cutting-out party step on board, and a deadly fear seized him. For that last man was the beachcomber.

He walked aft and stood over him. "Come on board, Captain Thomas Matson," he said, mockingly saluting him. Then he stepped back and surveyed his prisoner.

"You look well, Matson. You know me now, don't you?"

The red, bloated face of the skipper patched and mottled, and his breath came in quick, short gasps of rage and terror.

"Ah, of course you do! It's only three years ago since that Sunday at Vaté in the New Hebrides, when you had me triced up and Barton peeled the hide off me in strips. You said I'd never forget it—*and I've come to tell you that you were right*. I haven't. It's been meat and drink to me to think that we might meet again."

He stopped. His white teeth glistened beneath the black-bearded lips in a low laugh—a laugh that chilled the soul of his listener.

He seized the fated man by the hair

A light air rippled the water and filled the sails, and the brigantine moved. The man went to the wheel and gave it a turn to port.

"Yes," he resumed, casting his eye aloft, "I'm delighted to have a talk with you, Matson. You will see that your crew are working the ship for me. You don't mind, do you, eh? And we can talk a bit, can't we?"

No answer came.

"None of the old hands left, I see, Matson—except Barton. Do you know where he is now? No? He's dead. I hadn't any particular grudge against him. He was only your flogger. But I killed him, and I'm going to kill you." He crossed his bare, sinewy arms on the wheel, and smiled again at the bound and terrified wretch.

"You've had new bulwarks and spars since, I see. Making money fast now, I suppose. I hope your mate is a good navigator, Matson. *He's* going to take this ship to Honolulu."

Then the fear-stricken man found his tongue, and a wild, gasping appeal for mercy broke from him.

"Don't murder me, Hollis. I've been a bad man all my life. For God's sake, let me off! I was a brute to you. I've got a wife and children. For Christ's sake—!"

The man sprang from the wheel and kicked him savagely in the mouth with his bare foot.

"Ha! you've done it now. 'For Christ's sake. For Christ's sake!' Don't you remember when *I* used those words: 'For Christ's sake, sir, hear me! I did not run away. I got lost coming from the place where we were cutting the sandalwood.'" A flicker of foam fell on his tawny hand. "You dog, you bloody-minded fiend! For three years I have waited . . . and I have you now."

A choking groan of terror came from Matson.

"Hollis! Spare me! . . . my children."

The man had gone back to the wheel, calm again. A brisk puff was rippling over the water from the westward. His seaman's eye glanced aloft, and the wheel again spun round. "Ready, about!" he called. The brigantine went and stood in again—to meet the mate's boat.

"Come this way, Mr. Willis. Captain Matson and I have been having a chat about old times. You don't know me, do you? Captain Matson is a little upset just now, so I'll tell you who I am. My name is Hollis. I was one of the hands of this ship. I am owner now. Funny, isn't it? Now, now; don't get excited, Mr. Willis, and look about you in that way. There isn't a ghost of a chance; I can tell you that. If you make one step towards me, you and every man Jack will get his throat cut. And as soon as I have finished my business with our friend here you'll be captain—and owner, too, if you like. By the by, what's the cargo worth?"

The mate told him.

"Ah, quite a nice little sum—two thousand pounds. Now, Mr. Willis, that will be practically yours. With only one other white man on board, you can take the vessel to Honolulu and sell both her and the cargo, and no questions asked. Hard on our friend here, though; isn't it?"

"Good God, man, what are you going to do to the captain— murder him?"

"For God's sake, Willis, help me!" The mute agony in the skipper's face, more than the spoken words, moved even the rough and brutal nature of the mate, and he opened his lips to speak.

"No!" said the man at the wheel; "you shall not help him. Look at this!"

He tossed aside the mantle of tangled hair that fell down his shoulders, and presented his scarred and hideous back to the mate.

"Now, listen to me, Mr. Willis. Go below and pass up as much tobacco and trade as will fill the small boat. I don't want plunder. But these natives of mine do."

In a few minutes the goods were hoisted up and lowered into the boat. Then the two six-pounders on the main-deck were run overboard, and all the small arms taken from the cabin by the natives.

"Call your men aft," the white man said to Willis. They came along the deck and stood behind him.

"Carry that man on to the main hatch."

Two of the strongest of the native sailors picked up the burly figure of the captain and laid him on the spot the beach-comber indicated and cut his bonds.

A dead silence. The tall, sun-baked figure of the muscular beach-comber, naked save for his grass girdle, seemed, as he stood at the wheel, the only animate thing on board. He raised his finger and beckoned to a sailor to come and steer. Then with quick strides he reached the hatch and stood in front of his prey.

"Captain Tom Matson. Look at, me well; and see what you have made me. Your time . . . and *mine* . . . at last."

He extended his hand. A native placed in it the hilt of a knife, short, broad-bladed, heavy and keen-edged.

"Ha! Can't you speak? Can't *you* say 'for Christ's sake'? Don't the words stick in your throat?"

The sinewy left hand darted out and seized the fated man by the hair, and then with a savage backward jerk bent back his head, and drew taut the skin of the coarse, thick throat. Then he raised the knife. . . .

He wiped the knife on his girdle, and looked in silence at the bubbling arterial stream that poured down over the hatch-coamings.

"You won't forget my name, will you?" he said to the mate. "Hollis; Hollis, of Sydney; they know me there; the man that was flogged at Vaté by him, *there*—and left ashore to die at Santo."

He glanced down at the limp, huddled-up mass at his feet, got into the boat, and with his naked associates, paddled ashore.

The breeze had freshened up, and as the brigantine slowly sailed past the crowded huts of the native village a hundred yards distant, the mate saw the beachcomber standing by his thatched house. He was watching the ship.

A young native girl came up to him with a wooden water-bowl, and stood waiting. With his eyes still fixed on the ship he thrust his reddened hands into the water, moved them slowly to and fro, then dried them on his girdle of grass.

SMITH *VERSUS* LICHTENSTEIGER

WESTON MARTYR

Smith stood five feet five inches in his boots, weighed nearly ten stone in his winter clothes and an overcoat, and he had a flat chest and a round stomach. Smith was a clerk in a small branch bank in East Anglia; he was not an athlete or a fighting man, although he followed the fortunes of a professional football team in the newspapers with great interest, and he had fought for a year in France without ever seeing his enemy or achieving a closer proximity to him than one hundred and twenty yards. When a piece of shrapnel reduced his fighting efficiency by abolishing the biceps of one arm, Smith departed from the field of battle and (as he himself would certainly have put it) "in due course" returned to his branch bank.

For forty-nine weeks each year Smith laboured faithfully at his desk. In his free hours during the winter he read Joseph Conrad, Stevenson, and E. F. Knight; he did hardly anything else. But every year in early April, Smith suddenly came to life. For he was a yachtsman, and he owned a tiny yacht which he called the *Kate* and loved with a great love. The spring evenings he spent fitting out, painting and fussing over his boat. Thereafter, as early as possible every Saturday afternoon, he set sail and cruised alone amongst the tides and sandbanks of the Thames Estuary, returning again as late as possible on Sunday night. And every summer, when his three weeks' holiday came round, Smith and his *Kate* would sail away from East Anglia together and voyage afar. One year Smith cruised to Falmouth in the West Countree, and he likes to boast about that cruise still. Once he set out for Cherbourg, which is a port in foreign parts; but that time, thanks to a westerly gale, he got no farther than Dover. The year Smith encountered Lichtensteiger he had sailed as far east as Flushing, and he was on his way back when a spell of bad weather and head winds drove him into Ostend and detained him there three days.

Lichtensteiger was also detained at Ostend; but not by the weather. Lichtensteiger had come from Alexandria, with a rubber tube stuffed full of morphine wound round his waist next to his skin, and he was anxious to get to London as quickly as he could. He had already been as far as Dover, but there a Customs official (who had suspicions but no proof) whispered to a friend in the Immigration Department, and Lichtensteiger found himself debarred as an "undesirable alien" from entering the United Kingdom. He had therefore returned to Ostend in the steamer in which he had left that place.

Lichtensteiger stood six feet one inch in his socks, weighed fourteen stone stripped, and he had a round chest and a flat stomach. He was as strong as a gorilla, as quick in action as a mongoose, and he had never done an honest day's work in his life. There is reason to believe that Lichtensteiger was a Swiss, as he spoke Switzer-Deutsch, which is something only a German-Swiss can do. His nationality, however, is by no means certain, because he looked like a Lombard, carried Rumanian and Austrian passports, and in addition to the various dialects used in those two countries, he spoke French like a Marseillais, German like a Würtemberger, and English like a native of the lower Westside of New York.

When Smith and Lichtensteiger first set eyes on each other, Smith was sitting in the *Kate's* tiny cockpit, smoking his pipe and worrying about the weather. For Smith's holiday was nearly over; he was due at his bank again in three days, and he knew he could not hope to sail back while the strong northwesterly wind continued to blow straight from East Anglia towards Belgium. Said Smith to himself, "Hang it! I've got to sail to-morrow or get into a nasty fix. And if only I had two sound arms I *would* sail to-morrow and chance it; but a hundred-mile beat to wind'ard all by myself is going to be no joke. What I need is another man to help me; but there isn't an earthly hope of getting hold of any one in this filthy hole."

Lichtensteiger was walking along the quay. He glanced at the *Kate* and her owner with a disdainful eye and passed on, because neither the boat nor the man held any interest for him. But in Lichtensteiger's card-index-like mind, in which he filed without conscious effort most of the things he heard and saw, there were registered three impressions and one deduction: "A yacht. The British flag. An Englishman. A fool." Having filed these particulars, Lichtensteiger's mind was about to pass on to the problem of how to get Lichtensteiger to London, when an idea flashed like a blaze of light into his consciousness. To translate Lichtensteiger's multi-lingual thoughts is difficult; a free rendering of them must suffice. Said Lichtensteiger to himself, "Thunder and lightning. Species of a goose. You poor fish. Of course. It is *that*! If *you* had a yacht—if *you* were a sailor—*there* is the obvious solution. Then there no more need would be to risk placing oneself in the talons of the sacred bureaucrats of Customs or within the despicable jurisdiction of blood-sucking immigration officials. Why, say! If I had a little boat I guess I wouldn't worry myself about smuggling my dope through no Dovers and suchlike places. With a boat of my own then veritably would I be a smuggler classical and complete. But what's the use! I ain't got no boat and I ain't no sailor. But hold! Attention! The English yacht. That fool Englishman. There are possibilities in that direction there. Yes. I guess I go back and take another look at that guy."

Lichtensteiger's second survey of Smith was detailed and thorough, and it confirmed his previous judgment. "Easy meat," said Lichtensteiger to himself, and then, aloud, "Evening, stranger. Pardon me, but I see you're British, and I guess it'll sound good to me to hear some one talk like a Christian for a change. I'm from New York, and Otis T. Merritt's my name. I'm over this side on vacation; but I'll tell you the truth, I don't cotton to these darned Dagoes and Squareheads here, not at all. So I reckon to catch the next boat across to your good country, mister, and spend the balance of my trip there with white men. That's a peach of a little yacht you got. I'll say she certainly is. She's a pippin, and I guess you have a number one first-class time sailing around in her. It's just the kind of game I've always had in mind to try for myself. It 'd suit me down to the ground, I reckon. If you've no objections, I'll step aboard. I'd sure like to look her over. Where are you sailing to next after here?"

"Harwich," answered Smith. "Come aboard and look round if you like, by all means; but I'm afraid you won't find very much to see here."

"Why, she's the finest little ship I ever set eyes on," cried Lichtensteiger a few minutes later, settling himself on the cabin settee. "And to think you run her all alone. My gracious! Have a cigar?"

"Thanks," said Smith. "I do sail her by myself usually, but this time I'm afraid I've bitten off more than I can chew. You see, I've got to get back to Harwich within three days. If I had another man to help me I'd do it easily, but with this wind blowing it's a bit more than I care to tackle alone."

After that, of course, it was easy for Lichtensteiger. He did not ask Smith if he could sail with him; he led Smith on to make that suggestion himself. Then he hesitated awhile at the unexpectedness of the proposal, and when he finally yielded to persuasion, he left Smith with the impression that he was doing him a favour. It was very beautifully done.

That night Lichtensteiger transferred himself and two suitcases from his hotel and slept aboard the *Kate*. At daybreak next morning they sailed. Once outside the harbour entrance Smith found the wind had fallen to a moderate breeze, but it still blew out of the north-west, making the shaping of a direct course to Harwich impossible. Smith, therefore, did the best he could. He put the *Kate* on the starboard tack and sailed her to the westward along the Belgian coast.

It did not take Smith long to discover that Lichtensteiger was no sailor. He could not steer or even make fast a rope securely. In half an hour it became clear to Smith that Lichtensteiger literally did not know one end of the boat from the other, and within an hour he realised that his passenger, instead of helping him, was going to be a hindrance and an infernal nuisance as well. Lichtensteiger did all those things which must on no account be done if life is to be made livable in the confined space aboard a small boat. In addition to other crimes, Lichtensteiger grumbled at the motion, the hardness of the bunks and the lack of head-room in the cabin. He left his clothes scattered all over the yacht, he used the deck as a spittoon, and he sprawled at ease in the cockpit, so that every time Smith had to move in a hurry he tripped over Lichtensteiger's legs. By midday Smith had had as much of Lichtensteiger's company as he felt he could stand. Now that the weather was fine and looked like remaining so, he knew he could easily sail the *Kate* home by himself. He said, "Look here, Merrit; I'm afraid you don't find yachting in such a small boat is as much fun as you thought it was going to be. See those buildings sticking up on the shore there? Well, that's Dunkerque, and I'll sail in and land you, and then you can catch the night boat over to Tilbury nice and comfortably. I'll run you in there in half an hour."

Smith's suggestion astounded Lichtensteiger, and produced in him so profound an alarm that he forgot for a moment that he was Merritt. His eyes blazed, the colour vanished from his face, and tiny beads of sweat hopped out upon it. Then Lichtensteiger emitted some most extraordinary sounds which, had Smith but known it, were Switzer-Deutsch curses of a horrid and disgusting kind, coupled with an emphatic and blasphemous assertion that nothing, not even ten thousand flaming blue devils, could force him to set foot upon the suppurating soil of France. In fairness to Lichtensteiger it must be stated that he very rarely forgot himself, or any part he might happen to be playing, and it was also always difficult to frighten him. But the toughest ruffian may be, perhaps, excused if he shrinks from venturing into a country which he has betrayed in time of war. And this is what Lichtensteiger had done to France, or, more precisely, he had twice double-crossed the French Army Intelligence Department; Section Counter-Espionage, and Sub-section N.C.D. And the penalty for doing this, as Lichtensteiger well knew, is death. Since 1916, when Lichtensteiger succeeded in escaping from that country by the skin of his teeth, France was a place which he had taken the most sedulous pains to avoid, and at the sudden prospect of being landed there he lost his grip of himself for fifteen seconds. Then he pulled himself together and grinned at Smith and said, "Dunkerque nix! Nothing doing. I guess not. And don't you make any mistake, brother; I think this yachting stuff's just great. I'm getting a whale of a kick out of it. So we'll keep on a-going for Harwich. Sure, we will. You bet. And no Dunkerque. No, sir. No Dunkerque for mine. Forget it."

Smith said, "Oh! All right," and that was all he said. But he was thinking hard. He thought, "By God! That was queer. That was *damned* queer. The fellow was scared to death. Yes—to *death*! For I'll swear nothing else could make a man look like that so suddenly. He turned absolutely green. And he sweated. And his eyes... he was terrified. He yammered, panicked, and babbled—in German, too, by the sound of it. By gosh! I wonder who he is? *And what it is he's been up to?* Something damnable, by the look of it. And whatever it was, he did it in Dunkerque—or in France, anyway. That's plain. To look like that at the mere thought of landing in France! My God, he might be a murderer, or anything. Cleared out into Belgium and hanging about, waiting his chance to get away probably. And here I am, helping him to escape. Oh Lord, what a fool I was to let him come. I actually *asked* him to come. Or did I? Yes, I did; but it seems to me now, with *this* to open my eyes, that he meant to come all the time. He did! He led me on to ask him. I can see it all now. He's a clever crafty devil—and he's twice my size! Oh, hang it all. This is *nasty*."

Smith was so absorbed by his thoughts that he did not notice the change of wind coming. The *Kate* heeled suddenly to the puff, her sheets strained and creaked, and she began to string a wake of bubbles and foam behind her. "Hallo," said Smith, "wind's shifted and come more out of the north. We'll be able to lay our course a little better now; she's heading up as high as nor'-west. I'll just see where that course takes us to if you'll bring up the chart."

Lichtensteiger brought the chart from the cabin table, and Smith spread it out upon the deck. "Not so good," said he, after gazing at it for a while. "We can't fetch within forty miles of Harwich on this tack. A nor'-west course only just clears the Goodwins and the North Foreland. Look."

"Then why don't you point the boat straight for Harwich," said Lichtensteiger, "instead of going way off to the left like that?"

"Because this isn't a steamer, and we can't sail against the wind. But we'll get to Harwich all right, although if this wind holds we won't be there before to-morrow night."

"To-morrow night," said Lichtensteiger. "Well, that suits me. What sort of a kind of a place is this Harwich, anyway? Walk ashore there, I suppose, as soon as we get in, without any messing about?"

"Oh, yes. But we'll have to wait till the morning probably, for the Customs to come off and pass us."

"Customs!" said Lichtensteiger. "Customs! I thought—you'd think, in a one-hole dorp like Harwich, there wouldn't be no Customs and all that stuff. And anyways, you don't mean to tell me the Customs'll worry about a little bit of a boat like this?"

"Oh, yes, they will," Smith answered. "Harwich isn't the hole you seem to think it is. It's a big port. We're arriving from foreign, and if we went ashore before the Customs and harbour-master and so on passed us there'd be the very devil of a row."

"Well, crying out loud!" said Lichtensteiger. "What a hell of a country. Not that the blamed Customs worry me any; but—well, what about all this Free Trade racket you Britishers blow about? Seems to me, with your damned Customs and immigration sharps and passports an' God knows what all, you've got Great Britain tied up a blame sight tighter than the United States." Saying which, Lichtensteiger spat viciously upon the deck and went below to think things over.

Before Lichtensteiger finished his thinking the sun had set, and when he came on deck again, with his plan of action decided upon, it was night. Said he, "Gee! It's black. Say, how d'you know where you're going to when you can't see? And where the hell are we now, anyway?"

"A mile or so nor'-west of the Sandettie Bank."

"That don't mean nothing to me. Where is this Sandettie place?"

"It's about twenty miles from Ramsgate one way and eighteen from Calais the other."

"Twenty miles from Ramsgate?" said Lichtensteiger. "Well, listen here, brother. I guess I've kind of weakened on this Harwich idea. It's too far, and it's going to take too long getting there. And I find this yachting game ain't all it's cracked up to be by a long sight. To tell you the truth, without any more flim-flam, I'm fed right up to the gills with this, and the sooner you get me ashore and out of it the better. See? Twenty miles ain't far, and I reckon Ramsgate, or anywhere around that way, will do me fine. Get me? Now you point her for Ramsgate right away and let's get a move on."

"But, I say—look here!" protested Smith. "I don't want to go to Ramsgate. I mean, I've got to get back to Harwich by to-morrow night, and if we put into Ramsgate I'll lose hours and hours. We can't get there till after midnight, and you won't be able to land before daylight at the very earliest, because the Customs won't pass us till then. And. . . ."

"Oh, hell!" broke in Lichtensteiger. "Customs at Ramsgate, too, are there? Well, say, that's all right. I'll tell you what we'll do. We won't trouble no flaming Customs—and save time that way. You land me on the beach, somewheres outside the town, where it's quiet and there's no one likely to be around. I'll be all right then. I'll hump my suitcases into this Ramsgate place and catch the first train to London in the morning. That'll suit me down to the ground."

"But, look here! I can't do that," said Smith.

"What d'you mean, you can't? You can. What's stopping you?"

"Well, if you will have it, Merritt," answered Smith, "I'll tell you straight, I don't like being a party to landing a man—any man—in the way you want me to. It's illegal. I might get into trouble over it, and I can't afford to get into trouble. If they heard in the bank I'd lose my job. I'd be ruined. I'm sorry, but I can't risk it. Why, if we got caught they might put us in prison!"

"Caught! You poor fish," said Lichtensteiger. "How can you get caught! All you've got to do is to put me ashore in the dark in that little boat we're pulling behind us, and then you vamoose and go to Harwich—or hell if you like. I'll be damned if I care. And you can take it from me, now, brother, you've got to put me ashore whether you like it or not. And if you don't like it, I'm going to turn to right here and make you. See? All this darned shinanyking makes me tired. I'm through with it and it's time you tumbled to who's boss here—you one-armed, mutt-faced, sawn-off little son of a b. . . you. You steer this boat for Ramsgate, *now*, pronto, and land me like I said, or by Gor, I'll scrape that fool face off the front of your silly head and smear the rest of you all over the boat. So—jump to it! Let's see some action, quick!"

If Smith had not been born and bred in the midst of a habitually peaceful and law-abiding community, he might perhaps have understood that Lichtensteiger meant to do what he said. But Smith had never encountered a really *bad* and utterly unscrupulous human being in all his life before. In spite of the feeble imitations of the breed which he had seen inside the cinemas, Smith did not believe in such things as human wolves. It is even doubtful if Smith had ever envisaged himself as being involved in fight by the Marquis of Queensberry's rules. It is a fact that Smith would never have dreamed of kicking a man when he was down or of hitting any one below the belt, and he made the mistake of believing that Lichtensteiger must, after all, be more or less like himself. Smith believed that Lichtensteiger's threats, though alarming, were not to be taken seriously. He therefore said, "Here! I say! You can't say things like that, you know. This is my boat and I won't. . ."

But Smith did not get any further. Lichtensteiger interrupted him. He drove his heel with all his might into Smith's stomach, and Smith doubled up with a grunt and dropped on the cockpit floor. Lichtensteiger then kicked him in the back and the mouth, spat in his face and stamped on him. When Smith came to he heard Lichtensteiger saying, "You'll be wise, my buck, to get on to the fact that I took pains, that time, not to hurt you. Next time, though, I reckon to beat you up good. So—cut out the grunting and all that sob-stuff and let's hear if you're going to do what I say. Let's hear from you. Or do you want another little dose? Pipe up, you. . ."

Smith vomited. When he could speak, he said, "I can't. . . Ah, God! Don't kick me again. I'll do it. I'll do what you want. But—I can't—get up. Wait—and I'll do it—if I can. I think my back's—broken."

Smith lay still and gasped, until his breath and his wits returned to him. He explored his hurts with his fingers gingerly, and then he sat up and nursed his battered face in his hands. He was thinking. He was shocked and amazed at Lichtensteiger's strength and brutal ferocity, and he knew that, for the moment, he dare do nothing which might tempt Lichtensteiger to attack him again. Smith was sorely hurt and frightened, but he was not daunted. And deep down in the soul of that under-sized bank clerk there smouldered a resolute and desperate determination to have his revenge. Presently he said, "Better now. But it hurts me to move. Bring up the chart from the cabin. I'll find out a quiet place to land you and see what course to steer."

Lichtensteiger laughed. "That's right, my son," said he. "Pity you didn't see a light a bit sooner, and you'd have saved yourself a whole heap of grief." He brought the chart and Smith studied it carefully for some minutes. Then he put his finger on the coastline between Deal and Ramsgate and said, "There, that looks the best place. It's a stretch of open beach, with no houses shown anywhere near. It looks quiet and deserted enough on the chart. Look for yourself. Will that spot suit you?"

Lichtensteiger looked and grunted. He was no sailor, and that small-scale chart of the southern half of the North Sea did not convey very much to him. He said, "Huh! Guess that'll do. Nothing much doing around that way by the look of it. What's this black line running along here?"

"That's a road. I'll put you on the beach here, and you walk inland till you get to the road and then turn left. It's only two miles to Deal that way."

"Let her go then," said Lichtensteiger. "The sooner you get me ashore the sooner you'll get quit of me, which ought to please you some, I guess. And watch your step! I reckon you know enough now not to try and put anything over on me; but if you feel like playing any tricks—*look out*. If I have to start in on you again, my bucko, I'll tear you up in little bits."

"I'll play no tricks," replied Smith. "How can I? For my own sake, I can't risk you being caught. You're making me do this against my will, but nobody will believe that if they catch me doing it. I promise to do my best to land you where no one will see you. It shouldn't be hard. In four or five hours we'll be close to the land, and you'll see the lights of Ramsgate on one side and Deal on the other. In between there oughtn't to be many lights showing, and we'll run close inshore where it's darkest and anchor. Then I'll row you ashore in the dinghy, and after that it'll be up to you."

"Get on with it, then," said Lichtensteiger, and Smith trimmed the *Kate's* sails to the northerly wind and settled down to steer the compass course he had decided on. The yacht slipped through the darkness with scarcely a sound. Smith steered and said nothing, while Lichtensteiger looked at the scattered lights of the shipping which dotted the blackness around him and was silent too.

At the end of an hour Lichtensteiger yawned and stretched himself. "Beats me," he said, "how in hell you can tell where you're going to." And Smith said, "It's easy enough, when you know how."

At the end of the second hour Lichtensteiger said, "Gee, this is slow. Deader'n mud. How long now before we get there?" And Smith replied, "About three hours. Why don't you sleep. I'll wake you in time."

Lichtensteiger said, "Nothing doing. Don't you kid yourself. I'm keeping both eyes wide open, constant and regular. I've got 'em on you. Don't forget it either!"

Another hour went by before Lichtensteiger spoke again. He said, "What's that light in front there? The bright one that keeps on going in and out."

"Lighthouse," said Smith. "That's the South Foreland light. I'm steering for it. The lights of Deal will show up to the right of it presently, and then we'll pick out a dark patch of coast somewhere to the right of that again and I'll steer in for it."

By 2 A.M. the land was close ahead, a low black line looming against the lesser blackness of the sky. "Looks quiet enough here," said Lichtensteiger. "Just about right for our little job, I reckon. How about it?"

"Right," said Smith, sounding overside with the lead-line. "Four fathoms. We'll anchor here." He ran the *Kate* into the wind, lowered the jib and let go his anchor with a rattle and a splash.

"Cut out that flaming racket," hissed Lichtensteiger. "Trying to give the show away, are you, or what? You watch your step, damn you."

"You watch yours," said Smith, drawing the dinghy alongside. "Get in carefully or you'll upset."

"You get in first," replied Lichtensteiger. "Take hold of my two bags and then I'll get in after. And you want to take pains we don't upset. If we do, there'll be a nasty accident—to your neck! I guess I can wring it for you as quick under water as I can here. You watch out now and go slow. You haven't done with me yet, don't you kid yourself."

"No, not yet," said Smith. "I'll put you on shore all right. I'll promise that. It's all I can do under the circumstances; but, considering everything, I think it ought to be enough. I hope so, anyhow. Get in now and we'll go."

Smith rowed the dinghy towards the shore. Presently the boat grounded on the sand and Lichtensteiger jumped out. He looked around him for a while and listened intently; but, except for the sound of the little waves breaking and the distant lights of the town, there was nothing to be heard or seen. Then, "All right," said Lichtensteiger. And Smith said nothing. He pushed off from the beach and rowed away silently into the darkness.

Lichtensteiger laughed. He turned and walked inland with a suitcase in each hand. He felt the sand under his feet give way to shingle, the shingle to turf, and the turf to a hard road surface. Lichtensteiger laughed again. It amused him to think that the business of getting himself unnoticed into England should prove, after all, to be so ridiculously easy. He turned to the left and walked rapidly for half a mile before he came to a fork in the road and a signpost. It was too dark for him to see the sign; but he stacked his suitcases against the post and climbing on them struck a match. He read: "Calais—1 1/2."

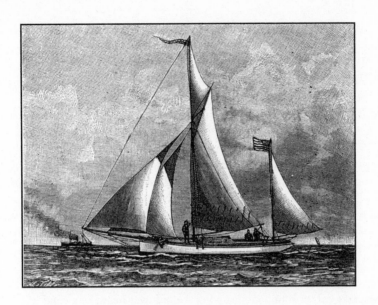

A CIGAR CAT

W. L. ALDEN

About forty years ago, said Captain Foster, settling himself comfortably in his arm-chair and taking a long pull at his pipe, I came
across one of the curiousest chaps that ever I was shipmates with. I was
before the mast in the old *Hendrick Hudson,* of the Black X line, and
she was about the leakiest old tub sailing the Western ocean. This man
I am speaking of came aboard about half an hour before we warped out
of London Dock, clean and sober, which was an unusual thing in those
days. He was a tall, lean, wiry fellow, with a shifty sort of look in his
eye. He carried a big canvas bag of dunnage on his shoulder, and in one
hand he had another bag that must have had some sort of frame inside
of it, for it was pretty near square in shape. I was in the fo'c's'le when he
came down and hove his bags into an empty bunk and sat down on my
chest to rest a bit.

"What might you have in that there bag?" says I, in a friendly sort of way.

"I've got my best friend there," says the chap.

"Then," says I, "suppose we have the cork out of him before the other chaps notice it. I'm everlastingly thirsty this morning."

"My friend ain't no bloomin' bottle," says the fellow, "and he ain't no sort of use to a thirsty man. But if you want to see him, here goes."

With that he opened the bag and hauled out a tremendous big black cat, who licked his face, and then curled up in the bunk and went to sleep as sudden as if he had just come below after twenty-four hours on deck.

"That," says the man, "is an old shipmate of mine, and I never goes to sea without him. He's a cigar cat, that's what he is; and you'll see what he can do to make a man comfortable, if you keep dark about his being aboard, so that the old man and the mates don't get a sight of him."

"Well!" said I. "Having been to sea, man and boy, for twenty years, I've seen some queer things; but this is the first time I ever knew a sailorman to carry a cat with him, and the first time I ever heard of a cigar cat."

"Live and learn," says the chap. "That's what Elexander the Great here has done. There was a time when he didn't know no more about tobacco than a baby, and now he knows where to find cigars, and how to bring 'em to me on the quiet. You keep mum about Elexander, and if the old man or either of the mates smokes cigars you'll have one of them now and again, and then you'll understand what a cigar cat is."

Well, we went on deck, leaving Elexander in the bunk, and as there was a lot of work to do, I didn't see any more of him till we knocked off for supper. We'd chose watches by that time, and the fellow with the cat, whose name was Harry, was with me in the starboard watch. The men naturally noticed that there was a cat in Harry's bunk, but they didn't take any interest in him. Harry brought out a bottle and invited all hands to have a tot, and then asked them not to say anything about there being a cat in the fo'c's'le. He had a pleasant kind of way with him, and the bottle was pretty near full, so we all promised not to let it be known aft that we had a cat for'ard.

For the next three or four days Elexander kept himself below all day, and didn't show up on deck until dark, or pretty near it. Then he'd come up for a little fresh air, and would generally sit on the lee cathead and meditate for an hour or two. I reckoned that he chose the cathead on account of the name of it, and fancied that it was meant for his convenience. Later on in the night he would take exercise by climbing up the forestay and having a little game with his tail in the foretop. He knew just as well as anybody that he wasn't to be seen by the officers, and he took such good precautions that not a soul outside of the fo'c's'le knew of his existence.

One evening, just after eight bells, when our side had gone below, Harry says to Elexander, "Now, old man, go and fetch me a cigar." The cat looked at him for a minute and then darted up the ladder out of the fo'c's'le and we didn't see him for the next ten minutes. I would have turned in before that time, but Harry whispered to me to wait and see what Elexander would do. Pretty soon back comes the cat, and, if you'll believe it, he carried a big cigar in his mouth—just such a one as the old man smoked. Harry took it, and patted the cat, and lighted the cigar. He took three or four pulls, and then passed it on to me, and so we smoked it turn and turn about, and it was prime.

"How on earth," says I, "did you ever learn that cat to steal cigars?"

"Never you mind," says Harry; "I done it, and that's all about it. Elexander has got a nose for cigars that no regular tobacconist ever dreamed of having. Put him aboard a ship where cigars are smoked, and he'll find out where they are kept, and he'll steal 'em, provided, of course, they ain't locked up or kept in a chest with a lid too heavy for him to lift. He's found out where the old man's cigars are, and unless he has the bad luck to get caught, he'll bring me a cigar every night till we sight Sandy Hook. I wouldn't go to sea without Elexander, not if you was to offer me double wages and all night below. The only fault with him is that his mouth ain't big enough to hold more than one cigar at a time. If he only had a mouth like the second mate, he'd bring me a dozen cigars a day—so long as the supply lasted."

Now, I'm telling you the cold truth when I tell you that Elexander brought Harry a cigar every night regular from that time on—that is to say, for the next three weeks or so. Nobody ever caught him on the quarter-deck during that time, and the officers never dreamed that there was a cat aboard. But one night, when we were coming up with the Banks, the old man caught a sight of Elexander bolting out of his room with a cigar in his mouth, and he called the steward and says to him: "Steward! What do you let the cat into my room for?"

"Cat, sah!" says the steward. "There ain't no sort nor description of cat aboard this vessel. Our cat fell overboard and was drownded just before we sailed, and I didn't have time to go ashore and get another."

"What do you mean by telling me that," says the old man, "when I see with my own eyes a black cat coming out of my room with a mouse, or something else, in his mouth?"

"Beggin' your pahdon, sah, all I can say is that there ain't no suspicion nor insinuation of a cat aboard here."

The steward was a nigger that was fond of using big words, but he always told the truth, except, of course, to passengers, and the captain couldn't very well help believing him. So he said no more about the cat, but went into his room, feeling considerable worried, as any man naturally would at seeing a black cat where he was sure that there wasn't any real cat. But he was a cool-headed man, was old Captain Barbour, and the next morning he made up his mind that he had seen a shadow and mistook it for a cat.

The next night Harry was sitting on the windlass, smoking one of the old man's cigars, which was a risky thing to do, for it wasn't dark yet, and there was always a chance that the old man might happen to come for'ard and catch him. Elexander was sitting alongside of Harry, rubbing his head against the man's leg and purring like a steam winch. All of a sudden Harry catches sight of the old man about amidships, coming for'ard with his usual quick step. Now, Harry didn't want to waste that cigar by heaving it overboard, for he had only smoked about half an inch of it. So he shoves it athwartship into Elexander's mouth and tells him to go below. But Elexander either didn't understand exactly what Harry said, or else he preferred to stop on deck; so he runs out on the cathead, and sits there as usual with the smoke curling up from the lighted end of the cigar.

"Where did that cat come from?" says the old man, as soon as he caught sight of Elexander.

"Cat, sir!" says Harry. "I haven't seen no cat aboard this ship."

"Do you mean to tell me," says the captain, "that there ain't a cat sitting at this identical minute on the port cathead?"

"Very sorry, sir," says Harry, who could be particular polite when he wanted to be, "I can't see no cat nowhere."

Just then the captain caught sight of the smoke curling up from Elexander's cigar, and that knocked him silly.

Harry said that the old man turned as white as a cotton skysail. He said to himself in a curious sort of way, as if he was talking in his sleep: "A cat, sitting up and smoking a cigar!—a cat smoking a cigar!—smoking a cigar!" And then he turned and went aft, walking as if his knees were sprung, and catching hold of the rail to steady himself. If ever a man was scared it was Captain Barbour, and it was probably the first time in his life that he really knew what it was to be scared all the way through.

The captain went up to the mate, who was on the quarter-deck, and says he, "Mr. Jones! If I don't live till we get into port, I want you to see my wife and break it to her easy."

"Why, what's the matter, sir?" says Jones. "You're all right, ain't you?"

"I've had an awful warning," says the old man. "What would you say if you'd been seeing cats when there wasn't a cat within a thousand miles?"

"I should say," says Jones, "that it was time for me to knock off rum, and go slow in future. But then you ain't much of a drinking man, and you can't have been seeing things."

"Mr. Jones," says the captain, solemnly, "I've seen a black cat twice since we sailed from London, and the last time that cat was sitting up and smoking a cigar—a cigar as big as the ones I smoke myself. Now, there ain't no cat aboard this ship; and there never was a cat since cats were first invented that smoked cigars. And what's more, as you say yourself, I ain't a man as drinks more than is good for him, especially when I'm at sea. That cat didn't mean drink. It meant something a sight worse; and I know, just as well as I stand here, that I'm not long for this world."

"You go below, sir, and try to sleep," said the mate. "And if I was you I'd overhaul the medicine chest, and take a good stiff dose of something."

"There's medicine for a lot of things in that chest," says the captain; "but there ain't no sort of medicine for black cats that sits up and smokes cigars. Salts and laudanum, and porous plasters wouldn't do me any good, not if I was to take them all at once. No, sir! I'm a doomed man, and that's all there is about it."

After the old man had gone aft Harry jumped up, and, being pretty mad at Elexander for stopping on deck after he had been told to go below, he lays hold of him by the tail and yanks him off the cathead and tosses him down the fo'c's'le ladder, giving him a few heavy cuffs over the head at the same time. Now, sir, I don't know if you are well acquainted with cats, but if you're not, I can tell you one curious thing about them. You can hit a cat, and hit him hard, and you can kick him clean across a room, and you can heave cold water on him, and if he judges that it's good policy for him to keep friends with you, he'll overlook it. But a cat always draws the line at his tail; he won't allow you to take the least liberty with his tail, and if you do he'll never forgive you. It hurts a cat's self-respect to have his tail meddled with, and a cat has a heap of self-respect.

Now, when Harry hauled Elexander off that cathead by his tail he made the biggest mistake of his life. Elexander couldn't have overlooked it with justice to himself, even if he had wanted to. When Harry went below there wasn't any Elexander in his bunk, and he couldn't find him nowhere. The next day he found him, but he found at the same time that Elexander wouldn't have anything to do with him. The cat had selected the boy Jim, who was in the port watch, for his new master, and he was snuggled up against him in his bunk, and letting on to be everlastingly fond of him. Harry tried to pick the cat up and take him over to his side of the fo'c's'le, but Elexander swore at him in a way that any second mate would have envied, and when Harry put a hand on him, he bit him clean to the bone. It was all over between Harry and Elexander, and after a while Harry gave up all hope of ever making up the quarrel.

Of course, Harry and me didn't have any more cigars. Elexander wouldn't have brought one to Harry not if there had been hundreds of cigars lying about the deck. Jim said that Elexander didn't bring him any, and he pretended to be astonished that Harry should think such a thing possible as that a cat should sneak cigars; but then Jim was an able liar, and what he said didn't convince either Harry or me. We watched Jim pretty close, but we couldn't catch him smoking anything but his pipe, and we watched Elexander, but we never saw him bringing any cigars for' ard. All the same, he brought them, and Jim, of course, had the benefit of them.

I noticed after a while that Jim got into a way of being missing some time in the course of the dog-watches, and Elexander was generally missing at the same time. Neither of them could be found in the fo'c's'le, and when I spoke of the matter to Harry he calculated that Jim had been sent for by the mate to clean out his room, the mate having a way of putting Jim at that job at all odd times.

But one day I saw a little whiff of smoke sailing up from the foretop, and I naturally thought that I had caught Jim out. So I went aloft, and when I got into the top there I found Jim, sure enough, with Elexander sleeping by the side of him. But Jim had his pipe in his hand, and there wasn't any sign of a cigar to be seen. He let on that he had come up there so as to have a quiet half-hour while he read over an old letter from his mother, and that was all I could get out of him.

One of the men—a chap from Nova Scotia, and a pretty mean one even at that—said one day that he had found Elexander alone in the foretop with the ashes of a cigar sprinkled around the place where he was lying. The chap said that he believed the cat smoked cigars, and another chap— an Irishman—who told the truth every now and then when he was feeling good and fit, said that he had seen Elexander more than once with a cigar in his mouth, though he had always calculated that it was the quality of the rum that he drank at his boarding-house in the Highway that made him see such a curious sight. Gradually it got round among the crew that the cat was a smoker, and they used to try him with pipes. Of course, Elexander wasn't going to come down to a pipe. He was a sight too aristocratic for that, but the men stuck to their theory that Elexander smoked cigars, and the wonder was where he got hold of them.

Captain Barbour had been feeling very low ever since he saw Elexander sitting on the cathead. He hardly ever swore at the men, and when he did it didn't seem to do him any real good. Once on a Sunday, when I was at the wheel, I saw him overhauling a prayer-book, and when a skipper comes to doing that it looks pretty bad for him. The captain had made up his mind that he had had a warning, and that he wouldn't live to see New York, and, of course, he didn't feel very cheerful at the prospect, partly because he wanted to see New York and his wife and the other captains of the Black X. line again, and partly because he hadn't the least idea where he would bring up if he slipped his cable.

One afternoon, in the first dog-watch, the old man, who had been walking the quarterdeck with the mate, suddenly stopped, and catching the mate by the arm said, "There's that cat again! He's sitting up in the foretop and smoking, just as he was doing the last time I saw him. This is the end of me, Mr. Jones."

The mate looked aloft and there he saw Elexander, sitting on the edge of the top and looking down around as if he was looking for a sail on the horizon. He didn't have any cigar in his mouth, but there wasn't the least doubt that smoke was drifting gently out of the top, there being just a breath of wind from the southward.

"I see him, sir," said the mate. "He's a sure enough cat, and if he's smoking I'll learn him what the regulations of this ship are." So saying the mate jumps into the rigging and runs up to the foretop in next to no time, he being an active man and a first-class sailor. The next thing was a yell from the foretop, and then we could see the mate holding Jim by the scruff of the neck and lecturing to him on the evils of smoking, there happening to be a rope's end in the top that was just the thing for lecturing purposes.

You never saw a happier man than Captain Barbour when the mate came down from aloft with Jim and introduced him to the old man as the real smoker. The captain cussed Jim as cheerful as ever he had cussed in his best days, and before he had got through he made the boy confess that the cat had been stealing cigars and bringing them for'ard. Jim swore that the cat never brought any to him and that they all went to Harry, who owned the cat and had trained him to sneak cigars, and he pretended that he had accidentally found one under a bunk in the fo'c's'le, and had gone into the top to smoke it on the quiet, thinking that it wouldn't be right to hand it over to Harry for fear of encouraging him and the cat in stealing cigars. Naturally nobody believed what Jim said, but, having already had his licking from the mate, the old man let him off with a cuff or two, and passed the word for Harry to come aft.

But he couldn't get anything out of Harry either. Harry swore that he had never laid eyes on the cat until four or five nights before, and that he never dreamed that Elexander stole cigars. "The cat belongs to that there boy Jim," said Harry, "and you can see for yourself, sir, that he won't have anything to say to me, if you call him aft."

The old man sent for Jim again and ordered him to bring the cat on to the quarter-deck, which Jim accordingly did, holding the cat in his arms and petting it while Elexander licked the boy's face. Harry went up to the cat and spoke to him fair and polite, but Elexander only swore at him and tried to hit him in the eye.

"You see, sir," said Harry, "how it is. Ain't it plain enough whose cat that is? As for me, I wouldn't allow no cat of no kind to come within a mile of me if I could help it. They're nasty, treacherous beasts, and I never see a cat yet who wasn't a thief."

Well, the upshot of it was that Jim got a first-class licking for lying about his cat, and another for training the cat to steal the old man's cigars, and he got thirty shillings stopped from his wages to pay for the cigars that Elexander had stole, and he was ordered to heave the cat overboard. He'd have done so then and there, but the mate being a sensible man, and as good a sailorman as ever trod a deck, sort of interceded for the cat, arguing that there was nothing in the world half so unlucky as drowning a cat. So the old man finally agreed that the cat should be put down in the run, with a pannikin of water, and told that unless he worked his passage by catching rats he might starve. And starve he did—not because there weren't plenty of rats in the run, but because Elexander was that aristocratic and high-toned that he made up his mind to starve sooner than turn to and work his passage. When we got to New York I saw the steward come on deck with the remains of a cat in his hand, and then I knew that Elexander wouldn't never steal anybody's cigars no more.

THE FLOATING BEACON

ANONYMOUS

One night we were on a voyage from Bergen to Christiansand in a small sloop. Our captain suspected that he had approached too near the Norwegian coast, though he could not discern any land, and the wind blew with such violence that we were in momentary dread of being driven upon a lee-shore.

We had endeavored, for more than an hour, to keep the vessel away; but our efforts proved unavailing, and we soon found that we could scarcely hold our own. A clouded sky, a hazy atmosphere, and irregular showers of sleety rain combined to deepen the obscurity of night, and nothing whatever was visible, except the sparkling of the distant waves, when their tops happened to break into a wreath of foam. The sea ran very high, and sometimes broke over the deck so furiously that the men were obliged to hold by the logging, lest they should be carried away.

Our captain was a person of timid and irresolute character, and the dangers that environed us made him gradually lose confidence in himself.

He often gave orders and countermanded them in the same moment, all the while taking small quantities of ardent spirits at intervals. Fear and intoxication soon stupefied him completely, and the crew ceased to consult him, or to pay any respect to his authority, in so far as regarded the management of the vessel.

About midnight our mainsail was split, and shortly after we found that the sloop had sprung a leak. We had before shipped a good deal of water through the hatches, and the quantity that now entered from below was so great that we thought she would go down every moment. Our only chance of escape lay in our boat, which was immediately lowered. After we had all got on board of her, except the captain, who stood leaning against the mast, we called to him, requesting that he would follow us without delay.

"How dare you quit the sloop without my permission?" cried he, staggering forwards. "This is not fit weather to go a-fishing. Come back— back with you all!"

"No, no," returned one of the crew; "we don't want to be sent to the bottom for your obstinacy. Bear a hand there, or we'll leave you behind."

"Captain, you are drunk," said another; "you cannot take care of yourself. You must obey *us* now."

"Silence! mutinous villain!" answered the captain. "What are you afraid of? This is a fine breeze—Up mainsail and steer her right in the wind's eye."

The sea knocked the boat so violently and constantly against the side of the sloop, that we feared the former would be injured or upset if we did not immediately row away; but, anxious as we were to preserve our lives, we could not reconcile ourselves to the idea of abandoning the captain, who grew more obstinate the more we attempted to persuade him to accompany us.

At length one of the crew leaped on board the sloop, and having seized hold of him, tried to drag him along by force; but he struggled resolutely, and soon freed himself from the grasp of the seaman, who immediately resumed his place among us, and urged that we should not any longer risk our lives for the sake of a drunkard and a madman. Most of the party declared they were of the same opinion, and began to push off the boat; but I entreated them to make one effort more to induce their infatuated commander to accompany us.

At that moment he came up from the cabin, to which he had descended a little time before, and we immediately perceived that he was more under the influence of ardent spirits than ever. He abused us all in the grossest terms, and threatened his crew with severe punishment, if they did not come on board, and return to their duty. His manner was so violent that no one seemed willing to attempt to constrain him to come on board the boat; and after vainly representing the absurdity of his conduct, and the danger of his situation, we bade him farewell, and rowed away.

The sea ran so high, and had such a terrific appearance, that I almost wished myself in the sloop again. The crew plied the oars in silence, and we heard nothing but the hissing of the enormous billows as they gently rose up, and slowly subsided again, without breaking. At intervals our boat was elevated far above the surface of the ocean, and remained for a few moments trembling upon the pinnacle of a surge, from which it would quietly descend into a gulf so deep and awful that we often thought the dense black mass of waters which formed its sides were on the point of overarching us, and bursting upon our heads. We glided with regular undulations from one billow to another; but every time we sank into the trough of the sea my heart died within me, for I felt as if we were going lower down than we had ever done before, and clung instinctively to the board on which I sat.

Notwithstanding my terrors, I frequently looked towards the sloop. The fragments of her mainsail, which remained attached to the yard, and fluttered in the wind, enabled us to discern exactly where she lay, and showed, by their motion, that she pitched about in a terrible manner. We occasionally heard the voice of her unfortunate commander, calling to us in tones of frantic derision, and by turns vociferating curses and blasphemous oaths, and singing sea-songs with a wild and frightful energy. I sometimes almost wished that the crew would make another effort to save him, but next moment the principle of self-preservation repressed all feelings of humanity, and I endeavored, by closing my ears, to banish the idea of his sufferings from my mind.

After a little while the shivering canvas disappeared, and we heard a tumultuous roaring and bursting of billows, and saw an unusual sparkling of the sea about a quarter of a mile from us. One of the sailors cried out that the sloop was new on her beam ends, and that the noise to which we listened was that of the waves breaking over her.

We could sometimes perceive a large black mass heaving itself up irregularly among the flashing surges, and then disappearing for a few moments, and knew but too well that it was the hull of the vessel. At intervals a shrill and agonized voice uttered some exclamations, but we could not distinguish what they were, and then a long-drawn shriek came across the ocean, which suddenly grew more furiously agitated near the spot where the sloop lay, and in a few moments she sank down, and a black wave formed itself out of the waters that had engulfed her, and swelled gloomily into a magnitude greater than that of the surrounding billows.

The seamen dropped their oars, as if by one impulse, and looked expressively at each other, without speaking a word. Awful forebodings of a fate similar to that of the captain appeared to chill every heart, and to repress the energy that had hitherto excited us to make unremitting exertions for our common safety. While we were in this state of hopeless inaction, the man at the helm called out that he saw a light ahead. We all strained our eyes to discern it, but at the moment the boat was sinking down between two immense waves, one of which closed the prospect, and we remained in breathless anxiety till a rising surge elevated us above the level of the surrounding ocean. A light like a dazzling star then suddenly flashed upon our view, and joyful exclamations burst from every mouth.

"That," cried one of the crew, "must be the floating beacon which our captain was looking out for this afternoon. If we can but gain it, we'll be safe enough yet." This intelligence cheered us all, and the men began to ply the oars with redoubled vigor, while I employed myself in baling out the water that sometimes rushed over the gunnel of the boat when a sea happened to strike her.

An hour's hard rowing brought us so near the lighthouse that we almost ceased to apprehend any further danger; but it was suddenly obscured from our view, and at the same time a confused roaring and dashing commenced at a little distance, and rapidly increased in loudness. We soon perceived a tremendous billow rolling towards us. Its top, part of which had already broke, overhung the base, as if unwilling to burst until we were within the reach of its violence. The man who steered the boat brought her head to the sea, but all to no purpose, for the water rushed furiously over us, and we were completely immersed. I felt the boat swept from under me, and was left struggling and groping about in hopeless desperation for something to catch hold of.

When nearly exhausted, I received a severe blow on the side from a small cask of water which the sea had forced against me. I immediately twined my arms round it, and after recovering myself a little, began to look for the boat, and to call to my companions; but I could not discover any vestige of them, or of the vessel. However, I still had a faint hope that they were in existence, and that the intervention of the billows concealed them from my view. I continued to shout as loud as possible, for the sound of my own voice in some measure relieved me from the feeling of awful and heart-chilling loneliness which my situation inspired; but not even an echo responded to my cries, and, convinced that my comrades had all perished, I ceased looking for them, and pushed towards the beacon in the best manner I could.

A long series of fatiguing exertions brought me close to the side of the vessel which contained it, and I called out loudly, in hopes that those on board might hear me and come to my assistance; but no one appearing, I waited patiently till a wave raised me on a level with the chains, and then caught hold of them, and succeeded in getting on board.

As I did not see any person on deck, I went forwards to the skylight and looked down. Two men were seated below at a table; and a lamp, which was suspended above them, being swung backwards and forwards by the rolling of the vessel, threw its light upon their faces alternately. One seemed agitated with passion, and the other surveyed him with a scornful look. They both talked very loudly, and used threatening gestures, but the sea made so much noise that I could not distinguish what was said. After a little time they started up, and seemed to be on the point of closing and wrestling together, when a woman rushed through a small door and prevented them.

I beat upon the deck with my feet at the same time, and the attention of the whole party was soon transferred to the noise. One of the men immediately came up the cabin stairs, but stopped short on seeing me, as if irresolute whether to advance or hasten below again. I approached him, and told my story in a few words, but instead of making any reply, he went down to the cabin, and began to relate to the others what he had seen. I soon followed him, and easily found my way into the apartment where they all were. They appeared to feel mingled sensations of fear and astonishment at my presence, and it was some time before any of them entered into conversation with me, or afforded those comforts which I stood so much in need of.

After I had refreshed myself with food, and been provided with a Change of clothing, I went upon deck, and surveyed the singular asylum in which Providence had enabled me to take refuge from the fury of the storm. It did not exceed thirty feet long, and was very strongly built, and completely decked over, except at the entrance to the cabin. It had a thick mast at midships, with a large lantern, containing several burners and reflectors, on the top of it; and this could be lowered and hoisted up again as often as required, by means of ropes and pulleys.

The vessel was firmly moored upon an extensive sand-bank, the beacon being intended to warn seamen to avoid a part of the ocean where many lives and vessels had been lost in consequence of the latter running aground. The accommodations below decks were narrow, and of an inferior description; however, I gladly retired to the berth that was allotted me by my entertainers, and fatigue and the rocking of billows combined to lull me into a quiet and dreamless sleep.

Next morning, one of the men, whose name was Angerstoff, came to my bedside, and called me to breakfast in a surly and imperious manner. The others looked coldly and distrustfully when I joined them, and I saw that they regarded me as an intruder and an unwelcome guest. The meal passed without almost any conversation, and I went upon deck whenever it was over. The tempest of the preceding night had in a great measure abated, but the sea still ran very high, and a black mist hovered over it, through which the Norwegian coast, lying at eleven miles distance, could be dimly seen.

I looked in vain for some remains of the sloop or boat. Not a bird enlivened the heaving expanse of waters, and I turned shuddering from the dreary scene, and asked Morvalden, the youngest of the men, when he thought I had any chance of getting ashore. "Not very soon, I'm afraid," returned he. "We are visited once a month by people from yonder land, who are appointed to bring us supply of provisions and other necessaries. They were here only six days ago, so you may count how long it will be before they return. Fishing boats sometimes pass us during fine weather, but we won't have much of that this moon at least."

No intelligence could have been more depressing to me than this. The idea of spending perhaps three weeks in such a place was almost insupportable, and the more so as I could not hasten my deliverance by any exertions of my own, but would be obliged to remain, in a state of inactive suspense, till good fortune, or the regular course of events, afforded me the means of getting ashore. Neither Angerstoff nor Morvalden seemed to sympathize with my distress, or even to care that I should have it in my power to leave the vessel, except in so far as my departure would free them from the expense of supporting me.

They returned indistinct and repulsive answers to all the questions I asked, and appeared anxious to avoid having the least communication with me. During the greater part of the forenoon, they employed themselves in trimming the lamps and cleaning the reflectors, but never conversed any. I easily perceived that a mutual animosity existed between them, but was unable to discover the cause of it. Morvalden seemed to fear Angerstoff, and at the same time to feel a deep resentment towards him, which he did not dare to express. Angerstoff apparently was aware of this, for he behaved to his companion with the undisguised fierceness of determined hate, and openly thwarted him in everything.

Marietta, the female on board, was the wife of Morvalden. She remained chiefly below decks, and attended to the domestic concerns of the vessel. She was rather good-looking, but so reserved and forbidding in her manners that she formed no desirable acquisition to our party, already so heartless and unsociable in its character.

When night approached, after the lapse of a wearisome and monotonous day, I went on deck to see the beacon lighted, and continued walking backwards and forwards till a late hour. I watched the lantern, as it swung from side to side, and flashed upon different portions of the sea alternately, and sometimes fancied I saw men struggling among the billows that tumbled around, and at other times imagined I could discern the white sail of an approaching vessel. Human voices seemed to mingle with the noise of the bursting waves, and I often listened intently, almost in the expectation of hearing articulate sounds.

My mind grew somber as the scene itself, and strange and fearful ideas obtruded themselves in rapid succession. It was dreadful to be chained in the middle of the deep—to be the continual sport of the quiet-less billows—to be shunned as a fatal thing by those who traversed the solitary ocean. Though within sight of the shore, our situation was more dreary than if we had been sailing a thousand miles from it. We felt not the pleasure of moving forwards, nor the hope of reaching port, nor the delights arising from favorable breezes and genial weather. When a billow drove us to one side, we were tossed back again by another; our imprisonment had no variety or definite termination; and the calm and the tempest were alike uninteresting to us.

I felt as if my fate had already become linked with that of those who were on board the vessel. My hopes of being again permitted to mingle with mankind died away, and I anticipated long years of gloom and despair in the company of these repulsive persons into whose hands fate had unexpectedly consigned me.

Angerstoff and Morvalden tended the beacon alternately during the night. The latter had the watch while I remained upon deck. His appearance and manner indicated much perturbation of mind, and he paced hurriedly from side to side, sometimes muttering to himself, and sometimes stopping suddenly to look through the skylight, as if anxious to discover what was going on below. He would then gaze intently upon the heavens, and next moment take out his watch and contemplate the motions of its hands. I did not offer to disturb these reveries, and thought myself altogether unobserved by him, till he suddenly advanced to the spot where I stood, and said, in a loud whisper:

"There's a villain below—a desperate villain—this is true—he is capable of anything—and the woman is as bad as him."

I asked what proof he had of all this.

"Oh, I know it," returned he; "that wretch Angerstoff, whom I once thought my friend, has gained my wife's affections. She has been faithless to me—yes, she has. They both wish I were out of the way. Perhaps they are now planning my destruction. What can I do? It is very terrible to be shut up in such narrow limits with those who hate me, and to have no means of escaping or defending myself from their infernal machinations."

"Why do you not leave the beacon," inquired I, "and abandon your companion and guilty wife?"

"Ah, that is impossible," answered Morvalden; "if I went on shore I would forfeit my liberty. I live here that I may escape the vengeance of the law, which I once outraged for the sake of her who has now withdrawn her love from me. What ingratitude! Mine is indeed a terrible fate, but I must bear it. And shall I never again wander through the green fields, and climb the rocks that encircle my native place? Are the weary dashings of the sea, and the moanings of the wind, to fill my ears continually, all the while telling me that I am an exile?—a hopeless, despairing exile. But it won't last long," cried he, catching hold of my arm; "they will murder me!—I am sure of it—I never go to sleep without dreaming that Angerstoff has pushed me overboard."

"Your lonely situation and inactive life dispose you to give way to these chimeras," said I; "you must endeavor to resist them. Perhaps things aren't so bad as you suppose."

"This is not a lonely situation," replied Morvalden, in a solemn tone. "Perhaps you will have proof of what I say before you leave us. Many vessels used to be lost here, and a few are wrecked still; and the skeletons and corpses of those who have perished lie all over the sand-bank. Sometimes, at midnight, I have seen crowds of human figures moving backwards and forwards upon the surface of the ocean, almost as far as the eye could reach. I neither knew who they were, nor what they did there. When watching the lantern alone, I often hear a number of voices talking together, as it were, under the waves; and I twice caught the very words they uttered, but I cannot repeat them—they dwell incessantly in my memory, but my tongue refuses to pronounce them, or to explain to others what they meant."

"Do not let your senses be imposed upon by a distempered imagination," said I; "there is no reality in the things you have told me."

"Perhaps my mind occasionally wanders a little, for it has a heavy burden upon it," returned Morvalden. "I have been guilty of a dreadful crime. Many that now lie in the deep below us might start up and accuse me of what I am just going to reveal to you. One stormy night, shortly after I began to take charge of this beacon, while watching on deck, I fell into a profound sleep. I know not how long it continued, but I was awakened by horrible shouts and cries. I started up, and instantly perceived that all the lamps in the lantern were extinguished.

"It was very dark, and the sea raged furiously; but notwithstanding all this, I observed a ship aground on the bank, a little way from me, her sails fluttering in the wind, and the waves breaking over her with violence. Half frantic with horror, I ran down to the cabin for a taper, and lighted the lamps as fast as possible. The lantern, when hoisted to the top of the mast, threw a vivid glare on the surrounding ocean, and showed me the vessel disappearing among the billows. Hundreds of people lay gasping in the water near her. Men, women, and children writhed together in agonizing struggles, and uttered soul-harrowing cries; and their countenances, as they gradually stiffened under the hand of death, were all turned towards me with glassy stare, while the lurid expression of their glistening eyes upbraided me with having been the cause of their untimely end.

"Never shall I forget these looks. They haunt me wherever I am—asleep and awake—night and day. I have kept this tale of horror secret till now, and do not know if I shall ever have courage to relate it again. The masts of the vessel projected above the surface of the sea for several months after she was lost, as if to keep me in recollection of the night in which so many human creatures perished, in consequence of my neglect and carelessness. Would to God I had no memory! I sometimes think I am getting mad. The past and present are equally dreadful to me; and I dare not anticipate the future."

I felt a sort of superstitious dread steal over me, while Morvalden related his story, and we continued walking the deck in silence till the period of his watch expired. I then went below, and took refuge in my berth, though I was but little inclined for sleep. The gloomy ideas and dark forebodings expressed by Morvalden weighed heavily upon my mind, without my knowing why; and my situation, which had at first seemed only dreary and depressing, began to have something indefinitely terrible in its aspect.

Next day, when Morvalden proceeded as usual to put the beacon in order, he called upon Angerstoff to come and assist him, which the latter peremptorily refused. Morvalden then went down to the cabin, where his companion was, and requested to know why his orders were not obeyed.

"Because I hate trouble," replied Angerstoff. "I am master here," said Morvalden, "and have been intrusted with the direction of everything. Do not attempt to trifle with me."

"Trifle with you!" exclaimed Angerstoff, looking contemptuously. "No, no, I am no trifler; and I advise you to walk upstairs again, lest I prove this to your cost."

"Why, husband," cried Marietta, "I believe there are no bounds to your laziness. You make this young man toil from morning to night, and take advantage of his good nature in the most shameful manner."

"Peace, infamous woman!" said Morvalden; "I know very well why you stand up in his defense; but I'll put a stop to the intimacy that exists between you. Go to your room instantly! You are my wife, and shall obey me." "Is this usage to be borne?" exclaimed Marietta. "Will no one step forward to protect me from his violence?" "Insolent fellow!" cried Angerstorff, "don't presume to insult my mistress."

"Mistress!" repeated Morvalden. "This to my face!" and struck him a severe blow.

Angerstorff sprung forward, with the intention of returning it, but I got between them, and prevented him. Marietta then began to shed tears, and applauded the generosity her paramour had evinced in sparing her husband, who immediately went upon deck, without speaking a word, and hurriedly resumed the work that had engaged his attention previous to the quarrel.

Neither of the two men seemed at all disposed for a reconciliation, and they had no intercourse during the whole day, except angry and revengeful looks. I frequently observed Marietta in deep consultation with Angerstoff, and easily perceived that the subject of debate had some relation to her injured husband, whose manner evinced much alarm and anxiety, although he endeavored to look calm and cheerful. He did not make his appearance at meals, but spent all his time upon deck. Whenever Angerstoff accidentally passed him, he shrank back with an expression of dread, and intuitively, as it were, caught hold of a rope, or any other object to which he could cling.

The day proved a wretched and fearful one to me, for I momentarily expected that some terrible affray would occur on board, and that I would be implicated in it. I gazed upon the surrounding sea almost without intermission, ardently hoping that some boat might approach near enough to afford me an opportunity of quitting the horrid and dangerous abode in which I was imprisoned.

It was Angerstoff's watch on deck till midnight; and as I did not wish to have any communication with him, I remained below. At twelve o'clock Morvalden got up and relieved him, and he came down to the cabin, and soon after retired to his berth. Believing, from this arrangement, that they had no hostile intentions, I lay down in bed with composure, and fell asleep.

It was not long before a noise overhead awakened me. I started up, and listened intently. The sound appeared to be that of two persons scuffling together, for a successsion of irregular footsteps beat the deck, and I could hear violent blows given at intervals. I got out of my berth, and entered the cabin, where I found Marietta standing alone, with a lamp in her hand.

"Do you hear that?" cried I.

"Hear what?" returned she; "I have had a dreadful dream—I am all trembling."

"Is Angerstoff below?" demanded I.

"No—yes, I mean," said Marietta. "Why do you ask that? He went upstairs."

"Your husband and he are fighting. We must part them instantly."

"How can that be?" answered Marietta; "Angerstoff is asleep."

"Asleep! Didn't you say he went upstairs?"

"I don't know," returned she; "I am hardly awake yet—Let us listen for a moment."

Everything was still for a few seconds; then a voice shrieked out, "Ah! that knife! you are murdering me! Draw it out! No help! Are you done? Now—now—now!" A heavy body fell suddenly along the deck, and some words were spoken in a faint tone, but the roaring of the sea prevented me from hearing what they were.

I rushed up the cabin stairs, and tried to push open the folding-doors at the head of them, but they resisted my utmost efforts. I knocked violently and repeatedly to no purpose.

"Some one is killed," cried I. "The person who barred these doors on the outside is guilty."

"I know nothing of that," returned Marietta. "We can't be of any use now.—Come here again!—how dreadfully quiet it is. My God!—a drop of blood has fallen through the skylight.—What faces are yon looking down upon us?—But this lamp is going out.—We must be going through the water at a terrible rate—how it rushes past us!—I am getting dizzy.—Do you hear these bells ringing? and strange voices—"

The cabin doors were suddenly burst open, and Angerstoff next moment appeared before us, crying out, "Morvalden has fallen overboard. Throw a rope to him!—he will be drowned." His hands and dress were marked with blood, and he had a frightful look of horror and confusion.

"You are a murderer!" exclaimed I, almost involuntarily.

"How do you know that?" said he, staggering back; "I'm sure you never saw—"

"Hush, hush," cried Marietta to him; "are you mad? Speak again!—What frightens you?—Why don't you run and help Morvalden?"

"Has anything happened to him?" inquired Angerstoff, with a gaze of consternation.

"You told us he had fallen overboard," returned Marietta; "must my husband perish?"

"Give me some water to wash my hands," said Angerstoff, growing deadly pale, and catching hold of the table for support.

I now hastened upon deck, but Morvalden was not there. I then went to the side of the vessel, and put my hands on the gunwale, while I leaned over, and looked downwards. On taking them off, I found them marked with blood. I grew sick at heart, and began to identify myself with Angerstoff the murderer.

The sea, the beacon, and the sky, appeared of a sanguine hue, and I thought I heard the dying exclamations of Morvalden sounding a hundred fathom below me, and echoing through the caverns of the deep. I advanced to the cabin door, intending to descend the stairs, but found that some one had fastened it firmly on the inside. I felt convinced that I was intentionally shut out, and a cold shuddering pervaded my frame. I covered my face with my hands, not daring to look around; for it seemed as if I was excluded from the company of the living, and doomed to be the associate of the spirits of drowned and murdered men.

After a little time, I began to walk hastily backwards and forwards; but the light of the lantern happened to flash on a stream of blood that ran along the deck, and I could not summon up resolution to pass the spot where it was a second time. The sky looked black and threatening—the sea had a fierceness in its sound and motions—and the wind swept over its bosom with melancholy sighs. Everything was somber and ominous; and I looked in vain for some object that would, by its soothing aspect, remove the dark impressions which crowded upon my mind.

While standing near the bows of the vessel, I saw a hand and arm rise slowly behind the stern, and wave from side to side. I started back as far as I could go in horrible affright, and looked again, expecting to behold the entire spectral figure of which I supposed they formed a part. But nothing more was visible. I struck my eyes till the light flashed from them, in hopes that my senses had been imposed upon by distempered vision. However, it was in vain, for the hand still motioned me to advance, and I rushed forwards with wild desperation, and caught hold of it.

I was pulled along a little way notwithstanding the resistance I made, and soon discovered a man stretched along the stern-cable, and clinging to it in a convulsive manner. It was Morvalden. He raised his head feebly, and said something, but I could only distinguish the words, "murdered—overboard—reached this rope—terrible death."

I stretched out my arms to support him, but at that moment the vessel plunged violently, and he was shaken off the cable, and dropped among the waves. He floated for an instant, and then disappeared under the keel.

I seized the first rope I could find, and threw one end of it over the stern, and likewise flung some planks into the sea, thinking that the unfortunate Morvalden might still retain strength enough to catch hold of them if they came within his reach. I continued on the watch for a considerable time, but at last abandoned all hopes of saving him, and made another attempt to get down to the cabin. The doors were now unfastened, and I opened them without any difficulty.

The first thing I saw on going below, was Angerstoff stretched along the floor, and fast asleep. His torpid look, flushed countenance, and uneasy respiration, convinced me that he had taken a large quantity of ardent spirits. Marietta was in her own apartment. Even the presence of a murderer appeared less terrible than the frightful solitariness of the deck, and I lay down upon a bench determining to spend the remainder of the night there. The lamp that hung from the roof soon went out, and left me in total darkness.

Imagination began to conjure up a thousand appalling forms, and the voice of Angerstoff, speaking in his sleep, filled my ears at intervals—"Hoist up the beacon!—the lamps won't burn—horrible!—they contain blood instead of oil. Is that a boat coming?—Yes, yes, I hear the oars.

Damnation!—why is that corpse so long of sinking?—if it doesn't go down soon they'll find me out. How terribly the wind blows!—we are driving ashore—See! see! Morvalden is swimming after us—how he writhes in the water!"

Marietta now rushed from her room, with a light in her hand, and seizing Angerstoff by the arm, tried to awake him. He soon rose up with chattering teeth and shivering limbs, and was on the point of speaking, but she prevented him, and he staggered away to his berth, and lay down in it.

Next morning, when I went upon deck, after a short and perturbed sleep, I found Marietta dashing water over it, that she might efface all vestige of the transactions of the preceding night. Angerstoff did not make his appearance till noon, and his looks were ghastly and agonized. He seemed stupefied with horror, and sometimes entirely lost all perception of the things around him for a considerable time. He suddenly came close up to me, and demanded, with a bold air, but quivering voice, what I had meant by calling him a murderer?

"Why, that you are one," replied I, after a pause,

"Beware what you say," returned he fiercely,—"you cannot escape my power now—I tell you, sir, Morvalden fell overboard."

"Whence, then, came that blood that covered the deck?" inquired I.

He grew pale, and then cried, "You lie—you lie infernally—there was none!"

"I saw it," said I. "I saw Morvalden himself—long after midnight. He was clinging to the stern-cable, and said—"

"Ha, ha, ha—devils!—curses!" exclaimed Angerstoff. "Did you hear me dreaming?—I was mad last night—Come, come, come!—We shall tend the beacon together—Let us make friends, and don't be afraid, for you'll find me a good fellow in the end."

He now forcibly shook hands with me, and then hurried down to the cabin.

In the afternoon, while sitting on deck, I discerned a boat far off, but I determined to conceal this from Angerstoff and Marietta, lest they should use some means to prevent its approach. I walked carelessly about, casting a glance upon the sea occasionally, and meditating how I could best take advantage of the means of deliverance which I had in prospect. After the lapse of an hour, the boat was not more than half a mile distant from us, but she suddenly changed her course, and bore away towards the shore.

I immediately shouted, and waved a handkerchief over my head, as signals for her to return. Angerstoff rushed from the cabin, and seized my arm, threatening at the same time to push me overboard if I attempted to hail her again. I disengaged myself from his grasp, and dashed him violently from me. The noise brought Marietta upon deck, who immediately perceived the cause of the affray, and cried:

"Does the wretch mean to make his escape? For Godsake, prevent the possibility of that!"

"Yes, yes," returned Angerstoff; "he never shall leave the vessel—He had as well take care, lest I do to him what I did to—"

"To Morvalden, I suppose you mean," said I.

"Well, well, speak it out," replied he ferociously; "there is no one here to listen to your damnable falsehoods, and I'll not be fool enough to give you an opportunity of uttering them elsewhere. I'll strangle you the next time you tell these lies about—"

"Come," interrupted Marietta, "don't be uneasy—the boat will soon be far enough way—If he wants to give you the slip, he must leap overboard."

I was irritated and disappointed beyond measure at the failure of the plan of escape I had formed, but thought it most prudent to conceal my feelings. I now perceived the rashness and bad consequences of my bold assertions respecting the murder of Morvalden; for Angerstoff evidently thought that his personal safety, and even his life, would be endangered, if I ever found an opportunity of accusing and giving evidence against him.

All my motions were now watched with double vigilance. Marietta and her paramour kept upon deck by turns during the whole day, and the latter looked over the surrounding ocean, through a glass, at intervals, to discover if any boat or vessel was approaching us. He often muttered threats as he walked past me, and, more than once, seemed waiting for an opportunity to push me overboard. Marietta and he frequently whispered together, and I always imagined I heard my name mentioned in the course of these conversations.

I now felt completely miserable, being satisfied that Angerstoff was bent upon my destruction. I wandered, in a state of fearful circumspection, from one part of the vessel to the other, not knowing how to secure myself from his designs. Every time he approached me, my heart palpitated dreadfully; and when night came on, I was agonized with terror, and could not remain in one spot, but hurried backwards and forwards between the cabin and the deck, looking wildly from side to side, and momentarily expecting to feel a cold knife entering my vitals.

My forehead began to burn, and my eyes dazzled; I became acutely sen-
sitive, and the slightest murmur, or the faintest breath of wind, set my whole
frame in a state of uncontrollable vibration. At first, I sometimes thought of
throwing myself into the sea; but I soon acquired such an intense feeling of
existence, that the mere idea of death was horrible to me.

Shortly after midnight I lay down in my berth, almost exhausted by the
harrowing emotions that had careered through my mind during the past
day. I felt a strong desire to sleep, yet dared not indulge myself; soul and
body seemed at war. Every noise excited my imagination, and scarcely a
minute passed, in the course of which I did not start up and look around.
Angerstoff paced the deck overhead, and when the sound of his footsteps
accidentally ceased at any time, I grew deadly sick at heart, expecting that
he was silently coming to murder me.

At length I thought I heard some one near my bed. I sprung from it,
and, having seized a bar of iron that lay on the floor, rushed into the cabin.
I found Angerstoff there, who started back when he saw me, and said:

"What is the matter? Did you think that—I want you to watch the
beacon, that I may have some rest. Follow me upon deck, and I will give
you directions about it."

I hesitated a moment, and then went up the gangway stairs behind him.
We walked forward to the mast together, and he showed how I was to lower
the lantern when any of the lamps happened to go out, and bidding me beware
of sleep, returned to the cabin. Most of my fears forsook me the moment he
disappeared. I felt nearly as happy as if I had been set at liberty, and, for a time,
forgot that my situation had anything painful or alarming connected with it.
Angerstoff resumed his station in about three hours, and I again took refuge
in my berth, where I enjoyed a short but undisturbed slumber.

Next day while I was walking the deck, and anxiously surveying the
expanse of ocean around, Angerstoff requested me to come down to the
cabin. I obeyed his summons, and found him there. He gave me a book,
saying it was very entertaining, and would serve to amuse me during my
idle hours; and then went above, shutting the doors carefully behind him.
I was struck with his behavior, but felt no alarm, for Marietta sat at work
near me, apparently unconscious of what had passed. I began to peruse
the volume I held in my hand, and found it so interesting that I paid little
attention to anything else, till the dashing of oars struck my ear.

I sprang from my chair, with the intention of hastening upon deck,
but Marietta stopped me, saying, "It is of no use—the gangway doors are
fastened."

Notwithstanding this information, I made an attempt to open them, but could not succeed. I was now convinced, by the percussion against the vessel, that a boat lay alongside, and I heard a strange voice addressing Angerstoff. Fired with the idea of deliverance, I leaped upon a table which stood in the middle of the cabin, and tried to push off the skylight, but was suddenly stunned by a violent blow on the back of my head. I staggered back and looked round. Marietta stood close behind me, brandishing an ax, as if in the act of repeating the stroke.

Her face was flushed with rage, and, having seized my arm, she cried, "Come down instantly, accursed villain! I know you want to betray us, but may we all go to the bottom if you find a chance of doing so."

I struggled to free myself from her grasp, but, being in a state of dizziness and confusion, I was unable to effect this, and she soon pulled me to the ground.

At that moment, Angerstoff hurriedly entered the cabin, exclaiming, "What noise is this? Oh, just as I expected! Has that devil—that spy—been trying to get above boards? Why haven't I the heart to dispatch him at once? But there's no time now. The people are waiting—Marietta, come and lend a hand."

They now forced me down upon the floor, and bound me to an iron ring that was fixed in it. This being done, Angerstoff directed his female accomplice to prevent me from speaking, and went up on deck again.

While in this state of bondage, I heard distinctly all that passed without. Some one asked Angerstoff how Morvalden did. "Well, quite well," replied the former; "but he's below, and so sick that he can't see any person." "Strange enough," said the first speaker, laughing. "Is he ill and in good health at the same time? he had as well be overboard as in that condition." "Overboard!" repeated Angerstoff, "what!—how do you mean?—all false!—but listen to me,—Are there any news stirring ashore?" "Why," said the stranger, "the chief talk there just now is about a curious thing that happened this morning.

"A dead man was found upon the beach, and they suspect, from the wounds on his body, that he hasn't got fair play. They are making a great noise about it, and Government means to send out a boat, with an officer on board, who is to visit all the shipping round this, that he may ascertain if any of them has lost a man lately. 'Tis a dark business; but they'll get to the bottom of it, I warrant ye. Why, you look as pale as if you knew more about this matter than you choose to tell."

"No, no, no," returned Angerstoff; "I never hear of a murder but I think of a friend of mine who—but I won't detain you, for the sea is getting up—we'll have a blowy night, I'm afraid."

"So you don't want any fish to-day?" cried the stranger. "Then I'll be off—Good morning, good morning. I suppose you'll have the Government boat alongside by-and-by."

I now heard the sound of oars, and supposed, from the conversation having ceased, that the fisherman had departed. Angerstoff came down to the cabin soon after, and released me without speaking a word.

Marietta then approached him, and, taking hold of his arm, said, "Do you believe what that man has told you?"

"Yes, by the eternal hell!" cried he, vehemently; "I suspect I will find the truth of it soon enough."

"My God!" exclaimed she, "what is to become of us?—How dreadful! We are chained here and cannot escape."

"Escape what?" interrupted Angerstoff; "girl, you have lost your senses. Why should we fear the officers of justice? Keep a guard over your tongue."

"Oh," returned Marietta, "I talk without thinking, or understanding my own words; but come upon deck, and let me speak with you there."

They now went up the gangway stairs together, and continued in deep conversation for some time.

Angerstoff gradually became more agitated as the day advanced. He watched upon deck almost without intermission, and seemed irresolute what to do, sometimes sitting down composedly, and at other times hurrying backwards and forwards, with clenched hands and bloodless cheeks. The wind blew pretty fresh from the shore, and there was a heavy swell; and I supposed, from the anxious looks with which he contemplated the sky, that he hoped the threatening aspect of the weather would prevent the government boat from putting out to sea. He kept his glass constantly in his hand, and surveyed the ocean through it in all directions.

At length he suddenly dashed the instrument away, and exclaimed, "God help us! they are coming now!"

Marietta, on hearing this, ran wildly towards him, and put her hands in his, but he pushed her to one side, and began to pace the deck, apparently in deep thought.

After a little time, he started, and cried, "I have it now!—It's the only plan—I'll manage the business—yes, yes—I'll cut the cables, and off we'll go—that's settled!"

He then seized an ax, and first divided the hawser at the bows, and afterwards the one attached to the stern.

The vessel immediately began to drift away, and having no sails or helm to steady her, rolled with such violence that I was dashed from side to side several times. She often swung over so much that I thought she would not regain the upright position, and Angerstoff all the while unconsciously strengthened this belief, by exclaiming, "She will capsize! shift the ballast, or we must go to the bottom!"

In the midst of this, I kept my station upon deck, intently watching the boat, which was still several miles distant. I waited in fearful expectation, thinking that every new wave against which we were impelled would burst upon our vessel and overwhelm us, while our pursuers were too far off to afford any assistance. The idea of perishing when on the point of being saved was inexpressibly agonizing.

As the day advanced, the hopes I had entertained of the boat making up with us gradually diminished. The wind blew violently, and we drifted along at a rapid rate, and the weather grew so hazy that our pursuers soon became quite undistinguishable. Marietta and Angerstoff appeared to be stupefied with terror. They stood motionless, holding firmly by the bulwarks of the vessel; and though the waves frequently broke over the deck, and rushed down the gangway, they did not offer to shut the companion door, which would have remained open had I not closed it.

The tempest, gloom, and danger that thickened around us, neither elicited from them any expressions of mutual regard, nor seemed to produce the slightest sympathetic emotion in their bosoms. They gazed sternly at each other and at me, and every time the vessel rolled, clung with convulsive eagerness to whatever lay within their reach.

About sunset our attention was attracted by a dreadful roaring, which evidently did not proceed from the waves around us; but the atmosphere being very hazy, we were unable to ascertain the cause of it for a long time. At length we distinguished a range of high cliffs, against which the sea beat with terrible fury. Whenever the surge broke upon them, large jets of foam started up to a great height, and flashed angrily over their black and rugged surfaces, while the wind moaned and whistled with fearful caprice among the projecting points of rock. A dense mist covered the upper part of the cliffs, and prevented us from seeing if there were any houses upon their summits, though this point appeared of little importance, for we drifted towards the shore so fast that immediate death seemed inevitable.

We soon felt our vessel bound twice against the sand, and in a little time after a heavy sea carried her up the beach, where she remained imbedded and hard aground. During the ebb of the waves there was not more than two feet of water round her bows.

I immediately perceived this, and, watching a favorable opportunity, swung myself down to the beach by means of part of the cable that projected through the hawse-hole. I began to run towards the cliffs the moment my feet touched the ground, and Angerstoff attempted to follow me, that he might prevent my escape; but while in the act of descending from the vessel, the sea flowed in with such violence that he was obliged to spring on board again to save himself from being overwhelmed by its waters.

I hurried on and began to climb up the rocks, which were very steep and slippery; but I soon grew breathless from fatigue, and found it necessary to stop. It was now almost dark, and when I looked around, I neither saw anything distinctly, nor could form the least idea how far I had still to ascend before I reached the top of the cliffs. I knew not which way to turn my steps, and remained irresolute, till the barking of a dog faintly struck my ear. I joyfully followed the sound, and, after an hour of perilous exertion, discovered a light at some distance, which I soon found to proceed from the window of a small hut.

After I had knocked repeatedly, the door was opened by an old man, with a lamp in his hand. He started back on seeing me, for my dress was wet and disordered, my face and hands had been wounded while scrambling among the rocks, and fatigue and terror had given me a wan and agitated look. I entered the house, the inmates of which were a woman and a boy, and having seated myself near the fire, related to my host all that had occurred on board the floating beacon, and then requested him to accompany me down to the beach, that we might search for Angerstoff and Marietta.

"No, no," cried he; "that is impossible. Hear how the storm rages! Worlds would not induce me to have any communication with murderers. It would be impious to attempt it on such a night as this. The Almighty is surely punishing them now! Come here and look out."

I followed him to the door, but the moment he opened it the wind extinguished the lamp. Total darkness prevailed without, and a chaos of rushing, bursting and moaning sounds swelled upon the ear with irregular loudness. The blast swept round the hut in violent eddyings, and we felt the chilly spray of the sea driving upon our faces at intervals.

I shuddered, and the old man closed the door, and then resumed his seat near the fire.

My entertainer made a bed for me upon the floor, but the noise of the tempest, and the anxiety I felt about the fate of Angerstoff and Marietta, kept me awake the greater part of the night. Soon after dawn my host accompanied me down to the beach. We found the wreck of the floating beacon, but were unable to discover any traces of the guilty pair whom I had left on board of it.

A GLORY DEPARTED

C. ERNEST FAYLE

We were discussing, soberly enough, certain problems of trade and shipping when I happened to mention my one long voyage in a sailing vessel. "Ah yes," said Captain——with a new animation in his voice, "but she wasn't a flyer like my old ship." His tone was so full of pride and affection that it was with an eager interest I enquired her name. "*Cutty Sark*," he replied, "I was in her when she made her last run home with tea from China." It was like meeting a man who had known King Arthur intimately.

Even among those who have made no special study of the sea, the name of *Cutty Sark* is known as one of the fastest and smartest—many would say *the* fastest and smartest—of the wonderful clippers with whom the old order at sea culminated, and passed away. Too late for the great years of the tea races from Foochow, she was for many years the crack ship of the wool fleet from Australia which carried on, right into the nineties, so gallant a fight against the competition of the steamer; but like most of her consorts, she was at length 'sold foreign,' and until her recent purchase brought her back to the British register she had been knocking about under the Portuguese flag, forgotten by all but a few who had known and loved her. To-day, when the windjammer has ceased almost entirely to count as a factor in ocean trade, the glories of the old clippers have acquired an almost legendary savour, and this chance meeting with one who had served in *Cutty Sark* in the days of her greatness brought home with something of a shock the narrowness of the gulf that separates us from an era now irrevocably past.

It set me trying to fathom the secret of that romance which clings around the names of the China and Colonial clippers—*Ariel, Sir Lancelot, Thermopylæ, Salamis*—and is denied, fairly or unfairly, to their successors, the ocean greyhounds of to-day. We all know what Kipling's old Scotch engineer thought of the amateur yachtsman who asked him, "Mister MacAndrews, don't you think steam spoils romance at sea?" and the creator of MacAndrews has proved, if it needed proving, that poetry and romance can be found in the engine-room as well as on the skysail yard; yet for most of us the white-winged clipper has a charm and personality that we cannot so fully associate with the masterpieces of modern marine architecture. I do not know whether a man would be moved, as Captain——was moved, in saying "I was in the *Mauretania* when she won the blue riband of the Atlantic." I am sure we should not listen to him with the same thrill.

It is not merely, as has sometimes been suggested, a question of beauty. True, the towering canvas, the tapering spars, the clipper bow are gone; but the lines of an *Olympic* or a *Mauretania* have a beauty of their own, a beauty firmly based on essential rightness and fitness for purpose. It is not 'the taint of commercialism.' *Ariel* and *Cutty Sark* were run to pay, and though success in the race home with tea from China or with wool from Australia was a matter of personal pride to owner, master, and crew, the main object of the race was to reach London in time for the first sales of the season. A reputation as a flyer had its cash value in the freight markets.

There are many other causes that have been advanced for the passing of the glamour that surrounds the sailing ship—the substitution of the big impersonal company for the individual owner, the smaller opportunities for human contacts on board a mammoth liner, the lesser value of instinctive seamanship and long experience in a steamer's crew. Almost all of them connect themselves in some way with a loss of that personality which the sailing ship possessed, and to which Joseph Conrad has given imperishable expression. There is one factor in this loss of personality, however, which has perhaps been insufficiently emphasized. The quality in the steamer that has done most to dim the romance of the sea is that which, from every other point of view, is her crowning glory. She suffers from the defect of reliability.

A ship is built to-day for a speed of 12, 15, 20 knots, and though her actual performance may vary a little from voyage to voyage, she will make passage after passage, in the liner trades, to a fixed schedule of dates, and with a variation of only a few hours in her actual time at sea. It is her boast that she may be depended on with almost mathematical certainty to make her port on the appointed day. The ratio of her speed to that of her rivals is known and recorded.

In the old days it was not so. When the clipper left port, it was never safe to calculate within a week the date of her arrival. Her passage was a matter of pluck and luck. *Cutty Sark*, of course, was a marvel, and the average of all her wool passages between 1874 and 1890 works out at 77 days, only five days above her best passage between port and port during that period; but *Serica*, one of the three who came home from Foochow in 99 days in the great race of 1866, took 120 in the following year, and four consecutive runs of *Salamis* from Melbourne to London give 94, 100, and 77 days respectively. These records, picked out at random from Mr. Basil Lubbock's fascinating volumes, *The China Clippers* and *The Colonial Clippers*, are only stray instances of a variation between voyage and voyage which, apart altogether from port delays or accidents, frequently presented still greater contrasts.

It was partly a matter of handling, of the smartness of the crew, of the tenacity with which the master would 'carry on,' when the gale drove others to shorten sail, the skill with which he could take advantage of the slightest puff of wind in the 'doldrums,' the judgment with which he shaped his course. It was partly a matter of luck; a long succession of contrary winds or baffling calms might nullify the effects of the most beautiful model and the most skilful seamanship. Hence there could be no reckoning with certainty on either the actual or the comparative performances of the ships. The cracks raced year after year with varying and often alternate success; a change of master or the favour of the elements might bring the laggard of the fleet into the first flight.

This it was that gave to the old sailing tradition a large part of its vitality and thrill. The modern liner may have the satisfaction of lowering a record established by her predecessors, but the largest share of the glory goes to those who designed her hull and engines, and from the standard set on her maiden voyage she will show but small variation. To a great extent—for the argument must not be pushed too far—she is like a watch, which, once set and regularly wound, will keep time until it wears out. The clipper was like a high-metalled horse, responsive with the responsiveness of a living thing to the touch of her master, capable of being coaxed into surprising efforts, subject, as all living things are subject, to strange inconsistencies and reversals of fortune. For her, each voyage was a contest with other ships and with the elements, to the result of which neither her own previous performances, nor those of her rivals, afforded any sure pointer. For master, officers, and crew, each passage was one long struggle, calling for daring, skill, endurance and ceaseless vigilance.

This element of struggle is essential to romance. We can admire the skill by which victory is assured, but it is only so long as the event of a contest is uncertain that it stirs the blood, and the longer the odds, the greater the thrill. Set in a world where arduous effort and uncertain reward are the normal conditions of our existence, we cannot easily recognize a kinship to humanity in the effortless certainty with which the machine performs its work. We have come to love the struggle for its own sake and to think more of the effort than of the attainment.

The heart of man revolts against the finality of accomplishment. The development of the steamship is a triumph over the elements; it enables man to sail at his own will, not the wind's; but for this triumph a price has been paid. The true romance of steam was in the days when the elements were still imperfectly subdued, when every ship was experimental, and the possibility of an Atlantic steamship service was a matter of bitter controversy. Now that we know what we can do, some of the savour has gone out of the doing.

It is for this reason that so large a proportion of our energy and inventiveness, so much of youth and daring and enterprise, are to-day directed not to the sea, but to the air, where unknown possibilities still remain to be explored. It is for this reason that, while the perils of the seas still surround every voyage with a halo of adventure, we look back with a special affection and pride to the doings of the *Cutty Sark* and her contemporaries, in days when the race was not always to the swift, and either personality or fortune could still upset the most careful calculations.

THE YACHT

ARNOLD BENNETT

When Mrs. Alice Thorpe, with her black Pomeranian, arrived at the Hard from the railway station she at once picked out a small motor-launch among the boats that were bobbing about the steps, and said:

"Is this Mr. Thorpe's?"

"Yes'm," said the sailor in charge of the launch.

She signalled to a lad who lingered in the rear with her valise perched on his head; the valise was dropped into the forward part of the launch, Mrs. Thorpe gave the boy sixpence, and placed herself and dog neatly in the stern-sheets; the engine suddenly began to fire and throb with great velocity and noise, and the launch threaded out from the concourse of craft into the middle of the creek, leaving a wake of boiling foam. There had been no delay, no misunderstanding, no bungling, no slip. The telegraphic arrangements for taking Mrs. Thorpe on board the yacht had worked to perfection. Efficiency reigned.

Aged twenty-seven, slim, not tall, Alice was a capable woman. Her eyes had the capable look which many men dislike, for while they appreciate the conveniences of efficiency in a girl they seem to prefer the efficiency to be modestly masked by an appearance of helplessness. Alice neither disguised nor flaunted the fact that she was capable. Her eyes had also the look of one accustomed to give orders that were obeyed. The dog was supposed to be the only Pomeranian on earth not given to habitual yapping; Alice had purged it of the hereditary Pomeranian curse by replying instantly to every yap with a sound smack on the head. She adored the dog, which was passionately and exclusively devoted to her, after the manner of Pomeranian ladies to their mistresses. This Pomeranian's mistress, if not beautiful, was attractive, especially in figure and in clothes. She was a fine dancer, with a body that always surprised her partners by its extraordinary yieldingness, responsiveness and flexibility. A man having danced with her for the first time would remember her physical elasticity for days—to say nothing of her sudden eager smiles that puckered all the skin round her eyes.

"Which is the yacht?" asked Alice of the sailor.

He was tidily dressed, but had an untidy mop of red hair escaping from his white cap, and a shapeless, ugly face; and his manner was somewhat gruff. She knew that he must be Peter, the steward and handy man, her husband's favourite, more than once referred to with laudation in her husband's letters. She did not care for him, and had already decided that he did not care for her. But she smiled amiably.

"Her's lying at the mouth of the creek, in the river," said Peter, pointing. "That's her, that ketch with the blue ensign at the mizzen."

Alice looked in vain along the vista of yachts and other craft in the creek. She did not know what a mizzen was, nor that the blue ensign was a flag—she fancied indeed that an ensign was a sort of three-cornered thing. Peter's incomprehensible indication, however, merely increased her sense of mystery and expectancy. The moment was thrilling for her.

She had met her husband when both of them were in uniform in France. She had married him in London impulsively because they were mad for each other. A week later he had been tragically swept off to Mesopotamia. Then, having got out of uniform, she had become organising secretary to a political body, and had had to go to America on its business. During her absence James Thorpe had received unexpected leave. But her tyrannous conscience would not allow her to depart from the United States until her work was done; and she exulted in her work. Some caprice of the political body ended it in an hour by cable. She had obtained a berth on a Liverpool-bound liner the very next day.

She might have cabled the grand news to her husband, but she found somewhere in her mind a piquant pleasure in the notion of surprising him. She surprised him by a telegram from Liverpool. She knew that he was out of the army and in business. The unconventional wording of his reply to her telegram enchanted her, besides providing diversion for telegraph operators (who are not easily diverted). He was yachting, alone. She remembered, vaguely, that he possessed a yacht (laid up for five years), and had spoken very enthusiastically of yachting. Of course he had been for meeting her in London; but she would have none of it. "You shall receive me on your yacht," she had telegraphed. As she was an expert organiser, and he was an expert organiser, the arrangements following this decision of hers were easy enough.

She was now afraid, and her fear was romantic and terrible. The creek was alarmingly short, the launch surged at an alarming speed through the dappled blue water. She had not seen her lover, who was incidentally her husband, for nearly two years. She knew him by his photographs, his handwriting, his turns of phrase, and the memory of his gestures and of the feel of his moustache—but did she know him? Would he prove on further acquaintance to be somebody quite other than the image established in her heart? The situation was acutely disconcerting as she approached it. She stroked the dog's silky hair, and the dog glanced up at her face.

"That's her," said Peter, to the composed and prim young lady opposite him, pointing again.

She almost exclaimed:

"It's a very small yacht, isn't it?" But restrained herself.

The yacht's stem was pointing up-creek, against the ebb-tide. Peter seemed to steer the launch very queerly. He was apparently passing the yacht. She caught sight of a name on a life-buoy hung in the yacht's rigging. The name was *Alice*.

"But I thought the yacht was called *Hermes*," she said.

"Guv'nor had her name changed last month," gloomily answered Peter, as it were with resentment. Peter was preoccupied with the manœuvring of the launch on the tide, and Alice perceived that he knew exactly what he was doing. The nose of the launch edged towards the yacht's side; the launch seemed to hang in the current; then it slowly swung round, the propeller stopped, and the whole affair came gently to rest against dazzlingly white cushiony fenders and a polished stairway, from the top of which hung two dazzlingly white ropes. The yacht had grown enormous. Its bulwark rose high above the tiny launch, and it was as solid and moveless as a rock.

"And now he's called it *Alice*," said Alice to herself; and the situation appeared to be rather disconcerting.

II

Her husband loomed perpendicularly over her.

"Hallo!" he cried, saluting.

She answered in a weak voice:

"Well?" Her face was burning.

She seized the white ropes and tripped neatly up the stairway, and the blanched deck of the yacht stretched out firm and vast; and tall Jim clutched at her hand.

"Come below and see the saloon," he murmured.

He pushed her to a mahogany staircase under the main boom, and no sooner were they out of sight of the deck than he kissed her with rather more than his old accustomed violence. And the situation was acutely disconcerting again, but differently.

There was a pattering of innumerable little feet on the staircase, and the dog, who under excitement produced in human ears the illusion that she was a centipede and not a quadruped, bounded into the saloon.

"Oh, Fifi! I'd forgotten you! . . . Jim, this is Fifi."

The dog sprang into her arms, and Jim praised the dog highly and stroked her.

Husband and wife sat side by side in the saloon, and talked rather self-consciously about nothing, which was rather strange, seeing that each of them had ten thousand exciting matters to impart to the other. Still, it was all right. Alice knew it was all right, and she knew that Jim knew it was all right. They were strangers in one way and the most intimate of intimates in another. It might be said that the saloon held four people, not two.

"Oh! What's that funny thing?" Alice demanded, pointing to a very complicated kind of dial with a finger on it that was screwed face downwards to the saloon ceiling.

"That? Oh! That's a compass so that I can see the course of the ship when I'm having my meals."

"But the finger's moving right round!"

"Then you may be sure the yacht's moving right round too."

"Then we are off—already?"

And Jim said in his stern, sardonic tone:

"Didn't you hear the anchor being hauled up? Can't you feel the propeller?"

The fact was that Alice had not noticed the loud clacking of the anchor chain, her powers of observation having been temporarily impaired by the surpassing interest of her own private sensations. As for the propeller, she had in a vague manner been aware of a general vibration, but had not attributed it to anything in particular; she did not even know that the yacht possessed a propeller. Jim took her by the shoulders and they ran up on deck. The yacht was gliding out to sea, magically, formidably, by its own secret force; for the sails were not yet set. The entire adventure was ecstatic, incredibly romantic. Alice had never been so happy, so troubled, so restless.

"I do want to see all the rooms," said she, like a curious child.

"You shall. Are you given to being seasick?"

"I have never been seasick in my life," the capable woman replied with confidence.

Jim's keen eyes wandered over her admiringly.

"No," he murmured. "You aren't the sort that's seasick, you aren't."

They descended again to the saloon. A beautiful tea, with real crockery and brilliant electro-plate and real cakes and real cream, all set out upon a brass tray, lay on the table.

"Oh! Pete's served the tea. Good! Will you pour out? You must. You're the mistress of this wigwam."

She poured out. As she leaned an elbow on the table, the table tipped downwards under the pressure of her arm. She gave a little squeal.

"All right! All right!" Jim reassured her grandly. "Pete's taken the pin out, you know. Leaves the table free to oscillate when the boat rolls. It's weighted with lead underneath, so it can't swing far."

"Oh! I see. Of course!" said Alice, who, however, was not completely reassured. Things were not after all quite what they seemed.

She admired tremendously the internal arrangements of the yacht— they were so cosy, they were so complete; the most home-like thing she had ever seen. She visited every bit of the home. There was the saloon, or drawing-room, and there were a large double sleeping-cabin and a small single one; also there was a tiny bathroom. The multiplicity of cupboards and drawers delighted her; only in Utopia could she have imagined there would be so many cupboards and drawers. And there was electric light. And there were electric bells. You rang a bell, and it was answered just as it would have been in a real house—but much more promptly. Indeed, life on the yacht might be described as playing at perfect housekeeping. Everything had a place, and everything had to be in its place; and every place was full—except the drawers and the mirrored wardrobe reserved for the use of the mistress of the floating home. In the pantry every cup was hung on a hook; every wine-glass was lightly wedged in a fitting so that it could not dash itself against another wine-glass; and the same with saucers and plates. One surmised that even if the yacht were to turn upside down nothing would break.

And the organism was complete in itself, and sufficient to itself. Before dinner Jim said:

"Like a cocktail, beloved infant?"

The notion of a cocktail appealed to her as something wild and wicked.

"Why not?" said she. And Jim rang a bell.

"Two cocktails, Pete."

In about two minutes Peter, in a white jacket, brought two cocktails out of the mysteries of the forecastle where the pantry was. If Jim had ordered two nectars doubtless Pete would have produced them.

The dinner was very sound. It was strictly plain—oxtail soup (tinned), herring, roast mutton, potatoes, rice pudding—but it was sound. Alice admitted that Pete, for all his defects, could not merely cook meat well—he could buy good meat.

But she pointed out to Jim that Pete did not know how to lay the table properly—the fellow had put the fish knife and fork within the meat knife and fork—and at Jim's suggestion she pointed out the sad lapse to Pete personally, with a bright smile. Pete received the correction with a tranquillity too perfect, indicating by his nonchalant demeanour that if it pleased madam to have the meat knife and fork within the fish knife and fork he had no objection to obliging her, but that for himself his soul was above trifles. Pete had been Jim's batman for nearly three years in the war, and Jim spoke with quiet enthusiasm of his qualities. Alice, however, did not quite see what that had to do with the knife-and-fork question. They went on deck. The yacht was now at anchor in another estuary, whose quiet waters were full of phosphorescence. A dinghy moving towards another yacht close by threw up marvellous silver fireworks at every stroke of the oars. The night was obscure and warm and incredible. A radiance came from the saloon skylight; and a brighter radiance, sharply rectangular, from the open hatch of the forecastle. The crew (four human beings) could be heard talking in the depths of the forecastle. The old skipper appeared and made an inspection in the gloom; and Jim addressed him as "Skipper" with affectionate respect, though he was naught but a fisherman in winter and spoke with a terrific Essex accent.

The skipper disappeared. When next Alice glanced round there was no radiance, and no sound, from the forecastle. The crew had gone to bed. She and Jim were alone in the vast and miraculous world, enveloped by the poetry of water and sky. . . .

III

Nevertheless the next morning, in the double cabin, when she awoke very early in the twilight, that singular young woman was not utterly happy. That is to say, she was utterly happy, but at the same time she was unhappy—her heart being a huge place where all kinds of contradictory emotions could roam in comfort without interfering with each other. Jim was not in his berth. Through the open skylight, across which a horizontal blue blind was drawn, she could hear him chatting with the skipper. Jim was disturbingly friendly with his crew. "Look lively with the tea, Pete," he cried out. "Very good, sir." In another minute she could hear him sipping tea in enormous sips. She had an impression that he was seated, in pyjamas and dressing-gown, on the very skylight itself.

The floating home, then, had already begun to function very perfectly for the day. It was precisely the perfect functioning of the organism that upset her. Every contrivance in it was a man's contrivance. Woman had had naught to do with its excellence. It would function with the same perfection whether she happened to be there or not. It was orderly, it was comfortable; it was luxurious; and men had accomplished it and were maintaining it all by themselves. And the five males appeared to have an understanding among themselves, as if they belonged to a secret monastic or masonic order. She was outside the understanding. She was a woman, ornamental no doubt, but unnecessary. Well, she resented this in her great happiness. And she petted Fifi, who was curled within her arm, and Fifi resented it also.

So that the next afternoon Alice had a headache. It was a genuine headache, of which the symptoms were genuine pain in the forehead and a general sense of impending calamity. Considering a headache to be the proper thing at this conjuncture, she had desired to have a headache, and she had a headache; for she was a capable and thoroughly efficient woman. Hence, with Fifi, she went and lay down in her bunk in the big cabin, and parted from Jim at the door thereof, telling him that she did not want him to tuck her up. She noticed that the general sense of impending calamity had already affected Jim's gaze, and she resented that. What justification had Jim to assume that all was not for the best on board of an ideal yacht, seeing that her behaviour towards him had been pluperfect? He had no justification. Therefore he was in the wrong.

In her happiness she gave herself up to unhappiness. And yet her second marriage—it must be deemed her second marriage to Jim, the first having been an experiment, a prelude, an overture to the authentic union—her second marriage was unquestionably a success. She was mad about him. He was mad about her. She admired his character. He admired hers. She knew that he was the man for her and she the woman for him. Nothing could have been more propitious, more delicious, more exciting, more solidly sure. But she gave herself up to unhappiness because she felt herself unnecessary to the smooth working of the material organism in which she lived, and also because she felt herself to be outside the monastic or masonic order of five mutually comprehending males. And here was the self-same woman who had commanded hundreds of fellow-creatures in France, saying to them Go and they went, and Come and they came; and who had positively frightened a British political body, and startled bigwigs in New York, by the calm, unsentimental power of her horse-sense. Most of the persons with whom she had come into contact would have been ready to assert that where a woman's heart usually is she carried a bundle of pure sagacity, and none would have admitted that she could be subject to fancies. If those people whose respect she had extorted could have seen the charming little creature as she lay all wires and springs and nerves in the bunk! And if they could have looked inside her head! Marriage is a most mysterious developer. The worst of it was that Fifi encouraged Alice in her morbidity. Fifi understood; she did not argue; she did not even yap; but the glance of her eyes was a plain statement of the thesis: "You are always right, and when the created universe is out of tune with you the created universe needs altering."

Then Alice became aware of a vibration, which increased till it affected the entire ship—the bunk, the water-glass, the skylight, the pillow, the mattress, her toes, her temples. The propeller was propelling! Never before had the propeller been set to work while Alice was lying in her bunk. Why was the propeller now propelling? The weather was magnificent; the sun slanted into the cabin; the water was calm. Did not everybody know that she had a headache and was trying to rest? It was an outrage that the propeller should be set to work in such circumstances. Soon the propeller was doing more than revolve behind the stern-post of the yacht; it was revolving right inside her poor head. She could not and would not stand it. She rang the bell. A red head appeared in the doorway.

"Come in, come in," she said pettishly.

But the red head, timid in spite of campaigns, would not come in.

"Yes'm?"

"Oh! Please ask Mr. Thorpe to have that propeller stopped."

Peter merely laughed—a sort of contemptuously amused grin—and shut the door.

The propeller was not stopped. In five minutes, which seemed rather like a century, there was nothing else on earth for Alice save the propeller. It became the sole mundane phenomenon. It was revolving not only in her head, but in every part of her lithe and attractive body. It monopolised her attention, her intelligence, and her emotions. It had been going on from everlasting, and it would go on to everlasting. As a method of torture it rivalled and surpassed the most devilish inventions of the Holy Office at Toledo. It was the very thing to manufacture lunatics. Why had not Jim had the propeller stopped? He owned the yacht. If you could not silence your own propeller, what point was there in owning a yacht? Enormous and inexplicable events were passing on deck—bumps, thuds, sudden rushes of feet, shouts, bangs, rattlings, thunderings, clackings. But none of the five members of the monastic or masonic order showed the least interest in Alice and her aching head. Ah! The door of the cabin opened.

"Better?" asked Jim, standing by the side of her bunk. He was perspiring.

"No," she said.

"Tea-time. Come and have tea on deck. Do you good."

"No," she said.

"Shall I bring it you here?"

"No," she said.

At that moment the propeller stopped.

"At last!" breathed Alice sardonically and even bitterly. "If you've got a headache it's the most horrible torment one can imagine. I rang for Peter hours ago and asked him to tell you to stop it."

"I'm so sorry, my dove. But you see the propeller couldn't be stopped. We were going up the Blackwater against the ebb. And it's some ebb, believe me. Wind fell to nothing. If we'd stopped the propeller we should certainly have drifted on to a mudbank—Blackwater's full of 'em—and stuck there till next tide. We might have heeled over and filled as the tide fell. Ticklish thing, a boat drawing eight feet odd on a falling tide in a river like the Blackwater."

"Well, I think some one might have told me. I'm quite capable of understanding, though perhaps you mayn't think it."

Jim's eyes glittered.

"My child, I never thought for a moment——

"Just so! Just so! And let me tell you your Peter's extremely rude. When I asked him, do you know what he did? He just laughed—his horrid sarcastic grin. And I'll thank you to speak to him about his manners to me."

Jim did a surprising thing. He laughed, heartily.

"Well, of course it *would* strike Peter as comic, asking for the propeller to be stopped in a dead calm against an ebb-tide in this old Blackwater. He laughed when he came on deck and told me. It appealed to his sense of humour."

"And I suppose you all laughed!" said Alice sharply, in a loud tone. "You would!" She raised herself too violently on one elbow, and her delightful, misguided head struck the ceiling above the bunk.

"Awfully sorry, darling!" said Jim, very quietly. But whether he was sorry about Peter's enormity, or sorry merely about the detail of the head-bumping, Alice could not decide. At any rate, the bumping of her head rendered her furious and—quaintly enough—quite cured the headache.

"Peter is a fool!" she almost shouted.

"Hush!" Jim murmured grimly and dangerously.

And at the same time the skipper's voice was heard on deck:

"Let out a couple o' fathoms more chain, Charlie."

Alice's brain grasped the great truth that if she could hear the skipper, the skipper and crew could hear her, and the still greater truth that voice-raising in anger was impossible on that yacht without open scandal. She would have given about ten pounds for the privilege of one unrestrained scream.

Jim whispered uncompromisingly:

"Pete certainly isn't a fool. Also, he's a particular friend of mine."

An awful silence descended upon the yacht, and in the silence the yacht's clock, placed over the saloon stairs, could be heard ticking with uncanny loudness. In the late afternoon and early evening Alice ranged and raged about the vessel, chewing the cud of the discovery that there was no real privacy aboard. There was privacy from eyes, and plenty of it; but there was absolutely no privacy from ears if you raised your tone beyond a certain degree. She wanted to do that more than she wanted to do anything else in the world. She examined the dispositions of the yacht again and again, with no satisfactory result. It was sixty feet from end to end of its wonderful deck, and it was full of secret compartments, but it held no compartment in which a grand quarrel, row, and upset could be comfortably conducted according to the rules of such encounters. As a honeymoon resort the yacht was merely absurd. None but an idiot could have had the preposterous notion of honeymooning on a fifty-ton yacht.

Alice did not reflect upon the dangerous folly and the bad form and the gross inefficiency of making a scene on the third day of your second honeymoon. She did not even reflect that man is held to be a reasoning animal. She reflected simply and exclusively upon her predicament, which was surely the most singular predicament that a bride had ever found herself in. But she did not disclose her thoughts. No, to external view she was a charming, capable, sensible little yachtswoman in an agreeable blue jumper and blue skirt, wandering to and fro in and on the yacht, interesting herself in its construction and its life, and behaving to all the men with the delicatest feminine sweetness. To Jim she was acquiescence embodied; the irritation shown in the bunk had completely vanished. Night fell, and a red eye shone forth from the land. She learned that it indicated a jetty on an island which, in mid-Blackwater, was devoted to the reclamation of habitual drunkards. She was suddenly inspired.

"Let's row ashore, shall we?" she suggested persuasively.

"But the island's private, you know," said Jim.

Here, referring to the affair of the propeller, she might have revolted, and said angrily:

"Of course you're against anything I want."

Many women in her place would have said just that. But Alice was determined to be efficient, and so she said with increased persuasiveness:

"Still, it would be a bit of a lark, wouldn't it?"

Jim gave the order to lower the launch, and they were taken ashore, and the launch instructed to return in an hour. Half an hour would have sufficed for Alice's purposes; but the captain and two of the crew were also in the launch and had to go down river to fill six beakers with fresh water from a well in the vicinity; which job could scarcely be accomplished in less than an hour.

IV

"Now," said Jim, "shall we take a stroll and look for reformed drunkards?"

"I think we'll just stay where we are," Alice answered. "I must have an understanding with you." She spoke firmly but quietly. The desire to make a noise seemed to have left her, now that she was free to make a noise without making a scandal. Both inside and out she was the self-possessed woman again, the model of efficiency and sagacity, not merely in appearance, but to her own secret judgment.

"Certainly," said Jim with calmness. "Let's understand."

She was nettled because she thought she detected irony in his powerful, almost brutal, masculine voice.

"I've already told you that I think Peter ought to apologise to me. He hasn't apologised to me. Quite the contrary."

"Ah!" Jim answered. "I knew that was on your mind. You're an A1 actress, but I'm an A1 dramatic critic." And he proceeded: "And what's more, I've already told you that Pete's a friend of mine, and I don't like to hear my wife call my friends fools."

She then burst out into one of the most voluptuous of human passions—over-righteous indignation. She didn't want any more to be self-possessed, efficient, sagacious; nor to be an exemplary wife, nor to teach a barbaric husband by the force of Christian example, nor to do any of the things that serious young wives very properly want to do. She just wanted to let herself go; and she did. The mysterious and terrible potion had been brewing for several hours; it now boiled over, surging magnificently upwards as a geyser shoots out of the ground. She was at last free of the captivity of the yacht. There was none to overhear and no eye to see except the red eye on the jetty.

"That's just like you," she cried. "That's just like you. You're ready to risk the whole of our married life in order to indulge your brutality. You once said you were a brute, and so you are. We've scarcely been three days together and yet you're spoiling for a row. You think you can browbeat me, you and your crew. You can't. You've all done nothing but laugh at me since I went on board. Look how you all stood round and smiled condescendingly when I steered. And heaven knows I only took the helm because you asked me to. You're all as thick as thieves together, and I'm nobody. I'm only a woman, a doll to be petted and laughed at. Do you imagine I wanted to steer your precious yacht? Indeed no! Give me an Atlantic liner, that's what I say. Your crew do what they like with you, and you're such a simpleton you can't see it. They flatter you, and you're so conceited you swallow it all. And shouldn't I just like to see the food bills for your precious yacht. Why, there's been as much meat cooked for us two in these three days as would keep a family for a fortnight. You pay your crew wages that include their food, and then instead of buying their own food they live on ours. It's as plain as a pikestaff."

In a short pause that followed Jim said:

"Don't let me interrupt you. Tell me when you've quite done, and then I'll make a short speech. But if you think I'm going to lose my temper, old woman, you're mistook."

Alice resumed.

"I said Peter was a fool. So he is. But he's also a lout. And what's worse, he's a thief. He steals your food."

Then Jim, taken unawares, lost his temper. The battle was joined. A big steam tug passed slowly up the river, a noisy but a noble phenomenon in the night. They did not notice it. They noticed nothing except their own dim forms, pale faces and glinting eyes; heard nothing but their own voices and the crunching of their restless feet on the caked mud of the foreshore. The old earth was whirling round with incredible velocity amid uncounted millions of starry bodies of which it was nearly the very least. The mystery of life was unfathomed the structure of society was shaken and cracked. Tens of thousands of children were starving in Europe. Frightful problems presented themselves on every side for solution. The future of the world was dark with fantastic menaces. And the great beauty and wistfulness of nature were unimpaired by all these horrors. But Alice and Jim ignored everything save the gratification of their base and petty instincts. They were indeed a shocking couple. The moon rose—the solemn lovely moon that was drawing incalculable volumes of water out of the ocean into the estuary of the Blackwater—and Alice snapped:

"What I say I stick to. And I tell you another thing—all red-headed men are the same."

A strange glow appeared on the yacht. They did not see it. Peter hailed faintly from the yacht. They did not hear him. They were indulging themselves after restraint. They had gone back to the neolithic age after too much civilisation. And the whole fracas was due to the fact that, on a small yacht, everybody can hear everything. The ignoble altercation was suddenly cut short by the grating of a boat's keel on the muddy shingle—Peter in the dinghy.

"Yacht's afire, sir!" Peter called grimly.

So it was. They could see flames coiling like snakes about the region of the saloon hatch.

Jim came back to civilisation in an instant.

"Well, why haven't you put it out, you fool, instead of coming here to tell me? Do you want the bally ship to be burnt to the water's edge?"

"Can't find the extinguisher, sir. It's supposed to hang in the small cabin, but it isn't on its hook. And we've run out of water on account of missis's baths. . . . Not as canvas buckets would be much good."

"My dog!" cried Alice. "She'll be roasted alive."

"I've brought her ashore," said Peter, pitching the animal out of the dinghy.

"Ah!"

Jim rushed to the boat's nose, shoved her back into the water, and sprang aboard.

"Pull like the devil."

"Stop!" shouted Alice. "I know where the extinguisher is." She plunged, Fifi in her arms, into the dark water, and was dragged into the dinghy.

Not only had she transgressed the rules of the yacht by taking fresh-water baths, but she had moved the Pyrene extinguisher from its hook into a locker in order to get another hook for her dresses. The small cabin had been allotted to her for a tiring-room, and her attire was all over it. Wonderful it was how one small valise could carry all she wore. She had taken things from the valise and more and more things, in the manner of a conjurer taking drapers' shops, flower shops, and zoological gardens out of one small hat.

Once aboard the vessel, she plunged devotedly through smoke into the bowels thereof and ascended again with the extinguisher. In three minutes the fire was out. It appeared that someone with a British sense of humour had thrown a piece of burning rope from the tug. The rope had dropped on to the saloon hatch. The roof of the said hatch was severely damaged and the coat of the mainsail a little charred; but that was the limit of the catastrophe.

V

The yacht was speeding up the Blackwater in the moonlight towards Maldon, James Thorpe, with all the dark fire of his nature, having determined at once to hunt the flame-scattering tug and get the law of it. He was in possession of what he considered to be sound circumstantial evidence of the tug's guilt. James himself had taken the wheel. Alice reclined at his feet. Fifi reclined at Alice's feet. The captain and crew were forward. Alice was perfectly happy. She had never really been unhappy—and especially had she not been unhappy in her nervous outpouring of riotous temper. But now she was in a kind of bliss—a bliss which was heightened by certain pin-pricks. These pin-pricks came from the facts, one, that she had upset the marvellous functioning of the ship by misplacing the fire-extinguisher; two, that she had upset the marvellous economy of the ship by using fresh water instead of salt water for her baths; and three, that James, in his enormous magnanimity, had refrained from twitting her about these lapses.

She reflected that, owing to pressure of patriotic and other business, she had not lost her temper for several years, and probably would not lose it again for several years, and at any rate to have lost it and safely found it so early in marriage, and with such an agreeable result, was not a bad thing, for it had amounted to a desirable and successful experiment. Her powerful common sense told her that there was a process in marriage known as "settling down," that this process had to be gone through by all couples and that she and Jim were getting through it quickly and brightly. She knew that she need not apologise to Jim, and indeed that he would hate her for apologising to him. She apologised by a touch, a glance, a tone, and by sitting at his feet.

Peter came aft to the little deck-larder that was forward of the saloon skylight.

"Pete."

"Sir?"

"Don't buy any more meat to-morrow until you've spoken to the mistress about it."

"No, sir."

Peter departed.

Jim lowered his face and murmured:

"You know you've got to admit that old Pete isn't a fool."

Alice had already fully absorbed the truth that Peter was not a fool. A man who, placed as Peter was placed, had had the presence of mind to think of the dog and bring the dog to safety ashore—such a man could not possibly be a fool. As for being the other thing that she had called him, of course that was absurd, and she had not meant it. No! She fully admitted, in the privacy of her mind, that she had been hopelessly wrong to call Peter a fool. But what she murmured to Jim in reply was:

"Why! You called him a fool yourself!"

Jim pinched her arm cruelly, but she dared not cry out lest she should be overheard. Therefore she suffered in silence and enjoyed the suffering.

THE MONKEY

EDEN PHILLPOTTS

They sat together forward, under scant shadows, while the *Land Crab*, a little coasting schooner, lay nearly becalmed in the Caribbean. Her sails flapped idly; hot air danced over the deck and along the bulwarks. Now and then a spar creaked lazily, or a block went "chip, chip," as the *Land Crab* rolled on a swell. The sun blazed over the foreyard-arm, the heat was tremendous, but Pete and Pete basked in it and loved it. Neither saw necessity for a straw of head covering; indeed Pete the greater wore no clothes at all. He sat watching Pete the less; anon he put forth a small black hand for a banana; then, with forehead puckered into a world of wrinkles and furrows, he inspected his namesake's work; and later, tired of squatting in the sun, hopped on to the bulwark and up the mizzen shrouds.

Peter the greater was a brown monkey, treasured property of the skipper; and Pete the less, now cleaning some flying-fish for the cook, was a negro boy, treasured property of nobody—a small lad, with a lean body, more of which appeared than was hidden by the rags of his shirt, and great black eyes like a dog's. He was, in fact, a very dog-like boy. When the men cursed him he cowered, and hung his head, and slunk away, sometimes showing a canine tooth; when they were in merry mood he frisked and fawned and went mad with delight. But chance for joy seldom offered. He had a stern master, and an awful responsibility in the shape of Pete the greater. This active beast, under God and the skipper, was Pete's boss. The sailors said that he always touched his wool to it, and everybody knew that he talked to it for hours at a time. When the lad first came aboard, Captain Spicer put the matter in a nutshell.

"See here, nig—this monkey's your pigeon; you've just got to watch it, an' feed it, an' think of it all the time. And bear in mind as he's a darned sight more valuable than anything else aboard this ship. So keep your weather eye lifting, and remember there'll be hell round here if harm comes to Pete."

"I's call Pete too, Cap'n sar," the boy had answered, grinning at what had struck him as a grand joke.

"Are you? Well, you get pals with Pete number one. That's what you've got to do."

But apes are capricious, and Pete the less found his pigeon aboard the *Land Crab* no bed of roses. For that matter the rest of the hands suffered too. Nathan Spicer was a bald-headed old man with an evil temper—one blighted by sorrow and affliction, hard to please, bad to sail with. Dick Bent, the mate, had known his captain in past years, when the sun shone on him, and he explained the position from his former knowledge.

"It's like this 'ere—Nature filled the old sweep with the milk of human kindness; then she up and sent a thunderstorm of troubles and turned it sour. I've sailed on and off with him these twenty year, and I mind when he kept his foot on his temper, an' were a very tidy member o' seafarin' society. But after his missis died and his kid died, then he—what had married old and was wrapped up in the woman—why, then he cast off all holds, and chucked religion, and wished he could see the world in hell, and done his little best to help send it there. Men gets that way when things turn contraiwise. Not but what there's good hid in him too."

But Bent's shipmates—three mongrel negroes and two Englishmen—failed to find the buried treasure. Skipper Spicer was always the same, with painful monotony. Only the man, Duck Bent, and the monkey, Pete, could pull with him. The rest of the crew suffered variously, for the captain, though no longer young, was rough and powerful. He had outbursts of passion that presented a sorry sight for gods and men. Such paroxysms seemed likely enough to end life for him some day; and just as likely to end life for another.

The negro boy scraped out his flying-fish and cut off their tails and wings, then he peeled a pannikin of sweet potatoes and talked to his charge.

"Marse Pete," he said gravely, "you's a dam lucky gem'man, sar—de mose lucky gem'man aboard de *Lan' Crab*. You frens wid cap'n a'ways. He nebber sharp wid you—nebber; but he dat sharp wid me, sar, dat I'se sore all over de backside all de time. I fink you might say word to cap'n for me, Marse Pete, for I'se mighty kind nigger to you, sar."

The monkey was chewing another banana. It stripped off the skin with quick black fingers, filled its mouth, stuffed its cheeks, and then munched and munched and looked at Pete. It held its head on one side as though thinking and weighing each word, and Pete felt quite convinced that it understood him. The boy himself was ten years old. He had entered the world undesired and knew little of it, save that sugar-cane was sweet in the mouth but hard to come by, honestly or otherwise. Pete the greater lived in his master's cabin, and Pete the less often heard the skipper talking to him. If the captain could exchange ideas with his monkey, surely a nigger might do so; and it comforted the boy to chatter his miseries and empty his heart to the beast. Nobody on board had time or inclination to attend to him.

"I wish you was me and me was you, sar, for I has berry bad time aboard dis boat, but you has all b'nana an' no work—an'—an'—don't be so spry, Marse Pete!" as the monkey went capering aloft. "One day you run 'long dem spars too often and fall in de sea to Marse Shark. Den what de boss do wid me?"

It happened that Bent was lying full sprawl behind a hatchway, smoking and grinning, as he listened to these remarks. Now he lifted a funny, small head, with a red beard, and answered the question.

"Old man'd skin you, nig, and then throw you after the monkey," he answered.

"I guess he would, sar."

"So keep alive. Why, you might as well steal skipper's watch as let that animal there get adrift."

The skipper came on deck and both Petes saw him at the same moment. One touched his wool and ambled forward to the galley; the other came down the ratlines head first, and leapt chattering to the captain's shoulder, a favourite perch. His master had owned the monkey five years. It belonged once to his mulattress wife; and when she was dying, she specially mentioned it and made it over to him. That and his watch were the only treasures he had in the world. With his brown wife and his home in Tobago, the man had been happy, even God-fearing, but the first baby killed its mother and, dying also, left a wrecked life behind. Nathan Spicer cared for nothing now, and consequently feared nothing. It is their interest on earth, not the stake in eternity, that makes men cowards.

II

The *Land Crab*, delayed by light winds, was some days overdue at Trinidad, and the skipper exploded in successive volcanoes from dawn till dusk. He was always in a rage, and, as Bent observed:

"If this sight o' energy, and cussing and swearing and to helling the ship's comp'ny, was only shoved into the elements we'd 'a' had half a gale o' wind by now. The old man'll bust 'is biler, sure as death, 'fore he's done with it."

But the winds kept baffling, and swearing did not mend them, nor yet blows, nor yet footfall with Pete the boy. There is no reason to suppose that Skipper Spicer disliked Pete overmuch—not more than he hated any boy; but he was brutal, and needed something to kick at times. Moreover, a kick does not show on a negro, and many imagine that it is the only way of explaining that you disagree with him.

Once the mate ventured to intercede by virtue of his long acquaintance.

"We're old pals, Cap'n," he said, "and meanin' no disrespect, it's like this 'ere—you're killing that little black devil. 'E's small, and you do welt that 'ard. It's 'cause he's a good boy I mention it. If he was a bad 'un, then I'd say, 'lather on,' and I'd help. But he minds his pigeon."

"Which you'd better do likewise," answered the skipper.

"All right, boss. Only it's generally allowed now that nigs is human, same as us, and has workin' souls also."

"Drivel and rot! I don't have none of that twaddle aboard this ship. I know—nobody better'n me—'cause I was a psalm-singer myself among the best. And what's come of it? There ain't no God in these latitoods any-way, else why did he play it so dirty on me? If there's any manner of God at all, He killed my wife and my child for fun, and I don't take no stock in a God that could do that. I'll rip forrard my own way now, till He calls for my checks, which He's quite welcome to, any time—damn Him. But 'tis all bunkum and mumbo-jumbo. Nobody's got a soul no more'n my monkey, so there's a end of the argument."

"Soul or none, 'e's a deal of sense for sartin," admitted the mate, "a 'maz-ing deal of sense. An' he takes kind to t'other Pete. If 'e could talk now, I bet he'd say to give the boy a chance, off and on, to get a whole skin over his bones for a change."

"Which if he did," answered the other, "I should say to him as I do to you: to mind his own blasted bus'ness."

But the men were friends in half an hour, for a fair wind came up out of the sea at dusk, the *Land Crab* plodded along and Spicer quickly thawed.

"Darn the old tub, she makes some of them new-fangled boats look silly yet!" he said to Bent, as, a day later, they lumbered through the Dragon's Teeth to Port of Spain.

After leaving Trinidad, the little coaster proceeded to Tobago for a cargo of coconuts, and the crew viewed that circumstance with gratification, for the most heavy-witted amongst them never failed to notice how a visit to his former home softened the old man. On this occasion, as upon past trips, the palm-crowned mountains of Tobago brought a measure of peace into the skipper's heart, whilst a fair wind and a good cargo tended to improve that condition. All hands reaped benefit and to Dick Bent the captain grew more communicative than usual.

They walked the deck together one morning on the homeward passage to Barbados, and Spicer lifted a corner of the curtain hiding his past.

"Then it was good to live like, but when my missus went 'west,' and took the baby along with her, life changed. Now there's only two things in all creation I care a red cent about. One's a beast, t'other an old gold watch—pretty mean goods to set your heart on, but all as I've got in the whole world."

"It's a mighty fine watch," said Bent.

"It is, and chain too, for that matter. I was lookin' at 'em in my cabin only half an hour past." He brightened as he thought of the trinket, and continued, "I doubt there's many better'n me would fancy that chain across their bellies, but she—"

"Lord deliver us, look aft!" sang out the mate suddenly, interrupting and pointing to the hatch of the companion.

Spicer's monkey had just hopped up on deck, and from his black paw hung the skipper's watch and chain. Pete the greater ambled along towards the bulwark, and a sweat burst from his master's face as he called to the brute in a strange voice. But Pete was perverse. He reached the bulwark and the skipper's nerve died in him, while Bent dared not to take a step towards hastening the threatened catastrophe, or identifying himself therewith. It was a trying moment as the monkey made for his favourite perch on the mizzen rigging, and while he careered forward on all fours, the watch bumped, bumped against the ship's side. The sound brought the blood with a rush to Skipper Spicer's head. Patience was no virtue of his at the best, and he jumped forward with a curse. The man had his hand within six inches of the watch when Pete squeaked and dropped it into the sea. There was a splash, a gleam of gold, and the treasure sank, flashing and twinkling down through the blue, dwindling to a bright, submerged snake, then vanishing for ever. A great gust of passion shook the skipper and tied his tongue. He tried to swear, but could only hiss and growl like an angry beast. Then he seized the monkey by the scruff of the neck as it jumped for his shoulder, shook it and flung it overboard with a shower of oaths. A red light blinded him, he felt his temples bursting, and he reeled away below, not stopping to see a brown head rise from the foam of the splash where Pete had fallen. The monkey fought for it, as one may see a rat driven off shipboard into the deep water. Two terrified eyes gazed upwards at his home, while the *Land Crab* swept by him; his red mouth opened with a yell, and his black paws began beating the water hard as he fell astern. Presently Pete sank for the first time. Then he came up again and went on fighting.

But the skipper saw nothing. He only felt the hot blood surging through his head as he flung himself on his bunk, face downwards. For a moment he thought death had gripped him; but the threatened evil passed, and his consciousness did not depart. He guessed that he had been near apoplexy. Then thoughts came and flooded his brain with abomination of desolation. He lay with his bald head on his arms and turned his mind back into the past. He remembered so much, and every shaft of memory brought him back with a round turn to the present. There was the lemon-tree with Pete's perch on it. His wife had loved the monkey. He could see her now kissing its nose. And she had died with the gold watch ticking under her head. Her wedding ring was upon the chain of it. She had tried to put it on his little finger before she went, but it would not get over the second joint, so she had slipped it upon the watch-chain. Now God in heaven could tell what loathsome fish was nosing it under the sea. And her monkey, her last gift to him, a live meal for a shark. Now the wide world remained to him, empty—save for the thought of what he had done.

He lay needless of time for near three hours. Then he sat up and looked round the cabin. As he did so the door opened, Bent's small head peeped in and the mate spoke:

"Fit as a fiddle, boss; only a flea or two missing."

Then the man shut the cabin door again. But he left something behind. Pete the greater chattered and jumped to his perch in the corner, and from there on to his master's berth. He was dry, warm and much as usual apparently; and he bore no malice whatever. Spicer glared and his breath caught in his throat. Then he grabbed the brute to him till it squeaked, while Nathan snuffled horrible but grateful oaths.

There was only one soul aboard the *Land Crab* who would have gone into a shark-haunted sea to save a monkey, and he did not think twice about it. He came on deck too late to see the catastrophe, though in time to note Pete the greater in the jaws of death. Had he known how the monkey came into the Caribbean he might have doubted the propriety of attempting a rescue; but he did not know, and so he joined it, feeling they might as well die together as perish apart. The boy could swim like a duck, and as Bent lowered a boat smartly, and the sharks held off, it was not long before Pete and Pete came aboard again. But, meantime, their master in his bunk did not even know that the ship had been hove to.

They emptied the water out of Pete the monkey and dried him, and they gave Pete the negro some rum. Both were jolly in an hour; and Skipper Spicer chose to take peculiar views of the gravity of the incident. He never kicked his cabin-boy again.

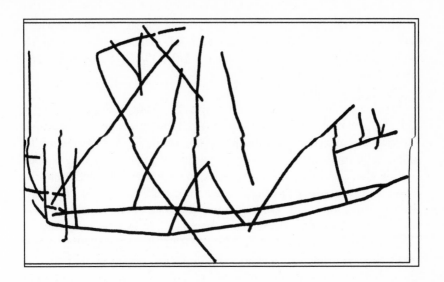

THE MURDERER

PERCEVAL GIBBON

From the open door of the galley, where the cross, sleepy cook was coaxing his stove to burn, a path of light lay across the deck, showing a slice of steel bulwark with ropes coiled on the pins, and above it the arched foot of the mainsail. In the darkness forward, where the port watch of the *Villingen* was beginning the sea day by washing down decks, the brooms swished briskly and the head-pump clacked like a great, clumsy clock.

The men worked in silence, though the mate was aft on the poop, and nothing prevented them from talking as they passed the buckets to and from the tub under the pump and drove their brooms along the planks. They laboured with the haste of men accustomed to be driven hard, with the shuffling, involuntary speed that has nothing in it of free strength or goodwill. The big German four-master had gathered from the boarding-houses of Philadelphia a crew representing all the nationalities which breed sailors, and carried officers skilled in the crude arts of getting the utmost out of it. And since the *lingua franca* of the sea, the tongue which has meaning for Swedish carpenters, Finn sail-makers, and Greek fo'c'sle hands alike, is not German, orders aboard the *Villingen* were given and understood in English.

"A hand com' aft here!"

It was the mate's voice from the poop, robust and peremptory. Conroy, one of the two Englishmen in the port watch, laid down the bucket he was carrying and moved aft in obedience to the summons. As he trod into the slip of light by the galley door he was visible as a fair youth, long-limbed and slender, clad in a serge shirt, with dungaree trousers rolled up to the knees, and girt with a belt which carried the usual sheath-knife. His pleasant face had a hint of uncertainty; it was conciliatory and amiable; he was an able seaman of the kind which is manufactured by a boarding-master short of men out of a runaway apprentice. The others, glancing after him while they continued their work, saw him suddenly clear by the galley door, then dim again as he stepped beyond it. He passed out of sight towards the lee poop ladder.

The silent, hurried sailors pressed on with their work, while the big barque purred through the water to the drone of wind thrusting in the canvas. The brooms were abaft of the galley when the outcry began which caused them to look apprehensively toward the poop without ceasing their business of washing down. First it was an oath in explosive German, the tongue which puts a cutting-edge on profanity; then the mate's roar:

"Is dat vat I tell you, you *verfluchter* fool? Vat? Vat? You don't understand ven I speak? I show you vat——"

The men who looked up were on the wrong side of the deck to make out what was happening, for the chart-house screened the drama from them. But they knew too well the meaning of that instantaneous silence which cut the words off. It was the mate biting in his breath as he struck. They heard the smack of the fist's impact and Conroy's faint, angry cry as he failed to guard it; then the mate again, bull-mouthed, lustful for cruelty: "Vat—you lift up your arm to me! You dog!" More blows, a rain of them, and then a noise as though Conroy had fallen or been knocked down. And after that a thud and a scream.

The men looked at one another, and nods passed among them. "He kicked him when he was down on the deck," the whisper went. The other Englishman in the watch swore in a low grunt and dropped his broom, meeting the wondering eyes of the "Dutchmen" and "Dagoes" with a scowl. He was white-haired and red-faced, a veteran among the nomads of the sea, the oldest man aboard, and the only one in the port watch who had not felt the weight of the mate's fist. Scowling still, as though in deep thought, he moved towards the ladder. The forlorn hope was going on a desperate enterprise of rescue.

It might have been an ugly business; there was a sense in the minds of his fellows of something sickening about to happen; but the mate had finished with Conroy. The youth came staggering and crying down the ladder, with tears and blood befouling his face, and stumbled as his foot touched the deck. The older man, Slade, saved him from falling, and held him by the upper arm with one gnarled, toil-roughened hand, peering at him through the early morning gloom.

"Kicked you when you was down, didn't he?" he demanded abruptly.

"Yes," blubbered Conroy, shivering and dabbing at his face. "With his sea-boots, too, the—the——"

Slade shook him. "Don't make that noise or he might kick you some more," he advised grimly. "You better go now an' swab that blood off your face."

"Yes," agreed Conroy tremulously, and Slade let him go.

The elder man watched him move forward on shambling and uncertain feet, with one hand pressed to his flank, where the mate's kick was still an agony. Slade was frowning heavily, with a tincture of thought in his manner, as though he halted on the brink of some purpose.

"Conroy," he breathed, and started after the other.

The younger man turned. Slade again put his hand on Conroy's arm.

"Say," he said, breathing short, "is that a knife in your belt?"

Conroy felt behind him, uncomprehending, for the sheath-knife which he wore, sailor fashion, in the middle of his back.

"What d'you mean?" he asked vacantly. "Here's my knife."

He drew it and showed it to Slade, the flat blade displayed in his palm.

The white-haired seaman thrust his keen old face toward Conroy's, so that the other could see the flash of the white of his eyes.

"And he kicked you, didn't he?" said Slade tensely. "You fool!"

He struck the knife to the deck, where it rattled and slid toward the scupper.

"Eh?" Conroy gaped, not understanding. "I don't see what——"

"Pick it up!" said Slade, with a gesture toward the knife. He spoke, as though he strangled an impulse to brandish his fists and scream, in a nasal whisper. "It's safe to kick you," he said. "A woman could do it."

"But——" Conroy flustered vaguely.

Slade drove him off with a wave of his arm and turned away with the abruptness of a man disgusted beyond bearing.

Conroy stared after him and saw him pick up his broom where he had dropped it and join the others. His intelligence limped; his thrashing had stunned him, and he could not think—he could only feel, like fire in his mind, the passion of the feeble soul resenting injustice and pain which it cannot resist or avenge. He stooped to pick up his knife and went forward to the tub under the head-pump, to wash his cuts in cold sea-water, the cheap balm for so many wrongs of cheap humanity.

It was an accident such as might serve to dedicate the day to the service of the owners of the *Villingen*. It was early and sudden; but, save in these respects, it had no character of the unusual. The men who plied the brooms and carried the buckets were not shocked or startled by it so much as stimulated; it thrust under their noses the always imminent danger of failing to satisfy the mate's ideal of seamanlike efficiency. They woke to a fresher energy, a more desperate haste, under its suggestion.

It was after the coffee interval, which mitigates the sourness of the morning watch, when daylight had brought its chill, grey light to the wide, wet decks, that the mate came forward to superintend the "pull all round," which is the ritual sequel to washing down.

"Lee fore-brace, dere!" his flat, voluminous voice ordered, heavy with the man's potent and dreaded personality. They flocked to obey, scurrying like scared rats, glancing at him in timid hate. He came striding along the weather side of the deck from the remote, august poop; he was like a dreadful god making a dreadful visitation upon his faithful. Short-legged, tending to bigness in the belly, bearded, vibrant with animal force and personal power, his mere presence cowed them. His gross face, the happy face of an egoist with a sound digestion, sent its lofty and sure regard over them; it had a kind of unconsciousness of their sense of humility, of their wrong and resentment—the innocence of an aloof and distant tyrant, who has not dreamed how hurt flesh quivers and seared minds rankle. He was bland and terrible; and they hated him after their several manners, some with dull fear, one or two—and Slade among them—with a ferocity that moved them like physical nausea.

He had left his coat on the wheel-box to go to his work, and was manifestly unarmed. The belief which had currency in the forecastle, that he came on watch with a revolver in his coat pocket, did not apply to him now; they could have seized him, smitten him on his blaspheming mouth, and hove him over the side without peril. It is a thing that has happened to a hated officer more than once or ten times, and a lie, solemnly sworn to by every man of the watch on deck, has been entered in the log, and closed the matter for all hands. He was barer of defence than they, for they had their sheath-knives; and he stood by the weather-braces, arrogant, tyrannical, overbearing, and commanded them. He seemed invulnerable, a thing too great to strike or defy, like the white squalls that swooped from the horizon and made of the vast *Villingen* a victim and a plaything. His full, boastful eye travelled over them absently, and they cringed like slaves.

"Belay, dere!" came his orders, overloud and galling to men surging with cowardly and insufferable hate. "Lower tobsail—haul! Belay! Ubber tobsail—haul, you sons of dogs! Haul, dere, blast you! You vant me to come over and show you?"

Servilely, desperately, they obeyed him, spending their utmost strength to placate him, while the naked spirit of murder moved in every heart among them. At the tail of the brace, Conroy, with his cuts stanched, pulled with them. His abject eyes, showing the white in sidelong glances, watched the great, squat figure of the mate with a fearful fascination.

Eight bells came at last, signalling the release of the port watch from the deck and the tension of the officer's presence. The forecastle received them, the stronghold of their brief and limited leisure. The unkempt, weather-stained men, to whom the shifting seas were the sole arena of their lives, sat about on chests and on the edges of the lower bunks, at their breakfast, while the pale sunlight travelled to and fro on the deck as the *Villingen* lurched in her gait. Conroy, haggard and drawn, let the coffee slop over the brim of his hook-pot as he found himself a seat.

"Well, an' what did he punch ye for this time?"

It was old Slade who put the question, seated on a chest with his back against the bulkhead. His pot was balanced on his knee, and his venerable, sardonic face, with the scanty white hair clinging about the temples, addressed Conroy with slow mockery.

Conroy hesitated. "It was over coilin' away some gear," he said. Slade waited, and he had to go on. He had misunderstood the mate's order to coil the ropes on the pins, where they would be out of the way of the deck-washing, and he had flemished them down on the poop instead. It was the mistake of a fool, and he knew it.

Slade nodded. "Ye-es," he drawled. "You earned a punch an' you got it. But he kicked you, too, didn't he?"

"Kicked me!" cried Conroy. "Why, I thought he was goin' to kill me! Look here—look at this, will you?"

With fumbling hands he cast loose his belt and flung it on the floor, and plucked his shirt up so as to leave his side bare. He stood up, with one arm raised above his head, showing his naked flank to the slow eyes of his shipmates. His body had still a boyish delicacy and slenderness; the labour of his trade had not yet built it and thickened it to a full masculinity of proportion. Measured by any of the other men in the watch, it was frail, immature, and tender. The moving sunlight that flowed around the door touched the fair skin and showed the great, puffed bruises that stood on it, swollen and horrid, like' some vampire fungus growing on the clean flesh.

A great Greek, all black hair and eyeball, clicked softly between his teeth.

"It looks like—a hell!" he said softly, in his purring voice.

"Dem is kicks, all right—*ja!*" said some one else, and yet another added the comment of a heavy oath.

Old Slade made no comment, but sat, balancing his hook-pot of coffee and watching the scene under his heavy white brows. Conroy lowered his arm and let the shirt fall to cover the bruises.

"You see?" he said to Slade.

"I see," answered the other, with a bitter twist of his old, malicious lips. Setting down the pot which he held, he stooped and lifted the belt which Conroy had thrown down. It seemed to interest him, for he looked at it for some moments.

"And here's yer knife," he said, reaching it to the youth, still with his manner of mockery. "There's some men it wouldn't be safe to kick, with a knife in their belts."

He and Conroy were the only Englishmen there; the rest were of the races which do not fight barehanded. The big Greek flashed a smile through the black, shining curls of his beard, and continued to smile without speaking. Through the tangle of incomprehensible conventions, he had arrived at last at a familiar principle.

Conroy flushed hotly, the blood rising hectic on his bruised and broken face.

"If he thinks it's safe with me," he cried, "he'll learn different. I didn't have a chance aft there; he came on me too quick, before I was expecting him, and it was dark, besides. Or else——"

"It'll be dark again," said Slade, with intent, significant eyes fixed on him, "and he needn't be expecting you. But—it don't do to talk too much. Talk's easy—talk is."

"I'll do more than talk," responded Conroy. "You'll see!"

Slade nodded. "Right, then; we'll see," he said, and returned to his breakfast.

His bunk was an upper one, lighted and aired by a brass-framed port-hole. Here, when his meal was at an end, he lay, his pipe in his mouth, his hands behind his head, smoking with slow relish, with his wry old face upturned, and the leathery, muscular forearms showing below the rolled shirtsleeves. His years had ground him to an edge; he had an effect, as he lay, of fineness, of subtlety, of keen and fastidious temper. Forty years of subjection to arbitrary masters had left him shrewd and secret, a Machiavelli of the forecastle.

Once Conroy, after seeming to sleep for an hour, rose on his elbow and stared across at him, craning his neck from his bunk to see the still mask of his face.

"Slade?" he said uncertainly.

"What?" demanded the other, unmoving.

Conroy hesitated. The forecastle was hushed; the seamen about them slumbered; the only noises were the soothing of the water overside, the stress of the sails and gear, and the irregular tap of a hammer aft. It was safe to speak, but he did not speak.

"Oh, nothing," he said, and lay down again. Slade smiled slowly, almost paternally.

It took less than eight hours for Conroy's rancour to wear dull, and he could easily have forgotten his threat against the mate in twelve, if only he had been allowed to. He was genuinely shocked when he found that his vapourings were taken as the utterance of a serious determination. Just before eight bells in the afternoon watch he went forward beneath the forecastle head in search of some rope-yarns, and was cutting an end off a bit of waste-line when the Greek, he of the curly beard and extravagant eyeballs, rose like a demon of pantomime from the forepeak. Conroy had his knife in his hand to cut the rope, and the Greek's sudden smile seemed to rest on that and nothing else.

"Sharp, eh?" asked the Greek, in a whisper that filled the place with dark drama.

Conroy paused, apprehending his meaning with a start.

"Oh, it's all right," he growled, and began to saw at the rope in his hand, while the Greek watched him with his fixed, bony smile.

"No," said the latter suddenly. "Dat-a not sharp—no! Look-a 'ere; you see dis?"

He drew his own knife, and showed it pointing toward Conroy in a damp, swarthy hand, whose knuckles bulged above the haft. His rough, spatulate thumb rasped along it, drawing from it the crepitation that proves an acute edge.

"Carve him like-a da pork," he said in his stage conspirator's whisper. "And da point—now, see!"

He glanced over his shoulder to be sure that none overlooked them; then, with no more than a jerk of his hand beside his hip, threw the keen blade toward the wooden door of the bo'sun's locker. It travelled through the air swiftly and stuck, quivering on its thin point, in the stout teak. The Greek turned his smile again for a moment on Conroy before he strode across and recovered it.

"You take 'im," he whispered. "Beter dan your little knife—yais."

By the mere urgency of his proffering it the exchange was made, and Conroy found himself with a knife in his hand that fell through the strands of the manila line as though they had been butter, an instrument made and perfected for a murder.

"Yes, but look here——" he began in alarm.

The broad, mirthless smile was turned on him.

"Just like-a da pork," purred the Greek, and nodded assuringly before he turned to go aft.

The bull-roar of the mate, who was awaiting his return with the rope-yarns, roused Conroy from a scared reverie over the knife. He started; the mate was bustling furiously forward in search of him, full of uproar and anger.

"Dam' lazy *Schwein*, you goin' to schleep dere? You vant me to come an' fetch you? You vant anodder schmack on de *Maul* to keep you avake—yes?"

He stamped into view round the forward house, while Conroy stood, convicted of idleness by the rope in his hand only half cut through. At the same moment a population of faces came into being behind him. A man who had been aloft shuffled down to the rail; a couple of others came into view on the deck; on top of the house, old Slade kneeled to see under the break of the forecastle head. It seemed as though a sceptical audience had suddenly been created out of his boast of the morning, every face threatening him with that shame which vanity will die rather than endure. In a panic of his faculties he took one step toward the mate.

"Hey?" The mate halted in his stride, with sheer amazement written on his face. "You vant yer head knocked off—yes?"

"No, I don't," said Conroy, out of a dry mouth.

According to the usage of ships, even that was defiance and a challenge.

He had forgotten the revolver with which the mate was credited; he had forgotten everything but the fact that eyes were on him. Even the knife in his hand passed from his mind; he was a mere tingling pretence at fortitude, expending every force to maintain his pose.

"Put dat knife avay!" ordered the mate suddenly.

He arrested an automatic movement to obey, fighting down a growing fear of his opponent.

"I've not finished with it yet," he answered.

The mate measured him with a practised eye. Though he had the crazy courage of a bulldog, he was too much an expert in warlike emergencies to overlook the risk of trying to rush a desperate man armed with a knife; the chances of the grapple were too ugly. There was something lunatic and strange in the youth's glare also; and it will sometimes happen that an oppressed and cowed man in his extremity will shrug his meekness from him and become, in a breath, a desperado. This had its place in the mate's considerations.

"Finish, den!" he rasped, with no weakening of his tone or manner. "You don't t'ink I'm goin' to vait all night for dem rope-yarns—hey?"

He turned his back at once lest Conroy should venture another retort, and make an immediate fight unavoidable. Before his eye the silent audience melted as swiftly as it had appeared, and Conroy was alone with his sick sense of having ventured too far, which stood him in place of the thrill of victory.

The thrill came later, in the forecastle, where he swelled to the adulation of his mates. They, at any rate, had been deceived by his attitude; they praised him by word and look; the big Greek infused a certain geniality into his smile. Only Slade said the wrong thing.

"I was ready for him as soon as he moved," Conroy was asserting. "And he knew it. You should ha' seen how he gaped when I wouldn't put the knife away."

The men were listening, crediting him. Old Slade, in the background, took his pipe from his lips.

"An' now I suppose you're satisfied," he inquired harshly.

"How d'you mean, satisfied?" demanded Conroy, colouring. "You saw what happened, didn't you?"

"You made him gape," said Slade. "That was because he made you howl, eh? Well, ain't you calling it quits, then—till the next time he kicks you?"

Some one laughed; Conroy raised his voice.

"He'll never kick me again," he cried. "His kicking days are over. He's kicked me once too often, he has. Quits—I guess not!"

Slade let a mouthful of smoke trickle between his lips; it swam in front of his face in a tenuous film of pale vapour.

"Well, talkin' won't do it, anyhow," he said.

"No," retorted Conroy, and collected all eyes to his gesture. "But this will!"

He showed them the thin-bladed knife which the Greek had given him, holding it before them by the hilt. He let a dramatic moment elapse.

"Like that!" he said, and stabbed at the air. "Like that—see? Like that!"

They came upon bad weather gradually, drawing into a belt of half-gales, with squalls that roared up from the horizon and made them for the time into whole gales. The *Villingen*, designed and built primarily for cargo capacity, was a wet ship, and upon any point of sailing had a way of scooping in water by the many tons. In nearly every watch came the roar, "Stand by yer to'gallant halliards!" Then the wait for ten seconds or ten minutes while the wind grew and the big four-masted barque lay over and bumped her bluff bows through racing seas, till the next order, shriller and more urgent, "Lower away!" and the stiff canvas fought and slatted as the yards came down. Sea-boots and oilskins were the wear for every watch; wet decks and the crash of water coming inboard over the rail, dull cold and the rasp of heavy, sodden canvas on numb fingers, became again familiar to the men, and at last there arrived the evening, gravid with tempest, on which all hands reefed topsails.

The mate had the middle watch, from midnight till four o'clock in the morning, and for the first two hours it was Conroy's turn on the look-out. The rest, in oilskins and sea-boots, were standing by under the break of the poop; save for the sleeping men in the shut forecastle, he had the fore part of the ship to himself. He leaned against the after rail of the forecastle head, where a ventilator somewhat screened him from the bitter wind that blew out of the dark, and gazed ahead at the murk. Now and again the big barque slid forward with a curtseying motion, and dipped up a sea that flowed aft over the anchors and cascaded down the ladders to the main-deck; spray that spouted aloft and drove across on the wind, sparkled red and green in the glare of the sidelights like brief fireworks.

The splash and drum of waters, the heavy drone of the wind in the sails, the clatter of gear aloft, were in his ears; he did not hear one bell strike from the poop, which he should have answered with a stroke on the big bell behind him and a shouted report on the lights.

"Hoy! You schleepin' up dere—hey?"

It was the mate, who had come forward in person to see why he had not answered. He was by the fore fife-rail, a mere black shape in the dark.

"Sleepin'—no, sir!"

"Don t you hear von bell shtrike?" cried the mate, slithering on the wet deck toward the foot of the ladder.

"No, sir," said Conroy, and stooped to strike the bell.

The mate came up the ladder, hauling himself by the handrails, for he was swollen beyond the ordinary with extra clothes under his long oilskin coat. A plume of spray whipped him in the face as he got to the top, and he swore shortly, wiping his eyes with his hands. At the same moment Conroy, still stooping to the bell-lanyard, felt the *Villingen* lower her nose and slide down in one of her disconcerting curtseys; he caught at the rail to steady himself. The dark water, marbled with white foam, rode in over the deck, slid across the anchors and about the capstan, and came aft toward the ladder and the mate. The ship rolled at the same moment.

Conroy saw what happened as a grotesque trick of circumstance. The mate, as the deck slanted, slipped and reached for the hand-rail with an ejaculation. The water flowed about his knees; he fell back against the hand-rail, which was just high enough for him to sit on. It was what, for one ridiculous moment, he seemed to be doing. The next, his booted feet swayed up and he fell over backward, amid the confusion of splashing water that leaped down the main-deck. Conroy heard him strike something below with a queer, smacking noise.

"Pity he didn't go overboard while he was about it," he said to himself, acting out his role. Really he was rather startled and dismayed.

He found the mate coiled in the scupper, very wet and still. He took hold of him to draw him under the forecastle head, where he would have shelter, and was alarmed at the inertness of the body under his hands.

"Sir!" he cried, "sir!—sir!"

He shook the great shoulders, but quickly desisted; there was something horrible, something that touched his nerves, in its irresponsiveness. He remembered that he might probably find matches in the lamp-locker, and staggered there to search. He had to grope in gross darkness about the place, touching brass and the uncanny smoothness of glass, before his hand fell on what he sought. At last he was on one knee by the mate's side, and a match shed its little illumination. The mate's face was odd in its quietude, and the sou'-wester of oilskin was still on his head, held there by the string under the chin. From under its edge blood flowed steadily, thickly, appallingly.

"But——" cried Conroy. The match-flame stung his fingers and he dropped it. "O Lord!" he said. It occurred to him then, for the first time, that the mate was dead.

The men aft, bunched up under the break of the poop, were aware of him as a figure that came sliding and tottering toward them and fell sprawling at the foot of the poop ladder. He floundered up and clutched the nearest of them, the Greek.

"The mate's dead," he broke out, in a kind of breathless squeal. "Somebody call the captain; the mate's dead."

There was a moment of silence; then a cackle of words from several of them together. The Greek's hands on his shoulders tightened. He heard the man's purring voice in his ear.

"How did you do it?"

Conroy thrust himself loose; the skies of his mind were split by a frightful lightning flash of understanding. He had been alone with the mate; he had seen him die; he was sworn to kill him. He could see the livid smile of the Greek bent upon him.

"I didn't do it," he choked passionately, and struck with a wild, feeble hand at the smile. "You liar—I didn't do it."

"Hush!" The Greek caught him again and held him.

Some of the men had started forward; others had slipped into the alley-way to rouse the second mate and captain. The Greek had him clutched to his bosom in a strong embrace and was hushing him as one might hush a scared child. Slade was at his side.

"He slipped, I tell you; he slipped at the top of the ladder! She'd shipped a dollop of water and then rolled, and over he went. I heard his head go smack and went down to him. I never touched him. I swear it—I never touched him."

"Hush!" It was Slade this time. "And yer sure he's dead?"

"Yes, he's dead."

"Well——" the old man exchanged nods with the Greek. "All right. Only—don't tell the captain that tale; it ain't good enough."

"But——" began Conroy. A hug that crushed his face against the Greek's oilskin breast silenced him.

"Vat is all dis?"

It was the captain, tall, august, come full-dressed from his cabin. At his back the second mate, with his oilskin coat over his pyjamas, thrust forward his red, cheerful face.

Slade told the matter briefly. "And it's scared young Conroy all to bits, sir," he concluded.

"Come for'ard," bade the captain. "Get a lamp, some vun!"

They followed him along the wet, slippery deck slowly, letting him pass ahead out of earshot.

"It was a belayin'-pin, ye-es?" queried the Greek softly of Conroy.

"He might have hit his head against a pin," replied Conroy.

"Eh?" The Greek stopped. "Might 'ave—might 'ave 'it 'is 'ead! Ah, dat is fine! 'E might 'ave 'it 'is 'ead, Slade! You 'ear dat?"

"Yes, it ain't bad!" replied Slade, and Conroy, staring in a wild attempt to see their faces clearly, realised that they were laughing, laughing silently and heartily. With a gesture of despair he left them.

A globe-lamp under the forecastle head lighted the captain's investigations, gleaming on wet oilskins, shadow-pitted faces, and the curious, remote thing that had been the mate of the *Villingen*. Its ampler light revealed much that the match-flame had missed from its field—the manner in which the sou'-wester and the head it covered were caved in at one side, the cut in the sou'-wester through which clotted hair protruded, the whole ghastliness of death that comes by violence. With all that under his eyes, Conroy had to give his account of the affair, while the ring of silent, hard-breathing men watched him and marvelled at the clumsiness of his story.

"It is strange," said the captain. "Fell ofer backvards, you said. It is very strange! And vere did you find de body?"

The scupper and deck had been washed clean by successive seas; there was no trace there of blood, and none on the rail. Even while they searched, water spouted down on them. But what Conroy noted was that no pin stood in the rail where the mate had fallen, and the hole that might have held one was empty.

"Ah, vell!" said the captain at last. "De poor fellow is dead. I do not understand, quite, how he should fall like dat, but he is dead. Four of you get de body aft."

"Please, sir," accosted Conroy, and the tall captain turned.

"Vell, vat is it?"

"Can I go below, sir? It was me that found him, sir. I feel rather—rather bad."

"So!" The tall captain considered him inscrutably, he, the final arbiter of fates. "You feel bad—yes? Vell, you can go below!"

He fell over backward

The little group that bore the mate's body shuffled aft, with the others following like a funeral procession. A man looked shivering out of the door of the starboard forecastle, and inquired in loud whispers: "*Was ist los? Sag' mal—was ist denn los?*" He put his inquiry to Conroy, who waved him off and passed to the port forecastle on the other side of the deckhouse.

The place was somehow strange, with its double row of empty bunks like vacant coffin-shelves in a vault, but solitude was what he desired. The slush-lamp swung and stank and made the shadows wander. From the other side of the bulkhead he could hear stirrings and a murmur of voices as the starboard watch grew aware that something had happened on deck. Conroy, with his oilskin coat half off, paused to listen for comprehensible words. The opening of the door behind him startled him, and he spun round to see Slade making a cautious entry. He recoiled.

"Leave me alone," he said, in a strangled voice, before the other could speak. "What are you following me for? You want to make me out a murderer. I tell you I never touched him."

The other stood just within the door, the upper half of his face shadowed by his sou'-wester, his thin lips curved in a faint smile. "No!" he said mockingly. "You didn't touch him? An' I make no doubts you'd take yer oath of it. But you shouldn't have put the pin back in the rail when you was through with it, all the same."

"There wasn't any pin there," said Conroy quickly. He had backed as far from Slade as he could, and was staring at him with horrified eyes.

"But there would ha' been if I hadn't took a look round while you were spinnin' your yarn to the Old Man," said Slade. "I knew you was a fool."

With a manner as of mild glee he passed his hand into the bosom of his coat, still keeping his sardonic gaze fixed on Conroy.

"Good thing you've got me to look after you," he went on. "Thinks I, 'He might easy make a mistake that 'ud cost him dear'; so I took a look round. An' I found this." From within his coat he brought forth an iron belaying-pin, and held it out to Conroy.

"See?" His finger pointed to it. "That's blood, that is—and that's hair. Look for yourself! *Now* I suppose you'll tell me you never touched him!"

"He hit his head against it when he fell," protested the younger man. "He did! Oh, God, I can't stand this!"

He sank to a seat on one of the chests and leaned his face against the steel plate of the wall.

"Hit his head!" snorted old Slade. "Couldn't you ha' fixed up a better yarn than that? What are you snivellin' at? D'ye think yer the only man as ever stove in a mate's head—an' him a murderin' man-driver? Keep them tales for the Old Man; he believes 'em seemingly; but don't you come them on me."

Conroy was moaning. "I never touched him; I never touched him!"

"Never touched him! Here, take the pin; it's yours!"

He shrank from it. "No, no!"

Slade pitched it to his bunk, where it lay on the blanket. "It's yours," he repeated. "If yer don't want it, heave it overboard yerself or stick it back in the rail. Never touched him—you make me sick with yer 'never touched him'!"

The door slammed on his scornful retreat; Conroy shuddered and sat up. The iron belaying-pin lay where it had fallen, on his bed, and even in that meagre light it carried the traces of its part in the mate's death. It had the look of a weapon rather than of a humble ship-fitting. It rolled a couple of inches where it lay as the ship leaned to a gust, and he saw that it left a mark where it had been, a stain.

He seized it in a panic and started for the door to be rid of it at once.

As if a malicious fate made him its toy, he ran full into the Greek outside.

"Ah!" The man's smile flashed forth, wise and livid "An' so you 'ad it in your pocket all de time, den!"

Conroy answered nothing. It was beyond striving against. He walked to the rail and flung the thing forth with hysterical violence to the sea.

The watch going below at four o'clock found him apparently asleep, with his face turned to the wall. They spoke in undertones, as though they feared to disturb him, but none of them mentioned the only matter which all had in mind. They climbed heavily to their bunks, there to smoke the brief pipe, and then to slumber. Only Slade, who slept little, would from time to time lean up on one elbow to look down and across to the still figure which hid its face throughout the night.

Conroy woke when the watch was called for breakfast by a man who thrust his head in and shouted. He had slept at last, and now as he sat up it needed an effort of mind to recall his trouble. He looked out at his mates, who stood about the place pulling on their clothes, with sleep still heavy on them. They seemed as usual. It was his turn to fetch the coffee from the galley, he remembered, and he slipped out of his bunk to dress and attend to it.

"I won't be a minute," he said to the others, as he dragged on his trousers.

A shaggy young Swede near the door was already dressed.

"I vill go," he said. "You don't bother," and forthwith slipped out.

The others were looking at him now, glancing with a queer, sharp interest and turning away when they met his eyes. It was as though he were a stranger.

"That was a queer thing last night," he said to the nearest.

"Yes," the other agreed, with a kind of haste.

They sat about at their meal, when the coffee had been brought by the volunteer, under the same constraint. He could not keep silent; he had to speak and make them answer.

"Where is he?" he asked abruptly.

"On de gratings," he was told. And the Swede who fetched the coffee added, "Sails is sowin' him up now already."

"We'll see the last of him to-day," said Slade. "He won't kick nobody again!"

There was a mutter of agreement, and eyes turned on Conroy again. Slade smiled slowly.

"Yes, he keeck once too many times," said the Greek.

The shaggy young Swede wagged his head. "He t'ink it was safe to kick Conroy, but it aindt," he observed profoundly. "No, it aindt safe."

"He got vat he ask for. . . . Didn't know vat he go up againdst. . . . No, it aindt—it aindt safe. . . . Maybe vish he aindt so handy mit his feet now."

They were all talking; their mixed words came to Conroy in broken sentences. He stared at them a little wildly, realising the fact that they were admiring him, praising him, and afraid of him. The blood rose in his face hotly.

"You fellers talk," he began, and was disconcerted at the manner in which they all fell silent to hear him—"you talk as if I'd killed him."

"Well! . . . *Ach was!*"

He faced their smiles, their conciliatory gestures, with a frown.

"You better stop it," he said. "He fell—see? He fell an' stove his head in. An' any feller that says he didn't——"

His regard travelled from face to face, giving force to his challenge.

"Ve aindt goin' to say nodings!" they assured him mildly. "You don't need to be scared of us, Conroy."

"I'm not scared," he said with meaning. "But—look out, that's all."

When breakfast was over, it was his turn to sweep up. But there was almost a struggle for the broom and the privilege of saving him that trouble. It comforted him and restored him; it would have been even better but for the presence of Slade, sitting aloft in his bunk, smiling over his pipe with malicious understanding.

The *Villingen* was still under reefed upper topsails, walking into the seas on a taut bowline, with water coming aboard freely. There was little for the watch to do save those trivial jobs which never fail on a ship. Conroy and some of the others were set to scrubbing teak on the poop, and he had a view of the sail-maker at his work on the gratings under the break of the poop, stitching on his knees to make the mate presentable for his last passage. The sail-maker was a bearded Finn, with a heavy, darkling face and the secret eyes of a faun. He bent over his task, and in his attitude and the slow rhythm of his moving hand there was a suggestion of ceremonial, of an act mysterious and ritual.

Half-way through the morning Conroy was sent for to the cabin, there to tell his tale anew, to see it taken down, and to sign it. The captain even asked him if he felt better.

"Thank you, sir," replied Conroy. "It was a shock, findin' him dead like that."

"Yes, yes," agreed the captain. "I can understand—a great shock. Yes!"

He was bending over his papers at the table; Conroy smiled over his bowed head. Returning on deck, he winked to the man at the wheel, who smiled uncomfortably in return. Later he borrowed a knife to scrape some spots of paint off the deck; he did not want to spoil the edge of his own.

They buried the mate at eight bells; the weather was thickening, and it might be well to have the thing done. The hands stood around, bareheaded, with the grating in the middle of them, one edge resting on the rail, the other supported by two men. There was a dark smudge on the sky up to windward, and several times the captain glanced up from his book towards it. He read in German slowly, with a dwelling upon the sonorous passages, and towards the end he closed the book and finished without its aid.

Conroy was at the foot of the ladder; the captain was above him, reading mournfully, solemnly, without looking at the men. They were rigid, only their eyes moving. Conroy collected their glances irresistibly. When the captain had finished his reading he sighed and made a sign, lifting his hand like a man who resigns himself. The men holding the grating tilted it; the mate of the *Villingen*, with a little jerk, went over the side.

"Shtand by der tobs'l halliards!" roared the second mate.

Conroy, in the flurry, found himself next to a man of his watch. He jerked a thumb in the direction of the second mate, who was still vociferating orders.

"Hark at him!" he said. "Before we're through I'll teach *him* manners too."

And he patted his knife.

THE FAIR EXCHANGE

ANNA McMULLEN

I've never before realised what it means to me. Even the familiar things: the murmur of talk in the bar downstairs; the hum of conversation from the groups of people on the Hard—all those commonplace sounds I am hearing now. And behind them all, the sea, slapping softly at the boats as the rising tide creeps up the mud.

Ever since I can remember I have found here everything that is *necessary* for my life. This place has been all-sufficient. The sea, so vast, and yet so small and intimate where it gurgles in the little creeks among the saltings. The saltings, so grey and dun, and then so beautiful when they are purple with sea lavender, in the summer, and green with the queer transparent samphire. Even the mud can be lovely at low tide, with lights and shades, and the different greens of the seaweeds that grow on the harder parts. And the winds: the east wind that brings the pure sea smell, a *deep* sea smell, and raises white horses up the river; and the south-west wind that brings the mud smell at low tide, a mixed smell of flowers and hedgerows, and a warm smell of cattle on the marshes.

Winter and summer it changes, but I love it. I have seen it on November evenings, very grey and colourless, and very still; the water like a mirror, hazy with mist; the marshes lying low and quiet. A flock of great saddle-back gulls standing motionless on the mud, the silence only broken as one or another of them flies up with a flapping of wings and a harsh cry. And on cold, frosty mornings the water blue and dancing in the sunlight, and flocks of oxbird wheeling and turning in the clear sky, flashing silver as they turn their white undersides to the sun; the saltings sparkling with frost, the fleets on the marshes frozen hard enough for skating.

But I can never make anyone understand what all this means to me. Except Peter; I think Peter would understand. With Peter I have never felt the need to explain, from the days when we used to wade after flounders up the creeks at low tide—feeling with our hands along the rill of water at the bottom. Then catching them and throwing them up on the mud. When the tide began to flow we would tramp along the mud to collect them, and stow them in Peter's canvas dinghy. I remember how our bare legs looked like long black stockings, and how we used to cut our feet on oyster shells.

Those days are still so vivid to me—the freedom and the timelessness. In fact, the only sort of time that mattered at all was the ebb and flow of the tides. Taking sandwiches, we would go out all day on the Old Barn Marsh. Walking till we were tired and hungry; then bathing in the creek over the seawall. After that we would eat our sandwiches; then lie on our backs in the sweet marsh grass, watching a heron flap slowly across the vast sky that stretches enormously from low horizon to horizon. And then we'd go to Holepenny Fleet, and creep up to the decoy to see how many duck we could surprise in it.

Or we'd take the dinghy and explore new, unknown creeks, following them right up to the end. Sometimes the tide would fall, leaving us stranded on the mud, with no choice but to get out and push the dinghy or wait until the water returned. And sometimes the creeks became so narrow at the end that we were squeezed between the banks of the saltings.

That was before Peter's father built me *The Fair Exchange*—cutter-rigged, eighteen feet long, and not very beautiful. But comfortable and easy to handle. He said she was only a fair exchange for my amusing Peter during his holidays. After that we could explore the larger and more distant creeks; could sail across the estuary to villages on the other side. And then, later still, I could sail *The Fair Exchange* in the club races, with Peter as crew.

Now I can hear Joe clearing the bar and father's voice saying good-night. I can hear other voices getting louder as they pass into the road. But to-night they are not so loud and cheerful as usual.

I cannot believe there might have come a time when all this would have gone on without me. When I could no longer have sat up here in my room at night, looking over the dark water, watching the yachts' lights and their shimmering reflections.

If I put my head out of the window I can see the few lights on the derelict tramp steamers lying up the river. Through the window comes the smell of the sea, and now and then a wailing cry from redshank on the marshes. Footsteps and voices are dying away now, some up the road and some down to the Hard. In a minute or two father will be coming upstairs. He will be very kind and tender. He has always been kind and tender. Ever since my mother died and he retired from the navy. So simple in his kind-ness. Just as he is simple in his queer pride at being an innkeeper.

He was so pleased and proud when I became engaged to Ralph. He had always wanted me to be mistress of a comfortable home: of luxuries and possessions that he could never give me—and that I have never wanted. And he had always been afraid that I should marry Peter. Not that he wasn't fond of him, but Peter was only the son of a boatbuilder. Poor Peter.

It was a Saturday when Ralph first came—one of those soft, warm days we sometimes get in very early spring. I remember Peter and I had *The Fair Exchange* up on the Hard and were scraping and painting her. Ralph's friends had arranged for him to put up with us at the Lord Nelson. I remember father coming down to see how we were getting on, and tell-ing us that an elder brother of Ralph's had served under him in the navy.

Ralph came down fairly often after that, and most week-ends his big grey car was in our garage. It is there now, I suppose. He seemed to enjoy coming, and was at first anxious for me to teach him to sail and to take him out in *The Fair Exchange*. By the end of May we were engaged; and to this day I don't know how it happened. I remember it only as part of the evening, for in itself it never seemed to make a real impression on me.

Father had been out of sorts all the week, depressed and anxious because business was slack; and I was worried about him. Ralph arrived in high spirits, and father seemed to cheer up at once. Somehow the sight of his big body with its strength and assurance relieved my worry. I was glad to listen to his jokes and talk at dinner. After dinner Ralph and I walked down the coast road to the old tarred wooden houses and ships' stores. Then on to the sea-wall that runs up the creek. The evening was warm and still. The thorn trees on Haye Island stood out black against a clear, green-blue sky. The tide was ebbing, the mud glimmering in the fading light. After walking along a little, we sat down on a derelict boat, upturned against the seawall. I think the beauty of the evening had stilled even Ralph's tongue—the silence was broken only by the gentle sucking noises the water makes as it runs out of the little creeks and holes in the saltings. Ralph turned to speak to me and I laid a finger on his rather full lips—I had always wanted to do that—and then I was in his arms. It was as if all my worry and tiredness were flowing away with the tide, leaving a sense of renewed strength that was yet peaceful and secure.

I don't remember feeling very different afterwards, or thinking much about it. Life went on as usual and father's health improved. He was in good spirits and especially affectionate to me. During the week I did my usual jobs about the house, bathed and walked, and sailed *The Fair Exchange*. The only difference was that I didn't see so much of Peter.

I used to look forward to the week-ends—to the strange, sweet excitement of being taken in Ralph's arms and kissed. I enjoyed taking him for walks, and out in *The Fair Exchange*, and trying to show him the ropes.

But he never had any sea sense. At first I think he genuinely tried to be interested and to like the things I liked. But he didn't like mud, and he didn't like getting wet and not having his meals at regular times. I think he was soon impatient of my preoccupation with it all, and would try to make me discuss the wedding and the house he was building for me. He liked to make me go out in the car with him instead of sailing. And yet he had only to touch me and I forgot all those things and would do as he liked.

Ralph came down last night. For the first time I was glad when he let me go. I don't know whether it was the faint smell of petrol on his clothes, or the strength with which he held me—he seemed so benevolently possessive. At dinner he began to plan a long drive for to-day. Father said it was a good idea, and would be a change for me. Somehow the fact of their both being in agreement made me resentful. I said it looked so fine that it would be a good opportunity to take Ralph for a long sail. He didn't like the idea, and was inclined to argue. But I had my way.

It is strange to think that it was only this morning we started out. It seems like something that happened a long time ago, or like a violent storm that has now drifted away.

The day was so fine when I woke this morning that I never gave Ralph a thought. It was a lovely day, and we were going sailing. I was up early, so that I could get my jobs done in good time and the food-basket ready. As I worked I whistled. Even Ralph seemed cheerful, and tried to help me in. his clumsy way.

We started down to the Hard, Ralph, in his clean white flannels, carrying the lunch-basket, and I carrying the oars and rowlocks for the dinghy, for since my new brass ones disappeared I have always brought the rowlocks up at night. I reckoned it would be high tide about 1.15, and I wondered whether last night I had left the dinghy anchor high enough up the beach to get it without wading.

I found the anchor without any trouble, and pulled the dinghy in against the stone part of the Hard so that Ralph and the lunch could embark without getting muddy. Then I pulled out from among the huddle of boats, and rowed to *The Fair Exchange*, rocking gently at her moorings in the middle of the creek.

I brought the dinghy alongside and went aboard, so that I could take the lunch-basket from Ralph, and make the dinghy fast. Ralph came aboard heavily, as he usually does, making both boats rock. I made him undo the tiers round the mainsail while I got the jib ready for hoisting. Then I gave him the tiller, and told him to keep her head to wind, and the mainsheet clear, while I hoisted the sails. I went forward and cast off from the buoy, ran back and took the tiller from Ralph, took in the jibsheet and mainsheet, and we were off, leaving the dinghy on the mooring. We had a soldier's wind down the creek—it was fair nearly all the way across the estuary to Stonewell, except for a short beat up Stonewell Creek.

Soon I forgot about Ralph. The boat was like a live thing under my hands, quivering as she forged ahead, the water slapping under herbow, and the wind thrumming through the stays. The smell of the sea was in my nostrils, and the wind in my hair.

It was about half-past twelve when we sailed up the creek to Stonewell, and brought up at the little tumbledown jetty, making fast to one of the wooden piles. I let down the sails, and we left *The Fair Exchange* snug and tidy and went ashore. As we walked along the grass lane to the Leather Bottle to buy beer, the sounds and smells were all of the country instead of the sea—the humming of insects and bees, the song of larks, and the smell of dusty roads and cow-dung. We ate our lunch and drank our beer in the shade of a haystack. It was soft and comfortable in the sweet-smelling hay, and I think I must have dozed for a moment after lunch, because when I closed my eyes Ralph was lighting a cigarette, and when I next opened them he was stubbing it out on the sole of his shoe.

"Go on, you fool!"

We got up and shook the hay out of our clothes, and walked back to the jetty. The spring tide was at its height, the saltings covered, with only a tuft of coarse grass here and there standing up out of the water, which had risen right up to the sea-walls.

Ralph took my hand in his, and we stood looking over the water. I remember Ralph asked me about some gulls that got up and flew along the creek, and I told him they were cob-gulls, which get their black heads from March to September, so the fishermen say, by dipping them in March water.

The tide turned while we were standing there, and I noticed that the sky had clouded over and the sun gone in. The wind, that had freshened, blew rather chilly, and we decided to set off. We went aboard *The Fair Exchange*, ran up the sails, and got under way. As we came out of the creek into the estuary the wind was against the tide, and the sea was quite rough. *The Fair Exchange* put her nose into it once or twice, sending a shower of water over us. We sailed for home.

I suppose if I'd not decided to turn and run up West Creek it might never have happened. But *The Fair Exchange* goes so well in a strong breeze; it was still early; and I'd caught sight of Peter's sail round a bend in the creek. Ralph wasn't very wet but he hated the taste of salt on his lips. For some reason he was always afraid of gybing, so to save his feelings I wended round, and we set off up the creek after Peter.

The tide was racing out of West Creek against the wind, and even there it was choppy. We were running by the lee and I knew we should have to gybe at the bend, so I warned Ralph. He asked, why couldn't we wend, and I explained there wasn't room. There was a pretty strong gust of wind as we came to the bend. I said: " 'Ware gybe!" to Ralph, put up the helm, and started to gather in the mainsheet.

About what happened then I shall never know. I suppose Ralph either fouled the mainsheet accidentally or seized it in a panic. At the time all I knew was that we were over, the sail flat in the water, and I was automatically bracing my feet against the gunwale, trying, to stop any loose gear going overboard.

Then I was aware of Ralph's feet scrabbling violently on the bottom boards, as he tried to climb on to the top side of the overturned boat.

"Hurry up and get there, Ralph," I said. "You'll have the bottom boards out in a minute."

I glanced down the creek and saw Peter about three minutes away. He waved his arm to us, and I waved back.

The Fair Exchange was getting lower in the water.

I said to Ralph, "You'd better abandon ship and swim ashore, or pot-ter about till Peter picks you up."

But he sat on, his face looking rather white.

"Hurry up, Ralph, do!" I said. "Your weight is sinking her."

He would not let go.

I said again, "Your weight is sinking her. What are you waiting for?"

But he still clung on.

Suddenly the look of panic in his eyes infuriated me. If he stayed there much longer he'd sink the boat. He'd only just got to drop into the water and swim about till Peter came; but there he sat like a great stuffed dummy, white and shivering.

"Go on, you fool!" I said, and gave him a push. He went into the water.

It was when I saw the look on his face and heard his frantic splash-ings that I first realised he couldn't swim. For a second or two I hesi-tated, amazed. Before I was in the water the race had caught him, and was sweeping him out of my reach.

When I had cleared the hair and water from my eyes I saw Peter dive in and seize him. Ralph was struggling furiously, and as Peter first caught hold of him they both went under. When they came up again they were farther from me, and as the tide hurried them along I heard Peter calling.

I swam with every ounce of energy I possessed—my lungs bursting, my clothes sodden and heavy. I can feel the ache in my limbs now. But I couldn't get near them, though I could see that Ralph had got Peter round the neck and was hanging on. I tried to shout, but my mouth was full of water and my hair was getting in my eyes. For a moment I thought I heard the chug-chug of a motor-boat. But soon that was drowned by the sound of water roaring in my ears.

The next thing I felt—as if to reassure me—was the familiar sensation of a boat under way. I was lying on the deck of a smack, while a fisherman tried to pour something down my throat. For a little I lay still, trying to remember. Then I remembered. I looked at his face and I knew they were gone.

I lay still and watched the top of the mast swaying against the sky. I listened to the throb of the engine and the wash of the dinghy astern. Overhead the gulls circled and screamed.

It was on the mud they found them, at low tide, their bodies locked together. There was mud in their eyes and ears when they brought them ashore two hours ago. The mud that to Peter and me has always been a friendly and familiar sort of joke. But Ralph, he would have hated to be found like that. He hated the mud, the way it oozes round your bare feet in the water, the way it sticks and clings and spreads to everything you touch.

Now I can hear father shutting and bolting the door. Soon he will be coming upstairs. I shall see the pain and bewilderment in his eyes. He will be appalled at the idea of my grief. He will be kind and very gentle, thinking I am numbed with shock, fearing the moment when the full realisation of my grief will come.

But I can feel no grief. And I believe no grief *will* come. Perhaps I am utterly heartless. Perhaps in my soul I have committed murder. But now suddenly all things are plain and clear. They are both gone—Ralph whom I desired, and, at the last moment, hated, and Peter who was part of all those things I love. But those other things have been returned to me. And now they will never be taken from me. To me it seems a fair exchange. The only thing I can't understand is how I ever came to be in such danger—I mean the danger of marrying Ralph, of going away and losing everything.

Father is coming upstairs now. I don't think I have seen so fine a night this summer. There is a shifting mist on the marshes behind the sea-wall. The moonlight is shining through it, giving it the milky appearance of pearls. Pearls and diamonds. I suppose I can take this ring off now? I should like to throw it away. To-morrow I think I *shall* throw it away. Into the sea, perhaps. Yes, into the sea.

THE RUNNING AMOK IN THE
"FRANK N. THAYER"

J. G. LOCKHART

The sea and the desert are akin in this—that each holds for those who travel it a supreme charm and a supreme danger. The charm is beyond debate, familiar to any one who has made even the shortest of voyages, or trod even the fringes of a desert. The danger is more elusive. I refer not to risks of shipwreck or drowning by sea, of thirst or loss of bearings by land, but to something psychological. A dreadful malady lingers about those great spaces. The French legionary with *le cafard*, who shoots his sergeant and then blows out his own brains, is fellow-sufferer to the Malay seaman who, without any warning, runs amok and knifes his comrades. We may not understand these things. We cannot explain them adequately, any more than we can deny them glibly. But they exist; and in them I find the only possible solution to the puzzling and horrible story of the *Frank N. Thayer*.

On the morning of Monday, January 14th, 1886, the small population of Jamestown, St. Helena, awoke to find that during the night an open boat containing seventeen castaways had come into harbour, freighted with as strange and gruesome a tale as any man could wish to hear. They were the survivors of the *Frank N. Thayer* of Boston, a fine American vessel of 1600 tons burden, sailing from Manila to New York with a cargo of hemp. The men had been taken to the office of the American Consul, Mr. McKnight, and, as details of their experiences leaked out, there was great excitement; the wildest rumours ran through the little town, and the truth, astounding though it was, became distorted beyond recognition. The account which I give here is taken from Mr. McKnight's report, following the official investigation which he held in the island.

Until the night of Saturday, January 2nd, when the *Frank N. Thayer* was about seven hundred miles south-east of St. Helena, her voyage had been entirely uneventful. There was not the least apprehension of impending danger in the minds either of Robert K. Clarke, her commander, or of his two officers. All was as it should be. Nothing unusual or disturbing had occurred. The officers knew their job and did it. The men were contented. The weather was fine. When the Captain went below at ten o'clock to join his wife and child in their cabin, all was shipshape aboard, the night was bright and starlit, and the *Frank N. Thayer* was bowling along under a fair, strong breeze. Two hours later the men on watch below had the first indication that something was amiss when, just before the change of watch, they noticed that a man of their number had gone on deck. This was one of two seamen shipped at Manila—they are described as Indian coolies—fine, stalwart fellows who had worked well and given no trouble. The irregularity was trifling, and none of the watch below was at all alarmed by the man's absence.

On deck the first and second mates were sitting and chatting on the booby hatch, when the two Manila men came up to them in the darkness, one of them beginning to explain that he had been taken ill. It was an odd hour at which to report sick, and the first mate was starting to question the man, when suddenly the Indians whipped out knives and fell upon their unarmed officers. A few yards away a white seaman, Maloney, was at the wheel. He saw everything that occurred, but was too terrified to utter a sound. The two mates were stabbed or slashed to death before his eyes.

The Captain, peacefully asleep below, awoke suddenly with a loud cry ringing in his ears. It was followed by a babble of voices as in altercation. He tumbled from his bunk and went out into the little passage to discover what had happened. He was clad in shirt and trousers; he was dazed with sleep; and he had a vague idea that one of the mates was calling him to see a vessel which had been ahead of them the previous evening and which they had been afraid of overhauling during the night. From the passage the deck was reached by a companion-way, and the Captain had hardly set foot on the lowest step when a man came tumbling down from above, cried out, "Captain Clarke! Captain Clarke!" in an agonised voice, and collapsed in a heap on the deck. It was the second mate. By the starlight which dropped through the open hatch the Captain could see that blood was pouring from him. Clarke's name was still on his lips when he died.

Had the Captain stopped to think he would now have gone back to his cabin and fetched his revolver. As it was, he seems to have been utterly bewildered by this sudden horror, and mounted the companion-way unarmed. At the top some one stabbed him on the head and then seized him by the throat. Though nearly blinded by a rush of blood, he turned and knocked his assailant over with a blow between the eyes. Then at last he tried to retire to his cabin for a weapon, but the coolie was up in a moment and grappled with him, and the pair of them fell struggling down the companion. The coolie strove to use his knife and managed to wound the Captain severely in the left side. At the bottom Clarke recovered his foothold, but slipped on the bloodstained deck and fell back into the open door of his cabin. Whereupon the coolie stabbed him again and left him, thinking him dead, and doubtless intending to return a little later to ransack the cabin and deal with the woman and child.

The Captain, however, though badly hurt, was not quite out of action. With the help of his wife he got his revolver and crawled out again into the passage. It must be remembered that he had still no idea what the trouble was. Some one had killed the mate and attacked him. It was mutiny beyond a doubt; but how many of his men were in it, and how many loyal men remained alive, he did not know. His first impulse, therefore, was to secure his own quarters against further attack. Looking up through the open hatch he could see the man Maloney still at the wheel and still too paralysed by fear to give the alarm. He called to him to shut the door at the top of the companion-way.

"I can't, sir," the man called tremulously back.

"Why not?"

"There's somebody there," objected Maloney.

"Who is it?"

"I don't know, sir."

The man was useless, obviously unwilling to stir from the wheel. Possibly, thought the Captain, he was in the mutiny, or had been overawed by the mutineers. He himself was too weak from loss of blood to climb the companion-way, but he shut and locked the door of the after-cabin, leading into the passage, and also the door of the fore-cabin. Then he returned to his wife; but hardly had he done so when he heard some one floundering down the companion-way outside. He opened the door once more, to find one of his white seamen, Hendricsen by name, outside. The Captain covered him with his revolver and demanded to be told what had happened. The man was apparently mad with fright. He could only stammer, "Oh, hide me, Captain, hide me."

Clarke was dizzy, faint, and bewildered. Hendricsen might be genuinely afraid, but again he might be privy to this extraordinary, murderous conspiracy and be intending treachery. It was better to take no risks, and the Captain slammed his door on the cowering man, leaving him in the passage. He then lay down on a mat in a corner of his cabin from which he could command with his revolver the door and the big portholes opening on to the deck outside, while Mrs. Clarke, who had behaved throughout with the greatest pluck and self control, washed and bandaged his wounds. The worst of these was the stab in his side, from which the lower lobe of the left lung protruded, but he had also some bad gashes on his head and temple; moreover, he was so exhausted from loss of blood that it was only by an effort of will that he could keep himself from fainting.

Mrs. Clarke was still dressing her husband's wounds when there was a further alarm. From one of the big portholes came a crash of shattered glass, and through the opening appeared the brown leg of one of the Indians. The Captain, who by now could hardly hold his revolver, fired twice, blindly and wide; but the shots served their purpose, for the coolie, who had supposed the Captain to be dead, was scared and quickly withdrew. In the cabin they heard the pair of mutineers go off cursing.

Silence followed, broken a little later by the noise of a scuffle and a single shrill scream from the deck. Half an hour later another scream rang out; and—at about five in the morning—yet another. The first was the death-cry of Maloney, the man at the wheel, whose timidity had not saved him; the second that of the carpenter, who was surprised and murdered while asleep in his shop; and the third that of the last man left alive on deck. The mutineers flung the three bodies overboard. These facts were afterwards elicited from Ah Say, the Chinese cook, who was a trembling witness of the crimes. The coolies spared his life because, as they explained, they wished him to cook for them.

What, meanwhile, had been happening elsewhere in the ship? Down in the fo'c'sle twelve men were asleep. When the watch was relieved a scuffle overhead was heard, and a moment later the first mate had tumbled in among them. He had taken advantage of the encounter between the Captain and the coolies to make his escape from the booby hatch where he had been surprised. He was desperately hurt, could give no clear account of what had passed, and, in fact, died three hours later. It was clear that something very serious had occurred, and while three of the men stayed with the mate, the other nine armed themselves with capstan-bars and went aft to investigate. Suddenly the two coolies appeared among them, cutting stabbing, slashing, and shouting that the Captain and mates were dead and the ship was now in their charge. In the darkness it was hard to distinguish friend from foe. There was a panic. The crew broke and fled in disorder back to the fo'c'sle. One man, Robert Sonnberg, alone remained outside. Cut off from safety, he made for the mizzen-rigging and climbed up to the cross-jack yard. From there he climbed along the stays towards the fo'c'sle, but by the time he reached it he found that the mutineers, following up the flying crew, had roughly barricaded them in. A little later, to his mortification, he saw the coolies return and make a sure job of it, battening down the hatch and securing it so strongly that it would be necessary for the men inside to hew a way out with axes.

Sonnberg returned to the rigging, from which he saw Maloney dragged shrieking from the wheel and butchered. The murder of Booth the carpenter followed; and worst of all was the death of Antonio Serrain, the third victim, who had often befriended the coolies during the voyage, and now pleaded hard for mercy; but none was shown him. The coolies then clad themselves in the carpenter's best clothes and called to Sonnberg to come down from the rigging, promising that if he did so they would not harm him. Sonnberg, wisely, remained aloft, and, detaching a block, tied it to a gasket, so that he might have a weapon of sorts. Thus he stayed through the long hours of Sunday.

Night fell once more, and at eight o'clock Sonnberg was nodding on his perch when he started awake as the rigging perceptibly shook. There, a couple of feet below, was the face of one of the mutineers, with a knife in his hand and murder in his eyes. Sonnberg dodged a blow and struck back at the man with his block. The coolie, baffled, returned to the deck, while Sonnberg climbed to the greater safety of the royal yard where he spent the rest of the night, descending to the topsail yard in the light of day.

Sonnberg struck at the man with his block

Let us return to the cabin. All through Sunday the Captain was prostrate, nursed by his wife. The mutineers, beyond screening the portholes with timber to cover them from revolver-fire, left him alone. In the small hours of Monday morning he was so much stronger that he was able to undertake a reconnaissance outside. In his lavatory he found the man Hendricsen, who had rushed down the companion-way twenty-four hours before. From him he was at last able to obtain an account of what had happened. The Captain also found the Chinese steward hiding in one of the cabins. He armed both these men, and prepared to take the offensive against the mutineers.

First of all, the Captain tried to get a sight of the enemy. This was not easy, as all portholes and hatches had been blocked and he had to use the skylight. Through it he obtained occasional fleeting glimpses. Apparently one of the coolies was watching the cabin, the other the fo'c'sle; they had armed themselves with harpoons and knives lashed to the ends of sticks, to be flung at any one who showed himself, or to be used for probing at random through the skylight. The Captain and his two men now opened fire whenever a target appeared, and when they heard footsteps on the deck they discharged their revolvers blindly through the partitions. A lucky shot at last found a mark. There was a shriek of pain, followed by sounds of a hurried retreat forward. At that moment Sonnberg, watching events from the rigging, seized his opportunity and made for the fo'c'sle.

For meanwhile the men below had been stirred to belated action. During Sunday they had remained unaccountably passive, preferring the security of their prison to the risks of the deck. The first mate was dead, and, to the best of their belief, the Captain and second mate had also been murdered. What was there for them to do? Indeed, the crew might have stayed inactive even longer than they did, had not Ah Say, the Chinese cook, who had just been compelled to prepare a meal of coffee, chickens, and rice for the mutineers, contrived to smuggle an axe through the fo'c'sle window. This put spirit into the men, and they began to hack their way out. As they toiled below, Sonnberg, who had found an axe lying on the deck, started to smash away the barricading over the hatches. And at the same time the Captain and his helpers, encouraged by that one successful shot, were battering down the cabin door. The two parties emerged from their respective prisons almost simultaneously.

But the mutineers had realised that their fun was finished. One of them was badly wounded in the breast, and their plans had so far miscarried that an unmanageable number of men remained alive and were growing in aggression. They decided to make a bolt from the ship. They rushed a heavy boom to the side and flung it overboard, the wounded coolie jumping in after it. But one last blow was to be struck, so, just as the cabin and fo'c'sle parties met, the other coolie made a sudden dash for a ventilating hatch and sprang through it into the hold. The Captain sent Hendricsen and the steward below with revolvers to hunt the man out, but they were too late or too cautious to stop the mischief. The coolie had set alight the cargo in several places before they found him, and presently dense volumes of smoke began to pour through the hatch.

Presently, too the atmosphere of the hold became unendurable. After firing at and wounding their man, Hendricsen and the steward groped their way on deck half-suffocated. A moment later the coolie followed, smoked out like a rat. With a wild yell he made for the side and jumped over, joining his fellow-mutineer, who was already in the water.

By this time the men on board, maddened by the traces of bloodshed which met them everywhere, were in no mood for mercy. They opened fire on the two wretches in the sea, and went on shooting until they had sunk from sight.

The murderers were dead, but a new danger now threatened. The fire in the hold had got a very strong purchase, and, although the crew fought it stoutly for four hours, they were unable to extinguish it. Slowly it crept through the ship, eating out her vitals and—a most serious matter—destroying her spare sails and all the provisions in store except those which were kept in the boats ready for emergencies. When the Captain saw that it was impossible to save the ship, he gave orders to lower away two boats. One of them capsized, but seventeen people managed to pack themselves into the other. During Monday night they stood by the blazing vessel, hoping that some passing craft, attracted by the glare, would pick them up. But on Tuesday morning there was not a sail in sight, and the *Frank N. Thayer* was burned almost to the water's edge.

The survivors had now no option but to make for the nearest land, the island of St. Helena, which was still some hundreds of miles distant. To men in their condition a voyage of such length in an open boat must have been a stern ordeal, and has not had the attention it deserved. It lasted for nine days. The supply of food and water was very scanty. Five of the party were suffering from wounds. As neither mast nor sail had survived the fire, a couple of oars were lashed together and blankets were fastened to them. Fortunately the wind was favourable; had it been otherwise the boat could never have reached harbour as it did, on the night of January 13th, without another life being lost.

That was the end of a queer tale, not altogether creditable—in its early phases—to the crew of the *Frank N. Thayer*. Not much could have been expected of the Captain after the wounds he had received, and undoubtedly he made a plucky recovery. The amazing fact remains that a pair of determined coolies, without firearms, mastered a company of twenty, killed five, wounded four, and overawed the remainder for a period of forty-eight hours; and that eleven active men were quite content during that period to remain imprisoned below-deck while their comrades were being murdered above.

The cause of the outbreak remains a mystery; in any case, we have the evidence of only one side. Captain Clarke, in a statement which he made to the harbourmaster at St. Helena, expressed his belief that the two coolies had plotted to murder every one on board and then take to a boat, posing to any one who might pick them up as the innocent survivors of a mutiny. This explanation, of course, shirks the real issue. Why should two men, apparently contented with their lot, outwardly at amity with their fellows, suddenly launch so murderous an attack? If we may assume that we have all the evidence, there can be only one answer. Madness is plainly stamped on each episode. The plan itself was mad, its execution was mad, its end was mad. Sane men could hardly have conceived such a scheme; certainly sane men could never have carried it out.

THE VOICE IN THE NIGHT

WILLIAM HOPE HODGSON

It was a dark, starless night. We were becalmed in the Northern Pacific. Our exact position I do not know; for the sun had been hidden during the course of a weary, breathless week, by a thin haze which had seemed to float above us, about the height of our mastheads, at whiles descending and shrouding the surrounding sea.

With there being no wind, we had steadied the tiller, and I was the only man on deck. The crew, consisting of two men and a boy, were sleeping forrard in their den; while Will—my friend, and the master of our little craft—was aft in his bunk on the port side of the little cabin.

Suddenly, from out of the surrounding darkness, there came a hail:—

"Schooner, ahoy!"

The cry was so unexpected that I gave no immediate answer, because of my surprise.

It came again—a voice curiously throaty and inhuman, calling from somewhere upon the dark sea away on our port broadside:—

"Schooner, ahoy!"

"Hullo!" I sung out, having gathered my wits somewhat. "What are you? What do you want?"

"You need not be afraid," answered the queer voice, having probably noticed some trace of confusion in my tone. "I am only an old—man."

The pause sounded oddly; but it was only afterwards that it came back to me with any significance.

"Why don't you come alongside, then?" I queried somewhat snappishly; for I liked not his hinting at my having been a trifle shaken.

"I—I—can't. It wouldn't be safe. I——" The voice broke off, and there was silence.

"What do you mean?" I asked, growing more and more astonished. "Why not safe? Where are you?"

I listened for a moment; but there came no answer. And then, a sudden indefinite suspicion, of I knew not what, coming to me, I stepped swiftly to the binnacle, and took out the lighted lamp. At the same time, I knocked on the deck with my heel to waken Will. Then I was back at the side, throwing the yellow funnel of light out into the silent immensity beyond our rail. As I did so, I heard a slight, muffled cry, and then the sound of a splash, as though some one had dipped oars abruptly. Yet I cannot say that I saw anything with certainty; save, it seemed to me, that with the first flash of the light, there had been something upon the waters, where now there was nothing.

"Hullo, there!" I called. "What foolery is this!"

But there came only the indistinct sounds of a boat being pulled away into the night.

Then I heard Will's voice, from the direction of the after scuttle:—

"What's up, George?"

"Come here, Will!" I said.

"What is it?" he asked, coming across the deck.

I told him the queer thing which had happened. He put several questions; then, after a moment's silence, he raised his hands to his lips, and hailed:—

"Boat, ahoy!"

From a long distance away, there came back to us a faint reply, and my companion repeated his call. Presently, after a short period of silence, there grew on our hearing the muffled sound of oars; at which Will hailed again.

This time there was a reply:—

"Put away the light."

"I'm damned if I will," I muttered; but Will told me to do as the voice bade, and I shoved it down under the bulwarks.

"Come nearer," he said, and the oar-strokes continued. Then, when apparently some half-dozen fathoms distant, they again ceased.

"Come alongside," exclaimed Will. "There's nothing to be frightened of aboard here!"

"Promise that you will not show the light?"

"What's to do with you," I burst out, "that you're so infernally afraid of the light?"

"Because——" began the voice, and stopped short.

"Because what?" I asked, quickly.

Will put his hand on my shoulder.

"Shut up a minute, old man," he said, in a low voice. "Let me tackle him."

He leant more over the rail.

"See here, Mister," he said, "this is a pretty queer business, you coming upon us like this, right out in the middle of the blessed Pacific. How are we to know what sort of a hanky-panky trick you're up to? You say there's only one of you. How are we to know, unless we get a squint at you—eh? What's your objection to the light, anyway?"

As he finished, I heard the noise of the oars again, and then the voice came; but now from a greater distance, and sounding extremely hopeless and pathetic.

"I am sorry—sorry! I would not have troubled you, only I am hungry, and—so is she."

The voice died away, and the sound of the oars, dipping irregularly, was borne to us.

"Stop!" sung out Will. "I don't want to drive you away. Come back! We'll keep the light hidden, if you don't like it."

He turned to me:—

"It's a damned queer rig, this; but I think there's nothing to be afraid of?"

There was a question in his tone, and I replied.

"No, I think the poor devil's been wrecked around here, and gone crazy." The sound of the oars drew nearer.

"Shove that lamp back in the binnacle," said Will; then he leaned over the rail, and listened. I replaced the lamp, and came back to his side. The dipping of the oars ceased some dozen yards distant.

"Won't you come alongside now?" asked Will in an even voice. "I have had the lamp put back in the binnacle."

"I—I cannot," replied the voice. "I dare not come nearer. I dare not even pay you for the—the provisions."

"That's all right," said Will, and hesitated. "You're welcome to as much grub as you can take——" Again he hesitated.

"You are very good," exclaimed the voice. "May God, Who understands everything, reward you——" It broke off huskily.

"The—the lady?" said Will, abruptly. "Is she——"

"I have left her behind upon the island," came the voice.

"What island?" I cut in.

"I know not its name," returned the voice. "I would to God——!" it began, and checked itself as suddenly.

"Could we not send a boat for her?" asked Will at this point.

"No!" said the voice, with extraordinary emphasis. "My God! No!" There was a moment's pause; then it added, in a tone which seemed a merited reproach:—

"It was because of our want I ventured—Because her agony tortured me."

"I am a forgetful brute," exclaimed Will. "Just wait a minute, whoever you are, and I will bring you up something at once."

In a couple of minutes he was back again, and his arms were full of various edibles. He paused at the rail.

"Can't you come alongside for them?" he asked.

"No—I *dare not*," replied the voice, and it seemed to me that in its tones I detected a note of stifled craving—as though the owner hushed a mortal desire. It came to me then in a flash, that the poor old creature out there in the darkness, was *suffering* for actual need of that which Will held in his arms; and yet, because of some unintelligible dread, refraining from dashing to the side of our little schooner, and receiving it. And with the lightning-like conviction, there came the knowledge that the Invisible was not mad; but sanely facing some intolerable horror.

"Damn it, Will!" I said, full of many feelings, over which predominated a vast sympathy. "Get a box. We must float off the stuff to him in it."

This we did—propelling it away from the vessel, out into the darkness, by means of a boathook. In a minute, a slight cry from the Invisible came to us, and we knew that he had secured the box.

A little later, he called out a farewell to us, and so heartful a blessing, that I am sure we were the better for it. Then, without more ado, we heard the ply of oars across the darkness.

"Pretty soon off," remarked Will, with perhaps just a little sense of injury.

"Wait," I replied. "I think somehow he'll come back. He must have been badly needing that food."

"And the lady," said Will. For a moment he was silent; then he continued:—

"It's the queerest thing ever I've tumbled across, since I've been fishing."

"Yes," I said, and fell to pondering.

And so the time slipped away—an hour, another, and still Will stayed with me; for the queer adventure had knocked all desire for sleep out of him.

The third hour was three parts through, when we heard again the sound of oars across the silent ocean.

"Listen!" said Will, a low note of excitement in his voice.

"He's coming, just as I thought," I muttered.

The dipping of the oars grew nearer, and I noted that the strokes were firmer and longer. The food had been needed.

They came to a stop a little distance off the broadside, and the queer voice came again to us through the darkness:—

"Schooner, ahoy!"

"That you?" asked Will.

"Yes," replied the voice. "I left you suddenly; but—but there was great need."

"The lady?" questioned Will.

"The—lady is grateful now on earth. She will be more grateful soon in—in heaven."

Will began to make some reply, in a puzzled voice; but became confused, and broke off short. I said nothing. I was wondering at the curious pauses, and, apart from my wonder, I was full of a great sympathy.

The voice continued:—

"We—she and I, have talked, as we shared the result of God's tenderness and yours——"

Will interposed; but without coherence.

"I beg of you not to—to belittle your deed of Christian charity this night," said the voice. "Be sure that it has not escaped His notice."

It stopped, and there was a full minute's silence. Then it came again:—

"We have spoken together upon that which—which has befallen us. We had thought to go out, without telling any, of the terror which has come into our——lives. She is with me in believing that to-night's happenings are under a special ruling, and that it is God's wish that we should tell to you all that we have suffered since—since——"

"Yes?" said Will, softly.

"Since the sinking of the 'Albatross.'"

"Ah!" I exclaimed, involuntarily. "She left Newcastle for 'Frisco some six months ago, and hasn't been heard of since."

"Yes," answered the voice. "But some few degrees to the North of the line she was caught in a terrible storm, and dismasted. When the day came, it was found that she was leaking badly, and, presently, it falling to a calm, the sailors took to the boats, leaving—leaving a young lady—my fiancée—and myself upon the wreck.

"We were below, gathering together a few of our belongings, when they left. They were entirely callous, through fear, and when we came up upon the decks, we saw them only as small shapes afar off upon the horizon. Yet we did not despair, but set to work and constructed a small raft. Upon this we put such few matters as it would hold, including a quantity of water and some ship's biscuit. Then, the vessel being very deep in the water, we got ourselves on to the raft, and pushed off.

"It was later, when I observed that we seemed to be in the way of some tide or current, which bore us from the ship at an angle; so that in the course of three hours, by my watch, her hull became invisible to our sight, her broken masts remaining in view for a somewhat longer period. Then, towards evening, it grew misty, and so through the night. The next day we were still encompassed by the mist, the weather remaining quiet.

"For four days, we drifted through this strange haze, until, on the evening of the fourth day, there grew upon our ears the murmur of breakers at a distance. Gradually it became plainer, and, somewhat after midnight, it appeared to sound upon either hand at no very great space. The raft was raised upon a swell several times, and then we were in smooth water, and the noise of the breakers was behind.

"When the morning came, we found that we were in a sort of great lagoon; but of this we noticed little at the time; for close before us, through the enshrouding mist, loomed the hull of a large sailing-vessel. With one accord, we fell upon our knees and thanked God; for we thought that here was an end to our perils. We had much to learn.

"The raft drew near to the ship, and we shouted on them, to take us aboard; but none answered. Presently, the raft touched against the side of the vessel, and, seeing a rope hanging downwards, I seized it and began to climb. Yet I had much ado to make my way up, because of a kind of grey, lichenous fungus, which had seized upon the rope, and which blotched the side of the ship, lividly.

"I reached the rail, and clambered over it, on to the deck. Here, I saw that the decks were covered, in great patches, with the grey masses, some of them rising into nodules several feet in height; but at the time, I thought less of this matter than of the possibility of there being people aboard the ship. I shouted; but none answered. Then I went to the door below the poop deck. I opened it, and peered in. There was a great smell of staleness, so that I knew in a moment that nothing living was within, and with the knowledge, I shut the door quickly; for I felt suddenly lonely.

"I went back to the side, where I had scrambled up. My—my sweetheart was still sitting quietly upon the raft. Seeing me look down, she called up to know whether there were any aboard of the ship. I replied that the vessel had the appearance of having been long deserted; but that if she would wait a little, I would see whether there was anything in the shape of a ladder, by which she could ascend to the deck. Then we would make a search through the vessel together. A little later, on the opposite side of the decks, I found a rope side-ladder. This I carried across, and a minute afterwards, she was beside me.

"Together, we explored the cabins and apartments in the after-part of the ship; but nowhere was there any sign of life. Here and there, within the cabins themselves, we came across odd patches of that queer fungus; but this, as my sweetheart said, could be cleansed away.

"In the end, having assured ourselves that the after portion of the vessel was empty, we picked our ways to the bows, between the ugly grey nodules of that strange growth; and here we made a further search, which told us that there was indeed none aboard but ourselves.

"This being now beyond any doubt, we returned to the stern of the ship, and proceeded to make ourselves as comfortable as possible. Together, we cleared out and cleaned two of the cabins; and, after that, I made examination whether there was anything eatable in the ship. This I soon found was so, and thanked God in my heart for His goodness. In addition to this, I discovered the whereabouts of the freshwater pump, and having fixed it, I found the water drinkable, though somewhat unpleasant to the taste.

"For several days, we stayed aboard the ship, without attempting to get to the shore. We were busily engaged in making the place habitable. Yet even thus early, we became aware that our lot was even less to be desired than might have been imagined; for though, as a first step, we scraped away the odd patches of growth that studded the floors and walls of the cabins and saloon, yet they returned almost to their original size within the space of twenty-four hours, which not only discouraged us, but gave us a feeling of vague unease.

"Still, we would not admit ourselves beaten, so set to work afresh, and not only scraped away the fungus, but soaked the places where it had been, with carbolic, a can-full of which I had found in the pantry. Yet, by the end of the week, the growth had returned in full strength, and, in addition, it had spread to other places, as though our touching it had allowed germs from it to travel elsewhere.

"On the seventh morning, my sweetheart woke to find a small patch of it growing on her pillow, close to her face. At that, she came to me, so soon as she could get her garments upon her. I was in the galley at the time, lighting the fire for breakfast.

"'Come here, John,' she said, and led me aft. When I saw the thing upon her pillow, I shuddered, and then and there we agreed to go right out of the ship, and see whether we could not fare to make ourselves more comfortable ashore.

"Hurriedly, we gathered together our few belongings, and even among these, I found that the fungus had been at work; for one of her shawls had a little lump of it growing near one edge. I threw the whole thing over the side, without saying anything to her.

"The raft was still alongside; but it was too clumsy to guide, and I lowered down a small boat that hung across the stern, and in this we made our way to the shore. Yet, as we drew near to it, I became gradually aware that here the vile fungus, which had driven us from the ship, was growing riot. In places it rose into horrible, fantastic mounds, which seemed almost to quiver, as with a quiet life, when the wind blew across them. Here and there, it took on the forms of vast fingers, and in others it just spread out flat and smooth and treacherous. Odd places, it appeared as grotesque stunted trees, seeming extraordinarily kinked and gnarled——The whole quaking vilely at times.

"At first, it seemed to us that there was no single portion of the sur-rounding shore which was not hidden beneath the masses of the hideous lichen; yet, in this, I found we were mistaken; for somewhat later, coasting along the shore at a little distance, we descried a smooth white patch of what appeared to be fine sand, and there we landed. It was not sand. What it was, I do not know. All that I have observed, is that upon it, the fun-gus will not grow; while everywhere else, save where the sand-like earth wanders oddly, path-wise, amid the grey desolation of the lichen, there is nothing but that loathsome greyness.

"It is difficult to make you understand how cheered we were to find one place that was absolutely free from the growth, and here we deposited our belongings. Then we went back to the ship for such things as it seemed to us we should need. Among other matters, I managed to bring ashore with me one of the ship's sails, with which I constructed two small tents, which, though exceedingly rough-shaped, served the purposes for which they were intended. In these, we lived and stored our various necessities, and thus for a matter of some four weeks, all went smoothly and without particular unhappiness. Indeed, I may say with much of happiness——for—for we were together.

"It was on the thumb of her right hand, that the growth first showed. It was only a small circular spot, much like a little grey mole. My God! how the fear leapt to my heart when she showed me the place. We cleansed it, between us, washing it with carbolic and water. In the morning of the following day, she showed her hand to me again. The grey warty thing had returned. For a little while, we looked at one another in silence. Then, still wordless, we started again to remove it. In the midst of the operation, she spoke suddenly.

" 'What's that on the side of your face, Dear!' Her voice was sharp with anxiety. I put my hand up to feel.

" 'There! Under the hair by your ear.—A little to the front a bit.' My finger rested upon the place, and then I knew.

" 'Let us get your thumb done first' I said. And she submitted, only because she was afraid to touch me until it was cleansed. I finished wash-ing and disinfecting her thumb, and then she turned to my face. After it was finished, we sat together and talked awhile of many things; for there had come into our lives sudden, very terrible thoughts. We were, all at once, afraid of something worse than death. We spoke of loading the boat with provisions and water, and making our way out on to the sea; yet we were helpless, for many causes, and—and the growth had attacked us already. We decided to stay. God would do with us what was His will. We would wait.

"A month, two months, three months passed, and the places grew somewhat, and there had come others. Yet we fought so strenuously with the fear, that its headway was but slow, comparatively speaking.

"Occasionally, we ventured off to the ship for such stores as we needed. There, we found that the fungus grew persistently. One of the nodules on the maindeck became soon as high as my head.

"We had now given up all thought or hope of leaving the island. We had realised that it would be unallowable to go among healthy humans, with the thing from which we were suffering.

"With this determination and knowledge in our minds, we knew that we should have to husband our food and water; for we did not know, at that time, but that we should possibly live for many years.

"This reminds me that I have told you that I am an old man. Judged by years this is not so. But—but——"

He broke off; then continued somewhat abruptly:—

"As I was saying, we knew that we should have to use care in the matter of food. But we had no idea then how little food there was left, of which to take care. It was a week later, that I made the discovery that all the other bread tanks—which I had supposed full—were empty, and that (beyond odd tins of vegetables and meat, and some other matters) we had nothing on which to depend, but the bread in the tank which I had already opened.

"After learning this, I bestirred myself to do what I could, and set to work at fishing in the lagoon; but with no success. At this, I was somewhat inclined to feel desperate, until the thought came to me to try outside the lagoon, in the open sea.

"Here, at times, I caught odd fish; but, so infrequently, that they proved of but little help in keeping us from the hunger which threatened. It seemed to me that our deaths were likely to come by hunger, and not by the growth of the thing which had seized upon our bodies.

"We were in this state of mind when the fourth month wore out. Then I made a very horrible discovery. One morning, a little before midday, I came off from the ship, with a portion of the biscuits which were left. In the mouth of her tent, I saw my sweetheart sitting, eating something.

" 'What is it, my Dear?' I called out as I leapt ashore. Yet, on hearing my voice, she seemed confused, and, turning, slyly threw something towards the edge of the little clearing. It fell short, and, a vague suspicion having arisen within me, I walked across and picked it up. It was a piece of the grey fungus.

"As I went to her, with it in my hand, she turned deadly pale; then a rose red.

"I felt strangely dazed and frightened.

"'My Dear! My Dear!' I said, and could say no more. Yet, at my words, she broke down and cried bitterly. Gradually, as she calmed, I got from her the news that she had tried it the preceding day, and—and liked it. I got her to promise on her knees not to touch it again, however great our hunger. After she had promised, she told me that the desire for it had come suddenly, and that, until the moment of desire, she had experienced nothing towards it, but the most extreme repulsion.

"Later in the day, feeling strangely restless, and much shaken with the thing which I had discovered, I made my way along one of the twisted paths—formed by the white, sand-like substance—which led among the fungoid growth. I had, once before, ventured along there; but not to any great distance. This time, being involved in perplexing thought, I went much further than hitherto.

"Suddenly, I was called to myself, by a queer hoarse sound on my left. Turning quickly, I saw that there was movement among an extraordinarily shaped mass of fungus, close to my elbow. It was swaying uneasily, as though it possessed life of its own. Abruptly, as I stared, the thought came to me that the thing had a grotesque resemblance to the figure of a distorted human creature. Even as the fancy flashed into my brain, there was a slight, sickening noise of tearing, and I saw that one of the branch-like arms was detaching itself from the surrounding grey masses, and coming towards me. The head of the thing—a shapeless grey ball, inclined in my direction. I stood stupidly, and the vile arm brushed across my face. I gave out a frightened cry, and ran back a few paces. There was a sweetish taste upon my lips, where the thing had touched me. I licked them, and was immediately filled with an inhuman desire. I turned and seized a mass of the fungus. Then more, and—more. I was insatiable. In the midst of devouring, the remembrance of the morning's discovery swept into my mazed brain. It was sent by God. I dashed the fragment I held, to the ground. Then, utterly wretched and feeling a dreadful guiltiness, I made my way back to the little encampment.

"I think she knew, by some marvellous intuition which love must have given, so soon as she set eyes on me. Her quiet sympathy made it easier for me, and I told her of my sudden weakness; yet omitted to mention the extraordinary thing which had gone before. I desired to spare her all unnecessary terror.

"But, for myself, I had added an intolerable knowledge, to breed an incessant terror in my brain; for I doubted not but that I had seen the end of one of those men who had come to the island in the ship in the lagoon; and in that monstrous ending, I had seen our own.

"Thereafter, we kept from the abominable food, though the desire for it had entered into our blood. Yet, our drear punishment was upon us; for, day by day, with monstrous rapidity, the fungoid growth took hold of our poor bodies. Nothing we could do would check it materially, and so—and so—we who had been human, became—Well, it matters less each day. Only—only we had been man and maid!

"And day by day, the fight is more dreadful, to withstand the hunger-lust for the terrible lichen.

"A week ago we ate the last of the biscuit, and since that time I have caught three fish. I was out here fishing to-night, when your schooner drifted upon me out of the mist. I hailed you. You know the rest, and may God, out of His great heart, bless you for your goodness to a—a couple of poor outcast souls."

There was the dip of an oar—another. Then the voice came again, and for the last time, sounding through the slight surrounding mist, ghostly and mournful.

"God bless you! Good-bye!"

"Good-bye," we shouted together, hoarsely, our hearts full of many emotions.

I glanced about me. I became aware that the dawn was upon us.

The sun flung a stray beam across the hidden sea; pierced the mist dully, and lit up the receding boat with a gloomy fire. Indistinctly, I saw something nodding between the oars. I thought of a sponge—a great, grey nodding sponge——The oars continued to ply. They were grey—as was the boat—and my eyes searched a moment vainly for the conjunction of hand and oar. My gaze flashed back to the—head. It nodded forward as the oars went backward for the stroke. Then the oars were dipped, the boat shot out of the patch of light, and the—the thing went nodding into the mist.

AT SEA

GUY DE MAUPASSANT

The following lines recently appeared in the press:

"Boulogne-Sur-Mer, January 22.

"From our correspondent.

"A frightful disaster has occurred which throws into consternation our maritime population, so grievously afflicted for the last two years. The fishing boat, commanded by Captain Javel, entering into port, was carried to the west, and broken upon the rocks of the breakwater near the pier. In spite of the efforts of the life-boat, and of life-lines shot out to them, four men and a cabin boy perished. The bad weather continues. Further wrecks are feared."

Who is this Captain Javel? Is he the brother of the one-armed Javel? If this poor man tossed by the waves, and dead perhaps, under the *débris* of his boat cut in pieces, is the one I think he is, he witnessed, eighteen years ago, another drama, terrible and simple as are all the formidable dramas of the sea.

Javel senior was then master of a smack. The smack is the fishing boat *par excellence.* Solid, fearing no kind of weather, with round body, rolled incessantly by the waves, like a cork, always lashed by the harsh, salty winds of the Channel, it travels the sea indefatigably, with sail filled, carrying in its wake a net which reaches the bottom of the ocean, detaching all the sleeping creatures from the rocks, the flat fishes glued to the sand, the heavy crabs with their hooked claws, and the lobster with his pointed mustaches.

When the breeze is fresh and the waves choppy, the boat puts about to fish. A rope is fastened to the end of a great wooden shank tipped with iron, which is let down by means of two cables slipping over two spools at the extreme end of the craft. And the boat, driving under wind and current, drags after her this apparatus, which ravages and devastates the bottom of the sea.

Javel had on board his younger brother, four men, and a cabin boy. He had set out from Boulogne in fair weather to cast the nets. Then, suddenly, the wind arose and a squall drove the boat before the wind. It reached the coast of England; but a tremendous sea was beating against the cliffs and the shore so that it was impossible to enter port. The little boat put to sea again and returned to the coast of France. The storm continued to make the piers unapproachable, enveloping with foam, noise and danger every place of refuge.

The fishing boat set out again, running along the tops of the billows, tossed about, shaken up, streaming, buffeted by mountains of water, but game in spite of all, accustomed to heavy weather, which sometimes kept it wandering for five or six days between the two countries, unable to land in the one or the other.

Finally, the hurricane ceased, when they came out into open sea, and although the sea was still high, the Old Man ordered them to cast the net. Then the great fishing tackle was thrown overboard, and two men at one side and two at the other began to unwind from windlasses the cable which held it. Suddenly it touched the bottom, but a high wave tipped the boat forward. Javel junior, who was in the prow directing the casting of the net, tottered and found his arm caught between the cable, slackened an instant by the motion, and the wood on which it was turning. He made a desperate effort with his other hand to lift the cable, but the net was dragging again and the taut cable would not yield.

Rigid with pain, he called. Every one ran to him. His brother left the helm. They threw their full force upon the rope, forcing it away from the arm it was grinding. It was in vain. "We must cut it," said a sailor, and he drew from his pocket a large knife which could, in two blows, save young Javel's arm. But to cut was to lose the net, and the net meant money, much money—fifteen hundred francs; it belonged to the elder Javel, who was keen on his property.

In anguish he cried out: "No, don't cut; I'll luff the ship." And he ran to the wheel, putting the helm about. The boat scarcely obeyed, paralyzed by the net, which counteracted its power, and driven besides by the force of the leeway and the wind.

Young Javel fell to his knees with set teeth and haggard eyes. He said nothing. His brother returned, still anxious about the sailor's knife.

"Wait! wait!" he said, "don't cut; we must cast anchor."

The anchor was thrown overboard, all the chain paid out, and they then tried to take a turn around the capstan with the cables in order to loosen them from the weight of the net. The cables finally relaxed, and they released the arm, which hung inert under a sleeve of bloody woolen cloth.

Young Javel seemed to have lost his mind. They removed his jersey, and then saw something horrible; a mass of bruised flesh, from which the blood was gushing, as if it were forced by a pump. The man himself looked at his arm and murmured: "Done for."

Then, as the hæmorrhage made a pool on the deck of the boat, the sailors cried: "He'll lose all his blood. We must bind the artery!"

They then took some twine, thick, black, tarred twine, and, twisting it around the limb above the wound, bound it with all their strength. Little by little the jets of blood stopped, and finally ceased altogether.

Young Javel arose, his arm hanging by his side. He took it by the other hand, raised it, turned it, shook it. Everything was broken; the bones were crushed completely; only the muscles held it to his body. He looked at it thoughtfully, with sad eyes. Then he seated himself on a folded sail, and his comrades came around him, advising him to soak it continually to prevent gangrene.

They put a bucket near him and every moment he would dip into it with a glass and bathe the horrible wound by letting a thin stream of clear water fall upon it.

"You would be better down below," said his brother. He went down, but after an hour he came up again, feeling better not to be alone. And then, he preferred the open air. He sat down again upon the sail and continued bathing his arm.

The fishing was good. The huge fish with white bodies were lying beside him, shaken by the spasms of death. He looked at them without ceasing to sprinkle the mangled flesh.

When they started to return to Boulogne, another gale of wind began to blow. The little boat resumed its mad course, bounding, and tumbling, shaking the poor wounded man.

Night came on. The weather was heavy until daybreak. At sunrise, they could see England again, but as the sea was a little less rough, they turned toward France, beating against the wind.

Toward evening, young Javel called his comrades and showed them black traces and the hideous signs of decay around that part of his arm which was no longer joined to his body.

The sailors looked at it, giving advice: "That must be gangrene," said one.

"It must have salt water on it," said another.

Then they brought salt water and poured it on the wound. The wounded man became livid, grinding his teeth, and twisting with pain; but he uttered no cry.

When the burning grew less, he said to his brother: "Give me your knife." The brother gave it to him.

"Hold this arm up for me, and pull it."

His brother did as he was asked.

Then he began to cut. He cut gently, with caution, severing the last tendons with the blade as sharp as a razor. Soon he had only a stump. He heaved a deep sigh and said: "That had to be done. Otherwise, it would be all up."

He seemed relieved and breathed energetically. He continued to pour water on the part of his arm remaining to him.

The night was still bad and they could not land. When the day appeared, young Javel took his severed arm and examined it carefully. Putrefaction had begun. His comrades came also and examined it, passing it from hand to hand, touching it, turning it over, and smelling it.

His brother said: "It's about time to throw that into the sea."

Young Javel was angry; he replied: "No, oh! no! I will not. It is mine, isn't it? Since it is my arm—" He took it and held it between his legs.

"It won't grow any less putrid," said the elder.

Then an idea came to the wounded man. In order to keep the fish when they remained a long time at sea, they had with them barrels of salt. "Couldn't I put it in there in the brine?" he asked.

"That's so," declared the others.

Then they emptied one of the barrels, already full of fish from the last few days, and, at the bottom, they deposited the arm. Then they turned salt upon it and replaced the fishes, one by one.

One of the sailors made a little joke: "Take care we don't happen to sell it at the fish market."

And everybody laughed except the Javel brothers.

The wind still blew. They beat about in sight of Boulogne until the next day at ten o'clock. The wounded man still poured water on his arm. From time to time he would get up and walk from one end of the boat to the other. His brother, who was at the wheel, shook his head and followed him with his eye.

Finally, they came into port.

The doctor examined the wound and declared it was doing well. He dressed it properly and ordered rest. But Javel could not go to bed without having his arm again, and went quickly back to the dock to find the barrel, which he had marked with a cross.

They emptied it in front of him, and he found his arm well preserved in the salt, wrinkled and in good condition. He wrapped it in a napkin brought for this purpose, and took it home.

His wife and children examined carefully this fragment of their father, touching the fingers, taking up the grains of salt that had lodged under the nails. Then they sent for the carpenter, who measured it for a little coffin.

The next day the complete crew of the fishing smack followed the funeral of the severed arm. The two brothers, side by side, conducted the ceremony. The parish beadle held the coffin under his arm.

Javel junior gave up going to sea. He obtained a small position in port, and, later, whenever he spoke of the accident, he would say to his auditor, in a low tone: "If my brother had been willing to cut the net, I should still have my arm, for certain. But he was thinking of his valuable property."

DAVY JONES'S GIFT

JOHN MASEFIELD

"Once upon a time," said the sailor, "the Devil and Davy Jones came to Cardiff, to the place called Tiger Bay. They put up at Tony Adams's, not far from Pier Head, at the corner of Sunday Lane. And all the time they stayed there they used to be going to the rum-shop, where they sat at a table, smoking their cigars, and dicing each other for different persons' souls. Now you must know that the Devil gets landsmen, and Davy Jones gets sailor-folk; and they get tired of having always the same, so then they dice each other for some of another sort.

"One time they were in a place in Mary Street, having some burnt brandy, and playing red and black for the people passing. And while they were looking out on the street and turning the cards, they saw all the people on the sidewalk breaking their necks to get into the gutter. And they saw all the shop-people running out and kowtowing, and all the carts pulling up, and all the police saluting. 'Here comes a big nob,' said Davy Jones. 'Yes,' said the Devil; 'it's the Bishop that's stopping with the Mayor.' 'Red or black?' said Davy Jones, picking up a card. 'I don't play for bishops,' said the Devil. 'I respect the cloth,' he said. 'Come on, man,' said Davy Jones. 'I'd give an admiral to have a bishop. Come on, now; make your game. Red or black?' 'Well, I say red,' said the Devil. 'It's the ace of clubs,' said Davy Jones 'I win; and it's the first bishop ever I had in my life.' The Devil was mighty angry at that—at losing a bishop. 'I'll not play any more,' he said; 'I'm off home. Some people gets too good cards for me. There was some queer shuffling when that pack was cut, that's my belief.'

" 'Ah, stay and be friends, man,' said Davy Jones. 'Look at what's coming down the street. I'll give you that for nothing.'

"Now, coming down the street there was a reefer—one of those apprentice fellows. And he was brass-bound fit to play music. He stood about six feet, and there were bright brass buttons down his jacket, and on his collar, and on his sleeves. His cap had a big gold badge, with a house-flag in seven different colours in the middle of it, and a gold chain cable of a chinstay twisted round it. He was wearing his cap on three hairs, and he was walking on both the sidewalks and all the road. His trousers were cut like wind-sails round the ankles. He had a fathom of red silk tie rolling out over his chest. He'd a cigarette in a twisted clay holder a foot and a half long. He was chewing tobacco over his shoulders as he walked. He'd a bottle of rum-hot in one hand, a bag of jam tarts in the other, and his pockets were full of love-letters from every port between Rio and Callao, round by the East.

" 'You mean to say you'll give me that?' said the Devil. 'I will,' said Davy Jones, 'and a beauty he is. I never see a finer.' 'He is, indeed, a beauty,' said the Devil. 'I take back what I said about the cards. I'm sorry I spoke crusty. What's the matter with some more burnt brandy?' 'Burnt brandy be it,' said Davy Jones. So then they rang the bell, and ordered a new jug and clean glasses.

"Now the Devil was so proud of what Davy Jones had given him, he couldn't keep away from him. He used to hang about the East Bute Docks, under the red-brick clock-tower, looking at the barque the young man worked aboard. Bill Harker his name was. He was in a West Coast barque, the *Coronel*, loading fuel for Hilo. So at last, when the *Coronel* was sailing, the Devil shipped himself aboard her, as one of the crowd in the fo'c'sle, and away they went down the Channel. At first he was very happy, for Bill Harker was in the same watch, and the two would yarn together. And though he was wise when he shipped, Bill Harker taught him a lot. There was a lot of things Bill Harker knew about. But when they were off the River Plate, they got caught in a pampero, and it blew very hard, and a big green sea began to run. The *Coronel* was a wet ship, and for three days you could stand upon her poop, and look forward and see nothing but a smother of foam from the break of the poop to the jib-boom. The crew had to roost on the poop. The fo'c'sle was flooded out. So while they were like this the flying jib worked loose. 'The jib will be gone in half a tick,' said the mate. 'Out there, one of you, and make it fast, before it blows away.' But the boom was dipping under every minute, and the waist was four feet deep, and green water came aboard all along her length. So none of the crowd would go forward. Then Bill Harker shambled out, and away he went forward, with the green seas smashing over him, and he lay out along the jib-boom and made the sail fast, and jolly nearly drowned he was. 'That's a brave lad, that Bill Harker,' said the Devil. 'Ah, come off,' said the sailors. 'Them reefers, they haven't got souls to be saved.' It was that that set the Devil thinking.

"By and by they came up with the Horn; and if it had blown off the Plate, it now blew off the roof. Talk about wind and weather. They got them both for sure aboard the *Coronel*. And it blew all the sails off her, and she rolled all her masts out, and the seas made a breach of her bulwarks, and the ice knocked a hole in her bows. So watch and watch they pumped the old *Coronel*, and the leak gained steadily, and there they were hove to under a weather cloth, five and a half degrees to the south of anything. And while they were like this, just about giving up hope, the old man sent the watch below, and told them they could start prayers. So the Devil crept on to the top of the half-deck, to look through the scuttle, to see what the reefers were doing, and what kind of prayers Bill Harker was putting up. And he saw them all sitting round the table, under the lamp, with Bill Harker at the head. And each of them had a hand of cards, and a length of knotted rope-yarn, and they were playing able-whackets. Each man in turn put down a card, and swore a new blasphemy, and if his swear didn't come as he played the card, then all the others hit him with their teasers. But they never once had a chance to hit Bill Harker. 'I think they were right about his soul,' said the Devil. And he sighed, like he was sad.

"Shortly after that the *Coronel* went down, and all hands drowned in her, saving only Bill and the Devil. They came up out of the smothering green seas, and saw the stars blinking in the sky, and heard the wind howling like a pack of dogs. They managed to get aboard the *Coronel's* hen-house, which had come adrift, and floated. The fowls were all drowned inside, so they lived on drowned hens. As for drink, they had to do without, for there was none. When they got thirsty they splashed their faces with salt water; but they were so cold they didn't feel thirst very bad. They drifted three days and three nights, till their skins were all cracked and salt-caked.

And all the Devil thought of was whether Bill Harker had a soul. And Bill kept telling the Devil what a thundering big feed they would have as soon as they fetched to port, and how good a rum-hot would be, with a lump of sugar and a bit of lemon peel.

"And at last the old hen-house came bump on to Terra del Fuego, and there were some natives cooking rabbits. So the Devil and Bill made a raid of the whole jing bang, and ate till they were tired. Then they had a drink out of a brook, and a warm by the fire, and a pleasant sleep, 'Now,' said the Devil, 'I will see if he's got a soul. I'll see if he give thanks.' So after an hour or two Bill took a turn up and down and came to the Devil. 'It's mighty dull on this forgotten continent,' he said. 'Have you got a ha'penny?' 'No,' said the Devil. 'What in joy d'ye want with a ha'penny?' 'I might have played you pitch and toss,' said Bill. 'It was better fun on the hen-coop than here.' 'I give you up,' said the Devil; 'you've no more soul than the inner part of an empty barrel.' And with that the Devil vanished in a flame of sulphur.

"Bill stretched himself, and put another shrub on the fire. He picked up a few round shells, and began a game of knucklebones."

"BLOW UP WITH THE BRIG!"

WILKIE COLLINS

I have got an alarming confession to make. I am haunted by a Ghost.

If you were to guess for a hundred years, you would never guess what my ghost is. I shall make you laugh to begin with—and afterward I shall make your flesh creep. My Ghost is the ghost of a Bedroom Candlestick.

Yes, a bedroom candlestick and candle, or a flat candlestick and candle—put it which way you like—that is what haunts me. I wish it was something pleasanter and more out of the common way; a beautiful lady, or a mine of gold and silver, or a cellar of wine and a coach and horses, and such like. But, being what it is, I must take it for what it is, and make the best of it; and I shall thank you kindly if you will help me out by doing the same.

I am not a scholar myself, but I make bold to believe that the haunting of any man with any thing under the sun begins with the frightening of him. At any rate, the haunting of me with a bedroom candlestick and candle began with the frightening of me with a bedroom candlestick and candle—the frightening of me half out of my life; and, for the time being, the frightening of me altogether out of my wits. That is not a very pleasant thing to confess before stating the particulars; but perhaps you will be the readier to believe that I am not a downright coward, because you find me bold enough to make a clean breast of it already, to my own great disadvantage so far.

Here are the particulars, as well as I can put them:

I was apprenticed to the sea when I was about as tall as my own walking-stick; and I made good enough use of my time to be fit for a mate's berth at the age of twenty-five years.

It was in the year eighteen hundred and eighteen or nineteen, I am not quite certain which, that I reached the before-mentioned age of twenty-five. You will please to excuse my memory not being very good for dates, names, numbers, places, and such like. No fear, though, about the particulars I have undertaken to tell you of; I have got them all shipshape in my recollection; I can see them, at this moment, as clear as noonday in my own mind. But there is a mist over what went before, and, for the matter of that, a mist likewise over much that came after—and it's not very likely to lift at my time of life, is it?

Well, in eighteen hundred and eighteen, or nineteen, when there was peace in our part of the world—and not before it was wanted, you will say—there was fighting, of a certain scampering, scrambling kind, going on in that old battle-field which we seafaring men know by the name of the Spanish Main.

The possessions that belonged to the Spaniards in South America had broken into open mutiny and declared for themselves years before. There was plenty of bloodshed between the new Government and the old; but the new had got the best of it, for the most part, under one General Bolivar—a famous man in his time, though he seems to have dropped out of people's memories now. Englishmen and Irishmen with a turn for fighting, and nothing particular to do at home, joined the general as volunteers; and some of our merchants here found it a good venture to send supplies across the ocean to the popular side. There was risk enough, of course, in doing this; but where one speculation of the kind succeeded, it made up for type? at the least, that failed. And that's the true principle of trade, wherever I have met with it, all the world over.

Among the Englishmen who were concerned in this Spanish-American business, I, your humble servant, happened, in a small way, to be one.

I was then mate of a brig belonging to a certain firm in the City, which drove a sort of general trade, mostly in queer out-of-the-way places, as far from home as possible; and which freighted the brig, in the year I am speaking of, with a cargo of gunpowder for General Bolivar and his volunteers. Nobody knew anything about our instructions, when we sailed, except the captain; and he didn't half seem to like them. I can't rightly say how many barrels of powder we had on board, or how much each barrel held—I only know we had no other cargo. The name of the brig was the *Good Intent*—a queer name enough, you will tell me, for a vessel laden with gunpowder, and sent to help a revolution. And as far as this particular voyage was concerned, so it was. I mean that for a joke, and I hope you will encourage me by laughing at it.

The *Good Intent* was the craziest tub of a vessel I ever went to sea in, and the worst found in all respects. She was two hundred and thirty, or two hundred and eighty tons burden, I forget which; and she had a crew of eight, all told—nothing like as many as we ought by rights to have had to work the brig. However, we were well and honestly paid our wages; and we had to set that against the chance of foundering at sea, and, on this occasion, likewise the chance of being blown up into the bargain.

In consideration of the nature of our cargo, we were harassed with new regulations, which we didn't at all like, relative to smoking our pipes and lighting our lanterns; and, as usual in such cases, the captain, who made the regulations, preached what he didn't practise. Not a man of us was allowed to have a bit of lighted candle in his hand when he went below—except the skipper; and he used his light, when he turned in, or when he looked over his charts on the cabin table, just as usual.

This light was a common kitchen candle or "dip," and it stood in an old battered flat candlestick, with all the japan worn and melted off, and all the tin showing through. It would have been more seaman-like and suitable in every respect if he had had a lamp or a lantern; but he stuck to his old candlestick; and that same old candlestick has ever afterward stuck to *me*. That's another joke, if you please, and a better one than the first, in my opinion.

Well (I said "well" before, but it's a word that helps a man on like), we sailed in the brig, and shaped our course, first, for the Virgin Islands, in the West Indies; and, after sighting them, we made for the Leeward Islands next, and then stood on due south, till the lookout at the masthead hailed the deck and said he saw land. That land was the coast of South America. We had had a wonderful voyage so far. We had lost none of our spars or sails, and not a man of us had been harassed to death at the pumps. It wasn't often the *Good Intent* made such a voyage as that, I can tell you.

I was sent aloft to make sure about the land, and I did make sure of it.

When I reported the same to the skipper, he went below and had a look at his letter of instructions and the chart. When he came on deck again, he altered our course a trifle to the eastward—I forget the point on the compass, but that don't matter. What I do remember is, that it was dark before we closed in with the land. We kept the lead going, and hove the brig to in from four to five fathoms water, or it might be six—I can't say for certain. I kept a sharp eye to the drift of the vessel, none of us knowing how the currents ran on that coast. We all wondered why the skipper didn't anchor; but he said No, he must first show a light at the foretopmast-head, and wait for an answering light on shore. We did wait, and nothing of the sort appeared. It was starlight and calm. What little wind there was came in puffs off the land. I suppose we waited, drifting a little to the westward, as I made it out, best part of an hour before anything happened—and then, instead of seeing the light on shore, we saw a boat coming toward us, rowed by two men only.

We hailed them, and they answered "Friends!" and hailed us by our name. They came on board. One of them was an Irishman, and the other was a coffee-coloured native pilot, who jabbered a little English.

The Irishman handed a note to our skipper, who showed it to me. It informed us that the part of the coast we were off was not oversafe for discharging our cargo, seeing that spies of the enemy (that is to say, of the old Government) had been taken and shot in the neighbourhood the day before. We might trust the brig to the native pilot; and he had his instructions to take us to another part of the coast. The note was signed by the proper parties; so we let the Irishman go back alone in the boat, and allowed the pilot to exercise his lawful authority over the brig. He kept us stretching off from the land till noon the next day—his instructions, seemingly, ordering him to keep up well out of sight of the shore. We only altered our course in the afternoon, so as to close in with the land again a little before midnight.

This same pilot was about as ill-looking a vagabond as ever I saw; a skinny, cowardly, quarrelsome mongrel, who swore at the men in the vilest broken English, till they were every one of them ready to pitch him overboard. The skipper kept them quiet, and I kept them quiet; for the pilot being given us by our instructions, we were bound to make the best of him. Near nightfall, however, with the best will in the world to avoid it, I was unlucky enough to quarrel with him.

He wanted to go below with his pipe, and I stopped him, of course, because it was contrary to orders. Upon that he tried to hustle by me, and I put him away with my hand. I never meant to push him down, but somehow I did. He picked himself up as quick as lightning, and pulled out his knife. I snatched it out of his hand, slapped his murderous face for him, and threw his weapon overboard. He gave me one ugly look, and walked aft. I didn't think much of the look then, but I remembered it a little too well afterward.

We were close in with the land again, just as the wind failed us, between eleven and twelve that night, and dropped our anchor by the pilot's directions.

It was pitch-dark, and a dead, airless calm. The skipper was on deck, with two of our best men for watch. The rest were below, except the pilot, who coiled himself up, more like a snake than a man, on the forecastle. It was not my watch till four in the morning. But I didn't like the look of the night, or the pilot, or the state of things generally, and I shook myself down on deck to get my nap there, and be ready for anything at a moment's notice. The last I remember was the skipper whispering to me that he didn't like the look of things either, and that he would go below and consult his instructions again. That is the last I remember, before the slow, heavy, regular roll of the old brig on the ground-swell rocked me off to sleep.

I was awoke by a scuffle on the forecastle and a gag in my mouth. There was a man on my breast and a man on my legs, and I was bound hand and foot in half a minute.

The brig was in the hands of the Spaniards. They were swarming all over her. I heard six heavy splashes in the water, one after another. I saw the captain stabbed to the heart as he came running up the companion, and I heard a seventh splash in the water. Except myself, every soul of us on board had been murdered and thrown into the sea. Why I was left I couldn't think, till I saw the pilot stoop over me with a lantern, and look, to make sure of who I was. There was a devilish grin on his face, and he nodded his head at me, as much as to say, *You* were the man who hustled me down and slapped my face, and I mean to play the game of cat and mouse with you in return for it!

I could neither move nor speak, but I could see the Spaniards take off the main hatch and rig the purchases for getting up the cargo. A quarter of an hour afterward I heard the sweeps of a schooner, or other small vessel, in the water. The strange craft was laid alongside of us, and the Spaniards set to work to discharge our cargo into her. They all worked hard except the pilot; and he came from time to time, with his lantern, to have another look at me, and to grin and nod, always in the same devilish way. I am old enough now not to be ashamed of confessing the truth, and I don't mind acknowledging that the pilot frightened me.

The fright, and the bonds, and the gag, and the not being able to stir hand or foot, had pretty nigh worn me out by the time the Spaniards gave over work. This was just as the dawn broke. They had shifted a good part of our cargo on board their vessel, but nothing like all of it, and they were sharp enough to be off with what they had got before daylight.

I need hardly say that I had made up my mind by this time to the worst I could think of. The pilot, it was clear enough, was one of the spies of the enemy, who had wormed himself into the confidence of our consignees without being suspected. He, or more likely his employers, had got knowledge enough of us to suspect what our cargo was; we had been anchored for the night in the safest berth for them to surprise us in; and we had paid the penalty of having a small crew, and consequently an insufficient watch. All this was clear enough—but what did the pilot mean to do with *me?*

On the word of a man, it makes my flesh creep now, only to tell you what he did with me.

After all the rest of them were out of the brig, except the pilot and two Spanish seamen, these last took me up, bound and gagged as I was, lowered me into the hold of the vessel, and laid me along on the floor, lashing me to it with ropes' ends, so that I could just turn from one side to the other, but could not roll myself fairly over, so as to change my place. They then left me. Both of them were the worse for liquor; but the devil of a pilot was sober—mind that!—as sober as I am at the present moment.

I lay in the dark for a little while, with my heart thumping as if it was going to jump out of me. I lay about five minutes or so when the pilot came down into the hold alone.

He had the captain's cursed flat candlestick and a carpenter's awl in one hand, and a long thin twist of cotton yarn, well oiled, in the other. He put the candlestick, with a new "dip" candle lighted in it, down on the floor about two feet from my face, and close against the side of the vessel. The light was feeble enough; but it was sufficient to show a dozen barrels of gunpowder or more left all round me in the hold of the brig. I began to suspect what he was after the moment I noticed the barrels. The horrors laid hold of me from head to foot, and the sweat poured off my face like water.

I saw him go next to one of the barrels of powder standing against the side of the vessel in a line with the candle, and about three feet, or rather better, away from it. He bored a hole in the side of the barrel with his awl, and the horrid powder came trickling out, as black as hell, and dripped into the hollow of his hand, which he held to catch it. When he had got a good handful, he stopped up the hole by jamming one end of his oiled twist of cotton-yarn fast into it, and he then rubbed the powder into the whole length of the yarn till he had blackened every hair-breadth of it.

The next thing he did—as true as I sit here, as true as the heaven above us all—the next thing he did was to carry the free end of his long, lean, black, frightful slow-match to the lighted candle alongside my face. He tied it (the bloody-minded villain!) in several folds round the tallow dip, about a third of the distance down, measuring from the flame of the wick to the lip of the candlestick. He did that; he looked to see that my lashings were all safe; and then he put his face close to mine, and whispered in my ear, "Blow up with the brig!"

He was on deck again the moment after, and he and the two others shoved the hatch on over me. At the farthest end from where I lay they had not fitted it down quite true, and I saw a blink of daylight glimmering in when I looked in that direction. I heard the sweeps of the schooner fall into the water—splash! splash! fainter and fainter, as they swept the vessel out in the dead calm, to be ready for the wind in the offing. Fainter and fainter, splash, splash! for a quarter of an hour or more.

While those receding sounds were in my ears, my eyes were fixed on the candle.

It had been freshly lighted. If left to itself, it would burn for between six and seven hours. The slow-match was twisted round it about a third of the way down, and therefore the flame would be about two hours reaching it. There I lay, gagged, bound, lashed to the floor; seeing my own life burning down with the candle by my side—there I lay, alone on the sea, doomed to be blown to atoms, and to see that doom drawing on, nearer and nearer with every fresh second of time, through nigh on two hours to come; powerless to help myself, and speechless to call for help to others.

The wonder to me is that I didn't cheat the flame, the slow-match, and the powder, and die of the horror of my situation before my first half-hour was out in the hold of the brig.

I can't exactly say how long I kept the command of my senses after I had ceased to hear the splash of the schooner's sweeps in the water. I can trace back everything I did and everything I thought up to a certain point; but, once past that, I get all abroad, and lose myself in my memory now, much as I lost myself in my own feelings at the time.

The moment the hatch was covered over me, I began, as every other man would have begun in my place, with a frantic effort to free my hands. In the mad panic I was in, I cut my flesh with the lashings as if they had been knife blades, but I never stirred them. There was less chance still of freeing my legs, or of tearing myself from the fastenings that held me to the floor. I gave in when I was all but suffocated for want of breath. The gag, you will be pleased to remember, was a terrible enemy to me; I could only breathe freely through my nose—and that is but a poor vent when a man is straining his strength as far as ever it will go.

I gave in and lay quiet, and got my breath again, my eyes glaring and straining at the candle all the time.

While I was staring at it, the notion struck me of trying to blow out the flame by pumping a long breath at it suddenly through my nostrils. It was too high above me, and too far away from me, to be reached in that fashion. I tried, and tried, and tried; and then I gave in again, and lay quiet again, always with my eyes glaring at the candle, and the candle glaring at *me*. The splash of the schooner's sweeps was very faint by this time. I could only just hear them in the morning stillness. Splash! splash!—fainter and fainter—splash! splash!

Without exactly feeling my mind going, I began to feel it getting queer as early as this. The snuff of the candle was growing taller and taller, and the length of tallow between the flame and the slow-match, which was the length of my life, was getting shorter and shorter. I calculated that I had rather less than an hour and a half to live.

An hour and a half! Was there a chance in that time of a boat pulling off to the brig from shore? Whether the land near which the vessel was anchored was in possession of our side, or in possession of the enemy's side, I made out that they must, sooner or later, send to hail the brig merely because she was a stranger in those parts. The question for *me* was, how soon? The sun had not risen yet, as I could tell by looking through the chink in the hatch. There was no coast village near us, as we all knew, before the brig was seized, by seeing no lights on shore. There was no wind, as I could tell by listening, to bring any strange vessel near. If I had had six hours to live, there might have been a chance for me, reckoning from sunrise to noon. But with an hour and a half, which had dwindled to an hour and a quarter by this time—or, in other words, with the earliness of the morning, the uninhabited coast, and the dead calm all against me—there was not the ghost of a chance. As I felt that, I had another struggle—the last—with my bonds, and only cut myself the deeper for my pains.

I gave in once more, and lay quiet, and listened for the splash of the sweeps.

Gone! Not a sound could I hear but the blowing of a fish now and then on the surface of the sea, and the creak of the brig's crazy old spars, as she rolled gently from side to side with the little swell there was on the quiet water.

An hour and a quarter. The wick grew terribly as the quarter slipped away, and the charred top of it began to thicken and spread out mushroom-shape. It would fall off soon. Would it fall off red-hot, and would the swing of the brig cant it over the side of the candle and let it down on the slow-match? If it would, I had about ten minutes to live instead of an hour.

This discovery set my mind for a minute on a new tack altogether. I began to ponder with myself what sort of a death blowing up might be. Painful! Well, it would be, surely, too sudden for that. Perhaps just one crash inside me, or outside me, or both; and nothing more! Perhaps not even a crash; that and death and the scattering of this living body of mine into millions of fiery sparks, might all happen in the same instant! I couldn't make it out; I couldn't settle how it would be. The minute of calmness in my mind left it before I had half done thinking; and I got all abroad again.

When I came back to my thoughts, or when they came back to me (I can't say which), the wick was awfully tall, the flame was burning with a smoke above it, the charred top was broad and red, and heavily spreading out to its fall.

My despair and horror at seeing it took me in a new way, which was good and right, at any rate, for my poor soul. I tried to pray—in my own heart, you will understand, for the gag put all lip-praying out of my power. I tried, but the candle seemed to burn it up in me. I struggled hard to force my eyes from the slow, murdering flame, and to look up through the chink in the hatch at the blessed daylight. I tried once, tried twice; and gave it up. I next tried only to shut my eyes, and keep them shut—once—twice—and the second time I did it. "God bless old mother, and sister Lizzie; God keep them both, and forgive me." That was all I had time to say, in my own heart, before my eyes opened again, in spite of me, and the flame of the candle flew into them, flew all over me, and burned up the rest of my thoughts in an instant.

I couldn't hear the fish blowing now; I couldn't hear the creak of the spars; I couldn't think; I couldn't feel the sweat of my own death agony on my face—I could only look at the heavy, charred top of the wick. It swelled, tottered, bent over to one side, dropped—red-hot at the moment of its fall—black and harmless, even before the swing of the brig had canted it over into the bottom of the candlestick.

I caught myself laughing.

Yes! laughing at the safe fall of the bit of wick. But for the gag, I should have screamed with laughter. As it was, I shook with it inside me—shook till the blood was in my head, and I was all but suffocated for want of breath. I had just sense enough left to feel that my own horrid laughter at that awful moment was a sign of my brain going at last. I had just sense enough left to make another struggle before my mind broke loose like a frightened horse, and ran away with me.

One comforting look at the blink of daylight through the hatch was what I tried for once more. The fight to force my eyes from the candle and to get that one look at the daylight was the hardest I had had yet; and I lost the fight. The flame had hold of my eyes as fast as the lashings had hold of my hands. I couldn't look away from it. I couldn't even shut my eyes, when I tried that next, for the second time. There was the wick growing tall once more. There was the space of unburned candle between the light and the slow-match shortened to an inch or less.

How much life did that inch leave me? Three-quarters of an hour? Half an hour? Fifty minutes? Twenty minutes? Steady! an inch of tallow candle would burn longer than twenty minutes. An inch of tallow! the notion of a man's body and soul being kept together by an inch of tallow! Wonderful! Why, the greatest king that sits on a throne can't keep a man's body and soul together; and here's an inch of tallow that can do what the king can't! There's something to tell mother when I get home which will surprise her more than all the rest of my voyages put together. I laughed inwardly again at the thought of that, and shook and swelled and suffocated myself, till the light of the candle leaped in through my eyes, and licked up the laughter, and burned it out of me, and made me all empty and cold and quiet once more.

Mother and Lizzie. I don't know when they came back; but they did come back—not, as it seemed to me, into my mind this time, but right down bodily before me, in the hold of the brig.

Yes: sure enough, there was Lizzie, just as lighthearted as usual, laughing at me. Laughing? Well, why not? Who is to blame Lizzie for thinking I'm lying on my back, drunk in the cellar, with the beer barrels all round me? Steady! she's crying now—spinning round and round in a fiery mist, wringing her hands, screeching out for help—fainter and fainter, like the splash of the schooner's sweeps. Gone—burned up in the fiery mist! Mist? fire? no; neither one nor the other. It's mother makes the light—mother knitting, with ten flaming points at the ends of her fingers and thumbs, and slow-matches hanging in bunches all round her face instead of her own grey hair. Mother in her old armchair, and the pilot's long skinny hands hanging over the back of the chair, dripping with gunpowder. No! no gunpowder, no chair, no mother—nothing but the pilot's face, shining red-hot, like a sun, in the fiery mist; turning upside down in the fiery mist; running backward and forward along the slow-match, in the fiery mist; spinning millions of miles in a minute, in the fiery mist—spinning itself smaller and smaller into one tiny point, and that point darting on a sudden straight into my head—and then, all fire and all mist—no hearing, no seeing, no thinking, no feeling—the brig, the sea, my own self, the whole world, all gone together!

After what I've just told you, I know nothing and remember nothing, till I woke up (as it seemed to me) in a comfortable bed, with two rough-and-ready men like myself sitting on each side of my pillow, and a gentleman standing watching me at the foot of the bed. It was about seven in the morning. My sleep (or what seemed like my sleep to me) had lasted better than eight months—I was among my own countrymen in the island of Trinidad—the men at each side of my pillow were my keepers, turn and turn about—and the gentleman standing at the foot of the bed was the doctor. What I said and did in those eight months I never have known, and never shall. I woke out of it as if it had been one long sleep—that's all I know.

It was another two months or more before the doctor thought it safe to answer the questions I asked him.

An American vessel, becalmed in the offing, had made out the brig as the sun rose; and the captain, seeing her anchored where no vessel had any reason to be, had manned one of his boats and sent his mate to look into the matter and report of what he saw.

What he saw, when he and his men found the brig deserted and boarded her, was a gleam of candlelight through the chink in the hatch-way. The flame was within about a thread's breadth of the slow-match when he lowered himself into the hold; and if he had not had the sense and coolness to cut the match in two with his knife before he touched the candle, he and his men might have been blown up along with the brig as well as me. The match caught, and turned into sputtering red fire, in the very act of putting the candle out. . . .

What became of the Spanish schooner and the pilot I have never heard from that day to this.

As for the brig, the Yankees took her, as they took me, to Trinidad, and claimed their salvage, and got it, I hope, for their own sakes. I was landed just in the same state as when they rescued me from the brig—that is to say, clean out of my senses. But please to remember, it was a long time ago; and, take my word for it, I was discharged cured, as I have told you. Bless your hearts, I'm all right now, as you may see. I'm a little shaken by telling the story, as is only natural—a little shaken, my good friends, that's all.

THE ADMIRAL

O. HENRY

Spilled milk draws few tears from an Anchurian administration. Many are its lacteal sources; and the clock's hands point for ever to milking time. Even the rich cream skimmed from the treasury by the bewitched

Miraflores did not cause the newly-installed patriots to waste time in unprofitable regrets. The government philosophically set about supplying the deficiency by increasing the import duties and by "suggesting" to wealthy private citizens that contributions according to their means would be considered patriotic and in order. Prosperity was expected to attend the reign of Losada, the new president. The ousted office-holders and military favourites organised a new "Liberal" party, and began to lay their plans for a re-succession. Thus the game of Anchurian politics began, like a Chinese comedy, to unwind slowly its serial length. Here and there Mirth peeps for an instant from the wings and illumines the florid lines.

A dozen quarts of champagne in conjunction with an informal sitting of the president and his cabinet led to the establishment of the navy and the appointment of Felipe Carrera as its admiral. Next to the champagne the credit of the appointment belongs to Don Sabas Placido, the newly confirmed Minister of War.

The president had requested a convention of his cabinet for the discussion of questions politic and for the transaction of certain routine matters of state. The session had been signally tedious; the business and the wine prodigiously dry. A sudden, prankish humour of Don Sabas, impelling him to the deed, spiced the grave affairs of state with a whiff of agreeable playfulness.

In the dilatory order of business had come a bulletin from the coast department of Orilla del Mar reporting the seizure by the customs-house officers at the town of Coralio of the sloop *Estrella del Noche* and her cargo of dry goods, patent medicines, granulated sugar and three-star brandy. Also six Martini rifles and a barrel of American whisky. Caught in the act of smuggling, the sloop with its cargo was now, according to law, the property of the republic.

The Collector of Customs, in making his report, departed from the conventional forms so far as to suggest that the confiscated vessel be converted to the use of the government. The prize was the first capture to the credit of the department in ten years. The collector took opportunity to pat his department.

It often happened that government officers required transportation from point to point along the coast, and means were usually lacking. Furthermore, the sloop could be manned by a loyal crew and employed as a coast guard to discourage the pernicious art of smuggling. The collector also ventured to nominate one to whom the charge of the boat could be safely entrusted— a young man of Coralio, Felipe Carrera—not, be it understood, one of extreme wisdom, but loyal and the best sailor along the coast.

It was upon this hint that the Minister of War acted, executing a rare piece of drollery that so enlivened the tedium of executive session.

In the constitution of this small, maritime banana republic was a forgotten section that provided for the maintenance of a navy. This provision—with many other wiser ones—had lain inert since the establishment of the republic. Anchuria had no navy and had no use for one. It was characteristic of Don Sabas—a man at once merry, learned, whimsical and audacious—that he should have disturbed the dust of this musty and sleeping statute to increase the humour of the world by so much as a smile from his indulgent colleagues.

With delightful mock seriousness the Minister of War proposed the creation of a navy. He argued its need and the glories it might achieve with such gay and witty zeal that the travesty overcame with its humour even the swart dignity of President Losada himself.

The champagne was bubbling trickily in the veins of the mercurial statesmen. It was not the custom of the grave governors of Anchuria to enliven their sessions with a beverage so apt to cast a veil of disparagement over sober affairs. The wine had been a thoughtful compliment tendered by the agent of the Vesuvius Fruit Company as a token of amicable relations—and certain consummated deals—between that company and the republic of Anchuria.

The jest was carried to its end. A formidable, official document was prepared, encrusted with chromatic seals and jaunty with fluttering ribbons, bearing the florid signatures of state. This commission conferred upon *el Señor* Don Felipe Carrera the title of Flag Admiral of the Republic of Anchuria. Thus within the space of a few minutes and the dominion of a dozen "extra dry" the country took its place among the naval powers of the world, and Felipe Carrera became entitled to a salute of nineteen guns whenever he might enter port.

The southern races are lacking in that particular kind of humour that finds entertainment in the defects and misfortunes bestowed by Nature. Owing to this defect in their constitution they are not moved to laughter (as are their northern brothers) by the spectacle of the deformed, the feeble-minded or the insane.

Felipe Carrera was sent upon earth with but half his wits. Therefore, the people of Coralio called him "*El pobrecito loco*"—"the poor little crazed one"—saying that God had sent but half of him to earth, retaining the other half.

A sombre youth, glowering, and speaking only at the rarest times, Felipe was but negatively "loco." On shore he generally refused all conversation.

He seemed to know that he was badly handicapped on land, where so many kinds of understanding are needed; but on the water his one talent set him equal with most men. Few sailors whom God had carefully and completely made could handle a sail-boat as well. Five points nearer the wind than the best of them he could sail his sloop. When the elements raged and set other men to cowering, the deficiencies of Felipe seemed of little importance. He was a perfect sailor, if an imperfect man. He owned no boat, but worked among the crews of the schooners and sloops that skimmed the coast, trading and freighting fruit out to the steamers where there was no harbour. It was through his famous skill and boldness on the sea, as well as for the pity felt for his mental imperfections, that he was recommended by the collector as a suitable custodian of the captured sloop.

When the outcome of Don Sabas' little pleasantry arrived in the form of the imposing and preposterous commission, the collector smiled. He had not expected such prompt and overwhelming response to his recommendation. He dispatched a *muchacho* at once to fetch the future admiral.

The collector waited in his official quarters. His office was in the Calle Grande, and the sea-breezes hummed through its windows all day. The collector, in white linen and canvas shoes, philandered with papers on an antique desk. A parrot, perched on a pen rack, seasoned the official tedium with a fire of choice Castilian imprecations. Two rooms opened into the collector's. In one the clerical force of young men of variegated complexions transacted with glitter and parade their several duties. Through the open door of the other room could be seen a bronze babe, guiltless of clothing, that rollicked upon the floor. In a grass hammock a thin woman, tinted a pale lemon, played a guitar and swung contentedly in the breeze. Thus surrounded by the routine of his high duties and the visible tokens of agreeable domesticity, the collector's heart was further made happy by the power placed in his hands to brighten the fortunes of the "innocent" Felipe.

Felipe came and stood before the collector. He was a lad of twenty, not ill-favoured in looks, but with an expression of distant and pondering vacuity. He wore white cotton trousers, down the seams of which he had sewn red stripes with some vague aim of military decoration. A flimsy blue shirt fell open at his throat; his feet were bare; he held in his hand the cheapest of straw hats from the States.

"*Señor* Carrera," said the collector gravely, producing the showy commission, "I have sent for you at the president's bidding. This document that I present to you confers upon you the title of Admiral of this great republic, and gives you absolute command of the naval forces and fleet of our country. You may think, friend Felipe, that we have no navy—but yes! The sloop the *Estrella del Noche*, that my brave men captured from the coast smugglers, is to be placed under your command. The boat is to be devoted to the services of your country. You will be ready at all times to convey officials of the government to points along the coast where they may be obliged to visit. You will also act as a coast-guard to prevent, as far as you may be able, the crime of smuggling. You will uphold the honour and prestige of your country at sea, and endeavour to place Anchuria among the proudest naval powers of the world. These are your instructions as the Minister of War desires me to convey them to you. *Por Dios*! I do not know how all this is to be accomplished, for not one word did the letter contain in respect to a crew or to the expenses of this navy. Perhaps you are to provide a crew yourself, *Señor* Admiral—I do not know—but it is a very high honour that has descended upon you. I now hand you your commission. When you are ready for the boat I will give orders that she shall be made over into your charge. That is as far as my instructions go."

Felipe took the commission that the collector handed to him. He gazed through the open window at the sea for a moment, with his customary expression of deep but vain pondering. Then he turned without having spoken a word, and walked swiftly away through the hot sand of the street.

"*Pobrecito loco!*" sighed the collector; and the parrot on the pen racks screeched, "Loco!—loco!—loco!"

The next morning a strange procession filed through the streets to the collector's office. At its head was the admiral of the navy. Somewhere Felipe had raked together a pitiful semblance of a military uniform—a pair of red trousers, a dingy blue short jacket heavily ornamented with gold braid, and an old fatigue cap that must have been cast away by one of the British soldiers in Belize and brought away by Felipe on one of his coasting voyages. Buckled around his waist was an ancient ship's cutlass contributed to his equipment by Pedro Lafitte, the baker, who proudly asserted its inheritance from his ancestor, the illustrious buccaneer. At the admiral's heels tagged his newly-shipped crew—three grinning, glossy, black Caribs, bare to the waist, the sand spurting in showers from the spring of their naked feet.

Briefly and with dignity Felipe demanded his vessel of the collector. And now a fresh honour awaited him. The collector's wife, who played the guitar and read novels in the hammock all day, had more than a little romance in her placid, yellow bosom. She had found in an old book an engraving of a flag that purported to be the naval flag of Anchuria. Perhaps it had so been designed by the founders of the nation; but, as no navy had ever been established, oblivion had claimed the flag. Laboriously with her own hands she had made a flag after the pattern—a red cross upon a blue-and-white ground. She presented it to Felipe with these words: "Brave sailor, this flag is of your country. Be true, and defend it with your life. Go you with God."

For the first time since his appointment the admiral showed a flicker of emotion. He took the silken emblem, and passed his hand reverently over its surface. "I am an admiral," he said to the collector's lady. Being on land he could bring himself to no more exuberant expression of sentiment. At sea with the flag at the masthead of his navy, some more eloquent exposition of feelings might be forthcoming.

Abruptly the admiral departed with his crew. For the next three days they were busy giving the *Estrella del Noche* a new coat of white paint trimmed with blue. And then Felipe further adorned himself by fastening a handful of brilliant parrot's plumes in his cap. Again he tramped with his faithful crew to the collector's office and formally notified him that the sloop's name had been changed to *El Nacional.*

During the next few months the navy had its troubles. Even an admiral is perplexed to know what to do without any orders. But none came. Neither did any salaries. *El Nacional* swung idly at anchor.

When Felipe's little store of money was exhausted he went to the collector and raised the question of finances.

"Salaries!" exclaimed the collector, with hands raised; "*Valgame Dios!* not one *centavo* of my own pay have I received for the last seven months. The pay of an admiral, do you ask? *Quién sabe?* Should it be less than three thousand *pesos? Mira!* you will see a revolution in this country very soon. A good sign of it is when the government calls all the time for *pesos, pesos, pesos,* and pays none out."

Felipe left the collector's office with a look almost of content on his sombre face. A revolution would mean fighting, and then the government would need his services. It was rather humiliating to be an admiral without anything to do, and have a hungry crew at your heels begging for *reales* to buy plantains and tobacco with.

When he returned to where his happy-go-lucky Caribs were waiting they sprang up and saluted, as he had drilled them to do.

"Come, *muchachos*," said the admiral; "it seems that the government is poor. It has no money to give us. We will earn what we need to live upon.

Thus we will serve our country. Soon"—his heavy eyes almost lighted up—"it may gladly call upon us for help."

Thereafter *El Nacional* turned out with the other coast craft and became a wage-earner. She worked with the lighters freighting bananas and oranges out to the fruit steamers that could not approach nearer than a mile from the shore. Surely a self-supporting navy deserves red letters in the budget of any nation.

After earning enough at freighting to keep himself and his crew in provisions for a week, Felipe would anchor the navy and hang about the little telegraph office, looking like one of the chorus of an insolvent comic opera troupe besieging the manager's den. A hope for orders from the capital was always in his heart. That his services as admiral had never been called into requirement hurt his pride and patriotism. At every call he would inquire, gravely and expectantly, for dispatches. The operator would pretend to make a search, and then reply:

"Not yet, it seems, *Senor el Almirante—poco tiempo!*"

Outside in the shade of the lime trees the crew chewed sugarcane or slumbered, well content to serve a country that was contented with so little service.

One day in the early summer the revolution predicted by the collector flamed out suddenly. It had long been smouldering. At the first note of alarm the admiral of the navy force and fleet made all sail for a larger port on the coast of a neighbouring republic, where he traded a hastily collected cargo of fruit for its value in cartridges for the five Martini rifles, the only guns that the navy could boast. Then to the telegraph office sped the admiral. Sprawling in his favourite corner, in his fast-decaying uniform, with his prodigious sabre distributed between his red legs, he waited for the long-delayed, but now soon expected, orders.

"Not yet, *Señor el Almirante,*" the telegraph clerk would call to him— "*poco tiempo!*"

At the answer the admiral would plump himself down with a great rattling of scabbard to await the infrequent tick of the little instrument on the table.

"They will come," would be his unshaken reply; "I am the admiral."

AT MORO CASTLE

MICHAEL SCOTT

When the day broke, with a strong breeze and a fresh shower, the *Firebrand* was about two miles off the Moro Castle, at the entrance of Santiago de Cuba.

I went aloft to look round me. The sea breeze blew strong until it reached within half a mile of the shore, where it stopped short, shooting in cat's-paws occasionally into the smooth belt of water beyond, where the long unbroken swell rolled like molten silver in the rising sun, without a ripple on its surface, until it dashed its gigantic undulations against the face of the precipitous cliffs on the shore and flew up in smoke. The entrance to the harbour is very narrow, and looked from my perch like a zigzag chasm in the rock, inlaid at the bottom with polished blue steel; so clear and calm and pellucid was the still water, wherein the frowning rocks, and magnificent trees on the banks, and the white Moro, rising with its grinning tiers of cannon, battery above battery, were reflected, as if it had been in a mirror.

We had shortened sail and fired a gun, and the signal for a pilot was flying, when the captain hailed me. "Does the sea breeze blow into the harbour yet, Mr. Cringle?"

"Not yet, sir; but it is creeping in fast."

"Very well. Let me know when we can run in. Mr. Yerk, back the main-topsail and heave the ship to."

Presently the pilot canoe, with the Spanish flag flying in the stern, came alongside; and the pilot, a tall brown man, a *Moreno*, as the Spaniards say, came on board. He wore a glazed cocked hat, rather an out-of-the-way finish to his figure, which was rigged in a simple Osnaburg shirt and pair of trousers. He came on the quarter-deck, and made his bow to the captain with all the ease in the world, wished him a good-morning, and taking his place by the quartermaster at the conn, he took charge of the ship. "Señor," quoth he to me, "is de harbour blow up yet? I mean, you see de *viento* walking into him?—de terral—dat is land wind—has he cease?"

"No," I answered; "the belt of smooth water is growing narrower fast; but the sea breeze does not blow into the channel yet. Now it has reached the entrance."

"Ah, den make sail, Señor Capitan; fill de main-topsail." We stood in, the scene becoming more and more magnificent as we approached the land.

The fresh green shores of this glorious island lay before us, fringed with white surf, as the everlasting ocean in its approach to it gradually changed its dark blue colour, as the water shoaled, into a bright joyous green under the blazing sun, before it tumbled in shaking thunders on the reefs. The undulating hills in the vicinity were all either cleared, and covered with the greenest verdure that imagination can picture, over which strayed large herds of cattle, or with forests of gigantic trees from amongst which, every now and then, peeped out some palm-thatched mountain settlement, with its small thread of blue smoke floating up into the calm clear morning air, while the blue hills in the distance rose higher and higher, and more and more blue, and dreamy, and indistinct, until their rugged summits could not be distinguished from the clouds through the glimmering hot haze of the tropics.

"By the mark seven," sung out the leadsman in the starboard, chains. "Quarter less three," responded he in the larboard, showing the inequalities of the surface at the bottom of the sea.

By this time, on our right hand, we were within pistol-shot of the Moro, where the channel is not above fifty yards across; indeed there is a chain, made fast to a rock on the opposite side, that can be hove up by a capstan until is is level with the water, so as to constitute an insurmountable obstacle to any attempt to force an entrance in time of war. As we stood in, the golden flag of Spain rose slowly on the staff at the Water Battery, and cast its large sleepy folds abroad in the breeze; but, instead of floating over mail-clad men, or Spanish soldiers in warlike array, three poor devils of half-naked mulattoes stuck their heads out of an embrasure under its shadow. We were mighty close upon leaving the bones of the old ship here, by the by; for at the very instant of entering the harbour's mouth, the land-wind checked us off, and very nearly hove us broadside on upon the rocks below the castle, against which the swell was breaking in thunder.

"Let go the anchor," sung out the captain.

"All gone, sir," promptly responded the boatswain from the forecastle. And as he spoke we struck once, twice, and very heavily the third time. But the breeze coming in strong, we fetched way again; and as the cable was promptly cut, we got safely off. However, on weighing the anchor afterwards, we found the water had been so shoal under the bows that the ship when she stranded had struck it and broken the stock short off by the ring.

The only laughable part of the story consisted in the old cook, an Irishman, with one leg and half an eye, scrambling out of the galley nearly naked, in his trousers, shirt, and greasy nightcap, and sprawling on all fours after two tubsful of yams, which the third thump had capsized all over the deck. "Oh, you scurvy-looking tief," said he, eyeing the pilot; "if it was running us ashore you were set on, why the blazes couldn't ye wait until the yams were in the copper, bad luck to ye—and them all scraped too! I do believe, *if they even had been taties it would have been all the same to you.*"

We stood on, the channel narrowing still more—the rocks rising to a height of a least five hundred feet from the water's edge, as sharply as if they had only yesterday been split asunder.

Noble trees shot out in all directions wherever they could find a little earth and a crevice to hold on by, almost meeting overhead in several places, and alive with all kinds of birds and beasts incidental to the climate; parrots of all sorts, great and small, *clomb*, and hung, and fluttered amongst the branches; and pigeons of numberless varieties; and the glancing woodpecker, with his small hammerlike *tap, tap, tap*; and the West India nightingale, and humming-birds of all hues; while cranes, black, white, and grey, frightened from their fishing-stations, stalked and peeped about, as awkwardly as a warrant-officer in his long-skirted coat on a Sunday; while whole flocks of ducks flew across the mastheads and through the rigging; and the dragon-like guanas, and lizards of many kinds, disported themselves amongst the branches.

And then the dark, transparent crystal depth of the pure waters under foot, reflecting all nature so steadily and distinctly, that in the hollows, where the overhanging foliage of the laurel-like bushes darkened the scene, you could not for your life tell where the elements met, so blended were earth and sea.

"Starboard," said I. I had now come on deck. "Starboard, or the main-topgallant-masthead *will be foul of the limb of that tree.* Foretop, there—lie out on the larboard foreyard-arm, and be ready to shove her off if she sheers too close."

"Let go the anchor," struck in the first lieutenant.

Splash—the cable rumbled through the hawse-hole.

"Now here are we brought up in paradise," quoth the doctor.

"Curukity coo—curukity coo," sung out a great bushy-whiskered sailor from the crows' nest, our old friend Timothy Tailtackle. "Here am I, Jack, a booby amongst the singing-birds," crowed he to one of his messmates in the maintop, as he clutched a branch of a tree in his hand, and swung himself up into it. But the ship, as Old Nick would have it, at the very instant dropped astern a few yards in swinging to her anchor, and that so suddenly, that she left him on his perch in the tree, converting his jest, poor fellow, into melancholy earnest.

"Oh Lord, sir!" sung out Timotheus, in a great quandary. "Captain, do heave ahead a bit—Murder—I shall never get down again! Do, Mr. Yerk, if you please, sir!" And there he sat twisting and craning himself about, and screwing his features into combinations evincing the most comical perplexity.

The captain, by way of a bit of fun, pretended not to hear him.

"Maintop, there," quoth he.

The midshipman in the top answered him, "Ay, ay, sir."

"Not you, Mr. Reefpoint; the captain of the top I want."

"He is not in the top, sir," responded little Reefpoint, chuckling like to choke himself.

"Where the devil is he, sir?"

"*Here,* sir," squealed Timothy, his usual gruff voice spindling into a small *cheep* through his great perplexity. "*Here,* sir."

"What are you doing there, sir? Come down this moment, sir. Rig out the main-topmast- studding-sail-boom, Mr. Reefpoint, and tell him to slew himself down by that long water-withe."

To hear was to obey. Poor Timothy clambered down to the fork of the tree, from which the withe depended, and immediately began to warp himself down, until he reached within three or four yards of the starboard fore-topsail-yard-arm; but the corvette *still* dropped astern, so that, after a vain attempt to hook on by his feet, he swung off into mid-air, hanging by his hands.

It was no longer a joke. "Here, you black fellows in the pilot canoe," shouted the captain, as he threw them a rope himself. "Pass the end of that line round the stump yonder—that one below the cliff, there—now pull like devils, pull."

They did not understand a word he said; but, comprehending his gestures, did what he wished.

"Now haul on the line, men—gently, that will do. Missed it again," continued the skipper, as the poor fellow once more made a fruitless attempt to swing himself on to the yard.

"Pay out the warp again," sung out Tailtackle—"quick, quick, let the ship swing from under, and leave me scope to dive, or I shall be obliged to let go, and be killed on the deck."

"God bless me, yes," said Transon, "stick out the warp, let her swing to her anchor."

In an instant all eyes were again fastened with intense anxiety on the poor fellow, whose strength was fast failing, and his grasp plainly relaxing.

"See all clear to pick me up, messmates."

Tailtackle slipped down to the extreme end of the black withe, that looked like a scorched snake, pressed his legs close together, pointing his toes downwards, and then steadying himself for a moment, with his hands right above his head, and his arms at the full stretch, he dropped, struck the water fairly, entering its dark blue depths without a splash, and instantly disappeared, leaving a white frothy mark on the surface.

"Did you ever see anything better done?" said Yerk. "Why, he clipped into the water with the speed of light, as clean and clear as if he had been a marlinspike."

"Thank heaven!" gasped the captain; for if he had struck the water horizontally, or fallen headlong, he would have been shattered in pieces—every bone would have been broken—he would have been as completely smashed as if he had dropped upon one of the limestone rocks on the ironbound shore.

"Ship, ahoy!" We were all breathlessly looking over the side where he fell, expecting to see him rise again; but the hail came from the water on t'other side. "Ship, ahoy—throw me a rope, good people—a rope, if you please. Do you mean to careen the ship, that you have all run to the starboard side, leaving me to be drowned to port here?"

"Ah, Tailtackle! well done, old boy," sung out a volley of voices, men and officers rejoiced to see the honest fellow alive. He clambered on board, in the bight of one of twenty ropes that were hove to him.

When he came on deck the captain slyly said, "I don't think you'll go a bird-nesting in a hurry again, Tailtackle."

Tim looked with a most quizzical expression at his captain all blue and breathless and dripping as he was; and then sticking his tongue slightly in his cheek, he turned away, without addressing him directly, but murmuring as he went, "A glass of grog now."

The captain, with whom he was a great favourite, took the hint. "Go below now, and turn in till eight bells, Tailtackle. Mafame," to his steward, "send him a glass of hot brandy grog."

Our instructions were to lie at St. Jago until three British ships, then loading, were ready for sea, and then to convoy them through the Caicos, or windward passage. As our stay was therefore likely to be ten days or a fortnight at the shortest, the boats were hoisted out, and we made our little arrangements and preparations for taking all the recreation in our power; and our worthy skipper, taut and stiff as he was at sea, always encouraged all kinds of fun and larking, both amongst the men and the officers, on occasions like the present.

Amongst his other pleasant qualities, he was a great boat-racer, constantly building and altering gigs and pulling-boats at his own expense, and matching the men against each other for small prizes. He had just finished what the old carpenter considered his *chef-d'œuvre*, and a curious affair this same masterpiece was. In the first place it was forty-two feet long over all, and only three and a half feet beam—the planking was not much above an eighth of an inch in thickness, so that if one of the crew had slipped his foot off the stretcher it must have gone through the bottom. There was a standing order that no man was to go into it with shoes on. She was to pull six oars, and her crew were the captains of the tops, the primest seamen in the ship, and the steersman, no less a character than the skipper himself.

Her name, for I love to be particular, was the *Dragonfly*; she was painted out and in of a bright red, amounting to a flame colour—oars red—the men wearing trousers and shirts of red flannel, and red net nightcaps—which common uniform the captain himself wore. I think I have said before that he was a very handsome man, but if I have not I say so now, and when he had taken his seat, and the *gigs*, all fine men, were seated each with his oar held upright upon his knees ready to be dropped into the water at the same instant, the craft and her crew formed to my eye as pretty a plaything for grown children as ever was seen.

"Give way, men," the oars dipped as clean as so many knives, without a sparkle, the gallant fellows stretched out, and away shot the *Dragonfly* like an arrow, the green water foaming into white smoke at the bows, and hissing away in her wake.

She disappeared in a twinkling round a reach of the canal where we were anchored, and we, the officers, for we must needs have our boat also, were making ready to be off, to have a shot at some beautiful cranes that, floating on there large pinions, slowly passed us with their long legs stuck straight out astern, and their longer necks gathered into their crops when we heard a loud shouting in the direction where the captain's boat had vanished.

Presently the *Devil's Darning Needle* as the Scottish part of the crew loved to call the *Dragonfly* stuck her long snout round the headland and came spinning along with a Spanish canoe manned by four negroes, and steered by an elderly gentleman, a sharp acute-looking little man in a gingham coat, in her wake, also pulling very fast; however, the Don seemed dead beat, and the captain was in great glee.

By this time both boats were alongside, and the old Spaniard, Don Ricardo Campana, addressed the captain, judging that he was one of the seamen. "Is the captain on board?" said he in Spanish. The captain, who understood the language, but did not speak it, answered him in French, which Don Ricardo seemed to speak fluently.

"No, sir, the captain is not on board; but there is Mr. Yerk, the first lieutenant, at the gangway." He had come for the letter-bag, he said, and if we had any newspapers, and could spare them, it would be conferring a great favour on him.

He got his letters and newspapers handed down, and very civilly gave the captain a dollar, who touched his cap, tipped the money to the men, and winking slightly to old Yerk and the rest of us, addressed himself to shove off. The old Don, drawing up his eyebrows a little (I *guess* he rather saw who was who, for all his make-believe innocence) bowed to the officers at the gangway, sat down, and desiring his people to use their broad-bladed, clumsy-looking oars, or paddles, began to move awkwardly away. We, that is, the gunroom officers, all except the second lieutenant, who had the watch, and the master, now got into our own gig also, rowed by ourselves, and away we all went in a covey; the purser and doctor, and three of the middies forward, Thomas Cringle, gent., pulling the stroke-oar, with old Moses Yerk as coxswain; and as the Dragonflies were all red, so we were all sea-green, boat, oars, trousers, shirts, and nightcaps.

We soon distanced the cumbrous-looking Don, and the strain was between the *Devil's Darning Needle* and our boat the *Watersprite*, which was making capital play, for although we had not the bottom of the top-men, yet we had more blood, so to speak, and we had already beaten them, in their last gig, all to sticks. But the *Dragonfly* was a new boat, and now in the water for the first time.

We were both of us so intent on our own match, that we lost sight of the Spaniard altogether, and the captain and the first lieutenant were bobbing in the stern-sheets of their respective gigs like a couple of *souple Tams*, as intent on the game as if all our lives had depended on it, when in an instant the long black dirty prow of the canoe was thrust in between us, the old Don singing out, "*Dexa mi lugar, paysanos, dexa mi lugar, mis hijos*" ("Leave me room, countrymen—leave me room, my children").

We kept away right and left, to look at the miracle; and there lay the canoe, rumbling and splashing, with her crew walloping about, and grinning and yelling like incarnate fiends, and as naked as the day they were born, and the old Don himself, so staid and so sedate and drawly as he was a minute before, now all alive, shouting "*Tira diablitos, tira!*" ("Pull, you devils, pull!"), flourishing a small paddle, with which he steered, about his head like a wheel, and dancing and jumping about in his seat.

"Zounds," roared the skipper—"why, topmen—why, gentlemen, give way for the honour of the ship—Gentlemen, stretch out—Men, pull like devils; twenty pounds if you beat him."

We pulled, and they pulled, and the water roared, and the men strained their muscles and sinews to cracking; and all was splash, splash, and *whiz, whiz*, and *pech, pech*, about us, *but it would not do*—the canoe headed us like a shot, and in passing, the cool old Don again subsided into a calm as suddenly as he had been roused from it, and sitting once more, stiff as a poker, turned round and touched his *sombrero*, "I will tell that you are coming, gentlemen."

It was now the evening, near nightfall, and we had been so intent on beating our awkward-looking opponent, that we had none of us time to look at the splendid scene that burst upon our view, on rounding a precipitous rock, from the crevices of which some magnificent trees shot up—their gnarled trunks and twisted branches overhanging the canal where we were pulling and anticipating the fast-falling darkness that was creeping over the fair face of nature; and there we floated, in the deep shadow of the cliff and trees—Dragonflies and Watersprites—motionless and silent, the boats floating so lightly that they scarcely seemed to touch the water, the men resting on their oars, and all of us rapt with the magnificence of the scenery around us, beneath us, and above us.

The left or western bank of the narrow entrance to the harbour from which we were now debouching, ran out in all its precipitousness and beauty (with its dark evergreen bushes overshadowing the deep blue waters, and its gigantic trees shooting forth high into the glowing western sky), until it joined the northern shore, when it sloped away gradually towards the east; the higher parts of the town sparkled in the evening sun, on this dun ridge, like golden turrets on the back of an elephant, while the houses that were in the shade covered the declivity with their dark masses, until it sank down to the water's edge.

On the right hand the haven opened boldly out into a basin about four miles broad by seven long, in which the placid waters spread out beyond the shadow of the western bank into one vast sheet of molten gold, with the canoe tearing along the shining surface, her side glancing in the sun, and her paddles flashing back his rays, and leaving a long train of living fire sparkling in her wake.

It was now about six o'clock in the evening; the sun had set to us, as we pulled along under the frowsing brow of the cliff, where the birds were fast settling on their nightly perches with small happy twitterings, and the lizards and numberless other chirping things began to send forth their evening hymn to the great Being who made them and us, and a solitary white-sailing owl would every now and then flit spectre-like from one green tuft, across the bald face of the cliff, to another, and the small divers around us were breaking up the black surface of the waters into little sparkling circles as they fished for their suppers. All was becoming brown and indistinct near us; but the level beams of the setting sun still lingered with a golden radiance upon the lovely city and the shipping at anchor before it, making their sails, where loosed to dry, glance like leaves of gold.

One half of every object, shipping, houses, trees, and hills, was gloriously illuminated; but even as we looked, the lower part of the town gradually sank into darkness, and faded from our sight—the deepening gloom cast by the high bank above us, like the dark shadow of a bad spirit, gradually crept on and on, and extended farther and farther; the sailing water-fowl in regular lines no longer made the water flash up like flame; the russet mantle of eve was fast extending over the entire hemisphere; the glancing minarets, and the tallest trees, and the topgallant-yards and masts of the shipping, alone flashed back the dying effulgence of the glorious orb, which every moment grew fainter and fainter, and redder and redder, until it shaded into purple, and the loud deep bell of the convent of La Merced swung over the still waters, announcing the arrival of evensong and the departure of day.

"Had we not better pull back to supper, sir?" quoth Moses Yerk to the captain. We all started, the men dipped their oars, our dreams were dispelled, the charm was broken—"Confound the matter-of-fact blockhead," or something very like it, grumbled the captain—"but give way, men," fast followed, and we returned towards the ship.

We had not pulled fifty yards, when we heard the distant rattle of the muskets of the sentries at the gangways, as they discharged them at sundown, and were remarking, as we were rowing leisurely along, upon the strange effect produced by the reports, as they were frittered away amongst the overhanging cliffs in chattering reverberations, when the captain suddenly sang out, "Oars!" All hands lay on them. "Look there," he continued—"There—between the gigs—saw you ever anything like that, gentlemen?" We all leant over; and although the boats, from the *way* they had, were skimming along nearer seven than five knots, *there* lay a large shark—he must have been twelve feet long at the shortest—swimming right in the middle, and equidistant from both, and keeping *way* with us most accurately.

He was distinctly visible, from the strong and vivid phosphorescence excited by his rapid motion through the sleeping waters of the dark creek, which lit up his jaws, head, and whole body; his eyes were especially luminous, while a long wake of sparkles streamed astern of him from the lashing of his tail. As the boats lost speed, the luminousness of his appearance faded gradually as he shortened sail also, until he disappeared altogether. He was then at rest, and suspended motionless in the water; and the only thing that indicated his proximity was an occasional sparkle from the motion of a fin.

We brought the boats nearer together, after pulling a stroke or two, but he seemed to sink as we closed, until at last we could merely perceive an indistinct halo far down in the clear black profound. But as we separated, and resumed our original position, he again rose near the surface; and although the ripple and dip of the oars rendered him invisible while we were pulling, yet the moment we again rested on them, there was the monster, like a persecuting fiend, once more right between us, glaring on us, and apparently watching every motion. It was a terrible spectacle.

"A water-kelpie," murmured one of the captain's gigs, a Scotsman, "an evil sprite."

The men were evidently alarmed. "Stretch out, men; never mind the shark. He can't jump into the boat surely," said the skipper. "What the deuce are you afraid of?"

We arrived within pistol-shot of the ship. As we approached, the sentry hailed, "Boat, ahoy!"

"Firebrand," sang out the skipper, in reply.

"Man the side—gangway lanterns there," quoth the officer on duty; and by the time we were close to, there were two sides-men over the side with the man-ropes ready stuck out to our grasp, and two boys with lanterns above them. We got on deck, the officers touching their hats, and speedily the captain dived down the ladder, saying, as he descended, "Mr. Yerk, I shall be happy to see you and your boat's-crew at supper, or rather to a late dinner, at eight o'clock; but come down a moment as you are. Tailtackle, bring the gigs into the cabin to get a glass of grog, will you?"

"Ay, ay, sir," responded Timothy. "Down with you, you flaming thieves."

So down we all trundled into the cabin, masters and men.

THE PHANTOM SHIP

CAPTAIN MARRYAT

The ship was ready to sail for Europe; and Philip Vanderdecken went on board—hardly caring whither he went. To return to Terneuse was not his object; he could not bear the idea of revisiting the scene of so much happiness and so much misery. Amine's form was engraven on his heart, and he looked forward with impatience to the time when he should be summoned to join her in the land of spirits.

He had awakened as from a dream, after so many years of aberration of intellect. He was no longer the sincere Catholic that he had been; for he never thought of religion without his Amine's cruel fate being brought to his recollection. Still he clung on to the relic—he believed in that—and that only. It was his god—his creed—his everything—the passport for himself and for his father into the next world—the means whereby he should join his Amine—and for hours would he remain holding in his hand that object so valued—gazing upon it—recalling every important event in his life, from the death of his poor mother, and his first sight of Amine; to the last dreadful scene. It was to him a journal of his existence, and on it were fixed all his hopes for the future.

"When! oh, when is it to be accomplished!" was the constant subject of his reveries. "Blessed, indeed, will be the day when I leave this world of hate, and seek that other in which 'the weary are at rest.'"

The vessel on board of which Philip was embarked as a passenger was the *Nostra Señora da Monte*, a brig of three hundred tons, bound for Lisbon. The captain was an old Portuguese, full of superstition, and fond of arrack—a fondness rather unusual with the people of his nation. They sailed from Goa, and Philip was standing abaft, and sadly contemplating the spire of the Cathedral, in which he had last parted with his wife, when his elbow was touched, and he turned round.

"Fellow-passenger again!" said a well-known voice—it was that of the pilot Schriften.

There was no alteration in the man's appearance; he showed no marks of declining years; his one eye glared as keenly as ever.

Philip started, not only at the sight of the man, but at the reminiscences which his unexpected appearance brought to his mind. It was but for a second, and he was again calm and pensive.

"You here again, Schriften?" observed Philip. "I trust your appearance forebodes the accomplishment of my task."

"Perhaps it does," replied the pilot; "we both are weary."

Philip made no reply; he did not even ask Shriften in what manner he had escaped from the fort; he was indifferent about it; for he felt that the man had a charmed life.

"Many are the vessels that have been wrecked, Philip Vanderdecken, and many the souls summoned to their account by meeting with your father's ship, while you have been so long shut up," observed the pilot.

"May our next meeting with him be more fortunate—may it be the last!" replied Philip.

"No, no! rather may he fulfil his doom, and sail till the day of judgment," replied the pilot with emphasis.

"Vile caitiff! I have a foreboding that you will not have your detestable wish. Away!—leave me! or you shall find that although this head is blanched by misery, this arm has still some power."

Schriften scowled as he walked away; he appeared to have some fear of Philip, although it was not equal to his hate. He now resumed his former attempts of stirring up the ship's company against Philip, declaring that he was a Jonas, who would occasion the loss of the ship, and that he was connected with the *Flying Dutchman*. Philip very soon observed that he was avoided; and he resorted to counter-statements, equally injurious to Schriften, whom he declared to be a demon. The appearance of Schriften was so much against him, while that of Philip, on the contrary, was so prepossessing, that the people on board hardly knew what to think. They were divided: some were on the side of Philip—some on that of Schriften; the captain and many others looking with equal horror upon both, and longing for the time when they could be sent out of the vessel.

The captain, as we have before observed, was very superstitious, and very fond of his bottle. In the morning he would be sober and pray; in the afternoon he would be drunk, and swear at the very saints whose protection he had invoked but a few hours before.

"May Holy Saint Antonio preserve us, and keep us from temptation," said he, on the morning after a conversation with the passengers about the Phantom Ship. "All the saints protect us from harm," continued he, taking off his hat reverentially, and crossing himself. "Let me but rid myself of these two dangerous men without accident, and I will offer up a hundred wax candles, of three ounces each, to the shrine of the Virgin, upon my safe anchoring off the tower of Belem." In the evening he changed his language.

"Now, if that Maldetto Saint Antonio don't help us, may he feel the coals of hell yet; damn him and his pigs too; if he has the courage to do his duty, all will be well; but he is a cowardly wretch, he cares for nobody, and will not help those who call upon him in trouble. Carambo! that for you," exclaimed the captain, looking at the small shrine of the saint at the bittacle, and snapping his fingers at the image—"that for you, you useless wretch, who never help us in our trouble. The Pope must canonise some better saints for us, for all we have now are worn out. They could do something formerly, but now I would not give two ounces of gold for the whole calendar; as for you, you lazy old scoundrel," continued the captain, shaking his fist at poor Saint Antonio.

The ship had now gained off the southern coast of Africa, and was about one hundred miles from the Lagullas coast; the morning was beautiful, a slight ripple only turned over the waves, the breeze was light and steady, and the vessel was standing on a wind, at the rate of about four miles an hour.

"Blessed be the holy saints," said the captain, who had just gained the deck; "another little slant in our favour, and we shall lay our course. Again I say, blessed be the holy saints, and particularly our worthy patron Saint Antonio, who has taken under his peculiar protection the *Nostra Señora da Monte*. We have a prospect of fine weather; come, signors, let us down to breakfast, and after breakfast we will enjoy our cigarros upon the deck."

But the scene was soon changed; a bank of clouds rose up from the eastward, with a rapidity that, to the seamen's eyes, was unnatural, and it soon covered the whole firmament; the sun was obscured, and all was one deep and unnatural gloom; the wind subsided, and the ocean was hushed. It was not exactly dark, but the heavens were covered with one red haze, which gave an appearance as if the world was in a state of conflagration.

In the cabin the increased darkness was first observed by Philip, who went on deck; he was followed by the captain and passengers, who were in a state of amazement. It was unnatural and incomprehensible. "Now, holy Virgin, protect us—what can this be?" exclaimed the captain in a fright. "Holy Saint Antonio, protect us—but this is awful."

"There! there!" shouted the sailors, pointing to the beam of the vessel. Every eye looked over the gunnel to witness what had occasioned such exclamations. Philip, Schriften, and the captain were side by side. On the beam of the ship, not more than two cables' length distant, they beheld, slowly rising out of the water, the tapering mast-head and spars of another vessel. She rose, and rose gradually; her topmasts and top-sail yards, with the sails set, next made their appearance; higher and higher she rose up from the element. Her lower masts and rigging, and, lastly, her hull showed itself above the surface. Still she rose up till her ports, with her guns, and at last the whole of her floatage was above water, and there she remained close to them, with her main-yard squared, and hove-to.

"Holy Virgin!" exclaimed the captain, breathless; "I have known ships to *go down*, but never to *come up* before. Now will I give one thousand candles, of ten ounces each, to the shrine of the Virgin to save us in this trouble. One thousand wax candles! Hear me, blessed lady; ten ounces each. Gentlemen," cried the captain to the passengers, who stood aghast, "why don't you promise? Promise, I say; *promise*, at all events."

"The Phantom Ship—*The Flying Dutchman*," shrieked Schriften; "I told you so, Philip Vanderdecken; there is your father. He! he!"

Philip's eyes had remained fixed on the vessel; he perceived that they were lowering down a boat from her quarter. "It is possible," thought he,

"I shall now be permitted!" and Philip put his hand into his bosom and grasped the relic.

The gloom now increased, so that the strange vessel's hull could but just be discovered through the murky atmosphere. The seamen and passengers threw themselves down on their knees, and invoked their saints. The captain ran down for a candle, to light before the image of St. Antonio, which he took out of its shrine, and kissed with much apparent affection and devotion, and then replaced.

Shortly afterwards the splash of oars was heard alongside, and a voice calling out, "I say, my good people, give us a rope from forward."

No one answered, or complied with the request. Schriften only went up to the captain, and told him that if they offered to send letters they must not be received or the vessel would be doomed, and all would perish.

A man now made his appearance from over the gunnel, at the gangway. "You might as well have let me had a side rope, my hearties," said he, as he stepped on deck; "where is the captain?"

"Here," replied the captain, trembling from head to foot. The man who accosted him appeared a weather-beaten seaman, dressed in a fur cap and canvas petticoats; he held some letters in his hand.

"What do you want?" at last screamed the captain.

"Yes—what do you want?" continued Schriften. "He! he!"

"What, you here, pilot?" observed the man; "well—I thought you had gone to Davy's locker, long enough ago."

"He! he!" replied Schriften, turning away.

"Why, the fact is, captain, we have had very foul weather, and we wish to send letters home; I do believe that we shall never get round this Cape."

"I can't take them," cried the captain.

"Can't take them! well, it's very odd—but every ship refuses to take our letters; it's very unkind—seamen should have a feeling for brother seamen, especially in distress. God knows, we wish to see our wives and families again; and it would be a matter of comfort to them, if they only could hear from us."

"I cannot take your letters—the saints preserve us," replied the captain.

"We have been a long while out," said the seaman, shaking his head.

"How long?" inquired the captain, not knowing what to say.

"We can't tell; our almanack was blown overboard, and we have lost our reckoning. We never have our latitude exact now for we cannot tell the sun's declination for the right day."

"Let *me* see your letters," said Philip, advancing, and taking them out of the seaman's hands.

"They must not be touched," screamed Schriften.

"Out, monster!" replied Philip, "who dares interfere with me?"

"Doomed—doomed—doomed!" shrieked Schriften, running up and down the deck, and then breaking into a wild fit of laughter.

"Touch not the letters," said the captain, trembling as if in an ague fit.

Philip made no reply, but held out his hand for the letters.

"Here is one from our second mate, to his wife at Amsterdam, who lives on Waser Quay."

"Waser Quay has long been gone, my good friend; there is now a large dock for ships where it once was," replied Philip.

"Impossible!" replied the man; "here is another from the boatswain to his father, who lives in the old market-place."

"The old market-place has long been pulled down, and there now stands a church upon the spot."

"Impossible!" replied the seaman; "here is another from myself to my sweetheart, Vrow Ketser—with money to buy her a new brooch."

Philip shook his head—"I remember seeing an old lady of that name buried some thirty years ago."

"Impossible! I left her young and blooming. Here's one for the house of Slutz & Co., to whom the ship belongs."

"There's no such house now," replied Philip; "but I have heard that many years ago there was a firm of that name."

"Impossible! you must be laughing at me. Here is a letter from our captain to his son—"

"Give it me," cried Philip, seizing the letter, he was about to break the seal when Schriften snatched it out of his hand, and threw it over the lee gunnel.

"That's a scurvy trick for an old shipmate," observed the seaman. Schriften made no reply, but catching up the other letters which Philip had laid down on the capstan, he hurled them after the first.

The strange seaman shed tears, and walked again to the side. "It is very hard—very unkind," observed he, as he descended; "the time may come when you may wish that your family should know your situation." So saying, he disappeared—in a few seconds was heard the sound of the oars, retreating from the ship.

"Holy St. Antonio!" exclaimed the captain, "I am lost in wonder and fright. Steward, bring me up the arrack."

The steward ran down for the bottle; being as much alarmed as his captain, he helped himself before he brought it up to his commander. "Now," said the captain, after keeping his mouth for two minutes to the bottle, and draining it to the bottom, "what is to be done next?"

"I'll tell you," said Schriften, going up to him. "That man there has a charm hung round his neck; take it from him and throw it overboard, and your ship will be saved; if not, it will be lost, with every soul on board."

"Yes, yes, it's all right, depend upon it," cried the sailors.

"Fools," replied Philip, "do you believe that wretch? Did you not hear the man who came on board recognise him, and call him shipmate? He is the party whose presence on board will prove so unfortunate."

"Yes, yes," cried the sailors, "it's all right, the man did call him shipmate."

"I tell you it's all wrong," cried Schriften; "that is the man, let him give up the charm."

"Yes, yes; let him give up the charm," cried the sailors, and they rushed upon Philip.

Philip started back to where the captain stood. "Madmen, know ye what ye are about? It is the holy cross that I wear round my neck. Throw it overboard if you dare, and your souls are lost for ever": and Philip took the relic from his bosom and showed it to the captain.

"No, no, men," exclaimed the captain, who was now more settled in his nerves; "that won't do—the saints protect us."

The seamen, however, became clamorous; one portion were for throwing Schriften overboard, the other for throwing Philip; at last, the point was decided by the captain, who directed the small skiff, hanging astern, to be lowered down, and ordered both Philip and Schriften to get into it. The seamen approved of this arrangement, as it satisfied both parties. Philip made no objection; Schriften screamed and fought, but he was tossed into the boat. There he remained trembling in the stern sheets, while Philip, who had seized the sculls, pulled away from the vessel in the direction of the Phantom Ship.

In a few minutes the vessel which Philip and Schriften had left was no longer to be discerned through the thick haze; the Phantom Ship was still in sight, but at a much greater distance from them than she was before. Philip pulled hard towards her, but although hove-to, she appeared to increase her distance from the boat. For a short time he paused on his oars to regain his breath, when Schriften rose up and took his seat in the stern sheets of the boat. "You may pull and pull, Philip Vanderdecken," observed Schriften; "but you will not gain that

With their hands raised to heaven.

ship—no, no, that cannot be—we may have a long cruise together, but you will be as far from your object at the end of it as you are now at the commencement. Why don't you throw me overboard again? You would be all the lighter—He! he!"

"I threw you overboard in a state of frenzy," replied Philip, "when you attempted to force from me my relic."

"And have I not endeavoured to make others take it from you this very day?—Have I not—He! he!"

"You have," rejoined Philip; "but I am now convinced, that you are as unhappy as myself, and that in what you are doing, you are only following your destiny, as I am mine. Why and wherefore I cannot tell, but we are both engaged in the same mystery;—if the success of my endeavours depends upon guarding the relic, the success of yours depends upon your obtaining it, and defeating my purpose by so doing. In this matter we are both agents, and you have been, as far as my mission is concerned, my most active enemy. But, Schriften, I have not forgotten, and never will, that you kindlily *did advise* my poor Amine; that you prophesied to her what would be her fate, if she did not listen to your counsel; that you were no enemy of hers, although you have been, and are still mine. Although my enemy, for her sake I *forgive you*, and will not attempt to harm you."

"You do then *forgive your enemy*, Philip Vanderdecken?" replied Schriften, mournfully, "for such, I acknowledge myself to be."

"I do, with *all my heart, with all my soul*," replied Philip.

"Then you have conquered me, Philip Vanderdecken; you have now made me your friend, and your wishes are about to be accomplished. You would know who I am. Listen:—when your father, defying the Almighty's will, in his rage took my life, he was vouchsafed a chance of his doom being cancelled, through the merits of his son. I had also my appeal, which was for *vengeance*; it was granted that I should remain on earth, and thwart your will. That as long as we were enemies, you should not succeed; but that when you had conformed to the highest attribute of Christianity, proved on the holy cross, that of *forgiving your enemy*, your task should be fulfilled. Philip Vanderdecken, you have forgiven your enemy, and both our destinies are now accomplished."

As Schriften spoke, Philip's eyes were fixed upon him. He extended his hand to Philip—it was taken; and as it was pressed, the form of the pilot wasted as it were into the air, and Philip found himself alone.

"Father of Mercy, I thank Thee," said Philip, "that my task is done, and that I again may meet my Amine."

Philip then pulled towards the Phantom Ship, and found that she no longer appeared to leave him; on the contrary, every minute he was nearer and nearer, and at last he threw in his oars, climbed her sides, and gained her deck.

The crew of the vessel crowded round him.

"Your captain," said Philip; "I must speak with your captain."

"Who shall I say, sir?" demanded one, who appeared to be the first mate.

"Who?" replied Philip. "Tell him his son would speak to him, his son Philip Vanderdecken."

Shouts of laughter from the crew followed this answer of Philip's; and the mate, as soon as they ceased, observed with a smile:

"You forget, sir, perhaps you would say his father."

"Tell him his son, if you please," replied Philip; "take no note of grey hairs."

"Well, sir, here he is coming forward," replied the mate, stepping aside, and pointing to the captain.

"What is all this?" inquired the captain.

"Are you Philip Vanderdecken, the captain of this vessel?"

"I am, sir," replied the other.

"You appear not to know me! But how can you? You saw me but when I was only three years old; yet may you remember a letter which you gave to your wife."

"Ha!" replied the captain; "and who then are you?"

"Time has stopped with you, but with those who live in the world he stops not! and for those who pass a life of misery, he hurries on still faster. In me, behold your son, Philip Vanderdecken, who has obeyed your wishes; and after a life of such peril and misery as few have passed, has at last fulfilled his vow, and now offers to his father the precious relic that he required to kiss."

Philip drew out the relic, and held it towards his father. As if a flash of lightning had passed through his mind, the captain of the vessel started back, clasped his hands, fell on his knees, and wept.

"My son, my son!" exclaimed he, rising, and throwing himself into Philip's arms, "my eyes are opened—the Almighty knows how long they have been obscured." Embracing each other, they walked aft, away from the men, who were still crowded at the gangway.

"My son, my noble son, before the charm is broken—before we resolve, as we must into the elements oh! let me kneel in thanksgiving and contrition: my son, my noble son, receive a father's thanks," exclaimed Vanderdecken. Then with tears of joy and penitence he humbly addressed himself to that Being whom he once so awfully defied.

The elder Vanderdecken knelt down: Philip did the same; still embracing each other with one arm, while they raised on high the other, and prayed.

For the last time the relic was taken from the bosom of Philip and handed to his father—and his father raised his eyes to heaven and kissed it. And as he kissed it, the long, tapering, upper spars of the Phantom vessel, the yards and sails that were set, fell into dust, fluttered in the air and sank upon the wave. Then mainmast, foremast, bowsprit, everything above the deck, crumbled into atoms and disappeared.

Again he raised the relic to his lips and the work of destruction continued, the heavy iron guns sank through the decks and disappeared; the crew of the vessel (who were looking on) crumbled down into skeletons, and dust, and fragments of ragged garments; and there were none left on board the vessel in the semblance of life but the father and the son.

Once more did he put the sacred emblem to his lips, and the beams and timber separated, the decks of the vessel slowly sank, and the remnants of the hull floated upon the water; and as the father and son—the one young and vigorous, the other old and decrepit—still kneeling, still embracing, with their hands raised to heaven, sank slowly under the deep blue wave the lurid sky was for a moment illumined by a lightning cross.

Then did the clouds which obscured the heavens roll away swift as thought—the sun again burst out in all his splendour—the rippling waves appeared to dance with joy. The screaming seagull again whirled in the air, and the scared albatross once more slumbered on the wing. The porpoise tumbled and tossed in his sportive play, the albicore and dolphin leaped from the sparkling sea. All nature smiled as if it rejoiced that the charm was dissolved for ever, and that "THE PHANTOM SHIP" WAS NO MORE.

THE SEED OF McCOY

JACK LONDON

The *Pyrenees*, her iron sides pressed low in the water by her cargo of wheat, rolled sluggishly, and made it easy for the man who was climbing aboard from out a tiny outrigger canoe. As his eyes came level with the rail, so that he could see inboard, it seemed to him that he saw a dim, almost indiscernible haze. It was more like an illusion, like a blurring film that had spread abruptly over his eyes. He felt an inclination to brush it away, and the same instant he thought that he was growing old and that it was time to send to San Francisco for a pair of spectacles.

As he came over the rail he cast a glance aloft at the tall masts, and next, at the pumps. They were not working. There seemed nothing the matter with the big ship, and he wondered why she had hoisted the signal of distress. He thought of his happy islanders, and hoped it was not disease. Perhaps the ship was short of water or provisions. He shook hands with the captain, whose gaunt face and careworn eyes made no secret of the trouble, whatever it was. At the same moment the new-comer was aware of a faint, indefinable smell. It seemed like that of burnt bread, but different.

He glanced curiously about him. Twenty feet away a weary-faced sailor was caulking the deck. As his eye lingered on the man, he saw suddenly arise from under his hands a faint spiral of haze that curled and twisted and was gone. By now he had reached the deck. His bare feet were pervaded by a dull warmth that quickly penetrated the thick calluses. He knew now the nature of the ship's distress. His eyes roved swiftly forward, where the full crew of weary-faced sailors regarded him eagerly. The glance from his liquid brown eyes swept over them like a benediction, soothing them, wrapping them about as in the mantle of a great peace. "How long has she been afire, captain?" he asked, in a voice so gentle and unperturbed that it was as the cooing of a dove.

At first the captain felt the peace and content of it stealing in upon him; then the consciousness of all that he had gone through and was going through smote him, and he was resentful. By what right did this ragged beach-comber, in dungaree trousers and a cotton shirt, suggest such a thing as peace and content to him and his overwrought, exhausted soul? The captain did not reason this; it was the unconscious process of emotion that caused his resentment.

"Fifteen days," he answered shortly. "Who are you?"

"My name is McCoy," came the answer, in tones that breathed tenderness and compassion.

"I mean, are you the pilot?"

McCoy passed the benediction of his gaze over the tall, heavy-shouldered man with the haggard, unshaven face who had joined the captain.

"I am as much a pilot as anybody," was McCoy's answer. "We are all pilots here, captain, and I know every inch of these waters."

But the captain was impatient.

"What I want is some of the authorities. I want to talk with them, and blame quick."

"Then I'll do just as well."

Again that insidious suggestion of peace, and his ship a raging furnace beneath his feet! The captain's eyebrows lifted impatiently and nervously, and his fist clenched as if he were about to strike a blow with it.

"Who the blazes are you?" he demanded.

"I am the chief magistrate," was the reply, in a voice that was still the softest and gentlest imaginable.

The tall, heavy-shouldered man broke out in a harsh laugh that was partly amusement, but mostly hysterical. Both he and the captain regarded McCoy with incredulity and amazement. That this barefooted beach-comber should possess such high-sounding dignity was inconceivable. His cotton shirt, unbuttoned, exposed a grizzled chest and the fact that there was no undershirt beneath. A worn straw hat failed to hide the ragged grey hair. Half-way down his chest descended an untrimmed patriarchal beard. In any slop-shop, two shillings would have outfitted him complete as he stood before them.

"Any relation to the McCoy of the *Bounty*?" the captain asked.

"He was my great grand-father."

"Oh," the captain said, then bethought himself. "My name is Davenport, and this is my first mate, Mr. Konig."

They shook hands.

"And now to business." The captain spoke quickly, the urgency of a great haste pressing his speech. "We've been on fire for over two weeks. She's ready to break all hell loose any moment. That's why I held for Pitcairn. I want to beach her, or scuttle her, and save the hull."

"Then you made a mistake, captain," said McCoy. "You should have slacked away for Mangareva. There's a beautiful beach there, in a lagoon where the water is like a mill-pond."

"But we're here, ain't we?" the first mate demanded. "That's the point. We're here, and we've got to do something."

McCoy shook his head kindly.

"You can do nothing here. There is no beach. There isn't even anchorage."

"Gammon!" said the mate. "Gammon!" he repeated loudly, as the captain signalled him to be more soft-spoken. "You can't tell me that sort of stuff. Where d'ye keep your own boats, hey—your schooner, or cutter, or whatever you have? Hey? Answer me that."

McCoy smiled as gently as he spoke. His smile was a caress, an embrace that surrounded the tired mate and sought to draw him into the quietude and rest of McCoy's tranquil soul.

"We have no schooner or cutter," he replied. "And we carry our canoes to the top of the cliff."

"You've got to show me," snorted the mate. "How d'ye get around to the other islands, hey? Tell me that."

"We don't get around. As governor of Pitcairn, I sometimes go. When I was younger I was away a great deal—sometimes on the trading schooners, but mostly on the missionary brig. But she's gone now, and we depend on passing vessels. Sometimes we have had as high as six calls in one year. At other times, a year, and even longer, has gone by without one passing ship. Yours is the first in seven months."

"And you mean to tell me——" the mate began.

But Captain Davenport interfered.

"Enough of this. We're losing time. What is to be done, Mr. McCoy?"

The old man turned his brown eyes, sweet as a woman's, shoreward, and both captain and mate followed his gaze around from the lonely rock of Pitcairn to the crew clustering forward and waiting anxiously for the announcement of a decision. McCoy did not hurry. He thought smoothly and slowly, step by step, with the certitude of a mind that was never vexed or outraged by life.

"The wind is light now," he said finally. "There is a heavy current setting to the westward."

"That's what made us fetch to leeward," the captain interrupted, desiring to vindicate his seamanship.

"Yes, that is what fetched you to leeward," McCoy went on. "Well, you can't work up against this current to-day. And if you did, there is no beach. Your ship will be a total loss."

He paused, and captain and mate looked despair at each other.

"But I will tell you what you can do. The breeze will freshen to-night around midnight—see those tails of cloud and that thickness to windward, beyond the point there? That's where she'll come from, out of the south-east, hard. It is three hundred miles to Mangareva. Square away for it. There is a beautiful bed for your ship there."

The mate shook his head.

"Come into the cabin and we'll look at the chart," said the captain.

McCoy found a stifling, poisonous atmosphere in the pent cabin. Stray waftures of invisible gases bit his eyes and made them sting. The deck was hotter, almost unbearably hot to his bare feet. The sweat poured out of his body. He looked almost with apprehension about him. This malignant, internal heat was astounding. It was a marvel that the cabin did not burst into flames. He had a feeling as of being in a huge bake-oven where the heat might at any moment increase tremendously and shrivel him up like a blade of grass.

As he lifted one foot and rubbed the hot sole against the leg of his trousers, the mate laughed in a savage, snarling fashion.

"The anteroom of hell," he said. "Hell herself is right down there under your feet."

"It's hot!" McCoy cried involuntarily, mopping his face with a bandana handkerchief.

"Here's Mangareva," the captain said, bending over the table and pointing to a black speck in the midst of the white blankness of the chart. "And here, in between, is another island. Why not run for that?"

McCoy did not look at the chart.

"That's Crescent Island," he answered. "It is uninhabited, and it is only two or three feet above water. Lagoon, but no entrance. No, Mangareva is the nearest place for your purpose."

"Mangareva it is, then," said Captain Davenport, interrupting the mate's growling objection. "Call the crew aft, Mr. Konig."

The sailors obeyed, shuffling wearily along the deck and painfully endeavouring to make haste. Exhaustion was evident in every movement. The cook came out of his galley to hear, and the cabin-boy hung about near him.

When Captain Davenport had explained the situation and announced his intention of running for Mangareva, an uproar broke out. Against a background of throaty rumbling arose inarticulate cries of rage, with here and there a distinct curse, or word, or phrase. A shrill Cockney voice soared and dominated for a moment, crying, "'Ear 'im! After bein 'in 'ell for fifteen days—an' now 'e wants us to sail this floatin''ell to sea again!"

The captain could not control them, but McCoy's gentle presence seemed to rebuke and calm them, and the muttering and cursing died away, until the full crew, save here and there an anxious face directed at the captain, yearned dumbly towards the green-clad peaks and beetling coast of Pitcairn.

Soft as a spring zephyr was the voice of McCoy:

"Captain, I thought I heard some of them say they were starving."

"Aye," was the answer, "and so we are. I've had a sea-biscuit and a spoonful of salmon in the last two days. We're on whack. You see, when we discovered the fire, we battened down immediately to suffocate the fire. And then we found how little food there was in the pantry. But it was too late. We didn't dare break out the lazarette. Hungry? I'm just as hungry as they are."

He spoke to the men again, and again the throat-rumbling and cursing arose, their faces convulsed and animal-like with rage. The second and third mates had joined the captain, standing behind him at the break of the poop. Their faces were set and expressionless; they seemed bored, more than anything else, by this mutiny of the crew. Captain Davenport glanced questioningly at his first mate, and that person merely shrugged his shoulders in token of his helplessness.

"You see," the captain said to McCoy, "you can't compel sailors to leave the safe land and go to sea on a burning vessel. She has been their floating coffin for over two weeks now. They are worked out, and starved out, and they've got enough of her. We'll beat up for Pitcairn."

But the wind was light, the *Pyrenees'* bottom was foul, and she could not beat up against the strong westerly current. At the end of two hours she had lost three miles. The sailors worked eagerly, as if by main strength they could compel the *Pyrenees* against the adverse elements. But steadily, port tack and starboard tack, she sagged off to the westward. The captain paced restlessly up and down, pausing occasionally to survey the vagrant smoke-wisps and to trace them back to the portions of the deck from which they sprang. The carpenter was engaged constantly in attempting to locate such places, and, when he succeeded, in caulking them tighter and tighter.

"Well, what do you think?" the captain finally asked McCoy, who was watching the carpenter with all a child's interest and curiosity in his eyes.

McCoy looked shoreward, where the land was disappearing in the thickening haze.

"I think it would be better to square away for Mangareva. With that breeze that is coming, you'll be there to-morrow evening."

"But what if the fire breaks out? It is liable to do it any moment."

"Have your boats ready in the falls. The same breeze will carry your boats to Mangareva if the ship burns out from under."

Captain Davenport debated for a moment, and then McCoy heard the question he had not wanted to hear, but which he knew was surely coming.

"I have no chart of Mangareva. On the general chart it is only a fly-speck. I would not know where to look for the entrance into the lagoon. Will you come along and pilot her in for me?"

McCoy's serenity was unbroken.

"Yes, captain," he said, with the same quiet unconcern with which he would have accepted an invitation to dinner, "I'll go with you to Mangareva."

Again the crew was called aft, and the captain spoke to them from the break of the poop.

"We've tried to work her up, but you see how we've lost ground. She's setting off in a two-knot current. This gentleman is the Honourable

McCoy, Chief Magistrate and Governor of Pitcairn Island. He will come along with us to Mangareva. So you see the situation is not so dangerous. He would not make such an offer if he thought he was going to lose his life. Besides, whatever risk there is, if he of his own free will come on board and take it, we can do no less. What do you say for Mangareva?"

This time there was no uproar. McCoy's presence, the surety and calm that seemed to radiate from him, had had its effect. They conferred with one another in low voices. There was little arguing. They were virtually unanimous, and they shoved the Cockney out as their spokesman. That worthy was overwhelmed with consciousness of the heroism of himself and his mates, and with flashing eyes he cried:

"If 'e will, we will!"

The crew mumbled its assent and started forward.

"One moment, captain," McCoy said, as the other was turning to give orders to the mate. "I must go ashore first."

Mr. Konig was thunderstruck, staring at McCoy as if he were a madman.

"Go ashore!" the captain cried. "What for? It will take you three hours to get there in your canoe."

McCoy measured the distance of the land away and nodded.

"Yes; it is six now. I won't get ashore till nine. The people cannot be assembled earlier than ten. As the breeze freshens up to-night, you can begin to work up against it, and pick me up at daylight to-morrow morning."

"In the name of reason and common sense," the captain burst forth, "what do you want to assemble the people for? Don't you realise that my ship is burning beneath me?"

McCoy was as placid as a summer sea, and the other's anger produced not the slightest ripple upon it.

"Yes, captain," he cooed in his dovelike voice, "I do realise that your ship is burning. That is why I am going with you to Mangareva. But I must get permission to go with you. It is our custom. It is an important matter when the governor leaves the island. The people's interests are at stake, and so they have the right to vote their permission or refusal. But they will give it, I know that."

"Are you sure?"

"Quite sure."

"Then if you know they will give it, why bother with getting it? Think of the delay—a whole night."

"It is our custom," was the imperturbable reply. "Also, I am the governor, and I must make arrangements for the conduct of the island during my absence."

"But it is only a twenty-four hour run to Mangareva," the captain objected. "Suppose it took you six times that long to return to windward that would bring you back by the end of a week."

McCoy smiled his large, benevolent smile.

"Very few vessels come to Pitcairn, and when they do, they are usually from San Francisco or from around the Horn. I shall be fortunate if I get back in six months. I may be away a year, and I may have to go to San Francisco in order to find a vessel that will bring me back. My father once left Pitcairn to be gone three months, and two years passed before he could get back. Then, too, you are short of food. If you have to take to the boats, and the weather comes up bad, you may be days in reaching land. I can bring off two canoe loads of food in the morning. Dried bananas will be best. As the breeze freshens, you beat up against it. The nearer you are, the bigger loads I can bring off. Good-bye."

He held out his hand. The captain shook it, and was reluctant to let go. He seemed to cling to it as a drowning sailor clings to a lifebuoy.

"How do I know you will come back in the morning?" he asked.

"Yes, that's it!" cried the mate. "How do we know but what he's skinning out to save his own hide?"

McCoy did not speak. He looked at them sweetly and benignantly, and it seemed to them that they received a message from his tremendous certitude of soul.

The captain released his hand, and, with a last sweeping glance that embraced the crew in its benediction, McCoy went over the rail and descended into his canoe.

The wind freshened, and the *Pyrenees*, despite the foulness of her bottom, won half a dozen miles away from the westerly current. At daylight, with Pitcairn three miles to windward, Captain Davenport made out two canoes coming off to him. Again McCoy clambered up the side and dropped over the rail to the hot deck. He was followed by many packages of dried bananas, each package wrapped in dry leaves.

"Now, captain," he said, "swing the yards and drive for dear life. You see, I am no navigator," he explained a few minutes later, as he stood by the captain aft, the latter with gaze wandering from aloft to overside as he estimated the *Pyrenees'* speed. "You must fetch her to Mangareva. When you have picked up the land, then I will pilot her in. What do you think she is making?"

"Eleven," Captain Davenport answered, with a final glance at the water rushing past.

"Eleven. Let me see, if she keeps up that gait, we'll sight Mangareva between eight and nine o'clock to-morrow morning. I'll have her on the beach by ten, or by eleven at latest. And then your troubles will be all over."

It almost seemed to the captain that the blissful moment had already arrived, such was the persuasive convincingness of McCoy. Captain Davenport had been under the fearful strain of navigating his burning ship for over two weeks, and he was beginning to feel that he had had enough.

A heavier flaw of wind struck the back of his neck and whistled by his ears. He measured the weight of it, and looked quickly overside.

"The wind is making all the time," he announced. "The old girl's doing nearer twelve than eleven right now. If this keeps up, we'll be shortening down to-night."

All day the *Pyrenees*, carrying her load of living fire, tore across the foaming sea. By nightfall, royals and topgallant-sails were in, and she flew on into the darkness, with great crested seas roaring after her. The auspicious wind had had its effect, and fore and aft a visible brightening was apparent. In the second dog-watch some careless soul started a song, and by eight bells the whole crew was singing.

Captain Davenport had his blankets brought up and spread on top of the house.

"I've forgotten what sleep is," he explained to McCoy. "I'm all in. But give me a call at any time you think necessary."

At three in the morning he was aroused by a gentle tugging at his arm. He sat up quickly, bracing himself against the skylight, stupid yet from his heavy sleep. The wind was thrumming its war-song in the rigging, and a wild sea was buffeting the *Pyrenees*. Amidships she was wallowing first one rail under and then the other, flooding the waist more often than not. McCoy was shouting something he could not hear. He reached out, clutched the other by the shoulder, and drew him close so that his own ear was close to the other's lips.

"It's three o'clock," came McCoy's voice, still retaining its dovelike quality, but curiously muffled, as if from a long way off. "We've run two hundred and fifty. Crescent Island is only thirty miles away, somewhere there dead ahead. There's no lights on it. If we keep running, we'll pile up, and lose ourselves as well as the ship."

"What d'ye think—heave to?"

"Yes; heave to till daylight. It will only put us back four hours."

So the *Pyrenees*, with her cargo of fire, was hove to, biting the teeth of the gale, and fighting, and smashing the pounding seas. She was a shell, filled with a conflagration, and on the outside of the shell, clinging precariously, the little motes of men, by pull and haul, helped her in the battle.

"It is most unusual, this gale," McCoy told the captain, in the lee of the cabin. "By rights there should be no gale at this time of the year. But everything about the weather has been unusual. There has been a stoppage of the trades, and now it's howling right out of the trade quarter." He waved his hand into the darkness, as if his vision could dimly penetrate for hundreds of miles. "It is off to the westward. There is something big making off there somewhere—a hurricane or something. We're lucky to be so far to the eastward. But this is only a little blow," he added. "It can't last. I can tell you that much."

By daylight the gale had eased down to normal. But daylight revealed a new danger. It had come on thick. The sea was covered by a fog, or, rather, by a pearly mist that was fog-like in density in so far as it obstructed vision, but that was no more than a film on the sea, for the sun shot through it and filled it with a glowing radiance.

The deck of the *Pyrenees* was making more smoke than on the preceding day, and the cheerfulness of officers and crew had vanished. In the lee of the galley the cabin-boy could be heard whimpering. It was his first voyage, and the fear of death was at his heart. The captain wandered about like a lost soul, nervously chewing his moustache, scowling, unable to make up his mind what to do.

"What do you think?" he asked, pausing by the side of McCoy, who was making a breakfast off fried bananas and a mug of water.

McCoy finished the last banana, drained the mug, and looked slowly around. In his eyes was a smile of tenderness as he said:

"Well, captain, we might as well drive as burn. Your decks are not going to hold out for ever. They are hotter this morning. You haven't a pair of shoes I can wear? It is getting uncomfortable for my bare feet."

The *Pyrenees* shipped two heavy seas as she was swung off and put once more before it, and the first mate expressed a desire to have all that water down in the hold, if only it could be introduced without taking off the hatches. McCoy ducked his head into the binnacle and watched the course set.

"I'd hold her up some more, captain," he said. "She's been making drift when hove to."

"I've set it to a point higher already," was the answer. "Isn't that enough?"

"I'd make it two points, captain. This bit of a blow kicked that westerly current ahead faster than you imagine."

Captain Davenport compromised on a point and a half, and then went aloft, accompanied by McCoy and the first mate, to keep a look-out for land. Sail had been made, so that the *Pyrenees* was doing ten knots. The following sea was dying down rapidly. There was no break in the pearly fog, and by ten o'clock Captain Davenport was growing nervous. All hands were at their stations, ready, at the first warning of land ahead, to spring like fiends to the task of bringing the *Pyrenees* up on the wind. That land ahead, a surf-washed outer reef, would be perilously close when it revealed itself in such a fog.

Another hour passed. The three watchers aloft stared intently into the pearly radiance.

"What if we miss Mangareva?" Captain Davenport asked abruptly.

McCoy, without shifting his gaze, answered softly:

"Why, let her drive, captain. That is all we can do. All the Paumotus are before us. We can drive for a thousand miles through reefs and atolls. We are bound to fetch up somewhere."

"Then drive it is." Captain Davenport evidenced his intention of descending to the deck. "We've missed Mangareva. God knows where the next land is. I wish I'd held up that other half-point," he confessed a moment later. "This cursed current plays the devil with a navigator."

"The old navigators called the Paumotus the Dangerous Archipelago," McCoy said when they had partly regained the poop. "This very current was partly responsible for that name."

"I was talking with a sailor chap in Sydney once," said Mr. Konig. "He'd been trading in the Pautomus. He told me insurance was eighteen per cent. Is that right?"

McCoy smiled and nodded.

"Except that they don't insure," he explained. "The owners write off twenty per cent of the cost of their schooners each year."

Captain Davenport groaned. "That makes the life of a schooner only five years!" He shook his head sadly, murmuring, "Bad waters! bad waters!"

Again they went into the cabin to consult the big general chart; but the poisonous vapours drove them coughing and gasping on deck.

"Here is Moerenhout Island." Captain Davenport pointed it out on the chart, which he had spread on the house. "It can't be more than a hundred miles to leeward."

"A hundred and ten." McCoy shook his head doubtfully. "It might be done, but it is very difficult. I might beach her, and then, again, I might put her on the reef. A bad place, a very bad place."

"We'll take the chance," was Captain Davenport's decision, as he set about working out the course.

Sail was shortened early in the afternoon, to avoid running past in the night; and in the second dog-watch the crew manifested its regained cheerfulness. Land was so very near, and their troubles would be over in the morning.

But morning broke clear, with a blazing tropic sun. The south-east trade had swung around to the eastward, and was driving the *Pyrenees* through the water at an eight-knot clip. Captain Davenport worked up his dead reckoning, allowing generously for drift, and announced Moerenhout Island to be not more than ten miles off. The *Pyrenees* sailed the ten miles; she sailed ten miles more; and the look-outs at the three mastheads saw naught but the naked, sun-washed sea.

"But the land is there, I tell you," Captain Davenport shouted to them from the poop.

McCoy smiled soothingly, but the captain glared about him like a madman, fetched his sextant, and took a chronometer sight.

"I knew I was right," he almost shouted, when he had worked up the observation. "Twenty-one, fifty-five, south; one-thirty-six, two, west. There you are. We're eight miles to windward yet. What did you make it out, Mr. Konig?"

The first mate glanced at his own figures, and said in a low voice:

"Twenty-one, fifty-five all right; but my longitude's one-thirty-six, forty-eight. That puts us considerably to leeward——"

But Captain Davenport ignored his figures with so contemptuous a silence as to make Mr. Konig grit his teeth and curse savagely under his breath.

"Keep her off," the captain ordered the man at the wheel. "Three points—steady there, as she goes!"

Then he returned to his figures and worked them over. The sweat poured from his face. He chewed his moustache, his lips, and his pencil, staring at the figures as a man might at a ghost. Suddenly, with a fierce, muscular outburst, he crumpled the scribbled paper in his fist and crushed it under foot. Mr. Konig grinned vindictively and turned away, while Captain Davenport leaned against the cabin and for half an hour spoke no word, contenting himself with gazing to leeward with an expression of musing hopelessness on his face.

"Mr. McCoy," he broke silence abruptly. "The chart indicates a group of islands, but not how many, off there to the north'ard, or nor'-nor'-westward, about forty miles—the Acteon Islands. What about them?"

"There are four, all low," McCoy answered. "First, to the south-east is Matueri—no people, no entrance to the lagoon. Then comes Tenarunga. There used to be about a dozen people there, but they may be all gone now. Anyway, there is no entrance for a ship—only a boat entrance, with a fathom of water. Vehauga and Teua-raro are the other two. No entrances, no people, very low. There is no bed for the *Pyrenees* in that group. She would be a total wreck."

"Listen to that!" Captain Davenport was frantic. "No people! No entrances! What in the devil are islands good for?

"Well, then," he barked suddenly, like an excited terrier, "the chart gives a whole mess of islands off to the nor'-west. What about them? What one has an entrance where I can lay my ship?"

McCoy calmly considered. He did not refer to the chart. All these islands, reefs, shoals, lagoons, entrances, and distances were marked on the chart of his memory. He knew them as the city dweller knows his buildings, streets, and alleys.

"Papakena and Vanavana are off there to the westward, or west-nor'-westward, a hundred miles, and a bit more," he said. "One is uninhabited, and I heard that the people on the other had gone off to Cadmus Island. Anyway, neither lagoon has an entrance. Ahunui is another hundred miles on to the nor'-west. No entrance, no people."

"Well, forty miles beyond them are two islands?" Captain Davenport queried, raising his head from the chart.

McCoy shook his head.

"Paros and Manuhungi—no entrances, no people. Nengo-Nengo is forty miles beyond them, in turn, and it has no people and no entrance. But there is Hao Island. It is just the place. The lagoon is thirty miles long and five miles wide. There are plenty of people. You can usually find water. And any ship in the world can go through the entrance."

He ceased, and gazed solicitously at Captain Davenport, who, bending over the chart with a pair of dividers in hand, had just emitted a low groan.

"Is there any lagoon with an entrance anywhere nearer than Hao Island?" he asked.

"No, captain; that is the nearest."

"Well, it's three hundred and forty miles." Captain Davenport was speaking very slowly, with decision. "I won't risk the responsibility of all these lives. I'll wreck her on the Acteons. And she's a good ship, too," he added regretfully, after altering the course, this time making more allowance than ever for the westerly current.

An hour later the sky was overcast. The south-east trade still held, but the ocean was a checker-board of squalls.

"We'll be there by one o'clock," Captain Davenport announced confidently—"by two o'clock at the outside. McCoy, you put her ashore on the one where the people are."

The sun did not appear again, nor, at one o'clock, was any land to be seen. Captain Davenport looked astern at the *Pyrenees'* canting wake.

"Good Lord!" he cried. "An easterly current! Look at that!"

Mr. Konig was incredulous. McCoy was non-committal, though he said that in the Paumotus there was no reason why it should not be an easterly current. A few minutes later a squall robbed the *Pyrenees* temporarily of all her wind, and she was left rolling heavily in the trough.

"Where's that deep lead? Over with it, you there!" Captain Davenport held the lead-line and watched it sag off to the north-east. "There, look at that! Take hold of it for yourself."

McCoy and the mate tried it, and felt the line thrumming and vibrating savagely to the grip of the tidal stream.

"A four-knot current," said Mr. Konig.

"An easterly current instead of a westerly," said Captain Davenport, glaring accusingly at McCoy, as if to cast the blame for it upon him.

"That is one of the reasons, captain, for insurance being eighteen per cent in these waters," McCoy answered cheerfully. "You never can tell. The currents are always changing. There was a man who wrote books, I forget his name, in the yacht *Casco*. He missed Takaroa by thirty miles and fetched Tikei, all because of the shifting currents. You are up to windward now, and you'd better keep off a few points."

"But how much has this current set me?" the captain demanded irately. "How am I to know how much to keep off?"

"I don't know, captain," McCoy said with great gentleness.

The wind returned, and the *Pyrenees*, her deck smoking and shimmering in the bright grey light, ran off dead to leeward. Then she worked back, port tack and starboard tack, crisscrossing her track, combing the sea for the Acteon Islands, which the masthead look-outs failed to sight.

Captain Davenport was beside himself. His rage took the form of sullen silence, and he spent the afternoon in pacing the poop or leaning against the weather-shrouds. At nightfall, without even consulting

McCoy, he squared away and headed into the north-west. Mr. Konig, surreptitiously consulting chart and binnacle, and McCoy, openly and innocently consulting the binnacle, knew that they were running for Hao Island. By midnight the squalls ceased, and the stars came out. Captain Davenport was cheered by the promise of a clear day.

"I'll get an observation in the morning," he told McCoy, "though what my latitude is, is a puzzler. But I'll use the Sumner method and settle that. Do you know the Sumner line?"

And thereupon he explained it in detail to McCoy.

The day proved clear, the trade blew steadily out of the east, and the *Pyrenees* just as steadily logged her nine knots. Both the captain and mate worked out the position on a Sumner line, and agreed, and at noon agreed again, and verified the morning sights by the noon sights.

"Another twenty-four hours and we'll be there," Captain Davenport assured McCoy. "It's a miracle the way the old girl's decks hold out. But they can't last. They can't last. Look at the smoke, more and more every day. Yet it was a tight deck to begin with, fresh-caulked in 'Frisco. I was surprised when the fire first broke out and we battened down. Look at that!"

He broke off to gaze with dropped jaw at a spiral of smoke that coiled and twisted in the lee of the mizzen-mast twenty feet above the deck.

"Now, how did that get there?" he demanded indignantly.

Beneath it there was no smoke. Crawling up from the deck, sheltered from the wind by the mast, by some freak it took form and visibility at that height. It writhed away from the mast, and for a moment overhung the captain like some threatening portent. The next moment the wind whisked it away, and the captain's jaw returned to place.

"As I was saying, when we first battened down, I was surprised. It was a tight deck, yet it leaked smoke like a sieve. And we've caulked and caulked ever since. There must be tremendous pressure underneath to drive so much smoke through."

That afternoon the sky became overcast again, and squally, drizzly weather set in. The wind shifted back and forth between south-east and north-east, and at midnight the *Pyrenees* was caught aback by a sharp squall from the south-west, from which point the wind continued to blow intermittently.

"We won't make Hao until ten or eleven," Captain Davenport complained at seven in the morning, when the fleeting promise of the sun had been erased by hazy cloud masses in the eastern sky. And the next moment he was plaintively demanding, "And what are the currents doing?"

Look-outs at the mastheads could report no land, and the day passed in drizzling calms and violent squalls. By nightfall a heavy sea began to make from the west. The barometer had fallen to 29.50. There was no wind, and still the ominous sea continued to increase. Soon the *Pyrenees* was rolling madly in the huge waves that marched in an unending procession from out of the darkness of the west. Sail was shortened as fast as both watches could work, and when a tired crew had finished, its grumbling and complaining voices, peculiarly animal-like and menacing, could be heard in the darkness. Once the starboard watch was called aft to lash down and make secure, and the men openly advertised their sullenness and unwillingness. Every slow movement was a protest and a threat. The atmosphere was moist and sticky like mucilage, and in the absence of wind all hands seemed to pant and gasp for air. The sweat stood out on faces and bare arms, and Captain Davenport for one, his face more gaunt and careworn than ever, and his eyes troubled and staring, was oppressed by a feeling of impending calamity.

"It's off to the westward," McCoy said encouragingly. "At worst, we'll only be on the edge of it."

But Captain Davenport refused to be comforted, and by the light of a lantern read up the chapter in his *Epitome* that related to the strategy of shipmasters in cyclonic storms. From somewhere amidships the silence was broken by a low whimpering from the cabin-boy.

"Oh, shut up!" Captain Davenport yelled suddenly and with such force as to startle every man on board and to frighten the offender into a wild wail of terror.

"Mr. Konig," the captain said in a voice that trembled with rage and nerves, "will you kindly step for'ard and stop that brat's mouth with a deck mop?"

But it was McCoy who went forward, and in a few minutes had the boy comforted and asleep.

Shortly before daybreak the first breath of air began to move from out the south-east, increasing swiftly to a stiff and stiffer breeze. All hands were on deck waiting for what might be behind it.

"We're all right now, captain," said McCoy, standing close to his shoulder. "The hurricane is to the west'ard, and we are south of it. This breeze is the in-suck. It won't blow any harder. You can begin to put sail on her."

"But what's the good? Where shall I sail? This is the second day without observations, and we should have sighted Hao Island yesterday morning. Which way does it bear, north, south, east, or what? Tell me that, and I'll make sail in a jiffy."

"I am no navigator, captain," McCoy said in his mild way.

"I used to think I was one," was the retort, "before I got into these Paumotus."

At midday the cry of "Breakers ahead!" was heard from the look-out. The *Pyrenees* was kept off and sail after sail was loosed and sheeted home. The *Pyrenees* was sliding through the water and fighting a current that threatened to set her down upon the breakers. Officers and men were working like mad, cook and cabin-boy, Captain Davenport himself, and McCoy all lending a hand. It was a close shave. It was a low shoal, a bleak and perilous place over which the seas broke unceasingly, where no man could live, and on which not even sea-birds could rest. The *Pyrenees* was swept within a hundred yards of it before the wind carried her clear, and at this moment the panting crew, its work done, burst out in a torrent of curses upon the head of McCoy—of McCoy who had come on board, and proposed the run to Mangareva, and lured them all away from the safety of Pitcairn Island to certain destruction in this baffling and terrible stretch of sea. But McCoy's tranquil soul was undisturbed. He smiled at them with simple and gracious benevolence, and, somehow, the exalted goodness of him seemed to penetrate to their dark and sombre souls, shaming them, and from very shame stilling the curses vibrating in their throats.

"Bad waters! bad waters!" Captain Davenport was murmuring as his ship forged clear; but he broke off abruptly to gaze at the shoal which should have been dead astern, but which was already on the *Pyrenees'* weather-quarter and working up rapidly to windward.

He sat down and buried his face in his hands. And the first mate saw, and McCoy saw, and the crew saw, what he had seen. South of the shoal an easterly current had set them down upon it; north of the shoal an equally swift westerly current had clutched the ship and was sweeping her away.

"I've heard of these Paumotus before," the captain groaned, lifting his blanched face from his hands. "Captain Moyendale told me about them after losing his ship on them. And I laughed at him behind his back. God forgive me, I laughed at him. What shoal is that?" he broke off to ask McCoy.

"I don't know, captain."

"Why don't you know?"

"Because I never saw it before, and because I never heard of it. I do know that it is not charted. These waters have never been thoroughly surveyed."

"Then you don't know where we are?"

"No more than you do," McCoy said gently.

At four in the afternoon coco-nut trees were sighted, apparently growing out of the water. A little later the low land of an atoll was raised above the sea.

"I know where we are now, captain." McCoy lowered the glasses from his eyes. "That's Resolution Island. We are forty miles beyond Hao Island, and the wind is in our teeth."

"Get ready to beach her, then. Where's the entrance?"

"There's only a canoe passage. But now that we know where we are, we can run for Barclay de Tolley. It is only one hundred and twenty miles from here, due nor'-nor'-west. With this breeze we can be there by nine o'clock to-morrow morning."

Captain Davenport consulted the chart and debated with himself.

"If we wreck her here," McCoy added, "we'd have to make the run to Barclay de Tolley in the boats just the same."

The captain gave his orders, and once more the *Pyrenees* swung off for another run across the inhospitable sea.

And the middle of the next afternoon saw despair and mutiny on her smoking deck. The current had accelerated, the wind had slackened, and the *Pyrenees* had sagged off to the west. The look-out sighted Barclay de Tolley to the eastward, barely visible from the masthead, and vainly and for hours the *Pyrenees* tried to beat up to it. Ever, like a mirage, the coco-nut trees hovered on the horizon, visible only from the masthead. From the deck they were hidden by the bulge of the world.

Again Captain Davenport consulted McCoy and the chart. Makemo lay seventy-five miles to the south-west. Its lagoon was thirty miles long, and its entrance was excellent. When Captain Davenport gave his orders, the crew refused duty. They announced that they had had enough of hell-fire under their feet. There was the land. What if the ship could not make it? They could make it in the boats. Let her burn, then. Their lives amounted to something to them. They had served faithfully the ship, now they were going to serve themselves.

They sprang to the boats, brushing the second and third mates out of the way, and proceeded to swing the boats out and to prepare to lower away. Captain Davenport and the first mate, revolvers in hand, were advancing to the break of the poop, when McCoy, who had climbed on top of the cabin, began to speak.

He spoke to the sailors, and at the first sound of his dovelike, cooing voice they paused to hear. He extended to them his own ineffable serenity and peace. His soft voice and simple thoughts flowed out to them in a magic stream, soothing them against their wills. Long-forgotten things came back to them, and some remembered lullaby songs of childhood and the content and rest of the mother's arm at the end of the day. There was no more trouble, no more danger, no more irk, in all the world. Everything was as it should be, and it was only a matter of course that they should turn their backs upon the land and put to sea once more with hell-fire hot beneath their feet.

McCoy spoke simply; but it was not what he spoke. It was his personality that spoke more eloquently than any word he could utter. It was an alchemy of soul occultly subtle and profoundly deep—a mysterious emanation of the spirit, seductive, sweetly humble, and terribly imperious. It was illumination in the dark crypts of their souls, a compulsion of purity and gentleness vastly greater than that which resided in the shining death-spitting revolvers of the officers.

The men wavered reluctantly where they stood, and those who had loosed the turns made them fast again. Then one, and then another, and then all of them, began to sidle awkwardly away.

McCoy's face was beaming with childlike pleasure as he descended from the top of the cabin. There was no trouble. For that matter there had been no trouble averted. There never had been any trouble, for there was no place for such in the blissful world in which he lived.

"You hypnotised 'em," Mr. Konig grinned at him, speaking in a low voice.

"Those boys are good," was the answer. "Their hearts are good. They have had a hard time, and they have worked hard, and they will work hard to the end."

Mr. Konig had no time to reply. His voice was ringing out orders, the sailors were springing to obey, and the *Pyrenees* was paying slowly off from the wind until her bow should point in the direction of Makemo.

The wind was very light, and after sun-down almost ceased. It was insufferably warm, and fore and aft men sought vainly to sleep. The deck was too hot to lie upon, the poisonous vapours, oozing through the seams, crept like evil spirits over the ship, stealing into the nostrils and windpipes of the unwary and causing fits of sneezing and coughing. The stars blinked lazily in the dim vault overhead; and the full moon, rising in the east, touched with its light the myriads of wisps and threads and spidery films of smoke that intertwined and writhed and twisted along the deck, over the rails, and up the masts and shrouds.

"Tell me," Captain Davenport said, rubbing his smarting eyes, "what happened with that *Bounty* crowd after they reached Pitcairn? The account I read said they burnt the *Bounty*, and that they were not discovered until many years later. But what happened in the meantime? I've always been curious to know. They were men with their necks in the rope. There were some native men, too. And then there were women. That made it look like trouble right from the jump."

"There was trouble," McCoy answered. "They were bad men. They quarrelled about the women right away. One of the mutineers, Williams, lost his wife. All the women were Tahitian women. His wife fell from the cliffs when hunting sea-birds. Then he took the wife of one of the native men away from him. All the native men were made very angry by this, and they killed off nearly all the mutineers. Then the mutineers that escaped killed off all the native men. The women helped. And the natives killed each other. Everybody killed everybody. They were terrible men.

"Timiti was killed by two other natives while they were combing his hair in friendship. The white men had sent them to do it. Then the white men killed them. The wife of Tullaloo killed him in a cave because she wanted a white man for husband. They were very wicked. God had hidden His face from them. At the end of two years all the native men were murdered, and all the white men except four. They were Young, John Adams, McCoy, who was my great-grandfather, and Quintal. He was a very bad man too. Once, just because his wife did not catch enough fish for him, he bit off her ear."

"They were a bad lot!" Mr. Konig exclaimed.

"Yes, they were very bad," McCoy agreed, and went on serenely cooing of the blood and lust of his iniquitous ancestry. "My great-grandfather escaped murder in order to die by his own hand. He made a still and manufactured alcohol from the roots of the ti-plant. Quintal was his chum, and they got drunk together all the time. At last McCoy got delirium tremens, tied a rock to his neck, and jumped into the sea.

"Quintal's wife, the one whose ear he bit off, also got killed by falling from the cliffs. Then Quintal went to Young and demanded his wife, and went to Adams and demanded his wife. Adams and Young were afraid of Quintal. They knew he would kill them. So they killed him, the two of them together, with a hatchet. Then Young died. And that was about all the trouble they had."

"I should say so," Captain Davenport snorted. "There was nobody left to kill."

"You see, God had hidden His face," McCoy said.

By morning no more than a faint air was blowing from the eastward, and, unable to make appreciable southing by it, Captain Davenport hauled up full-and-by on the port tack. He was afraid of that terrible westerly current which had cheated him out of so many ports of refuge. All day the calm continued, and all night, while the sailors, on a short ration of dried banana, were grumbling. Also, they were growing weak, and complaining of stomach pains caused by the straight banana diet. All day the current swept the *Pyrenees* to the westward, while there was no wind to bear her south. In the middle of the first dog-watch, coco-nut trees were sighted due south, their tufted heads rising above the water and marking the low-lying atoll beneath.

"That is Taenga Island," McCoy said. "We need a breeze to-night, or else we'll miss Makemo."

"What's become of the south-east trade?" the captain demanded. "Why don't it blow? What's the matter?"

"It is the evaporation from the big lagoons—there are so many of them," McCoy explained. "The evaporation upsets the whole system of trades. It even causes the wind to back up and blow gales from the south-west. This is the Dangerous Archipelago, captain."

Captain Davenport faced the old man, opened his mouth, and was about to curse, but paused and refrained. McCoy's presence was a rebuke to the blasphemies that stirred in his brain and trembled in his larynx. McCoy's influence had been growing during the many days they had been together. Captain Davenport was an autocrat of the sea, fearing no man, never bridling his tongue, and now he found himself unable to curse in the presence of this old man with the feminine brown eyes and the voice of a dove. When he realized this, Captain Davenport experienced a distinct shock. This old man was merely the seed of McCoy, of McCoy of the *Bounty*, the mutineer fleeing from the hemp that waited him in England, the McCoy who was a power for evil in the early days of blood and lust and violent death on Pitcairn Island.

Captain Davenport was not religious, yet in that moment he felt a mad impulse to cast himself at the other's feet—and to say he knew not what. It was an emotion that so deeply stirred him, rather than a coherent thought, and he was aware in some vague way of his own unworthiness and small-ness in the presence of this other man who possessed the simplicity of a child and the gentleness of a woman.

Of course he could not humble himself so before the eyes of his officers and men. And yet the anger that had prompted the blasphemy still raged in him. He suddenly smote the cabin with his clenched hand and cried:

"Look here, old man, I won't be beaten. These Paumotus have cheated and tricked me and made a fool of me. I refuse to be beaten. I am going to drive this ship, and drive and drive and drive clear through the Paumotus to China but what I find a bed for her. If every man deserts, I'll stay by her. I'll show the Paumotus. They can't fool me. She's a good girl, and I'll stick by her as long as there's a plank to stand on. You hear me?"

"And I'll stay with you, captain," McCoy said.

During the night, light, baffling airs blew out of the south, and the frantic captain, with his cargo of fire, watched and measured his westward drift, and went off by himself at times to curse softly so that McCoy should not hear.

Daylight showed more palms growing out of the water to the south.

"That's the leeward point of Makemo," McCoy said. "Katiu is only a few miles to the west. We may make that."

But the current, sucking between the two islands, swept them to the north-west, and at one in the afternoon they saw the palms of Katiu rise above the sea and sink back into the sea again.

A few minutes later, just as the captain had discovered that a new cur-rent from the north-east had gripped the *Pyrenees*, the masthead look-outs raised coco-nut palms in the north-west.

"It is Raraka," said McCoy. "We won't make it without wind. The cur-rent is drawing us down to the south-west. But we must watch out. A few miles farther on a current flows north and turns in a circle to the north-west. This will sweep us away to Fakarava, and Fakarava is the place for the *Pyrenees* to find her bed."

"They can sweep all they—all they well please," Captain Davenport remarked with heat. "We'll find a bed for her somewhere just the same."

But the situation on the *Pyrenees* was reaching a culmination. The deck was so hot that it seemed an increase of a few degrees would cause it to burst into flames. In many places even the heavy-soled shoes of the men were no protection, and they were compelled to step lively to avoid scorching their feet. The smoke had increased and grown more acrid. Every man on board was suffering from inflamed eyes, and they coughed and strangled like a crew of tuberculosis patients. In the afternoon the boats were swung out and equipped. The last several packages of dried bananas were stored in them, as well as the instruments of the officers. Captain Davenport even put the chronometer into the long-boat, fearing the blowing up of the deck at any moment.

All night this apprehension weighed heavily on all, and in the first morning light, with hollow eyes and ghastly faces, they stared at one another as if in surprise that the, *Pyrenees* still held together and that they still were alive.

Walking rapidly at times, and even occasionally breaking into an undignified hop-skip-and-run, Captain Davenport inspected his ship's deck.

"It is a matter of hours now, if not of minutes," he announced on his return to the poop.

The cry of land came down from the masthead. From the deck the land was invisible, and McCoy went aloft, while the captain took advantage of the opportunity to curse some of the bitterness out of his heart. But the cursing was suddenly stopped by a dark line on the water which he sighted to the north-east. It was not a squall, but a regular breeze—the disrupted trade-wind, eight points out of its direction, but resuming business once more.

"Hold her up, captain," McCoy said as soon as he reached the poop. "That's the easterly point of Fakarava, and we'll go in through the passage full tilt, and wind abeam, and every sail drawing."

At the end of an hour, the coco-nut trees and the low-lying land were visible from the deck. The feeling that the end of the *Pyrenees'* resistance was imminent weighed heavily on everybody. Captain Davenport had the three boats lowered and dropped short astern, a man in each to keep them apart. The *Pyrenees* closely skirted the shore, the surf-whitened atoll a bare two cable-lengths away.

"Get ready to wear her, captain," McCoy warned.

And a minute later the land parted, exposing a narrow passage and the lagoon beyond, a great mirror, thirty miles in length and a third as broad.

"Now, captain."

For the last time the yards of the *Pyrenees* swung around as she obeyed the wheel and headed into the passage. The turns had scarcely been made, and nothing had been coiled down, when the men and mates swept back to the poop in panic terror. Nothing had happened, yet they averred that something was going to happen. They could not tell why. They merely knew that it was about to happen. McCoy started forward to take up his position on the bow in order to con the vessel in; but the captain gripped his arm and whirled him around.

"Do it from here," he said. "That deck's not safe. What's the matter?" he demanded the next instant. "We're standing still."

McCoy smiled.

"You are bucking a seven-knot current, captain," he said. "That is the way the full ebb runs out of this passage."

At the end of another hour the *Pyrenees* had scarcely gained her length, but the wind freshened and she began to forge ahead.

"Better get into the boats, some of you," Captain Davenport commanded.

His voice was still ringing, and the men were just beginning to move in obedience, when the amidship deck of the *Pyrenees*, in a mass of flame and smoke, was flung upward into the sails and rigging, part of it remaining there and the rest falling into the sea. The wind being abeam was what had saved the men crowded aft. They made a blind rush to gain the boats, but McCoy's voice, carrying its convincing message of vast calm and endless time, stopped them.

"Take it easy," he was saying. "Everything is all right. Pass that boy down somebody, please."

The man at the wheel had forsaken it in a funk, and Captain Davenport had leaped and caught the spokes in time to prevent the ship from yawing in the current and going ashore.

"Better take charge of the boats," he said to Mr. Konig. "Tow one of them short, right under the quarter. . . . When I go over, it'll be on the jump."

Mr. Konig hesitated, then went over the rail and lowered himself into the boat.

"Keep her off half a point, captain."

Captain Davenport gave a start. He had thought he had the ship to himself.

"Ay, ay; half a point it is," he answered.

Amidships, the *Pyrenees* was an open, flaming furnace, out of which poured an immense volume of smoke which rose high above the masts and completely hid the forward part of the ship. McCoy, in the shelter of the mizzen-shrouds, continued his difficult task of conning the ship through the intricate channel. The fire was working aft along the deck from the seat of explosion, while the soaring tower of canvas on the main-mast went up and vanished in a sheet of flame. Forward, though they could not see them, they knew that the headsails were still drawing.

"If only she don't burn all her canvas off before she makes inside," the captain groaned.

"She'll make it," McCoy assured him with supreme confidence. "There is plenty of time. She is bound to make it. And once inside, we'll put her before it; that will keep the smoke away from us and hold back the fire from working aft."

A tongue of flame sprang up the mizzen, reached hungrily for the lowest tier of canvas, missed it, and vanished. From aloft a burning shred of ropestuff fell square on the back of Captain Davenport's neck. He acted with the celerity of one stung by a bee as he reached up and brushed the offending fire from his skin.

"How is she heading, captain?"

"Nor'-west by west."

"Keep her west-nor'-west."

Captain Davenport put the wheel up and steadied her.

"West by north, captain."

"West by north she is."

"And now west."

Slowly, point by point, as she entered the lagoon, the *Pyrenees* described the circle that put her before the wind; and point by point, with all the calm certitude of a thousand years of time to spare, McCoy chanted the changing course.

"Another point, captain."

"A point it is."

Captain Davenport whirled several spokes over suddenly reversing and coming back one to check her.

"Steady."

"Steady she is—right on it."

Despite the fact that the wind was now astern, the heat was so intense that Captain Davenport was compelled to steal sidelong glances into the binnacle, letting go the wheel, now with one hand, now with the other, to rub or shield his blistering cheeks. McCoy's beard was crinkling and shrivelling, and the smell of it, strong in the other's nostrils, compelled him to look toward McCoy with sudden solicitude. Captain Davenport was letting go the spokes alternately with his hands in order to rub their blistering backs against his trousers. Every sail on the mizzen-mast vanished in a rush of flame, compelling the two men to crouch and shield their faces.

"Now," said McCoy, stealing a glance ahead at the low shore, "four points up, captain, and let her drive."

Shreds and patches of burning rope and canvas were falling about them and upon them. The tarry smoke from a smouldering piece of rope at the captain's feet set him off into a violent coughing fit, during which he still clung to the spokes.

The *Pyrenees* struck, her bow lifted, and she ground ahead gently to a stop. A shower of burning fragments, dislodged by the shock, fell about them. The ship moved ahead again and struck a second time. She crushed the fragile coral under her keel, drove on, and struck a third time.

"Hard over," said McCoy. "Hard over?" he questioned gently, a minute later.

"She won't answer," was the reply.

"All right. She is swinging around." McCoy peered over the side. "Soft, white sand. Couldn't ask better. A beautiful bed."

As the *Pyrenees* swung around, her stern away from the wind, a fearful blast of smoke and flame poured aft. Captain Davenport deserted the wheel in blistering agony. He reached the painter of the boat that lay under the quarter, then looked for McCoy, who was standing aside to let him go down.

"You first," the captain cried, gripping him by the shoulder and almost throwing him over the rail. But the flame and smoke were too terrible, and he followed hard after McCoy, both men wriggling on the rope and sliding down into the boat together. A sailor in the bow, without waiting for orders, slashed the painter through with his sheath-knife. The oars, poised in readiness, bit into the water, and the boat shot away.

"A beautiful bed, captain," McCoy murmured, looking back.

"Ay, a beautiful bed, and all thanks to you," was the answer.

The three boats pulled away for the white beach of pounded coral, beyond which, on the edge of a coco-nut grove, could be seen a half-dozen grasshouses, and a score or more of excited natives, gazing wide-eyed at the conflagration that had come to land.

The boats grounded and they stepped out on the white beach.

"And now," said McCoy, "I must see about getting back to Pitcairn."

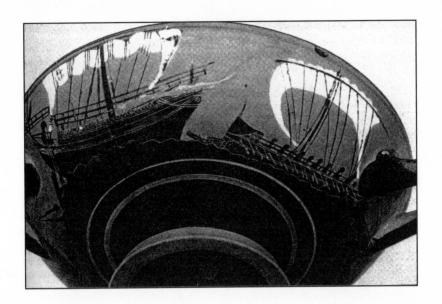

"BOOK XII" OF HOMER'S *ODYSSEY*

TRANS. SAMUEL BUTLER

After we were clear of the river Oceanus, and had got out into the open sea, we went on till we reached the Aeaean island where there is dawn and sunrise as in other places. We then drew our ship on to the sands and got out of her on to the shore, where we went to sleep and waited till day should break.

"Then, when the child of morning, rosy-fingered Dawn, appeared, I sent some men to Circe's house to fetch the body of Elpenor. We cut firewood from a wood where the headland jutted out into the sea, and after we had wept over him and lamented him we performed his funeral rites. When his body and armor had been burned to ashes, we raised a cairn, set a stone over it, and at the top of the cairn we fixed the oar that he had been used to row with.

"While we were doing all this, Circe, who knew that we had got back from the house of Hades, dressed herself and came to us as fast as she could; and her maidservants came with her bringing us bread, meat, and wine. Then she stood in the midst of us and said, 'You have done a bold thing in going down alive to the house of Hades, and you will have died twice, to other people's once. Now, then, stay here for the rest of the day, feast your fill, and go on with your voyage at daybreak tomorrow morning. In the meantime I will tell Odysseus about your course, and will explain everything to him so as to prevent your suffering from misadventure either by land or sea.'

"We agreed to do as she had said, and feasted through the livelong day to the going down of the sun, but when the sun had set and it came on dark, the men laid themselves down to sleep by the stern cables of the ship. Then Circe took me by the hand and bade me be seated away from the others, while she reclined by my side and asked me all about our adventures.

" 'So far so good,' said she, when I had ended my story, 'and now pay attention to what I am about to tell you—heaven itself, indeed, will recall it to your recollection. First you will come to the Sirens who enchant all who come near them. If anyone unwarily draws in too close and hears the singing of the Sirens, his wife and children will never welcome him home again, for they sit in a green field and warble him to death with the sweetness of their song. There is a great heap of dead men's bones lying all around, with the flesh still rotting off them. Therefore pass these Sirens by, and stop your men's ears with wax that none of them may hear; but if you like you can listen yourself, for you may get the men to bind you as you stand upright on a cross-piece halfway up the mast, and they must lash the rope's ends to the mast itself, that you may have the pleasure of listening. If you beg and pray the men to unloose you, then they must bind you faster.

" 'When your crew have taken you past these Sirens, I cannot give you coherent directions as to which of two courses you are to take; I will lay the two alternatives before you, and you must consider them for yourself. On the one hand there are some overhanging rocks against which the deep blue waves of Amphitrite beat with terrific fury; the blessed gods call these rocks the Wanderers. Here not even a bird may pass, no, not even the timid doves that bring ambrosia to Father Zeus, but the sheer rock always carries off one of them, and Father Zeus has to send another to make up their number. No ship that ever yet came to these rocks has got away again, but the waves and whirlwinds of fire are freighted with wreckage and with the bodies of dead men. The only vessel that ever sailed and got through was the famous Argo on her way from the house of Aeetes, and she too would have gone against these great rocks, only that Hera piloted her past them for the love she bore to Jason.

" 'Of these two rocks the one reaches heaven and its peak is lost in a dark cloud. This never leaves it, so that the top is never clear not even in summer and early autumn. No man, though he had twenty hands and twenty feet, could get a foothold on it and climb it, for it runs sheer up, as smooth as though it had been polished. In the middle of it there is a large cavern, looking west and turned towards Erebus; you must take your ship this way, but the cave is so high up that not even the stoutest archer could send an arrow into it. Inside it Scylla sits and yelps with a voice that you might take to be that of a young hound, but in truth she is a dreadful monster and no one—not even a god—could face her without being terror-struck. She has twelve misshapen feet, and six necks of the most prodigious length; and at the end of each neck she has a frightful head with three rows of teeth in each, all set very close together, so that they would crunch anyone to death in a moment. She sits deep within her shady cell thrusting out her heads and peering all round the rock, fishing for dolphins or dogfish or any larger monster that she can catch, of the thousands with which Amphitrite teems. No ship ever yet got past her without losing some men, for she shoots out all her heads at once, and carries off a man in each mouth.

" 'You will find the other rock lies lower, but they are so close together that there is not more than a bow-shot between them. A large fig tree in full leaf grows upon it, and under it lies the sucking whirlpool of Charybdis. Three times in the day does she vomit forth her waters, and three times she sucks them down again. See that you be not there when she is sucking, for if you are, Poseidon himself could not save you; you must hug the Scylla side and drive your ship by as fast as you can, for you had better lose six men than your whole crew.'

" 'Is there no way,' said I, 'of escaping Charybdis, and at the same time keeping Scylla off when she is trying to harm my men?'

" 'You daredevil,' replied the goddess, 'you are always wanting to fight somebody or something; you will not let yourself be beaten even by the immortals. For Scylla is not mortal; moreover she is savage, extreme, rude, cruel and invincible. There is no help for it; your best chance will be to get by her as fast as ever you can, for if you dawdle about her rock while you are putting on your armor, she may catch you with a second cast of her six heads, and snap up another half dozen of your men. So drive your ship past her at full speed, and roar out lustily to Crataiis who is Scylla's dam, bad luck to her; she will then stop her from making a second raid upon you.

" 'You will now come to the Thrinacian island, and here you will see many herds of cattle and flocks of sheep belonging to the sun-god—seven herds of cattle and seven flocks of sheep, with fifty head in each flock. They do not breed, nor do they become fewer in number, and they are tended by the goddesses Phaethusa and Lampetie, who are children of the sun-god Hyperion by Neaera. Their mother, when she had borne them and had done suckling them, sent them to the Thrinacian island, which was a long way off, to live there and look after their father's flocks and herds. If you leave these flocks unharmed, and think of nothing but getting home, you may yet after much hardship reach Ithaca. But if you harm them, then I forewarn you of the destruction both of your ship and of your comrades; and even though you may yourself escape, you will return late, in bad plight, after losing all your men.'

"Here she ended, and dawn enthroned in gold began to show in heaven, whereon she returned inland. I then went on board and told my men to loose the ship from her moorings; so they at once got into her, took their places, and began to smite the gray sea with their oars. Presently the great and cunning goddess Circe befriended us with a fair wind that blew dead aft, and stayed steadily with us, keeping our sails well filled, so we did whatever wanted doing to the ship's gear, and let her go as wind and helmsman headed her.

"Then, being much troubled in mind, I said to my men, 'My friends, it is not right that one or two of us alone should know the prophecies that Circe has made me, I will therefore tell you about them, so that whether we live or die we may do so with our eyes open. First she said we were to keep clear of the Sirens, who sit and sing most beautifully in a field of flowers; but she said I might hear them myself so long as no one else did. Therefore, take me and bind me to the crosspiece halfway up the mast; bind me as I stand upright, with a bond so fast that I cannot possibly break away, and lash the rope's ends to the mast itself. If I beg and pray you to set me free, then bind me more tightly still.'

"I had hardly finished telling everything to the men before we reached the island of the two Sirens, for the wind had been very favorable. Then all of a sudden it fell dead calm; there was not a breath of wind or a ripple upon the water, so the men furled the sails and stowed them; then taking to their oars they whitened the water with the foam they raised in rowing. Meanwhile I took a large wheel of wax and cut it up small with my sword. Then I kneaded the wax in my strong hands till it became soft, which it soon did between the kneading and the rays of the sun-god son of Hyperion. Then I stopped the ears of all my men, and they bound me hands and feet to the mast as I stood upright on the crosspiece; but they went on rowing themselves. When we had got within earshot of the land, and the ship was going at a good rate, the Sirens saw that we were getting in shore and began with their singing.

"'Come here,' they sang, 'renowned Odysseus, honor to the Achaean name, and listen to our two voices. No one ever sailed past as without staying to hear the enchanting sweetness of our song—and he who listens will go on his way not only charmed, but wiser, for we know all the ills that the gods laid upon the Argives and Trojans before Troy, and can tell you everything that is going to happen over the whole world.'

"They sang these words most musically, and as I longed to hear them further I made signs by frowning to my men that they should set me free; but they quickened their stroke, and Eurylochus and Perimedes bound me with still stronger bonds till we had got out of hearing of the Sirens' voices. Then my men took the wax from their ears and unbound me.

"Immediately after we had got past the island I saw a great wave from which spray was rising, and I heard a loud roaring sound. The men were so frightened that they loosed hold of their oars, for the whole sea resounded with the rushing of the waters, but the ship stayed where it was, for the men had left off rowing. I went round, therefore, and exhorted them man by man not to lose heart.

"'My friends,' said I, 'this is not the first time that we have been in danger, and we are in nothing like so bad a case as when the Cyclops shut us up in his cave; nevertheless, my courage and wise counsel saved us then, and we shall live to look back on all this as well. Now, therefore, let us all do as I say, trust in Zeus and row on with might and main. As for you, coxswain, these are your orders—attend to them, for the ship is in your hands: turn her head away from these steaming rapids and hug the rock, or she will give you the slip and be over yonder before you know where you are, and you will be the death of us.'

"So they did as I told them; but I said nothing about the awful monster Scylla, for I knew the men would not go on rowing if I did, but would huddle together in the hold. In one thing only did I disobey Ciree's strict instructions—I put on my armor. Then seizing two strong spears I took my stand on the ship's bows, for it was there that I expected first to see the monster of the rock, who was to do my men so much harm; but I could not make her out anywhere, though I strained my eyes with looking the gloomy rock all over and over.

"Then we entered the Straits[1] in great fear of mind, for on the one hand was Scylla, and on the other dread Charybdis kept sucking up the salt water. As she vomited it up, it was like the water in a cauldron when it is boiling over upon a great fire, and the spray reached the top of the rocks on either side. When she began to suck again, we could see the water all inside whirling round and round, and it made a deafening sound as it broke against the rocks. We could see the bottom of the whirlpool all black with sand and mud, and the men were at their wits ends for fear. While we were taken up with this, and were expecting each moment to be our last, Scylla pounced down suddenly upon us and snatched up my six best men. I was looking at once after both ship and men, and in a moment I saw their hands and feet ever so high above me, struggling in the air as Scylla was carrying them off, and I heard them call out my name in one last despairing cry. As a fisherman, seated, spear in hand, upon some jutting rock,[2] throws bait into the water to deceive the poor little fishes, and spears them with the ox's horn with which his spear is shod, throwing them gasping on to the land as he catches them one by one—even so did Scylla land these panting creatures on her rock and munch them up at the mouth of her den, while they screamed and stretched out their hands to me in their mortal agony. This was the most sickening sight that I saw throughout all my voyages.

"When we had passed the [Wandering] rocks, with Scylla and terrible Charybdis, we reached the noble island of the sun-god, where were the goodly cattle and sheep belonging to the sun Hyperion. While still at sea in my ship I could hear the cattle lowing as they came home to the yards, and the sheep bleating. Then I remembered what the blind Theban prophet Teiresias had told me, and how carefully Aeaean Circe had warned me to shun the island of the blessed sun-god. So being much troubled, I said to the men, 'My men, I know you are hard pressed, but listen while I tell you the prophecy that Teiresias made me, and how carefully Aeaean Circe warned me to shun the island of the blessed sun-god, for it was here, she said, that our worst danger would lie. Head the ship, therefore, away from the island.'

---

[1] These straits are generally understood to be the Straits of Messina.
[2] In the islands of Favognana and Marettimo off Sicily I have seen men fish exactly as here described. They chew bread into a paste and throw it into the sea to attract the fish, which they then spear. No line is used. (B.)

"The men were in despair at this, and Eurylochus at once gave me an insolent answer. 'Odysseus,' said he, 'you are cruel. You are very strong yourself and never get worn out; you seem to be made of iron, and now, though your men are exhausted with toil and want of sleep, you will not let them land and cook themselves a good supper upon this island, but bid them put out to sea and go faring fruitlessly on through the watches of the flying night. It is by night that the winds blow hardest and do so much damage. How can we escape should one of those sudden squalls spring up from southwest or west, which so often wreck a vessel when our lords the gods are unpropitious? Now, therefore, let us obey the behests of night and prepare our supper here hard by the ship; tomorrow morning we will go on board again and put out to sea.'

"Thus spoke Eurylochus, and the men approved his words. I saw that heaven meant us a mischief and said, 'You force me to yield, for you are many against one, but at any rate each one of you must take his solemn oath that if he meet with a herd of cattle or a large flock of sheep, he will not be so mad as to kill a single head of either, but will be satisfied with the food that Circe has given us.'

"They all swore as I bade them, and when they had completed their oath we made the ship fast in a harbor that was near a stream of fresh water, and the men went ashore and cooked their suppers. As soon as they had had enough to eat and drink, they began talking about their poor comrades whom Scylla had snatched up and eaten; this set them weeping, and they went on crying till they fell off into a sound sleep.

"In the third watch of the night when the stars had shifted their places, Zeus raised a great gale of wind that blew a hurricane so that land and sea were covered with thick clouds, and night sprang forth out of the heavens. When the child of morning, rosy-fingered Dawn, appeared, we brought the ship to land and drew her into a cave wherein the sea-nymphs hold their courts and dances, and I called the men together in council.

" 'My friends,' said I, 'we have meat and drink in the ship, let us mind, therefore, and not touch the cattle, or we shall suffer for it; for these cattle and sheep belong to the mighty sun, who sees and gives ear to everything.' And again they promised that they would obey.

"For a whole month the wind blew steadily from the south, and there was no other wind, but only south and east.[3] As long as corn and wine held out

---

[3] The writer evidently regards Odysseus as on a coast that looked east at no great distance south of the Straits of Messina somewhere, say, near Tauromeniuin, now

the men did not touch the cattle when they were hungry. When, however, they had eaten all there was in the ship, they were forced to go further afield, fishing with hook and line, catching birds, and taking whatever they could lay their hands on, for they were starving. One day, therefore, I went up inland that I might pray heaven to show me some means of getting away. When I had gone far enough to be clear of all my men, and had found a place that was well sheltered from the wind, I washed my hands and prayed to all the gods in Olympus till by and by they sent me off into a sweet sleep.

"Meanwhile Eurylochus had been giving evil counsel to the men. 'listen to me,' said he, 'my poor comrades. All deaths are bad enough, but there is none so bad as famine. Why should not we drive in the best of these cows and offer them in sacrifice to the immortal gods? If we ever get back to Ithaca, we can build a fine temple to the sun-god and enrich it with every kind of ornament. If, however, he is determined to sink our ship out of revenge for these horned cattle, and the other gods are of the same mind, I for one would rather drink salt water once for all and have done with it than be starved to death by inches in such a desert island as this is.'

"Thus spoke Eurylochus, and the men approved his words. Now the cattle, so fair and goodly, were feeding not far from the ship; the men, therefore, drove in the best of them, and they all stood round them saying their prayers, and using young oak-shoots instead of barley meal, for there was no barley left. When they had done praying they killed the cows and dressed their carcasses; they cut out the thighbones, wrapped them round in two layers of fat, and set some pieces of raw meat on the top of them. They had no wine with which to make drink offerings over the sacrifice while it was cooking, so they kept pouring on a little water from time to time while the inward meats were being grilled. Then, when the thigh bones were burned and they had tasted the inward meats, they cut the rest up small and put the pieces upon the spits.

"By this time my deep sleep had left me, and I turned back to the ship and to the seashore. As I drew near I began to smell hot roast meat, so I groaned out a prayer to the immortal gods. 'Father Zeus,' I exclaimed, 'and all you other gods who live in everlasting bliss, you have done me a cruel mischief by the sleep into which you have sent me. See what fine work these men of mine have been making in my absence.'

"Meanwhile Lampetie went straight off to the sun and told him we had been killing his cows, whereon he flew into a great rage, and said to

Taormina. (B.)

the immortals, 'Father Zeus, and all you other gods who live in everlasting bliss, I must have vengeance on the crew of Odysseus' ship. They have had the insolence to kill my cows, which were the one thing I loved to look upon, whether I was going up heaven or down again. If they do not square accounts with me about my cows, I will go down to Hades and shine there among the dead.'

" 'Sun,' said Zeus, 'go on shining upon us gods and upon mankind over the fruitful earth. I will shiver their ship into little pieces with a bolt of white lightning as soon as they get out to sea.'

"I was told all this by Calypso, who said she had heard it from the mouth of Hermes.

"As soon as I got down to my ship and to the seashore, I rebuked each one of the men separately, but we could see no way out of it, for the cows were dead already. And indeed the gods began at once to show signs and wonders among us, for the hides of the cattle crawled about, and the joints upon the spits began to low like cows, and the meat, whether cooked or raw, kept on making a noise just as cows do.

"For six days my men kept driving in the best cows and feasting upon them, but when Zeus the son of Cronus had added a seventh day, the fury of the gale abated; we therefore went on board, raised our masts, spread sail, and put out to sea. As soon as we were well away from the island, and could see nothing but sky and sea, the son of Cronus raised a black cloud over our ship, and the sea grew dark beneath it. We did not get on much further, for in another moment we were caught by a terrific squall from the west that snapped the forestays of the mast so that it fell aft, while all the ship's gear tumbled about at the bottom of the vessel. The mast fell upon the head of the helmsman in the ship's stern, so that the bones of his head were crushed to pieces, and he fell overboard as though he were diving, with no more life left in him.

"Then Zeus let fly with his thunderbolts, and the ship went round and round, and was filled with fire and brimstone as the lightning struck it. The men all fell into the sea; they were carried about in the water round the ship, looking like so many sea gulls, but the god presently deprived them of all chance of getting home again.

"I stuck to the ship till the sea knocked her sides from her keel (which drifted about by itself) and struck the mast out of her in the direction of the keel; but there was a backstay of stout ox-thong still hanging about it, and with this I lashed the mast and keel together, and getting astride of them was carried wherever the winds chose to take me.

"The gale from the west had now spent its force, and the wind got into the south again, which frightened me lest I should be taken back to the terrible whirlpool of Charybdis. This indeed was what actually happened, for I was borne along by the waves all night, and by sunrise had reached the rock of Scylla, and the whirlpool. She was then sucking down the salt sea water, but I was carried aloft toward the fig tree, which I caught hold of and clung on to like a bat. I could not plant my feet anywhere so as to stand securely, for the roots were a long way off and the boughs that overshadowed the whole pool were too high, too vast, and too far apart for me to reach them; so I hung patiently on, waiting till the pool should discharge my mast and raft again—and a very long while it seemed. A juryman is not more glad to get home to supper, after having been long detained in court by troublesome cases, than I was to see my raft beginning to work its way out of the whirlpool again. At last I let go with my hands and feet, and fell heavily into the sea, hard by my raft on to which I then got, and began to row with my hands. As for Scylla, the father of gods and men would not let her get further sight of me—otherwise I should have certainly been lost.

"Hence I was carried along for nine days till on the tenth night the gods stranded me on the Ogygian island, where dwells the great and powerful goddess Calypso. She took me in and was kind to me, but I need say no more about this, for I told you and your noble wife all about it yesterday, and I hate saying the same thing over and over again."

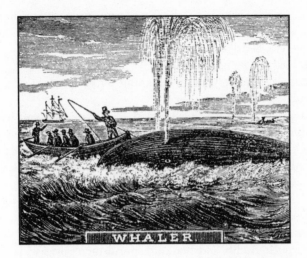

THE FIRST LOWERING

HERMAN MELVILE

The phantoms, for so they then seemed, were flitting on the other side of the deck, and, with a noiseless celerity, were casting loose the tackles and bands of the boat which swung there. This boat had always been deemed one of the spare boats, though technically called the captain's, on account of its hanging from the starboard quarter. The figure that now stood by its bows was tall and swart, with one white tooth evilly protruding from its steel-like lips. A rumpled Chinese jacket of black cotton funereally invested him, with wide black trowsers of the same dark stuff. But strangely crowning his ebonness was a glistening white plaited turban, the living hair braided and coiled round and round upon his head. Less swart in aspect, the companions of this figure were of that vivid, tiger-yellow complexion peculiar to some of the aboriginal natives of the Manillas;—a race notorious for a certain diabolism of subtilty, and by some honest white mariners supposed to be the paid spies and secret confidential agents on the water of the devil, their lord, whose counting-room they suppose to be elsewhere.

While yet the wondering ship's company were gazing upon these strangers, Ahab cried out to the white-turbaned old man at their head, 'All ready there, Fedallah?'

'Ready,' was the half-hissed reply.

'Lower away then; d'ye hear?' shouting across the deck. 'Lower away there, I say.'

Such was the thunder of his voice, that spite of their amazement the men sprang over the rail; the sheaves whirled round in the blocks; with a wallow, the three boats dropped into the sea; while, with a dexterous, off-handed daring, unknown in any other vocation, the sailors, goat-like, leaped down the rolling ship's side into the tossed boats below.

Hardly had they pulled out from under the ship's lee, when a fourth keel, coming from the windward side, pulled round under the stern, and showed the five strangers rowing Ahab, who, standing erect in the stern, loudly hailed Starbuck, Stubb, and Flask, to spread themselves widely, so as to cover a large expanse of water but with all their eyes again riveted upon the swart Fedallah and his crew, the inmates of the other boats obeyed not the command.

'Captain Ahab?—' said Starbuck.

'Spread yourselves,' cried Ahab; 'give way, all four boats. Thou, Flask, pull out more to leeward!'

'Aye, aye, sir,' cheerily cried little King-Post, sweeping round his great steering oar. 'Lay back!' addressing his crew. 'There!—there!—there again! There she blows right ahead, boys! — lay back!'

'Never heed yonder yellow boys, Archy.'

'Oh, I don't mind 'em, sir,' said Archy; 'I knew it all before now. Didn't I hear 'em in the hold? And didn't I tell Cabaco here of it? What say ye, Cabaco? They are stowaways, Mr. Flask.'

'Pull, pull, my fine hearts-alive; pull, my children; pull, my little ones,' drawingly and soothingly sighed Stubb to his crew, some of whom still showed signs of uneasiness. 'Why don't you break your backbones, my boys? What is it you stare at? Those chaps in yonder boat? Tut! They are only five more hands come to help us—never mind from where—the more the merrier. Pull, then, do pull; never mind the brimstone—devils are good fellows enough. So, so; there you are now; that's the stroke for a thousand pounds; that's the stroke to sweep the stakes! Hurrah for the gold cup of sperm oil, my heroes! Three cheers, men—all hearts alive! Easy, easy; don't be in a hurry—don't be in a hurry. Why don't you snap your oars, you rascals? Bite something, you dogs! So, so, so, then;—softly,

softly! That's it—that's it! long and strong. Give way there, give way! The devil fetch ye, ye ragamuffin rapscallions; ye are all asleep. Stop snoring, ye sleepers, and pull. Pull, will ye? pull, can't ye? pull, won't ye? Why in the name of gudgeons and ginger-cakes don't ye pull?—pull and break something! pull, and start your eyes out! Here! whipping out the sharp knife from his girdle; every mother's son of ye draw his knife, and pull with the blade between his teeth. That's it—that's it. Now ye do something; that looks like it, my steel-bits. Start her—start her, my silver-spoons! Start her, marling-spikes!'

Stubb's exordium to his crew is given here at large, because he had rather a peculiar way of talking to them in general, and especially in inculcating the religion of rowing. But you must not suppose from this specimen of his sermonizings that he ever flew into downright passions with his congregation. Not at all; and therein consisted his chief peculiarity. He would say the most terrific things to his crew, in a tone so strangely compounded of fun and fury, and the fury seemed so calculated merely as a spice to the fun, that no oarsman could hear such queer invocations without pulling for dear life, and yet pulling for the mere joke of the thing. Besides he all the time looked so easy and indolent himself, so loungingly managed his steering-oar, and so broadly gaped— open-mouthed at times—that the mere sight of such a yawning commander, by sheer force of contrast, acted like a charm upon the crew. Then again, Stubb was one of those odd sort of humorists, whose jollity is sometimes so curiously ambiguous, as to put all inferiors on their guard in the matter of obeying them.

In obedience to a sign from Ahab, Starbuck was now pulling obliquely across Stubb's bow; and when for a minute or so the two boats were pretty near to each other, Stubb hailed the mate.

'Mr. Starbuck! larboard boat there, ahoy! a word with ye, sir, if ye please!'

'Halloa!' returned Starbuck, turning round not a single inch as he spoke; still earnestly but whisperingly urging his crew; his face set like a flint from Stubb's.

'What think ye of those yellow boys, sir!'

'Smuggled on board, somehow, before the ship sailed. (Strong, strong, boys!') in a whisper to his crew, then speaking out loud again: 'A sad business, Mr. Stubb! (seethe her, seethe her, my lads!) but never mind, Mr. Stubb, all for the best. Let all your crew pull strong, come what will. (Spring, my men, spring!) There's hogsheads of sperm ahead, Mr. Stubb, and that's what ye came for. (Pull, my boys!) Sperm, sperm's the play! This at least is duty; duty and profit hand in hand!'

'Aye, aye, I thought as much,' soliloquized Stubb, when the boats diverged, 'as soon as I clapt eye on 'em, I thought so. Aye, and that's what he went into the after hold for, so often, as Dough-Boy long suspected. They were hidden down there. The White Whale's at the bottom of it. Well, well, so be it! Can't be helped! All right! Give way, men! It ain't the White Whale to-day! Give way!'

Now the advent of these outlandish strangers at such a critical instant as the lowering of the boats from the deck, this had not unreasonably awakened a sort of superstitious amazement in some of the ship's company; but Archy's fancied discovery having some time previous got abroad among them, though indeed not credited then, this had in some small measure prepared them for the event. It took off the extreme edge of their wonder; and so what with all this and Stubb's confident way of accounting for their appearance, they were for the time freed from superstitious surmisings; though the affair still left abundant room for all manner of wild conjectures as to dark Ahab's precise agency in the matter from the beginning. For me, I silently recalled the mysterious shadows I had seen creeping on board the Pequod during the dim Nantucket dawn, as well as the enigmatical hintings of the unaccountable Elijah.

Meantime, Ahab, out of hearing of his officers, having sided the furthest to windward, was still ranging ahead of the other boats; a circumstance bespeaking how potent a crew was pulling him. those tiger yellow creatures of his seemed all steel and whale-bone; like five trip-hammers they rose and fell with regular strokes of strength, which periodically started the boat along the water like a horizontal burst boiler out of a Mississippi steamer. As for Fedallah, who was seen pulling the harpooneer oar, he had thrown aside his black jacket, and displayed his naked chest with the whole part of his body above the gunwale, clearly cut against the alternating depressions of the watery horizon; while at the other end of the boat Ahab, with one arm, like a fencer's, thrown half backward into the air, as if to counterbalance any tendency to trip: Ahab was seen steadily managing his steering oar as in a thousand boat lowerings ere the White Whale had torn him. All at once the out-stretched arm gave a peculiar motion and then remained fixed, while the boat's five oars were seen simultaneously peaked. Boat and crew sat motionless on the sea. Instantly the three spread boats in the rear paused on their way. The whales had irregularly settled bodily down into the blue, thus giving no distantly discernible token of the movement, though from his closer vicinity Ahab had observed it.

'Every man look out along his oars!' cried Starbuck. 'Thou, Queequeg, stand up!'

Nimbly springing up on the triangular raised box in the bow, the savage stood erect there, and with intensely eager eyes gazed off towards the spot where the chase had last been descried. Likewise upon the extreme stern of the boat where it was also triangularly platformed level with the gunwale, Starbuck himself was seen coolly and adroitly balancing himself to the jerking tossings of his chip of a craft, and silently eyeing the vast blue eye of the sea.

Not very far distant Flask's boat was also lying breathlessly still; its commander recklessly standing upon the top of the loggerhead, a stout sort of post rooted in the keel, and rising some two feet above the level of the stern platform. it is used for catching turns with the whale line. Its top is not more spacious than the palm of a man's hand, and standing upon such a base as that, Flask seemed perched at the mast-head of some ship which had sunk to all but her trucks. But little King-Post was small and short, and at the same time little King-Post was full of a large and tall ambition, so that this loggerhead stand-point of his did by no means satisfy King-Post.

'I can't see three seas off; tip us up an oar there, and let me on to that.'

Upon this, Daggoo, with either hand upon the gunwale to steady his way, swiftly slid aft, and then erecting himself volunteered his lofty shoulders for a pedestal.

'Good a mast-head as any, sir. Will you mount?'

'That I will, and thank ye very much, my fine fellow; only I wish you fifty feet taller.'

Whereupon planting his feet firmly against two opposite planks of the boat, the gigantic negro, stooping a little, presented his flat palm to Flask's foot, and then putting Flask's hand on his hearse-plumed head and bidding him spring as he himself should toss, with one dexterous fling landed the little man high and dry on his shoulders. And here was Flask now standing, Daggoo with one lifted arm furnishing him with a breast-band to lean against and steady himself by.

At any time it is a strange sight to the tyro to see with what wondrous habitude of unconscious skill the whaleman will maintain an erect posture in his boat, even when pitched about by the most riotously perverse and cross-running seas. Still more strange to see him giddily perched upon the loggerhead itself, under such circumstances. But the sight of little Flask mounted upon gigantic Daggoo was yet more curious; for sustaining himself with a cool, indifferent, easy, unthought of, barbaric majesty, the noble negro to every roll of the sea harmoniously rolled his fine form. On his broad back, flaxen-haired flask seemed a snow-flake. The bearer looked nobler than the rider. Though truly vivacious, tumultuous, ostentatious little Flask would now and then stamp with impatience; but not one added heave did he thereby give to the negro's lordly chest. So have I seen Passion and Vanity stamping the living magnanimous earth, but the earth did not alter her tides and her seasons for that.

Meanwhile Stubb, the third mate, betrayed no such far-gazing solicitudes. The whales might have made one of their regular soundings, not a temporary dive from mere fright; and if that were the case, Stubb, as his wont in such cases, it seems, was resolved to solace the languishing interval with his pipe. He withdrew it from his hatband, where he always wore it aslant like a feather. He loaded it, and rammed home the loading with his thumb-end; but hardly had he ignited his match across the rough sand-paper of his hand, when Tashtego, his harpooneer, whose eyes had been setting to windward like two fixed stars, suddenly dropped like light from his erect attitude to his seat, crying out in a quick phrensy of hurry, 'Down, down all, and give way!—there they are!'

To a landsman, no whale, nor any sign of a herring, would have been visible at that moment; nothing but a troubled bit of greenish white water, and thin scattered puffs of vapor hovering over it, and suffusingly blowing off to leeward, like the confused scud from white rolling billows. The air around suddenly vibrated and tingled, as it were, like the air over intensely heated plates of iron. Beneath this atmospheric waving and curling, and partially beneath a thin layer of water, also, the whales were swimming. Seen in advance of all the other indications, the puffs of vapor they spouted, seemed their forerunning couriers and detached flying outriders.

All four boats were now in keen pursuit of that one spot of troubled water and air. But it bade far to outstrip them; it flew on and on, as a mass of interblending bubbles borne down a rapid stream from the hills.

'Pull, pull, my good boys,' said Starbuck, in the lowest possible but intensest concentrated whisper to his men; while the sharp fixed glance from his eyes darted straight ahead of the bow, almost seemed as two visible needles in two unerring binnacle compasses. He did not say much to his crew, though, nor did his crew say anything to him. Only the silence of the boat was at intervals startlingly pierced by one of his peculiar whispers, now harsh with command, now soft with entreaty.

How different the loud little King-Post. 'Sing out and say something, my hearties. Roar and pull, my thunderbolts! Beach me, beach me on their black backs, boys; only do that for me, and I'll sign over to you my Martha's Vineyard plantation, boys; including wife and children, boys. Lay me on—lay me on! O Lord, Lord! but I shall go stark, staring mad: See! see that white water!' And so shouting, he pulled his hat from his head, and stamped up and down on it; then picking it up, flirted it far off upon the sea; and finally fell to rearing and plunging in the boat's stern like a crazed colt from the prairie.

'Look at that chap now,' philosophically drawled Stubb, who, with his unlighted short pipe, mechanically retained between his teeth, at a short distance, followed after—'He's got fits, that Flask has. Fits? yes, give him fits—that's the very word—pitch fits into 'em. Merrily, merrily, hearts-alive. Pudding for supper, you know;—merry's the word. Pull, babes—pull, sucklings—pull, all. But what the devil are you hurrying about? Softly, softly, and steadily, my men. Only pull, and keep pulling; nothing more. Crack all your backbones, and bite your knives in two—that's all. Take it easy—why don't ye take it easy, I say, and burst all your livers and lungs!'

But what it was that inscrutable Ahab said to that tiger-yellow crew of his—these were words best omitted here; for you live under the blessed light of the evangelical land.

Only the infidel sharks in the audacious seas may give ear to such words, when, with tornado brow, and eyes of red murder, and foam-glued lips, Ahab leaped after his prey.

Meanwhile, all the boats tore on. The repeated specific allusions of Flask to 'that whale', as he called the fictitious monster which he declared to be incessantly tantalizing his boat's bow with its tail—these allusions of his were at times so vivid and life-like, that they would cause some one or two of his men to snatch a fearful look over the shoulder. But this was against all rule; for the oarsmen must put out their eyes, and ram a skewer through their necks; usage pronouncing that they must have no organs but ears, and no limbs but arms, in these critical moments.

It was a sight full of quick wonder and awe! The vast swells of the omnipotent sea; the surging, hollow roar they made, as they rolled along the eight gunwales, like gigantic bowls in a boundless bowling-green; the brief suspended agony of the boat, as it would tip for an instant on the knife-like edge of the sharper waves, that almost seemed threatening to cut it in two; the sudden profound dip into the watery glens and hollows; the keen spurrings and goadings to gain the top of the opposite hill; the headlong, sled-like slide down its other side;—all these, with the cries of the headsmen and harpooneers, and the shuddering gasps of the oarsmen, with the wondrous sight of the ivory Pequod bearing down upon her boats with outstretched sails, like a wild hen after her screaming brood;—all this was thrilling. Not the raw recruit, marching from the bosom of his wife into the fever heat of his first battle; not the dead man's ghost encountering the first unknown phantom in the other world;—neither of these can feel stranger and stronger emotions than that man does, who for the first time finds himself pulling into the charmed, churned circle of the hunted Sperm Whale.

The dancing white water made by the chase was now becoming more and more visible, owing to the increasing darkness of the dun cloud-shadows flung upon the sea. The jets of vapor no longer blended, but tilted everywhere to right and left; the whales seemed separating their wakes. The boats were pulled more apart; Starbuck giving chase to three whales running dead to leeward. Our sail was now set, and, with the still rising wind, we rushed along; the boat going with such madness through the water, that the lee oars could scarcely be worked rapidly enough to escape being torn from the row-locks.

Soon we were running through a suffusing wide veil of mist; neither ship nor boat to be seen.

'Give way, men,' whispered Starbuck, drawing still further aft the sheet of his sail; 'there is time to kill a fish yet before the squall comes. There's white water again!—close to! Spring!'

Soon after, two cries in quick succession on each side of us denoted that the other boats had got fast; but hardly were they overheard, when with a lightning-like hurtling whisper Starbuck said: 'Stand up!' and Queequeg, harpoon in hand, sprang to his feet.

Though not one of the oarsmen was then facing the life and death peril so close to them ahead, yet with their eyes on the intense countenance of the mate in the stern of the boat, they knew that the imminent instant had come; they heard, too, an enormous wallowing sound as of fifty elephants stirring in their litter. Meanwhile the boat was still booming through the mist, the waves curling and hissing around us like the erected crests of enraged serpents.

'That's his hump. There, there, give it to him!' whispered Starbuck.

A short rushing sound leaped out of the boat; it was the darted iron of Queequeg. Then all in one welded commotion came an invisible push from astern, while forward the boat seemed striking on a ledge; the sail collapsed and exploded; a gush of scalding vapor shot up near by; something rolled and tumbled like an earthquake beneath us. The whole crew were half suffocated as they were tossed helter-skelter into the white curdling cream of the squall. Squall, whale, and harpoon had all blended together; and the whale, merely grazed by the iron, escaped.

Though completely swamped, the boat was nearly unharmed. Swimming round it we picked up the floating oars, and lashing them across the gunwale, tumbled back to our places. There we sat up to our knees in the sea, the water covering every rib and plank, so that to our downward gazing eyes the suspended craft seemed a coral boat grown up to us from the bottom of the ocean.

The wind increased to a howl; the waves dashed their bucklers together; the whole squall roared, forked, and crackled around us like a white fire upon the prairie, in which, unconsumed, we were burning; immortal in these jaws of death! In vain we hailed the other boats; as well roar to the live coals down the chimney of a flaming furnace as hail those boats in that storm. Meanwhile the driving scud, rack, and mist, grew darker with the shadows of night; no sign of the ship could be seen. The rising sea forbade all attempts to bale out the boat. The oars were useless as propellers, performing now the office of life-preservers. So, cutting the lashing of the water-proof match keg, after many failures Starbuck contrived to ignite the lamp in the lantern; then stretching it on a waif pole, handed it to Queequeg as the standard-bearer of this forlorn hope. There, then, he sat, holding up that imbecile candle in the heart of that almighty forlornness. There, then, he sat, the sign and symbol of a man without faith, hopelessly holding up hope in the midst of despair.

Wet, drenched through, and shivering cold, despairing of ship or boat, we lifted up our eyes as the dawn came on. The mist still spread over the sea, the empty lantern lay crushed in the bottom of the boat. Suddenly Queequeg started to his feet, hollowing his hand to his ear. We all heard a faint creaking, as of ropes and yards hitherto muffled by the storm. The sound came nearer and nearer; the thick mists were dimly parted by a huge, vague form. Affrighted, we all sprang into the sea as the ship at last loomed into view, bearing right down upon us within a distance of not much more than its length.

Floating on the waves we saw the abandoned boat, as for one instant it tossed and gaped beneath the ship's bows like a chip at the base of a cataract; and then the vast hull rolled over it, and it was seen no more till it came up weltering astern. Again we swam for it, were dashed against it by the seas, and were at last taken up and safely landed on board. Ere the squall came close to, the other boats had cut loose from their fish and returned to the ship in good time. The ship had given us up, but was still cruising, if haply it might light upon some token of our perishing,—an oar or a lance pole.

YOUTH

JOSEPH CONRAD

This could have occurred nowhere but in England, where men and sea interpenetrate, so to speak—the sea entering into the life of most men, and the men knowing something or everything about the sea, in the way of amusement, of travel, or of bread-winning.

We were sitting round a mahogany table that reflected the bottle, the claret-glasses, and our faces as we leaned on our elbows. There was a director of companies, an accountant, a lawyer, Marlow, and myself. The director had been a *Conway* boy, the accountant had served four years at sea, the lawyer—a fine crusted Tory, High Churchman, the best of old fellows, the soul of honour—had been chief officer in the P. & O. service in the good old days when mail-boats were square-rigged at least on two masts, and used to come down the China Sea before a fair monsoon with stun'-sails set alow and aloft. We all began life in the merchant service. Between the five of us there was the strong bond of the sea, and also the fellowship of the craft, which no amount of enthusiasm for yachting, cruising, and so on can give, since one is only the amusement of life and the other is life itself.

Marlow (at least I think that is how he spelt his name) told the story, or rather the chronicle, of a voyage:—

"Yes, I have seen a little of the Eastern seas; but what I remember best is my first voyage there. You fellows know there are those voyages that seem ordered for the illustration of life, that might stand for a symbol of existence. You fight, work, sweat, nearly kill yourself, sometimes do kill yourself, trying to accomplish something—and you can't. Not from any fault of yours. You simply can do nothing, neither great nor little—not a thing in the world—not even marry an old maid, or get a wretched 600-ton cargo of coal to its port of destination.

"It was altogether a memorable affair. It was my first voyage to the East, and my first voyage as second mate; it was also my skipper's first command. You'll admit it was time. He was sixty if a day; a little man, with a broad, not very straight back, with bowed shoulders and one leg more bandy than the other, he had that queer twisted-about appearance you see so often in men who work in the fields. He had a nut-cracker face—chin and nose trying to come together over a sunken mouth—and it was framed in iron-gray fluffy hair, that looked like a chin-strap of cotton-wool sprinkled with coal-dust. And he had blue eyes in that old face of his, which were amazingly like a boy's, with that candid expression some quite common men preserve to the end of their days by a rare internal gift of simplicity of heart and rectitude of soul. What induced him to accept me was a wonder. I had come out of a crack Australian clipper, where I had been third officer, and he seemed to have a prejudice against crack clippers as aristocratic and high-toned. He said to me, 'You know, in this ship you will have to work.' I said I had to work in every ship I had ever been in. 'Ah, but this is different, and you gentlemen out of them big ships; . . . but there! I dare say you will do. Join to-morrow.'

"I joined to-morrow. It was twenty-two years ago; and I was just twenty. How time passes! It was one of the happiest days of my life. Fancy! Second mate for the first time—a really responsible officer! I wouldn't have thrown up my new billet for a fortune. The mate looked me over carefully. He was also an old chap, but of another stamp. He had a Roman nose, a snow-white, long beard, and his name was Mahon, but he insisted that it should be pronounced Mann. He was well connected; yet there was something wrong with his luck, and he had never got on.

"As to the captain, he had been for years in coasters, then in the Mediterranean, and last in the West Indian trade. He had never been round the Capes. He could just write a kind of sketchy hand, and didn't care for writing at all. Both were thorough good seamen of course, and between those two old chaps I felt like a small boy between two grandfathers.

"The ship also was old. Her name was the *Judea*. Queer name, isn't it? She belonged to a man Wilmer, Wilcox—some name like that; but he has been bankrupt and dead these twenty years or more, and his name don't matter. She had been laid up in Shadwell basin for ever so long. You may imagine her state. She was all rust, dust, grime—soot aloft, dirt on deck. To me it was like coming out of a palace into a ruined cottage. She was about 400 tons, had a primitive windlass, wooden latches to the doors, not a bit of brass about her, and a big square stern. There was on it, below her name in big letters, a lot of scrollwork, with the gilt off, and some sort of a coat of arms, with the motto 'Do or Die' underneath. I remember it took my fancy immensely. There was a touch of romance in it, something that made me love the old thing—something that appealed to my youth:

"We left London in ballast—sand ballast—to load a cargo of coal in a northern port for Bankok. Bankok! I thrilled. I had been six years at sea, but had only seen Melbourne and Sydney, very good places, charming places in their way—but Bankok!

"We worked out of the Thames under canvas, with a North Sea pilot on board. His name was Jermyn, and he dodged all day long about the galley drying his handkerchief before the stove. Apparently he never slept. He was a dismal man, with a perpetual tear sparkling at the end of his nose, who either had been in trouble, or was in trouble, or expected to be in trouble—couldn't be happy unless something went wrong. He mistrusted my youth, my common-sense, and my seamanship, and made a point of showing it in a hundred little ways. I dare say he was right. It seems to me I knew very little then, and I know not much more now; but I cherish a hate for that Jermyn to this day.

"We were a week working up as far as Yarmouth Roads, and then we got into a gale—the famous October gale of twenty-two years ago. It was wind, lightning, sleet, snow, and a terrific sea. We were flying light, and you may imagine how bad it was when I tell you we had smashed bulwarks and a flooded deck. On the second night she shifted her ballast into the lee bow, and by that time we had been blown off somewhere on the Dogger Bank. There was nothing for it but go below with shovels and try to right her, and there we were in that vast hold, gloomy like a cavern, the tallow dips stuck and flickering on the beams, the gale howling above, the ship tossing about like mad on her side; there we all were, Jermyn, the captain, every one, hardly able to keep our feet, engaged on that gravedigger's work, and trying to toss shovelfuls of wet sand up to windward. At every tumble of the ship you could see vaguely in the dim light men falling down with a great flourish of shovels. One of the ship's boys (we had two), impressed by the weirdness of the scene, wept as if his heart would break. We could hear him blubbering somewhere in the shadows.

"On the third day the gale died out, and by and by a north-country tug picked us up. We took sixteen days in all to get from London to the Tyne! When we got into dock we had lost our turn for loading, and they hauled us off to a tier where we remained for a month. Mrs. Beard (the captain's name was Beard) came from Colchester to see the old man. She lived on board. The crew of runners had left, and there remained only the officers, one boy and the steward, a mulatto who answered to the name of Abraham. Mrs. Beard was an old woman, with a face all wrinkled and ruddy like a winter apple, and the figure of a young girl. She caught sight of me once, sewing on a button, and insisted on having my shirts to repair. This was something different from the captains' wives I had known on board crack clippers. When I brought her the shirts, she said: 'And the socks? They want mending, I am sure, and John's—Captain Beard's—things are all in order now. I would be glad of something to do.' Bless the old woman. She overhauled my outfit for me, and meantime I read for the first time *Sartor Resartus* and Burnaby's *Ride to Khiva*. I didn't understand much of the first then; but I remember I preferred the soldier to the philosopher at the time; a preference which life has only confirmed. One was a man, and the other was either more—or less. However, they are both dead and Mrs. Beard is dead, and youth, strength, genius, thoughts, achievements, simple hearts—all die. . . . No matter.

"They loaded us at last. We shipped a crew. Eight able seamen and two boys. We hauled off one evening to the buoys at the dock-gates, ready to go out, and with a fair prospect of beginning the voyage next day. Mrs. Beard was to start for home by a late train. When the ship was fast we went to tea. We sat rather silent through the meal—Mahon, the old couple, and I. I finished first, and slipped away for a smoke, my cabin being in a deck-house just against the poop. It was high water, blowing fresh with a drizzle; the double dock-gates were opened, and the steam-colliers were going in and out in the darkness with their lights burning bright, a great plashing of propellers, rattling of winches, and a lot of hailing on the pier-heads. I watched the procession of head-lights gliding high and of green lights gliding low in the night, when suddenly a red gleam flashed at me, vanished, came into view again, and remained. The fore-end of a steamer loomed up close. I shouted down the cabin, 'Come up, quick!' and then heard a startled voice saying afar in the dark, 'Stop her, sir.' A bell jingled. Another voice cried warningly, 'We are going right into that barque, sir.' The answer to this was a gruff 'All right,' and the next thing was a heavy crash as the steamer struck a glancing blow with the bluff of her bow about our fore-rigging. There was a moment of confusion, yelling, and running about. Steam roared. Then somebody was heard saying, 'All clear, sir.' . . . 'Are you all right?' asked the gruff voice. I had jumped forward to see the damage, and hailed back, 'I think so.' 'Easy astern,' said the gruff voice. A bell jingled. 'What steamer is that?' screamed Mahon. By that time she was no more to us than a bulky shadow manœuvring a little way off. They shouted at us some name—a woman's name, Miranda or Melissa— or some such thing. 'This means another month in this beastly hole,' said Mahon to me, as we peered with lamps about the splintered bulwarks and broken braces. 'But where's the captain?'

'We had not heard or seen anything of him all that time. We went aft to look. A doleful voice arose hailing somewhere in the middle of the dock, '*Judea* ahoy!' . . . How the devil did he get there? . . . 'Hallo!' we shouted. 'I am adrift in our boat without oars,' he cried. A belated water-man offered his services, and Mahon struck a bargain with him for half-a-crown to tow our skipper alongside; but it was Mrs. Beard that came up the ladder first. They had been floating about the dock in that mizzly cold rain for nearly an hour. I was never so surprised in my life.

"It appears that when he heard my shout 'Come up' he understood at once what was the matter, caught up his wife, ran on deck, and across, and down into our boat, which was fast to the ladder. Not bad for a sixty-year-old. Just imagine that old fellow saving heroically in his arms that old woman—the woman of his life. He set her down on a thwart, and was ready to climb back on board when the painter came adrift somehow, and away they went together. Of course in the confusion we did not hear him shouting. He looked abashed. She said cheerfully, 'I suppose it does not matter my losing the train now?' 'No, Jenny—you go below and get warm,' he growled. Then to us: 'A sailor has no business with a wife—I say.

There I was, out of the ship. Well, no harm done this time. Let's go and look at what that fool of a steamer smashed.'

"It wasn't much, but it delayed us three weeks. At the end of that time, the captain being engaged with his agents, I carried Mrs. Beard's bag to the railway-station and put her all comfy into a third-class carriage. She lowered the window to say, 'You are a good young man. If you see John—Captain Beard—without his muffler at night, just remind him from me to keep his throat well wrapped up.' 'Certainly, Mrs. Beard,' I said. 'You are a good young man; I noticed how attentive you are to John—to Captain——' The train pulled out suddenly; I took my cap off to the old woman: I never saw her again. . . Pass the bottle.

"We went to sea next day. When we made that start for Bankok we had been already three months out of London. We had expected to be a fortnight or so—at the outside.

"It was January, and the weather was beautiful—the beautiful sunny winter weather that has more charm than in the summer-time, because it is unexpected, and crisp, and you know it won't, it can't, last long. It's like a windfall, like a godsend, like an unexpected piece of luck.

"It lasted all down the North Sea, all down Channel; and it lasted till we were three hundred miles or so to the westward of the Lizards: then the wind went round to the sou'west and began to pipe up. In two days it blew a gale. The *Judea*, hove to, wallowed on the Atlantic like an old candle-box. It blew day after day: it blew with spite, without interval, without mercy, without rest. The world was nothing but an immensity of great foaming waves rushing at us, under a sky low enough to touch with the hand and dirty like a smoked ceiling. In the stormy space surrounding us there was as much flying spray as air. Day after day and night after night there was nothing round the ship but the howl of the wind, the tumult of the sea, the noise of water pouring over her deck. There was no rest for her and no rest for us. She tossed, she pitched, she stood on her head, she sat on her tail, she rolled, she groaned, and we had to hold on while on deck and cling to our bunks when below, in a constant effort of body and worry of mind.

One night Mahon spoke through the small window of my berth. It opened right into my very bed, and I was lying there sleepless, in my boots, feeling as though I had not slept for years, and could not if I tried. He said excitedly—

" 'You got the sounding-rod in here, Marlow? I can't get the pumps to suck. By God! it's no child's play.'

"I gave him the sounding-rod and lay down again, trying to think of various things—but I thought only of the pumps. When I came on deck they were still at it, and my watch relieved at the pumps. By the light of the lantern brought on deck to examine the sounding-rod I caught a glimpse of their weary, serious faces. We pumped all the four hours. We pumped all night, all day, all the week—watch and watch. She was working herself loose, and leaked badly—not enough to drown us at once, but enough to kill us with the work at the pumps. And while we pumped the ship was going from us piecemeal: the bulwarks went, the stanchions were torn out, the ventilators smashed, the cabin-door burst in. There was not a dry spot in the ship. She was being gutted bit by bit. The long-boat changed, as if by magic, into matchwood where she stood in her gripes. I had lashed her myself, and was rather proud of my handiwork, which had withstood so long the malice of the sea. And we pumped. And there was no break in the weather. The sea was white like a sheet of foam, like a caldron of boiling milk; there was not a break in the clouds, no—not the size of a man's hand—no, not for so much as ten seconds. There was for us no sky, there were for us no stars, no sun, no universe—nothing but angry clouds and an infuriated sea. We pumped watch and watch, for dear life; and it seemed to last for months, for years, for all eternity, as though we had been dead and gone to a hell for sailors. We forgot the day of the week, the name of the month, what year it was, and whether we had ever been ashore. The sails blew away, she lay broadside on under a weather-cloth, the ocean poured over her, and we did not care. We turned those handles, and had the eyes of idiots. As soon as we had crawled on deck I used to take a round turn with a rope about the men, the pumps, and the mainmast, and we turned, we turned incessantly, with the water to our waists, to our necks, over our heads. It was all one. We had forgotten how it felt to be dry.

"And there was somewhere in me the thought: By Jove! this is the deuce of an adventure—something you read about; and it is my first voyage as second mate—and I am only twenty—and here I am lasting it out as well as any of these men, and keeping my chaps up to the mark. I was pleased. I would not have given up the experience for worlds. I had moments of exultation. Whenever the old dismantled craft pitched heavily with her counter high in the air, she seemed to me to throw up, like an appeal, like a defiance, like a cry to the clouds without mercy, the words written on her stern: '*Judea*, London. Do or Die.'

"O youth! The strength of it, the faith of it, the imagination of it! To me she was not an old rattletrap carting about the world a lot of coal for a freight—to me she was the endeavour, the test, the trial of life I think of her with pleasure, with affection, with regret—as you would think of someone dead you have loved. I shall never forget her. . . Pass the bottle.

"One night when tied to the mast, as I explained, we were pumping on, deafened with the wind, and without spirit enough in us to wish ourselves dead, a heavy sea crashed aboard and swept clean over us. As soon as I got my breath I shouted, as in duty bound, 'Keep on, boys!' when suddenly I felt something hard floating on deck strike the calf of my leg. I made a grab at it and missed. It was so dark we could not see each other's faces within a foot—you understand.

"After that thump the ship kept quiet for a while, and the thing, whatever it was, struck my leg again. This time I caught it—and it was a saucepan. At first, being stupid with fatigue and thinking of nothing but the pumps, I did not understand what I had in my hand. Suddenly it dawned upon me, and I shouted, 'Boys, the house on deck is gone. Leave this, and let's look for the cook.'

"There was a deck-house forward, which contained the galley, the cook's berth, and the quarters of the crew. As we had expected for days to see it swept away, the hands had been ordered to sleep in the cabin—the only safe place in the ship. The steward, Abraham, however, persisted in clinging to his berth, stupidly, like a mule—from sheer fright I believe, like an animal that won't leave a stable falling in an earthquake. So we went to look for him. It was chancing death, since once out of our lashings we were as exposed as if on a raft. But we went. The house was shattered as if a shell had exploded inside. Most of it had gone overboard—stove, men's quarters, and their property, all was gone; but two posts, holding a portion of the bulkhead to which Abraham's bunk was attached, remained as if by a miracle. We groped in the ruins and came upon this, and there he was, sitting in his bunk, surrounded by foam and wreckage, jabbering cheerfully to himself. He was out of his mind; completely and for ever mad, with this sudden shock coming upon the fag-end of his endurance. We snatched him up, lugged him aft, and pitched him head-first down the cabin companion. You understand there was no time to carry him down with infinite precautions and wait to see how he got on. Those below would pick him up at the bottom of the stairs all right. We were in a hurry to go back to the pumps. That business could not wait. A bad leak is an inhuman thing.

"One would think that the sole purpose of that fiendish gale had been to make a lunatic of that poor devil of a mulatto. It eased before morning, and next day the sky cleared, and as the sea went down the leak took up. When it came to bending a fresh set of sails the crew demanded to put back—and really there was nothing else to do. Boats gone, decks swept clean, cabin gutted, men without a stitch but what they stood in, stores spoiled, ship strained. We put her head for home, and—would you believe it? The wind came east right in our teeth. It blew fresh, it blew continuously. We had to beat up every inch of the way, but she did not leak so badly, the water keeping comparatively smooth. Two hours' pumping in every four is no joke—but it kept her afloat as far as Falmouth.

"The good people there live on casualties of the sea, and no doubt were glad to see us. A hungry crowd of shipwrights sharpened their chisels at the sight of that carcass of a ship. And, by Jove! they had pretty pickings off us before they were done. I fancy the owner was already in a tight place. There were delays. Then it was decided to take part of the cargo out and caulk her topsides. This was done, the repairs finished, cargo reshipped; a new crew came on board, and we went out—for Bankok. At the end of a week we were back again. The crew said they weren't going to Bankok—a hundred and fifty days' passage—in a something hooker that wanted pumping eight hours out of the twenty-four; and the nautical papers inserted again the little paragraph: '*Judea*. Barque. Tyne to Bankok; coals; put back to Falmouth leaky and with crew refusing duty.'

"There were more delays—more tinkering. The owner came down for a day, and said she was as right as a little fiddle. Poor old Captain Beard looked like the ghost of a Geordie skipper—through the worry and humiliation of it. Remember he was sixty, and it was his first command. Mahon said it was a foolish business, and would end badly. I loved the ship more than ever, and wanted awfully to get to Bankok. To Bankok! Magic name, blessed name. Mesopotamia wasn't a patch on it. Remember I was twenty, and it was my first second-mate's billet, and the East was waiting for me.

"We went out and anchored in the outer roads with a fresh crew—the third. She leaked worse than ever. It was as if those confounded shipwrights had actually made a hole in her. This time we did not even go outside. The crew simply refused to man the windlass.

"They towed us back to the inner harbour, and we became a fixture, a feature, an institution of the place. People pointed us out to visitors as 'That 'ere barque that's going to Bankok—has been here six months—put back three times.' On holidays the small boys pulling about in boats would hail, '*Judea*, ahoy!' and if a head showed above the rail shouted, 'Where you bound to?—Bankok?' and jeered. We were only three on board. The poor old skipper mooned in the cabin. Mahon undertook the cooking, and unexpectedly developed all a Frenchman's genius for preparing nice little messes. I looked languidly after the rigging. We became citizens of Falmouth. Every shopkeeper knew us. At the barber's or tobacconist's they asked familiarly. 'Do you think you will ever get to Bankok?' Meantime the owner, the underwriters, and the charterers squabbled amongst themselves in London, and our pay went on. . . . Pass the bottle.

"It was horrid. Morally it was worse than pumping for life. It seemed as though we had been forgotten by the world, belonged to nobody, would get nowhere; it seemed that, as if bewitched, we would have to live for ever and ever in that inner harbour, a derision and a byword to generations of long-shore loafers and dishonest boatmen. I obtained three months' pay and a five days' leave, and made a rush for London. It took me a day to get there and pretty well another to come back—but three months' pay went all the same. I don't know what I did with it. I went to a music-hall, I believe, lunched, dined, and supped in a swell place in Regent Street, and was back to time, with nothing but a complete set of Byron's works and a new railway rug to show for three months' work. The boat-man who pulled me off to the ship said: 'Hallo! I thought you had left the old thing. *She* will never get to Bankok.' 'That's all *you* know about it,' I said scornfully—but I didn't like that prophecy at all.

"Suddenly a man, some kind of agent to somebody, appeared with full powers. He had grog-blossoms all over his face, an indomitable energy, and was a jolly soul. We leaped into life again. A hulk came alongside, took our cargo, and then we went into dry dock to get our copper stripped. No wonder she leaked. The poor thing, strained beyond endurance by the gale, had, as if in disgust, spat out all the oakum of her lower seams. She was recaulked, new coppered, and made as tight as a bottle. We went back to the hulk and reshipped our cargo.

"Then, on a fine moonlight night, all the rats left the ship.

"We had been infested with them. They had destroyed our sails, consumed more stores than the crew, affably shared our beds and our dangers, and now, when the ship was made seaworthy, concluded to clear out. I called Mahon to enjoy the spectacle. Rat after rat appeared on our rail, took a last look over his shoulder, and leaped with a hollow thud into the empty hulk. We tried to count them, but soon lost the tale. Mahon said:

'Well, well! don't talk to me about the intelligence of rats. They ought to have left before, when we had that narrow squeak from foundering. There you have the proof how silly is the superstition about them. They leave a good ship for an old rotten hulk, where there is nothing to eat, too, the fools! . . . I don't believe they know what is safe or what is good for them, any more than you or I.'

"And after some more talk we agreed that the wisdom of rats had been grossly overrated, being in fact no greater than that of men.

"The story of the ship was known, by this, all up the Channel from Land's End to the Forelands, and we could get no crew on the south coast. They sent us one all complete from Liverpool, and we left once more—for Bankok.

"We had fair breezes, smooth water right into the tropics, and the old *Judea* lumbered along in the sunshine. When she went eight knots everything cracked aloft, and we tied our caps to our heads; but mostly she strolled on at the rate of three miles an hour. What could you expect? She was tired—that old ship. Her youth was where mine is—where yours is—you fellows who listen to this yarn; and what friend would throw your years and your weariness in your face? We didn't grumble at her. To us aft, at least, it seemed as though we had been born in her, reared in her, had lived in her for ages, had never known any other ship. I would just as soon have abused the old village church at home for not being a cathedral.

"And for me there was also my youth to make me patient. There was all the East before me, and all life, and the thought that I had been tried in that ship and had come out pretty well. And I thought of men of old who, centuries ago, went that road in ships that sailed no better, to the land of palms, and spices, and yellow sands, and of brown nations ruled by kings more cruel than Nero the Roman, and more splendid than Solomon the Jew. The old bark lumbered on, heavy with her age and the burden of her cargo, while I lived the life of youth in ignorance and hope. She lumbered on through an interminable procession of days; and the fresh gilding flashed back at the setting sun, seemed to cry out over the darkening sea the words painted on her stern, '*Judea*, London. Do or Die.'

"Then we entered the Indian Ocean and steered northerly for Java Head. The winds were light. Weeks slipped by. She crawled on, do or die, and people at home began to think of posting us as overdue.

"One Saturday evening, I being off duty, the men asked me to give them an extra bucket of water or so—for washing clothes. As I did not wish to screw on the fresh-water pump so late, I went forward whistling, and with a key in my hand to unlock the forepeak scuttle, intending to serve the water out of a spare tank we kept there.

"The smell down below was as unexpected as it was frightful. One would have thought hundreds of paraffin-lamps had been flaring and smoking in that hole for days. I was glad to get out. The man with me coughed and said, 'Funny smell, sir.' I answered negligently, 'It's good for the health they say,' and walked aft.

"The first thing I did was to put my head down the square of the midship ventilator. As I lifted the lid a visible breath, something like a thin fog, a puff of faint haze, rose from the opening. The ascending air was hot, and had a heavy, sooty, paraffiny smell. I gave one sniff, and put down the lid gently. It was no use choking myself. The cargo was on fire.

"Next day she began to smoke in earnest. You see it was to be expected, for though the coal was of a safe kind, that cargo had been so handled, so broken up with handling, that it looked more like smithy coal than anything else. Then it had been wetted—more than once. It rained all the time we were taking it back from the hulk, and now with this long passage it got heated, and there was another case of spontaneous combustion.

"The captain called us into the cabin. He had a chart spread on the table, and looked unhappy. He said, 'The coast of West Australia is near, but I mean to proceed to our destination. It is the hurricane month, too; but we will just keep her head for Bankok, and fight the fire. No more putting back anywhere, if we all get roasted. We will try first to stifle this 'ere damned combustion by want of air.'

"We tried. We battened down everything, and still she smoked. The smoke kept coming out through imperceptible crevices; it forced itself through bulkheads and covers; it oozed here and there and everywhere in slender threads, in an invisible film, in an incomprehensible manner. It made its way into the cabin, into the forecastle; it poisoned the sheltered places on the deck, it could be sniffed as high as the mainyard. It was clear that if the smoke came out the air came in. This was disheartening. This combustion refused to be stifled.

"We resolved to try water, and took the hatches off. Enormous volumes of smoke, whitish, yellowish, thick, greasy, misty, choking, ascended as high as the trucks. All hands cleared out aft. Then the poisonous cloud blew away, and we went back to work in a smoke that was no thicker now than that of an ordinary factory chimney.

"We rigged the force-pump, got the hose along, and by and by it burst. Well, it was as old as the ship—a prehistoric hose, and past repair. Then we pumped with the feeble head-pump, drew water with buckets, and in this way managed in time to pour lots of Indian Ocean into the main hatch. The bright stream flashed in sunshine, fell into a layer of white crawling smoke, and vanished on the black surface of coal. Steam ascended mingling with the smoke. We poured salt water as into a barrel without a bottom. It was our fate to pump in that ship, to pump out of her, to pump into her; and after keeping water out of her to save ourselves from being drowned, we frantically poured water into her to save ourselves from being burnt.

"And she crawled on, do or die, in the serene weather. The sky was a miracle of purity, a miracle of azure. The sea was polished, was blue, was pellucid, was sparkling like a precious stone, extending on all sides, all round to the horizon—as if the whole terrestrial globe had been one jewel, one colossal sapphire, a single gem fashioned into a planet. And on the lustre of the great calm waters the *Judea* glided imperceptibly, enveloped in languid and unclean vapours, in a lazy cloud that drifted to leeward, light and slow; a pestiferous cloud defiling the splendour of sea and sky.

"All this time of course we saw no fire. The cargo smouldered at the bottom somewhere. Once Mahon, as we were working side by side, said to me with a queer smile: 'Now, if she only would spring a tidy leak—like that time when we first left the Channel—it would put a stopper on this fire. Wouldn't it?' I remarked irrelevantly, 'Do you remember the rats?'

"We fought the fire and sailed the ship too as carefully as though nothing had been the matter. The steward cooked and attended on us. Of the other twelve men, eight worked while four rested. Everyone took his turn, captain included. There was equality, and if not exactly fraternity, then a deal of good feeling. Sometimes a man, as he dashed a bucketful of water down the hatchway, would yell out, 'Hurrah for Bankok!' and the rest laughed. But generally we were taciturn and serious—and thirsty. Oh! how thirsty! And we had to be careful with the water. Strict allowance. The ship smoked, the sun blazed... Pass the bottle.

"We tried everything. We even made an attempt to dig down to the fire. No good, of course. No man could remain more than a minute below. Mahon, who went first, fainted there, and the man who went to fetch him out did likewise. We lugged them out on deck. Then I leaped down to show how easily it could be done. They had learned wisdom by that time, and contented themselves by fishing for me with a chain-hook tied to a broom-handle, I believe. I did not offer to go and fetch up my shovel, which was left down below.

"Things began to look bad. We put the long-boat into the water. The second boat was ready to swing out. We had also another, a 14-foot thing, on davits aft, where it was quite safe.

"Then, behold, the smoke suddenly decreased. We redoubled our efforts to flood the bottom of the ship. In two days there was no smoke at all. Everybody was on the broad grin. This was on a Friday. On Saturday no work, but sailing the ship of course, was done. The men washed their clothes and their faces for the first time in a fortnight, and had a special dinner given them. They spoke of spontaneous combustion with contempt, and implied *they* were the boys to put out combustions. Somehow we all felt as though we each had inherited a large fortune. But a beastly smell of burning hung about the ship. Captain Beard had hollow eyes and sunken cheeks. I had never noticed so much before how twisted and bowed he was. He and Mahon prowled soberly about hatches and ventilators, sniffing. It struck me suddenly poor Mahon was a very, very old chap. As to me, I was as pleased and proud as though I had helped to win a great naval battle. O! Youth!

"The night was fine. In the morning a homeward-bound ship passed us hull down—the first we had seen for months; but we were nearing the land at last, Java Head being about 190 miles off, and nearly due north.

"Next day it was my watch on deck from eight to twelve. At breakfast the captain observed, 'It's wonderful how that smell hangs about the cabin.' About ten, the mate being on the poop, I stepped down on the main-deck for a moment. The carpenter's bench stood abaft the mainmast: I leaned against it sucking at my pipe, and the carpenter, a young chap, came to talk to me. He remarked, 'I think we have done very well, haven't we?' and then I perceived with annoyance the fool was trying to tilt the bench. I said curtly, 'Don't, Chips,' and immediately became aware of a queer sensation, of an absurd delusion,—I seemed somehow to be in the air. I heard all round me like a pent-up breath released—as if a thousand giants simultaneously had said Phoo!—and felt a dull concussion which made my ribs ache suddenly. No doubt about it—I was in the air, and my body was describing a short parabola. But short as it was, I had the time to think several thoughts in, as far as I can remember, the following order: 'This can't be the carpenter—What is it?—Some accident—Submarine volcano?—Coals, gas!—By Jove! we are being blown up—Everybody's dead—I am falling into the after-hatch—I see fire in it.'

"The coal-dust suspended in the air of the hold had glowed dull-red at the moment of the explosion. In the twinkling of an eye, in an infinitesimal fraction of a second since the first tilt of the bench, I was sprawling full length on the cargo. I picked myself up and scrambled out. It was quick like a rebound. The deck was a wilderness of smashed timber, lying crosswise like trees in a wood after a hurricane; an immense curtain of soiled rags waved gently before me—it was the mainsail blown to strips. I thought, The masts will be toppling over directly; and to get out of the way bolted on all-fours towards the poop-ladder. The first person I saw was Mahon, with eyes like saucers, his mouth open, and the long white hair standing straight on end round his head like a silver halo. He was just about to go down when the sight of the main-deck stirring, heaving up, and changing into splinters before his eyes, petrified him on the top step. I stared at him in unbelief, and he stared at me with a queer kind of shocked curiosity. I did not know that I had no hair, no eyebrows, no eyelashes, that my young moustache was burnt off, that my face was black, one cheek laid open, my nose cut, and my chin bleeding. I had lost my cap one of my slippers, and my shirt was torn to rags. Of all this I was not aware. I was amazed to see the ship still afloat, the poop-deck whole— and, most of all, to see anybody alive. Also the peace of the sky and the serenity of the sea were distinctly surprising. I suppose I expected to see them convulsed with horror. . . Pass the bottle.

"There was a voice hailing the ship from somewhere—in the air, in the sky—I couldn't tell. Presently I saw the captain—and he was mad. He asked me eagerly, 'Where's the cabin-table?' and to hear such a question was a frightful shock. I had just been blown up, you understand, and vibrated with that experience,—I wasn't quite sure whether I was alive. Mahon began to stamp with both feet and yelled at him, 'Good God! don't you see the deck's blown out of her?' I found my voice, and stammered out as if conscious of some gross neglect of duty, 'I don't know where the cabin-table is.' It was like an absurd dream.

"Do you know what he wanted next? Well, he wanted to trim the yards. Very placidly, and as if lost in thought, he insisted on having the foreyard squared. 'I don't know if there's anybody alive,' said Mahon, almost tearfully. 'Surely,' he said, gently, 'there will be enough left to square the foreyard.'

"The old chap, it seems, was in his own berth winding up the chronometers, when the shock sent him spinning. Immediately it occurred to him—as he said afterwards—that the ship had struck something, and he ran out into the cabin. There, he saw, the cabin-table had vanished some-where. The deck being blown up, it had fallen down into the lazarette of course. Where we had our breakfast that morning he saw only a great hole in the floor. This appeared to him so awfully mysterious, and impressed him so immensely, that what he saw and heard after he got on deck were mere trifles in comparison. And, mark, he noticed directly the wheel deserted and his barque off her course—and his only thought was to get that miser-able, stripped, undecked, smouldering shell of a ship back again with her head pointing at her port of destination. Bankok! That's what he was after. I tell you this quiet, bowed, bandy-legged, almost deformed little man was immense in the singleness of his idea and in his placid ignorance of our agitation. He motioned us forward with a commanding gesture, and went to take the wheel himself.

"Yes; that was the first thing we did—trim the yards of that wreck! No one was killed, or even disabled, but everyone was more or less hurt. You should have seen them! Some were in rags, with black faces, like coal-heavers, like sweeps, and had bullet heads that seemed closely cropped, but were in fact singed to the skin. Others, of the watch below, awakened by being shot out from their collapsing bunks, shivered inces-santly, and kept on groaning even as we went about our work. But they all worked. That crew of Liverpool hard cases had in them the right stuff. It's my experience they always have. It is the sea that gives it—the vastness, the loneliness surrounding their dark stolid souls. Ah! Well! we stumbled, we crept, we fell, we barked our shins on the wreckage, we hauled. The masts stood, but we did not know how much they might be charred down below. It was nearly calm, but a long swell ran from the west and made her roll. They might go at any moment. We looked at them with apprehen-sion. One could not foresee which way they would fall.

"Then we retreated aft and looked about us. The deck was a tangle of planks on edge, of planks on end, of splinters, of ruined woodwork. The masts rose from that chaos like big trees above a matted undergrowth. The interstices of that mass or wreckage were full of something whitish, slug-gish, stirring—of something that was like a greasy fog. The smoke of the invisible fire was coming up again, was trailing, like a poisonous thick mist in some valley choked with dead wood. Already lazy wisps were beginning to curl upwards amongst the mass of splinters. Here and there a piece of timber, stuck upright, resembled a post. Half of a fife-rail had been shot through the foresail, and the sky made a patch of glorious blue in the ignobly soiled canvas. A portion of several boards holding together had fallen across the rail, and one end protruded overboard, like a gangway leading upon nothing, like a gangway leading over the deep sea, leading to death—as if inviting us to walk the plank at once and be done with our ridiculous troubles. And still the air, the sky—a ghost, something invisible was hailing the ship.

"Someone had the sense to look over, and there was the helmsman, who had impulsively jumped overboard, anxious to come back. He yelled and swam lustily like a merman, keeping up with the ship. We threw him a rope, and presently he stood amongst us streaming with water and very crestfallen. The captain had surrendered the wheel, and apart, elbow on rail and chin in hand, gazed at the sea wistfully. We asked ourselves, What next? I thought, Now, this is something like. This is great. I wonder what will happen. O youth!

"Suddenly Mahon sighted a steamer far astern. Captain Beard said, 'We may do something with her yet.' We hoisted two flags, which said in the international language of the sea, 'On fire. Want immediate assistance.' The steamer grew bigger rapidly, and by and by spoke with two flags on her foremast, 'I am coming to your assistance.'

"In half an hour she was abreast, to windward, within hail, and rolling slightly, with her engines stopped. We lost our composure, and yelled all together with excitement, 'We've been blown up'. A man in a white helmet, on the bridge, cried, 'Yes! All right! all right!' and he nodded his head, and smiled, and made soothing motions with his hand as though at a lot of frightened children. One of the boats dropped in the water, and walked towards us upon the sea with her long oars. Four Calashes pulled a swinging stroke. This was my first sight of Malay seamen. I've known them since, but what struck me then was their unconcern: they came alongside, and even the bowman standing up and holding to our main-chains with the boat-hook did not deign to lift his head for a glance. I thought people who had been blown up deserved more attention.

"A little man, dry like a chip and agile like a monkey, clambered up. It was the mate of the steamer. He gave one look, and cried, 'O boys—you had better quit.'

"We were silent. He talked apart with the captain for a time—seemed to argue with him. Then they went away together to the steamer.

"When our skipper came back we learned that the steamer was the *Somerville*, Captain Nash, from West Australia to Singapore *via* Batavia with mails, and that the agreement was she should tow us to Anjer or Batavia, if possible, where we could extinguish the fire by scuttling, and then proceed on our voyage—to Bankok! The old man seemed excited. 'We will do it yet,' he said to Mahon, fiercely. He shook his fist at the sky. Nobody else said a word.

"At noon the steamer began to tow. She went ahead slim and high, and what was left of the *Judea* followed at the end of seventy fathom of tow-rope,—followed her swiftly like a cloud of smoke with mast-heads protruding above. We went aloft to furl the sails. We coughed on the yards, and were careful about the bunts. Do you see the lot of us there, putting a neat furl on the sails of that ship doomed to arrive nowhere? There was not a man who didn't think that at any moment the masts would topple over. From aloft we could not see the ship for smoke, and they worked carefully, passing the gaskets with even turns. 'Harbour furl—aloft there!' cried Mahon from below.

"You understand this? I don't think one of those chaps expected to get down in the usual way. When we did I heard them saying to each other, 'Well, I thought we would come down overboard, in a lump—sticks and all—blame me if I didn't.' 'That's what I was thinking to myself,' would answer wearily another battered and bandaged scarecrow. And, mind, these were men without the drilled-in habit of obedience. To an onlooker they would be a lot of profane scallywags without a redeeming point. What made them do it—what made them obey me when I, thinking consciously how fine it was, made them drop the bunt of the foresail twice to try and do it better? What? They had no professional reputation—no examples, no praise. It wasn't a sense of duty; they all knew well enough how to shirk, and laze, and dodge—when they had a mind to it—and mostly they had. Was it the two pounds ten a-month that sent them there? They didn't think their pay half good enough. No; it was some-thing in them, something inborn and subtle and everlasting. I don't say positively that the crew of a French or German merchantman wouldn't have done it, but I doubt whether it would have been done in the same way. There was a completeness in it, something solid like a principle, and masterful like an instinct—a disclosure of something secret—of that hid-den something, that gift of good or evil that makes racial difference, that shapes the face of nations.

"It was that night at ten that, for the first time since we had been fight-ing it, we saw the fire. The speed of the towing had fanned the smoulder-ing destruction. A blue gleam appeared forward, shining below the wreck of the deck. It wavered in patches, it seemed to stir and creep like the light of a glowworm. I saw it first, and told Mahon. 'Then the game's up,' he said. 'We had better stop this towing, or she will burst out suddenly fore and aft before we can clear out.' We set up a yell; rang bells to attract their attention; they towed on. At last Mahon and I had to crawl forward and cut the rope with an axe. There was no time to cast off the lashings. Red tongues could be seen licking the wilderness of splinters under our feet as we made our way back to the poop.

"Of course they very soon found out in the steamer that the rope was gone. She gave a loud blast of her whistle, her lights were seen sweeping in a wide circle, she came up ranging close along-side, and stopped. We were all in a tight group on the poop looking at her. Every man had saved a little bundle or a bag. Suddenly a conical flame with a twisted top shot up forward and threw upon the black sea a circle of light, with the two vessels side by side and heaving gently in its centre. Captain Beard had been sitting on the gratings still and mute for hours, but now he rose slowly and advanced in front of us, to the mizzen-shrouds. Captain Nash hailed: 'Come along! Look sharp. I have mail-bags on board. I will take you and your boats to Singapore.'

" 'Thank you! No!' said our skipper. 'We must see the last of the ship.'

" 'I can't stand by any longer,' shouted the other. 'Mails—you know.'

" 'Ay! ay! We are all right.'

" 'Very well! I'll report you in Singapore... Good-bye!'

"He waved his hand. Our men dropped their bundles quietly. The steamer moved ahead, and passing out of the circle of light, vanished at once from our sight, dazzled by the fire which burned fiercely. And then I knew that I would see the East first as commander of a small boat. I thought it fine; and the fidelity to the old ship was fine. We should see the last of her. Oh, the glamour of youth! Oh, the fire of it, more dazzling than the flames of the burning ship, throwing a magic light on the wide earth, leaping audaciously to the sky, presently to be quenched by time, more cruel, more pitiless, more bitter than the sea—and like the flames of the burning ship surrounded by an impenetrable night.

"The old man warned us in his gentle and inflexible way that it was part of our duty to save for the underwriters as much as we could of the ship's gear. Accordingly we went to work aft, while she blazed forward to give us plenty of light. We lugged out a lot of rubbish. What didn't we save? An old barometer fixed with an absurd quantity of screws nearly cost me my life: a sudden rush of smoke came upon me, and I just got away in time. There were various stores, bolts of canvas, coils of rope; the poop looked like a marine bazaar, and the boats were lumbered to the gunwales. One would have thought the old man wanted to take as much as he could of his first command with him. He was very, very quiet, but off his balance evidently. Would you believe it? He wanted to take a length of old stream-cable and a kedge-anchor with him in the long-boat. We said, 'Ay, ay, sir,' deferentially, and on the quiet let the things slip overboard. The heavy medicine-chest went that way, two bags of green coffee, tins of paint—fancy, paint!—a whole lot of things. Then I was ordered with two hands into the boats to make a stowage and get them ready against the time it would be proper for us to leave the ship.

"We put everything straight, stepped the long-boat's mast for our skipper, who was to take charge of her, and I was not sorry to sit down for a moment. My face felt raw, every limb ached as if broken, I was aware of all my ribs, and would have sworn to a twist in the backbone. The boats, fast astern, lay in a deep shadow, and all around I could see the circle of the sea lighted by the fire. A gigantic flame arose forward straight and clear. It flared fierce, with noises like the whirr of wings, with rumbles as of thunder. There were cracks, detonations, and from the cone of flame the sparks flew upwards, as man is born to trouble, to leaky ships, and to ships that burn.

"What bothered me was that the ship, lying broadside to the swell and to such wind as there was—a mere breath—the boats would not keep astern where they were safe, but persisted, in a pig-headed way boats have, in getting under the counter and then swinging alongside. They were knocking about dangerously and coming near the flame, while the ship rolled on them, and, of course, there was always the danger of the masts going over the side at any moment. I and my two boat-keepers kept them off as best we could, with oars and boat-hooks; but to be constantly at it became exasperating, since there was no reason why we should not leave at once. We could not see those on board, nor could we imagine what caused the delay. The boatkeepers were swearing feebly, and I had not only my share of the work but also had to keep at it two men who showed a constant inclination to lay themselves down and let things slide.

"At last I hailed, 'On deck there,' and someone looked over. 'We're ready here,' I said. The head disappeared, and very soon popped up again. 'The captain says, All right, sir, and to keep the boats well clear of the ship.'

"Half an hour passed. Suddenly there was a frightful racket, rattle, clanking of chain, hiss of water, and millions of sparks flew up into the shivering column of smoke that stood leaning slightly above the ship.

The cat-heads had burned away, and the two red-hot anchors had gone to the bottom, tearing out after them two hundred fathom of red-hot chain. The ship trembled, the mass of flame swayed as if ready to collapse, and the fore top-gallant-mast fell. It darted down like an arrow of fire, shot under, and instantly leaping up within an oar's-length of the boats, floated quietly, very black on the luminous sea. I hailed the deck again. After some time a man in an unexpectedly cheerful but also muffled tone, as though he had been trying to speak with his mouth shut, informed me, 'Coming directly, sir,' and vanished. For a long time I heard nothing but the whirr and roar of the fire. There were also whistling sounds. The boats jumped, tugged at the painters, ran at each other playfully, knocked their sides together, or, do what we would, swung in a bunch against the ship's side. I couldn't stand it any longer, and swarming up a rope, clambered aboard over the stern.

"It was as bright as day. Coming up like this, the sheet of fire facing me was a terrifying sight, and the heat seemed hardly bearable at first. On a settee cushion dragged out of the cabin Captain Beard, his legs drawn up and one arm under his head, slept with the light playing on him. Do you know what the rest were busy about? They were sitting on deck right aft, round an open case, eating bread and cheese and drinking bottled stout.

"On the background of flames twisting in fierce tongues above their heads they seemed at home like salamanders, and looked like a band of desperate pirates. The fire sparkled in the whites of their eyes, gleamed on patches of white skin seen through the torn shirts. Each had the marks as of a battle about him—bandaged heads, tied-up arms, a strip of dirty rag round a knee—and each man had a bottle between his legs and a chunk of cheese in his hand. Mahon got up. With his handsome and disreputable head, his hooked profile, his long white beard, and with an uncorked bottle in his hand, he resembled one of those reckless sea-robbers of old making merry amidst violence and disaster. 'The last meal on board,' he explained solemnly. 'We had nothing to eat all day, and it was no use leaving all this.' He flourished the bottle and indicated the sleeping skipper. 'He said he couldn't swallow anything, so I got him to lie down,' he went on; and as I stared, 'I don't know whether you are aware, young fellow, the man had no sleep to speak of for days—and there will be dam' little sleep in the boats.' 'There will be no boats by-and-by if you fool about much longer,' I said, indignantly. I walked up to the skipper and shook him by the shoulder. At last he opened his eyes, but did not move. 'Time to leave her, sir,' I said quietly.

"He got up painfully, looked at the flames, at the sea sparkling round the ship, and black, black as ink farther away; he looked at the stars shining dim through a thin veil of smoke in a sky black, black as Erebus.

" 'Youngest first,' he said.

"And the ordinary seaman, wiping his mouth with the back of his hand, got up, clambered over the taffrail, and vanished. Others followed. One, on the point of going over, stopped short to drain his bottle, and with a great swing of his arm flung it at the fire. 'Take this!' he cried.

"The skipper lingered disconsolately, and we left him to commune alone for a while with his first command. Then I went up again and brought him away at last. It was time. The ironwork on the poop was hot to the touch.

"Then the painter of the long-boat was cut, and the three boats, tied together, drifted clear of the ship. It was just sixteen hours after the explosion when we abandoned her. Mahon had charge of the second boat, and I had the smallest—the 14-foot thing. The longboat would have taken the lot of us; but the skipper said we must save as much property as we could—for the underwriters—and so I got my first command. I had two men with me, a bag of biscuits, a few tins of meat, and a breaker of water. I was ordered to keep close to the long-boat, that in case of bad weather we might be taken into her.

"And do you know what I thought? I thought I would part company as soon as I could. I wanted to have my first command all to myself. I wasn't going to sail in a squadron if there were a chance for independent cruising. I would make land by myself. I would beat the other boats. Youth! All youth! The silly, charming, beautiful youth.

"But we did not make a start at once. We must see the last of the ship. And so the boats drifted about that night, heaving and setting on the swell. The men dozed, waked, sighed, groaned. I looked at the burning ship.

"Between the darkness of earth and heaven she was burning fiercely upon a disc of purple sea shot by the blood-red play of gleams; upon a disc of water glittering and sinister. A high, clear flame, an immense and lonely flame, ascended from the ocean, and from its summit the black smoke poured continuously at the sky. She burned furiously; mournful and imposing like a funeral pile kindled in the night, surrounded by the sea, watched over by the stars. A magnificent death had come like a grace, like a gift, like a reward to that old ship at the end of her laborious days. The surrender of her weary ghost to the keeping of stars and sea was stirring like the sight of a glorious triumph. The masts fell just before daybreak, and for a moment there was a burst and turmoil of sparks that seemed to fill with flying fire the night patient and watchful, the vast night lying silent upon the sea. At daylight she was only a charred shell, floating still under a cloud of smoke and bearing a glowing mass of coal within.

"Then the oars were got out, and the boats forming in a line moved round her remains as if in procession—the long-boat leading. As we pulled across her stern a slim dart of fire shot out viciously at us, and suddenly she went down, head first, in a great hiss of steam. The unconsumed stern was the last to sink; but the paint had gone, had cracked, had peeled off, and there were no letters, there was no word, no stubborn device that was like her soul, to flash at the rising sun her creed and her name.

"We made our way north. A breeze sprang up, and about noon all the boats came together for the last time. I had no mast or sail in mine, but I made a mast out of a spare oar and hoisted a boat-awning for a sail, with a boat-hook for a yard. She was certainly over-masted, but I had the satisfaction of knowing that with the wind aft I could beat the other two. I had to wait for them. Then we all had a look at the captain's chart, and, after a sociable meal of hard bread and water, got our last instructions. These were simple: steer north, and keep together as much as possible. 'Be careful with that jury-rig, Marlow,' said the captain; and Mahon, as I sailed proudly past his boat, wrinkled his curved nose and hailed, 'You will sail that ship of yours under water, if you don't look out, young fellow.' He was a malicious old man—and may the deep sea where he sleeps now rock him gently, rock him tenderly to the end of time!

"Before sunset a thick rain-squall passed over the two boats, which were far astern, and that was the last I saw of them for a time. Next day I sat steering my cockle-shell—my first command—with nothing but water and sky around me. I did sight in the afternoon the upper sails of a ship far away, but said nothing, and my men did not notice her. You see I was afraid she might be homeward bound, and I had no mind to turn back from the portals of the East. I was steering for Java—another blessed name—like Bankok, you know. I steered many days.

"I need not tell you what it is to be knocking about in an open boat. I remember nights and days of calm, when we pulled, we pulled, and the boat seemed to stand still, as if bewitched within the circle of the sea horizon. I remember the heat, the deluge of rainsqualls that kept us baling for dear life (but filled our water-cask), and I remember sixteen hours on end with a mouth dry as a cinder and a steering-oar over the stern to keep my first command head on to a breaking sea. I did not know how good a man

I was till then. I remember the drawn faces, the dejected figures of my two men, and I remember my youth and the feeling that will never come back any more—the feeling that I could last for ever, outlast the sea, the earth, and all men; the deceitful feeling that lures us on to joys, to perils, to love, to vain effort—to death; the triumphant conviction of strength, the heat of life in the handful of dust, the glow in the heart that with every year grows dim, grows cold, grows small, and expires—and expires, too soon, too soon—before life itself.

"And this is how I see the East. I have seen its secret places and have looked into its very soul; but now I see it always from a small boat, a high outline of mountains, blue and afar in the morning; like faint mist at noon; a jagged wall of purple at sunset. I have the feel of the oar in my hand, the vision of a scorching blue sea in my eyes. And I see a bay, a wide bay, smooth as glass and polished like ice, shimmering in the dark. A red light burns far off upon the gloom of the land, and the night is soft and warm. We drag at the oars with aching arms, and suddenly a puff of wind, a puff faint and tepid and laden with strange odours of blossoms, of aromatic wood, comes out of the still night—the first sigh of the East on my face. That I can never forget. It was impalpable and enslaving, like a charm, like a whispered promise of mysterious delight.

"We had been pulling this finishing spell for eleven hours. Two pulled, and he whose turn it was to rest sat at the tiller. We had made out the red light in that bay and steered for it, guessing it must mark some small coasting port. We passed two vessels, outlandish and high-sterned, sleeping at anchor, and, approaching the light, now very dim, ran the boat's nose against the end of a jutting wharf. We were blind with fatigue. My men dropped the oars and fell off the thwarts as if dead. I made fast to a pile. A current rippled softly. The scented obscurity of the shore was grouped into vast masses, a density of colossal clumps of vegetation, probably—mute and fantastic shapes. And at their foot the semicircle of a beach gleamed faintly, like an illusion. There was not a light, not a stir, not a sound. The mysterious East faced me, perfumed like a flower, silent like death, dark like a grave.

"And I sat weary beyond expression, exulting like a conqueror, sleepless and entranced as if before a profound, a fateful enigma.

"A splashing of oars, a measured dip reverberating on the level of water, intensified by the silence of the shore into loud claps, made me jump up. A boat, a European boat, was coming in. I invoked the name of the dead; I hailed: *Judea* ahoy! A thin shout answered.

"It was the captain. I had beaten the flagship by three hours, and I was glad to hear the old man's voice again, tremulous and tired. 'Is it you, Marlow?' 'Mind the end of that jetty, sir,' I cried.

"He approached cautiously, and brought up with the deep-sea lead-line which we had saved—for the underwriters. I eased my painter and fell alongside. He sat, a broken figure at the stern, wet with dew, his hands clasped in his lap. His men were asleep already. 'I had a terrible time of it,' he murmured. 'Mahon is behind—not very far.' We conversed in whispers, in low whispers, as if afraid to wake up the land. Guns, thunder, earthquakes would not have awakened the men just then.

"Looking round as we talked, I saw away at sea a bright light travelling in the night. 'There's a steamer passing the bay,' I said. She was not passing, she was entering, and she even came close and anchored. 'I wish,' said the old man, 'you would find out whether she is English. Perhaps they could give us a passage somewhere.' He seemed nervously anxious. So by dint of punching and kicking I started one of my men into a state of somnambulism, and giving him an oar, took another and pulled towards the lights of the steamer.

"There was a murmur of voices in her, metallic hollow clangs of the engine-room, footsteps on the deck. Her ports shone, round like dilated eyes. Shapes moved about, and there was a shadowy man high up on the bridge. He heard my oars.

"And then, before I could open my lips, the East spoke to me, but it was in a Western voice. A torrent of words was poured into the enigmatical, the fateful silence; outlandish, angry words, mixed with words and even whole sentences of good English, less strange but even more surprising. The voice swore and cursed violently; it riddled the solemn peace of the bay by a volley of abuse. It began by calling me Pig, and from that went crescendo into unmentionable adjectives—in English. The man up there raged aloud in two languages, and with a sincerity in his fury that almost convinced me I had, in some way, sinned against the harmony of the universe. I could hardly see him, but began to think he would work himself into a fit.

"Suddenly he ceased, and I could hear him snorting and blowing like a porpoise. I said—

" 'What steamer is this, pray?'

" 'Eh? What's this? And who are you?'

" 'Castaway crew of an English barque burnt at sea. We came here to-night. I am the second mate. The captain is in the long-boat, and wishes to know if you would give us a passage somewhere.'

" 'Oh, my goodness! I say. . . This is the *Celestial* from Singapore on her return trip. I'll arrange with your captain in the morning. . . and. . . I say. . . did you hear me just now?'

" 'I should think the whole bay heard you.'

" 'I thought you were a shore-boat. Now, look here—this infernal lazy scoundrel of a caretaker has gone to sleep again—curse him. The light is out, and I nearly ran foul of the end of this damned jetty. This is the third time he plays me this trick. Now, I ask you, can anybody stand this kind of thing? It's enough to drive a man out of his mind. I'll report him. . . . I'll get the Assistant Resident to give him the sack, by. . . ! See—there's no light. It's out, isn't it? I take you to witness the light's out. There should be a light, you know. A red light on the——'

" 'There was a light,' I said, mildly.

" 'But it's out, man! What's the use of talking like this? You can see for yourself it's out—don't you? If you had to take a valuable steamer along this Godforsaken coast you would want a light, too. I'll kick him from end to end of his miserable wharf. You'll see if I don't. I will——'

" 'So I may tell my captain you'll take us?' I broke in.

" 'Yes, I'll take you. Good-night,' he said, brusquely

"I pulled back, made fast again to the jetty, and then went to sleep at last. I had faced the silence of the East. I had heard some of its language. But when I opened my eyes again the silence was as complete as though it had never been broken. I was lying in a flood of light, and the sky had never looked so far, so high, before. I opened my eyes and lay without moving.

"And then I saw the men of the East—they were looking at me. The whole length of the jetty was full of people. I saw brown, bronze, yellow faces, the black eyes, the glitter, the colour of an Eastern crowd. And all these beings stared without a murmur, without a sigh, without a move-ment. They stared down at the boats, at the sleeping men who at night had come to them from the sea. Nothing moved. The fronds of palms stood still against the sky. Not a branch stirred along the shore, and the brown roofs of hidden houses peeped through the green foliage, through the big leaves that hung shining and still like leaves forged of heavy metal. This was the East of the ancient navigators, so old, so mysterious, resplendent and sombre, living and unchanged, full of danger and promise. And these were the men. I sat up suddenly. A wave of movement passed through the crowd from end to end, passed along the heads, swayed the bodies, ran along the jetty like a ripple on the water, like a breath of wind on a field—and all was still again. I see it now—the wide sweep of the bay, the glittering sands, the wealth of green infinite and varied, the sea blue like the sea of a dream, the crowd of attentive faces, the blaze of vivid colour—the water reflecting it all, the curve of the shore, the jetty, the high-sterned outlandish craft floating still, and the three boats with the tired men from the West sleeping, unconscious of the land and the people and of the violence of sunshine. They slept thrown across the thwarts, curled on bottom-boards, in the careless attitudes of death. The head of the old skipper, leaning back in the stern of the long-boat, had fallen on his breast, and he looked as though he would never wake. Farther out old Mahon's face was upturned to the sky, with the long white beard spread out on his breast, as though he had been shot where he sat at the tiller; and a man, all in a heap in the bows of the boat, slept with both arms embracing the stem-head and with his cheek laid on the gunwale. The East looked at them without a sound.

"I have known its fascination since; I have seen the mysterious shores, the still water, the lands of brown nations, where a stealthy Nemesis lies in wait, pursues, overtakes so many of the conquering race, who are proud of their wisdom, of their knowledge, of their strength. But for me all the East is contained in that vision of my youth. It is all in that moment when I opened my young eyes on it. I came upon it from a tussle with the sea— and I was young—and I saw it looking at me. And this is all that is left of it! Only a moment; a moment of strength, of romance, of glamour—of youth! A flick of sunshine upon a strange shore, the time to remember, the time for a sigh, and—good-bye!—Night—Good-bye!"

He drank.

"Ah! The good old time—the good old time. Youth and the sea. Glamour and the sea! The good, strong sea, the salt, bitter sea, that could whisper to you and roar at you and knock your breath out of you."

He drank again.

"By all that's wonderful it is the sea, I believe, the sea itself—or is it youth alone? Who can tell? But you here—you all had something out of life: money, love—whatever one gets on shore—and, tell me, wasn't that the best time, that time when we were young at sea; young and had nothing, on the sea that gives nothing, except hard knocks—and sometimes a chance to feel your strength—that only—what you all regret?"

And we all nodded at him: the man of finance, the man of accounts, the man of law, we all nodded at him over the polished table that like a still sheet of brown water reflected our faces, lined, wrinkled; our faces marked by toil, by deceptions, by success, by love; our weary eyes looking still, looking always, looking anxiously for something out of life, that while it is expected is already gone—has passed unseen, in a sigh, in a flash— together with the youth, with the strength, with the romance of illusions.

THE SINGULAR FATE OF THE BRIG POLLY

RALPH D. PAINE

Steam has not banished from the deep sea the ships that lift tall spires of canvas to win their way from port to port. The gleam of their top-sails recalls the centuries in which men wrought with stubborn courage to fashion fabrics of wood and cordage that should survive the enmity of the implacable ocean and make the winds obedient. Their genius was unsung, their hard toil forgotten, but with each generation the sailing ship became nobler and more enduring, until it was a perfect thing. Its great days live in memory with a peculiar atmosphere of romance. Its humming shrouds were vibrant with the eternal call of the sea, and in a phantom fleet pass the towering East Indiaman, the hard-driven Atlantic packet, and the gracious clipper that fled before the Southern trades.

A hundred years ago every bay and inlet of the New England coast was building ships which fared bravely forth to the West Indies, to the roadsteads of Europe, to the mysterious havens of the Far East. They sailed in peril of pirate and privateer, and fought these rascals as sturdily as they battled with wicked weather. Coasts were unlighted, the seas uncharted, and navigation was mostly by guesswork, but these seamen were the flower of an American merchant marine whose deeds are heroic in the nation's story. Great hearts in little ships, they dared and suffered with simple, uncomplaining fortitude. Shipwreck was an incident, and to be adrift in lonely seas or cast upon a barbarous shore was sadly commonplace. They lived the stuff that made fiction after they were gone.

Your fancy may be able to picture the brig *Polly* as she steered down Boston harbour in December, 1811, bound to Santa Cruz with lumber and salted provisions for the slaves of the sugar plantations. She was only a hundred and thirty tons burden and perhaps eighty feet long. Rather clumsy to look at and roughly built was the *Polly* as compared with the larger ships that brought home the China tea and silks to the warehouses of Salem. Such a ship was a community venture. The blacksmith, the rigger, and the calker took their pay in shares, or 'pieces.' They became part owners, as did likewise the merchant who supplied stores and material; and when the brig was afloat, the master, the mate, and even the seamen were allowed cargo space for commodities that they might buy and sell to their own advantage. A voyage directly concerned a whole neighbourhood.

Every coastwise village had a row of keel-blocks sloping to the tide. In winter weather too rough for fishing, when the farms lay idle, the Yankee Jack-of-all-trades plied with his axe and adze to shape the timbers and peg together such a little vessel as the *Polly*, in which to trade to London or Cadiz or the Windward Islands. Hampered by an unfriendly climate, hard put to it to grow sufficient food, with land immensely difficult to clear, the New Englander was between the devil and the deep sea, and he sagaciously, chose the latter. Elsewhere, in the early days, the forest was an enemy to be destroyed with great pains. The pioneers of Massachusetts, New Hampshire, and Maine regarded it with favour as the stuff with which to make stout ships and the straight masts they 'stepped' in them.

Nowadays, such a little craft as the *Polly* would be rigged as a schooner. The brig is obsolete, along with the quaint array of scows, ketches, pinks, brigantines and sloops which once filled the harbours and hove their hempen cables short to the clank of the windlass or capstan-pawl, while the brisk seamen sang a chanty to help the work along. The *Polly* had yards on both masts, and it was a bitter task to lay out in a gale of wind and reef the unwieldy single topsails. She would try for no record passages, but jogged sedately, and snugged down when the weather threatened.

On this tragic voyage she carried a small crew, Captain W. L. Cazneau, a mate, four sailors, and a cook who was a native Indian. No mention is to be found of any ill omens that forecasted disaster, such as a black cat, or a cross-eyed Finn in the forecastle. Two passengers were on board, "Mrs. J. S. Hunt and a negro girl nine years old." We know nothing whatever about Mr. Hunt, who may have been engaged in some trading 'adventure' of his own. Perhaps his kinsfolk had waved him a fare-ye-well from the pier-head when the *Polly* warped out of her berth.

The lone piccaninny is more intriguing. She appeals to the imagination and inspires conjecture. Was she a waif of the slave traffic whom some benevolent merchant of Boston was sending to Santa Cruz to find a home beneath kindlier skies? Had she been entrusted to the care of Mr. Hunt? She is unexplained, a pitiful atom visible for an instant on the tide of human destiny. She amused the sailors, no doubt, and that austere, copper-hued cook may have unbent to give her a doughnut when she grinned at the galley-door.

Four days out from Boston, on December 15, the *Polly* had cleared the perilous sands of Cape Cod and the hidden shoals of the Georges. Mariners were profoundly grateful when they, had safely worked off shore in the wintertime and were past Cape Cod, which bore a very evil repute in those days of square-rigged vessels. Captain Cazneau could recall that sombre day of 1802 when three fine ships, the *Ulysses, Brutus,* and *Volusia,* sailing together from Salem for European ports, were wrecked next day on Cape Cod. The fate of those who were washed ashore alive was most melancholy. Several died of the cold, or were choked by the sand which covered them after they fell exhausted.

As in other regions where shipwrecks were common, some of the natives of Cape Cod regarded a ship on the beach as their rightful plunder. It was old Parson Lewis of Wellfleet, who, from his pulpit window, saw a vessel drive ashore on a stormy Sunday morning. "He closed his Bible, put on his outside garment, and descended from the pulpit, not explaining his intention until he was in the aisle, and then he cried out 'Start fair' and took to his legs. The congregation understood and chased pell-mell after him."

The brig *Polly* laid her course to the southward and sailed into the safer, milder waters of the Gulf Stream. The skipper's load of anxiety was lightened. He had not been sighted and molested by the British men-of-war that cruised off Boston and New York to hold up Yankee merchantmen and impress stout seamen. This grievance was to flame in a righteous war only a few months later. Many a voyage was ruined, and ships had to limp back to port short-handed, because their best men had been kidnapped to serve in British ships. It was an age when might was right on the sea.

The storm which overwhelmed the brig *Polly* came out of the south-east, when she was less than a week on the road to Santa Cruz. To be dismasted and water logged was no uncommon fate. It happens often nowadays, when little schooners creep along the coast, from Maine and Nova Scotia ports, and dare the winter blows to earn their bread. Men suffer in open boats, as has been the seafarer's hard lot for ages, and they drown with none to hear their cries, but they are seldom adrift more than a few days. The story of the *Polly* deserves to be rescued from oblivion because, so far as I am able to discover, it is unique in the spray-swept annals of maritime disaster.

Seamanship was helpless to ward off the attack of the storm that left the brig a sodden hulk. Courageously her crew shortened sail and made all secure when the sea and sky presaged a change of weather. There were no green hands, but men seasoned by the continual hazards of their calling. The wild gale smote them in the darkness of the night. They tried to heave the vessel to, but she was battered and wrenched without mercy. Stout canvas was whirled away in fragments. The seams of the hull opened as she laboured, and six feet of water flooded the hold. Leaking like a sieve, the *Polly* would never see port again.

Worse was to befall her. At midnight she was capsized, or thrown on her beam-ends, as the sailor's lingo has it. She lay on her side while the clamorous seas washed clean over her. The skipper, the mate, the four seamen, and the cook somehow clung to the rigging and grimly refused to be drowned. They were of the old breed, "every hair a rope-yarn and every finger a fish-hook." They even managed to find an axe and grope their way to the shrouds in the faint hope that the brig might right if the masts went overside. They hacked away, and came up to breathe now and then, until the foremast and mainmast fell with a crash, and the wreck rolled level. Then they slashed with their knives at the tangle of spars and ropes until they drifted clear. As the waves rush across a half-tide rock, so they broke over the shattered brig, but she no longer wallowed on her side.

At last the stormy daylight broke. The mariners had survived, and they looked to find their two passengers, who had no other refuge than the cabin. Mr. Hunt was gone, blotted out with his affairs and his ambitions, whatever they were. The coloured child they had vainly tried to find in the night. When the sea boiled into the cabin and filled it, she had climbed to the sky-light in the roof, and there she clung like a bat. They hauled her out through a splintered gap, and sought tenderly to shelter her in a corner of the streaming deck, but she lived no more than a few hours. It was better that this bit of human flotsam should flutter out in this way than to linger a little longer in this forlorn derelict of a ship. The *Polly* could not sink, but she drifted as a mere bundle of boards with the ocean winds and currents, while seven men tenaciously fought off death and prayed for rescue.

The gale blew itself out, the sea rolled blue and gentle, and the wreck moved out into the Atlantic, having veered beyond the eastern edge of the Gulf Stream. There was raw salt pork and beef to eat, nothing else, barrels of which they fished out of the cargo. A keg of water which had been lashed to the quarter-deck was found to contain thirty gallons. This was all there was to drink, for the other water-casks had been smashed or carried away. The diet of meat pickled in brine aggravated the thirst of these castaways. For twelve days they chewed on this salty raw stuff, and then the Indian cook, Moho by name, actually succeeded in kindling a fire by rubbing two sticks together in some abstruse manner handed down by his ancestors. By splitting pine spars and a bit of oaken rail he was able to find in the heart of them wood which had not been dampened by the sea, and he sweated and grunted until the great deed was done. It was a trick which he was not at all sure of repeating unless the conditions were singularly favourable. Fortunately for the hapless crew of the *Polly*, their Puritan grandsires had failed in their amiable endeavour to extinguish the aborigine.

The tiny galley, or 'camboose' as they called it, was lashed to ring-bolts in the deck, and had not been washed into the sea when the brig was swept clean. So now they patched it up and got a blaze going in the brick oven. The meat could be boiled, and they ate it without stint, assuming that a hundred barrels of it remained in the hold. It had not been discov-ered that the stern-post of the vessel was staved in under water and all of the cargo excepting some of the lumber had floated out.

The cask of water was made to last eighteen days by serving out a quart a day to each man. Then an occasional rain-squall saved them for a little longer from perishing of thirst. At the end of the forty days they had come to the last morsel of salt meat. The *Polly* was following an aimless course to the eastward, drifting slowly under the influence of ocean winds and currents. These gave her also a southerly slant, so that she was caught by the vast movement of water which is known as the Gulf Stream Drift. It sets over toward the coast of Africa and sweeps into the Gulf of Guinea.

The derelict was moving away from the routes of trade to Europe into the almost trackless spaces beneath the tropic sun, where the sea glittered empty to the horizon. There was a remote chance that she might be descried by a low-hulled slaver crowding for the West Indies under a mighty press of sail, with her human freightage jammed between decks to endure the unspeakable horrors of the Middle Passage. Although the oceans were populous with ships a hundred years ago, trade flowed on habitual routes. Moreover, a wreck might pass unseen two or three miles away. From the quarter-deck of a small sailing ship there was no such circle of vision as extends from the bridge of a steamer forty or sixty feet above the water, where the officers gaze through high-powered binoculars.

The crew of the *Polly* stared at skies which yielded not the merciful gift of rain. They had strength to build them a sort of shelter of lumber, but whenever the weather was rough, they were drenched by the waves which played over the wreck. At the end of fifty days of this hardship and torment the seven were still alive, but then the mate, Mr. Paddock, languished and died. It surprised his companions, for, as the old record runs,

> he was a man of robust constitution who had spent his life in fishing on the Grand Banks, was accustomed to endure privations, and appeared the most capable of standing the shocks of misfortune of any of the crew. In the meridian of life, being about thirty-five years old, it was reasonable to suppose that, instead of the first, he would have been the last to fall a sacrifice to hunger and thirst and exposure, but Heaven ordered it otherwise.

Singularly enough, the next to go was a young seaman, spare and active, who was also a fisherman by trade. His name was Howe. He survived six days longer than the mate, and "likewise died delirious and in dreadful distress." Fleeting thunder-showers had come to save the others, and they had caught a large shark by means of a running bowline slipped over his tail while he nosed about the weedy hull. This they cut up and doled out for many days. It was certain, however, that unless they could obtain water to drink they would soon all be dead men on the *Polly*.

Captain Cazneau seems to have been a sailor of extraordinary resource and resolution. His was the unbreakable will to live and to endure which kept the vital spark flickering in his shipmates. Whenever there was strength enough among them, they groped in the water in the hold and cabin in the desperate hope of finding something to serve their needs. In this manner they salvaged an iron tea-kettle and one of the captain's flint-lock pistols. Instead of flinging them away, he sat down to cogitate, a gaunt, famished wraith of a man who had kept his wits and knew what to do with them.

At length he took an iron pot from the galley, turned the tea-kettle upside down on it, and found that the rims failed to fit together. Undismayed, the skipper whittled a wooden collar with a seaman's sheath-knife, and so joined the pot and the kettle. With strips of cloth and pitch scraped from the deck-beams, he was able to make a tight union where his round wooden frame set into the flaring rim of the pot. Then he knocked off the stock of the pistol and had the long barrel to use for a tube. This he rammed into the nozzle of the tea-kettle, and calked them as well as he could. The result was a crude apparatus for distilling sea-water, when placed upon the bricked oven of the galley.

Imagine those three surviving seamen and the stolid redskin of a cook watching the skipper while he methodically tinkered and puttered! It was absolutely the one and final chance of salvation. Their lips were black and cracked and swollen, their tongues lolled, and they could no more than wheeze when they tried to talk. There was now a less precarious way of making fire than by rubbing dry sticks together. This had failed them most of the time. The captain had saved the flint and steel from the stock of his pistol. There was tow or tarry oakum to be shredded fine and used for tinder. This smouldered and then burst into a tiny blaze when the sparks flew from the flint, and they knew that they would not lack the blessed boon of fire.

Together they lifted the precious contrivance of the pot and the kettle and tottered with it to the galley. There was an abundance of fuel from the lumber, which was hauled through a hatch and dried on deck. Soon the steam was gushing from the pistol-barrel, and they poured cool salt water over the upturned spout of the tea-kettle to cause condensation. Fresh water trickled from the end of the pistol-barrel, and they caught it in a tin cup. It was scarcely more than a drop at a time, but they stoked the oven and lugged buckets of salt water, watch and watch, by night and day. They roused in their sleep to go on with the task with a sort of dumb instinct. They were like wretched automatons.

So scanty was the allowance of water obtained that each man was limited to "four small wine glasses" a day, perhaps a pint. It was enough to permit them to live and suffer and hope. In the warm seas which now cradled the *Polly* the barnacles grew fast. The captain, the cook, and the three seamen scraped them off and for some time had no other food. They ate these shell-fish mostly raw, because cooking interfered with that tiny trickle of condensed water.

The faithful cook was the next of the five to succumb. He expired in March, after they had been three months adrift, and the manner of his death was quiet and dignified, as befitted one who might have been a painted warrior in an earlier day. The account says of him:

> On the 15th of March, according to their computation, poor Moho gave up the ghost, evidently from want of water, though with much less distress than the others, and in full exercise of his reason. He very devoutly prayed and appeared perfectly resigned to the will of God who had so sorely afflicted him.

The story of the *Polly* is unstained by any horrid episode of cannibalism, which occurs now and then in the old chronicles of shipwreck. In more than one seaport the people used to point at some weather-beaten mariner who was reputed to have eaten the flesh of a comrade. It made a marked man of him, he was shunned, and the unholy notoriety followed him to other ships and ports. The sailors of the *Polly* did cut off a leg of the poor, departed Moho, and used it as bait for sharks, and they actually caught a huge shark by so doing.

It was soon after this that they found the other pistol of the pair, and employed the barrel to increase the capacity of the still. By lengthening the tube attached to the spout of the tea-kettle, they gained more cooling surface for condensation, and the flow of fresh water now amounted to "eight junk bottles full" every twenty-four hours. Besides this, wooden gutters were hung at the eaves of the galley and of the rough shed in which they lived, and whenever rain fell, it ran into empty casks.

The crew was dwindling fast. In April, another seaman, Johnson by name, slipped his moorings and passed on to the haven of Fiddler's Green, where the souls of all dead mariners may sip their grog and spin their yarns and rest from the weariness of the sea. Three men were left aboard the *Polly*, the captain and two sailors.

The brig drifted into that fabled area of the Atlantic that is known as the Sargasso Sea, which extends between 16° and 38° North, between the Azores and the Antilles. Here the ocean currents are confused and seem to move in circles, with a great expanse of stagnant ocean, where the sea-weed floats in tangled patches of red and brown and green. It was an old legend that ships once caught in the Sargasso Sea were unable to extricate themselves, and so rotted miserably and were never heard of again. Columbus knew better, for his caravels sailed through these broken carpets of weed, where the winds were so small and fitful that the Genoese sailors despaired of reaching anywhere. The myth persisted, and it was not dispelled until the age of steam. The doldrums of the Sargasso Sea were the dread of sailing ships.

The days and weeks of blazing calms in this strange wilderness of ocean mattered not to the blindly errant wreck of the *Polly*. She was a dead ship that had outwitted her destiny. She had no masts and sails to push her through these acres of leathery kelp and bright masses of weed which had drifted from the Gulf and the Caribbean to come to rest in this solitary, watery waste. And yet to the captain and his two seamen this dreaded Sargasso Sea was beneficent. The stagnant weed swarmed with fish and gaudy crabs and molluscs. Here was food to be had for the mere harvesting of it. They hauled masses of weed over the broken bulwarks and picked off the crabs by hundreds. Fishing gear was an easy problem for these handy sailor-men. They had found nails enough; hand-forged and malleable. In the galley they heated and hammered them to make fish-hooks, and the lines were of small stuff 'unrove' from a length of halyard. And so they caught fish, and cooked them while the oven could be spared. Otherwise they ate them raw, which was not distasteful after they had become accustomed to it. The natives of the Hawaiian Islands prefer their fish that way. Besides this, they split a large number of small fish and dried them in the hot sun upon the roof of the shelter. The sea-salt which collected in the bottom of the still was rubbed into the fish. It was a bitter condiment, but it helped to preserve them against spoiling.

The season of spring advanced until the derelict *Polly* had been four months afloat and wandering, and the end of the voyage was a long way off. The minds and bodies of the castaways had adjusted themselves to the intolerable situation. The most amazing aspect of the experience is that these men remained sane. They must have maintained a certain order and routine of distilling water, of catching fish, of keeping track of the indistinguishable procession of the days and weeks. Captain Cazneau's recollection was quite clear when he came to write down his account of what had happened. The one notable omission is the death of another sailor, name unknown, which must have occurred after April. The only seaman who survived to keep the skipper company was Samuel Badger.

By way of making the best of it, these two indomitable seafarers continued to work on their rough deckhouse, "which by constant improvement had become much more commodious." A few bundles of hewn shingles were discovered in the hold, and a keg of nails was found lodged in a corner of the forecastle. The shelter was finally made tight and water-proof, but, alas! there was no need of having it "more commodious." It is obvious, also, that "when reduced to two only, they had a better supply of water." How long they remained in the Sargasso Sea it is impossible to ascertain. Late in April it is recounted that "no friendly breeze wafted to their side the sea-weed from which they could obtain crabs or insects."

The mysterious impulse of the currents plucked at the keel of the *Polly* and drew her clear of this region of calms and of ancient, fantastic sea-tales. She moved in the open Atlantic again, without guidance or destination, and yet she seemed inexplicably to be following an appointed course, as though fate decreed that she should find rescue waiting somewhere beyond the horizon.

The brig was drifting toward an ocean more frequented, where the Yankee ships bound out to the River Plate sailed in a long slant far over to the African coast to take advantage of the booming trade-winds. She was also wallowing in the direction of the route of the East India-men, which departed from English ports to make the far-distant voyage around the Cape of Good Hope. None of them sighted the speck of a derelict, which floated almost level with the sea and had no spars to make her visible. Captain Cazneau and his companion saw sails glimmer against the sky-line during the last thousand miles of drift, but they vanished like bits of cloud, and none passed near enough to bring salvation.

June found the *Polly* approaching the Canary Islands. The distance of her journey had been about two thousand miles, which would make the average rate of drift something more than three hundred miles a month, or ten miles per day. The season of spring and its apple blossoms had come and gone in New England, and the brig had long since been mourned as missing with all hands. It was on the 20th of June that the skipper and his companion—two hairy, ragged apparitions—saw three ships which appeared to be heading in their direction. This was in latitude 28° North and longitude 13° West, and if you will look at a chart you will note that the wreck would soon have stranded on the coast of Africa. The three ships, in company, bore straight down at the pitiful little brig, which trailed fathoms of sea-growth along her hull. She must have

seemed uncanny to those who beheld her and wondered at the living figures that moved upon the weather-scarred deck. She might have inspired
"The Ancient Mariner."

Not one ship, but three, came bowling down to hail the derelict. They
manned the braces and swung the main-yards aback, beautiful, tall ships
and smartly handled, and presently they lay hove to. The captain of the
nearest one shouted a hail through his brass trumpet, but the skipper of
the *Polly* had no voice to answer back. He sat weeping upon the coaming
of a hatch. Although not given to emotion, he would have told you that it
had been a hard voyage. A boat was dropped from the davits of this nearest ship, which flew the red ensign from her spanker-gaff. A few minutes
later Captain Cazneau and Samuel Badger, able seaman, were alongside
the good ship *Fame* of Hull, Captain Featherstone, and lusty arms pulled
them up the ladder. It was six months to a day since the *Polly* had been
thrown on her beam-ends and dismasted.

The three ships had been near together in light winds for several days,
it seemed, and it occurred to their captains to dine together on board of
the *Fame*. And so the three skippers were there to give the survivors of
the *Polly* a welcome and to marvel at the yarn they spun. The *Fame* was
homeward bound from Rio Janeiro. It is pleasant to learn that Captain
Cazneau and Samuel Badger "were received by these humane Englishmen
with expressions of the most exalted sensibility." The musty old narrative
concludes:

> Thus was ended the most shocking catastrophe which our seafar-
> ing history has recorded for many years, after a series of distresses
> from December 20 to the 20th of June, a period of one hundred
> and ninety-two days. Every attention was paid to the sufferers that
> generosity warmed with pity and fellow-feeling could dictate, on
> board the *Fame*. They were transferred from this ship to the brig
> *Dromio* and arrived in the United States in safety.

Here the curtain falls. I for one should like to hear more incidents of
this astonishing cruise of the derelict *Polly* and also to know what happened to Captain Cazneau and Samuel Badger after they reached the
port of Boston. Probably they went to sea again, and more than likely in
a privateer to harry British merchantmen, for the recruiting officer was
beating them up to the rendezvous with fife and drum, and in August of
1812 the frigate *Constitution*, with ruddy Captain Isaac Hull walking the

poop in a gold-laced coat, was pounding the *Guerrière* to pieces in thirty minutes, with broadsides whose thunder echoed round the world.

"Ships are all right. It is the men in them," said one of Joseph Conrad's wise old mariners. This was supremely true of the little-brig that endured and suffered so much, and among the humble heroes of blue water by no means the least worthy to be remembered are Captain Cazneau and Samuel Badger, able seaman, and Moho, the Indian cook.

THE STRANGE STORY OF THE
EMILY BRAND

ANDREW HUSSEY ALLEN

I hardly suppose that any one will believe this story. Indeed I would hesitate to tell it were it not that its principal events are to be found recorded in the correspondence of the Department of State at Washington, and in the official reports of the Vice-Admiralty Court at Gibraltar, both of which sources of verification are, I have no doubt, accessible to the reader. I have myself seen the dispatches of our consul at Gibraltar and can vouch for their substantial correctness.

I was at Nice, where I had been sent a month earlier a tardy and restless convalescent, when, on the morning of November 20th, I found among my letters at breakfast one from my old friend Jack Drayton, dated two days earlier "On board the *Nomad*, Marseilles Harbor," and begging me to go for a cruise to the Azores with him. His fellow-voyagers, he wrote, had deserted him at Malta to go crusading to Jerusalem with some friends they had met there, and he urged me to go on this cruise with him as well on account of my health as on his account.

I called on my doctor, who agreed with Drayton that the voyage would set me squarely on my feet again, and as I knew of nothing that I would like better, I decided to go. I packed my trunks, took the early train for Marseilles, and boarded the yacht on the afternoon of the next day at five o'clock, and by eight the following morning we were under way.

The *Nomad* was a schooner of 230 tons, stanchly built for ocean cruising, and luxuriously equipped and furnished. Besides the captain, two mates, steward, cook, and Jack Drayton's servant, she carried a crew of seventeen men. Her owner was himself an able seaman, and his yacht was his home. He and I were such old friends and had lived together for so many years that we not only did not fear tiring of each other, but were reasonably sure of very good company.

On this occasion, however, we had a companion in Roy, a thoroughbred English mastiff that Drayton, who was very fond of animals, had taken to sea with him for the two preceding years. I never had appreciated before this cruise how much of a companion a dog could be. Roy quite won my heart. Unprejudiced by my affection for him, I think he was the noblest animal I have ever known. Stately, high-bred, intelligent, and lovable, he was "a gentleman and a scholar" from the jet of his handsome muzzle to the tip of his tawny tail.

We ran down the Mediterranean to the Straits with a fair, fast wind, feeling, as we passed the fortress, that we were well started on our voyage. But outside, on the ocean, Æolus became capricious, as is his wont, and bestowed his favors elsewhere. From that time on, until the fifth of December, we loitered sadly and uneventfully, with light northerly winds.

On the morning of that day, however, the breeze freshened somewhat, the smooth surface of the sea began to glitter with little ripples, our spirits rose with the prospect, and soon after nine o'clock we sighted a sail about three points off the port bow—the only thing in sight on the broad expanse of blue, shining ocean. By noon we had approached the stranger near enough to see that she was a brigantine under short sail, and in a little while we were within hailing distance.

Taking the glass, I made her out to be a smart-looking and beautifully modeled craft, and after a few minutes I read the name in gilt letters on her quarter as *Emily Brand*. Except her jib and a staysail, she had not a stitch of canvas set. As I looked she impressed me with a sense of deathlike stillness, desolation, and mystery, and I could see that her wheel was loose, and that there was no one on her deck. The slight breeze that still prevailed was from the north, and the brigantine was on the starboard tack, while the yacht, as she had been for several days, was on the port tack.

I handed the glass to Drayton, who, after a short survey, told Captain Parker to hail. The captain, as we neared her, called repeatedly in stentorian tones, but no answer came, and no sign of life appeared on board the strange vessel. Finally, when within three hundred yards of her, we shortened sail, had a boat lowered away, and Drayton and I, with the first mate of the *Nomad* and two seamen, rowed alongside.

Slowly drifting to leeward, she was barely moving, and Jamieson, the mate, clambered aboard by the gear of the bowsprit. He threw us a line, and, making the boat fast, we quickly followed him. He and the two men went forward, while Drayton and I, crossing the deck to the companionway, which we found open, entered the cabin. It was empty. The men forward likewise finding no one, we all five searched the vessel fore and aft, and high and low. There was not a living being besides ourselves on board. She had evidently been deserted. But why?

She was seemingly perfectly sound, and we failed to discover the least apparent cause for her abandonment. Her hold was exceptionally dry, there not being as much bilge in it as would fill a hogshead. Her cargo consisted of casks marked as containing alcohol, all of which were stowed in good order and condition except one, which had been started. The exterior of the hull above the water line did not exhibit the slightest trace of damage, nor was there the least evidence on the interior that the vessel had been repaired in any way or was at that time in need of any repairs.

Among the seamen's effects were found a number of articles of not inconsiderable value, going to show that the men were comparatively well-to-do and apparently in a great measure free from the too common prodigality of their class. We also found that the vessel was amply provisioned and that she had plenty of good water in her casks.

Of her cabin I must say that I had no idea there was a merchantman afloat so comfortably and attractively equipped in this respect. The apartment was large, high, and well lighted, with four staterooms opening from it—two forward and two aft. On either side, along the bunks, were broad, thick hair cushions of crimson stuff. In the center the table with leaves was stationary, while in the space between the staterooms forward was a harmonium, open; and aft, in the corresponding space, stood a sewing-machine, also uncovered. On a chair beside the harmonium lay several music books and loose sheets of music, and on the sewing-machine we found a pattern in muslin, evidently a child's garment in process of making, besides a small phial of machine oil, a spool of cotton, and a thimble, all three in a perpendicular position: a fact which afforded additional proof that the vessel could not have encountered any stress of weather—not even enough, indeed, to upset these lightly balanced articles.

In the forward port stateroom, under the berth, we found an open box containing panes of glass packed in hay and unbroken. Hanging on the partition opposite the berth, in the starboard stateroom forward, we found a cutlass of somewhat ancient pattern, which, on extracting it from its scabbard, I discovered to be stained with what seemed to me to be blood.

I called Drayton's attention to this, and, after examining it, he agreed with me and concluded that we had perhaps found a clew to the mystery. Later along we discovered marks on the main rail, apparently of blood, but by that time we had been forced to give up the idea that there had been any violence on board the vessel, by the perfect order in which we had found everything on board. The remaining articles of furniture in the cabin were two large easy-chairs upholstered in leather, and several smaller, lighter chairs. The carpet was a heavy Brussels, and the woodwork was painted a pale, soft gray, with bluish trimmings. All the brass mountings and the lamps were bright and shining, and, in fact, the apartment was pervaded no less by an air of quiet order than of mystery. It was clear that it had been occupied in part by a woman and child, and these we naturally supposed to be the wife and child of the captain.

Our charts showed that we had boarded the derelict in latitude 38° 20' north, longitude 17° 15' west. In its proper place we found her log-book, but her chronometer, manifest, and bills of lading were missing. The log showed that the last day's work of the vessel had been on the twenty-fourth of November, sea time, when the weather had allowed an observation to be taken that placed her in latitude 36° 56' north, longitude 27° 20' west.

The entries on her slate log were, however, carried down to eight o'clock of the morning of the twenty-fifth, at which hour she had passed from west to east to the north of the island of St. Mary's (Azores), the eastern point of which then bore south-southwest, six miles distant. The distance in longitude from the island of St. Mary's to the point at which we fell in with the *Emily Brand* is 7° 54'; the corrected distance of the latitude from the position last indicated in the log is 1° 18' north; and the brigantine had apparently held on her course for ten days after the twenty-fifth of November, the wheel being loose all the time.

But during the period from the twenty-fifth of November to the fifth of December the wind had been more or less from the north continuously, and it appeared to us impossible that the derelict could have covered within that time a distance of 7° 54' east, at any rate on the starboard tack. The obvious inference was, therefore, that she had not been abandoned until several days after the last entry made in the log.

Drayton, who was nothing if not practical when occasion required, at once set about making his arrangements to work our prize to Gibraltar.

He dispatched the mate and the two men back to the yacht with orders to have Parker select five men from the crew, one to be in authority as sailing master, and send them aboard the brigantine prepared to take up their quarters. Meanwhile he returned to the cabin to look over the log-book again, and some papers we had found in the captain's room, and I went forward to poke about in the seamen's quarters, which were to be occupied by the *Nomad's* men.

Fifteen minutes later, standing by the foremast facing aft, I struck a match to light my cigar. As I raised my eyes from doing so, I distinctly saw a man step from the rail at the port quarter, move quickly across the deck, and disappear in the companionway.

At the moment I caught but the briefest glimpse of his face and figure; but they were not to be forgotten. He seemed to have clambered aboard from the sea, for he was dripping wet and hatless, and his light hair was matted or glued about his head and face by the water, while his clothes clung to his body and limbs, and glistened and dripped in the sunlight. His figure was gigantic. His face and trunk were bloated or distended, like those of a man who has been drowned, and the former, without a vestige of color, was ghastly horrible and expressionless, even to the eyes, beyond the possibility of description.

I was naturally startled and shocked by the suddenness of his appearance and his extraordinary condition; but not so much so that I failed to shout "Hallo there!" as I got sight of him. He neither answered nor hesitated; he did not even look towards me, but, almost as I uttered the words, disappeared, as I have said, down the companionway. I hurried aft and entered the cabin. There alone, with his feet on a chair before him and the log-book on his knees, was Drayton, quite calm, and half-facing the companionway. I looked around, saw no one else (all the stateroom doors were wide open), and exclaimed in amazement, "Where is he?"

"Where is who?" drawled Drayton.

"The fellow," I replied, "who just came in here. Wake up, Jack! I saw the man come in here this moment. He is here somewhere," I added, searching from room to room in vain, and trying to open a door in the forward starboard stateroom, leading, as I supposed, into the between-decks space. The door was fast, and bolted on my side of it. No one had gone through there.

I turned back to the cabin, where my companion stood gazing at me curiously. He stepped towards me, looked at me very closely, and then said sharply:

"What's the matter with you, old man; are you out of your mind? How could any one have come in here without my seeing him?"

I described the man, and added that I could swear I had seen him enter the cabin three seconds before me.

Finally, somewhat impressed by my positiveness, Drayton, in spite of himself, went on deck, I following, and hailing the yacht, he called out: "Let the men, when the boat comes over, bring the dog with them." And then, to me, "If there is any one on board here Roy will find him though we can't."

As we turned back to the cabin I noticed that that part of the deck over which I had seen the stranger pass, dripping with water, five minutes before, was perfectly dry, as were also the brass plates on the companion-ladder down which I had seen him disappear. This discovery bothered me not a little, as may be readily imagined. Still I remained firm in my conviction that I had actually seen the man, and had not, as Drayton evidently believed, simply suffered an optical illusion.

I paced the deck until the yacht's boat arrived with the men and Roy. When they had boarded the brigantine Drayton came on deck again, and we made another thorough search of her with the dog running on ahead and with the aid of two bull's-eye lanterns that the men had brought over. This second search was as fruitless of result as the first. By the time we had finished it was after five o'clock, and we were at the point of returning to the yacht, to prepare for dinner, when we decided that it would be best to lock the cabin. We entered it for that purpose, and after having secured the doors of the staterooms, and closed the ports, we turned to leave it, Drayton preceding me towards the deck.

Halfway up the companionway it suddenly occurred to me that I had left my cigar-case on the table, and I returned to get it. As I again stepped into the apartment I saw, clearly defined, at the upper end of the bunk on the starboard side upon the partition, close by the stateroom door, the shadow in profile of the face and figure of a man. The shadow appeared to be cast by some very tall person sitting on the bunk to my right, forward; but there was no one there, as a matter of course. I began to doubt the evidence of my senses, and stood for a moment looking about me in bewilderment.

Recovering myself, however, I approached the corner, convinced that the dark gray shadow was a stain upon the paint. Apparently it was not. From the chair near the harmonium I took a loose sheet of music, and, holding it between the shadow and the light, I looked behind it and perceived that that portion of the shadow—a part of the head and face—

between which and the light I had interposed the obstacle had been oblit-
erated. On looking at the surface of the paper in my hand, I beheld the
missing portion of the shadow clearly silhouetted thereon.

Having thus satisfied myself that it was a shadow, and one cast by some
(to me) invisible and impalpaole thing or substance, I hardly need add that
I became somewhat excited. I shouted to Drayton, who immediately ran
back into the cabin, followed by the dog. His examination of the phenomenon resulted exactly as mine had. On turning, at its conclusion, to speak to
Roy, we found to our surprise that he had left us. Although we tried our best,
neither by persuasion nor command could we move him to enter the cabin
again.

We looked at each other nonplused, Drayton and I, and I am willing to
confess that mingled with my feeling of triumph at having thus convinced
him that there were others at work besides ourselves aboard the mysterious
derelict, was an uncomfortable consciousness that the weird annoyance was
beginning to tell on my nerves and to excite my imagination disagreeably as
to what was to come next.

Still I entertained not the least doubt that we were the victims of some
vulgar jugglery practiced upon us for some unexplained reason by hidden
human agents. I was morally positive that this was the case. I had not, of
course, had time to reason with myself as to the logic of the conclusion,
but it was the only natural one, and certainly no other explanation of what
I had seen occurred to me. Consideration of possible supernatural causes
or solutions was out of the question with both of us. Jack Drayton was as
free from all superstitious fancies as he was incapable of fear, and I may
claim to have been his counterpart in the former respect.

Slowly, as we looked upon it, the strange shadow faded out. After a
vain search of half an hour, and fruitless experiments with the lights and
shadows of the cabin, we locked the companionway and returned to the
yacht to dine.

By eight o'clock, having completed our arrangements, we went back to
the brigantine to pass the night in her cabin. Roy received us on deck, and
we tried again, but in vain, to induce him to enter the apartment with us.
His refusal annoyed us both. It was incomprehensible. We, however, prepared ourselves for the night. Drayton established himself in the forward
starboard corner on the bunk, looking after—the shadow's corner. I made
myself comfortable in the port corner aft, diagonally opposite and facing
him. We thus between us commanded a full view of the cabin and the four
staterooms, the doors of which we had reopened.

The dog roamed restlessly about the decks until a little before midnight, when I heard him lie down across the entrance to the companionway.

At a quarter to one o'clock—I looked at my watch at the moment—without any premonition, the three cabin lamps—one over Drayton's head, one over mine, and one in the center over the table—suddenly became dim. This was surprising, as we had carefully filled and trimmed them all before lighting them. I got up to examine that nearest me, turning my back to Drayton.

As I did so I heard the peculiar double click of the hammer of a pistol. Turning again, I saw my companion, with his cocked revolver in hand, step to the floor.

His face was pale and rigid, and his eyes fierce and fixed. He moved to the table and raised the weapon. With an indescribable sensation of dread I looked in the direction of his aim, and there, not five feet from where I stood, on the inside edge of one of the ports, I saw a large, coarse, bloated hand clinging, and behind it, outside, at the shoulder, the ghastly, brutal face of the man I had seen cross the deck in the afternoon.

The dull, lead-colored eyes seemed peering into the cabin. Almost overcome by mingled horror and disgust (I can convey no idea of the loathesomeness of this man's appearance), I was somewhat relieved by the cold, clear tones of Drayton's voice, as I heard him say:

"Now, my man, I have you in range. I'm a passable shot, and if you move, I shall fire. Who are you? and what deviltry are you engaged in here?"

There was no reply. After a pause, Drayton spoke again:

"I intend to have an answer. If you don't speak up before I say three, I shall fire, anyway. We are not to be trifled with."

Still there was no reply; and after a pause of about ten seconds, Drayton counted very slowly, "one—two—three," and then followed the flash and report of a pistol.

The man at the porthole did not move. Drayton, with wonderful nerve, raised the weapon again; but even as he did so the face and hand disappeared. Not instantly; but, as if drawn slowly back, they seemed to be swallowed up in the darkness without. As they faded away, the light in the cabin waned again; and crying to me, "Stay where you are, and keep the dog with you" (the dog had bounded into the cabin, half involuntarily, I suppose, at the report of the pistol), Drayton hurried on deck.

I seized Roy's collar, and, at the moment, the doors of all four staterooms, although there was not the slightest lurch of the vessel, slowly but steadily swung and silently closed, as did also the skylights, the ports, and the sliding hatch and doors of the companionway, shutting me in alone with the dog.

My recollection of what followed is perfectly clear—nay, vivid—but it is not in my power to write an adequate description of it. All I can do is to relate what occurred as I actually saw and felt it. Appreciation of the horror of my position I must leave, with but an intimation of it, to the imagination of the reader.

On finding myself thus closed in, my first undefined idea, naturally, was to reach the deck and call Drayton. I was startled, but I do not think that I was afraid at first. Some new trick was about to be played upon us, and I wanted him to see what it was with me. It did not occur to me that the companion-hatch could have been made fast, so I turned to the steps, the dog accompanying me closely—too closely, in fact. As I raised my foot I felt that I was unable to place it on the first stair. It was as though the exit from the cabin had been walled up. A second attempt was equally in vain. I endeavored to precipitate myself into the companionway. I might as well have tried to walk through a wall of solid rock, and still, in extending my hands and looking before me, I felt nothing but a soft though forbidding pressure, and saw nothing but the open stairway. I cannot say whether my sensation was one of terror or bewilderment—perhaps it was a mingling of the two.

I called aloud with the full strength of my lungs, but the sound of my voice seemed strangely muffled, even while I was perfectly conscious that I had full possession of my senses. During all this time the dog had been pressing close against me, trembling like a leaf, shuddering. I laid my hand on his head. It was hot to the touch. I looked down at him. With his ears laid back, his eyes protruding, and his tongue hanging out, he was the picture of terror—such a picture as I hope never to see again. A great, fearless, noble mastiff utterly abject, and cowering like any little cur.

And now the cabin lamps were suddenly extinguished, and only a small lantern left burning on the table. The atmosphere became oppressively hot, and a musty, moldy odor pervaded the apartment. In the deepened darknss I turned to look behind me with an added foreboding—if my horror may be said not to have reached its acme already. Beneath the door of the starboard stateroom, forward, I saw a brilliant line of light, and in the same place as before, the weird shadow of the afternoon, now bent over as though he who cast it there were listening at the door.

With my hand still on the mastiff's head, and impelled by some power not my own and stronger than my will, I moved towards the shade. My third step placed me directly in front of one of the large leather lounging chairs, which was so situated as to squarely face the dreadful corner. Into this chair I sank not only involuntarily, but seemingly by physical compulsion, the dog standing against it beside me. As again I laid my hand upon him I felt that he was rigid and strained in every muscle.

As I gazed at the shadow it slowly became upright and huge, and cast itself clearly upon the door, which immediately swung open without sound. With this phenomenon an indefinable sensation of almost intolerable pressure came upon me. I felt as though bound with iron or encased in lead. The chair seemed to hold me in a vise-like embrace. All power of motion left me. I tried to speak. I was dumb. The silence was awful; my sense of loneliness appalling. My mind, however, was most active and acute, and after a moment, every faculty seemed to be concentrated upon attention to what was going on before me.

Within the stateroom I saw a short, thick-set man seated on a camp-stool beside the berth, under a hanging lamp which shed a brilliant light. With his face in his hands and his head leaning against the partition before him, he seemed asleep; but I could not see that he breathed.

Behind him and half turned from me, I saw one standing who seemed to me to be the original of the shadow, and who, as I looked, raised his right arm in the air, and dealt the sleeping man a terrible blow at the back of the head with a heavy marline-spike, crushing the skull and killing the victim instantly.

No blood followed the stroke, and, although, as I have said, the room was brilliantly illuminated, I saw no shadows. The murderer seized the dead man's body before it fell to the floor, and opening the forward door of the stateroom, which led into the between-decks space, passed out, dragging the corpse with him, and disappeared in the darkness. Almost at once, however, he returned, and as he came towards me into the cabin, I again recognized the horrible face of the giant I had seen cross the deck above in the afternoon—the face of the man at whose hand I believed that Drayton with unerring aim had fired in the open porthole a little while before.

He entered the apartment, and, following with my eyes the direction of his movements, I saw him extend his hand and take up from the bunk, where he might have been sitting a few moments earlier, what appeared to me to be a carpenter's chisel or screw-driver. With this he again vanished into the darkness between decks. As he did so the forward door of the stateroom closed behind him, and simultaneously the light within went out, and the lamps in the cabin were relighted, while the doors and portholes, skylight, and companion-hatch were, I felt, reopened.

My hand being still upon the dog, I perceived a tremor or shudder pass through his entire frame, as with a deep sigh he instantly thereafter dashed from the cabin to the deck.

I heard Drayton's voice call loudly, "Roy! Roy!" and then a splash in the silent sea.

Freed from the terrible pressure, I now arose blindly to make my own way to the deck from the stifling atmosphere of the cabin; but the walls and furniture seemed to whirl and spin around and around me—and I remembered no more.

When I recovered consciousness I was again seated in the heavy chair, the cabin was cool, and there was the odor of brandy about. Drayton was standing over me with his hand on my forehead, and I heard the tramp of feet on the deck above. I looked at my watch, which I had laid open on the table several hours earlier, and it told me that I had been in the cabin alone with the dog but ten minutes at the uttermost.

From my companion I learned that after leaving me he had called the forward watch and one of the men from the deckhouse, and searched fruitlessly for a trace of the man at the porthole. As he had approached the companionway, the dog had dashed from it, foaming at the mouth, and in his madness leaped into the sea. Every effort was made to save him, but we never saw the poor fellow again.

The remaining hours of the night passed without incident. I related to Drayton what I had seen in the cabin, and we agreed that whatever the power that was exhibiting itself on board the brigantine—whether human or superhuman, natural or supernatural—it was one that we certainly could not account for, theorize as we might. Drayton, however, held to his purpose of taking the vessel to Gibraltar, there to turn her over, with as much of her story as we could tell, to the Vice- Admiralty Court for investigation.

In the morning we made an examination of the room in which I had seen the phantom murder committed (if I may describe as "phantom" those who seemed no less real flesh and blood than myself) and of the between-decks space forward of it, but we discovered nothing. At the edge of the porthole, however, at the spot where the hand had been, we found the bullet from the revolver buried in the wood.

By this time the seamen had gotten an inkling of the character of the ship's mystery; but as none of them had actually seen anything (nor, strangely enough, had heard the shot) Drayton's good sense and firmness triumphed over their superstition, and we were enabled to work the derelict to port without difficulty and without further incident. A second night passed in her cabin by both of us was quiet and uneventful in every way, but we were satisfied that we had discovered the cause of her abandonment. The sailors would have said that she was haunted.

We made Gibraltar on the morning of the thirteenth of December, and immediately reporting the circumstances under which we had found the *Emily Brand* we turned her over to the authorities.

The Queen's Proctor in Admiralty at once ordered a special survey of the vessel by the surveyor of shipping, assisted by the marshal of the court and an expert diver. The result of this survey was a report substantially embodying the facts as to the finding of the vessel and her condition here related by me. In addition to this, however, the stains on the old cutlass and on the vessel's rail were subjected to a chemical analysis by which it was proved that they were not bloodstains, and this fact was made an item of the report.

Upon this unsatisfactory conclusion Drayton and I determined to communicate to the authorities an account of the almost incredible events of our first day and night aboard the mysterious vessel. This we were enabled to do without making ourselves ridiculous, through the good offices of the governor of the fortress, to whom Drayton was well known. Thereupon a second survey was ordered, during which the entire cargo was removed.

At the request of one of the officials engaged in this second survey, I accompanied him aboard the brigantine for the purpose of pointing out the movements of the phantom murderer. This official developed a rather remarkable detective ingenuity. He subjected me, in the course of our conversation, to a close cross-examination concerning the chisel or screw-driver, for which the assassin had returned after the murder. On my remaining firm in my conviction as to what the tool appeared to be, he confided to me his theory of the terrible mock murder I had witnessed.

He believed, he told me, that the crime which had caused the vessel's abandonment had been revealed to me "by the spirits," as he expressed it, "of the principal actors." Proceeding on this theory, he personally (permitting me to accompany him) made a careful examination of the fatal stateroom and of the now empty between-decks space forward, his object being to discover some evidence of the use of such a tool, to the appearance of which he attached the greatest importance.

At a point about fifteen feet distant from the stateroom he found a narrow strip of oak about an inch in thickness and five feet in length, projecting, by its thickness, beyond the smooth surface of the vessel's inner shell. On scrutinizing it closely we perceived that it had been fixed in its place by means of five screws, apparently of brass, as the heads were incrusted with bright green rust or mold. We immediately summoned assistance, procured a screw-driver, and removed the strip. Having accomplished this, we discovered that the strip had been affixed over a perpendicular succession of the joints of the narrow planks of the vessel's interior hull, which sprang outward as they were released, far enough for my companion to insert his fingers behind them.

Wrenching them off, we found to our horror, wedged in the inner space, the grinning skeleton of a man, upon which hung shreds of clothing. As this skeleton was lifted out, something dropped to the deck with a metallic sound, and rolled to my feet. I stooped and picked it up. It was a plain band of gold—a ring. On the inside was engraved: "From H. M. to J. B."

The clothing of the unfortunate man appeared to have been partially eaten by rats. At the time it seemed to me a fortunate thing that it had not been entirely destroyed, as otherwise the ring, which had been retained in one of the folds, would long before have slipped from the bony finger to the bottom of the hold, and rendered positive identification, perhaps, impossible. The skeleton was clean, dry, and white, and on further examination we found that the back of the skull had been fractured, apparently by a blow from a club.

Since our arrival at Gibraltar, and about a week before the finding of the skeleton, Drayton had written to the owners of the brigantine at New York, having learned who they were from the surveyor of shipping, to whom her missing captain had been well and favorably known. In his letter to these gentlemen Drayton had asked for such a history of the *Emily Brand* as her owners were willing and prepared to give. He particularly required a full account of her missing company, and the details of any mutiny or other crime that might have occurred on board within their knowledge, with a description of the participants.

At the end of about three weeks from the date on which the skeleton was found (we in the meanwhile having had a run up the Mediterranean and back) a new captain and new crew arrived from New York, sent out by Messrs. Barnes and Spaulding, to take the brigantine on to Genoa, for which port she had been originally bound. The captain, Mr. Church, presented himself on board the *Nomad* the day of his arrival, as the bearer of a long letter to Drayton from Mr. Barnes, the senior member of the owning firm. From that letter I transcribed the ensuing account of the *Emily Brand.*

"The brigantine was built for us about two years ago at Portland, Maine. Including her present voyage she has made four in all. The first two were prosperous, and on neither of them did anything out of the ordinary run occur. A year ago last November, however, she sailed from this port, with a miscellaneous cargo, for Lisbon, taken out by Captain James Blaisdel, who had been in our employ for many years, and who had commanded her on her two preceding voyages.

"Among her crew was a Swede or Norwegian of the name of Peterson, a gigantic, ill-favored fellow, who had been injured in our service some time before by a fall from the rigging, in which he sustained a severe contusion of the brain. For several months he lay in the hospital here, in what was believed to be a hopeless condition of imbecility; but finally, having recovered, or apparently recovered, he applied for a berth on the *Emily Brand.*

"On the eleventh of December we received news by cable from Mr. Riggs, the mate, of the death of Captain Blaisdel and the man Peterson. On the twenty-sixth a letter came, giving the particulars, which were briefly as follows: About the eighth day out from New York Peterson developed symptoms of a relapse of this disease (caused by the fall), which seemed, however, to affect his mind only with a sort of intermittent stupor. He exhibited no signs of mania or violence, and was capable of performing his light duties about one half the time. He was accordingly not confined, and the master did what he could for him, treating him with the utmost kindness, and advising him to lay off from his work. This he did for several days, but apparently without beneficial effect.

"On the night of December 5, Mr. Blaisdel turned in at eight bells (twelve o'clock). The weather was clear, the wind over the port quarter, and the moon lighted up the deck. The vessel was then about latitude 38° north, longitude 17° west, near the point at which you picked her up. Just before two bells (one o'clock) the man at the wheel saw Peterson, whom he recognized by his great size, cross the deck amidship to the starboard rail and throw something into the sea. On being hailed by this man, Peterson went aft, and said that he had thrown a pair of old shoes overboard. He was in his stocking feet.

"In the morning the master failed to appear, and after waiting a reasonable time the steward knocked at his door. Receiving no response, he called

Mr. Riggs, the mate, who entered the stateroom and found it empty. The berth had not been occupied. When after a search it became evident that the captain could not be found, Miller, the man who had taken the wheel at midnight, told the mate of Peterson's appearance and his conversation with him. Peterson was sent for, and found in his bunk, apparently sleeping. He was aroused, and brought on deck in a very excited condition, and on being interrogated by Mr. Riggs he became incoherent and violent.

"The mate thereupon ordered two of the men to seize him; but as they approached to do so, he eluded them, and darting to the vessel's side, went overboard. They put her about and lowered a boat immediately, but he was never seen again. It seems clear that in a fit of insanity he murdered the captain and threw his body into the sea during the night. How this was accomplished no one knows, for no noise was heard, nor were any traces of violence found about the vessel.

"On her present voyage Mr. Riggs, the former mate, went as master of the vessel. He was, I believe, thirty-six years of age, married, and had one child—a little girl of five or six years. It is our custom to allow our masters to purchase an interest in the vessels they command, and Mr. Riggs and his wife owned two-sixteenths of the *Emily Brand*. He was a man of the highest character and thoroughly competent to go as master. On this last voyage his wife and child accompanied him.

"I cannot form the slightest conjecture concerning the strange disappearance of poor Riggs and his family, with all on board, and I have but little belief that they will ever be heard of again."

From this letter it became evident that the skeleton found up in the between-decks space was that of Captain James Blaisdel, with whose name the initials engraved in the ring corresponded.

The remains thus identified were interred at Gibraltar.

Some hope of the rescue of the castaways was for a time entertained, as it was learned that the boat (the brigantine had but one) in which they were presumed to have left the vessel was a lifeboat, new, light, and incapable of sinking. Moreover, it was known that they could not have encountered any bad weather for many days after parting from the *Emily Brand*.

Accordingly the widest publicity was given to the fact of their having disappeared, and for more than a year the civilized world was searched throughout with all the facilities at the disposal of our own government and that of England, upon the chance that they had made some land or had been picked up by some passing vessel. But no trace of the lifeboat or of any of its occupants was ever discovered.

JONAH

THE BIBLE

Jonah, 1

1: Now the word of the LORD came unto Jonah the son of Amittai, saying,

2: Arise, go to Nineveh, that great city, and cry against it; for their wickedness is come up before me.

3: But Jonah rose up to flee unto Tarshish from the presence of the LORD, and went down to Joppa; and he found a ship going to Tarshish: so he paid the fare thereof, and went down into it, to go with them unto Tarshish from the presence of the LORD.

4: But the LORD sent out a great wind into the sea, and there was a mighty tempest in the sea, so that the ship was like to be broken.

5: Then the mariners were afraid, and cried every man unto his god, and cast forth the wares that were in the ship into the sea, to lighten it of them. But Jonah was gone down into the sides of the ship; and he lay, and was fast asleep.

6: So the shipmaster came to him, and said unto him, What meanest thou, O sleeper? arise, call upon thy God, if so be that God will think upon us, that we perish not.

7: And they said every one to his fellow, Come, and let us cast lots, that we may know for whose cause this evil is upon us. So they cast lots, and the lot fell upon Jonah.

8: Then said they unto him, Tell us, we pray thee, for whose cause this evil is upon us; What is thine occupation? and whence comest thou? what is thy country? and of what people art thou?

9: And he said unto them, I am an Hebrew; and I fear the LORD, the God of heaven, which hath made the sea and the dry land.

10: Then were the men exceedingly afraid, and said unto him, Why hast thou done this? For the men knew that he fled from the presence of the LORD, because he had told them.

11: Then said they unto him, What shall we do unto thee, that the sea may be calm unto us? for the sea wrought, and was tempestuous.

12: And he said unto them, Take me up, and cast me forth into the sea; so shall the sea be calm unto you: for I know that for my sake this great tempest is upon you.

13: Nevertheless the men rowed hard to bring it to the land; but they could not: for the sea wrought, and was tempestuous against them.

14: Wherefore they cried unto the LORD, and said, We beseech thee, O LORD, we beseech thee, let us not perish for this man's life, and lay not upon us innocent blood: for thou, O LORD, hast done as it pleased thee.

15: So they took up Jonah, and cast him forth into the sea: and the sea ceased from her raging.

16: Then the men feared the LORD exceedingly, and offered a sacrifice unto the LORD, and made vows.

17: Now the LORD had prepared a great fish to swallow up Jonah. And Jonah was in the belly of the fish three days and three nights.

Jonah, 2

1: Then Jonah prayed unto the LORD his God out of the fish's belly,

2: And said, I cried by reason of mine affliction unto the LORD, and he heard me; out of the belly of hell cried I, and thou heardest my voice.

3: For thou hadst cast me into the deep, in the midst of the seas; and the floods compassed me about: all thy billows and thy waves passed over me.

4: Then I said, I am cast out of thy sight; yet I will look again toward thy holy temple.

5: The waters compassed me about, even to the soul: the depth closed me round about, the weeds were wrapped about my head.

6: I went down to the bottoms of the mountains; the earth with her bars was about me for ever: yet hast thou brought up my life from corruption, O LORD my God.

7: When my soul fainted within me I remembered the LORD: and my prayer came in unto thee, into thine holy temple.

8: They that observe lying vanities forsake their own mercy.

9: But I will sacrifice unto thee with the voice of thanksgiving; I will pay that that I have vowed. Salvation is of the LORD.

10: And the LORD spake unto the fish, and it vomited out Jonah upon the dry land.

A NIGHTMARE OF THE DOLDRUMS

W. CLARK RUSSELL

The *Justitia* was a smart little barque of 395 tons. I had viewed her with something of admiration as she lay in midstream in the Hooghly—somewhere off the Coolie Bazaar.

I—representing in those days a large Birmingham firm of dealers in the fal-lal industries—had wished to make my way from Calcutta to Capetown. I saw the *Justitia* and took a fancy to her; I admired the long, low, piratic run of her hull, as she lay with straining hawsepipes on the rushing stream of the Hooghly; upon which, as you watched, there might go by in the space of an hour some halfscore at least of dead natives made ghastly canoes of by huge birds, erect upon the corpses, burying their beaks as they sailed along.

I called upon the agents, was told that the *Justitia* was not a passenger ship, but that I could hire a cabin for the run to Capetown if I chose; a sum in rupees, trifling compared with the cost of transit by steam, was named. I went on board, found the captain walking up and down under the awning, and agreeably killed an hour in a chat with as amiable a seaman as ever it was my good fortune to meet.

We sailed in the middle of July. Nothing worth talking about happened during our run down the Bay of Bengal. The crew aforemast were all of them Englishmen; there were twelve, counting the cook and steward. The captain was a man named Cayzer; the only mate of the vessel was one William Perkins. The boatswain, a rough, short, hairy, immensely strong man, acted as second mate and kept a look-out when Perkins was below. But he was entirely ignorant of navigation, and owned to me that he read with difficulty words of one syllable, and could not write.

I was the only passenger. My name, I may as well say here, is Thomas Barron. Our run to the south Ceylon parallels was slow and disappointing. The monsoon was light and treacherous, sometimes dying out in a sort of laughing, mocking gust till the whole ocean was a sheet-calm surface, as though the dependable trade wind was never again to blow.

"Oh, yes," said Captain Cayzer to me, "we're used to the unexpected hereabouts. Monsoon or no monsoon, I'll tell you what: you're always safe in standing by for an Irishman's hurricane down here."

"And what sort of breeze is that?" I asked.

"An up-and-down calm," said he; "as hard to know where it begins as to guess where it'll end."

However, thanks to the frequent trade puffs and other winds, which tasted not like the monsoon, we crawled through those latitudes which Ceylon spans and fetched within a few degrees of the Equator.

I left my cabin one morning some hours after the sun had risen, by which time the decks had been washed down, and were already dry, with a salt sparkle as of bright white sand on the face of the planks, so roasting was it. I went into the head to get a bath under the pump there.

It was a true tropic morning. The courses swung to the swell without response to the breathings of the air; and on high the light cotton-white royals were scarcely curved by the delicate passage of the draught.

Yet the barque had steerage way. When I looked through the grating at her metalled forefoot I saw the ripples plentiful as harpstrings threading aft, and whilst I dried myself I watched the slow approach of a piece of timber hoary with barnacles and venerable with long hairs of seaweed, amid and around which a thousand little fish were sporting, many-colored as though a rainbow had been shivered.

I returned to my cabin, dressed, and stepped on to the quarter-deck, where I found some men spreading the awning, and the captain viewing an object out upon the water through a telescope, and talking to the boatswain, who stood alongside.

"What do you see?" I asked.

"Something that resembles a raft," answered the captain.

The thing he looked at was about a mile distant, some three points on the starboard bow. On pointing the telescope, I distinctly made out the fabric of a raft, fitted with a short mast, to which midway a bundle—it resembled a parcel—was attached. A portion of the raft was covered by a white sheet or cloth, whence dangled a short length of something chocolate-coloured, indistinguishable even with the glass, lifting and sinking as the raft rose and fell upon the flowing heave of the sea.

"This ocean," said the captain, taking the glass from me, "is a big volume of tragic stories, and the artist who illustrates the book does it in that fashion," and he nodded in the direction of the raft.

"What do you make of it, boatswain?" I asked.

"It looks to me," he answered in his strong, harsh, deep voice, "like a religious job—one of them rafts the Burma covies float away their dead on. I never see one afore, sir, but I've heard tell of such things."

We sneaked stealthily towards the raft. It was seven bells—half-past seven—and the sailors ate their breakfast on the forecastle, that they might view the strange contrivance. The mate, Mr. Perkins, came on deck to relieve the boatswain, and, after inspecting the raft through the telescope, gave it as his opinion that it was a Malay floating bier—"a Mussulman trick of ocean burial, anyhow," said he. "There should be a jar of water aboard the raft, and cakes and fruit for the corpse to regale on, if he ha'n't been dead long."

The steward announced breakfast; the captain told him to hold it back awhile. He was as curious as I to get a close view of the queer object, but the wind was nearly gone, the barque scarcely responded to the motion of her rudder, the thread-like lines at the cutwater had faded, and a roasting, oppressive calm was upon the water, whitening it out into a tingling sheen of quicksilver with a fiery shaft of blinding dazzle, solitary and splendid.

The raft was about six cables' lengths off us when the barque came to a dead stand, with a soft, universal hollowing in of her canvas from royal to course, as though, like something sentient, she delivered one final sigh before the swoon of the calm seized her. But now we were near enough to resolve the floating thing with the naked eye into details.

It was a raft formed of bamboo canes. A mast about six feet tall was erected upon it; the dark thing over the edge proved a human leg, and, when the fabric lifted with the swell and raised the leg clear, we saw that the foot had been eaten away by fish, a number of which were swimming about the raft, sending little flashes of foam over the pale surface as they darted along with their back or dorsal fins exposed. They were all little fish; I saw no sharks. The body to which the leg belonged was covered by a white cloth. The captain called my attention to the parcel attached to the mast, and said that it possibly contained the food which the Malays leave beside their dead after burial.

"But let's go to breakfast now, Mr. Barron," said he, with a slow, reproachful, impatient look round the breathless scene of ocean. "If there's any amusement to be got out of that thing yonder there's a precious long, quiet day before us, I fear, for the entertainment."

We breakfasted, and in due course returned on deck. The slewing of the barque had caused the raft to shift its bearings, otherwise its distance remained as it was when we went below.

"Mr. Perkins," said the captain, "lower a boat and bring aboard that parcel from the raft's jury-mast, and likewise take a peep at the figure under the cloth, and report its sex and what it looks like."

I asked leave to go in the boat, and when she was lowered, with three men in her, I followed Mr. Perkins and we rowed over to the raft. All about the frail bamboo contrivance the water was beautiful with the colors and movements of innumerable fish. As we approached we were greeted by an evil smell. The raft seemed to have been afloat for a considerable period; its submerged portion was green with marine adhesions or growths. The fellow in the bows of the boat, maneuvering with the boathook, cleverly snicked the parcel from the jury-mast and handed it along to the mate, who put it beside him without opening it, for that was the captain's privilege.

"Off with that cloth," said Mr. Perkins, "and then back water a bit out of this atmosphere."

The bowman jerked the cloth clear of the raft with his boathook; the white sheet floated like a snowflake upon the water for a few breaths, then slowly sank. The body exposed was stark-naked and tawny. It was a male. I saw nothing revolting in the thing; it would have been otherwise perhaps had it been white. The hair was long and black, the nose aquiline, the mouth puckered into the aspect of a harelip; the gleam of a few white teeth painted a ghastly contemptuous grim upon the dead face. The only shocking part was the footless leg.

"Shall I hook him overboard, sir?" said the bowman.

"No, let him take his ease as he lies," answered the mate, and with that we returned to the barque.

We climbed over the side, the boat was hoisted to the davits, and Mr. Perkins took the parcel out of the stern-sheets and handed it to the captain. The cover was a kind of fine canvas, very neatly stitched with white thread. Captain Cayzer ripped through the stitching with his knife and exposed a couple of books bound in some kind of skin or parchment. They were probably the Koran, but the characters none of us knew. The captain turned them about for a bit, and I stood by looking at them; he then replaced them in their canvas cover and put them down upon the skylight, and, by and by, on his leaving the deck, he took them below to his cabin.

There had not been a stir of wind all day; not the faintest breathing of breeze had tarnished the sea down to the hour of midnight when, feeling weary, I withdrew to my cabin. I slept well, spite of the heat and the cockroaches, and rose at seven. I found the steward in the cabin. His face wore a look of concern; and on seeing me he instantly exclaimed:

"The captain seems very ill, sir. Might you know anything of physic? Neither Mr. Perkins nor me can make out what's the matter."

"I know nothing of physic," I answered, "but I'll look in on him."

I stepped to the door, knocked and entered. Captain Cayzer lay in a bunk under a middling-sized porthole; the cabin was full of the morning light. I started and stood at gaze, scarce crediting my sight, so shocked and astounded was I by the dreadful change which had happened in the night in the poor man's appearance.

His face was blue, and I remarked a cadaverous sinking in of the eyeballs; the lips were livid, the hands likewise blue, but strangely wrinkled like a washerwoman's. On seeing me he asked in a husky whispering voice for a drink of water. I handed him a full pannikin, which he drained feverishly, and then began to moan and cry out, making some weak, miserable efforts to rub first one arm, then the other, then his legs.

The steward stood in the doorway. I turned to him, sensible that my face was ashen, and asked some questions. I then said, "Where is Mr. Perkins?"

He was on deck. I bade the steward attend to the captain, and passed through the hatch to the quarterdeck, where I found the mate.

"Do you know that the captain is very ill?" said I.

"Do I know it, sir? Why, yes. I've been sitting by him chafing his limbs and giving him water to drink, and attending to him in other ways. What is it, d'ye know, sir?"

"*Cholera!*" said I.

"Oh, my God, I hope not!" he exclaimed. "How could it be cholera? How could cholera come aboard?"

"A friend of mine died of cholera at Rangoon when I was there," said I. "I recognize the looks and will swear to the symptoms."

"But how could it have come aboard?" he exclaimed in a voice low but agitated.

My eyes, as he asked the question, were upon the raft. I started and cried, "Is that thing still there?"

"Ay," said the mate, "we haven't budged a foot all night."

The suspicion rushed upon me whilst I looked at the raft and ran my eyes over the bright, hot morning sky and the burnished surface of sea, sheeting into dimness in the misty junction of heaven and water.

"I shouldn't be surprised," said I, "to discover that we brought the cholera aboard with us yesterday from that dead man's raft yonder."

"How is cholera to be caught in that fashion?" exclaimed Mr. Perkins, pale and a bit wild in his way of staring at me.

"We may have brought the poison aboard in the parcel of books."

"Is cholera to be caught so?"

"Undoubtedly. The disease may be propagated by human intercourse. Why not then by books which have been handled by cholera-poisoned people, or by the atmosphere of a body dead of the plague?" I added, pointing at the raft.

"No man amongst us is safe, then, now?" cried the mate.

"I'm no doctor," said I; "but I know this, that contagious poisons such as scarlet fever, glanders, and so on may retain their properties in a dormant state for years. I've heard tell of scores of instances of cholera being propagated through articles of dress. Depend upon it," said I, "that we brought the poison aboard with us yesterday from that accursed death-raft yonder."

"Aren't the books in the captain's cabin?" said the mate.

"Are they?"

"He took them below yesterday, sir."

"The sooner they're overboard the better," I exclaimed, and returned to the cabin.

I went to the captain and found the steward rubbing him. The disease appeared to be doing its work with horrible rapidity; the eyes were deeply sunk and red; every feature had grown sharp and pinched as after a long wasting disease; the complexion was thick and muddy. Those who have watched beside cholera know that terrific changes may take place in a few minutes. I cast my eyes about for the parcel of books, and, spying it, took a stick from a corner of the berth, hooked up the parcel, and, passing it through the open porthole, shook it overboard.

The captain lived till the evening, and seldom spoke save to call upon God to release him. I had found an opportunity to tell him that he was ill of the cholera, and explained how it happened that the horrible distemper was on board, for I was absolutely sure we had brought it with us in that parcel of books; but his anguish was so keen, his death so close then, that I cannot be sure he understood me. He died shortly after seven o'clock, and I have since learned that that time is one of the critical hours in cholera.

When the captain was dead I went to the mate and advised him to cast the body overboard at once. He called to some of the hands. They brought the body out just as the poor fellow had died, and, securing weight to the feet, they lifted the corpse over the rail and dropped it. No burial service was read. We were all too panic-stricken for reverence.

We got rid of the body quickly, the men handling the thing as though they felt the death in it stealing into them through their fingers—hoping and praying that with it the cholera would go. It was almost dark when this hurried funeral was ended. I stood beside the mate, looking round the sea for the shadow of wind in any quarter. The boatswain, who had been one of the men that handled the body, came up to us.

"Ain't there nothing to be done with that corpus out there?" he exclaimed, pointing with a square hand to the raft. "The men are agreed that there'll come no wind whilst that there dead blackie keeps afloat. And ain't he enough to make a disease of the hatmosphere itself, from horizon to horizon?"

I waited for the mate to answer. He said gloomily, "I'm of the poor captain's mind. You'll need to make something fast to the body to sink it. Who's to handle it? I'll ask no man to do what I wouldn't do myself, and rat me if I'd do *that!*"

"We brought the poison aboard by visiting the raft, bo'sun," said I. "Best leave the thing alone. The corpse is too far off to corrupt the air, as you suppose; though the imagination's nigh as bad as the reality," said I, spitting.

"If there's any of them game to sink the thing, may they do it?" said the boatswain. "For if there's ne'er a breeze of wind to come while it's there—"

"Chaw!" said the mate. "But try 'em, if you will. They may take the boat when the moon's up, should there come no wind first."

An hour later the steward told me that two of the sailors were seized with cramps and convulsions. After this no more was said about taking the boat and sinking the body. The mate went into the forecastle. On his return he begged me to go and look at the men.

"Better make sure that it's cholera with them too, sir," said he. "You know the signs;" and folding his arms, he leaned against the bulwarks in a posture of profound dejection.

I went forward and descended the forescuttle, and found myself in a small cave. The heat was overpowering; there was no air to pass through the little hatch; the place was dimly lighted by an evil-smelling lamp hanging under a beam, but, poor as the illumination was, I could see by it, and when I looked at the two men and spoke to them, I saw how it was, and came away sick at heart, and half dead with the hot foul air of the forecastle, and in deepest distress of mind, moreover, through perceiving that the two men had formed a part of the crew of the boat when we visited the raft.

One died at six o'clock next morning and the other at noon; but before this second man was dead three others had been attacked, and one of them was the mate. And still never a breath of air stirred the silver surface of the sea.

The mate was a strong man, and his fear of death made the conflict dreadful to behold. I was paralyzed at first by the suddenness of the thing and the tremendous character of our calamity, and, never doubting that I must speedily prove a victim as being one who had gone in the boat, I cast myself down upon a sofa in the cabin and there sat, waiting for the first signal of pain.

But a keen and biting sense of my cowardice came to my rescue. I sprang to my feet and went to the mate's berth, and nursed him till he died, which was shortly before midnight of the day of his seizure—so swift and sure was the poison we had brought from the raft.

He was dropped over the side, and in a few hours later he was followed by three others. I cannot be sure of my figures; it was a time of delirium, and I recall some details of it with difficulty, but I am pretty sure that by the morning of the fourth day of our falling in with the accursed raft the ship's company had been reduced to the boatswain and five men, making, with myself, seven survivors of fifteen souls who had sailed from Calcutta.

It was some time about the middle of the fifth day—two men were then lying stricken in the forecastle—the boatswain and a couple of seamen came aft to the quarter-deck where I was standing. The ocean floated in liquid glass; the smell of frying paint, bubbled into cinders by the roasting rays, rose like the stench of a second plague to the nostrils.

They had been drinking; no doubt they had broached the rum casks below. The boatswain carried a heavy weight of some sort, bound in canvas, with a long lanyard attached to it. He flung the parcel into the quar-ter-boat and roared out:

"If that don't drag the blistered cuss out of sight I'll show the fired carcass the road myself. Cholera or no cholera, here goes!"

"What are you going to do?" said I.

"Do?" he cried. "Why, sink that there plague out of it, so as to give us the chance of a breeze. Ain't this hell's delight? What's a-going to blow us clear whilst *he* keeps watch?" And he nodded with a fierce drunken gesture towards the raft.

"You'll have to handle the body to sink it," said I. "You're well, men, now; keep well, won't you? The two who are going may be the last taken."

The three of them roared out drunkenly together, so muddling their speech with oaths that I did not understand them. I walked aft, not liking their savage looks. Shouting and cursing plentifully, they lowered the boat, got into her by descending the falls, and shoved off for the raft.

They drew alongside the bamboo contrivance, and I looked to see the boat capsize, so wildly did they sway her in their wrath and drink as they fastened the weight to the foot of the body, sank it, and with the loom of their oars, hammered at the raft till the bamboos were scat-tered like a sheaf of walking-sticks cut adrift. They then returned to the barque, clambered aboard, and hoisted the boat.

The two sick men in the forecastle were at this time looked after by a seaman named Archer. I have said it was the fifth day of the calm; of the ship's company the boatswain and five men were living, but two were dying, and that, not counting me, left three as yet well and able to get about.

This man Archer, when the boatswain and his companions went for-ward, came out of the forecastle and drank at the scuttle-butt in the waist. He walked unsteadily, with that effort after stateliness which is peculiar to tipsy sailors; his eyes wandered, and he found some difficulty in hitting the bunghole with the dipper. Yet he was a civil sort of man when sober; I had occasionally chatted with him during his tricks at the wheel; and, feeling the need of some one to talk to about our frightful situation, I walked up to him and asked how the sick men did.

"Dying fast," he answered, steadying himself by leaning against the scuttle-butt, "and a-ravin' like screech-owls."

"What's to be done, Archer?"

"Oh, God alone He knows!" answered the man, and here he put his knuckles into his eyes and began to cry and sob.

"Is it possible that this calm can last much longer?"

"It may last six weeks," he answered, whimpering. "Down here, when the wind's drawed away by the sun, it may take six weeks afore it comes on to blow. Six weeks of calm down here ain't thought nothen of," and here he burst out blubbering again.

"Drinking 'll not help you," said I; "you'll all be the likelier to catch the malady for drinking. This is a sort of time, I should think, when a man most wants his senses. A breeze may come, and we ought to decide where to steer the barque to. The vessel's under all plain sail, too, and here we are, four men and a useless passenger, should it come on to blow suddenly—"

"We didn't sign on under you," he interrupted, with a tipsy scowl, "and as ye ain't no good either as sailor or doctor, you can keep your blooming sarmons to yourself till they're asked for."

I had now not only to fear the cholera but to dread the men. My mental distress was beyond all power of words to convey; I wonder it did not quickly drive me crazy and hurry me overboard. I lurked in the cabin to be out of sight of the fellows, and all the while my imagination was tormenting me with the first pangs of the cholera, and every minute I was believing I had the mortal malady. Sometimes I would creep up the companion steps and cautiously peer around, and always I beheld the same dead, faint blue surface of sea stretching like an ocean in a dream into the faint indefinable distances.

But shocking as that calm was to me, I very well knew there was nothing wonderful or preternatural in it. Our forefoot five days before had struck the equatorial zone called the Doldrums, and at a period of the year when a fortnight or even a month of atmospheric lifelessness might be as confidently looked for as the rising and setting of the sun.

At nine o'clock that night I was sitting at the cabin table with biscuit and a little weak brandy and water before me, when I was hailed by some one at the open skylight above. It was a black night, though the sky was glorious with stars; the moon did not rise till after eleven. I had lighted the cabin lamp, and the sheen of it was upon the face of Archer.

"The two men are dead and gone," said he, "and now the bo'sun and Bill are down. There's Jim dead drunk in his hammock. I can't stand the cries of sick men. What with liquor and pain, the air below suffocates me. Let me come aft, sir, and keep along with you. I'm sober, now. Oh, Christ, have mercy upon me! It's my turn next, ain't it?"

I passed a glass of brandy to him through the skylight, then joined him on deck, and told him that the two dead bodies must be thrown overboard and the sick men looked to. For some time he refused to go forward with me, saying that he was already poisoned and deadly sick, and a dying man, and that I had no right to expect that one dying man should wait upon another.

However, I was determined to turn the dead out of the ship in any case, for in freeing the vessel of the remains of the victims might lie my salvation. He consented to help me at last, and we went into the forecastle and between us got the bodies out of their bunks and dropped them, weighted, over the rail.

The boatswain and the other men lay groaning and writhing and crying for water; cursing at intervals. A coil of black smoke went up from the lamp-flame to the blackened beam under which the light was burning. The atmosphere was horrible. I bade Archer help me to carry a couple of mattresses on to the forecastle, and we got the sick men through the hatch, and they lay there in the coolness with plenty of cold water beside them and a heaven of stars above, instead of a low-pitched ceiling of grimy beam and plank dark with processions of cockroaches and dim with the smoke of the stinking slush lamp.

All this occupied us till about half-past ten. When I went aft I was seized with nausea, and, sinking upon the skylight, dabbled my brow in the dew betwixt the lifted lids for the refreshment of the moisture.

I believed that my time had come, and that this sickness was the cholera. Archer followed me, and seeing me in a posture of torment, as he supposed, concluded that I was a dead man. He flung himself upon the deck with a groan, and lay motionless, crying out at intervals, "God have mercy! God have mercy!" and that was all.

In about half an hour's time the sensation of sickness passed. I went below for some brandy, swallowed half a glass, and returned with a dram for Archer, but the man had either swooned or fallen asleep, and I let him lie. I had my senses perfectly, but felt shockingly weak in body. Indeed, the capacity of realization grew unendurably poignant. I imagined too well, I figured too clearly. I pictured myself as lying dead upon the deck of the barque, found a corpse by some passing vessel after many days; and so I dreamed, often breaking away from my horrible imaginations with moans and starts, then pacing the deck to rid me of the nightmare hag of thought till I was in a fever, then cooling my head by laying my cheek upon the dew-covered skylight.

By and by the moon rose, and I sat watching it. In half an hour she was a bright light in the east, and the shaft of silver that slept under her stretched to the barque's side. It was just then that one of the two sick men on the forecastle sent up a yell. The dreadful note rang through the vessel and dropped back to the deck in an echo from the canvas.

A moment after I saw a figure get on to the forecastle rail and spring overboard. I heard the splash of his body, and, bounding over to Archer, who lay on the deck, I pulled and hauled at him, roaring out that one of the sick men had jumped overboard, and then rushed forward and looked over into the water in the place where the man had leaped, but saw nothing, not even a ripple.

I turned and peered close at the man who lay on the forecastle, and discovered that the fellow who had jumped was the boatswain. I went again to the rail to look, and lifted a coil of rope from a pin, ready to fling the fakes to the man, should he rise. The moonlight was streaming along the ocean on this side of the ship, and now, when I leaned over the rail for the second time, I saw a figure close under the bows.

I stared a minute or two; the color of the body blended with the gloom, yet the moonlight was upon him too, and then it was that after looking awhile and observing the thing to lie motionless, I perceived that it was the body that had been upon the raft! No doubt the extreme horror raised in me by the sight of the poisonous thing beheld in that light and under such conditions crazed me.

I have a recollection of laughing wildly and of defying the dark floating shape in insane language. I remember that I shook my fist and spat at it, and that I turned to seek for something to hurl at the body, and it may have been that in the instant of turning my senses left me, for after this I can recall no more.

The sequel to this tragic and extraordinary experience will be found in the following statement made by the people of the ship *For fars hire*, from Calcutta to Liverpool:

"When in latitude 2° 15' N. and longitude 79° 40' E. we sighted a barque under all plain sail, apparently abandoned. The breeze was very scanty, and though we immediately shifted our helm for her on judging that she was in distress, it took us all the morning to approach her within hailing distance.

"Everything looked right with her aloft, but the wheel was deserted, and there were no signs of anything living in her. We sent a boat in charge of the second officer, who returned and informed us that the barque was the *Justitia*, of London.

"We knew that she was from Calcutta, for we had seen her lying in the river. The second officer stated that there were three dead bodies aboard, one in a hammock in the forecastle, a second on a mattress on the forecastle, and a third against the coamings of the main-hatch; there was also a fourth man lying at the heel of the port cathead—he did not seem to be dead.

"On this, Dr. Davison was requested to visit the barque, and he was put aboard by the second officer.

"He returned quickly with one of the men, whom he instantly ordered to be stripped and put into a warm bath and his clothes thrown overboard. He said that the dead showed unmistakable signs of having died from cholera.

"We proceeded, not deeming it prudent to have anything further to do with the ill-fated craft. The person we had rescued remained insensible for two days; his recovery was then slow, but sure, thanks to the skillful treatment of Dr. Davison. There were fifteen souls when the vessel left Calcutta, and all perished except the passenger, Thomas Barron."

WRECKED IN THE ANTARCTIC

W. CLARK RUSSELL

I lay for a long while insensible; and that I should have recovered my mind instead of dying in that swoon I must ever account as the greatest wonder of a life that has not been wanting in the marvellous. I had no sooner sat up than all that had happened and my present situation instantly came to me. My hair was stiff with ice; there was no more feeling in my hands than had they been of stone; my clothes weighed upon me like a suit of armour, so inflexibly hard were they frozen. Yet I got upon my legs, and found that I could stand and walk, and that life flowed warm in my veins, for all that I had been lying motionless for an hour or more, laved by water that would have become ice had it been still.

It was intensely dark; the binnacle lamp was extinguished, and the light in the cabin burned too dimly to throw the faintest colour upon the hatchway. One thing I quickly noticed, that the gale had broken and blew no more than a fresh breeze. The sea still ran very high, but though every surge continued to hurl its head of snow, and the heavens to resemble ink from contrast with the passage, as it seemed, close under them of these pallid bodies, there was less spite in its wash, less fury in its blow. The multitudinous roaring of the heaving blackness had sobered into a hard and sullen growling, a sound as of thunder among mountains heard in a valley.

The brig pitched and rolled heavily. Much of the buoyancy of her earlier dance was gone out of her. Nevertheless, I could not persuade myself that this sluggishness was altogether due to the water she had taken in. It was wonderful, however, that she should still be afloat. No man could have heard the rending and grating of her side against the ice without supposing that every plank in it was being torn out.

Finding that I had the use of my voice, I halloaed as loudly as I could, but no human note responded. Three or four times I shouted, giving some of the people their names, but in vain. Father of mercy! I thought, what has come to pass? Is it possible that all my companions have been washed overboard? Certainly, five men at least were living before we fouled the ice. And again I cried out, "Is there any one alive?" looking wildly along the black decks, and putting so much force into my voice with the consternation that the thought of my being alone raised in me, that I had like to have burst a blood-vessel.

My loneliness was more terrible to me than any other condition of my situation. It was dreadful to be standing, nearly dead with cold, in utter darkness, upon the flooded decks of a hull wallowing miserably amid the black hollows and eager foaming peaks of the labouring sea, convinced that she was slowly filling, and that at any moment she might go down with me; it was dreadful, I say, to be thus placed, and to feel that I was in the heart of the rudest, most desolate space of sea in the world, into which the commerce of the earth dispatched but few ships all the year round. But no feature of my lamentable situation so affrighted me, so worked upon the passions of my mind, as my loneliness. Oh, for one companion, even one only, to make me an echo for mine own speech! Nay, God Himself, the merciful Father of all, even He seemed not! The blackness lay like a pall upon the deep, and upon my soul. Misery and horror were within that shadow, and beyond it nothing that my spirit could look up to!

I stood for some moments as one stunned, and then my manhood—trained to some purpose by the usage of the sea—reasserted itself; and maybe I also got some slender comfort from observing that, dull and heavy as was the motion of the brig, there was yet the buoyancy of vitality in her manner of mounting the seas, and that, after all, her case might not be so desperate as was threatened by the way in which she had been torn and precipitated past the iceberg. At moments when she plunged the whiteness of the water creaming upon the surges on either hand threw out a phantom light of sufficient power to enable me to see that the forward part of the brig was littered with wreckage, which served to a certain extent as a breakwater by preventing the seas, which washed on to the forecastle, from cascading with their former violence aft; also that the whole length of the main and top masts lay upon the larboard rail and over the side, held in that position by the gear attached to them. This was all that I could distinguish, and of this only the most elusive glimpse was to be had.

Feeling as though the very marrow in my bones were frozen, I crawled to the companion and, pulling open the door, descended. The lamp in the companion burnt faintly. There was a clock fixed to a beam over the table; my eyes directly sought it, and found the time twenty minutes after ten. This signified that I had ten or eleven hours of darkness before me!

I took down the lamp, trimmed it, and went to the lazarette hatch at the after end of the cabin. Here were kept the stores for the crew. I lifted the hatch and listened, and could hear the water in the hold gurgling and rushing with every lift of the brig's bows; and I could not question from the volume of water which the sound indicated that the vessel was steadily taking it in, but not rapidly. I swallowed half a pannikin of the hollands for the sake of the warmth and life of the draught, and entering my cabin, put on thick dry stockings, first chafing my feet till I felt the blood in them; and I then, with a seaman's dispatch, shifted the rest of my apparel, and cannot express how greatly I was comforted by the change, though the jacket and trousers I put on were still damp with the soaking of previous days. To render myself as waterproof as possible—for it was the wet clothes against the skin that made the cold so cruel—I took from the captain's cabin a stout cloak and threw it over me, enveloping my head, which I had cased in a warm fur cap, with the hood of it; and thus equipped I lighted a small hand-lantern that was used on dark nights for heaving the log, that is, for showing how the sand runs in the glass, and carried it on deck.

The lantern made the scene a dead, grave-like black outside its little circle of illumination; nevertheless its rays suffered me to guess at the picture of ruin the decks offered. The main mast was snapped three or four feet above the deck, and the stump of it showed as jagged and barbed as a wild beast's teeth. But I now noticed that the weight of the hamper being on the larboard side, balanced the list the vessel took from her shifted ballast, and that she floated on a level keel with her bows fair at the sea, whence I concluded that a sort of sea-anchor had been formed ahead of her by the wreckage, and that it held her in that posture, otherwise she must certainly have fallen into the trough.

I moved with extreme caution, casting the lantern light before me, sometimes starting at a sound that resembled a groan, then stopping to steady myself during some particular wild leap of the hull; until, coming abreast of the main hatch, the rays of the lantern struck upon a man's body, which, on my bringing the flame to his face, proved to be Captain Rosy. There was a wound over his right brow; and as if that had not sufficed to slay him, the fall of the masts had in some wonderful manner whipped a rope several times round his body, binding his arms and encircling his throat so tightly, that no executioner could have gone more artistically to work to pinion and choke a man.

Under a mass of rigging in the larboard scuppers lay two bodies, as I could just faintly discern; it was impossible to put the lantern close enough to either one of them to distinguish his face, nor had I the strength even if I had possessed the weapons to extricate them, for they lay under a whole body of shrouds, complicated by a mass of other gear, against which leaned a portion of the caboose. I viewed them long enough to satisfy my mind that they were dead, and then with a heart of lead turned away.

I crossed to the starboard side, where the deck was comparatively clear, and found the body of a seaman named Abraham Wise near the fore-hatch. This man had probably been stunned and drowned by the sea that filled the deck after I loosed the staysail. These were all of our people that I could find; the others I supposed had been washed by the water or knocked by the falling spars overboard.

I returned to the quarter-deck, and sat down in the companion-way for the shelter of it and to think. No language that I have command of could put before you the horror that possessed me as I sat meditating upon my situation and recalling the faces of the dead. The wind was rapidly falling, and with it the sea, but the motion of the brig continued very heavy, a large swell having been set running by the long, fierce gale that was gone; and there being no uproar of tempest in the sky to confound the senses, I could hear a hundred harsh and melancholy groaning and straining sounds rising from the hull, with now and again a mighty blow as from some spar or lump of ice alongside, weighty enough, you would have supposed, to stave the ship. But though the *Laughing Mary* was not a new vessel, she was one of the stoutest of her kind ever launched, built mainly of oak, and put together by an honest artificer. Nevertheless her continuing to float in her miserably torn and mangled condition was so great a miracle, that, spite of my poor shipmates having perished and my own state being as hopeless as the sky was starless, I could not but consider that God's hand was very visible in this business.

I will not pretend to remember how I passed the hours till the dawn came. I recollect of frequently stepping below to lift the hatch of the lazarette, to judge by the sound of the quantity of water in the vessel. That she was filling I knew well, yet not leaking so rapidly but that, had our crew been preserved, we might easily have kept her free, and made shift to rig up jury masts and haul us as best we could out of these desolate parallels. There was, however, nothing to be done till the day broke. I had noticed the jolly-boat bottom up near the starboard gangway, and so far as I could make out by throwing the dull lantern light upon her she was sound; but I could not have launched her without seeing what I was doing, and even had I managed this, she stood to be swamped and I to be drowned. And, in sober truth, so horrible was the prospect of going adrift in her without preparing for the adventure with oars, sail, mast, provisions, and water—most of which, by the lamplight only, were not to be come at amid the hideous muddle of wreckage—that sooner than face it I was perfectly satisfied to take my chance of the hulk sinking with me in her before the sun rose.

II

The east grew pale and grey at last. The sea rolled black as the night from it, with a rounded smooth- backed swell; the wind was spent; only a small air, still from the north-east, stirred. There were a few stars dying out in the dark west; the atmosphere was clear, and when the sun rose I knew he would turn the sable pall overhead into blueness.

The hull lay very deep. I had at one time, during the black hours, struck into a mournful calculation, and reckoned that the brig would float some two or three hours after sunrise; but when the glorious beam flashed out at last, and transformed the ashen hue of dawn into a cerulean brilliance and a deep of rolling sapphire, I started with sudden terror to observe how close the covering-board sat upon the water, and how the head of every swell ran past as high as the bulwark rail.

Yet for a few moments I stood contemplating the scene of ruin. It was visible now to its most trifling detail. The foremast was gone smooth off at the deck; it lay over the starboard bow; and the topmast floated ahead of the hull, held by the gear. Many feet of bulwarks were crushed level; the pumps had vanished; the caboose was gone! A completer nautical ruin I had never viewed.

One extraordinary stroke I quickly detected. The jolly-boat had lain stowed in the long-boat; it was thus we carried those boats, the little one lying snugly enough in the other. The sea that had flooded our decks had floated the jolly-boat out of the long-boat, and swept it bottom up to the gangway where it lay, as though God's mercy designed it should be preserved for my use; for, not long after it had been floated out, the brig struck the berg, the masts fell—and there lay the long-boat crushed into staves!

This signal and surprising intervention filled my heart with thankfulness, though my spirits sank again at the sight of my poor drowned shipmates. But, unless I had a mind to join them, it was necessary I should speedily bestir myself. So after a minute's reflection I whipped out my knife, and cutting a couple of blocks away from the raffle on deck, I rove a line through them, and so made a tackle, by the help of which I turned the jolly-boat over: I then with a handspike prised her nose to the gangway, secured a bunch of rope on either side her to act as fenders or buffers when she should be launched and lying alongside, ran her midway out by the tackle, and, attaching a line to a ring-bolt in her bow, shoved her over the side, and she fell with a splash, shipping scarce a hatful of water.

I found her mast and sail—the sail furled to the mast, as it was used to lie in her—close against the stump of the mainmast; but though I sought with all the diligence that hurry would permit for her rudder, I nowhere saw it, but I met with an oar that had belonged to the other boat, and this with the mast and sail I dropped into her, the swell lifting her up to my hand when the blue fold swung past.

My next business was to victual her. I ran to the cabin, but the lazarette was full of water, and none of the provisions in it to be come at. I thereupon ransacked the cabin, and found a whole Dutch cheese, a piece of raw pork, half a ham, eight or ten biscuits, some candles, a tinder-box, several lemons, a little bag of flour, and thirteen bottles of beer. These things I rolled up in a cloth and placed them in the boat, then took from the captain's locker four jars of spirits, two of which I emptied that I might fill them with fresh water. I also took with me from the captain's cabin a small boat compass.

The heavy, sluggish, sodden movement of the hull advised me to make haste. She was now barely lifting to the swell that came brimming in broad liquid blue brows to her stem. It seemed as though another ton of water would sink her; and if the swell fell over her bows and filled the decks, down she would go. I had a small parcel of guineas in my chest, and was about to fetch this money, when a sort of staggering sensation in the upward slide of the hull gave me a fright, and, watching my chance, I jumped into the boat and cast the line that held her adrift.

The sun was an hour above the horizon. The sea was a deep blue, heaving very slowly, though you felt the weight of the mighty ocean in every fold; and eastwards, the shoulders of the swell, catching the glorious reflection of the sun, hurled the splendour along, till all that quarter of the sea looked to be a mass of leaping dazzle. Upon the eastern sea-line lay a range of white clouds, compact as the chalk cliffs of Dover; threads, crescents, feather-shapes of vapour of the daintiest sort, shot with pearly lustre, floated overhead very high. It was in truth a fair and pleasant morning—of an icy coldness indeed, but the air being dry, its shrewdness was endurable. Yet was it a brightness to fill me with anguish by obliging me to reflect how it would have been with us had it dawned yesterday instead of to-day. My companions would have been alive, and yonder sinking ruined fabric a trim ship capable of bearing us stoutly into warm seas and to our homes at last.

I threw the oar over the stern of the boat to keep her near to the brig, not so much because I desired to see the last of her, as because of the shrinking of my soul within me from the thought of heading in my loneliness into those prodigious leagues of ocean which lay stretched under the sky. Whilst the hull floated she was something to hold on to, so to say, something for the eye amid the vastness of water to rest upon, something to take out of the insufferable feeling of solitude the poisonous sting of conviction.

But her end was at hand. I had risen to step the boat's mast, and was standing and grasping it whilst I directed a slow look round the horizon in God knows what vain hope of beholding a sail, when my eye coming to the brig, I observed that she was sinking. She went down very slowly; there was a horrible gurgling sound of water rushing into her, and her main deck blew up with a loud clap or blast of noise. I could follow the line of her bulwarks fluctuating and waving in the clear dark blue when she was some feet under. A number of whirlpools spun round over her, but the slowness of her foundering was solemnly marked by the gradual descent of the ruins of masts and yards which were attached to the hull by their rigging, and which she dragged down with her. On a sudden, when the last fragment of mast had disappeared, and when the hollows of the whirlpools were flattening to the level surface of the sea, up rose a body, with a sort of leap. It was the sailor that had lain drowned on the starboard side of the forward deck. Being frozen stiff he rose in the posture in which he had expired, that is, with his arms extended; so that, when he jumped to the surface, he came with his hands lifted up to heaven, and thus he stayed a minute, sustained by the eddies which also revolved him.

The shock occasioned by this melancholy object was so great, it came near to causing me to swoon. He sank when the water ceased to twist him, and I was unspeakingly thankful to see him vanish, for his posture had all the horror of a spectral appeal, and such was the state of my mind that imagination might quickly have worked the apparition, had it lingered, into an instrument for the unsettling of my reason.

I rose from the seat on to which I had sunk and loosed the sail, and hauling the sheet aft, put the oar over the stern, and brought the little craft's head to an easterly course. The draught of air was extremely weak, and scarce furnished impulse enough to the sail to raise a bubble along-side. The boat was about fifteen feet long; she would be but a small boat for summer pleasuring in English July lake-waters, yet here was I in her in the heart of a vast ocean, many leagues south and west of the stormi-est, most inhospitable point of land in the world, with distances before me almost infinite for such a boat as this to measure ere I could heave a civilised coast or a habitable island into view!

At the start I had a mind to steer north-west and blow, as the wind would suffer, into the South Sea, where perchance I might meet a whaler or a Southseaman from New Holland; but my heart sank at the pros-pect of the leagues of water which rolled between me and the islands and the western American seaboard. Indeed I understood that my only hope of deliverance lay in being picked up; and that, though by head-ing east I should be clinging to the stormy parts, I was more likely to meet with a ship hereabouts than by sailing into the great desolation of the north-west. The burden of my loneliness weighed down upon me so crushingly that I cannot but consider my senses must have been some-what dulled by suffering, for had they been active to their old accustomed height, I am persuaded my heart must have broken and that I should have died of grief.

Faintly as the wind blew, it speedily wafted me out of sight of the floating relics of the wreck, and then all was bare, bald, swelling sea and empearled sky, darkening in lagoons of azure down to the soft moun-tainous masses of white vapour lying like the coast of a continent on the larboard horizon. But one living thing there was besides myself a grey-breasted albatross, of a princely width of pinion. I had not observed it till the hull went down, and then, lifting my eyes with involuntary sympathy in the direction pointed to by the upraised arms of the sailor, I observed the great royal bird hanging like a shape of marble directly over the frothing eddies. It was as though the spirit of the deep had taken form in the substance of the noblest of all the fowls of its dominions, and, poised on tremorless wings, was surveying with the cold curiosity of an intelligence empty of human emotion the destruction of one of those fabrics whose unequal contests and repeated triumphs had provoked its haughty surprise. The bird quitted the spot of the wreck after a while and followed me. Its eyes had the sparkling blood-red gleam of rubies. It was as silent as a phantom, and with arched neck and motionless plumes seemed to watch me with an earnestness that presently grew insufferable. So far from finding any comfort of companionship in the creature, methought if it did not speedily break from the motionless posture in which it rested on its seat of air, and remove its piercing gaze, it would end in crazing me. I felt a sudden rage, and, jumping up, shouted and shook my fist at it. This frightened the thing. It uttered a strange salt cry—the very note of a gust of wind splitting upon a rope—flapped its wings, and after a turn or two sailed away into the north.

I watched it till its figure melted into the blue atmosphere; and then sank trembling into the sternsheets of the boat.

III

Four days did I pass in that little open boat.

The first day was fine till sunset; it then blew fresh from the north-west, and I was obliged to keep the boat before the wind. The next day was dark and turbulent, with heavy falls of snow and a high swell from the north, and the wind a small gale. On the third day the sun shone, and it was a fair day, but horribly cold, and I saw two icebergs like clouds upon the far western sea-line. There followed a cruel night of clouded skies, sleet and snow, and a very troubled sea; and then broke the fourth day, as softly brilliant as an English May day, but cold—great God, how cold!

Thus might I epitomise this passage; and I do so to spare you the weariness of a relation of uneventful suffering.

In those four days I mainly ran before the wind, and in this way drove many leagues south, though whenever a chance offered I hauled my sheet for the east. I know not, I am sure, how the boat lived. I might pretend it was due to my clever management—I do not say I had no share in my own preservation, but to God belongs all the praise.

In the blackness of the first night the sea boiled all about me. The boat leapt into hollows in which the sail slapped the mast. One look behind me at the high dark curl of the oncoming surge had so affrighted me that I never durst turn my head again lest the sight should deprive me of the nerve to hold the oar with which I steered. I sat as squarely as the task of steering would suffer, trusting that if a sea should tumble over the stern my back would serve as a breakwater, and save the boat from being swamped. The whole sail was on her, and I could not help myself; for it would have been certain death to quit the steering oar for an instant. It was this that saved me, perhaps; for the boat blew along with such prodigious speed, running to the height of a sea as though she meant to dart from that eminence into the air, that the slope of each following surge swung like a pendulum under her, and though her sail was becalmed in the trough, her momentum was so great that she was speeding up the acclivity and catching the whole weight of the wind afresh before there was time for her to lose way.

I was nearly dead with cold and misery when the morning came, but the sparkling sun and the blue sky cheered me, and as wind and sea fell with the soaring of the orb, I was enabled to flatten aft the sheet and let the boat steer herself whilst I beat my arms about for warmth and broke my fast. When I look back I wonder that I should have taken any pains to live. That it is possible for the human mind at any period of its existence to be absolutely hopeless, I do not believe; but I can very honestly say that when I gazed round upon the enormous sea I was in, and considered the size of my boat, the quantity of my provisions, and my distance (even if I was heading that way) from the nearest point of land, I was not sensible of the faintest stirring of hope, and viewed myself as a dead man.

No bird came near me. Once I spied the back of a great black fish about a quarter of a mile off. The wetness of it caught the sunshine and reflected it like a mirror of polished steel, and the flash was so brilliant it might have passed for a bed of white fire floating on the blue heavings. But nothing more that was living did I meet, and such was the vastness of the sea over which my little keel glided, in the midst of which I sat abandoned by the angels, that for utter loneliness I might have been the very last of the human race.

When the third night came down with sullen blasts sweeping into a steady storming of wind, that swung a strong melancholy howl through the gloom, it found me so weak with cold, watching and anxiety, and the want of space wherein to rid my limbs of the painful cramp which weighted them with an insupportable leaden sensation, that I had barely power to control the boat with the oar. I pined for sleep; one hour of slumber would, I felt, give me new life, but I durst not close my eyes. The boat was sweeping through the dark and seething seas, and her course had to be that of an arrow, or she would capsize and be smothered in a breath.

Maybe I fell something delirious, for I had many strange and frightful fancies. Indeed I doubt not it was the spirit of madness—that is certainly tonical when small—which furnished strength enough to my arm to steer with. It was like the action of a powerful cordial in my blood, and the very horrors it fed my brain with were an animation to my physical qualities. The gale became a voice; it cried out my name, and every shout of it past my ear had the sound of the word "Despair!" I witnessed the forms of huge phantoms flying over the boat; I watched the beating of their giant wings of shadow and heard the thunder of their laughter as they fled ahead, leaving scores of like monstrous shapes to follow. There was a faint lightning of phosphor in the creaming heads of the ebon surges, and my sick imagination twisted that pallid complexion into the dim reflection of the lamps of illuminated pavilions at the bottom of the sea; mystic palaces of green marble, radiant cities in the measureless kingdoms of the ocean gods. I had a fancy of roofs of pearl below, turrets of milk-white coral, pavements of rainbow lustre like to the shootings and dartings of the hues of shells inclined and trembled to the sun. I thought I could behold the movements of shapes as indeterminable as the forms which swarm in dreams, human brows crowned with gold, the cold round emerald eyes of fish, the creamy breasts of women, large outlines slowly floating upwards, making a deeper blackness upon the blackness like the dye of the electric storm upon the velvet bosom of midnight. Often would I shrink from side to side, starting from a fancied apparition leaping into terrible being out of some hurling block of liquid obscurity.

Once a light shone upon the masthead. At any other time I should have known this to be a St. Elmo's fire, a corposant, the ignis fatuus of the deep, and hailed it with a seaman's faith in its promise of gentle weather. But to my distempered fancy it was a lanthorn hung up by a spirit hand; I traced the dusky curve of an arm and observed the busy twitching of visionary fingers by the rays of the ghostly light; the outline of a large face of a bland and sorrowful expression, pallid as any foam flake whirling past, came into the sphere of those graveyard rays. I shrieked and shut my eyes, and when I looked again the light was gone.

Long before daybreak I was exhausted. Mercifully, the wind was scant; the stars shone very gloriously; on high sparkled the Cross of the southern world. A benign influence seemed to steal into me out of its silver shining; the craze fell from me, and I wept.

Shortly afterwards, worn out by three days and nights of suffering, I fell into a deep sleep, and when I awoke my eyes opened right upon the blinding sun.

This was the morning of the fourth day. I was without a watch. By the height of the sun I reckoned the hour to be ten. I threw a languid glance at the compass and found the boat's head pointing north-west; she fell off and came to, being without governance, and was scarcely sailing therefore. The wind was west, a very light breeze just enough to put a bright twinkling into the long, smooth folds of the wide and weighty swell that was rolling up from the north-east. I tried to stand, but was so benumbed that many minutes passed before I had the use of my legs. Brightly as the sun shone there was no more warmth in his light than you find in a moonbeam on a frosty night, and the bite in the air was like the pang of ice itself pressed against the cheek. My right hand suffered most; I had fallen asleep clasping the loom of the steering oar, and when I awoke my fingers still gripped it, so that, on withdrawing them, they remained curved like talons, and I believed I had lost their use, and even reckoned they would snap off and so set up a mortification, till by much diligent rubbing I grew sensible of a small glow which, increasing, ended in rendering the joints supple.

I stood up to take a view of the horizon, and the first sight that met my eye forced a cry from me. Extending the whole length of the south-west seaboard lay what I took to be a line of white coast melting at either extremity into the blue airy distance. Even at the low elevation of the boat my eye seemed to measure thirty miles of it. It was not white as chalk is; there was something of a crystalline complexion upon the face of its solidity. It was too far off to enable me to remark its outline; yet on straining my sight—the atmosphere being very exquisitely clear—I thought I could distinguish the projections of peaks, of rounded slopes, and aerial angularities in places which, in the refractive lens of the air, looked, with their hue of glassy azure, like the loom of high land behind the coastal line.

The notion that it was ice came into my head after the first prospect of it; and then I returned to my earlier belief that it was land. Methought if it were ice, it must be the borderland of the Antarctic circle, the limits of the unfrozen ocean, for it was incredible that so mighty a body could signify less than the capes and terraces of a continent of ice glazing the circumference of the pole for leagues and leagues; but then I also knew that, though first the brig and then my boat had been for days steadily blown south, I was still to the north of the South Shetland parallels, and many degrees therefore removed from the polar barrier. Hence I concluded that what I saw was land, and that the peculiar crystal shining of it was caused by the snow that covered it.

But what land? Some large island that had been missed by the explorers and left uncharted? I put a picture of the map of this part of the world before my mind's eye, and fell to an earnest consideration of it, but could recollect of no land hereabouts, unless indeed we had been wildly wrong in our reckoning aboard the brig, and I in the boat had been driven four or five times the distance I had calculated—things not to be entertained.

Yet even as a mere break in the frightful and enduring continuity of the sea-line—even as something that was not sea nor sky nor the cold silent and mocking illusion of clouds—it took a character of blessedness in my eyes; my gaze hung upon it joyously, and my heart swelled with a new impulse of life in my breast. It would be strange, I thought, if on approaching it something to promise me deliverance from this dreadful situation did not offer itself—some whaler or trader at anchor, signs of habitation and of the presence of men, nay, even a single hut to serve as a refuge from the pitiless cold, the stormy waters, the black, lonely, delirious watches of the night, till help should heave into view with the white canvas of a ship.

I put the boat's head before the wind, and steered with one hand whilst I got some breakfast with the other. I thanked God for the brightness of the day and for the sight of that strange white line of land, that went in glimmering blobs of faintness to the trembling horizon where the southern end of it died out. The swell rose full and brimming ahead, rolling in sapphire hills out of the north-east, as I have said, whence I inferred that that extremity of the land did not extend very much farther than I could see it, otherwise there could not have been so much weight of water as I found in the heaving.

The breeze blew lightly and was the weaker for my running before it; but the little line of froth that slipped past either side the boat gave me to know that the speed would not be less than four miles in the hour; and as I reckoned the land to be but a few leagues distant, I calculated upon being ashore some little while before sundown.

In this way two hours passed. By this time the features of the coast were tolerably distinct. Yet I was puzzled. There was a peculiar sheen all about the irregular skyline; a kind of pearly whitening, as it were, of the heavens beyond, like to the effect produced by the rising of a very delicate soft mist melting from a mountain's brow into the air. This dismayed me. Still I cried to myself, "It must be land! All that whiteness is snow, and the luminous tinge above it is the reflection of the glaring sunshine thrown upwards from the dazzle. It cannot be ice! 'tis too mighty a barrier. Surely no single iceberg ever reached to the prodigious proportions of that coast. And it cannot be an assemblage of bergs, for there is no break—it is leagues of solid conformation. Oh, yes, it is land, sure enough! some island whose tops and seaboard are covered with snow. But what of that? It may be populated all the same. Are the northern kingdoms of Europe bare of life because of the winter rigours?" And then I thought to myself, if that island have natives, I would rather encounter them as the savages of an icebound country than as the inhabitants of a land of sunshine and spices and radiant vegetation; for it is the denizens of the most gloriously fair ocean seats in the world who are man-eaters; not the Patagonian, giant though he be, nor the blubber-fed anatomies of the ice-climes.

Thus I sought to reassure and comfort myself. Meanwhile my boat sailed quietly along, running up and down the smooth and foamless hills of water very buoyantly, and the sun slided into the north-west sky and darted a reddening beam upon the coast towards which I steered.

THE PLAGUE SHIP

HERMAN MELVILLE

"Mammy! mammy! come and see the sailors eating out of little troughs, just like our pigs at home." Thus exclaimed one of the steerage children, who at dinner-time was peeping down into the forecastle, where the crew were assembled, helping themselves from the "kids", which, indeed, resemble hog-troughs not a little.

"Pigs, is it?" coughed Jackson, from his bunk, where he sat presiding over the banquet, but not partaking, like a devil who had lost his appetite by chewing sulphur.—"Pigs, is it?—And the day is close by, ye spalpeens, when you'll want to be after taking a sup at our troughs!"

This malicious prophecy proved true.

As day followed day without glimpse of shore or reef, and head-winds drove the ship back, as hounds a deer; the improvidence and shortsightedness of the passengers in the steerage, with regard to their outfits for the voyage, began to be followed by the inevitable results.

Many of them at last went aft to the mate, saying that they had nothing to eat, their provisions were expended, and they must be supplied from the ship's stores, or starve.

This was told to the captain, who was obliged to issue a ukase from the cabin, that every steerage passenger, whose destitution was demonstrable, should be given one sea-biscuit and two potatoes a day; a sort of substitute for a muffin and a brace of poached eggs.

But this scanty ration was quite insufficient to satisfy their hunger: hardly enough to satisfy the necessities of a healthy adult. The consequence was, that all day long, and all through the night, scores of the emigrants went about the decks, seeking what they might devour. They plundered the chicken-coop; and disguising the fowls, cooked them at the public galley. They made inroads upon the pig-pen in the boat, and carried off a promising young shoat: *him* they devoured raw, not venturing to make an incognito of his carcass; they prowled about the cook's caboose, till he threatened them with a ladle of scalding water; they waylaid the steward on his regular excursions from the cook to the cabin; they hung round the forecastle, to rob the bread-barge; they beset the sailors, like beggars in the streets, craving a mouthful in the name of the Church.

At length, to such excesses were they driven, that the Grand Russian, Captain Riga, issued another ukase, and to this effect: Whatsoever emigrant is found guilty of stealing, the same shall be tied into the rigging and flogged.

Upon this, there were secret movements in the steerage, which almost alarmed me for the safety of the ship; but nothing serious took place, after all; and they even acquiesced in, or did not resent, a singular punishment which the captain caused to be inflicted upon a culprit of their clan, as a substitute for a flogging. For no doubt he thought that such rigorous discipline as *that* might exasperate five hundred emigrants into an insurrection.

A head was fitted to one of the large deck-tubs—the half of a cask; and into this head a hole was cut; also, two smaller holes in the bottom of the tub. The head—divided in the middle, across the diameter of the orifice— was now fitted round the culprit's neck; and he was forthwith coopered up into the tub, which rested on his shoulders, while his legs protruded through the holes in the bottom.

It was a burden to carry; but the man could walk with it; and so ridiculous was his appearance, that in spite of the indignity, he himself laughed with the rest at the figure he cut.

"Now, Pat, my boy," said the mate, "fill that big wooden belly of yours, if you can."

Compassionating his situation, our old "doctor" used to give him alms of food, placing it upon the cask-head before him; till at last, when the time for deliverance came, Pat protested against mercy, and would fain have continued playing Diogenes in the tub for the rest of this starving voyage.

Although fast-sailing ships, blest with prosperous breezes, have frequently made the run across the Atlantic in eighteen days; yet, it is not uncommon for other vessels to be forty, or fifty, and even sixty, eighty, and ninety days, in making the same passage. Though in these cases, some signal calamity or incapacity must occasion so great a detention. It is also true, that generally the passage out from America is shorter than the return; which is to be ascribed to the prevalence of westerly winds.

We had been outside of Cape Clear upward of twenty days, still harassed by head-winds, though with pleasant weather upon the whole, when we were visited by a succession of rain-storms, which lasted the greater part of a week.

During the interval, the emigrants were obliged to remain below; but this was nothing strange to some of them; who, not recovering, while at sea, from their first attack of seasickness, seldom or never made their appearance on deck, during the entire passage.

During the week, now in question, fire was only once made in the public galley. This occasioned a good deal of domestic work to be done in the steerage, which otherwise would have been done in the open air. When the lulls of the rain-storms would intervene, some unusually cleanly emigrant would climb to the deck, with a bucket of slops, to toss into the sea. No experience seemed sufficient to instruct some of these ignorant people in the simplest, and most elemental principles of ocean-life. Spite of all lectures on the subject, several would continue to shun the leeward side of the vessel, with their slops. One morning, when it was blowing very fresh, a simple fellow pitched over a gallon or two of something to windward. Instantly it flew back in his face; and also, in the face of the chief mate, who happened to be standing by at the time. The offender was collared, and shaken on the spot; and ironically commanded, never, for the future, to throw anything to windward at sea, but fine ashes and scalding hot water.

During the frequent hard blows we experienced, the hatchways on the steerage were, at intervals, hermetically closed; sealing down in their noisome den, those scores of human beings. It was something to be marvelled at, that the shocking fate, which, but a short time ago, overtook the poor passengers in a Liverpool steamer in the Channel, during similar stormy weather, and under similar treatment, did not overtake some of the emigrants of the *Highlander*.

Nevertheless, it was, beyond question, this noisome confinement in so close, unventilated, and crowded a den: joined to the deprivation of sufficient food, from which many were suffering; which, helped by their personal uncleanliness, brought on a malignant fever.

The first report was, that two persons were affected. No sooner was it known, than the mate promptly repaired to the medicine-chest in the cabin: and with the remedies deemed suitable, descended into the steerage. But the medicines proved of no avail; the invalids rapidly grew worse; and two more of the emigrants became infected.

Upon this, the captain himself went to see them; and returning, sought out a certain alleged physician among the cabin-passengers; begging him to wait upon the sufferers; hinting that, thereby, he might prevent the disease from extending into the cabin itself. But this person denied being a physician; and from fear of contagion—though he did not confess that to be the motive—refused even to enter the steerage.

The cases increased: the utmost alarm spread through the ship: and scenes ensued, over which, for the most part, a veil must be drawn; for such is the fastidiousness of some readers, that, many times, they must lose the most striking incidents in a narrative like mine.

Many of the panic-stricken emigrants would fain now have domiciled on deck; but being so scantily clothed, the wretched weather—wet cold, and tempestuous—drove the best part of them again below. Yet any other human beings, perhaps, would rather have faced the most outrageous storm, than continued to breathe the pestilent air of the steerage. But some of these poor people must have been so used to the most abasing calamities, that the atmosphere of a lazar-house almost seemed their natural air.

The first four cases happened to be in adjoining bunks; and the emigrants who slept in the farther part of the steerage, threw up a barricade in front of those bunks so as to cut off communication. But this was no sooner reported to the captain, than he ordered it to be thrown down; since it could be of no possible benefit; but would only make still worse, what was already direful enough.

It was not till after a good deal of mingled threatening and coaxing, that the mate succeeded in getting the sailors below, to accomplish the captain's order.

The sight that greeted us, upon entering, was wretched indeed. It was like entering a crowded jail. From the rows of rude bunks, hundreds of meagre, begrimed faces were turned upon us; while seated upon the chests, were scores of unshaven men, smoking tea-leaves, and creating a suffocating vapour. But this vapour was better than the native air of the place, which from almost unbelievable causes, was fetid in the extreme. In every corner, the females were huddled together, weeping and lamenting; children were asking bread from their mothers, who had none to give; and old men, seated upon the floor, were leaning back against the heads of the water-casks, with closed eyes and fetching their breath with a gasp.

At one end of the place was seen the barricade, hiding the invalids; while—notwithstanding the crowd—in front of it was a clear area, which the fear of contagion had left open.

"That bulkhead must come down," cried the mate, in a voice that rose above the din. "Take hold of it, boys."

But hardly had we touched the chests composing it, when a crowd of palefaced, infuriated men rushed up; and with terrific howls, swore they would slay us, if we did not desist.

"Haul it down!" roared the mate.

But the sailors fell back, murmuring something about merchant seamen having no pensions in case of being maimed, and they had no out shipped to fight fifty to one. Further efforts were made by the mate who at last had recourse to entreaty; but it would not do; and we were obliged to depart, without achieving our object.

About four o'clock that morning, the first four died. They were all men; and the scenes which ensued were frantic in the extreme. Certainly, the bottomless profound of the sea, over which we were sailing, concealed nothing more frightful.

Orders were at once passed to bury the dead. But this was unnecessary. By their own countrymen, they were torn from the clasp of their wives, rolled in their own bedding, with ballast-stones, and with hurried rites, were dropped into the ocean.

At this time, ten more men had caught the disease; and with a degree of devotion worthy all praise, the mate attended them with his medicines; but the captain did not again go down to them.

It was all-important now that the steerage should be purified; and had it not been for the rains and squalls, which would have made it madness to turn such a number of women and children upon the wet and unsheltered decks, the steerage passengers would have been ordered above, and their den have been given a thorough cleansing. But, for the present, this was out of the question. The sailors peremptorily refused to go among the defilements to remove them; and so besotted were the greater part of the emigrants themselves, that though the necessity of the case was forcibly painted to them, they would not lift a hand to assist in what seemed their own salvation.

The panic in the cabin was now very great; and for fear of contagion to themselves, the cabin passengers would fain have made a prisoner of the captain, to prevent him from going forward beyond the mainmast. Their clamours at last induced him to tell the two mates that for the present they must sleep and take their meals elsewhere than in their old quarters, which communicated with the cabin.

On land, a pestilence is fearful enough; but there, many can flee from an infected city; whereas, in a ship, you are locked and bolted in the very hospital itself. Nor is there any possibility of escape from it; and in so small and crowded a place, no precaution can effectually guard against contagion.

Horrible as the sights of the steerage now were, the cabin, perhaps, presented a scene equally despairing. Many, who had seldom prayed before, now implored the merciful heavens, night and day, for fair winds and fine weather. Trunks were opened for Bibles; and at last, even prayer-meetings were held over the very table across which the loud jest had been so often heard.

Strange, though almost universal, that the seemingly nearer prospect of that death which anybody at any time may die, should produce these spasmodic devotions, when an everlasting Asiatic Cholera is forever thinning our ranks; and die by death we all must at last.

On the second day, seven died, one of whom was the little tailor; on the third, four; on the fourth, six, of whom one was the Greenland sailor, and another, a woman in the cabin, whose death, however, was afterward supposed to have been purely induced by her fears. These last deaths brought the panic to its height; and sailors, officers, cabin-passengers, and emigrants—all looked upon each other like lepers. All but the only true leper among us—the mariner Jackson, who seemed elated with the thought, that for *him*—already in the deadly clutches of another disease—no danger was to be apprehended from a fever which only swept off the comparatively healthy. Thus, in the midst of the despair of the healthful, this incurable invalid was not cast down; not, at least, by the same considerations that appalled the rest.

And still, beneath a gray, gloomy sky, the doomed craft beat on; now on this tack, now on that; battling against hostile blasts, and drenched in rain and spray; scarcely making an inch of progress toward her port.

On the sixth morning, the weather merged into a gale, to which we stripped our ship to a storm-stay-sail. In ten hours' time, the waves ran in mountains; and the *Highlander* rose and fell like some vast buoy on the water. Shrieks and lamentations were driven to leeward and drowned in the roar of the wind among the cordage; while we gave to the gale the blackened bodies of five more of the dead.

But as the dying departed, the places of two of them were filled in the rolls of humanity, by the birth of two infants, whom the plague, panic, and gale had hurried into the world before their time. The first cry of one of these infants, was almost simultaneous with the splash of its father's body in the sea. Thus we come and we go. But, surrounded by death, both mothers and babes survived.

At midnight, the wind went down; leaving a long, rolling sea; and, for the first time in a week, a clear, starry sky.

In the first morning-watch, I sat with Harry on the windlass, watching the billows; which, seen in the night, seemed real hills, upon which fortresses might have been built; and real valleys, in which villages, and groves, and gardens, might have nestled. It was like a landscape in Switzerland; for down into those dark, purple glens, often tumbled the white foam of the wavecrests, like avalanches; while the seething and boiling that ensued, seemed the swallowing up of human beings.

By the afternoon of the next day this heavy sea subsided; and we bore down on the waves, with all our canvas set; stun'-sails alow and aloft; and our best steersman at the helm; the captain himself at his elbow;— bowling along, with a fair, cheering breeze over the taffrail.

The decks were cleared, and swabbed bone-dry; and then, all the emigrants who were not invalids, poured themselves out on deck, snuffing the delightful air, spreading their damp bedding in the sun, and regaling themselves with the generous charity of the captain, who of late had seen fit to increase their allowance of food. A detachment of them now joined a band of the crew, who proceeding into the steerage, with buckets and brooms, gave it a thorough cleansing, sending on deck, I know not how many bucketsful of defilements. It was more like cleaning out a stable than a retreat for men and women. This day we buried three; the next day one, and then the pestilence left us, with seven convalescent; who, placed near the opening of the hatchway, soon rallied under the skilful treatment, and even tender care of the mate.

But even under this favorable turn of affairs, much apprehension was still entertained, lest in crossing the Grand Banks of Newfoundland, the fogs, so generally encountered there, might bring on a return of the fever. But, to the joy of all hands, our fair wind still held on; and we made a rapid run across these dreaded shoals, and southward steered for New York.

Our days were now fair and mild, and though the wind abated, yet we still ran our course over a pleasant sea. The steerage-passengers—at least by far the greater number—wore a still, subdued aspect, though a little cheered by the genial air, and the hopeful thought of soon reaching their port. But those who had lost fathers, husbands, wives, or children, needed no crêpe, to reveal to others who they were. Hard and bitter indeed was their lot; for with the poor and desolate, grief is no indulgence of mere sentiment, however sincere, but a gnawing reality, that eats into their vital beings; they have no kind condo-lers, and bland physicians, and troops of sympathizing friends; and they must toil, though to-morrow be the burial and their pallbearers throw down the hammer to lift up the coffin.

How, then, with these emigrants, who, three thousand miles from home, suddenly found themselves deprived of brothers and husbands, with but a few pounds, or perhaps but a few shillings, to buy food in a strange land?

As for the passengers in the cabin, who now so jocund as they, draw-ing nigh, with their long purses and goodly portmanteaus to the prom-ised land, without fear of fate? One and all were generous and gay, the jelly-eyed old gentleman, before spoken of, gave a shilling to the steward.

One lady who had died, was an elderly person, an American, returning from a visit to an only brother in London. She had no friend or relative on board, hence, as there is little mourning for a stranger dying among strangers, her memory had been buried with her body.

But the thing most worthy of note among these now light-hearted people in feathers, was the gay way in which some of them bantered oth-ers, upon the panic into which nearly all had been thrown.

And since, if the extreme fear of a crowd in a panic of peril, proves grounded on causes sufficient, they must then indeed come to perish;— therefore it is, that at such times they must make up their minds either to die, or else survive to be taunted by their fellow-men with their fear. For except in extraordinary instances of exposure, there are few living men, who, at bottom, are not very slow to admit that any other living men have ever been very much nearer death than themselves. Accordingly, *craven* is the phrase too often applied to anyone who, with however good rea-son, has been appalled at the prospect of sudden death, and yet lived to escape it. Though, should he have perished in conformity with his fears, not a syllable of *craven* would you hear. This is the language of one, who more than once has beheld the scenes, whence these principles have been deduced. The subject invites much subtle speculation; for in every being's ideas of death, and his behavior when it suddenly menaces him, lies the best index to his life and his faith. Though the Christian era had not then begun, Socrates died the death of the Christian; and though Hume was not a Christian in theory, yet he, too, died the death of the Christian— humble, composed, without bravado; and thought the most skeptical of philosophical skeptics, yet full of that firm, creedless faith, that embraces the spheres. Seneca died dictating to posterity; Petronius lightly discours- ing of essences and love-songs; and Addison, calling upon Christendom to behold how calmly a Christian could die; but not even the last of these three, perhaps, died the best death of the Christian.

The cabin passenger who had used to read prayers while the rest kneeled against the transoms and settees, was one of the merry young sparks, who had occasioned such agonies of jealousy to the, poor tailor, now no more. In his rakish vest, and dangling watch-chain, this same youth, with all the awfulness of fear, had led the earnest petitions of his companions, supplicating mercy, where before he had never solicited the slightest favour. More than once had he been seen thus engaged by the observant steersman at the helm: who looked through the little glass in the cabin bulk-head.

But this youth was an April man; the storm had departed; and now he shone in the sun, none braver than he.

One of his jovial companions ironically advised him to enter into holy orders upon his arrival in New York.

"Why so?" said the other, "have I such an orotund voice?"

"No;" profanely returned his friend—"but you are a coward—just the man to be a parson, and pray."

However this narrative of the circumstances attending the fever among the emigrants on the *Highlander* may appear; and though these things happened so long ago; yet just such events, nevertheless, are perhaps tak- ing place to-day. But the only account you obtain of such events, is gener- ally contained in a newspaper paragraph, under the shipping-head. *There* is the obituary of the destitute dead, who die on the sea. They die, like the billows that break on the shore, and no more are heard or seen. But in the events, thus merely initialized in the catalogue of passing occurrences, and but glanced at by the readers of news, who are more taken up with paragraphs of fuller flavour; what a world of life and death, what a world of humanity and its woes, lies shrunk into a three-worded sentence!

You see no plague-ship driving through a stormy sea; you hear no groans of despair; you see no corpses thrown over the bulwarks; you mark not the wringing hands and torn hair of widows and orphans:—all is a blank. And one of these blanks I have but filled up, in recounting the details of the *Highlander's* calamity.

HURRICANE

WILLIAM WATSON

One day it fell dead calm, and about noon a large circle was observed round the sun of a purple colour, which some of the men declared indicated the approach of a heavy gale, and that we might in a short time look out for a violent norther. Anything would be a relief to this suspense, and a norther would be welcomed if it did not come too severe.

As it was about dead calm, sails were taken down, and every strop, hook, and cringle examined and made as secure as possible. Flying jib and small sails stowed, and everything about deck firmly lashed and made snug. Double reefs put in mainsail and foresail, and single reef in jib, and sails hoisted again, and we looked for the change in the weather.

We did not have long to wait. About 3 P.M. the sky darkened all round, and by 4 P.M. it was fearfully dark, the sky to the northward being black as ink. There was now no mistake but that we were going to have a heavy gale, but whether it was going to be a West India hurricane or a Texas norther we did not know.

It was not just yet the season for the regular northers, but there were often in those latitudes heavy gales about the equinox which sometimes took the form of northers, and blew with great violence, but they were generally of short duration, and might be said to be something between the Texas norther and the West India hurricane.

There could now be seen under the black cloud to the northward what appeared to be snow hillocks on the horizon, which soon spread out, and was coming towards us. This of course was the sea lashed into a foam by the fury of the wind, but still not a breath of wind had reached us, and the vessel still rolled in a dead calm.

It soon came on, however, direct from the north, and first a few drops of rain struck the vessel, and then the cold wind which indicated, to all appearance at least, it was a norther. It struck the vessel with such violence that I thought it would have torn the masts out of her before she gathered headway.

I was not sure how the *Rob Roy* would lay to under a close-reefed I foresail, and I determined, as the wind was fair for us, to make the best of it, and scud before it.

The vessel was now rushing through the water at a great rate, but when the full force of the gale came up it struck her with such violence that it seemed as if it would tumble her stern overhead.

"Get the mainsail off her," I cried.

This was easier said than done. The sheet had been eased off to run before the wind, and the belly of the sail was pressing against the shrouds, and with the awful force of the wind it was impossible to move it. To ease her in the meantime the peak purchase was cast off, and the peak dropped. This did ease her a little, but the gale kept increasing in violence, and the mainsail must come off her.

To handle such a large sail in such a tempest was no easy task, and as the boom was eased off it must be got aboard. No strength could haul it in against the force of such wind; the vessel must be rounded to.

"Hard down your helm!" was the word. The helm was put hard down, but the peak having been dropped she would not come up, but rushed along in the trough of the sea with the full force of the hurricane on her beam. That she did not lose her masts or capsize showed great strength and stability.

"Let go the jib halliards." This was done and the jib hauled down. This had the desired effect, and she came up into the wind. The fore sheet was hauled in, and she was held up till the main sheet could be hauled in, the sail lowered and stowed securely.

The gale had now become terrific, and the wind being directly against the current of the Gulf Stream, the waves rose very fast and to a great height. While we had the vessel thus rounded to, we thought to try if she would lay to in the gale, but the seas having got to a great height, and coming with great force, and the vessel having such a light hold on the water, she was thrown back stern on with every wave, causing her to fall heavily on her rudder, which I feared might be carried away; we thought it best to scud before the wind under a close reefed foresail.

The last reef was then put in the foresail, the jib tack hauled to windward, and part of the jib run up. She payed off quickly, and bounded off before the wind. The jib was then taken down and cleared so as to be run up quickly in case of necessity.

She now scudded along beautifully, but the wind increased far beyond our imagination, and was something appalling, but it did not vary a point in its direction. We steered about due south; everything depended upon the steersman; to have broached to would have been destruction.

The night was very dark, and the terrible roaring of the wind and the hissing of the spray off the tops of the waves seemed at times high over our heads. No one sought to sleep that night; the men were gathered aft, where they stood in silence with their eyes alternately upon the foresail and the man at the helm. Sometimes the silence would be broken by the expression—"Well, that is blowing pretty stiff."

Up till midnight all went well enough, but there was no abatement of the gale; it was rather increasing, and the seas were breaking more. Our only fears were for the foresail splitting.

About 1 A.M. a tremendous sea caused the vessel to yaw a little, and the foreboom jibed from starboard to port like the shot of a cannon, and as she recovered herself it jibed back again with the same force. This was dangerous work, as each time it struck against the fore-shrouds, and might have carried them away. I went with the mate to examine, but found no harm done. The fore-sheet, which worked in a traveller on deck, was taut as a bar, although the boom was pressing hard against the shrouds. Thinking to ease the boom off the shrouds a little, we got all hands to try a pull on the fore-sheet, but such was the pressure of the wind on the sail that we could not gain an inch. To have put a back-tackle on the boom to prevent it jibing would have been madness. So the hauling part of the sheet was made fast to the block at the traveller, and the boom allowed to have its play, and every one warned to keep out from the sweep of the boom, as one blow from it would have sent them beyond hail.

Shortly after this the boom jibed again with a loud report, and as quickly jibed back again, but in jibing back the jaw rope parted, and the boom unshipped from the mast, and lay across ship, with one end pressing against the mast, and the other against the fore-shrouds.

This was a bad state of things, but it was impossible to do anything with it, as such was the force of the wind, and the boom adrift and flying about, that it was dangerous to go near it.

It was evident that we were going to lose the foresail, and as our last resource we must try and get the jib upon her; but just as the men were trying to get forward to loose the jib a tremendous sea came rolling up astern, and a large body of water, detached from the top of it by the fury of the wind, fell on board right amidships, filling the large boat with water, and causing the vessel to reel over almost on her beam end. She quickly recovered herself again, but singularly and fortunately the sudden jerk started the foreboom from where it lay pressing against the mast and shrouds, and shipped it back into its place again. Lucky event!

"Well done, *Rob Roy!*" shouted the mate, as he seized a short piece of rope used as a stopper and darted forward to secure the boom in its place. I was quickly with him with more hands, warning them to keep forward of the mast out of the sweep of the boom. The rope was quickly passed round the neck of the boom, and brought round the mast to hold it in its place till a new jaw rope was got ready, when as many of the purls as could be picked up were strung upon it, and it was rove in its place, and the boom was all right again.

The vessel was now found to be staggering under the weight of the large boat full of water on deck. This must be emptied out; to bail it out would be dangerous work, as the boat was just under the sweep of the fore-boom. The mate remembered that there was a large plug in the boat, but the stopper was in. We tried to get the stopper out, but there were difficulties in the way. It could not be got at from the outside for the deck-load, and the fowls having been all used up, the then coop had been broken up, and an empty water-cask placed in the boat where it had been.

This water-cask was right over the stopper, and the foreboom was just above the water-cask, so that it could not be moved.

The water-cask must be sacrificed. A hammer was got, and the cask knocked to pieces, and the mate, to avoid a stroke of the boom, sprawled along in the water, dived down and withdrew the stopper, and the water rushed out, and very soon the vessel was relieved of that unsteady top weight, and she bounded on all right again.

The gale had now reached its height, but still blew steady from the same point, and we began to imagine that it was abating a little.

As daylight began to appear we observed a small slit in the foresail, which, on being examined from the back or lee side of the sail, was found to be one of the seams which was just beginning to open. A piece of strong canvas was got, which, with a bent needle, was stitched strongly over the back of the place to help it a little.

When daylight broke clear the scene was truly grand. The most experienced man on board had never seen such a sea, but though the o waves were tremendously high it could not be called a dangerous cross chop of a sea. It was perfectly regular, and if from our position in it we could not afford to call it sublimely beautiful, we had at least to admit that it was grand and awful.

It seemed like a succession of mountain ridges perfectly straight and parallel to each other, rolling furiously in one direction, and between each a level plain about an eighth of a mile wide covered with white foam. This, I presume, was caused by the violent gale blowing steady from one point directly against the Gulf Stream.

About half-past seven the gale had somewhat abated, and soon after the cook managed to have some breakfast ready. Father Ryan, who had been up most of the night, was gazing on the scene.

"What do you think of that gale, Father Ryan?" said I.

"Awful! Truly awful," said he. "What kind of a gale do you call that? Is that a hurricane?"

"It blows hard enough for one," said I, "although it is too steady from one point for that. I think it is a sort of equinoctial norther. What do you think of that sea?"

"Oh, that is terrible," said he. "I would not think it safe for a small vessel like this."

"Many would think the same, and it is hard enough upon her, but she is buoyant, and rises finely upon it, and has come through it very well so far, and the worst is now past, for the gale has about spent itself."

"Oh, yes," said he, "it is calming down now, but when I looked out upon that awful sea this morning and thought of the calm sea of yesterday, I said, 'Surely awful are the works of the Almighty, and how suddenly He can send on the calmest sea such a storm as will raise it into angry mountains, and yet with the same hand He can guide safely through it a small, helpless vessel like this.'"

I agreed with him, and said we ought to be grateful.

By 9 A.M. the gale had much abated, and the morning, which up till now had been dark and cloudy, began to clear up, and soon after the sun broke through, and I got an observation, and assuming our latitude, found our longitude to be about 97° 20', which placed us about thirty miles from the coast of Mexico.

We now got more sail upon the vessel, and soon after we observed that the northerly wind of the gale had entirely spent itself, and we were into a light steady breeze from the eastward, although there was still a heavy swell from the northward. This indicated that the gale had not extended much further south, and we were now into the usual weather again.

The danger from the seas being for the time past, the old standing danger again cropped up, which was danger from the enemy, and, as we were now getting near to Tampico, it was exceedingly probable that some of their cruisers would be hovering in the neighbourhood with the view of picking up any blockade runner bound for that port. We, therefore, stood more to the westward, intending to sight the land, and then crawl down along the coast as we had done last trip.

We now began to wonder how it had fared with the *Mary Elizabeth,* which must have caught the gale at the same time with us. I knew that in point of management she would not lack, as she had a master and crew well experienced in these seas and in the management of this class of vessels. She was better provided in that respect than the *Roy Roy,* but she was a smaller vessel, and I knew that her sails were not of the same strength. We looked in all directions from the mast-head, but could see nothing of her.

As we stood to the westward, we saw something that looked like wreckage, but on steering towards it we found it to be large trees floating, which appeared to have been quite recently brought down some river, indicating that there had been heavy rain and floods in the northern parts of Mexico.

I may here anticipate, and say that of the *Mary Elizabeth* nothing was ever heard. Captain Shaeffer's brother afterwards called upon me in Havana to get the last and only information that he could ever obtain, and that was of her being seen by us on the day before the gale, and I have no doubt but that she foundered in that gale; and though she was larger, a better sea-boat, better found, and better managed than a great many of the craft which engaged in that rough and reckless trade, it was, strange to say, the only instance I ever knew of one of them being lost at sea. There was no doubt, however, that the gale, so far as it extended, was the heaviest which had been for some years.

We soon sighted the land, and at noon I got the latitude, and found that we were about fifteen miles to the northward of Tampico River, and we arrived off the mouth of the river about 3 P.M.

We found anchored there two vessels, both schooners. One of them was just such a vessel as the *Sylvia*, which we had met here six months before, and, like her, was from St. John with a cargo of lumber for Tampico. The other was a larger vessel, but she seemed light, as in ballast, and was anchored further out, some little distance away.

The former vessel we sailed up to and spoke with. I cannot remember her name, but will call her the *St. John*, as she was from that port. She had passed to the south of Cuba, and came in from the eastward, and had experienced nothing of the gale, but judged from the swell from the northward that there had been a heavy gale in that direction. They drew about six feet of water, and they wished to cross the bar and go up to Tampico Town.

The pilot's boat had been off in the morning, but it was impossible to take them over the bar at that time owing to the very high sea caused by the heavy swell from the northward, meeting in the channel the strong current of the Tampico River, which was then very high owing to great floods in the interior. The pilots had promised, however, to come out again in the afternoon, when, if the swell had gone down a little, they would be able to take them over.

As this bar at Tampico is of shifting quicksand, the channel through it keeps constantly changing, and it is necessary for the pilots to take soundings regularly—almost every day. It is sometimes very crooked and difficult to pass through, and if a vessel gets on to the shoal it is generally a total loss, and if it should be rough weather it is often attended with the loss of all hands, as no boat can live in the breakers. The entrance to this channel from seaward was supposed at this time to be about half a mile to the southward of where it was when we were here six months before, but it was very difficult to define the exact place.

As the pilots had promised to take over in the afternoon the *St. John*, which drew six feet of water, I conceived they could have no difficulty with the *Rob Roy*, which drew only four feet nine inches. We, therefore, dropped anchor and signalled for a pilot. After waiting about an hour there was no appearance of any pilot-boat coming off, and the sky had suddenly changed, and towards the north-east looked black and threatening. This was alarming.

Any one who knows anything of Tampico Roads knows what a dangerous place it is in a heavy north-easterly wind. A very high sea sets in, and with such violence that no amount of ground- tackling will I hold the vessel; and I have known large steamers with both anchors down and working propellers at full speed scarcely able to hold against it and keep off the breakers, while with a sailing vessel it is impossible to claw off.

As soon as I saw this appearance of a change in the weather I set about getting the anchor up to try and get out to sea, and I saw the other vessels doing the same, but it was too late. We had scarcely got sails set when it was down upon us. We set every bit of canvas, and gave full centre-board to see if we could weather the reefs to the southward, but we soon saw that we could not clear them on that stretch, and we tacked and stood to the northward as far as we could reach for the breakers, and then stood back to try again to weather the reefs to the southward; but to our dismay we found that we had not gained an inch, and the sea was now getting up and throwing us more to leeward, and we saw that the other two vessels were not making any more of it than ourselves.

This was something terrible to realize so suddenly and unexpected. To leeward and on each side were the shoals which hemmed us in, and on them the mountainous waves broke with great fury; to windward was the threatening cloud which betokened a heavy gale, and coming it was with certainty, and not the slightest chance of a lull or change in the wind, and night coming on. The gale did not come on with such violence as on the previous day, but it mattered little in the position we were in; it was sufficient to bring on our destruction, and that with certainty and in a very short time, and what would we not have given for the same sea room we had last night, even with the gale in all its fury.

What to do I did not know. The men looked at me, but no one spoke. I pointed to the deck-load of cotton.

"Men," said I, "the charge of every life is mine. Do you think it would help us any to throw over that deckload? If you think so, we will throw it over at once."

"It will do no good," they cried out together; "it eases her aloft and gives her a better hold on the water; and if at last we go on the bar there is a chance of saving our lives by clinging to bales of cotton."

"Then," said I, "we cannot claw off. The gale is increasing, night is upon us, and, do our best, we will be in these breakers before an hour. Now, I propose to make an attempt to run the gauntlet. I have been observing with the glass, and I fancy I see what I take to be the opening to the channel, and I propose to make the attempt to cross the bar. I know it is a desperate and dangerous undertaking, but it is the only chance for our lives. What do you all say?"

"I say try it," said the mate; "it is our only chance."

The men all acquiesced, and said they were ready to obey.

One man then spoke up, and said: "I am ready to leave it to your own judgment, Captain; but if you take my advice when crossing you will steer through where you see the highest seas and the bluest water."

"I believe you are right," I said, "and I intend to do so."

Father Ryan, who stood with an expression something between composure and anxiety on his countenance, looked at me seriously and said, "Try it, Captain, and may the hand of God guide you."

For once at least in my life, I implored the aid of a higher hand. I went to the cabin and took the chronometer and cushioned it in one of the beds; as is usually done in crossing bars, in case of a sudden touch on the ground shaking it, and, going on deck, told the men that everything now depended upon their coolness and prompt action.

The greatest difficulty in crossing a bar through a narrow channel before a heavy sea was to keep the vessel straight in the channel, and prevent her stern being swung round by the heavy seas rolling up astern.

In placing the men, the first point to be determined was who was the best steersman. This was accorded to Hagan. To the cook was assigned the charge of the centre-board, the bar of which being near the door of the galley he had been accustomed to work, and lower or raise as required. The mate would take charge aft, with another man at the peak purchase, and be ready to drop the peak of the mainsail if a heavy sea rolling up astern swung her stern round; while two men would be stationed at the jibsheet to haul to windward and make her pay off, and I would take my station on the top of the cotton amidships, and with my glass look out ahead for the best water, and direct with my hand to the right or left the pourse to steer. The helmsman would keep his eye on me and steer by the direction of my hand. The mate would also be ready to assist the man at the helm, or to take the helm in case of the steersman being knocked down by a heavy sea coming over the stern. Father Ryan wished to know where he could be of service. I directed him to watch the companion doors, and keep them shut to prevent a sea going down in the cabin.

The most important part was to find the proper entrance to the channel; and we were now approaching the place which I supposed to be the entrance, and as soon as it was under our lee the gaff-topsail was taken in, but everything else was carried full.

Every man now took his place, and I got upon the top of the cotton with my glass and directed with my hand. As we approached the place, it looked awful; the waves toppled up like the walls of a fortress. Sheets were eased off, and under a full pressure of canvas the vessel rushed at it. She plunged violently, every spar and timber seemed to quiver. There was evidently a strong current against her, while the tremendous seas breaking on each side seemed above our heads. Sometimes I thought we were completely locked in, but still some higher and bluer waves gave indication of the deepest water. Sometimes a tremendous sea would come rolling up astern and throw her stern forward and bring her almost broadside on across the channel; but the peak would be quickly dropped and jib hauled to windward, and she payed off again before another sea came, when the same thing was repeated. We were nearly to the midst of it, but we were not making fast progress owing to the strong current of the river against us. This, however, made her steer better, and convinced me that we were in the right channel; but I feared that the shallowest and worst-defined part of it would be the end next the shore, and often the flying spray blinded me and dimmed the glass in my hand so that I had to keep wiping it with my handkerchief. I could only see ahead when lifted on the top of a huge wave, as, when that passed on, the mountain of water shut off for a time the view forward.

I fancied that the water was getting shallower on each side, the breakers worse, and the channel less defined. When looking forward my eye caught the shore in the distance, and I saw a Mexican flag—the pilot's flag—and I saw they were waving directions. First inclined to the north, we altered course to the north, then held up straight—steady; then inclined to the south. We altered course to the south, then up straight again—steady.

I had now some hopes. We continued on, and soon after all in front seemed breakers, and I saw no appearance of a channel or deep water; but the pilot's flag was held up steady to come straight on. It looked fearful, but on we must go. Several heavy broken waves came up, two of which came over our stern. Another heavier one came up, and, nearly burying us, carried us forward some distance, and when it passed she touched the ground, but it was just lightly and for a moment. She payed off again. Another heavy and broken wave followed, and a violent gust of wind at the same time carried us along through a mass of foam into the deep and smooth water inside of the bar.

"Round her to, haul down staysail and jib, and let go anchor," said I.

This was soon done. The men stood round, but said nothing. Father Ryan, whose hat had blown overboard, came up to me bareheaded, drenched with salt-water, and with tears in his eyes. He grasped me warmly by the hand, and said seriously, "Captain, the finger of God was there."

"It was," I said; and I never said two words with more sincerity in all my life. Of the many incidents in my somewhat adventurous life I do not think that any made a greater impression on me than the fortune of the last twenty-four hours, and especially this last hour.

THE LOSS OF THE *"WHITE SHIP"*

CHARLES DICKENS

One of the most famous wrecks in English history is that of the "White Ship" in which Prince William, son and heir of King Henry 1, was lost.

Henry the First went over to Normandy with Prince William and a great retinue, to have the Prince acknowledged as his successor by the Norman nobles, and to contract the promised marriage—this was one of the many promises the King had broken—between him and the daughter of the Count of Anjou. Both these things were triumphantly done, with great show and rejoicing; and on the 25th of November, in the year 1120, the whole retinue prepared to embark at the port of Barfleur, on the voyage home.

On that day, and at that place, there came to the King, Fitz-Stephen, a sea captain, and said:

"My liege, my father served your father all his life upon the sea. He steered the ship with the golden boy upon the prow, in which your father sailed to conquer England. I beseech you to grant me the same office. I have a fair vessel in the harbour here, called the *White Ship*, manned by fifty sailors of renown. I pray you, sire, to let your servant have the honour of steering you in the *White Ship* to England!"

"I am sorry, friend," replied the King, "that my vessel is already chosen, and that I cannot, therefore, sail with the son of the man who served my father. But the Prince and all his company shall go along with you, in the fair *White Ship*, manned by the fifty sailors of renown."

An hour or two afterwards, the King set sail in the vessel he had chosen, accompanied by other vessels, and sailing all night with a fair and gentle wind, arrived upon the coast of England in the morning. While it was yet night, the people in some of those ships heard a faint, wild cry come over the sea, and wondered what it was.

Now, the Prince was a young man of eighteen, who bore no love to the English, and had declared that, when he came to the throne, he would yoke them to the plough like oxen. He went aboard the *White Ship*, with one hundred and forty youthful nobles like himself, among whom were eighteen noble ladies of the highest rank. All this gay company, with their servants and the fifty sailors, made three hundred souls aboard the fair *White Ship*.

"Give three casks of wine, Fitz-Stephen," said the Prince, "to the fifty sailors of renown! My father the King has sailed out of the harbour. What time is there to make merry here, and yet reach England with the rest?"

"Prince," said Fitz-Stephen, "before morning, my fifty and the *White Ship* shall overtake the swiftest vessel in attendance on your father, the King, if we sail at midnight!"

Then the Prince commanded to make merry; and the sailors drank out the three casks of wine; and the Prince and all the noble company danced in the moonlight on the deck of the *White Ship*.

When, at last, she shot out of the harbour of Barfleur, there was not a sober seaman on board. But the sails were all set, and the oars all going merrily. Fitz-Stephen had the helm. The gay young nobles and the beautiful ladies, wrapped in mantles of various bright colours to protect them from the cold, talked, laughed, and sang. The Prince encouraged the fifty sailors to row harder yet, for the honour of the *White Ship*.

Crash! A terrific cry broke from three hundred hearts. It was the cry the people in the distant vessels of the King heard faintly on the water. The *White Ship* had struck upon a rock—was filling—going down.

Fitz-Stephen hurried the Prince into a boat, with some few nobles.

"Push off," he whispered, "and row to the land. It is not far, and the sea is smooth. The rest of us must die."

But, as they rowed away fast from the sinking ship, the Prince heard the voice of his sister Marie, the Countess of Perche, calling for help. He never in his life had been so good as he was then.

"Row back at any risk! I cannot bear to leave her!" he cried.

They rowed back. As the Prince held out his arms to catch his sister such numbers leaped in, that the boat was overset. And in the same instant the *White Ship* went down.

Only two men floated. They both clung to the main yard of the ship, which had broken from the mast, and now supported them. One asked the other who he was. He said:

"I am a nobleman, Godrey by name, the son of Gilbert de l'Aigle. And you?"

"I am Berold, a poor butcher of Rouen," was the answer.

Then they said together, "Lord be merciful to us both!" and tried to encourage one another, as they drifted in the cold, benumbing sea on that unfortunate November night.

By-and-by, another man came swimming towards them, whom they knew, when he pushed aside his long wet hair, to be Fitz-Stephen.

"Where is the Prince?" said he.

"Gone! Gone!" the two cried together. "Neither he, nor his brother, nor his sister, nor the King's niece, nor her brother, nor any one of all the brave three hundred, noble or commoner, except we three, has risen above the water!"

Fitz-Stephen, with a ghastly face, cried, "Woe! Woe to me!" and sank to the bottom.

The other two clung to the yard for some hours. At length the young noble said faintly:

"I am exhausted, and chilled with the cold, and can hold no longer. Farewell, good friend! God preserve you!"

So, he dropped and sank; and of all the brilliant crowd, the poor butcher of Rouen alone was saved. In the morning some fishermen saw him floating in his sheepskin coat, and got him into their boat—the sole relater of the dismal tale.

For three days, no one dared to carry the intelligence to the King. At length, they sent into his presence a little boy, who, weeping bitterly and kneeling at his feet, told him that the *White Ship* was lost with all on board. The King was never afterwards seen to smile.

MAN OVERBOARD

W. H. G. KINGSTON

We were on our return home, by the way of the Cape of Good Hope, when, on the 8th of May of that year, we were off Cape L'Agullus. It was blowing a heavy gale of wind, with a tremendous sea running, such a sea as one rarely meets with anywhere but off the Cape, when just at nightfall, as we were taking another reef in the top-sails, a young seaman, a mizen-topman, James Miles by name, fell from the mizen-topsail-yard, and away he went overboard. In his descent he came across the chain-span of the weather-quarter davits, and with such force that he actually broke it. I could scarcely have supposed that he would have escaped being killed in his fall; but as the ship flew away from him, he was seen rising on the crest of a foaming wave, apparently unhurt. The life-buoy was let go as soon as possible, but by that time the ship had already got a considerable distance from him; and even could he reach it, I felt that the prospect of saving him was small indeed, as I had no hope, should we find him, of being able to pick him out of that troubled sea; and I had strong fears that a boat would be unable to swim to go to his rescue, should I determine to lower one. I was very doubtful as to what was my duty. I might, by allowing a boat to be lowered, sacrifice the lives of the officer and crew, who would, I was very certain, at all events volunteer to man her. It was a moment of intense anxiety. I instantly, however, wore the ship round; and while we stood towards the spot, as far as we could guess, where the poor fellow had fallen, the thoughts I have mentioned passed through my mind. The sad loss of the gallant Lieutenant Gore and a whole boat's crew a short time before, about the same locality, was present to my thoughts. To add to the chances of our not finding the man, it was now growing rapidly dusk. As we reached the spot, every eye on board was straining through the gloom to discern the object of our search, but neither Miles nor the life-buoy were to be seen. Still, I could not bring myself to leave him to one of the most dreadful of fates. He was a good swimmer, and those who knew him best asserted that he would swim to the last. For my part, I almost hoped that the poor fellow had been stunned, and would thus have sunk at once, and been saved the agony of despair he must be feeling were he still alive. Of one thing I felt sure, from the course we had steered, that we were close to the spot where he had fallen. Anxiously we waited,—minute after minute passed by,—still no sound was heard; not a speck could be seen to indicate his position. At least half an hour had passed by. The strongest man alive could not support himself in such a sea as this for so long, I feared. Miles must long before this have sunk, unless he could have got hold of the life-buoy, and of that I had no hope. I looked at my watch by the light of the binnacle lamp. "It is hopeless," I thought, "we must give the poor fellow up." When I had come to this melancholy resolve, I issued the orders for wearing ship in somewhat a louder voice than usual, as under the circumstances was natural, to stifle my own feelings. Just then I thought I heard a human voice borne down upon the gale. I listened; it was, I feared, but the effect of imagination; yet I waited a moment. Again the voice struck my ear, and this time several of the ship's company heard it. "There he is, sir! There he is away to windward!" exclaimed several voices; and then in return they uttered a loud hearty cheer, to keep up the spirits of the poor fellow. Now came the most trying moment; I must decide whether I would allow a boat to be lowered. "If I refuse," I felt, "my crew will say that I am careless of their lives. It is not their nature to calculate the risk they themselves must run." At once, Mr. Christopher, one of my lieutenants, nobly volunteered to make the attempt, and numbers of the crew came forward anxious to accompany him. At last, anxiety to save a drowning man prevailed over prudence, and I sanctioned the attempt.

The boat, with Mr. Christopher and a picked crew, was lowered, not without great difficulty and, sad to say, with the loss of one of the brave fellows. He was the bowman; and, as he stood up with his boathook in his hand to shove off, the boat give a terrific pitch and sent him over the bow. He must have struck his head against the side of the ship, for he went down instantly, and was no more seen. Thus, in the endeavour to save the life of one man, another was already sent to his long account. With sad forebodings for the fate of the rest of the gallant fellows, I saw the boat leave the ship's side. Away she pulled into the darkness, where she was no longer visible; and a heavy pull I knew she must have of it in that terrible sea, even if she escaped destruction. It was one of the most trying times of my life. We waited in suspense for the return of the boat; the minutes, seeming like hours, passed slowly by, and she did not appear. I began at length to dread that my fears would be realized, and that we should not again see her, when, after half an hour had elapsed since she had left the ship's side on her mission of mercy, a cheer from her gallant crew announced her approach with the success of their bold enterprise. My anxiety was not, however, entirely relieved till the falls were hooked on, and she and all her crew were hoisted on board, with the rescued man Miles. To my surprise I found that he was perfectly naked. As he came up the side, also, he required not the slightest assistance, but dived below at once to dry himself and to get out of the cold. I instantly ordered him to his hammock, and, with the doctor's permission, sent him a stiff glass of grog. I resolved also to relieve him from duty, believing that his nervous system would have received a shock from which it would take long to recover. After I had put the ship once more on her course, being anxious to learn the particulars of his escape, as soon as I heard that he was safely stowed away between the blankets, I went below to see him. His voice was as strong as ever; his pulse beat as regularly, and his nerves seemed as strong as usual. After pointing out to him how grateful he should feel to our Almighty Father for his preservation from an early and dreadful death, I begged him to tell me how he had contrived to keep himself so long afloat. He replied to me in the following words:—"Why, sir, you see as soon as I came up again, after I had first struck the water, I looked out for the ship, and, getting sight of her running away from me, I remembered how it happened I was there, and knew there would be no use swimming after her or singing out. Then, sir, I felt very certain you would not let me drown without an attempt to pick me up, and that there were plenty of fine fellows on board who would be anxious to man a boat to come to my assistance, if you thought a boat could swim. Then, thinks I to myself, a man can die but once, and if it's my turn to-day, why, there's no help for it. Yet I didn't think all the time that I was likely to lose the number of my mess, do ye see, sir. The next thought that came to me was, if I am to drown, it's as well to drown without clothes as with them; and if I get them off, why, there's a better chance of my keeping afloat till a boat can be lowered to pick me up; so I kicked off my shoes; then I got off my jacket, and then, waiting till I could get hold of the two legs at once, I drew off my trousers in a moment. My shirt was soon off me, but I took care to roll up the tails, so as not to get them over my face. As I rose on the top of the sea, I caught sight of the ship as you wore her round here, and that gave me courage, for I felt I was not to be deserted; indeed, I had no fear of that. Then I knew that there would be no use swimming; so all I did was to throw myself on my back and float till you came up to me. I thought the time was somewhat long, I own. When the ship got back, I saw her hove to away down to leeward, but I did not like to sing out for fear of tiring myself, and thought you would not hear me; and I fancied also that a boat would at once have been lowered to come and look for me. Well, sir, I waited, thinking the time was very long, and hearing no sound, yet still I could see the ship hove to, and you may be sure I did not take my eyes from off her; when at last I heard your voice give the order to wear ship again. Then thinks I to myself, now or never's the time to sing out. And, raising myself as high as I could out of the water, I sang out at the top of my voice. There was a silence on board, but no answer, and I did begin to feel that there was a chance of being lost after all. 'Never give in, though,' thinks I; so I sang out again, as loud, you may be sure, as I could sing. This time the answering cheers of my shipmates gave me fresh spirits; but still I knew full well that I wasn't safe on board yet. If I had wanted to swim, there was too much sea on to make any way; so I kept floating on my back as before, just keeping an eye to leeward to see if a boat was coming to pick me up. Well, sir, when the boat did come at last, with Mr. Christopher and the rest in her, I felt strong and hearty, and was well able to help myself on board. I now can scarcely fancy I was so long in the water."

I was much struck with the extraordinary coolness of Miles. He afterwards had another escape, which was owing less to his own self-possession, though he took it as coolly as the first. On our passage home, the ship was running with a lightish breeze and almost calm sea across the Bay of Biscay, when Miles was sent on the fore-top-gallant-yard. By some carelessness he fell completely over the yard, and those aloft expected to see him dashed to pieces on the forecastle. Instead of that, the foresail at that moment swelled out with a sudden breeze, and, striking the bulge of the sail, he was sent forward clear of the bows and hove into the water. A rope was towing overboard. He caught hold of it, and, hauling himself on board, was again aloft within a couple of minutes attending to his duty, which had so suddenly been interrupted. On his arrival in England, Lieutenant Christopher received the honorary silver medal from the Royal Humane Society for his gallant conduct on the occasion of saving Miles' life.

THROUGH THE VORTEX OF A CYCLONE

WILLIAM HOPE HODGSON

(The Cyclone—"The most fearful enemy which the mariner's perilous calling obliges him to encounter.")

It was in the middle of November that the four-masted barque, *Golconda*, came down from Crockett and anchored off Telegraph Hill, San Francisco. She was loaded with grain, and was homeward bound round Cape Horn. Five days later she was towed out through the Golden Gates, and cast loose off the Heads, and so set sail upon the voyage that was to come so near to being her last.

For a fortnight we had baffling winds; but after that time, got a good slant that carried us down to within a couple of degrees of the Line. Here it left us, and over a week passed before we had managed to tack and drift our way into the Southern Hemisphere.

About five degrees South of the Line, we met with a fair wind that helped us Southward another ten or twelve degrees, and there, early one morning, it dropped us, ending with a short, but violent, thunder storm, in which, so frequent were the lightning flashes, that I managed to secure a picture of one, whilst in the act of snapshotting the sea and clouds upon our port side.

During the day, the wind, as I have remarked, left us entirely, and we lay becalmed under a blazing hot sun. We hauled up the lower sails to prevent them from chafing as the vessel rolled lazily on the scarce perceptible swells, and busied ourselves, as is customary on such occasions, with much swabbing and cleaning of paint-work.

As the day proceeded, so did the heat seem to increase; the atmosphere lost its clear look, and a low haze seemed to lie about the ship at a great distance. At times, the air seemed to have about it a queer, unbreathable quality; so that one caught oneself breathing with a sense of distress.

And, hour by hour, as the day moved steadily onward, the sense of oppression grew ever more acute.

Then, it was, I should think, about three-thirty in the afternoon, I became conscious of the fact that a strange, unnatural, dull, brick-red glare was in the sky. Very subtle it was, and I could not say that it came from any particular place; but rather it seemed to shine *in* the atmosphere. As I stood looking at it, the Mate came up beside me. After about half a minute, he gave out a sudden exclamation:—

"Hark!" he said. "Did you hear that?"

"No, Mr. Jackson," I replied. "What was it like?"

"Listen!" was all his reply, and I obeyed; and so perhaps for a couple of minutes we stood there in silence.

"There!——There it is again!" he exclaimed, suddenly; and in the same instant I heard it . . . a sound like low, strange growling far away in the North-East. It lasted for about fifteen seconds, and then died away in a low, hollow, moaning noise, that sounded indescribably dree.

After that, for a space longer, we stood listening; and so, at last, it came again . . . a far, faint, wild-beast growling, away over the North-Eastern horizon. As it died away, with that strange hollow note, the Mate touched my arm:—

"Go and call the Old Man," he said, meaning the Captain. "And while you're down, have a look at the barometer."

In both of these matters I obeyed him, and in a few moments the Captain was on deck, standing beside the Mate—listening.

"How's the glass?" asked the Mate, as I came up.

"Steady," I answered, and at that, he nodded his head, and resumed his expectant attitude. Yet, though we stood silent, maybe for the better part of half an hour, there came no further repetition of that weird, far-off growling, and so, as the glass was steady, no serious notice was taken of the matter.

That evening, we experienced a sunset of quite indescribable gorgeousness, which had, to me, an unnatural glow about it, especially in the way in which it lit up the surface of the sea, which was, at this time, stirred by a slight evening breeze. Evidently, the Mate was of the opinion that it foreboded something in the way of ill weather; for he gave orders for the watch on deck to take the three royals off her.

By the time the men had got down from aloft, the sun had set, and the evening was fading into dusk; yet, despite that, all the sky to the North-East was full of the most vivid red and orange; this being, it will be remembered, the direction from which we had heard earlier that sullen growling.

It was somewhat later, I remember, that I heard the Mate remark to the Captain that we were in for bad weather, and that it was his belief a Cyclone was coming down upon us; but this, the Captain—who was quite a young fellow—poo-poohed; telling him that he pinned *his* faith to the barometer, which was perfectly steady. Yet, I could see that the Mate was by no means so sure; but forebore to press further his opinion against his superior's.

Presently, as the night came down upon the world, the orange tints went out of the sky, and only a sombre, threatening red was left, with a strangely bright rift of white light running horizontally across it, about twenty degrees above the North-*Eastern* horizon.

This lasted for nigh on to half an hour, and so did it impress the crew with a sense of something impending, that many of them crouched, staring over the port rail, until long after it had faded into the general greyness.

That night, I recollect, it was my watch on deck from midnight until four in the morning. When the boy came down to wake me, he told me that it had been lightning during the past watch. Even as he spoke, a bright, bluish glare lit up the porthole; but there was no succeeding thunder.

I sprang hastily from my bunk, and dressed; then, seizing my camera, ran out on deck. I opened the shutter, and the next instant—flash! a great stream of electricity sprang out of the zenith.

Directly afterwards, the Mate called to me from the break of the poop to know whether I had managed to secure *that* one. I replied, Yes, I thought I had, and he told me to come up on to the poop, beside him, and have a further try from there; for he, the Captain and the Second Mate were much interested in my photographic hobby, and did all in their power to aid me in the securing of successful snaps.

That the Mate was uneasy, I very soon perceived; for, presently, a little while after he had relieved the Second Mate, he ceased his pacing of the poop deck, and came and leant over the rail, alongside of me.

"I wish to goodness the Old Man would have her shortened right down to lower topsails," he said, a moment later, in a low voice. "There's some rotten, dirty weather knocking around. I can smell it." And he raised his head, and sniffed at the air.

"Why not shorten her down, on your own?" I asked him.

"Can't!" he replied. "The Old Man's left orders not to touch anything; but to call him if any change occurs. He goes *too* d——n much by the barometer, to suit me, and won't budge a rope's end, because it's steady."

All this time, the lightning had been playing at frequent intervals across the sky; but now there came several gigantic flashes, seeming extraordinarily near to the vessel, pouring down out of a great rift in the clouds— veritable torrents of electric fluid. I switched open the shutter of my camera, and pointed the lens upward; and the following instant, I secured a magnificent photograph of a great flash, which, bursting down from the same rift, divided to the East and West in a sort of vast electric arch.

For perhaps a minute afterwards, we waited, thinking that such a flash *must* be followed by thunder; but none came. Instead, from the darkness to the North-East, there sounded a faint, far-drawn- out wailing noise, that seemed to echo queerly across the quiet sea. And after that, silence.

The Mate stood upright, and faced round at me.

"Do you know," he said, "only once before in my life have I heard anything like that, and that was before the Cyclone in which the *Lancing* and the *Eurasian* were lost, in the Indian Ocean.

"Do you think then there's *really* any danger of a Cyclone now?" I asked him, with something of a little thrill of excitement.

"I think——" he began, and then stopped, and swore suddenly. "Look!" he said, in a loud voice. "Look! 'Stalk' lightning, as I'm a living man!" And he pointed to the North-East. "Photograph that, while you've got the chance; you'll never have another as long as you live!"

I looked in the direction which he indicated, and there, sure enough, were great, pale, flickering streaks and tongues of flame *rising apparently out of the sea.* They remained steady for some ten or fifteen seconds, and in that time I was able to take a snap of them.

This photograph, as I discovered when I came to develop the negative, has not, I regret to say, taken regard of a strange, indefinable dull-red glare that lit up the horizon at the same time; but, as it is, it remains to me a treasured record of a form of electrical phenomenon but seldom seen, even by those whose good, or ill, fortune has allowed them to come face to face with a Cyclonic Storm. Before leaving this incident, I would once more impress upon the reader that this strange lightning was *not* descending from the atmosphere; but *rising from the sea.*

It was after I had secured this last snap, that the Mate declared it to be his conviction that a great Cyclonic Storm was coming down upon us from the North-East, and, with that—for about the twentieth time that watch—he went below to consult the barometer.

He came back in about ten minutes, to say that it was still steady; but that he had called the Old Man, and told him about the upward "Stalk" lightning; yet the Captain, upon hearing from him that the glass was still steady, had refused to be alarmed, but had promised to come up and take a look round. This, in a while, he did; but, as Fate would have it, there was no further display of the "Stalk" lightning, and, as the other kind had now become no more than an occasional dull glare behind the clouds to the North-East, he retired once more, leaving orders to be called if there were any change either in the glass or the weather.

With the sunrise there came a change, a low, slow-moving scud driving down from the North-East, and drifting across the face of the newly-risen sun, which was shining with a queer, unnatural glare. Indeed, so stormy and be-burred looked the sun, that I could have applied to it with truth the line:—

"And the red Sun all bearded with the Storm," to describe its threatening aspect.

The glass also showed a change at last, rising a little for a short while, and then dropping about a tenth, and, at that, the Mate hurried down to inform the Skipper, who was speedily up on deck.

He had the fore and mizzen t'gallants taken off her; but nothing more; for he declared that he wasn't going to throw away a fine fair wind for any Old Woman's fancies.

Presently, the wind began to freshen; but the orange-red burr about the sun remained, and also it seemed to me that the tint of the water had a "bad weather" look about it. I mentioned this to the Mate, and he nodded agreement; but said nothing in so many words, for the Captain was standing near.

By eight bells (4 A.M.) the wind had freshened so much that we were lying over to it, with a big cant of the decks, and making a good twelve knots, under nothing higher than the main t'gallant.

We were relieved by the other watch, and went below for a short sleep. At eight o'clock, when again I came on deck, I found that the sea had begun to rise somewhat; but that otherwise the weather was much as it had been when I left the decks; save that the sun was hidden by a heavy squall to windward, which was coming down upon us.

Some fifteen minutes later, it struck the ship, making the foam fly, and carrying away the main topsail sheet. Immediately upon this, the heavy iron ring in the clew of the sail began to thrash and beat about, as the sail flapped in the wind, striking great blows against the steel yard; but the clewline was manned, and some of the men went aloft to repair the damage, after which the sail was once more sheeted home, and we continued to carry on.

About this time, the Mate sent me down into the saloon to take another look at the glass, and I found that it had fallen a further tenth. When I reported this to him, he had the main t'gallant taken in; but hung on to the mainsail, waiting for eight bells, when the whole crowd would be on deck to give a hand.

By that time, we had begun to ship water, and most of us were speedily very thoroughly soused; yet, we got the sail off her, and she rode the easier for the relief.

A little after one o'clock in the afternoon, I went out on deck to have a final "squint" at the weather, before turning-in for a short sleep, and found that the wind had freshened considerably, the seas striking the counter of the vessel at times, and flying to a considerable height in foam.

At four o'clock, when once more I appeared on deck, I discovered the spray flying over us with a good deal of freedom, and the solid water coming aboard occasionally in odd tons.

Yet, so far there was, *to a sailorman*, nothing worthy of note in the severity of the weather. It was merely blowing a moderately heavy gale, before which, under our six topsails and foresail, we were making a good twelve knots an hour to the Southward. Indeed, it seemed to me, at this time, that the Captain was right in his belief that we were not in for any very dirty weather, and I said as much to the Mate; whereat he laughed somewhat bitterly.

"Don't you make any sort of mistake!" he said, and pointed to leeward, where continual flashes of lightning darted down from a dark bank of cloud. "We're already within the borders of the Cyclone We are travelling, so I take it, about a knot slower an hour to the South than the bodily forward movement of the Storm; so that you may reckon it's overtaking us at the rate of something like a mile an hour. Later on, I expect, it'll get a move on it, and then a torpedo boat wouldn't catch it! This bit of a breeze that we're having now"—and he gestured to windward with his elbow—"is only fluff—nothing more than the outer fringe of the advancing Cyclone! Keep your eye lifting to the North-East, and keep your ears open. Wait until you hear the thing yelling at you as loud as a million mad tigers!"

He came to a pause, and knocked the ashes out of his pipe; then he slid the empty "weapon" into the side pocket of his long oilskin coat. And all the time, I could see that he was ruminating.

"Mark my words," he said, at last, and speaking with great deliberation. "Within twelve hours it'll be upon us!"

He shook his head at me. Then he added:—

"Within twelve hours, my boy, you and I and every other soul in this blessed packet may be down there in the cold!" And the brute pointed downward into the sea, and grinned cheerfully at me.

It was our watch that night from eight to twelve; but, except that the wind freshened a trifle, hourly, nothing of note occurred during our watch. The wind was just blowing a good fresh gale, and giving us all we wanted, to keep the ship doing her best under topsails and foresail.

At midnight, I went below for a sleep. When I was called at four o'clock, I found a very different state of affairs. The day had broken, and showed the sea in a very confused state, with a tendency to run up into heaps, and there was a good deal less wind; but what struck me as most remarkable, and brought home with uncomfortable force the Mate's warning of the previous day, was the colour of the sky, which seemed to be everywhere one great glare of gloomy, orange-coloured light, streaked here and there with red. So intense was this glare that the seas, as they rose clumsily into heaps, caught and reflected the light in an extraordinary manner, shining and glittering gloomily, like vast moving mounds of liquid flame. The whole presenting an effect of astounding and uncanny grandeur.

I made my way up on to the poop, carrying my camera. There, I met the Mate.

"You'll not want that pretty little box of yours," he remarked, and tapped my camera. "I guess you'll find a coffin more useful."

"Then it's coming?" I said.

"Look!" was all his reply, and he pointed into the North-East.

I saw in an instant what it was at which he pointed. It was a great black wall of cloud that seemed to cover about seven points of the horizon, extending almost from North to East, and reaching upward some fifteen degrees towards the zenith. The intense, solid blackness of this cloud was astonishing, and threatening to the beholder, seeming, indeed, to be more like a line of great black cliffs standing out of the sea, than a mass of thick vapour.

I glanced aloft, and saw that the other watch were securing the mizzen upper topsail. At the same moment, the Captain appeared on deck, and walked over to the Mate.

"Glass has dropped another tenth, Mr. Jackson," he remarked, and glanced to windward. "I think we'd better have the fore and main upper topsails off her."

Scarcely had he given the order, before the Mate was down on the maindeck, shouting:—"Fore and main topsail hal'yards! Lower away! Man clewlines and spillinglines!" So eager was he to have the sail off her.

By the time that the upper topsails were furled, I noted that the red glare had gone out of the greater part of the sky to windward, and a stiffish looking squall was bearing down upon us. Away more to the North, I saw that the black rampart of cloud had disappeared, and, in place thereof, it seemed to me that the clouds in that quarter were assuming a hard, tufted appearance, and changing their shapes with surprising rapidity.

The sea also at this time was remarkable, acting uneasily, and hurling up queer little mounds of foam, which the passing squall caught and spread.

All these points, the Mate noted; for I heard him urging the Captain to take in the foresail and mizzen lower topsail. Yet, this, the Skipper seemed unwilling to do; but finally agreed to have the mizzen topsail off her. Whilst the men were up at this, the wind dropped abruptly in the tail of the squall, the vessel rolling heavily, and taking water and spray with every roll.

Now, I want the Reader to try and understand exactly how matters were at this particular and crucial moment. The wind had dropped entirely, and, with the dropping of the wind, a thousand different sounds broke harshly upon the ear, sounding almost unnatural in their distinctness, and impressing the ear with a sense of discomfort. With each roll of the ship, there came a chorus of creaks and groans from the swaying masts and gear, and the sails slatted with a damp, disagreeable sound. Beyond the ship, there was the constant, harsh murmur of the seas, occasionally changing to a low roar, as one broke near us. One other sound there was that punctuated all these, and that was the loud, slapping blows of the seas, as they hove themselves clumsily against the ship; and, for the rest, there was a strange sense of silence.

Then, as sudden as the report of a heavy gun, a great bellowing came out of the North and East, and died away into a series of monstrous grumbles of sound. It was not thunder. *It was the Voice of the approaching Cyclone.*

In the same instant, the Mate nudged my shoulder, and pointed, and I saw, with an enormous feeling of surprise, that a large waterspout had formed about four hundred yards astern, and was coming towards us. All about the base of it, the sea was foaming in a strange manner, and the whole thing seemed to have a curious luminous quality.

Thinking about it now, I cannot say that I perceived it to be in rotation; but nevertheless, I had the impression that it was revolving swiftly. Its general onward motion seemed to be about as fast as would be attained by a well-manned gig.

I remember, in the first moments of astonishment, as I watched it, hearing the Mate shout something to the Skipper about the foresail, then I realised suddenly that the spout was coming straight for the ship. I ran hastily to the taffrail, raised my camera, and snapped it, and then, as it seemed to tower right up above me, gigantic, I ran backwards in sudden fright. In the same instant, there came a blinding flash of lightning, almost in my face, followed instantaneously by a tremendous roar of thunder, and I saw that the thing had burst within about fifty yards of the ship. The sea, immediately beneath where it had been, leapt up in a great hummock of solid water, and foam, as though something as great as a house had been cast into the ocean. Then, rushing towards us, it struck the stern of the vessel, flying as high as our topsail yards in spray, and knocking me backwards on to the deck.

As I stood up, and wiped the water hurriedly from my camera, I heard the Mate shout out to know if I were hurt, and then, in the same moment, and before I could reply, he cried out:—

"It's coming! Up helium! Up hellum! Look out everybody! Hold on for your lives!"

Directly afterwards, a shrill, yelling noise seemed to fill the whole sky with a deafening, piercing sound. I glanced hastily over the port quarter. *In that direction the whole surface of the ocean seemed to be torn up into the air in monstrous clouds of spray.* The yelling sound passed into a vast scream, and the next instant the Cyclone was upon us.

Immediately, the air was so full of flying spray that I could not see a yard before me, and the wind slapped me back against the teak companion, pinning me there for a few moments, helpless. The ship heeled over to a terrible angle, so that, for some seconds, I thought we were going to capsize. Then, with a sudden lurch, she hove herself upright, and I became able to see about me a little, by switching the water from my face, and shielding my eyes. Near to me, the helmsman—a little Dago—was clinging to the wheel, looking like nothing so much as a drowned monkey, and palpably frightened to such an extent that he could hardly stand upright.

From him, I looked round at so much of the vessel as I could see, and up at the spars, and so, presently, I discovered how it was that she had righted. The mizzen topmast was gone just below the heel of the t'gallantmast, and the fore topmast a little above the cap. The main topmast alone stood. It was the losing of these spars which had eased her, and allowed her to right so suddenly. Marvellously enough, the foresail—a small, new, No. 1 canvas stormsail—had stood the strain, and was now bellying out, with a high foot, the sheets evidently having surged under the wind pressure. What was more extraordinary, was that the fore and main lower topsails were standing and this, despite the fact that the bare upper spars, on both the fore and mizzen masts, had been carried away.

And now, the first awful burst of the Cyclone having passed with the righting of the vessel, the three sails stood, though tested to their utmost, and the ship, under the tremendous urging force of the Storm, was tearing forward at a high speed through the seas.

I glanced down now at myself and camera. Both were soaked; yet, as I discovered later, the latter would still take photographs. I struggled forward to the break of the poop, and stared down on to the maindeck. The seas were breaking aboard every moment, and the spray flying over us continually in huge white clouds. And in my ears was the incessant, wild, roaring-scream of the monster Whirl-Storm.

Then I saw the Mate. He was up against the lee rail, chopping at something with a hatchet. At times the water left him visible to his knees; anon he was completely submerged; but ever there was the whirl of his weapon amid the chaos of water, as he hacked and cut at the gear that held the mizzen t'gallant mast crashing against the side.

I saw him glance round once, and he beckoned with the hatchet to a couple of his watch who were fighting their way aft along the streaming decks. He did not attempt to shout; for no shout could have been heard in the incredible roaring of the wind. Indeed, so vastly loud was the noise made by this element, that I had not heard even the topmasts carry away; though the sound of a large spar breaking will make as great a noise as the report of a big gun. The next instant, I had thrust my camera into one of the hencoops upon the poop, and turned to struggle aft to the companionway; for I knew it was no use going to the Mate's aid without axes.

Presently, I was at the companion, and had the fastenings undone; then I opened the door, and sprang in on to the stairs. I slammed-to the door, bolted it, and made my way below, and so, in a minute, had possessed myself of a couple of axes. With these, I returned to the poop, fastening the companion doors carefully behind me, and, in a little, was up to my neck in water on the maindeck, helping to clear away the wreckage. The second axe, I had pushed into the hands of one of the men.

Presently, we had the gear cleared away.

Then we scrambled away forrard along the decks, through the boiling swirls of water and foam that swept the vessel, as the seas thundered aboard; and so we came to the assistance of the Second Mate, who was desperately busied, along with some of his watch, in clearing away the broken foretopmast and yards that were held by their gear, thundering against the side of the ship.

Yet, it must not be supposed that we were to manage this piece of work, without coming to some harm; for, just as we made an end of it, an enormous sea swept aboard, and dashed one of the men against the spare topmast that was lashed along, inside the bulwarks, below the pin-rail. When we managed to pull the poor senseless fellow out from underneath the spar, where the sea had jammed him, we found that his left arm and collar-bone were broken. We took him forrard to the fo'cas'le, and there, with rough surgery, made him so comfortable as we could; after which we left him, but half conscious, in his bunk.

After that, several wet, weary hours were spent in rigging rough preventer-stays. Then the rest of us, men as well as officers, made our way aft to the poop; there to wait, desperately ready to cope with any emergency where our poor, futile human strength might aid to our salvation.

With great difficulty, the Carpenter had managed to sound the well, and, to our delight, had found that we were not making any water; so that the blows of the broken spars had done us no vital harm.

By midday, the following seas had risen to a truly formidable height, and two hands were working half naked at the wheel; for any carelessness in steering would, most certainly, have had horrible consequences.

In the course of the afternoon, the Mate and I went down into the saloon to get something to eat, and here, out of the deafening roar of the wind, I managed to get a short chat with my senior officer.

Talking about the waterspout which had so immediately preceded the first rush of the Cyclone, I made mention of its luminous appearance; to which he replied that it was due probably to a vast electric action going on between the clouds and the sea.

After that, I asked him why the Captain did not heave to, and ride the Storm out, instead of running before it, and risking being pooped, or broaching to.

To this, the Mate made reply that we were right in the line of translation; in other words, that we were directly in the track of the vortex, or centre, of the Cyclone, and that the Skipper was doing his best to edge the ship to leeward, before the centre, with the awful Pyramidal Sea, should overtake us.

"If we can't manage to get out of the way," he concluded, grimly, "you'll probably have a chance to photograph something that you'll never have time to develop!"

I asked him how he knew that the ship was directly in the track of the vortex, and he replied that the facts that the wind was not hauling, but getting steadily worse, with the barometer constantly falling, were sure signs.

And soon after that we returned to the deck.

As I have said, at midday, the seas were truly formidable; but by four P.M. they were so much worse that it was impossible to pass fore or aft along the decks, the water breaking aboard, as much as a hundred tons at a time, and sweeping all before it.

All this time, the roaring and *howling* of the Cyclone was so incredibly loud, that no word spoken, or shouted, out on deck—even though right into one's ear—could be heard distinctly, so that the utmost we could do to convey ideas to one another, was to make signs. And so, because of this, and to get for a little out of the painful and exhausting pressure of the wind, each of the officers would, in turn (sometimes singly and sometimes two at once), go down to the saloon, for a short rest and smoke.

It was in one of these brief "smoke-ohs" that the Mate told me the vortex of the Cyclone was probably within about eighty or a hundred miles of us, and coming down on us at something like twenty or thirty knots an hour, which—as this speed enormously exceeded ours—made it probable that it would be upon us before midnight.

"Is there no chance of getting out of the way?" I asked. "Couldn't we haul her up a trifle, and cut across the track a bit quicker than we are doing?"

"No," replied the Mate, and shook his head, thoughtfully. "The seas would make a clean breach over us, if we tried that. It's a case of 'run till you're blind, and pray till you bust'!" he concluded, with a certain despondent brutalness.

I nodded assent; for I knew that it was true. And after that we were silent. A few minutes later, we went up on deck. There we found that the wind had increased, and blown the foresail bodily away; yet, despite the greater weight of the wind, there had come a rift in the clouds, through which the sun was shining with a queer brightness.

I glanced at the Mate, and smiled; for it seemed to me a good omen; but he shook his head, as one who should say:— "It is no good omen; but a sign of something worse coming."

That he was right in refusing to be assured, I had speedy proof; for within ten minutes the sun had vanished, and the clouds seemed to be right down upon our mast-heads—great bellying webs of black vapour, that seemed almost to mingle with the flying clouds of foam and spray. The wind appeared to gain strength minute by minute, rising into an abominable scream, so piercing at times as to seem to pain the ear drums.

In this wise an hour passed, the ship racing onward under her two topsails, seeming to have lost no speed with the losing of the foresail; though it is possible that she was more under water forrard than she had been.

Then, about five-thirty P.M., I heard a louder roar in the air above us, so deep and tremendous that it seemed to daze and stun one; and, in the same instant, the two topsails were blown out of the bolt-ropes, and one of the hen-coops was lifted bodily off the poop, and hurled into the air, descending with an *inaudible* crash on to the maindeck. Luckily, it was not the one into which I had thrust my camera.

With the losing of the topsails, we might be very truly described as running under bare poles; for now we had not a single stitch of sail set anywhere. Yet, so furious was the increasing wind, so tremendous the weight of it, that the vessel, though urged forward only by the pressure of the element upon her naked spars and hull, managed to keep ahead of the monstrous following seas, which now were grown to truly awesome proportions.

The next hour or two, I remember only as a time that spread out monotonously. A time miserable and dazing, and dominated always by the deafening, roaring scream of the Storm. A time of wetness and dismalness, in which I knew, more than saw, that the ship wallowed on and on through the interminable seas. And so, hour by hour, the wind increased as the Vortex of the Cyclone—the "Death-Patch"—drew nearer and ever nearer.

Night came on early, or, if not night, a darkness that was fully its equivalent. And now I was able to see how tremendous was the electric action that was going on all about us. There seemed to be no lightning flashes; but, instead, there came at times across the darkness, queer luminous shudders of light. I am not acquainted with any word that better describes this extraordinary electrical phenomenon, than 'shudders' of light—broad, dull shudders of light, that came in undefined belts across the black, thunderous canopy of clouds, which seemed so low that our main-truck must have "puddled" them with every roll of the ship.

A further sign of electric action was to be seen in the "corpse candles," which ornamented every yard-arm. Not only were they upon the yardarms; but occasionally several at a time would glide up and down one or more of the fore and aft stays, at whiles swinging off to one side or the other; as the ship rolled. The sight having in it a distinct touch of weirdness.

It was an hour or so later, I believe a little after nine P.M., that I witnessed the most striking manifestation of electrical action that I have ever seen; this being neither more nor less than a display of Aurora Borealis lightning—a sight dree and almost frightening, with the sense of unearthliness and mystery that it brings.

I want you to be very clear that I am *not* talking about the Northern Lights—which, indeed, could never be seen at that distance to the Southward—; but of an extraordinary electrical phenomenon which occurred when the vortex of the Cyclone was within some twenty or thirty miles of the ship. It occurred suddenly. First, a ripple of "Stalk" lightning showed right away over the oncoming seas to the Northward; then, abruptly, a red glare shone out in the sky, and, immediately afterwards, vast streamers of greenish flame appeared above the red glare. These lasted, perhaps, half a minute, expanding and contracting over the sky with a curious quivering motion. The whole forming a truly awe-inspiring spectacle.

And then, slowly, the whole thing faded, and only the blackness of the night remained, slit in all directions by the phosphorescent crests of the seas.

I don't know whether I can convey to you any vivid impression of our case and chances at this time. It is so difficult—unless one had been through a similar experience—even to comprehend fully the incredible loudness of the wind. Imagine a noise as loud as the loudest thunder you have ever heard; then imagine this noise to last hour after hour, without intermission, and to have in it a hideously threatening hoarse note, and, blending with this, a constant yelling scream that rises at times to such a pitch that the very ear drums seem to experience pain, and then, perhaps, you will be able to conprehend merely the amount of *sound* that has to be endured during the passage of one of these Storms. And then, the *force* of the wind! Have you ever faced a wind so powerful that it splayed your lips apart, whether you would or not, laying your teeth bare to view? This is only a little thing; but it may help you to conceive something of the strength of a wind that will play such antics with one's mouth. The sensation it gives is extremely disagreeable—a sense of foolish impotence, is how I can best describe it.

Another thing; I learned that, with my face to the wind, I could not breathe. This is a statement baldly put; but it should help me somewhat in my endeavour to bring home to you the force of the wind, as exemplified in the minor details of my experience.

To give some idea of the wind's power, as shown in a larger way, one of the lifeboats on the after skids was up-ended against the mizzen mast, and there crushed flat by the wind, as though a monstrous invisible hand had pinched it. Does this help you a little to gain an idea of wind-force never met with in a thousand ordinary lives?

Apart from the wind, it must be borne in mind that the gigantic seas pitch the ship about in a most abominable manner. Indeed, I have seen the stern of a ship hove up to such a height that I could see the seas ahead over the fore topsail yards, and when I explain that these will be something like seventy to eighty feet above the deck, you may be able to imagine what manner of Sea is to be met with in a great Cyclonic Storm.

Regarding this matter of the size and ferocity of the seas, I possess a photograph that was taken about ten o'clock at night. This was photographed by the aid of flashlight, an operation in which the Captain assisted me. We filled an old, percussion pistol with flashlight powder, with an air-cone of paper down the centre. Then, when I was ready, I opened the shutter of the camera, and pointed it over the stern into the darkness. The Captain fired the pistol, and, in the instantaneous great blaze of light that followed, I saw what manner of sea it was that pursued us. To say it was a mountain, is to be futile. *It was like a moving cliff.*

As I snapped-to the shutter of my camera, the question flashed into my brain:—"Are we going to live it out, after all?" And, suddenly, it came home to me that I was a little man in a little ship, in the midst of a very great sea.

And then fresh knowledge came to me; I knew, abruptly, that it would not be a difficult thing to be very much afraid. The knowledge was new, and took me more in the stomach than the heart. Afraid! I had been in so many storms that I had forgotten they might be things to fear. Hitherto, my sensation at the thought of bad weather had been chiefly a feeling of annoyed repugnance, due to many memories of dismal wet nights, in wetter oilskins; with everything about the vessel reeking with damp and cheerless discomfort. But *fear*——No! A sailor has no more normal fear of bad weather, than a steeple-jack fears height. It is, as you might say, his vocation. And now this hateful sense of insecurity!

I turned from the taffrail, and hurried below to wipe the lens and cover of my camera; for the whole air was full of driving spray, that soaked everything, and hurt the face intolerably; being driven with such force by the storm.

Whilst I was drying my camera, the Mate came down for a minute's breathing space.

"Still at it?" he said.

"Yes," I replied, and I noticed, half-consciously, that he made no effort to light his pipe, as he stood with his arm crooked over an empty, brass candle bracket.

"You'll never develop them," he remarked.

"Of course I shall!" I replied, half-irritably; but with a horrid little sense of chilliness at his words, which came so unaptly upon my mind, so lately perturbed by uncomfortable thoughts.

"You'll see," he replied, with a sort of brutal terseness. "We shan't be above water by midnight!"

"You *can't* tell," I said. "What's the use of meeting trouble! Vessels have lived through worse than this?"

"Have they?" he said, very quietly. "Not many vessels have lived through worse than what's to come. I suppose you realise we expect to meet the Centre in less than an hour?"

"Well," I replied, "anyway, I shall go on taking photos. I guess if we come through all right, I shall have something to show people ashore."

He laughed, a queer, little, bitter laugh.

"You may as well do that as anything else," he said. "We can't do anything to help ourselves. If we're not pooped before the Centre reaches us, IT'll finish us in quick time!"

Then that cheerful officer of mine turned slowly, and made his way on deck, leaving me, as may be imagined, particularly exhilarated by his assurances. Presently, I followed, and, having barred the companion-way behind me, struggled forward to the break of the poop, clutching blindly at any holdfast in the darkness.

And so, for a space, we waited in the Storm—the wind bellowing fiendishly, and our maindecks one chaos of broken water, swirling and roaring to and fro in the darkness.

It was a little later that some one plucked me hard by the sleeve, and, turning, I made out with difficulty that it was the Captain, trying to attract my attention. I caught his wrist, to show that I comprehended what he desired, and, at that, he dropped on his hands and knees, and crawled aft along the streaming poop deck, I following, my camera held between my teeth by the handle.

He reached the companion-way, and unbarred the starboard door; then crawled through, and I followed after him. I fastened the door, and made my way, in his wake, to the saloon. Here he turned to me. He was a curiously devil-may-care sort of man, and I found that he had brought me down to explain that the Vortex would be upon us very soon, and that I should have the chance of a life-time to get a snap of the much talked of Pyramidal Sea. And, in short, that he wished me to have everything prepared, and the pistol ready loaded with flashlight powder; for, as he remarked:—

"*If* we get through, it'll be a rare curiosity to show some of those unbelieving devils ashore."

In a little, we had everything ready, and then we made our way once more up on deck; the Captain placing the pistol in the pocket of his silk oilskin coat.

There, together, under the after weather-cloth, we waited. The Second Mate, I could not see; but occasionally I caught a vague sight of the First Mate, standing near the after binnacle, and obviously watching the steering. Apart from the puny halo that emanated from the binnacle, all else was blind darkness, save for the phosphorescent lights of the overhanging crests of the seas.

And above us and around us, filling all the sky with sound, was the incessant mad yowling of the Cyclone; the noise so vast, and the volume and mass of the wind so enormous that I am impressed now, looking back, with a sense of having been in a semi-stunned condition through those last minutes.

I am conscious now that a vague time passed. A time of noise and wetness and lethargy and immense tiredness. Abruptly, a tremendous flash of lightning burst through the clouds. It was followed, almost directly, by another, which seemed to rive the sky apart. Then, so quickly that the succeeding thunderclap was *audible* to our wind-deafened ears, the wind ceased, and, in the comparative, but hideously unnatural, silence, I caught the Captain's voice shouting:—

"The Vortex—quick!"

Even as I pointed my camera over the rail, and opened the shutter, my brain was working with a preternatural avidity, drinking in a thousand uncanny sounds and echoes that seemed to come upon me from every quarter, brutally distinct against the background of the Cyclone's distant howling. There were the harsh, bursting, frightening, intermittent noises of the seas, making tremendous, slopping crashes of sound; and, mingling with these, the shrill, hissing scream of the foam; the dismal sounds, that suggested dankness, of water swirling over our decks; and, oddly, the faintly-heard creaking of the gear and shattered spars; and then—*Flash*, in the same instant in which I had taken in these varied impressions, the Captain had fired the pistol, and I saw the Pyramidal Sea. . . . A sight never to be forgotten. A sight rather for the Dead than the Living. A sea such as I could never have imagined. Boiling and bursting upward in monstrous hillocks of water and foam as big as houses. I heard, without knowing I heard, the Captain's expression of amazement. Then a thunderous roar was in my ears. One of those vast, flying hills of water had struck the ship, and, for some moments, I had a sickening feeling that she was sinking beneath me. The water cleared, and I found myself clinging to the iron weather-cloth staunchion; the weather-cloth itself had gone. I wiped my eyes, and coughed dizzily for a little; then I stared round for the Captain. I could see something dimly up against the rail; something that moved and stood upright. I sung out to know whether it was the Captain, and whether he was all right? To which he replied, heartily enough, but with a gasp, that he was all right so far.

From him, I glanced across to the wheel. There was no light in the binnacle, and, later, I found that it had been washed away, and with it one of the helmsmen. The other man also was gone; but we discovered him, nigh an hour later, jammed half through the rail that ran round the poop. To leeward, I heard the Mate singing out to know whether we were safe; to which both the Captain and I shouted a reply, so as to assure him. It was then I became aware that my camera had been washed out of my hands. I found it eventually among a tangle of ropes and gear to leeward.

Again and again the great hills of water struck the vessel, seeming to rise up on every side at once—towering, live pyramids of brine, in the darkness, hurling upward with a harsh unceasing roaring.

From her taffrail to her knight-heads, the ship was swept, fore and aft, so that no living thing could have existed for a moment down upon the main-deck, which was practically submerged. Indeed, the whole vessel seemed at times to be lost beneath the chaos of water that thundered down and over her in clouds and cataracts of brine and foam, so that each moment seemed like to be our last.

Occasionally, I would hear the hoarse voice of the Captain or the Mate, calling through the gloom to one another, or to the figures of the clinging men. And then again would come the thunder of water, as the seas burst over us. And all this in an almost impenetrable darkness, save when some unnatural glare of lightning sundered the clouds, and lit up the thirty-mile cauldron that had engulfed us.

And, anon, all this while, round about, seeming to come from every point of the horizon, sounded a vast, but distant, bellowing and screaming noise, that I caught sometimes above the harsh, slopping roarings of the bursting water-hills all about us. The sound appeared now to be growing louder upon our port beam. It was the Storm circling far round us.

Some time later, there sounded an intense roar in the air above the ship, and then came a far-off shrieking, that grew rapidly into a mighty whistling-scream, and a minute afterwards a most tremendous gust of wind struck the ship on her port side, hurling her over on to her starboard broadside. For many minutes she lay there, her decks under water almost up to the coamings of the hatches. Then she righted, sullenly and slowly, freeing herself from, maybe, half a thousand tons of water.

Again there came a short period of windlessness and then once more the yelling of an approaching gust. It struck us; but now the vessel had paid off before the wind, and she was not again forced over on to her side.

From now onward, we drove forward over vast seas, with the Cyclone bellowing and wailing over us in one unbroken roar. . . . *The Vortex had passed*, and, could we but last out a few more hours, then might we hope to win through.

With the return of the wind, the Mate and one of the men had taken the wheel; but, despite the most careful steering, we were pooped several times; for the seas were hideously broken and confused, we being still in the wake of the Vortex, and the wind not having had time as yet to smash the Pyramidal Sea into the more regular storm waves, which, though huge in size, give a vessel a chance to rise to them.

It was later that some of us, headed by the Mate—who had relinquished his place at the wheel to one of the men—ventured down on to the main-deck with axes and knives, to clear away the wreckage of some of the spars which we had lost in the Vortex. Many a grim risk was run in that hour; but we cleared the wreck, and after that, scrambled back, dripping, to the poop, where the Steward, looking woefully white and scared, served out rum to us from a wooden deck-bucket.

It was decided now that we should bring her head to the seas, so as to make better weather of it. To reduce the risk as much as possible, we had already put out two fresh oil-bags, which we had prepared, and which, indeed, we ought to have done earlier; for though they were being constantly washed aboard again, we had begun at once to take less water.

Now, we took a hawser from the bows, outside of everything, and right away aft to the poop, where we bent on our sea-anchor, which was like an enormous log-bag, or drogue, made of triple canvas.

We bent on our two oil-bags to the sea-anchor, and then dropped the whole business over the side. When the vessel took the pull of it, we put down our helm, and came up into the wind, very quick, and without taking any great water. And a risk it was; but a deal less than some we had come through already.

Slowly, with an undreamt of slowness, the remainder of the night passed, minute by minute, and at last the day broke in a weary dawn; the sky full of a stormy, sickly light. One very side tumbled an interminable chaos of seas. And the vessel herself——! A wreck, she appeared. The mizzenmast had gone, some dozen feet above the deck; the main-topmast had gone, and so had the jigger-topmast. I struggled forrard to the break of the poop, and glanced along the decks. The boats had gone. All the iron scupper-doors were either bent, or had disappeared. On the starboard side, opposite to the stump of the mizzenmast, was a great ragged gap in the steel bulwarks, where the mast must have struck, when it carried away. In several other places, the t'gallant rail was smashed or bent, where it had been struck by falling spars. The side of the teak deck-house had been stove, and the water was roaring in and out with each roll of the ship. The sheep-pen had vanished, and so—as I discovered later—had the pigsty.

Further forrard, my glance went, and I saw that the sea had breached the bulkshead, across the after end of the fo'cas'le, and, with each biggish sea that we shipped, a torrent of water drove in, and then flowed out, sometimes bearing with it an odd board, or perhaps a man's boot, or some article of wearing apparel. In two places on the maindeck, I saw men's sea-chests, washing to and fro in the water that streamed over the deck. And, suddenly, there came into my mind a memory of the poor fellow who had broken his arm when we were cutting loose the wreck of the fore-topmast.

Already, the strength of the Cyclone was spent, so far, at least, as we were concerned; and I was thinking of making a try for the fo'cas'le, when, close beside me, I heard the Mate's voice. I turned, with a little start. He had evidently noticed the breach in the bulkshead; for he told me to watch a chance, and see if we could get forrard.

This, we did; though not without a further thorough sousing; as we were still shipping water by the score of tons. Moreover, the risk was considerably greater than might be conceived; for the doorless scupper-ports offered uncomfortable facilities for gurgling out into the ocean, along with a ton or two of brine from the decks.

We reached the fo'cas'le, and pulled open the lee door. We stepped inside. It was like stepping into a dank, gloomy cavern. Water was dripping from every beam and staunchion. We struggled across the slippery deck, to where we had left the sick man in his bunk. In the dim light, we saw that man and bunk, everything, had vanished; only the bare steel sides of the vessel remained. Every bunk and fitting in the place had been swept away, and all of the men's sea-chests. Nothing remained, save, it might be, an odd soaked rag of clothing, or a sodden bunk-board.

The Mate and I looked at one another, in silence.

"Poor devil!" he said. He repeated his expression of pity, staring at the place where had been the bunk. Then, grave of face, he turned to go out on deck. As he did so, a heavier sea than usual broke aboard; flooded roaring along the decks, and swept in through the broken bulkshead and the lee doorway. It swirled round the sides, caught us, and threw us down in a heap; then swept out through the breach and the doorway, carrying the

Mate with it. He managed to grasp the lintel of the doorway, else, I do believe, he would have gone out through one of the open scupper traps. A doubly hard fate, after having come safely through the Cyclone.

Outside of the fo'cas'le, I saw that the ladders leading up to the fo'cas'le head had both gone; but I managed to scramble up. Here, I found that both anchors had been washed away, and the rails all round; only the bare staunchions remaining.

Beyond the bows, the jibboom had gone, and all the gear was draggled inboard over the fo'cas'le head, or trailing in the sea.

We made our way aft, and reported; then the roll was called, and we found that one else was missing, besides the two I have already mentioned, and the man we found jammed half through the poop rails, who was now under the Steward's care.

From that time on, the sea went down steadily, until, presently, it ceased to threaten us, and we proceeded to get the ship cleared up a bit; after which, one watch turned-in on the floor of the saloon, and the other was told to "stand easy."

Hour by hour, through that day and the next, the sea went down, until it was difficult to believe that we had so lately despaired for our lives. And so the second evening came, calm and restful, the wind no more than a light summer's breeze, and the sea calming steadily.

About seven bells that second night, a big steamer crossed our stern, and slowed down to ask us if we were in need of help; for, even by moonlight, it was easy to see our dismantled condition. This offer, however, the Captain refused; and with many good wishes, the big vessel swung off into the moon-wake, and so, presently, we were left alone in the quiet night; safe at last, and rich in a completed experience.

SHIPWRECK

CAPTAIN JAMES RILEY

We set sail from the bay of Gibraltar on the 23rd of August, 1815, intending to go by way of the Cape de Verd Islands, to complete the lading of the vessel with salt. We passed Capt Spartel on the morning of the 24th, giving it a berth of from ten to twelve leagues, and steered off to the W. S. W. I intended to make the Canary Islands, and pass between Teneriffe and Palma, having a fair wind; but it being very thick and foggy weather, though we got two observations at noon, neither could be much depended upon. On account of the fog, we saw no land, and found, by good meridian altitudes on the twenty-eighth, that we were in the latitude of 27. 30. N. having differed our latitude by the force of current, one hundred and twenty miles; thus passing the Canaries without seeing any of them. I concluded we must have passed through the intended passage without discovering the land on either side, particularly, as it was in the night, which was very dark, and black as pitch; nor could I believe otherwise from having had a fair wind all the way, and having steered one course ever since we took our departure from Cape Spartel. Soon after we got an observation on the 28th, it became as thick as ever, and the darkness seemed (if possible) to increase. Towards evening I got up my reckoning, and examined it all over, to be sure that I had committed no error, and caused the mates to do the same with theirs. Having thus ascertained that I was correct in calculation, I altered our course to S. W. which ought to have carried us nearly on the course I wished to steer, that is, for the easternmost of the Cape de Verds; but finding the weather becoming more foggy towards night, it being so thick that we could scarcely see the end of the jib-boom, I rounded the vessel to, and sounded with one hundred and twenty fathoms of line, but found no bottom, and continued on our course, still reflecting on what should be the cause of our not seeing land, (as I never had passed near the Canaries before without seeing them, even in thick weather or in the night.) I came to a determination to haul off to the N. W. by the wind at 10 P.M.. as I should then be by the log only thirty miles north of Cape Bajador. I concluded on this at nine, and thought my fears had never before so much prevailed over my judgment and my reckoning. I ordered the light sails to be handed, and the steering sail booms to be rigged in snug, which was done as fast as it could be by one watch, under the immediate direction of Mr. Savage.

We had just got the men stationed at the braces for hauling off, as the man at helm cried "ten o'clock." Our try-sail boom was on the starboard side, but ready for jibing; the helm was put to port, dreaming of no danger near. I had been on deck all the evening myself; the vessel was running at the rate of nine or ten knots, with a very strong breeze, and high sea, when the main boom was jibed over, and I at that instant heard a roaring; the yards were braced up—all hands were called. I imagined at first it was a squall, and was near ordering the sails to be lowered down; but I then discovered breakers foaming at a most dreadful rate under our lee. Hope for a moment flattered me that we could fetch off still, as there were no breakers in view ahead: the anchors were made ready; but these hopes vanished in an instant, as the vessel was carried by a current and a sea directly towards the breakers, and she struck! We let go the best bower anchor; all sails were taken in as fast as possible: surge after surge came thundering on, and drove her in spite of anchors, partly with her head on shore. She struck with such violence as to start every man from the deck. Knowing there was no possibility of saving her, and that she must very soon bilge and fill with water, I ordered all the provisions we could get at to be brought on deck, in hopes of saving some, and as much water to be drawn from the large casks as possible. We started several quarter casks of wine, and filled them with water. Every man worked as if his life depended upon his present exertions; all were obedient to every order I gave, and seemed perfectly calm;—The vessel was stout and high, as she was only in ballast trim;—The sea combed over her stern and swept her decks; but we managed to get the small boat in on deck, to sling her and keep her from staving. We cut away the bulwark on the larboard side so as to prevent the boast from staving when we should get them out; cleared away the long boat and hung her in tackles, the vessel continuing to strike very heavy, and filling fast. We however, had secured five or six barrels of water, and as many of wine,—three barrels of bread, and three or four salted provisions. I had as yet been so busily employed, that no pains had been taken to ascertain what distance we were from the land, nor had any of us yet seen it; and in the meantime all the clothing, chests, trunks, &c. were got up, and the books, charts, and sea instruments, were stowed in them, in the hope of their being useful to us in future.

The vessel being now nearly full of water, the surf making a fair breach over her, and fearing she would go to pieces, I prepared a rope, and put it in the small boat, having got a glimpse of the short, at no great distance, and taking Porter with me, we were lowered down on the larboard or lee side of the vessel, where she broke the violence of the sea, and made it comparatively smooth; we shoved off, but on clearing away from the bow of the vessel, the boat was overwhelmed with a surf, and we were plunged into the foaming surges: we were driven along by the current, aided by what seamen call the undertow, (or recoil of the sea) to the distance of three hundred yards to the westward, covered nearly all the time by the billows, which, following each other in quick succession, scarcely gave us time to catch a breath before we were again literally swallowed by them, till at length we were thrown, together with our boat, upon a sandy beach. After taking breath a little, and ridding our stomachs of the salt water that had forced its way into them, my first care was to turn the water out of the boat, and haul her up out of the reach of the surf. We found the rope that was made fast to her still remaining; this we carried up along the beach, directly to leeward of the wreck, where we fastened it to sticks about the thickness of handspikes, that had drifted on the shore from the vessel, and which we drove into the sand by the help of other pieces of wood. Before leaving the vessel, I had directed that all the chests, trunks, and everything that would float, should be hove overboard: this all hands were busied in doing. The vessel lay about one hundred fathoms from the beach, at high tide. In order to save the crew, a hawser was made fast to the rope we had on shore, one end of which we hauled to us, and made it fast to a number of sticks we had driven into the sand for the purpose. It was then tautened on board the wreck, and made fast. This being done, the long-boat (in order to save the provisions already in her) was lowered down, and two hands steadied her by ropes fastened to the rings in her stem and stern posts over the hawser, so as to slide, keeping her bow to the surf. In this manner they reached the beach, carried on the top of a heavy wave. The boat was stove by the violence of the shock against the beach; but by great exertions we saved the three barrels of bread in her before they were much damaged; and two barrels of salted provisions were also saved. We were now, four of us, on shore, and busied in picking up the clothing and other things which drifted from the vessel, and carrying them up out of the surf. It was by this time daylight, and high water; the vessel careened deep off shore, and I made signs to have the mast cut away, in the hope of easing her, that she might not go to pieces. They were accordingly cut away, and fell on her starboard side, making a better lee for a boat alongside the wreck, as they projected considerably beyond her bows. The masts and rigging being gone, the sea breaking very high over the wreck, and nothing left to hold on by, the mates and six men still on board, though secured, as well as they could be, on the bowsprit and in the larboard fore-channels, were yet in imminent danger of being washed off by every surge. The long-boat was stove, and it being impossible for the small one to live, my great object was now to save the lives of the crew by means of the hawser. I therefore made signs to them to come, one by one, on the hawser, which had been stretched taut for that purpose. John Hogan ventured first, and having pulled off his jacket, took to the hawser, and made for the shore. When he had got clear of the immediate lee of the wreck, every surf buried him, combing many feet above his head; but he still held fast to the rope with a death-like grasp, and as soon as the surf was passed, proceeded on towards the shore, until another surf, more powerful than the former, unclenched his hands, and threw him within our reach; when we laid hold of him and dragged him to the beach; we then rolled him on the sand, until he discharged the salt water from his stomach, and revived. I kept in the water up to my chin, steadying myself by the hawser, while the surf passed over me, to catch the others as they approached, and thus, with the assistance of those already on shore, was enabled to save all the rest from a watery grave.

THE WRECK OF THE
GOLDEN MARY

CHARLES DICKENS WITH WILKIE COLLINS

The Wreck

I was apprenticed to the Sea when I was twelve years old, and I have encountered a great deal of rough weather, both literal and metaphorical. It has always been my opinion since I first possessed such a thing as an opinion, that the man who knows only one subject is next tiresome to the man who knows no subject. Therefore, in the course of my life I have taught myself whatever I could, and although I am not an educated man, I am able, I am thankful to say, to have an intelligent interest in most things.

A person might suppose, from reading the above, that I am in the habit of holding forth about number one. That is not the case. Just as if I was to come into a room among strangers, and must either be introduced or introduce myself, so I have taken the liberty of passing these few remarks, simply and plainly that it may be known who and what I am. I will add no more of the sort than that my name is William George Ravender, that I was born at Penrith half a year after my own father was drowned, and that I am on the second day of this present blessed Christmas week of one thousand eight hundred and fifty-six, fifty-six years of age.

When the rumour first went flying up and down that there was gold in California—which, as most people know, was before it was discovered in the British colony of Australia—I was in the West Indies, trading among the Islands. Being in command and likewise part-owner of a smart schooner, I had my work cut out for me, and I was doing it. Consequently, gold in California was no business of mine.

But, by the time when I came home to England again, the thing was as clear as your hand held up before you at noonday. There was Californian gold in the museums and in the goldsmiths' shops, and the very first time I went upon 'Change, I met a friend of mine (a seafaring man like myself), with a Californian nugget hanging to his watch-chain. I handled it. It was as like a peeled walnut with bits unevenly broken off here and there, and then electrotyped all over, as ever I saw anything in my life.

I am a single man (she was too good for this world and for me, and she died six weeks before our marriage-day), so when I am ashore, I live in my house at Poplar. My house at Poplar is taken care of and kept ship-shape by an old lady who was my mother's maid before I was born. She is as handsome and as upright as any old lady in the world. She is as fond of me as if she had ever had an only son, and I was he. Well do I know wherever I sail that she never lays down her head at night without having said, "Merciful Lord! bless and preserve William George Ravender, and send him safe home, through Christ our Saviour!" I have thought of it in many a dangerous moment, when it has done me no harm, I am sure.

In my house at Poplar, along with this old lady, I lived quiet for best part of a year: having had a long spell of it among the Islands, and having (which was very uncommon in me) taken the fever rather badly. At last, being strong and hearty, and having read every book I could lay hold of, right out, I was walking down Leadenhall Street in the City of London, thinking of turning-to again, when I met what I call Smithick and Watersby of Liverpool. I chanced to lift up my eyes from looking in at a ship's chronometer in a window, and I saw him bearing down upon me, head on.

It is, personally, neither Smithick, nor Watersby, that I here mention, nor was I ever acquainted with any man of either of those names, nor do I think that there has been any one of either of those names in that Liverpool House for years back. But, it is in reality the House itself that I refer to; and a wiser merchant or a truer gentleman never stepped.

"My dear Captain Ravender," says he. "Of all the men on earth, I wanted to see you most. I was on my way to you."

"Well!" says I. "That looks as if you *were* to see me, don't it?" With that I put my arm in his, and we walked on towards the Royal Exchange, and when we got there, walked up and down at the back of it where the Clock-Tower is. We walked an hour and more, for he had much to say to me. He had a scheme for chartering a new ship of their own to take out cargo to the diggers and emigrants in California, and to buy and bring back gold. Into the particulars of that scheme I will not enter, and I have no right to enter. All I say of it is, that it was a very original one, a very fine one, a very sound one, and a very lucrative one beyond doubt.

He imparted it to me as freely as if I had been a part of himself. After doing so, he made me the handsomest sharing offer that ever was made to me, boy or man—or I believe to any other captain in the Merchant Navy—and he took this round turn to finish with:

"Ravender, you are well aware that the lawlessness of that coast and country at present, is as special as the circumstances in which it is placed. Crews of vessels outward-bound, desert as soon as they make the land; crews of vessels homewardbound, ship at enormous wages, with the express intention of murdering the captain and seizing the gold freight; no man can trust another, and the devil seems let loose. Now," says he, "you know my opinion of you, and you know I am only expressing it, and with no singularity, when I tell you that you are almost the only man on whose integrity, discretion, and energy—" &c. &c. For, I don't want to repeat what he said, though I was and am sensible of it.

Notwithstanding my being, as I have mentioned, quite ready for a voyage, still I had some doubts of this voyage. Of course I knew, without being told, that there were peculiar difficulties and dangers in it, a long way over and above those which attend all voyages. It must not be supposed that I was afraid to face them; but, in my opinion a man has no manly motive or sustainment in his own breast for facing dangers, unless he has well considered what they are, and is able quietly to say to himself, "None of these perils can now take me by surprise; I shall know what to do for the best in any of them; all the rest lies in the higher and greater hands to which I humbly commit myself." On this principle I have so attentively considered (regarding it as my duty) all the hazards I have ever been able to think of, in the ordinary way of storm, shipwreck, and fire at sea, that I hope I should be prepared to do, in any of those cases, whatever could be done, to save the lives intrusted to my charge.

As I was thoughtful, my good friend proposed that he should leave me to walk there as long as I liked, and that I should dine with him by-and-by at his club in Pall Mall. I accepted the invitation and I walked up and down there, quarter-deck fashion, a matter of a couple of hours; now and then looking up at the weathercock as I might have looked up aloft; and now and then taking a look into Cornhill, as I might have taken a look over the side.

All dinner-time, and all after dinner-time, we talked it over again. I gave him my views of his plan, and he very much approved of the same. I told him I had nearly decided, but not quite. "Well, well," says he, "come down to Liverpool to-morrow with me, and see the Golden Mary." I liked the name (her name was Mary, and she was golden, if golden stands for good), so I began to feel that it was almost done when I said I would go to Liverpool. On the next morning but one we were on board the Golden Mary. I might have known, from his asking me to come down and see her, what she was. I declare her to have been the completest and most exquisite Beauty that ever I set my eyes upon.

We had inspected every timber in her, and had come back to the gang-way to go ashore from the dock-basin, when I put out my hand to my friend. "Touch upon it," says I, "and touch heartily. I take command of this ship, and I am hers and yours, if I can get John Steadiman for my chief mate."

John Steadiman had sailed with me four voyages. The first voyage John was third mate out to China, and came home second. The other three voyages he was my first officer. At this time of chartering the Golden Mary, he was aged thirty-two. A brisk, bright, blue-eyed fellow, a very neat figure and rather under the middle size, never out of the way and never in it, a face that pleased everybody and that all children took to, a habit of going about singing as cheerily as a blackbird, and a perfect sailor.

We were in one of those Liverpool hackney-coaches in less than a minute, and we cruised about in her upwards of three hours, looking for John.

John had come home from Van Diemen's Land barely a month before, and I had heard of him as taking a frisk in Liverpool. We asked after him, among many other places, at the two boarding-houses he was fondest of, and we found he had had a week's spell at each of them; but, he had gone here and gone there, and had set off "to lay out on the main-to'-gallant-yard of the highest Welsh mountain" (so he had told the people of the house), and where he might be then, or when he might come back, nobody could tell us. But it was surprising, to be sure, to see how every face brightened the moment there was mention made of the name of Mr. Steadiman.

We were taken aback at meeting with no better luck, and we had wore ship and put her head for my friends, when as we were jogging through the streets, I clap my eyes on John himself coming out of a toyshop! He was carrying a little boy, and conducting two uncommon pretty women to their coach, and he told me afterwards that he had never in his life seen one of the three before, but that he was so taken with them on looking in at the toyshop while they were buying the child a cranky Noah's Ark, very much down by the head, that he had gone in and asked the ladies' permission to treat him to a tolerably correct Cutter there was in the window, in order that such a handsome boy might not grow up with a lubberly idea of naval architecture.

We stood off and on until the ladies' coachman began to give way, and then we hailed John. On his coming aboard of us, I told him, very gravely, what I had said to my friend. It struck him, as he said himself, amidships. He was quite shaken by it. "Captain Ravender," were John Steadiman's words, "such an opinion from you is true commendation, and I'll sail round the world with you for twenty years if you hoist the signal, and stand by you for ever!" And now indeed I felt that it was done, and that the Golden Mary was afloat.

Grass never grew yet under the feet of Smithick and Watersby. The riggers were out of that ship in a fortnight's time, and we had begun taking in cargo. John was always aboard, seeing everything stowed with his own eyes; and whenever I went aboard myself early or late, whether he was below in the hold, or on deck at the hatchway, or overhauling his cabin, nailing up pictures in it of the Blush Roses of England, the Blue Bells of Scotland, and the female Shamrock of Ireland: of a certainty I heard John singing like a blackbird.

We had room for twenty passengers. Our sailing advertisement was no sooner out, than we might have taken these twenty times over. In entering our men, I and John (both together) picked them, and we entered none but good hands—as good as were to be found in that port. And so, in a good ship of the best build, well owned, well arranged, well officered, well manned, well found in all respects, we parted with our pilot at a quarter past four o'clock in the afternoon of the seventh of March, one thousand eight hundred and fifty-one, and stood with a fair wind out to sea.

It may be easily believed that up to that time I had had no leisure to be intimate with my passengers. The most of them were then in their berths sea-sick; however, in going among them, telling them what was good for them, persuading them not to be there, but to come up on deck and feel the breeze, and in rousing them with a joke, or a comfortable word, I made acquaintance with them, perhaps, in a more friendly and confidential way from the first, than I might have done at the cabin table.

Of my passengers, I need only particularise, just at present, a bright-eyed blooming young wife who was going out to join her husband in California, taking with her their only child, a little girl of three years old, whom he had never seen; a sedate young woman in black, some five years older (about thirty as I should say), who was going out to join a brother; and an old gentleman, a good deal like a hawk if his eyes had been better and not so red, who was always talking, morning, noon, and night, about the gold discovery. But, whether he was making the voyage, thinking his old arms could dig for gold, or whether his speculation was to buy it, or to barter for it, or to cheat for it, or to snatch it anyhow from other people, was his secret. He kept his secret.

These three and the child were the soonest well. The child was a most engaging child, to be sure, and very fond of me: though I am bound to admit that John Steadiman and I were borne on her pretty little books in reverse order, and that he was captain there, and I was mate. It was beautiful to watch her with John, and it was beautiful to watch John with her. Few would have thought it possible, to see John playing at bo-peep round the mast, that he was the man who had caught up an iron bar and struck a Malay and a Maltese dead, as they were gliding with their knives down the cabin stair aboard the barque Old England, when the captain lay ill in his cot, off Saugar Point. But he was; and give him his back against a bulwark, he would have done the same by half-a-dozen of them. The name of the young mother was Mrs. Atherfield, the name of the young lady in black was Miss Coleshaw, and the name of the old gentleman was Mr. Rarx.

As the child had a quantity of shining fair hair, clustering in curls all about her face, and as her name was Lucy, Steadiman gave her the name of the Golden Lucy. So, we had the Golden Lucy and the Golden Mary; and John kept up the idea to that extent as he and the child went playing about the decks, that I believe she used to think the ship was alive somehow—a sister or companion, going to the same place as herself. She liked to be by the wheel, and in fine weather, I have often stood by the man whose trick it was at the wheel, only to hear her, sitting near my feet, talking to the ship. Never had a child such a doll before, I suppose; but she made a doll of the Golden Mary, and used to dress her up by tying ribbons and little bits of finery to the belaying-pins; and nobody ever moved them, unless it was to save them from being blown away.

Of course I took charge of the two young women, and I called them "my dear," and they never minded, knowing that whatever I said was said in a fatherly and protecting spirit. I gave them their places on each side of me at dinner; Mrs. Atherfield on my right and Miss Coleshaw on my left; and I directed the unmarried lady to serve out the breakfast, and the married lady to serve out the tea. Likewise I said to my black steward in their presence, "Tom Snow, these two ladies are equally the mistresses of this house, and do you obey their orders equally;" at which Tom laughed, and they all laughed.

Old Mr. Rarx was not a pleasant man to look at, nor yet to talk to, or to be with, for no one could help seeing that he was a sordid and selfish character, and that he had warped further and further out of the straight with time. Not but what he was on his best behaviour with us, as everybody was; for we had no bickering among us, for'ard or aft. I only mean to say, he was not the man one would have chosen for a messmate. If choice there had been, one might even have gone a few points out of one's course, to say, "No! Not him!" But, there was one curious inconsistency in Mr. Rarx. That was, that he took an astonishing interest in the child. He looked, and I may add, he was, one of the last of men to care at all for a child, or to care much for any human creature. Still, he went so far as to be habitually uneasy, if the child was long on deck, out of his sight. He was always afraid of her falling overboard, or falling down a hatchway, or of a block or what not coming down upon her from the rigging in the working of the ship, or of her getting some hurt or other. He used to look at her and touch her, as if she was something precious to him. He was always solicitous about her not injuring her health, and constantly entreated her mother to be careful of it. This was so much the more curious, because the child did not like him, but used to shrink away from him, and would not even put out her hand to him without coaxing from others. I believe that every soul on board frequently noticed this, and not one of us understood it. However, it was such a plain fact, that John Steadiman said more than once when old Mr. Rarx was not within earshot, that if the Golden Mary felt a tenderness for the dear old gentleman she carried in her lap, she must be bitterly jealous of the Golden Lucy.

Before I go any further with this narrative, I will state that our ship was a barque of three hundred tons, carrying a crew of eighteen men, a second mate in addition to John, a carpenter, an armourer or smith, and two apprentices (one a Scotch boy, poor little fellow). We had three boats; the Long-boat, capable of carrying twenty-five men; the Cutter, capable of carrying fifteen; and the Surf-boat, capable of carrying ten. I put down the capacity of these boats according to the numbers they were really meant to hold.

We had tastes of bad weather and head-winds, of course; but, on the whole we had as fine a run as any reasonable man could expect, for sixty days. I then began to enter two remarks in the ship's Log and in my Journal; first, that there was an unusual and amazing quantity of ice; second, that the nights were most wonderfully dark, in spite of the ice.

For five days and a half, it seemed quite useless and hopeless to alter the ship's course so as to stand out of the way of this ice. I made what southing I could; but, all that time, we were beset by it. Mrs. Atherfield after standing by me on deck once, looking for some time in an awed manner at the great bergs that surrounded us, said in a whisper, "O! Captain Ravender, it looks as if the whole solid earth had changed into ice, and broken up!" I said to her, laughing, "I don't wonder that it does, to your inexperienced eyes, my dear." But I had never seen a twentieth part of the quantity, and, in reality, I was pretty much of her opinion.

However, at two P.M. on the afternoon of the sixth day, that is to say, when we were sixty-six days out, John Steadiman who had gone aloft, sang out from the top, that the sea was clear ahead. Before four P.M. a strong breeze springing up right astern, we were in open water at sunset. The breeze then freshening into half a gale of wind, and the Golden Mary being a very fast sailer, we went before the wind merrily, all night.

I had thought it impossible that it could be darker than it had been, until the sun, moon, and stars should fall out of the Heavens, and Time should be destroyed; but, it had been next to light, in comparison with what it was now. The darkness was so profound, that looking into it was painful and oppressive—like looking, without a ray of light, into a dense black bandage put as close before the eyes as it could be, without touching them. I doubled the look-out, and John and I stood in the bow side-by-side, never leaving it all night. Yet I should no more have known that he was near me when he was silent, without putting out my arm and touching him, than I should if he had turned in and been fast asleep below. We were not so much looking out, all of us, as listening to the utmost, both with our eyes and ears.

Next day, I found that the mercury in the barometer, which had risen steadily since we cleared the ice, remained steady. I had had very good observations, with now and then the interruption of a day or so, since our departure. I got the sun at noon, and found that we were in Lat. 58° S., Long. 60° W., off New South Shetland; in the neighbourhood of Cape Horn. We were sixty-seven days out, that day. The ship's reckoning was accurately worked and made up. The ship did her duty admirably, all on board were well, and all hands were as smart, efficient, and contented, as it was possible to be.

When the night came on again as dark as before, it was the eighth night I had been on deck. Nor had I taken more than a very little sleep in the daytime, my station being always near the helm, and often at it, while we were among the ice. Few but those who have tried it can imagine the difficulty and pain of only keeping the eyes open—physically open— under such circumstances, in such darkness. They get struck by the darkness, and blinded by the darkness. They make patterns in it, and they flash in it, as if they had gone out of your head to look at you. On the turn of midnight, John Steadiman, who was alert and fresh (for I had always made him turn in by day), said to me, "Captain Ravender, I entreat of you to go below. I am sure you can hardly stand, and your voice is getting weak, Sir. Go below, and take a little rest. I'll call you if a block chafes." I said to John in answer, "Well, well, John! Let us wait till the turn of one o'clock, before we talk about that." I had just had one of the ship's lanterns held up, that I might see how the night went by my watch, and it was then twenty minutes after twelve.

At five minutes before one, John sang out to the boy to bring the lantern again, and when I told him once more what the time was, entreated and prayed of me to go below. "Captain Ravender," says he, "all's well; we can't afford to have you laid up for a single hour; and I respectfully and earnestly beg of you to go below." The end of it was, that I agreed to do so, on the understanding that if I failed to come up of my own accord within three hours, I was to be punctually called. Having settled that, I left John in charge. But I called him to me once afterwards, to ask him a question.

I had been to look at the barometer, and had seen the mercury still perfectly steady, and had come up the companion again to take a last look about me—if I can use such a word in reference to such darkness—when I thought that the waves, as the Golden Mary parted them and shook them off, had a hollow sound in them; something that I fancied was a rather unusual reverberation. I was standing by the quarter-deck rail on the starboard side, when I called John aft to me, and bade him listen. He did so with the greatest attention. Turning to me he then said, "Rely upon it, Captain Ravender, you have been without rest too long, and the novelty is only in the state of your sense of hearing." I thought so too by that time, and I think so now, though I can never kow for absolute certain in this world, whether it was or not.

When I left John Steadiman in charge, the ship was still going at a great rate through the water. The wind still blew right, astern. Though she was making great way, she was under shortened sail, and had no more than she could easily carry. All was snug, and nothing complained. There was a pretty sea running, but not a very high sea neither, nor at all a confused one.

I turned in, as we seamen say, all standing. The meaning of that is, I did not pull my clothes off—no, not even so much as my coat: though I did my shoes, for my feet were badly swelled with the deck. There was a little swing-lamp alight in my cabin. I thought, as I looked at it before shutting my eyes, that I was so tired of darkness, and troubled by darkness, that I could have gone to sleep best in the midst of a million of flaming gas-lights. That was the last thought I had before I went off, except the prevailing thought that I should not be able to get to sleep at all.

I dreamed that I was back at Penrith again, and was trying to get round the church, which had altered its shape very much since I last saw it, and was cloven all down the middle of the steeple in a most singular manner. Why I wanted to get round the church I don't know; but I was as anxious to do it as if my life depended upon it. Indeed, I believe it did in the dream. For all that, I could not get round the church. I was still trying, when I came against it with a violent shock, and was flung out of my cot against the ship's side. Shrieks and a terrific outcry struck me far harder than the bruising timbers, and amidst sounds of grinding and crashing, and a heavy rushing and breaking of water—sounds I understood too well—I made my way on deck. It was not an easy thing to do, for the ship heeled over frightfully, and was beating in a furious manner.

I could not see the men as I went forward, but I could hear that they were hauling in sail, in disorder. I had my trumpet in my hand, and, after directing and encouraging them in this till it was done, I hailed first John Steadiman, and then my second mate, Mr. William Rames. Both answered clearly and steadily. Now, I had practised them and all my crew, as I have ever made it a custom to practise all who sail with me, to take certain stations and wait my orders, in case of any unexpected crisis. When my voice was heard hailing, and their voices were heard answering, I was aware, through all the noises of the ship and sea, and all the crying of the passengers below, that there was a pause. "Are you ready, Rames?"—"Ay, ay, Sir!"—"Then light up, for God's sake!" In a moment he and another were burning blue-lights, and the ship and all on board seemed to be enclosed in a mist of light, under a great black dome.

The light shone up so high that I could see the huge Iceberg upon which we had struck, cloven at the top and down the middle, exactly like Penrith Church in my dream. At the same moment I could see the watch last relieved, crowding up and down on deck; I could see Mrs. Atherfield and Miss Coleshaw thrown about on the top of the companion as they struggled to bring the child up from below; I could see that the masts were going with the shock and the beating of the ship; I could see the frightful breach stove in on the starboard side, half the length of the vessel, and the sheathing and timbers spirting up; I could see that the Cutter was disabled, in a wreck of broken fragments; and I could see every eye turned upon me. It is my belief that if there had been ten thousand eyes there, I should have seen them all, with their different looks. And all this in a moment. But you must consider what a moment.

I saw the men, as they looked at me, fall towards their appointed stations, like good men and true. If she had not righted, they could have done very little there or anywhere but die—not that it is little for a man to die at his post—I mean they could have done nothing to save the passengers and themselves. Happily, however, the violence of the shock with which we had so determinedly borne down direct on that fatal Iceberg, as if it had been our destination instead of our destruction, had so smashed and pounded the ship that she got off in this same instant and righted. I did not want the carpenter to tell me she was filling and going down; I could see and hear that. I gave Rames the word to lower the Long-boat and the Surf-boat, and I myself told off the men for each duty. Not one hung back, or came before the other. I now whispered to John Steadiman, "John, I stand at the gangway here, to see every soul on board safe over the side.

You shall have the next post of honour, and shall be the last but one to leave the ship. Bring up the passengers, and range them behind me; and put what provision and water you can get at, in the boats. Cast your eye for'ard, John, and you'll see you have not a moment to lose."

My noble fellows got the boats over the side as orderly as I ever saw boats lowered with any sea running, and, when they were launched, two or three of the nearest men in them as they held on, rising and falling with the swell, called out, looking up at me, "Captain Ravender, if anything goes wrong with us, and you are saved, remember we stood by you!"—"We'll all stand by one another ashore, yet, please God, my lads!" says I. "Hold on bravely, and be tender with the women."

The women were an example to us. They trembled very much, but they were quiet and perfectly collected. "Kiss me, Captain Ravender," says Mrs. Atherfield, "and God in heaven bless you, you good man!" "My dear," says I, "those words are better for me than a lifeboat." I held her child in my arms till she was in the boat, and then kissed the child and handed her safe down. I now said to the people in her, "You have got your freight, my lads, all but me, and I am not coming yet awhile. Pull away from the ship, and keep off!"

That was the Long-boat. Old Mr. Rarx was one of her complement, and he was the only passenger who had greatly misbehaved since the ship struck. Others had been a little wild, which was not to be wondered at, and not very blamable; but, he had made a lamentation and uproar which it was dangerous for the people to hear, as there is always contagion in weakness and selfishness. His incessant cry had been that he must not be separated from the child, that he couldn't see the child, and that he and the child must go together. He had even tried to wrest the child out of my arms, that he might keep her in his. "Mr. Rarx," said I to him when it came to that, "I have a loaded pistol in my pocket; and if you don't stand out of the gangway, and keep perfectly quiet, I shall shoot you through the heart, if you have got one." Says he, "You won't do murder, Captain Ravender!" "No, Sir," says I, "I won't murder forty-four people to humour you, but I'll shoot you to save them." After that he was quiet, and stood shivering a little way off, until I named him to go over the side.

The Long-boat being cast off, the Surf-boat was soon filled. There only remained aboard the Golden Mary, John Mullion, the man who had kept on burning the blue-lights (and who had lighted every new one at every old one before it went out, as quietly as if he had been at an illumination); John Steadiman; and myself. I hurried those two into the Surf-boat, called to them to keep off, and waited with a grateful and relieved heart for the Long-boat to come and take me in, if she could. I looked at my watch, and it showed me, by the blue-light, ten minutes past two. They lost no time. As soon as she was near enough, I swung myself into her, and called to the men, "With a will, lads! She's reeling!" We were not an inch too far out of the inner vortex of her going down, when, by the blue-light which John Mullion still burnt in the bow of the Surf-boat, we saw her lurch, and plunge to the bottom head-foremost. The child cried, weeping wildly, "O the dear Golden Mary! O look at her! Save her! Save the poor Golden Mary!" And then the light burnt out, and the black dome seemed to come down upon us.

I suppose if we had all stood a-top of a mountain, and seen the whole remainder of the world sink away from under us, we could hardly have felt more shocked and solitary than we did when we knew we were alone on the wide ocean, and that the beautiful ship in which most of us had been securely asleep within half an hour was gone for ever. There was an awful silence in our boat, and such a kind of palsy on the rowers and the man at the rudder, that I felt they were scarcely keeping her before the sea. I spoke out then, and said, "Let every one here thank the Lord for our preservation!" All the voices answered (even the child's), "We thank the Lord!" I then said the Lord's Prayer, and all hands said it after me with a solemn murmuring. Then I gave the word "Cheerily, O men, Cheerily!" and I felt that they were handling the boat again as a boat ought to be handled.

The Surf-boat now burnt another blue-light to show us where they were, and we made for her, and laid ourselves as nearly alongside of her as we dared. I had always kept my boats with a coil or two of good stout stuff in each of them, so both boats had a rope at hand. We made a shift, with much labour and trouble, to get near enough to one another to divide the blue-lights (they were no use after that night, for the sea-water soon got at them), and to get a tow-rope out between us. All night long we kept together, sometimes obliged to cast off the rope, and sometimes getting it out again, and all of us wearying for the morning—which appeared so long in coming that old Mr. Rarx screamed out, in spite of his fears of me, "The world is drawing to an end, and the sun will never rise any more!"

When the day broke, I found that we were all huddled together in a miserable manner. We were deep in the water; being, as I found on mustering, thirty-one in number, or at least six too many. In the Surf-boat they were fourteen in number, being at least four too many. The first thing I did, was to get myself passed to the rudder—which I took from that time—and to get Mrs. Atherfield, her child, and Miss Coleshaw, passed on to sit next me. As to old Mr. Rarx, I put him in the bow, as far from us as I could. And I put some of the best men near us in order that if I should drop there might be a skilful hand ready to take the helm.

The sea moderating as the sun came up, though the sky was cloudy and wild, we spoke the other boat, to know what stores they had, and to overhaul what we had. I had a compass in my pocket, a small telescope, a double-barrelled pistol, a knife, and a fire-box and matches. Most of my men had knives, and some had a little tobacco: some, a pipe as well. We had a mug among us, and an iron spoon. As to provisions, there were in my boat two bags of biscuit, one piece of raw beef, one piece of raw pork, a bag of coffee, roasted but not ground (thrown in, I imagine, by mistake, for something else), two small casks of water, and about half-a-gallon of rum in a keg. The Surf-boat, having rather more rum than we, and fewer to drink it, gave us, as I estimated, another quart into our keg. In return, we gave them three double handfuls of coffee, tied up in a piece of a handkerchief; they reported that they had aboard besides, a bag of biscuit, a piece of beef, a small cask of water, a small box of lemons, and a Dutch cheese. It took a long time to make these exchanges, and they were not made without risk to both parties; the sea running quite high enough to make our approaching near to one another very hazardous. In the bundle with the coffee, I conveyed to John Steadiman (who had a ship's compass with him), a paper written in pencil, and torn from my pocket-book, containing the course I meant to steer, in the hope of making land, or being picked up by some vessel—I say in the hope, though I had little hope of either deliverance. I then sang out to him, so as all might hear, that if we two boats could live or die together, we would; but, that if we should be parted by the weather, and join company no more, they should have our prayers and blessings, and we asked for theirs. We then gave them three cheers, which they returned, and I saw the men's heads droop in both boats as they fell to their oars again.

These arrangements had occupied the general attention advantageously for all, though (as I expressed in the last sentence) they ended in a sorrowful feeling. I now said a few words to my fellow-voyagers on the subject of the small stock of food on which our lives depended if they were preserved from the great deep, and on the rigid necessity of our eking it out in the most frugal manner. One and all replied that whatever allowance I thought best to lay down should be strictly kept to. We made a pair of scales out of a thin strap of iron-plating and some twine, and I got together for weights such of the heaviest buttons among us as I calculated made up some fraction over two ounces. This was the allowance of solid food served out once a-day to each, from that time to the end; with the addition of a coffee-berry, or sometimes half a one, when the weather was very fair, for breakfast. We had nothing else whatever, but half a pint of water each per day, and sometimes, when we were coldest and weakest, a teaspoonful of rum each, served out as a dram. I know how learnedly it can be shown that rum is poison, but I also know that in this case, as in all similar cases I have ever read of—which are numerous—no words can express the comfort and support derived from it. Nor have I the least doubt that it saved the lives of far more than half our number. Having mentioned half a pint of water as our daily allowance, I ought to observe that sometimes we had less, and sometimes we had more; for much rain fell, and we caught it in a canvas stretched for the purpose.

Thus, at that tempestuous time of the year, and in that tempestuous part of the world, we shipwrecked people rose and fell with the waves. It is not my intention to relate (if I can avoid it) such circumstances appertaining to our doleful condition as have been better told in many other narratives of the kind than I can be expected to tell them. I will only note, in so many passing words, that day after day and night after night we received the sea upon our backs to prevent it from swamping the boat; that one party was always kept baling, and that every hat and cap among us soon got worn out, though patched up fifty times, as the only vessels we had for that service; that another party lay down in the bottom of the boat, while a third rowed; and that we were soon all in boils and blisters and rags.

The other boat was a source of such anxious interest to all of us that I used to wonder whether, if we were saved, the time could ever come when the survivors in this boat of ours could be at all indifferent to the fortunes of the survivors in that. We got out a tow-rope whenever the weather permitted, but that did not often happen, and how we two parties kept within the same horizon, as we did, He, who mercifully permitted it to be so for our consolation, only knows. I never shall forget the looks with which, when the morning light came, we used to gaze about us over the stormy waters, for the other boat. We once parted company for seventy-two hours, and we believed them to have gone down, as they did us. The joy on both sides when we came within view of one another again, had something in a manner Divine in it; each was so forgetful of individual suffering, in tears of delight and sympathy for the people in the other boat.

I have been wanting to get round to the individual or personal part of my subject, as I call it, and the foregoing incident puts me in the right way. The patience and good disposition aboard of us, was wonderful. I was not surprised by it in the women; for all men born of women know what great qualities they will show when men will fail; but, I own I was a little surprised by it in some of the men. Among one-and-thirty people assembled at the best of times, there will usually, I should say, be two or three uncertain tempers. I knew that I had more than one rough temper with me among my own people, for I had chosen those for the Long-boat that I might have them under my eye. But, they softened under their misery, and were as considerate of the ladies, and as compassionate of the child, as the best among us, or among men—they could not have been more so. I heard scarcely any complaining. The party lying down would moan a good deal in their sleep, and I would often notice a man—not always the same man, it is to be understood, but nearly all of them at one time or other—sitting moaning at his oar, or in his place, as he looked mistily over the sea. When it happened to be long before I could catch his eye, he would go on moaning all the time in the dismallest manner; but, when our looks met, he would brighten and leave off. I almost always got the impression that he did not know what sound he had been making, but that he thought he had been humming a tune.

Our sufferings from cold and wet were far greater than our sufferings from hunger. We managed to keep the child warm; but, I doubt if any one else among us ever was warm for five minutes together; and the shivering, and the chattering of teeth, were sad to hear. The child cried a little at first for her lost playfellow, the Golden Mary; but hardly ever whimpered afterwards; and when the state of the weather made it possible, she used now and then to be held up in the arms of some of us, to look over the sea for John Steadiman's boat. I see the golden hair and the innocent face now, between me and the driving clouds, like an angel going to fly away.

It had happened on the second day, towards night, that Mrs. Atherfield, in getting Little Lucy to sleep, sang her a song. She had a soft, melodious voice, and, when she had finished it, our people up and begged for another. She sang them another, and after it had fallen dark ended with the Evening Hymn. From that time, whenever anything could be heard above the sea and wind, and while she had any voice left, nothing would serve the people but that she should sing at sunset. She always did, and always ended with the Evening Hymn. We mostly took up the last line, and shed tears when it was done, but not miserably. We had a prayer night and morning, also, when the weather allowed of it.

Twelve nights and eleven days we had been driving in the boat, when old Mr. Rarx began to be delirious, and to cry out to me to throw the gold overboard or it would sink us, and we should all be lost. For days past the child had been declining, and that was the great cause of his wildness. He had been over and over again shrieking out to me to give her all the remaining meat, to give her all the remaining rum, to save her at any cost, or we should all be ruined. At this time, she lay in her mother's arms at my feet. One of her little hands was almost always creeping about her mother's neck or chin. I had watched the wasting of the little hand, and I knew it was nearly over.

The old man's cries were so discordant with the mother's love and submission, that I called out to him in an angry voice, unless he held his peace on the instant, I would order him to be knocked on the head and thrown overboard. He was mute then, until the child died, very peacefully, an hour afterwards: which was known to all in the boat by the mother's breaking out into lamentations for the first time since the wreck—for, she had great fortitude and constancy, though she was a little gentle woman. Old Mr. Rarx then became quite ungovernable, tearing what rags he had on him, raging in imprecations, and calling to me that if I had thrown the gold overboard (always the gold with him!) I might have saved the child. "And now," says he, in a terrible voice, "we shall founder, and all go to the Devil, for our sins will sink us, when we have no innocent child to bear us up!" We so discovered with amazement, that this old wretch had only cared for the life of the pretty little creature dear to all of us, because of the influence he superstitiously hoped she might have in preserving him! Altogether it was too much for the smith or armourer, who was sitting next the old man, to bear. He took him by the throat and rolled him under the thwarts, where he lay still enough for hours afterwards.

All that thirteenth night, Miss Coleshaw, lying across my knees as I kept the helm, comforted and supported the poor mother. Her child, covered with a pea-jacket of mine, lay in her lap. It troubled me all night to think that there was no Prayer-Book among us, and that I could remember but very few of the exact words of the burial service. When I stood up at broad day, all knew what was going to be done, and I noticed that my poor fellows made the motion of uncovering their heads, though their heads had been stark bare to the sky and sea for many a weary hour. There was a long heavy swell on, but otherwise it was a fair morning, and there were broad fields of sunlight on the waves in the east. I said no more than this: "I am the Resurrection and the Life, saith the Lord. He raised the daughter of Jairus the ruler, and said she was not dead but slept. He raised the widow's son. He arose Himself, and was seen of many. He loved little children, saying, suffer them to come unto Me, and rebuke them not, for of such is the kingdom of heaven. In His name, my friends, and committed to His merciful goodness!" With those words I laid my rough face softly on the placid little forehed, and buried the Golden Lucy in the grave of the Golden Mary.

Having had it on my mind to relate the end of this dear little child, I have omitted something from its exact place, which I will supply here. It will come quite as well here as anywhere else.

Foreseeing that if the boat lived through the stormy weather, the time must come, and soon come, when we should have absolutely no morsel to eat, I had one momentous point often in my thoughts. Although I had, years before that, fully satisfied myself that the instances in which human beings in the last distress have fed upon each other, are exceedingly few, and have very seldom indeed (if ever) occurred when the people in distress, however dreadful their extremity, have been accustomed to moderate for bearance and restraint; I say, though I had long before quite satisfied my mind on this topic, I felt doubtful whether there might not have been in former cases some harm and danger from keeping it out of sight and pretending not to think of it. I felt doubtful whether some minds, growing weak with fasting and exposure and having such a terrific idea to dwell upon in secret, might not magnify it until it got to have an awful attraction about it. This was not a new thought of mine, for it had grown out of my reading. However, it came over me stronger than it had ever done before—as it had reason for doing—in the boat, and on the fourth day I decided that I would bring out into the light that unformed fear which must have been more or less darkly in every brain among us. Therefore, as a means of beguiling the time and inspiring hope, I gave them the best summary in my power of Bligh's voyage of more than three thousand miles, in an open boat, after the Mutiny of the Bounty, and of the wonderful preservation of that boat's crew. They listened throughout with great interest, and I concluded by telling them, that, in my opinion, the happiest circumstance in the whole narrative was, that Bligh, who was no delicate man either, had solemnly placed it on record therein that he was sure and certain that under no conceivable circumstances whatever would that emaciated party, who had gone through all the pains of famine, have preyed on one another. I cannot describe the visible relief which this spread through the boat, and how the tears stood in every eye. From that time I was as well convinced as Bligh himself that there was no danger, and that this phantom, at any rate, did not haunt us.

Now, it was a part of Bligh's experience that when the people in his boat were most cast down, nothing did them so much good as hearing a story told by one of their number. When I mentioned that, I saw that it struck the general attention as much as it did my own, for I had not thought of it until I came to it in my summary. This was on the day after Mrs. Atherfield first sang to us. I proposed that, whenever the weather would permit, we should have a story two hours after dinner (I always issued the allowance I have mentioned at one o'clock, and called it by that name), as well as our song at sunset. The proposal was received with a cheerful satisfaction that warmed my heart within me; and I do not say too much when I say that those two periods in the four-and-twenty hours were expected with positive pleasure, and were really enjoyed by all hands. Spectres as we soon were in our bodily wasting, our imaginations did not perish like the gross flesh upon our bones. Music and Adventure, two of the great gifts of Providence to mankind, could charm us long after that was lost.

The wind was almost always against us after the second day; and for many days together we could not nearly hold our own. We had all varieties of bad weather. We had rain, hail, snow, wind, mist, thunder and lightning. Still the boats lived through the heavy seas, and still we perishing people rose and fell with the great waves.

Sixteen nights and fifteen days, twenty nights and nineteen days, twenty-four nights and twenty-three days. So the time went on. Disheartening as I knew that our progress, or want of progress, must be, I never deceived them as to my calculations of it. In the first place, I felt that we were all too near eternity for deceit; in the second place, I knew that if I failed, or died, the man who followed me must have a knowledge of the true state of things to begin upon. When I told them at noon, what I reckoned we had made or lost, they generally received what I said in a tranquil and resigned manner, and always gratefully towards me. It was not unusual at any time of the day for some one to burst out weeping loudly without any new cause; and, when the burst was over, to calm down a little better than before. I had seen exactly the same thing in a house of mourning.

During the whole of this time, old Mr. Rarx had had his fits of calling out to me to throw the gold (always the gold!) overboard, and of heaping violent reproaches upon me for not having saved the child; but now, the food being all gone, and I having nothing left to serve out but a bit of coffee-berry now and then, he began to be too weak to do this, and consequently fell silent. Mrs. Atherfield and Miss Coleshaw generally lay, each with an arm across one of my knees, and her head upon it. They never complained at all. Up to the time of her child's death, Mrs. Atherfield had bound up her own beautiful hair every day; and I took particular notice that this was always before she sang her song at night, when every one looked at her. But she never did it after the loss of her darling; and it would have been now all tangled with dirt and wet, but that Miss Coleshaw was careful of it long after she was herself, and would sometimes smooth it down with her weak thin hands.

We were past mustering a story now; but one day, at about this period, I reverted to the superstition of old Mr. Rarx, concerning the Golden Lucy, and told them that nothing vanished from the eye of God, though much might pass away from the eyes of men. "We were all of us," says I, "children once; and our baby feet have strolled in green woods ashore; and our baby hands have gathered flowers in gardens, where the birds were singing. The children that we were, are not lost to the great knowledge of our Creator. Those innocent creatures will appear with us before Him, and plead for us. What we were in the best time of our generous youth will arise and go with us too. The purest part of our lives will not desert us at the pass to which all of us here present are gliding. What we were then, will be as much in existence before Him, as what we are now." They were no less comforted by this consideration, than I was myself; and Miss Coleshaw, drawing my ear nearer to her lips, said, "Captain Ravender, I was on my way to marry a disgraced and broken man, whom I dearly loved when he was honourable and good. Your words seem to have come out of my own poor heart." She pressed my hand upon it, smiling.

Twenty-seven nights and twenty-six days. We were in no want of rainwater, but we had nothing else. And yet, even now, I never turned my eyes upon a waking face but it tried to brighten before mine. O, what a thing it is, in a time of danger and in the presence of death, the shining of a face upon a face! I have heard it broached that orders should be given in great new ships by electric telegraph. I admire machinery as much as any man, and am as thankful to it as any man can be for what it does for us. But it will never be a substitute for the face of a man, with his soul in it, encouraging another man to be brave and true. Never try it for that. It will break down like a straw.

I now began to remark certain changes in myself which I did not like. They caused me much disquiet. I often saw the Golden Lucy in the air above the boat. I often saw her I have spoken of before, sitting beside me. I saw the Golden Mary go down, as she really had gone down, twenty times in a day. And yet the sea was mostly, to my thinking, not sea neither, but moving country and extraordinary mountainous regions, the like of which have never been beheld. I felt it time to leave my last words regarding John Steadiman, in case any lips should last out to repeat them to any living ears. I said that John had told me (as he had on deck) that he had sung out "Breakers ahead!" the instant they were audible, and had tried to wear ship, but she struck before it could be done. (His cry, I dare say, had made my dream.) I said that the circumstances were altogether without warning, and out of any course that could have been guarded against; that the same loss would have happened if I had been in charge; and that John was not to blame, but from first to last had done his duty nobly, like the man he was. I tried to write it down in my pocket-book, but could make no words, though I knew what the words were that I wanted to make. When it had come to that, her hands—though she was dead so long—laid me down gently in the bottom of the boat, and she and the Golden Lucy swung me to sleep.

All that follows, was written by John Steadiman, Chief Mate:

On the twenty-sixth day, after the foundering of the Golden Mary at sea, I, John Steadiman, was sitting in my place in the stern-sheets of the Surfboat, with just sense enough left in me to steer—that is to say, with my eyes strained, wide-awake, over the bows of the boat, and my brains fast asleep and dreaming—when I was roused upon a sudden by our second mate, Mr. William Rames.

"Let me take a spell in your place," says he. "And look you out for the Long-boat astern. The last time she rose on the crest of a wave, I thought I made out a signal flying aboard her."

We shifted our places, clumsily and slowly enough, for we were both of us weak and dazed with wet, cold, and hunger. I waited some time, watching the heavy rollers astern, before the Long-boat rose a-top of one of them at the same time with us. At last, she was heaved up for a moment well in view, and there, sure enough, was the signal flying aboard of her—a strip of rag of some sort, rigged to an oar, and hoisted in her bows.

"What does it mean?" says Rames to me in a quavering, trembling sort of voice. "Do they signal a sail in sight?"

"Hush, for God's sake!" says I, clapping my hand over his mouth. "Don't let the people hear you. They'll all go mad together if we mislead them about that signal. Wait a bit, till I have another look at it."

I held on by him, for he had set me all of a tremble with his notion of a sail in sight, and watched for the Long-boat again. Up she rose on the top of another roller. I made out the signal clearly, that second time, and saw that it was rigged half-mast high.

"Rames," says I, "it's a signal of distress. Pass the word forward to keep her before the sea, and no more. We must get the Long-boat within hailing distance of us, as soon as possible."

I dropped down into my old place at the tiller without another word—for the thought went through me like a knife that something had happened to Captain Ravender. I should consider myself unworthy to write another line of this statement, if I had not made up my mind to speak the truth, the whole truth, and nothing but the truth—and I must, therefore, confess plainly that now, for the first time, my heart sank within me. This weakness on my part was produced in some degree, as I take it, by the exhausting effects of previous anxiety and grief.

Our provisions—if I may give that name to what we had left—were reduced to the rind of one lemon and about a couple of handsfull of coffee-berries. Besides these great distresses, caused by the death, the danger, and the suffering among my crew and passengers, I had had a little distress of my own to shake me still more, in the death of the child whom I had got to be very fond of on the voyage out—so fond that I was secretly a little jealous of her being taken in the Long-boat instead of mine when the ship foundered. It used to be a great comfort to me, and I think to those with me also, after we had seen the last of the Golden Mary, to see the Golden Lucy, held up by the men in the Long-boat, when the weather allowed it, as the best and brightest sight they had to show. She looked, at the distance we saw her from, almost like a little white bird in the air. To miss her for the first time, when the weather lulled a little again, and we all looked out for our white bird and looked in vain, was a sore disappointment. To see the men's heads bowed down and the captain's hand pointing into the sea when we hailed the Long-boat, a few day's after, gave me as heavy a shock and as sharp a pang of heartache to bear as ever I remember suffering in all my life. I only mention these things to show that if I did give way a little at first, under the dread that our captain was lost to us, it was not without having been a good deal shaken beforehand by more trials of one sort or another than often fall to one man's share.

I had got over the choking in my throat with the help of a drop of water, and had steadied my mind again so as to be prepared against the worst, when I heard the hail (Lord help the poor fellows, how weak it sounded!)—

"Surf-boat ahoy!"

I looked up, and there were our companions in misfortune tossing abreast of us; not so near that we could make out the features of any of them, but near enough, with some exertion for people in our condition, to make their voices heard in the intervals when the wind was weakest.

I answered the hail, and waited a bit, and heard nothing, and then sung out the captain's name. The voice that replied did not sound like his; the words that reached us were:

"Chief-mate wanted on board!"

Every man of my crew knew what that meant as well as I did. As second officer in command, there could be but one reason for wanting me on board the Long-boat. A groan went all round us, and my men looked darkly in each other's faces, and whispered under their breaths:

"The captain is dead!"

I commanded them to be silent, and not to make too sure of bad news, at such a pass as things had now come to with us. Then, hailing the Long-boat, I signified that I was ready to go on board when the weather would let me—stopped a bit to draw a good long breath—and then called out as loud as I could the dreadful question:

"Is the captain dead?"

The black figures of three or four men in the after-part of the Long-boat all stooped down together as my voice reached them. They were lost to view for about a minute; then appeared again—one man among them was held up on his feet by the rest, and he hailed back the blessed words (a very faint hope went a very long way with people in our desperate situation): "Not yet!"

The relief felt by me, and by all with me, when we knew that our captain, though unfitted for duty, was not lost to us, it is not in words—at least, not in such words as a man like me can command—to express. I did my best to cheer the men by telling them what a good sign it was that we were not as badly off yet as we had feared; and then communicated what instructions I had to give, to William Rames, who was to be left in command in my place when I took charge of the Long-boat. After that, there was nothing to be done, but to wait for the chance of the wind dropping at sunset, and the sea going down afterwards, so as to enable our weak crews to lay the two boats alongside each other, without undue risk—or, to put it plainer, without saddling ourselves with the necessity for any extraordinary exertion of strength or skill. Both the one and the other had now been starved out of us for days and days together.

At sunset the wind suddenly dropped, but the sea, which had been running high for so long a time past, took hours after that before it showed any signs of getting to rest. The moon was shining, the sky was wonderfully clear, and it could not have been, according to my calculations, far off midnight, when the long, slow, regular swell of the calming ocean fairly set in, and I took the responsibility of lessening the distance between the Long-boat and ourselves.

It was, I dare say, a delusion of mine; but I thought I had never seen the moon shine so white and ghastly anywhere, either at sea or on land, as she shone that night while we were approaching our companions in misery. When there was not much more than a boat's length between us, and the white light streamed cold and clear over all our faces, both crews rested on their oars with one great shudder, and stared over the gunwale of either boat, panic-stricken at the first sight of each other.

"Any lives lost among you?" I asked, in the midst of that frightful silence. The men in the Long-boat huddled together like sheep at the sound of my voice.

"None yet, but the child, thanks be to God!" answered one among them.

And at the sound of his voice, all my men shrank together like the men in the Long-boat. I was afraid to let the horror produced by our first meeting at close quarters after the dreadful changes that wet, cold, and famine had produced, last one moment longer than could be helped; so, without giving time for any more questions and answers, I commanded the men to lay the two boats close alongside of each other. When I rose up and committed the tiller to the hands of Rames, all my poor fellows raised their white faces imploringly to mine. "Don't leave us, Sir," they said, "don't leave us." "I leave you," says I, "under the command and the guidance of Mr. William Rames, as good a sailor as I am, and as trusty and kind a man as ever stepped. Do your duty by him, as you have done it by me; and remember to the last, that while there is life there is hope. God bless and help you all!" With those words I collected what strength I had left, and caught at two arms that were held out to me, and so got from the stern-sheets of one boat into the stern-sheets of the other.

"Mind where you step, Sir," whispered one of the men who had helped me into the Long-boat. I looked down as he spoke. Three figures were huddled up below me, with the moonshine falling on them in ragged streaks through the gaps between the men standing or sitting above them. The first face I made out was the face of Miss Coleshaw; her eyes were wide open and fixed on me. She seemed still to keep her senses, and, by the alternate parting and closing of her lips, to be trying to speak, but I could not hear that she uttered a single word. On her shoulder rested the head of Mrs. Atherfield. The mother of our poor little Golden Lucy must, I think, have been dreaming of the child she had lost; for there was a faint smile just ruffling the white stillness of her face, when I first saw it turned upward, with peaceful closed eyes towards the heavens. From her, I looked down a little, and there, with his head on her lap, and with one of her hands resting tenderly on his cheek—there lay the Captain, to whose help and guidance, up to this miserable time, we had never looked in vain,—there, worn out at last in our service, and for our sakes, lay the best and bravest man of all our company. I stole my hand in gently through his clothes and laid it on his heart, and felt a little feeble warmth over it, though my cold dulled touch could not detect even the faintest beating. The two men in the stern-sheets with me, noticing what I was doing— knowing I loved him like a brother—and seeing, I suppose, more distress in my face than I myself was conscious of its showing, lost command over themselves altogether, and burst into a piteous moaning, sobbing lamentation over him. One of the two drew aside a jacket from his feet, and showed me that they were bare, except where a wet, ragged strip of stocking still clung to one of them. When the ship struck the Iceberg, he had run on deck leaving his shoes in his cabin. All through the voyage in the boat his feet had been unprotected; and not a soul had discovered it until he dropped! As long as he could keep his eyes open, the very look of them had cheered the men, and comforted and upheld the women. Not one living creature in the boat, with any sense about him, but had felt the good influence of that brave man in one way or another. Not one but had heard him, over and over again, give the credit to others which was due only to himself; praising this man for patience, and thanking that man for help, when the patience and the help had really and truly, as to the best part of both, come only from him. All this, and much more, I heard pouring confusedly from the men's lips while they crouched down, sobbing and crying over their commander, and wrapping the jacket as warmly and tenderly as they could over his cold feet. It went to my heart to check them; but I knew that if this lamenting spirit spread any further, all chance of keeping alight any last sparks of hope and resolution among the boat's company would be lost for ever. Accordingly I sent them to their places, spoke a few encouraging words to the men forward, promising to serve out, when the morning came, as much as I dared, of any eatable thing left in the lockers; called to Rames, in my old boat, to keep as near us as he safely could; drew the garments and coverings of the two poor suffering women more closely about them; and, with a secret prayer to be directed for the best in bearing the awful responsibility now laid on my shoulders, took my Captain's vacant place at the helm of the Long-boat.

This, as well as I can tell it, is the full and true account of how I came to be placed in charge of the lost passengers and crew of the Golden Mary, on the morning of the twenty-seventh day after the ship struck the Iceberg, and foundered at sea.

ICE AGAIN!

RICHARD HENRY DANA, JR.

In our first attempt to double the Cape, when we came up to the latitude of it, we were nearly seventeen hundred miles to the westward, but, in running for the straits of Magellan, we stood so far to the eastward, that we made our second attempt at a distance of not more than four or five hundred miles; and we had great hopes, by this means, to run clear of the ice; thinking that the easterly gales, which had prevailed for a long time, would have driven it to the westward. With the wind about two points free, the yards braced in a little, and two close-reefed topsails and a reefed foresail on the ship, we made great way toward the southward; and, almost every watch, when we came on deck, the air seemed to grow colder, and the sea to run higher. Still, we saw no ice, and had great hopes of going clear of it altogether, when, one afternoon, about three o'clock, while we were taking a *siesta* during our watch below, "All hands!" was called in a loud and fearful voice. "Tumble up here, men!—tumble up!—don't stop for your clothes— before we're upon it!" We sprang out of our berths and hurried upon deck. The loud, sharp voice of the captain was heard giving orders, as though for life or death, and we ran aft to the braces, not waiting to look ahead, for not a moment was to be lost. The helm was hard up, the after yards shaking, and the ship in the act of wearing. Slowly, with the stiff ropes and iced rigging, we swung the yards round, everything coming hard, and with a creaking and rending sound, like pulling up a plank which has been frozen into the ice. The ship wore round fairly, the yards were steadied, and we stood off on the other tack, leaving behind us, directly under our larboard quarter, a large ice island, peering out of the mist, and reaching high above our tops, while astern; and on either side of the island, large tracts of field-ice were dimly seen, heaving and rolling in the sea. We were now safe, and standing to the northward; but, in a few minutes more, had it not been for the sharp look-out of the watch, we should have been fairly upon the ice, and left our ship's old bones adrift in the Southern ocean. After standing to the northward a few hours, we wore ship, and, the wind having hauled, we stood to the southward and eastward. All night long, a bright look-out was kept from every part of the deck; and whenever ice was seen on the one bow or the other, the helm was shifted and the yards braced, and by quick working of the ship she was kept clear. The accustomed cry of "Ice ahead!"—"Ice on the lee bow!"—"Another island!" in the same tones, and with the same orders following them, seemed to bring us directly back to our old position of the week before. During our watch on deck, which was from twelve to four, the wind came out ahead, with a pelting storm of hail and sleet, and we lay hove-to, under a close-reefed main topsail, the whole watch. During the next watch it fell calm, with a drenching rain, until daybreak, when the wind came out to the westward, and the weather cleared up, and showed us the whole ocean, in the course which we should have steered, had it not been for the head wind and calm, completely blocked up with ice. Here then our progress was stopped, and we wore ship, and once more stood to the northward and eastward; not for the straits of Magellan, but to make another attempt to double the Cape, still farther to the eastward; for the captain was determined to get round if perseverance could do it; and the third time, he said, never failed.

With a fair wind we soon ran clear of the field-ice, and by noon had only the stray islands floating far and near upon the ocean. The sun was out bright, the sea of a deep blue, fringed with the white foam of the waves which ran high before a strong south-wester; our solitary ship tore on through the water, as though glad to be out of her confinement; and the ice islands lay scattered upon the ocean here and there, of various sizes and shapes, reflecting the bright rays of the sun, and drifting slowly northward before the gale. It was a contrast to much that we had lately seen, and a spectacle not only of beauty, but of life; for it required but little fancy to imagine these islands to be animate masses which had broken loose from the "thrilling regions of thick-ribbed ice," and were working their way, by wind and current, some alone, and some in fleets, to milder climes. No pencil has ever yet given anything like the true effect of an iceberg. In a picture, they are huge, uncouth masses, stuck in the sea, while their chief beauty and grandeur,—their slow, stately motion; the whirling of the snow about their summits, and the fearful groaning and cracking of their parts,—the picture cannot give. This is the large iceberg; while the small and distant islands, floating on the smooth sea, in the light of a clear day, look like little floating fairy isles of sapphire.

From a north-east course we gradually hauled to the eastward, and after sailing about two hundred miles, which brought us as near to the western coast of Terra del Fuego as was safe, and having lost sight of the ice altogether,—for the third time we put the ship's head to the south-ward, to try the passage of the Cape. The weather continued clear and cold, with a strong gale from the westward, and we were fast getting up with the latitude of the Cape, with a prospect of soon being round. One fine afternoon, a man who had gone into the fore-top to shift the roll-ing tackles, sung out, at the top of his voice, and with evident glee,— "Sail ho!" Neither land nor sail had we seen since leaving San Diego; and any one who has traversed the length of a whole ocean alone, can imagine what an excitement such an announcement produced on board. "Sail ho!" shouted the cook, jumping out of his galley; "Sail ho!" shouted a man, throwing back the slide of the scuttle, to the watch below, who were soon out of their berths and on deck; and "Sail ho!" shouted the captain down the companion-way to the passenger in the cabin. Beside the pleasure of seeing a ship and human beings in so desolate a place, it was important for us to speak a vessel, to learn whether there was ice to the eastward, and to ascertain the longitude; for we had no chronometer, and had been drifting about so long that we had nearly lost our reck-oning, and opportunities for lunar observations are not frequent or sure in such a place as Cape Horn. For these various reasons, the excitement in our little community was running high, and conjectures were made, and everything thought of for which the captain would hail, when the man aloft sung out—"Another sail, large on the weather bow!" This was a little odd, but so much the better, and did not shake our faith in their being sails. At length the man in the top hailed, and said he believed it was land, after all. "Land in your eye!" said the mate, who was looking through the telescope; "they are ice islands, if I can see a hole through a ladder;" and a few moments showed the mate to be right; and all our expectations fled; and instead of what we most wished to see, we had what we most dreaded, and what we hoped we had seen the last of. We soon, however, left these astern, having passed within about two miles of them; and at sundown the horizon was clear in all directions.

Having a fine wind, we were soon up with and passed the latitude of the Cape, and having stood far enough to the southward to give it a wide berth, we began to stand to the eastward, with a good prospect of being round and steering to the northward on the other side, in a very few days. But ill luck seemed to have lighted upon us. Not four hours had we been standing on in this course, before it fell dead calm; and in half an hour it clouded up; a few straggling blasts, with spits of snow and sleet, came from the eastward; and in an hour more, we lay hove-to under a close-reefed main topsail, drifting bodily off to leeward before the fiercest storm that we had yet felt, blowing dead ahead, from the eastward. It seemed as though the genius of the place had been roused at finding that we had nearly slipped through his fingers, and had come down upon us with tenfold fury. The sailors said that every blast, as it shook the shrouds, and whistled through the rigging, said to the old ship, "No, you don't!"—"No, you don't!"

For eight days we lay drifting about in this manner. Sometimes,—generally towards noon,—it fell calm; once or twice a round copper ball showed itself for a few moments in the place where the sun ought to have been; and a puff or two came from the westward, giving some hope that a fair wind had come at last. During the first two days, we made sail for these puffs, shaking the reefs out of the topsails and boarding the tacks of the courses; but finding that it only made work for us when the gale set in again, it was soon given up, and we lay-to under our close-reefs. We had less snow and hail than when we were farther to the westward, but we had an abundance of what is worse to a sailor in cold weather—drenching rain. Snow is blinding, and very bad when coming upon a coast, but, for genuine discomfort, give me rain with freezing weather. A snow-storm is exciting, and it does not wet through the clothes (which is important to a sailor); but a constant rain there is no escaping from. It wets to the skin, and makes all protection vain. We had long ago run through all our dry clothes, and as sailors have no other way of drying them than by the sun, we had nothing to do but to put on those which were the least wet. At the end of each watch, when we came below, we took off our clothes and wrung them out; two taking hold of a pair of trowsers,—one at each end,—and jackets in the same way. Stockings, mittens, and all, were wrung out also and then hung up to drain and chafe dry against the bulkheads. Then, feeling of all our clothes, we picked out those which were the least wet, and put them on, so as to be ready for a call, and turned-in, covered ourselves up with blankets, and slept until three knocks on the scuttle and the dismal sound of "All starbowlines ahoy! Eight bells, there below! Do you hear the news?" drawled out from on deck, and the sulky answer of "Aye, aye!" from below, sent us up again.

On deck, all was as dark as a pocket, and either a dead calm, with the rain pouring steadily down, or, more generally, a violent gale dead ahead, with rain pelting horizontally, and occasional variations of hail and sleet;—decks afloat with water swashing from side to side, and constantly wet feet; for boots could not be wrung out like drawers, and no composition could stand the constant soaking. In fact, wet and cold feet are inevitable in such weather, and are not the least of those little items which go to make up the grand total of the discomforts of a winter passage round the Cape. Few words were spoken between the watches as they shifted, the wheel was relieved, the mate took his place on the quarter-deck, the lookouts in the bows; and each man had his narrow space to walk fore and aft in, or, rather, to swing himself forward and back in, from one belaying pin to another,—for the decks were too slippery with ice and water to allow of much walking. To make a walk, which is absolutely necessary to pass away the time, one of us hit upon the expedient of sanding the deck; and afterwards, whenever the rain was not so violent as to wash it off, the weatherside of the quarter-deck, and a part of the waist and forecastle were sprinkled with the sand which we had on board for holystoning; and thus we made a good promenade, where we walked fore and aft, two and two, hour after hour, in our long, dull, and comfortless watches. The bells seemed to be an hour or two apart, instead of half an hour, and an age to elapse before the welcome sound of eight bells. The sole object was to make the time pass on. Any change was sought for, which would break the monotony of the time; and even the two hours' trick at the wheel, which came round to each of us, in turn, once in every other watch, was looked upon as a relief. Even the never-failing resource of long yarns, which eke out many a watch, seemed to have failed us now; for we had been so long together that we had heard each other's stories told over and over again, till we had them by heart; each one knew the whole history of each of the others, and we were fairly and literally talked out. Singing and joking, we were in no humor for, and, in fact, any sound of mirth or laughter would have struck strangely upon our ears, and would not have been tolerated, any more than whistling, or a wind instrument. The last resort, that of speculating upon the future, seemed now to fail us, for our discouraging situation, and the danger we were really in, (as we expected every day to find ourselves drifted back among the ice) "clapped a stopper" upon all that. From saying—"*when* we get home"—we began insensibly to alter it to—"*if* we get home"—and at last the subject was dropped by a tacit consent.

In this state of things, a new light was struck out, and a new field opened, by a change in the watch. One of our watch was laid up for two or three days by a bad hand, (for in cold weather the least cut or bruise ripens into a sore,) and his place was supplied by the carpenter. This was a windfall, and there was quite a contest, who should have the carpenter to walk with him. As "Chips" was a man of some little education, and he and I had had a good deal of intercourse with each other, he fell in with me in my walk. He was a Fin, but spoke English very well, and gave me long accounts of his country;—the customs, the trade, the towns, what little he knew of the government, (I found he was no friend of Russia,) his voyages, his first arrival in America, his marriage and courtship;— he had married a countrywoman of his, a dress-maker, whom he met with in Boston. I had very little to tell him of my quiet, sedentary life at home; and, in spite of our best efforts, which had protracted these yarns through five or six watches, we fairly talked one another out, and I turned him over to another man in the watch, and put myself upon my own resources.

I commenced a deliberate system of time-killing, which united some profit with a cheering up of the heavy hours. As soon as I came on deck, and took my place and regular walk, I began with repeating over to myself a string of matters which I had in my memory, in regular order. First, the multiplication table and the tables of weights and measures; then the states of the Union, with their capitals; the counties of England, with their shire towns; the kings of England in their order; and a large part of the peerage, which I committed from an almanac that we had on board; and then the Kanaka numerals. This carried me through my facts, and, being repeated deliberately, with long intervals, often eked out the two first bells. Then came the ten commandments; the thirty-ninth chapter of Job, and a few other passages from Scripture. The next in the order, that I never varied from, came Cowper's Castaway, which was a great favorite with me; the solemn measure and gloomy character of which, as well as the incident that it was founded upon, made it well suited to a lonely watch at sea. Then his lines to Mary, his address to the jackdaw, and a short extract from Table Talk; (I abounded in Cowper, for I happened to have a volume of his poems in my chest;) "Ille et nefasto" from Horace, and Gœthe's Erl King. After I had got through these, I allowed myself a more general range among everything that I could remember, both in prose and verse. In this way, with an occasional break by relieving the wheel, heaving the log, and going to the scuttlebutt for a drink of water, the longest watch was passed away; and I was so regular in my silent recitations, that if there was no interruption by ship's duty, I could tell very nearly the number of bells by my progress.

Our watches below were no more varied than the watch on deck. All washing, sewing, and reading was given up; and we did nothing but eat, sleep, and stand our watch, leading what might be called a Cape Horn life. The forecastle was too uncomfortable to sit up in; and whenever we were below, we were in our berths. To prevent the rain, and the sea-water which broke over the bows, from washing down, we were obliged to keep the scuttle closed, so that the forecastle was nearly air-tight. In this little, wet, leaky hole, we were all quartered, in an atmosphere so bad that our lamp, which swung in the middle from the beams, sometimes actually burned blue, with a large circle of foul air about it. Still, I was never in better health than after three weeks of this life. I gained a great deal of flesh, and we all ate like horses. At every watch, when we came below, before turning-in, the bread barge and beef kid were overhauled. Each man drank his quart of hot tea night and morning; and glad enough we were to get it, for no nectar and ambrosia were sweeter to the lazy immortals, than was a pot of hot tea, a hard biscuit, and a slice of cold salt beef, to us after a watch on deck. To be sure, we were mere animals, and had this life lasted a year instead of a month, we should have been little better than the ropes in the ship. Not a razor, nor a brush, nor a drop of water, except the rain and the spray, had come near us all the time; for we were on an allowance of fresh water; and who would strip and wash himself in salt water on deck, in the snow and ice, with the thermometer at zero?

After about eight days of constant easterly gales, the wind hauled occasionally a little to the southward, and blew hard, which, as we were well to the southward, allowed us to brace in a little and stand on, under all the sail we could carry. These turns lasted but a short while, and sooner or later it set in again from the old quarter; yet at each time we made something, and were gradually edging along to the eastward. One night, after one of these shifts of the wind, and when all hands had been up a great part of the time, our watch was left on deck, with the mainsail hanging in the buntlines, ready to be set if necessary. It came on to blow worse and worse, with hail and snow beating like so many furies upon the ship, it being as dark and thick as night could make it. The mainsail was blowing and slatting with a noise like thunder, when the captain came on deck, and ordered it to be furled. The mate was about to call all hands, when the captain stopped him, and said that the men would be beaten out if they were called up so often; that as our watch must stay on deck, it might as well be doing that as anything else. Accordingly, we went upon the yard; and never shall I forget that piece of work. Our watch had been so reduced by sickness, and by some having been left in California, that, with one man at the wheel, we had only the third mate and three beside myself to go aloft; so that, at most, we could only attempt to furl one yard-arm at a time. We manned the weather yard-arm, and set to work to make a furl of it. Our lower masts being short, and our yards very square, the sail had a head of nearly fifty feet, and a short leach, made still shorter by the deep reef which was in it, which brought the clue away out on the quarters of the yard, and made a bunt nearly as square as the mizen royal-yard. Beside this difficulty, the yard over which we lay was cased with ice, the gaskets and rope of the foot and leach of the sail as stiff and hard as a piece of suction-hose, and the sail itself about as pliable as though it had been made of sheets of sheathing copper. It blew a perfect hurricane, with alternate blasts of snow, hail, and rain. We had to *fist* the sail with bare hands. No one could trust himself to mittens, for if he slipped, he was a gone man. All the boats were hoisted in on deck, and there was nothing to be lowered for him. We had need of every finger God had given us. Several times we got the sail upon the yard, but it blew away again before we could secure it. It required men to lie over the yard to pass each turn of the gaskets, and when they were passed, it was almost impossible to knot them so that they would hold. Frequently we were obliged to leave off altogether and take to beating our hands upon the sail, to keep them from freezing. After some time,—which seemed forever,—we got the weather side stowed after a fashion, and went over to leeward for another trial. This was still worse, for the body of the sail had been blown over to leeward, and as the yard was a-cock-bill by the lying over of the vessel, we had to light it all up to windward. When the yard-arms were furled, the bunt was all adrift again, which made more work for us. We got all secure at last, but we had been nearly an hour and a half upon the yard, and it seemed an age. It had just struck five bells when we went up, and eight were struck soon after we came down. This may seem slow work, but considering the state of everything, and that we had only five men to a sail with just half as many square yards of canvas in it as the mainsail of the Independence, sixty-gun ship, which musters seven hundred men at her quarters, it is not wonderful that we were no quicker about it. We were glad enough to get on deck, and still more, to go below. The oldest sailor in the watch said, as he went down,—"I shall never forget that main yard;—it beats all my going a fishing. Fun is fun, but furling one yard-arm of a course, at a time, off Cape Horn, is no better than man-killing."

During the greater part of the next two days, the wind was pretty steady from the southward. We had evidently made great progress, and had good hope of being soon up with the Cape, if we were not there already. We could put but little confidence in our reckoning, as there had been no opportunities for an observation, and we had drifted too much to allow of our dead reckoning being anywhere near the mark. If it would clear off enough to give a chance for an observation, or if we could make land, we should know where we were; and upon these, and the chances of falling in with a sail from the eastward, we depended almost entirely.

Friday, July 22nd. This day we had a steady gale from the southward, and stood on under close sail, with the yards eased a little by the weather braces, the clouds lifting a little, and showing signs of breaking away. In the afternoon, I was below with Mr. H—, the third mate, and two others, fill-ing the bread locker in the steerage from the casks, when a bright gleam of sunshine broke out and shone down the companion-way and through the sky-light, lighting up everything below, and sending a warm glow through the heart of every one. It was a sight we had not seen for weeks,—an omen, a God-send. Even the roughest and hardest face acknowledged its influence. Just at that moment we heard a loud shout from all parts of the deck, and the mate called out down the companion-way to the captain, who was sitting in the cabin. What he said, we could not distinguish, but the captain kicked over his chair, and was on deck at one jump. We could not tell what it was; and, anxious as we were to know, the discipline of the ship would not allow of our leaving our places. Yet, as we were not called, we knew there was no danger. We hurried to get through with our job, when, seeing the steward's black face peering out of the pantry, Mr. H— hailed him, to know what was the matter. "Lan' o, to be sure, sir! No you hear 'em sing out, 'Lan' o?' De cap'em say 'im Cape Horn!"

This gave us a new start, and we were soon through our work, and on deck; and there lay the land, fair upon the larboard beam, and slowly edging away upon the quarter. All hands were busy looking at it,—the captain and mates from the quarter-deck, the cook from his galley, and the sailors from the forecastle; and even Mr. N., the passenger, who had kept in his shell for nearly a month, and hardly been seen by anybody, and who we had almost forgotten was on board, came out like a butterfly, and was hopping round as bright as a bird.

The land was the island of Staten Land, just to the eastward of Cape Horn; and a more desolate- looking spot I never wish to set eyes upon;—bare, broken, and girt with rocks and ice, with here and there, between the rocks and broken hillocks, a little stunted vegetation of shrubs. It was a place well suited to stand at the junction of the two oceans, beyond the reach of human cultivation, and encounter the blasts and snows of a perpetual winter. Yet, dismal as it was, it was a pleasant sight to us; not only as being the first land we had seen, but because it told us that we had passed the Cape,—were in the Atlantic,—and that, with twenty-four hours of this breeze, might bid defiance to the Southern ocean. It told us, too, our latitude and longitude better than any observation; and the captain now knew where we were, as well as if we were off the end of Long wharf.

In the general joy, Mr. N. said he should like to go ashore upon the island and examine a spot which probably no human being had ever set foot upon; but the captain intimated that he would see the island—speci-mens and all,—in—another place, before he would get out a boat or delay the ship one moment for him.

We left the land gradually astern; and at sundown had the Atlantic ocean clear before us.

THE OPEN BOAT

A Tale Intended to be After the Fact. Being the Experience of Four Men Sunk From the Steamer Commodore

STEPHEN CRANE

I

None of them knew the color of the sky. Their eyes glanced level, and were fastened upon the waves that swept toward them. These waves were of the hue of slate, save for the tops, which were of foaming white, and all of the men knew the colors of the sea. The horizon narrowed and widened, and dipped and rose, and at all times its edge was jagged with waves that seemed thrust up in points like rocks.

Many a man ought to have a bath-tub larger than the boat which here rode upon the sea. These waves were most wrongfully and barbarously abrupt and tall, and each froth-top was a problem in small boat navigation.

The cook squatted in the bottom and looked with both eyes at the six inches of gunwale which separated him from the ocean. His sleeves were rolled over his fat forearms, and the two flaps of his unbuttoned vest dangled as he bent to bail out the boat. Often he said: "Gawd! That was a narrow clip." As he remarked it he invariably gazed eastward over the broken sea.

The oiler, steering with one of the two oars in the boat, sometimes raised himself suddenly to keep clear of water that swirled in over the stern. It was a thin little oar and it seemed often ready to snap.

The correspondent, pulling at the other oar, watched the waves and wondered why he was there.

The injured captain, lying in the bow, was at this time buried in that profound dejection and indifference which comes, temporarily at least, to even the bravest and most enduring when, willy nilly, the firm fails, the army loses, the ship goes down. The mind of the master of a vessel is rooted deep in the timbers of her, though he command for a day or a decade, and this captain had on him the stern impression of a scene in the grays of dawn of seven turned faces, and later a stump of a top-mast with a white ball on it that slashed to and fro at the waves, went low and lower, and down. Thereafter there was something strange in his voice. Although steady, it was deep with mourning, and of a quality beyond oration or tears.

"Keep'er a little more south, Billie," said he.

" 'A little more south,' sir," said the oiler in the stern.

A seat in this boat was not unlike a seat upon a bucking broncho, and, by the same token, a broncho is not much smaller. The craft pranced and reared, and plunged like an animal. As each wave came, and she rose for it, she seemed like a horse making at a fence outrageously high. The manner of her scramble over these walls of water is a mystic thing, and, moreover, at the top of them were ordinarily these problems in white water, the foam racing down from the summit of each wave, requiring a new leap, and a leap from the air. Then, after scornfully bumping a crest, she would slide, and race, and splash down a long incline and arrive bobbing and nodding in front of the next menace.

A singular disadvantage of the sea lies in the fact that after successfully surmounting one wave you discover that there is another behind it just as important and just as nervously anxious to do something effective in the way of swamping boats. In a ten-foot dingey one can get an idea of the resources of the sea in the line of waves that is not probable to the average experience, which is never at sea in a dingey. As each slaty wall of water approached, it shut all else from the view of the men in the boat, and it was not difficult to imagine that this particular wavewas the final outburst of the ocean, the last effort of the grim water.

There was a terrible grace in the move of the waves, and they came in silence, save for the snarling of the crests.

In the wan light, the faces of the men must have been gray. Their eyes must have glinted in strange ways as they gazed steadily astern. Viewed from a balcony, the whole thing would doubtlessly have been weirdly picturesque. But the men in the boat had no time to see it, and if they had had leisure there were other things to occupy their minds. The sun swung steadily up the sky, and they knew it was broad day because the color of the sea changed from slate to emerald-green, streaked with amber lights, and the foam was like tumbling snow. The process of the breaking day was unknown to them. They were aware only of this effect upon the color of the waves that rolled toward them.

In disjointed sentences the cook and the correspondent argued as to the difference between a life-saving station and a house of refuge. The cook had said: "There's a house of refuge just north of the Mosquito Inlet Light, and as soon as they see us, they'll come off in their boat and pick us up."

"As soon as who see us?" said the correspondent.

"The crew," said the cook.

"Houses of refuge don't have crews," said the correspondent. "As I understand them, they are only places where clothes and grub are stored for the benefit of shipwrecked people. They don't carry crews."

"Oh, yes, they do," said the cook.

"No, they don't," said the correspondent.

"Well, we're not there yet, anyhow," said the oiler, in the stern.

"Well," said the cook, "perhaps it's not a house of refuge that I'm thinking of as being near Mosquito Inlet Light. Perhaps it's a life-saving station."

"We're not there yet," said the oiler, in the stern.

II

As the boat bounced from the top of each wave, the wind tore through the hair of the hatless men, and as the craft plopped her stern down again the spray slashed past them. The crest of each of these waves was a hill, from the top of which the men surveyed, for a moment, a broad tumultuous expanse; shining and wind-riven. It was probably splendid. It was probably glorious, this play of the free sea, wild with lights of emerald and white and amber.

"Bully good thing it's an on-shore wind," said the cook. "If not, where would we be? Wouldn't have a show."

"That's right," said the correspondent.

The busy oiler nodded his assent.

Then the captain, in the bow, chuckled in a way that expressed humor, contempt, tragedy, all in one. "Do you think we've got much of a show, now, boys?" said he.

Whereupon the three were silent, save for a trifle of hemming and hawing. To express any particular optimism at this time they felt to be childish and stupid, but they all doubtless possessed this sense of the situation in their mind. A young man thinks doggedly at such times. On the other hand, the ethics of their condition was decidedly against any open suggestion of hopelessness. So they were silent.

"Oh, well," said the captain, soothing his children, "we'll get ashore all right."

But there was that in his tone which made them think, so the oiler quoth: "Yes! If this wind holds!"

The cook was bailing: "Yes! If we don't catch hell in the surf."

Canton flannel gulls flew near and far. Sometimes they sat down on the sea, near patches of brown sea-weed that rolled over the waves with a movement like carpets on line in a gale. The birds sat comfortably in groups, and they were envied by some in the dingey, for the wrath of the sea was no more to them than it was to a covey of prairie chickens a thousand miles inland. Often they came very close and stared at the men with black bead-like eyes. At these times they were uncanny and sinister in their unblinking scrutiny, and the men hooted angrily at them, telling them to be gone. One came, and evidently decided to alight on the top of the captain's head. The bird flew parallel to the boat and did not circle, but made short sidelong jumps in the air in chicken-fashion. His black eyes were wistfully fixed upon the captain's head. "Ugly brute," said the oiler to the bird. "You look as if you were made with a jack-knife." The cook and the correspondent swore darkly at the creature. The captain naturally wished to knock it away with the end of the heavy painter, but he did not dare do it, because anything resembling an emphatic gesture would have capsized this freighted boat, and so with his open hand, the captain gently and carefully waved the gull away. After it had been discouraged from the pursuit the captain breathed easier on account of his hair, and others breathed easier because the bird struck their minds at this time as being somehow grewsome and ominous.

In the meantime the oiler and the correspondent rowed. And also they rowed.

They sat together in the same seat, and each rowed an oar. Then the oiler took both oars; then the correspondent took both oars; then the oiler; then the correspondent. They rowed and they rowed. The very ticklish part of the business was when the time came for the reclining one in the stern to take his turn at the oars. By the very last star of truth, it is easier to steal eggs from under a hen than it was to change seats in the dingey. First the man in the stern slid his hand along the thwart and moved with care, as if he were of Sevres. Then the man in the rowing seat slid his hand along the other thwart. It was all done with the most extraordinary care. As the two sidled past each other, the whole party kept watchful eyes on the coming wave, and the captain cried: "Look out now! Steady there!"

The brown mats of sea-weed that appeared from time to time were like islands, bits of earth. They were travelling, apparently, neither one way nor the other. They were, to all intents stationary. They informed the men in the boat that it was making progress slowly toward the land.

The captain, rearing cautiously in the bow, after the dingey soared on a great swell, said that he had seen the lighthouse at Mosquito Inlet. Presently the cook remarked that he had seen it. The correspondent was at the oars, then, and for some reason he too wished to look at the lighthouse but his back was toward the far shore and the waves were important, and for some time he could not seize an opportunity to turn his head. But at last there came a wave more gentle than the others, and when at the crest of it he swiftly scoured the western horizon.

"See it?" said the captain.

"No," said the correspondent, slowly, "I didn't see anything."

"Look again," said the captain. He pointed. "It's exactly in that direction."

At the top of another wave, the correspondent did as he was bid, and this time his eyes chanced on a small still thing on the edge of the swaying horizon. It was precisely like the point of a pin. It took an anxious eye to find a lighthouse so tiny.

"Think we'll make it, captain?"

"If this wind holds and the boat don't swamp, we can't do much else," said the captain.

The little boat, lifted by each towering sea, and splashed viciously by the crests, made progress that in the absence of sea-weed was not apparent to those in her. She seemed just a wee thing wallowing, miraculously, top-up, at the mercy of five oceans. Occasionally, a great spread of water, like white flames, swarmed into her.

"Bail her, cook," said the captain, serenely.

"All right, captain," said the cheerful cook.

III

It would be difficult to describe the subtle brotherhood of men that was here established on the seas. No one said that it was so. No one mentioned it. But it dwelt in the boat, and each man felt it warm him. They were a captain, an oiler, a cook, and a correspondent, and they were friends, friends in a more curiously iron-bound degree than may be common. The hurt captain, lying against the water-jar in the bow, spoke always in a low voice and calmly, but he could never command a more ready and swiftly obedient crew than the motley three of the dingey. It was more than a mere recognition of what was best for the common safety. There was surely in it a quality that was personal and heartfelt. And after this devotion to the commander of the boat there was this comradeship that the correspondent, for instance, who had been taught to be cynical of men, knew even at the time was the best experience of his life. But no one said that it was so. No one mentioned it.

"I wish we had a sail," remarked the captain. "We might try my overcoat on the end of an oar and give you two boys a chance to rest." So the cook and the correspondent held the mast and spread wide the overcoat. The oiler steered, and the little boat made good way with her new rig. Sometimes the oiler had to scull sharply to keep a sea from breaking into the boat, but otherwise sailing was a success.

Meanwhile the light-house had been growing slowly larger. It had now almost assumed color, and appeared like a little gray shadow on the sky. The man at the oars could not be prevented from turning his head rather often to try for a glimpse of this little gray shadow.

At last, from the top of each wave the men in the tossing boat could see land. Even as the light-house was an upright shadow on the sky, this land seemed but a long black shadow on the sea. It certainly was thinner than paper. "We must be about opposite New Smyrna," said the cook, who had coasted this shore often in schooners. "Captain, by the way, I believe they abandoned that life-saving station there about a year ago."

"Did they?" said the captain.

The wind slowly died away. The cook and the correspondent were not now obliged to slave in order to hold high the oar. But the waves continued their old impetuous swooping at the dingey, and the little craft, no longer under way, struggled woundily over them. The oiler or the correspondent took the oars again.

Shipwrecks are apropos of nothing. If men could only train for them and have them occur when the men had reached pink condition, there would be less drowning at sea. Of the four in the dingey none had slept any time worth mentioning for two days and two nights previous to embarking in the dingey, and in the excitement of clambering about the deck of a foundering ship they had also forgotten to eat heartily.

For these reasons, and for others, neither the oiler nor the correspondent was fond of rowing at this time. The correspondent wondered ingenuously how in the name of all that was sane could there be people who thought it amusing to row a boat. It was not an amusement; it was a diabolical punishment, and even a genius of mental aberrations could never conclude that it was anything but a horror to the muscles and a crime against the back. He mentioned to the boat in general how the amusement of rowing struck him, and the weary-faced oiler smiled in full sympathy. Previously to the foundering, by the way, the oiler had worked double-watch in the engine-room of the ship.

"Take her easy, now, boys," said the captain. "Don't spend yourselves. If we have to run a surf you'll need all your strength, because we'll sure have to swim for it. Take your time."

Slowly the land arose from the sea. From a black line it became a line of black and a line of white, trees, and sand. Finally, the captain said that he could make out a house on the shore. "That's the house of refuge, sure," said the cook. "They'll see us before long, and come out after us."

The distant light-house reared high. "The keeper ought to be able to make us out now, if he's looking through a glass," said the captain. "He'll notify the life-saving people."

"None of those other boats could have got ashore to give word of the wreck," said the oiler, in a low voice. "Else the life-boat would be out hunting us."

Slowly and beautifully the land loomed out of the sea. The wind came again. It had veered from the northeast to the southeast. Finally, a new sound struck the ears of the men in the boat. It was the low thunder of the surf on the shore. "We'll never be able to make the light-house now," said the captain. "Swing her head a little more north, Billie," said the captain.

"'A little more north,' sir," said the oiler.

Whereupon the little boat turned her nose once more down the wind, and all but the oarsman watched the shore grow. Under the influence of this expansion doubt and direful apprehension was leaving the minds of the men. The management of the boat was still most absorbing, but it could not prevent a quiet cheerfulness. In an hour, perhaps, they would be ashore.

Their back-bones had become thoroughly used to balancing in the boat and they now rode this wild colt of a dingey like circus men. The correspondent thought that he had been drenched to the skin, but happening to feel in the top pocket of his coat, he found therein eight cigars. Four of them were soaked with sea-water; four were perfectly scatheless. After a search, somebody produced three dry matches, and thereupon the four waifs rode in their little boat, and with an assurance of an impending rescue shining in their eyes, puffed at the big cigars and judged well and ill of all men. Everybody took a drink of water.

IV

"Cook," remarked the captain, "there don't seem to be any signs of life about your house of refuge."

"No," replied the cook. "Funny they don't see us!"

A broad stretch of lowly coast lay before the eyes of the men. It was of low dunes topped with dark vegetation. The roar of the surf was plain, and sometimes they could see the white lip of a wave as it spun up the beach. A tiny house was blocked out black upon the sky. Southward, the slim light-house lifted its little gray length.

Tide, wind, and waves were swinging the dingey northward. "Funny they don't see us," said the men.

The surf's roar was here dulled, but its tone was, nevertheless, thunderous and mighty. As the boat swam over the great rollers, the men sat listening to this roar. "We'll swamp sure," said everybody.

It is fair to say here that there was not a life-saving station within twenty miles in either direction, but the men did not know this fact and in consequence they made dark and opprobrious remarks concerning the eyesight of the nation's life-savers. Four scowling men sat in the dingey and surpassed records in the invention of epithets.

"Funny they don't see us."

The light-heartedness of a former time had completely faded. To their sharpened minds it was easy to conjure pictures of all kinds of incompetency and blindness and indeed, cowardice. There was the shore of the populous land, and it was bitter and bitter to them that from it came no sign.

"Well," said the captain, ultimately, "I suppose we'll have to make a try for ourselves. If we stay out here too long, we'll none of us have strength left to swim after the boat swamps."

And so the oiler, who was at the oars, turned the boat straight for the shore. There was a sudden tightening of muscles. There was some thinking.

"If we don't all get ashore—" said the captain. "If we don't all get ashore, I suppose you fellows know where to send news of my finish?"

They then briefly exchanged some addresses and admonitions. As for the reflections of the men, there was a great deal of rage in them. Perchance they might be formulated thus: "If I am going to be drowned—if I am going to be drowned—if I am going to be drowned, why, in the name of the seven mad gods who rule the sea, was I allowed to come thus far and contemplate sand and trees? Was I brought here merely to have my nose dragged away as I was about to nibble the sacred cheese of life? It is preposterous. If this old ninny-woman, Fate, cannot do better than this, she should be deprived of the management of men's fortunes. She is an old hen who knows not her intention. If she has decided to drown me, why did she not do it in the beginning and save me all this trouble. The whole affair is absurd.... But, no, she cannot mean to drown me. She dare not drown me. She cannot drown me. Not after all this work." Afterward the man might have had an impulse to shake his fist at the clouds: "Just you drown me, now, and then hear what I call you!"

The billows that came at this time were more formidable. They seemed always just about to break and roll over the little boat in a turmoil of foam. There was a preparatory and long growl in the speech of them. No mind unused to the sea would have concluded that the dingey could ascend these sheer heights in time. The shore was still afar. The oiler was a wily surfman. "Boys," he said, swiftly, "she won't live three minutes more and we're too far out to swim. Shall I take her to sea again, captain?"

"Yes! Go ahead!" said the captain.

This oiler, by a series of quick miracles, and fast and steady oarsmanship, turned the boat in the middle of the surf and took her safely to sea again.

There was a considerable silence as the boat bumped over the furrowed sea to deeper water. Then somebody in gloom spoke. "Well, anyhow, they must have seen us from the shore by now."

The gulls went in slanting flight up the wind toward the gray desolate east. A squall, marked by dingy clouds, and clouds brick-red, like smoke from a burning building, appeared from the southeast.

"What do you think of those life-saving people? Ain't they peaches?"

"Funny they haven't seen us."

"Maybe they think we're out here for sport! Maybe they think we're fishin'. Maybe they think we're damned fools."

It was a long afternoon. A changed tide tried to force them southward, but wind and wave said northward. Far ahead, where coast-line, sea, and sky formed their mighty angle, there were little dots which seemed to indicate a city on the shore.

"St. Augustine?"

The captain shook his head. "Too near Mosquito Inlet."

And the oiler rowed, and then the correspondent rowed. Then the oiler rowed. It was a weary business. The human back can become the seat of more aches and pains than are registered in books for the composite anatomy of a regiment. It is a limited area, but it can become the theatre of innumerable muscular conflicts, tangles, wrenches, knots, and other comforts.

"Did you ever like to row, Billie?" asked the correspondent.

"No," said the oiler. "Hang it."

When one exchanged the rowing-seat for a place in the bottom of the boat, he suffered a bodily depression that caused him to be careless of everything save an obligation to wiggle one finger. There was cold sea-water swashing to and fro in the boat, and he lay in it. His head, pillowed on a thwart, was within an inch of the swirl of a wave crest, and sometimes a particularly obstreperous sea came in-board and drenched him once more. But these matters did not annoy him. It is almost certain that if the boat had capsized he would have tumbled comfortably out upon the ocean as if he felt sure it was a great soft mattress.

"Look! There's a man on the shore!"

"Where?"

"There! See 'im? See 'im?"

"Yes, sure! He's walking along."

"Now he's stopped. Look! He's facing us!"

"He's waving at us!"

"So he is! By thunder!"

"Ah, now, we're all right! Now we're all right! There'll be a boat out here for us in half an hour."

"He's going on. He's running. He's going up to that house there."

The remote beach seemed lower than the sea, and it required a searching glance to discern the little black figure. The captain saw a floating stick and they rowed to it. A bath-towel was by some weird chance in the boat, and, tying this on the stick, the captain waved it. The oarsman did not dare turn his head, so he was obliged to ask questions.

"What's he doing now?"

"He's standing still again. He's looking, I think. . . . There he goes again. Toward the house. . . . Now he's stopped again."

"Is he waving at us?"

"No, not now! he was, though."

"Look! There comes another man!"

"He's running."

"Look at him go, would you."

"Why, he's on a bicycle. Now he's met the other man. They're both waving at us. Look!"

"There comes something up the beach."

"What the devil is that thing?"

"Why, it looks like a boat."

"Why, certainly it's a boat."

"No, it's on wheels."

"Yes, so it is. Well, that must be the life-boat. They drag them along shore on a wagon."

"That's the life-boat, sure."

"No, by——, it's—it's an omnibus."

"I tell you it's a life-boat."

"It is not! It's an omnibus. I can see it plain. See? One of these big hotel omnibuses."

"By thunder, you're right. It's an omnibus, sure as fate. What do you suppose they are doing with an omnibus? Maybe they are going around collecting the life-crew, hey?"

"That's it, likely. Look! There's a fellow waving a little black flag. He's standing on the steps of the omnibus.

There come those other two fellows. Now they're all talking together. Look at the fellow with the flag. Maybe he ain't waving it."

"That ain't a flag, is it? That's his coat. Why, certainly, that's his coat."

"So it is. It's his coat. He's taken it off and is waving it around his head. But would you look at him swing it."

"Oh, say, there isn't any life-saving station there. That's just a winter resort hotel omnibus that has brought over some of the boarders to see us drown."

"What's that idiot with the coat mean? What's he signaling, anyhow?"

"It looks as if he were trying to tell us to go north. There must be a life-saving station up there."

"No! He thinks we're fishing. Just giving us a merry hand. See? Ah, there, Willie."

"Well, I wish I could make something out of those signals. What do you suppose he means?"

"He don't mean anything. He's just playing."

"Well, if he'd just signal us to try the surf again, or to go to sea and wait, or go north, or go south, or go to hell — there would be some reason in it. But look at him. He just stands there and keeps his coat revolving like a wheel. The ass!"

"There come more people."

"Now there's quite a mob. Look! Isn't that a boat?"

"Where? Oh, I see where you mean. No, that's no boat."

"That fellow is still waving his coat."

"He must think we like to see him do that. Why don't he quit it. It don't mean anything."

"I don't know. I think he is trying to make us go north. It must be that there's a life-saving station there somewhere."

"Say, he ain't tired yet. Look at 'im wave."

"Wonder how long he can keep that up. He's been revolving his coat ever since he caught sight of us. He's an idiot. Why aren't they getting men to bring a boat out. A fishing boat—one of those big yawls—could come out here all right. Why don't he do something?"

"Oh, it's all right, now."

"They'll have a boat out here for us in less than no time, now that they've seen us."

A faint yellow tone came into the sky over the low land. The shadows on the sea slowly deepened. The wind bore coldness with it, and the men began to shiver.

"Holy smoke!" said one, allowing his voice to express his impious mood, "if we keep on monkeying out here! If we've got to flounder out here all night!"

"Oh, we'll never have to stay here all night! Don't you worry. They've seen us now, and it won't be long before they'll come chasing out after us."

The shore grew dusky. The man waving a coat blended gradually into this gloom, and it swallowed in the same manner the omnibus and the group of people. The spray, when it dashed uproariously over the side, made the voyagers shrink and swear like men who were being branded.

"I'd like to catch the chump who waved the coat. I feel like soaking him one, just for luck."

"Why? What did he do?"

"Oh, nothing, but then he seemed so damned cheerful."

In the meantime the oiler rowed, and then the correspondent rowed, and then the oiler rowed. Gray-faced and bowed forward, they mechanically, turn by turn, plied the leaden oars. The form of the light-house had vanished from the southern horizon, but finally a pale star appeared, just lifting from the sea. The streaked saffron in the west passed before the all-merging darkness, and the sea to the east was black. The land had vanished, and was expressed only by the low and drear thunder of the surf.

"If I am going to be drowned—if I am going to be drowned—if I am going to be drowned, why, in the name of the seven mad gods, who rule the sea, was I allowed to come thus far and contemplate sand and trees? Was I brought here merely to have my nose dragged away as I was about to nibble the sacred cheese of life?"

The patient captain, drooped over the water-jar, was sometimes obliged to speak to the oarsman.

"Keep her head up! Keep her head up!"

" 'Keep her head up,' sir." The voices were weary and low.

This was surely a quiet evening. All save the oarsman lay heavily and listlessly in the boat's bottom. As for him, his eyes were just capable of noting the tall black waves that swept forward in a most sinister silence, save for an occasional subdued growl of a crest.

The cook's head was on a thwart, and he looked without interest at the water under his nose. He was deep in other scenes. Finally he spoke. "Billie," he murmured, dreamfully, "what kind of pie do you like best?"

V

"Pie," said the oiler and the correspondent, agitatedly. "Don't talk about those things, blast you!"

"Well," said the cook, "I was just thinking about ham sandwiches, and—"

A night on the sea in an open boat is a long night. As darkness settled finally, the shine of the light, lifting from the sea in the south, changed to full gold. On the northern horizon a new light appeared, a small bluish gleam on the edge of the waters. These two lights were the furniture of the world. Otherwise there was nothing but waves.

Two men huddled in the stern, and distances were so magnificent in the dingey that the rower was enabled to keep his feet partly warmed by thrusting them under his companions. Their legs indeed extended far under the rowing-seat until they touched the feet of the captain forward. Sometimes, despite the efforts of the tired oarsman, a wave came piling into the boat, an icy wave of the night, and the chilling water soaked them anew. They would twist their bodies for a moment and groan, and sleep the dead sleep once more, while the water in the boat gurgled about them as the craft rocked.

The plan of the oiler and the correspondent was for one to row until he lost the ability, and then arouse the other from his sea-water couch in the bottom of the boat.

The oiler plied the oars until his head drooped forward, and the overpowering sleep blinded him. And he rowed yet afterward. Then he touched a man in the bottom of the boat, and called his name. "Will you spell me for a little while?" he said, meekly.

"Sure, Billie," said the correspondent, awakening and dragging himself to a sitting position. They exchanged places carefully, and the oiler, cuddling down to the sea-water at the cook's side, seemed to go to sleep instantly.

The particular violence of the sea had ceased. The waves came without snarling. The obligation of the man at the oars was to keep the boat headed so that the tilt of the rollers would not capsize her, and to preserve her from filling when the crests rushed past. The black waves were silent and hard to be seen in the darkness. Often one was almost upon the boat before the oarsman was aware.

In a low voice the correspondent addressed the captain. He was not sure that the captain was awake, although this iron man seemed to be always awake. "Captain, shall I keep her making for that light north, sir?"

The same steady voice answered him. "Yes. Keep it about two points off the port bow."

The cook had tied a life-belt around himself in order to get even the warmth which this clumsy cork contrivance could donate, and he seemed almost stove-like when a rower, whose teeth invariably chattered wildly as soon as he ceased his labor, dropped down to sleep.

The correspondent, as he rowed, looked down at the two men sleeping under foot. The cook's arm was around the oiler's shoulders, and, with their fragmentary clothing and haggard faces, they were the babes of the sea, a grotesque rendering of the old babes in the wood.

Later he must have grown stupid at his work, for suddenly there was a growling of water, and a crest came with a roar and a swash into the boat, and it was a wonder that it did not set the cook afloat in his life-belt. The cook continued to sleep, but the oiler sat up, blinking his eyes and shaking with the new cold.

"Oh, I'm awful sorry, Billie," said the correspondent, contritely.

"That's all right, old boy," said the oiler, and lay down again and was asleep.

Presently it seemed that even the captain dozed, and the correspondent thought that he was the one man afloat on all the oceans. The wind had a voice as it came over the waves, and it was sadder than the end.

There was a long, loud swishing astern of the boat, and a gleaming trail of phosphorescence, like blue flame, was furrowed on the black waters. It might have been made by a monstrous knife.

Then there came a stillness, while the correspondent breathed with the open mouth and looked at the sea.

Suddenly there was another swish and another long flash of bluish light, and this time it was alongside the boat, and might almost have been reached with an oar. The correspondent saw an enormous fin speed like a shadow through the water, hurling the crystalline spray and leaving the long glowing trail.

The correspondent looked over his shoulder at the captain. His face was hidden, and he seemed to be asleep. He looked at the babes of the sea. They certainly were asleep. So, being bereft of sympathy, he leaned a little way to one side and swore softly into the sea.

But the thing did not then leave the vicinity of the boat. Ahead or astern, on one side or the other, at intervals long or short, fled the long sparkling streak, and there was to be heard the whiroo of the dark fin. The speed and power of the thing was greatly to be admired. It cut the water like a gigantic and keen projectile.

The presence of this biding thing did not affect the man with the same horror that it would if he had been a picnicker. He simply looked at the sea dully and swore in an undertone.

Nevertheless, it is true that he did not wish to be alone with the thing. He wished one of his companions to awaken by chance and keep him company with it. But the captain hung motionless over the water-jar and the oiler and the cook in the bottom of the boat were plunged in slumber.

VI

"If I am going to be drowned—if I am going to be drowned—if I am going to be drowned, why, in the name of the seven mad gods, who rule the sea, was I allowed to come thus far and contemplate sand and trees?"

During this dismal night, it may be remarked that a man would conclude that it was really the intention of the seven mad gods to drown him, despite the abominable injustice of it. For it was certainly an abominable injustice to drown a man who had worked so hard, so hard. The man felt it would be a crime most unnatural. Other people had drowned at sea since galleys swarmed with painted sails, but still—

When it occurs to a man that nature does not regard him as important, and that she feels she would not maim the universe by disposing of him, he at first wishes to throw bricks at the temple, and he hates deeply the fact that there are no bricks and no temples. Any visible expression of nature would surely be pelleted with his jeers.

Then, if there be no tangible thing to hoot he feels, perhaps, the desire to confront a personification and indulge in pleas, bowed to one knee, and with hands supplicant, saying: "Yes, but I love myself."

A high cold star on a winter's night is the word he feels that she says to him. Thereafter he knows the pathos of his situation.

The men in the dingey had not discussed these matters, but each had, no doubt, reflected upon them in silence and according to his mind. There was seldom any expression upon their faces save the general one of complete weariness. Speech was devoted to the business of the boat.

To chime the notes of his emotion, a verse mysteriously entered the correspondent's head. He had even forgotten that he had forgotten this verse, but it suddenly was in his mind.

A soldier of the Legion lay dying in Algiers,

There was lack of woman's nursing, there was dearth of woman's tears;

But a comrade stood beside him, and he took that comrade's hand

And he said: "I shall never see my own, my native land."

In his childhood, the correspondent had been made acquainted with the fact that a soldier of the Legion lay dying in Algiers, but he had never regarded the fact as important. Myriads of his school-fellows had informed him of the soldier's plight, but the dinning had naturally ended by making him perfectly indifferent. He had never considered it his affair that a soldier of the Legion lay dying in Algiers, nor had it appeared to him as a matter for sorrow. It was less to him than breaking of a pencil's point.

Now, however, it quaintly came to him as a human, living thing. It was no longer merely a picture of a few throes in the breast of a poet, meanwhile drinking tea and warming his feet at the grate; it was an actuality—stern, mournful, and fine.

The correspondent plainly saw the soldier. He lay on the sand with his feet out straight and still. While his pale left hand was upon his chest in an attempt to thwart the going of his life, the blood came between his fingers. In the far Algerian distance, a city of low square forms was set against a sky that was faint with the last sunset hues. The correspondent, plying the oars and dreaming of the slow and slower movements of the lips of the soldier, was moved by a profound and perfectly impersonal comprehension. He was sorry for the soldier of the Legion who lay dying in Algiers.

The thing which had followed the boat and waited had evidently grown bored at the delay. There was no longer to be heard the slash of the cut-water, and there was no longer the flame of the long trail. The light in the north still glimmered, but it was apparently no nearer to the boat. Sometimes the boom of the surf rang in the correspondent's ears, and he turned the craft seaward then and rowed harder. Southward, someone had evidently built a watch-fire on the beach. It was too low and too far to be seen, but it made a shimmering, roseate reflection upon the bluff back of it, and this could be discerned from the boat. The wind came stronger, and sometimes a wave suddenly raged out like a mountain-cat and there was to be seen the sheen and sparkle of a broken crest.

The captain, in the bow, moved on his water-jar and sat erect. "Pretty long night," he observed to the correspondent. He looked at the shore. "Those life-saving people take their time."

"Did you see that shark playing around?"

"Yes, I saw him. He was a big fellow, all right."

"Wish I had known you were awake."

Later the correspondent spoke into the bottom of the boat.

"Billie!" There was a slow and gradual disentanglement. "Billie, will you spell me?"

"Sure," said the oiler.

As soon as the correspondent touched the cold comfortable sea-water in the bottom of the boat, and had huddled close to the cook's life-belt he was deep in sleep, despite the fact that his teeth played all the popular airs. This sleep was so good to him that it was but a moment before he heard a voice call his name in a tone that demonstrated the last stages of exhaustion. "Will you spell me?"

"Sure, Billie."

The light in the north had mysteriously vanished, but the correspondent took his course from the wide-awake captain.

Later in the night they took the boat farther out to sea, and the captain directed the cook to take one oar at the stern and keep the boat facing the seas. He was to call out if he should hear the thunder of the surf. This plan enabled the oiler and the correspondent to get respite together. "We'll give those boys a chance to get into shape again," said the captain. They curled down and, after a few preliminary chatterings and trembles, slept once more the dead sleep. Neither knew they had bequeathed to the cook the company of another shark, or perhaps the same shark.

As the boat caroused on the waves, spray occasionally bumped over the side and gave them a fresh soaking, but this had no power to break their repose. The ominous slash of the wind and the water affected them as it would have affected mummies.

"Boys," said the cook, with the notes of every reluctance in his voice, "she's drifted in pretty close. I guess one of you had better take her to sea again." The correspondent, aroused, heard the crash of the toppled crests.

As he was rowing, the captain gave him some whiskey and water, and this steadied the chills out of him. "If I ever get ashore and anybody shows me even a photograph of an oar—"

At last there was a short conversation.

"Billie. . . . Billie, will you spell me?"

"Sure," said the oiler.

VII

When the correspondent again opened his eyes, the sea and the sky were each of the gray hue of the dawning. Later, carmine and gold was painted upon the waters. The morning appeared finally, in its splendor with a sky of pure blue, and the sunlight flamed on the tips of the waves.

On the distant dunes were set many little black cottages, and a tall white wind-mill reared above them. No man, nor dog, nor bicycle appeared on the beach. The cottages might have formed a deserted village.

The voyagers scanned the shore. A conference was held in the boat. "Well," said the captain, "if no help is coming, we might better try a run through the surf right away. If we stay out here much longer we will be too weak to do anything for ourselves at all." The others silently acquiesced in this reasoning. The boat was headed for the beach. The correspondent wondered if none ever ascended the tall wind-tower, and if then they never looked seaward. This tower was a giant, standing with its back to the plight of the ants. It represented in a degree, to the correspondent, the serenity of nature amid the struggles of the individual—nature in the wind, and nature in the vision of men. She did not seem cruel to him, nor beneficent, nor treacherous, nor wise. But she was indifferent, flatly indifferent. It is, perhaps, plausible that a man in this situation, impressed with the unconcern of the universe, should see the innumerable flaws of his life and have them taste wickedly in his mind and wish for another chance. A distinction between right and wrong seems absurdly clear to him, then, in this new ignorance of the grave-edge, and he understands that if he were given another opportunity he would mend his conduct and his words, and be better and brighter during an introduction, or at a tea.

"Now, boys," said the captain, "she is going to swamp sure. All we can do is to work her in as far as possible, and then when she swamps, pile out and scramble for the beach. Keep cool now and don't jump until she swamps sure."

The oiler took the oars. Over his shoulders he scanned the surf. "Captain," he said, "I think I'd better bring her about, and keep her head-on to the seas and back her in."

"All right, Billie," said the captain. "Back her in." The oiler swung the boat then and, seated in the stern, the cook and the correspondent were obliged to look over their shoulders to contemplate the lonely and indifferent shore.

The monstrous inshore rollers heaved the boat high until the men were again enabled to see the white sheets of water scudding up the slanted beach. "We won't get in very close," said the captain. Each time a man could wrest his attention from the rollers, he turned his glance toward the shore, and in the expression of the eyes during this contemplation there was a singular quality. The correspondent, observing the others, knew that they were not afraid, but the full meaning of their glances was shrouded.

As for himself, he was too tired to grapple fundamentally with the fact. He tried to coerce his mind into thinking of it, but the mind was dominated at this time by the muscles, and the muscles said they did not care. It merely occurred to him that if he should drown it would be a shame.

There were no hurried words, no pallor, no plain agitation. The men simply looked at the shore. "Now, remember to get well clear of the boat when you jump," said the captain.

Seaward the crest of a roller suddenly fell with a thunderous crash, and the long white comber came roaring down upon the boat.

"Steady now," said the captain. The men were silent. They turned their eyes from the shore to the comber and waited. The boat slid up the incline, leaped at the furious top, bounced over it, and swung down the long back of the waves. Some water had been shipped and the cook bailed it out.

But the next crest crashed also. The tumbling boiling flood of white water caught the boat and whirled it almost perpendicular. Water swarmed in from all sides. The correspondent had his hands on the gunwale at this time, and when the water entered at that place he swiftly withdrew his fingers, as if he objected to wetting them.

The little boat, drunken with this weight of water, reeled and snuggled deeper into the sea.

"Bail her out, cook! Bail her out," said the captain.

"All right, captain," said the cook.

"Now, boys, the next one will do for us, sure," said the oiler. "Mind to jump clear of the boat."

The third wave moved forward, huge, furious, implacable. It fairly swallowed the dingey, and almost simultaneously the men tumbled into the sea. A piece of life-belt had lain in the bottom of the boat, and as the correspondent went overboard he held this to his chest with his left hand.

The January water was icy, and he reflected immediately that it was colder than he had expected to find it off the coast of Florida. This appeared to his dazed mind as a fact important enough to be noted at the time. The coldness of the water was sad; it was tragic. This fact was somehow mixed and confused with his opinion of his own situation that it seemed almost a proper reason for tears. The water was cold.

When he came to the surface he was conscious of little but the noisy water. Afterward he saw his companions in the sea. The oiler was ahead in the race. He was swimming strongly and rapidly. Off to the correspondent's left, the cook's great white and corked back bulged out of the water, and in the rear the captain was hanging with his one good hand to the keel of the overturned dingey.

There is a certain immovable quality to a shore, and the correspondent wondered at it amid the confusion of the sea.

It seemed also very attractive, but the correspondent knew that it was a long journey, and he paddled leisurely. The piece of life-preserver lay under him, and sometimes he whirled down the incline of a wave as if he were on a hand-sled.

But finally he arrived at a place in the sea where travel was beset with difficulty. He did not pause swimming to inquire what manner of current had caught him, but there his progress ceased. The shore was set before him like a bit of scenery on a stage, and he looked at it and understood with his eyes each detail of it.

As the cook passed, much farther to the left, the captain was calling to him, "Turn over on your back, cook! Turn over on your back and use the oar."

"All right, sir!" The cook turned on his back, and, paddling with an oar, went ahead as if he were a canoe.

Presently the boat also passed to the left of the correspondent with the captain clinging with one hand to the keel. He would have appeared like a man raising himself to look over a board fence, if it were not for the extraordinary gymnastics of the boat. The correspondent marvelled that the captain could still hold to it.

They passed on, nearer to shore—the oiler, the cook, the captain—and following them went the water-jar, bouncing gayly over the seas.

The correspondent remained in the grip of this strange new enemy—a current. The shore, with its white slope of sand and its green bluff, topped with little silent cottages, was spread like a picture before him. It was very near to him then, but he was impressed as one who in a gallery looks at a scene from Brittany or Algiers.

He thought: "I am going to drown? Can it be possible? Can it be possible? Can it be possible?" Perhaps an individual must consider his own death to be the final phenomenon of nature.

But later a wave perhaps whirled him out of this small deadly current, for he found suddenly that he could again make progress toward the shore. Later still, he was aware that the captain, clinging with one hand to the keel of the dingey, had his face turned away from the shore and toward him, and was calling his name. "Come to the boat! Come to the boat!"

In his struggle to reach the captain and the boat, he reflected that when one gets properly wearied, drowning must really be a comfortable arrangement, a cessation of hostilities accompanied by a large degree of relief, and he was glad of it, for the main thing in his mind for some moments had been horror of the temporary agony. He did not wish to be hurt.

Presently he saw a man running along the shore. He was undressing with most remarkable speed. Coat, trousers, shirt, everything flew magically off him.

"Come to the boat," called the captain.

"All right, captain." As the correspondent paddled, he saw the captain let himself down to bottom and leave the boat. Then the correspondent performed his one little marvel of the voyage. A large wave caught him and flung him with ease and supreme speed completely over the boat and far beyond it. It struck him even then as an event in gymnastics, and a true miracle of the sea. An overturned boat in the surf is not a plaything to a swimming man.

The correspondent arrived in water that reached only to his waist, but his condition did not enable him to stand for more than a moment. Each wave knocked him into a heap, and the under-tow pulled at him.

Then he saw the man who had been running and undressing, and undressing and running, come bounding into the water. He dragged ashore the cook, and then waded toward the captain, but the captain waved him away, and sent him to the correspondent. He was naked, naked as a tree in winter, but a halo was about his head, and he shone like a saint. He gave a strong pull, and a long drag, and a bully heave at the correspondent's hand. The correspondent, schooled in the minor formulae, said: "Thanks, old man." But suddenly the man cried: "What's that?" He pointed a swift finger. The correspondent said: "Go."

In the shallows, face downward, lay the oiler. His forehead touched sand that was periodically, between each wave, clear of the sea.

The correspondent did not know all that transpired afterward. When he achieved safe ground he fell, striking the sand with each particular part of his body. It was as if he had dropped from a roof, but the thud was grateful to him.

It seems that instantly the beach was populated with men with blankets, clothes, and flasks, and women with coffee-pots and all the remedies sacred to their minds. The welcome of the land to the men from the sea was warm and generous, but a still and dripping shape was carried slowly up the beach, and the land's welcome for it could only be the different and sinister hospitality of the grave.

When it came night, the white waves paced to and fro in the moonlight, and the wind brought the sound of the great sea's voice to the men on shore, and they felt that they could then be interpreters.

BEING ASHORE

JOHN MASEFIELD

In the nights, in the winter nights, in the nights of storm when the wind howls, it is then that I feel the sweet of it, Aha, I say, you howling catamount, I say, you may blow. wind, and crack your cheeks, for all I care. Then I listen to the noise of the elm trees and to the creak in the old floorings, and, aha, I say, you whining rantipoles, you may crack and you may creak, but here I shall lie till daylight.

There is a solid comfort in a roaring storm ashore here. But on a calm day, when it is raining, when it is muddy underfoot, when the world is the colour of a drowned rat, one calls to mind more boisterous days, the days of effort and adventure; and wasn't I a fool, I say, to come ashore to a life like this life. And I surely was daft, I keep saying, to think the sea as bad as I always thought it. And if I were in a ship now, I say, I wouldn't be doing what I'm trying to do. And, ah! I say, if I'd but stuck to the sea I'd have been a third in the Cunard, or perhaps a second in a P.S.N. coaster. I wouldn't be hunched at a desk, I say, but I'd be up on a bridge—up on a bridge with a helmsman, feeling her do her fifteen knots.

It is at such times that I remember the good days, the exciting days, the days of vehement and spirited living. One day stands out, above nearly all my days, as a day of joy.

We were at sea off the River Plate, running south like a stag. The wind had been slowly freshening for twenty-four hours, and for one whole day we had whitened the sea like a battleship. Our run for the day had been 271 knots, which we thought a wonderful run, though it has, of course, been exceeded by many ships. For this ship it was an exceptional run. The wind was on the quarter, her best point of sailing, and there was enough wind for a glutton. Our captain had the reputation of being a "cracker-on," and on this one occasion he drove her till she groaned. For that one wonderful day we staggered and swooped, and bounded in wild leaps, and burrowed down and shivered, and anon rose up shaking. The wind roared up aloft and boomed in the shrouds, and the sails bellied out as stiff as iron. We tore through the seas in great jumps—there is no other word for it. She seemed to leap clear from one green roaring ridge to come smashing down upon the next. I have been in a fast steamer—a very fast turbine steamer—doing more than twenty knots, but she gave me no sense of great speed. In this old sailing ship the joy of the hurry was such that we laughed and cried aloud. The noise of the wind booming, and the clack, clack, clack of the sheet-blocks, and the ridged seas roaring past us, and the groaning and whining of every block and plank, were like tunes for a dance. We seemed to be tearing through it at ninety miles an hour. Our wake whitened and broadened, and rushed away aft in a creamy fury. We were running here, and hurrying there, taking a small pull of this, and getting another inch of that, till we were weary. But as we hauled we sang and shouted. We were possessed of the spirits of the wind. We could have danced and killed each other. We were in an ecstasy. We were possessed. We half believed that the ship would leap from the waters and hurl herself into the heavens, like a winged god. Over her bows came the spray in showers of sparkles. Her foresail was wet to the yard. Her scuppers were brooks. Her swing-ports spouted like cataracts. Recollect, too, that it was a day to make your heart glad. It was a clear day, a sunny day, a day of brightness and splendour. The sun was glorious in the sky. The sky was of a blue unspeakable. We were tearing along across a splendour of sea that made you sing. Far as one could see there was the water shining and shaking. Blue it was, and green it was, and of a dazzling brilliance in the sun. It rose up in hills and in ridges. It smashed into foam and roared. It towered up again and toppled. It mounted and shook in a rhythm, in a tune, in a music. One could have flung one's body to it as a sacrifice. One longed to be in it, to be a part of it, to be beaten and banged by it. It was a wonder and a glory and a terror. It was a triumph, it was royal, to see that beauty.

And later, after a day of it, as we sat below, we felt our mad ship taking yet wilder leaps, bounding over yet more boisterous hollows, and shivering and exulting in every inch of her. She seemed filled with a fiery, unquiet life. She seemed inhuman, glorious, spiritual. One forgot that she was man's work. We forgot that we were men. She was alive, immortal, furious. We were her minions and servants. We were the star-dust whirled in the train of the comet. We banged our plates with the joy we had in her. We sang and shouted, and called her the glory of the seas.

There is an end to human glory. "Greatness a period hath, no sta-ti-on." The end to our glory came when, as we sat at dinner, the door swung back from its hooks and a mate in oilskins bade us come on deck "without stopping for our clothes." It was time. She was carrying no longer; she was dragging. To windward the sea was blotted in a squall. The line of the horizon was masked in a grey film. The glory of the sea had given place to greyness and grimness. Her beauty had become savage. The music of the wind had changed to a howl as of hounds.

And then we began to "take it off her," to snug her down, to check her in her stride. We went to the clew-lines and clewed the royals up. Then it was, "Up there, you boys, and make the royals fast." My royal was the mizzen-royal, a rag of a sail among the clouds, a great grey rag, which was leaping and slatting a hundred and sixty feet above me. The wind beat me down against the shrouds, it banged me and beat me, and blew the tears from my eyes. It seemed to lift me up the futtocks into the top, and up the topmast rigging to the cross-trees. In the cross-trees I learned what wind was.

It came roaring past with a fervour and a fury which struck me breathless. I could only look aloft to the yard I was bound for and heave my panting body up the rigging. And there was the mizzen-royal. There was the sail I had come to furl. And a wonder of a sight it was. It was blowing and bellying in the wind, and leaping around "like a drunken colt," and flying over the yard, thrashing and flogging. It was roaring like a bull with its slatting and thrashing. The royal mast was bending to the strain of it. To my eyes it was buckling like a piece of whalebone. I lay out on the yard, and the sail hit me in the face and knocked my cap away. It beat me and banged me, and blew from my hands. The wind pinned me flat against the yard, and seemed to be blowing all my clothes to shreds. I felt like a king, like an emperor. I shouted aloud with the joy of that "rastle" with the sail. Forward of me was the main mast, with another lad fighting another royal; and beyond him was yet another, whose sail seemed tied in knots. Below me was the ship, a leaping mad thing, with little silly figures, all heads and shoulders, pulling silly strings along the deck. There was the sea, sheer under me, and it looked grey and grim, and streaked with the white of our smother.

Then, with a lashing swish, the rain squall caught us. It beat down the sea. It blotted out the view. I could see nothing more but grey, driving rain, grey spouts of rain, grey clouds which burst rain, grey heavens which opened and poured rain, Cold rain. Icy-cold rain. Rain which drove the dye out of my shirt till I left blue tracks where I walked. For the next two hours I was clewing up, and furling, and snugging her down. By nightfall we were under our three lower topsails and a reefed fore-course. The next day we were hove-to under a weather cloth.

There are varieties of happiness; and, to most of us, that variety called excitement is the most attractive. On a grey day such as this, with the grass rotting in the mud, the image and memory of that variety are a joy to the heart. They are a joy for this, if for no other reason. They teach us that a little thing, a very little thing, a capful of wind even, is enough to make us exalt in, and be proud of, our parts in the pageant of life.

THE MATE'S STORY

ANONYMOUS

The sealing steamer *Greenland*, when berthed in Glasgow harbour, became a vessel of more than usual interest. The terrible disaster which befell her crew in March, 1898 when, of some 150 men who were sent out on the ice to "pan" seals, almost a third lost their lives, excited a great deal of attention.

The reports which appeared in the newspapers gave but a faint idea of the real nature of the disaster. It felt very different when one went down to the dock and looked at the blackened, battered, yet hardy-looking sealer, and talked to the second mate, who shared in the dangers of the memorable trip, and told so vividly of the storm and the search for his comrades on the ocean of ice.

The *Greenland*, a wood screw barque, was an ideal sealer. There was no new-fangled nonsense about her. A steamer, but with sails enough to make her independent of steam when on the fishing ground, one reminded one of the vessels described in the stories of adventure in which we revelled in our schoolboy days.

Ambrose Critch, the second mate, by birth a Newfoundlander, was the ideal of a sealing fisherman, and gave the impression, which is no doubt true, that he was more at home on the deck, or even on ice, than on a city's streets. Bronzed and weather-beaten, yet hardy and earnest, he spoke seriously, but without restraint, of the terrible three weeks spent on and among the ice off the coast of Newfoundland.

"You want to hear about the disaster?" he said to a visitor who boarded the *Greenland*. "I am not sure that I can tell the story very well. It is too terrible a story.

"We left St. John's on the 10th of March: a Thursday, it was. There were, I think, 207 of us on board altogether. Steering N.N.E., we made the Funks' the following day. About 60 miles, maybe, N.E. of the island, we struck seals—on the 12th, I think—it was the Saturday, anyhow. We kept getting seals from then-till the 20th—that was a Sunday, and, as perhaps you may know, we don't seal on Sundays.

"At three o'clock on Monday morning, Captain Barbour sent a watch out on the ice to kill and pan seals. At five he sent two other watches."

(Here Captain Vine, then in command of the *Greenland*, interposed to dispel the notetaker's puzzled look, by explaining that a watch generally consisted of from forty to fifty men, and that to "pan" seals was to gather them into heaps on the ice floes, so that they could be taken to the ship more conveniently.)

"The men were on the ice all day," the mate continued. "About five o'clock at night the storm came on—snow and drift. We could hardly see across the ship. It was like that from five on Monday till three on Tuesday afternoon, and we knew nothing of the poor men who were blindly wandering—perhaps frozen—among the ice and water. We knew the storm had made an opening that they could not get across. The ship was thrown on her beam ends by the wind, and the coal and provisions and seals had to be shifted to right her.

"At three on Tuesday the weather was better, and at five three men were seen on the ice, trying to make for the ship. Those on board were sent to search for the rest. Boats were provisioned and sent out, and before night we had found about eighty of the men. They were frostbitten, all of them, and some so badly injured that they had to be led on board. You see it was smooth ice, not the humpy, loose kind, on which the men could have built huts and sheltered themselves. So they could only stand or lie all the time. They were a mile or so from the ship—"

"A mile from the ship, and on ice?"

"A mile!" the sailor repeated, and he smiled a smile of pity at the ignorance of the man who had never been seal fishing. "Man, we are sometimes a dozen miles from the ship. Ay, a mile!"

Interruptions were few afterwards.

"The men were in extremity, and could not have lasted much longer. We got no bodies on the Tuesday. On Wednesday the drift had cleared, and more searchers were sent out, and on that day many of the dead men were found. Captain Barbour had hoisted flags at half-mast and men from the *Diana* and the *Iceland,* two other sealers, were sent to help us. The *Diana's* men found six bodies, and the *Iceland's* men four. The bodies were found scattered all over the ice, in ones and twos and threes. Many of the men seemed to have been crawling. They would know of the open water that was between them and the ship, and in the blinding drift they would be afraid to walk. One man, who was found alive, was creeping away from the ship. He had lost his mittens, and he had no feeling in his hands.

"The searchers got out the small boats, and hauled them over the ice with ropes. When they found bodies, they put them into the boat and hauled them back to our ship. Our own men did not use boats; they made 'drays'—things like lorries, but without wheels—and hauled them over the ice. We found twenty-four bodies in all."

"Was that the total number lost?"

"Over twenty-four. They must have suffered terribly. I never saw such a storm. It was a wonder how men could have lived at all on the pans. Some of them that the survivors told of actually went mad, and thought the ship was near, and ran into the open water to reach her, and were drowned. There was water all around them, you know.

"There were two boys saved, who had spent fifty-two hours on the ice, in the storm. We found them on the Wednesday, when the storm was over. They had been alone for a while, but they were joined by one of the men, and the three kept together.

"One curious thing there was. It was not the big, hardy-looking men who lived through the storm on the ice. They died, and those who survived were the slight and weak-looking kind.

"The last body we got was found on the Friday, about two miles from the ship. We cruised about for a while, but gave up the search on Saturday, and made for Bay de Verde. The twenty-four bodies were on board here, and I made a pound—a big box, you know—along by this stanchion, and put them all in. I iced them—you have seen salmon iced, a row of fish and a fold of ice—to keep them till we should reach port. We left Bay de Verde on Sunday morning, and after an uneventful voyage, we got to St. John's the same afternoon."

"And the bodies?"

"We saw them buried, of course. I had to take them out of the ice. When I put them in I had put tickets on them, so that we would know them again. No one of us knew them all, but among us we managed to find all their names. It was terrible work taking them out of the ice. The pound was one solid mass. I had to cut each body out in a square piece.

"It was an awful day in St. John's when we arrived. Not many of the lost and dead men belonged there, but there were other ships out, and the folks were frightened. They knew of the disaster, because our captain had telegraphed from Bay de Verde. The Governor did all he could, and the members of council all took part in the work of providing for the suffering, and disposing of the dead. We buried them in the cemeteries of their different churches.

"A relief fund was started, and the Glasgow owners of the ship, as well as the agent in St. John's, contributed handsomely. The crew all belonged to Newfoundland; most of them to Bonavista Bay.

"About the seals? The voyage was abandoned when the disaster happened. It lasted three weeks. We had 14,500 seals on board, and we left as many on the ice as would have loaded the ship. We landed the seals on Tuesday at Harbour Grace, after the bodies were buried and the ship stayed there until we took on board a cargo of oil and skins for Glasgow.

"You don't often have a sealer in your harbour, I daresay. No, I thought not. We had to come here because the vessel needed a new boiler. No, I don't think I can tell you much more about the disaster. There is plenty more to tell, but somehow I can't tell it. It was terrible."

A SAILOR'S GLOSSARY

ABACK: When a sailing ship is suddenly taken with the wind filling her sails from forward, pressing them back against the masts and spars. A very dangerous predicament, liable to dismast her. Usually caused by careless handling or lack of seamanship and happening with devastating suddenness. Hence the expression, "taken aback" - "taken flat aback" indicating one's being perilously surprised.

ABAFT: Towards the sternmost part of the ship from amidships. It is also used to indicate the bearing of some object from the vessel. "Ship three points abaft the starboard beam" indicates that it bears approximately 124 degrees from right ahead.

AFORE or FOR'ARD OF: The opposite of ABAFT.

AMIDSHIPS: In the centre, or the middle of the vessel.

ATHWART: Lying across—for instance, a boat that has drifted against a ship's anchor-cables as it lies moored is said to be "athwart her hawse."

AVAST: The command to stop. "Avast hauling" indicates to stop pulling at a rope.

BACKSTAYS: Ropes running from a mast-head, lower, top, or topgallant mast in a fore-and-aft direction, secured to the ship's sides, designed to stay the spar against longitudinal stresses and strains (see *Shrouds*) from aft. FORESTAYS do the same for stresses from forward.

BARE POLES (under): Indicates a ship driving before a storm with no canvas set. Only the bare poles of her yards or gaffs are showing.

BARQUE: A three- or four-masted ship square-rigged on all the masts except the aftermost one, which carries only fore-and-aft sail (see *Full-rigged Ship*).

BARQUENTINE: Three- or four-masted, with square rig on only her foremast, all the rest being fore-and-aft rigged (see *Schooner*).

BATTENS: Thin strips of wood or metal engaging in cleats around the hatch-coamings to hold down the tarpaulin coverings. They are secured by hammered-in wedges. Hence the term indicating everything is secured: "battened-down."

BEAMS: The strong cross-members running from side to side in the hull which support her ribs, knees and outer hull, and also her decks. Thus when a ship is said to be "over on her beam-ends" she is lying on her broadside in a state of complete capsize. But "the beam" also means a direction, at right angles from her fore-and-aft line. Thus "on the lee-beam" means something at right angles from the ship on the side sheltered from the wind: on the windward side at right angles, it would be "on the weather-beam."

BEND: To make fast a line or rope.

BIGHT: The loop or the doubled part of a rope when held. It also means a bay or an inlet. The Bight of Benin is perhaps the largest of these, as usually they indicate a small inlet or bend in a coastline.

BINNACLE: The case containing the compass by which the ship is steered. Originally it was a square, rough box, but later became a helmet-shaped brass container, fitted with a permanent lamp.

BLOCK: A pulley. A piece of wood with one or more sheaves, or wheels in it, through which ropes run, or are rove, to ease the labour involved in lifting heavy objects, or those under severe strains. Usually blocks are made to take a specified size of rope but SNATCH BLOCK is specially adapted, with a lifting slide, to accommodate several thicknesses at will.

BOBSTAY: The line holding the bowsprit down to the stem, preventing it being lifted or destroyed by the upward tugging of the jibs or headsails.

BOLTS: Large nails or bars of metal used to unite various parts of the ship. Bolts made of wood, used in ancient times more than nowadays, were TREE-NAILS. It is also a measure of canvas.

BOLT-ROPE: The rope surrounding a sail to which the canvas is sewn.

BOOM: A soar, rigged fore and aft when stretching a sail set in that direction. Also used in olden days for studding-sails, spread from the end of the yardarms when the wind was fair. Booms were also used to hold boats when at anchor out from the ship's side. TO BOOM OFF means to thrust something away with the aid of a pole or boom. BOOMs were also used as floating obstructions in harbour defence.

BRACES: Ropes at the yardarms by which the yards where swung, or "braced" to bring them to the correct angle to set the sail to the wind.

BRAILS: The ropes by which the lower corners of fore-and-aft sails are hauled up and so shortened.

BRIG: A two-masted sailing-ship carrying square-rig on both.

BRIGANTINE: Two-masted ship square-rigged on the foremast only.

BULKHEAD: Temporary or permanent partitions dividing a ship into separated compart ments. Some are "watertight" and meant to act as dams in case of flooding.

BULWARK: The wood or metal solid protection around the outer and upper edging of the upper deck.

BUNT: The middle section, or belly, of a sail.

BUNTLINES: The ropes for hauling up the bunt.

CABLE: Until the 1820's these were almost invariably of thick hemp rope. Now normally of chain cable, securing the ship to her anchor. The cable is also a unit of measurement, but one that varies greatly, ranging from 120 fathoms or 720 feet in American ships to 200 fathoms in the Royal Navy of Nelson's time.

CAT-HEAD: A large, usually squared baulk of timber projecting from the side of the forecastle, or the fore-part, to which the anchor was hoisted and secured (catted) by its ring, the flukes being led further aft.

CHAFING-GEAR: Old rope-yarns and other material wrapped around the rigging or the spars at friction-points to minimise chafing.

CLEAT: A piece of timber secured to the deck or the bulwarks, fashioned with projecting arms from the centre, around which ropes could be turned-up, or belayed, to secure them.

CLEW: The after lower corner of a fore-and-aft sail and the lower corners of square ones.

CLOSE HAULED: A ship with her sails trimmed to creep as close to the wind's flow as possible. She is trying to make headway against an unfavourable breeze without losing ground by being drifted down to leeward.

COIL: Rope stowed away in a ring. The act of stowing it in this fashion.

CRINGLE: The rope that runs around a sail but varying from a *Bolt-rope* (q.v.).

CROSS-TREES: Small projecting timbers supported by the "trestle-trees" and "cheeks." supporting-timbers, at the mast-head to hold the "tops" at the head of the lower-mast and also at the top-mast head to spread more widely the topgallant rigging.

DAVITS: Timbers or metal cranes, with sheaves at their ends outboard, meant to support and hoist the ship's boats so they project clear of her sides to enable them to be lowered in safety.

DEAD RECKONING: A calculation of the ship's various courses and speeds, taken at fixed and frequent intervals, if possible with due note of tides, currents and winds, which can give some indication of her position. The method is very prone to inaccuracy, but was essential in olden times, when it was impossible, or very difficult, to fix the longitude, either because of the lack of a chronometer or inability to "shoot" the stars, moon or the sun.

DOG WATCHES: Half-watches of two hours instead of the normal four. They came between 16.00 and 20.00 each day. Their purpose was to vary the actual hours so that the same watch was not on duty from midnight until 04.00 every day of the voyage. The watches changed at each four-hour period after midnight, when eight bells were struck. Thereafter each half-hour added a stroke to the bell, thus at 15.00 six bells were struck; at 15.30 seven. The custom arose in the days when times at sea were measured in thirty-minute sand-glasses, the quartermaster striking a bell for the number of the glass just emptying itself; eight of the sand glasses were kept in the rack before him and reversed as needed. The term "dog watch" has the same connotation as the "dog" in "dog roses." "dog violet." etc., i.e. pseudo. Thus four bells were struck at 18.00, but only one at 18.30. But instead of four following the three at 19.30 the full eight were sounded at 20.00 to mark the ending of a watch. At midnight on December 31st/ January 1st sixteen bells were struck — eight for the Old and eight for the New Year.

DOWN-HAUL: A rope to haul down jibs, staysails and other canvas such as studding-sails.

DROGUE: A canvas sleeve, or drag, towed astern to slow a ship. This was also often used by privateers or men-of-war under sail when they wanted to lure an enemy to destruction.

EARRING: The rope attached to the CRINGLE (q.v.) of a sail by which it is bent or netted. (A network of small lines by which sails and hammocks are lashed and stowed away).

EYE-BOLT: An iron bar with a loop or an eye at one end driven through the side or deck of a ship with the eye projecting to allow a hook to be affixed. If there is a ring through this eye it is called a RINGBOLT.

EYE-SPLICE: A rope with a permanent loop formed at one end by tucking individual strands in succession into the lay of the rope. A SHORT SPLICE is used to join two ends of a rope by interweaving the opposing strands. A LONG SPLICE is the same, but, by a system of halving the strands, the joined rope is no thicker than the original, so allowing it to be rove through a similar sheaved block. A BACK SPLICE is formed by tucking the strands back into the lay to prevent the end of the line being frayed by remaining loose.

FID: A wooden pin of various sizes employed to lift the lay of ropes while a strand is being tucked through to form one part of a splice. Also a fid can be a block of metal, usually of iron, or wood, which was thrust through the heel of a mast to support it. The metal counterpart of the fid used in splicing is a marline-spike.

FISH: To repair or strengthen a damaged spar or yard by passing cordage arund it. TO FISH AN ANCHOR entails raising its flukes upon the gunwale or bulwarks, the flukes being the point at each end of the bill, which is at the end of the upright shank, which is surmounted at right angles by the stock.

FOOT-ROPE: Formerly called the "horse." It is the looped rope slung beneath a yard on which the seamen stand while reefing, furling or doing any other work upon the sail.

FORECASTLE: The part of the deck, usually raised in sailing-ships, right in the bows forward of the foremast. It is the name used, as a rule, to designate the accommodation for the seamen, which was in this part of the vessel.

FOUNDERING: The act of sinking when a ship fills with water.

FURL: The rolling up of a sail and securing it.

GAFF: The spar to which the head of a fore-and-aft sail is bent. BOOM is the name for the lower spar.

GASKETS: The ropes securing a sail to a spar or a yard when it has been furled.

GRAPNEL: Small anchor with several flukes, or claws, usually found in boats and very small craft. Used for grappling.

GRATING: A wooden lattice-work used for covering open hatches in fine weather. In old men-of-war, the place where flogging was carried out.

GUNWALE: The uppermost part of the side of a boat or small ship.

GUY: A rope used for steadying a spar or mast, or to swing a derrick or spar either way when hoisting something from its upper end.

HALYARDS: Ropes and tackles employed in hoisting and lowering yards, sails and gaffs. Also thinner ones for hoisting flags, known as the SIGNAL HALYARDS.

HATCH OR HATCHWAY: Opening in the decks to allow passage to spaces beneath. The coverings of the holds are also called HATCHES.

HAWSE PIPE or HOLE: The holes in the bows through which the anchor-cables run.

HAWSER: A larger and much stronger rope used for towing, warping and other heavy 'duties where more slender ones would not suffice.

HAZE: Bullying a man.

HEAD SAILS: Used for all canvas setting forward of the fore-mast.

HEEL: The part of the keel nearest the rudder-post. TO HEEL means to list, or to lean over.

HELM: The complete mechanism by which a ship is steered.

HITCH: To secure; or a particular form of knots used for a special purpose.

HOLD: The interior, open part of a ship, where, for instance, her cargo or stores are stowed.

HOLY-STONE: A block of sandstone used for scrubbing and whitening wooden decks by abrasion. There were names for their various shapes and sizes, e.g. "Boston Bible." "Bristol Prayer-book." the eccleciastical implication being appropriate because holystoning was a chore often performed kneeling on the deck.

IRONS: A ship was "in irons" when, after messing up an attempt to tack and come around on the opposite course, she failed to swing through the wind's eye and hung there unable to help herself and usually "caught flat a-back." a position of considerable danger in a strong breeze. TO PUT A MAN IN IRONS was to fetter him.

JACKSTAYS: Ropes stretched tautly along a yard, or elsewhere, to bend sails or other ropes on to.

JIB: A triangular head-sail set fore and aft. Set on a stay forward of the foremast.

JIB-BOOM: The spar or boom rigged out beyond the bowsprit to which the tack of the jib is lashed.

JOLLYBOAT: One of the smallest boats carried, usually lashed across the stern in merchantmen.

JURY RIG: Temporary repairs to masts and sails and spars executed at sea. Jury masts and other replacements were erected to replace those damaged, but vitally needed.

KEDGE: A small anchor with an iron stock used for warping a vessel out of a narrow channel or to gain an offing when required.

KEEL and KEELSON: The keel is the spine of a ship, the lowermost of her timbers, running her entire length, the backbone on which she rests. The keelson is a timber sheath over the keel.

KNEES: The crooked timbers, or ribs, of a ship used to connect the beams to the rest of her framework.

KNOT: The nautical unit of speed which means the time needed to cover one nautical mile in terms of the number made good in one hour. Its name comes from the knots formed at certain intervals in the log-line which was streamed astern to find the speed. By measuring the time taken, using a sand-glass, for a certain number of these knots to run out from the reel, the hourly speed at that moment could be calculated. It is as wrong to speak of distances as being so many knots as it is to say a ship travels at so many knots *an hour*. The knot is a combined time-distance unit of measurement.

LANYARDS: Ropes rove through the DEAD EYES to set up the rigging and hold it taut. DEAD EYES are round pieces of timber, usually pierced with three holes and used in pairs. By tautening the lanyard between the upper and lower lanyard, the proper tension needed to keep the SHROUDS (q.v.) can be maintained. In vessels with hemp rigging the shrouds and stays would be stretched while to windward and require tightening after the ship came on to the other tack.

LARBOARD: The old name for port, or the left side of a ship when one looks forward from aft.

LAUNCH: A large boat. Often the LONG-BOAT.

LAY: To come or go. To LAY-TO is to heave-to, bring the ship up to ride to wind and sea, seeking safety untill a storm abates.

LEAD: The hand-lead is a small version used for soundings in not more than 20 fathoms. It has a hollow at its lower end meant to be charged with a piece of tallow to recover a specimen of the sea-floor. The DEEP-SEA LEAD was much larger and could sound depths up to 100 fathoms. The LEAD-LINE attached to it was marked at intervals to indicate the depths attained.

LEE: The side opposite to the one from which the wind is blowing. That would be the WEATHER SIDE. LEEWAY is the distance lost by a ship's drift to leeward. In a small craft it may easily be calculated by the angle between the wake and the fore-and-aft line of the vessel. This shows how far she is being set down from the course she appears to be lying and can be corrected with ease, once known.

LIFE LINES: Ropes carried along yard, or decks, to help men to their footings.

LOG: The log-book is the official diary and record of all that happens aboard a ship. In merchantmen it is usually kept by the Second Officer nowadays, though in earlier times it was the Mate's sole responsibility. The LOG, however, is a piece of timber, thrown overboard and secured by a rope, by means of which the speed is calculated in knots (q.v.)

LUFF: To alter the helm so as to bring the ship's head closer to the direction of the wind. "To bring her up."

MARTINGALE: A short, perpendicular spar set under the end of the bowsprit and used for a guy for the head-sails to prevent the bowsprit and jib-boom from being sprung upwards by their pull.

MESS: Any number of men who eat together.

MIZEN or MIZZEN MAST: the aftermost of the three masts of a three-master. In ships with four, the after one is usually called the JIGGER, though there are variations. In a BRIG (q.v.) the after of the two masts is the MAINMAST and there is no mizzen.

PAINTER: The rope from the bow of a boat for the purpose of attaching her to a wharf, to a stake, or to her parent-ship.

QUARTER-DECK: That part of the upper deck abaft the mainmast, the second mast. The name stems from the sixteenth century, when ships had half- and quarter-decks as well as a poop. The HALF-DECK is now the name given to quarters of the apprentices or cadets.

RATLINES: The rope lying across the shrouds (q.v.), like the rungs of a ladder, used to help men get aloft.

ROYALS: Light sails for fine weather set above the top gallant sails.

SCHOONER: Fore-and-aft rigged ship without tops, but with two or more masts. There were variants, such as the TOPSAIL SCHOONER, which carried a pair of topsails on her foremast. One that was two-masted and had a pair of topsails on each of her masts was an HERMAPHRODITEBRIG.

SCUPPERS: Holes cut in the waterways to enable the decks to clear themselves.

SHEET: The rope used to set a sail by keeping the CLEW (q.v.) down to its place.

SHEET ANCHOR: The ship's largest anchor.

SHROUDS: The ropes from the mastheads of lower, top and topgallant masts secured to the ship's sides and intended to sustain all lateral strains and stresses, as opposed to STAYS, which take those longitudinally applied.

SKY-SAIL: A light sail setting above the royals.

SLOOP: A small, one-masted fore-and-aft rigged vessel. A KETCH had a tall foremast and a short mizzen, its difference from a YAWL being that the ketch's steering gear was placed forward of the mizzen-mast, while a yawl had hers abaft it. A CUTTER was also one-masted, but differed in several particulars from a SLOOP.

SPANKER: The aftermost sail, fore and aft, of any ship of size. It set with BOOM and GAFF.

STANCHIONS: Upright posts meant to support the BEAMS, or the bulwarks.

STANDING RIGGING: The parts of a ship's rigging intended to remain fast and immovable, as opposed to the RUNNING RIGGING used to manoeuvre her.

STAYSAIL: A triangular, fore-and-aft sail which sets upon a STAY (q.v.).

STEERAGE: The parts below decks just forward of the after cabin.

STEM: The cutwater; a piece of staunch timber from the forward end of the keel up to the bowsprit heel.

STERN POST: The aftermost timber of a ship or the after-end of the vessel.

STRAND: A number of yarns twisted together to form part of a rope.

STRIKE: To lower sails or colours.

STUDDING-SALES (often written STUNSAILS): Light sails set outside the ordinary sails on the yards, set from booms sliding along the yard themselves and used only in fair weather. Nelson carried his fleet into action at Trafalgar under studding-sails because of the light favourable S.W. wind.

TACK: To put the ship about by turning head to wind and so bringing it on to the other side. By turning stern to wind, one WEARED or WORE ship. The TACK is also one of the ropes used to control fore-and-aft sails.

TAFFRAIL: The rail running around a ship's rails astern.

TAUNT or ATAUNTO: Meaning high or tall, and usually applied to a ship's masts.

TAUT: Tight.

TILLER: The bar of wood or metal which moves the rudder by means of the TILLER ROPES, which lead from the tiller-head to the barrel of the steering wheel, from whence she is controlled by the helmsmen.

TOPMAST: The second mast above the deck, above the lower mast. Above is sometimes stepped the third or TOPGALLANT MAST.

TOPSAILS (lower and upper): Usually the second and third sails above the deck. Over them went the upper and lower topgallants in ships rigged after 1885. Above them again were some variants, such as royals and skysails. All were square sails.

TRANSOMS: The timbers crossing the stern-post to strengthen the hull.

TRAVELLER: An iron ring fitted to slide up and down a rope or along a bar.

TRESTLE TREES: Two strong pieces of timber placed horizontally and fore-and-aft on opposite sides of the lower masthead to support the cross-trees (q.v.) and tops. In ancient times seamen stricken with mortal injuries and dying on deck without a confessor or chaplain believed they could win remission of all the punishment due to sin and complete absolution by turning their eyes to the cross-trees and expressing their contrition.

TRYSAIL: Fore-and-aft sail, setting with boom and gaff.

UNBEND: To cast-off or untie a line.

WAIST: The part of the upper-deck between the quarter-deck and the forecastle.

WARE or WEAR: See TACK.

WEATHER GAUGE; TO WEATHER: A vessel which is to windward of another holds the weather gauge of her. To weather a cape or an obstruction means a ship can claw far enough up into the wind not to be driven on to the rocks. WEATHER HELM signified that an individual ship had a tendency to bring her head up into the wind and needed constant correction of the helm and much vigilance if she was not to be caught aback.

WEIGH: To raise anchor or to lift a mast or spar.

WINDLASS: The machine used, like capstan, to weigh the anchor.

WRING BOLTS: Bolts securing the planks to the timbers.

YAWING: The motion of a ship lurching off her course.

VOYAGE IN THE PILOT-BOAT SCHOONER SEA-SERPENT

GEORGE COGGESHALL

After having settled the last voyage I made in the Volusia from New Orleans to Truxillo and Bonaco, and disposed of that vessel, I decided to make up a voyage to the Pacific. By recent accounts from Peru we learned that Lord Cochrane, with a Chilian fleet, was blockading Lima, aided by a strong land force under the command of General San Martin; that the Spaniards had concentrated their armies in Lima and its vicinity, and had strongly fortified themselves there and at the castles of Callao, and would probably hold out for at least six months longer. We also heard that the inhhabitants of Lima were in great want of every thing, especially provisions of almost every description. On the receipt of this information, Mr. H., a merchant of New-York, proposed to me in the month of October, 1821, to purchase a fast-sailing pilot-boat schooner and fit her out for Lima, with a view of evading the blockade, and profiting by the high prices which could be obtained for almost every thing sent to that place.

We soon made arrangements to purchase a suitable vessel, to be owned by Mr. H., Mr. B., an Italian gentleman and myself. I agreed to take one fifth interest in the schooner and cargo, and to command the vessel, and act as supercargo during the voyage. The enterprise was well planned, and had the cargo been laid in with good judgment, the voyage would have proved eminently successful. As it was managed by Mr. H. and Mr. B. it proved in the end rather a failure.

I had never been in Lima and knew nothing of its wants; Mr. B. had resided there several years, but as he was not a merchant, his information proved of little service. I relied entirely on the judgment of my two associates, and therefore took many articles not at all adapted to the market. Such articles as were wanted at Lima paid an enormous profit.

After searching about for a week or two, we at length found a sharp pilot-boat built schooner called the "Sea-Serpent." Her burthen was 139 tons. Though only three years old, she was soft and defective, and subsequently proved to be rotten, and, in bad weather, very leaky. The schooner had just returned from a voyage to Chagres, where she had lost her captain and officers and nearly all her crew by the yellow fever, and while in that hot climate she was not properly ventilated, and had thus suffered from dry rot.

The defect was not discovered by the carpenter who was sent to examine her before she was purchased by Mr. H. I think we gave seven thousand five hundred dollars for the schooner, and on or about the 20th of October we commenced loading. We first took in ten or twelve tons of English and Swedish iron and 100 flasks of quicksilver, which cost over $3,500. Six hogsheads containing 234 kegs of butter, about 2,500 pounds, and other articles of French, English and German goods, not at all adapted to the market, situated as the people of Lima were, in the midst of war and threatened with famine.

The whole cost of the vessel and cargo, including the insurance out, was $30,726.

Mr. B.'s interest amounted to $5,000, my own was one fifth of the adventure, and the remainder belonged to Mr. H. I subsequently, before sailing, sold to my friend Richard M. Lawrence, Esq., of New-York, half of my interest in both vessel and cargo, leaving for my account only about $3,000. Beside this amount, I had, however, for my own private adventure about $1,500 in jewelry and silk stockings. These articles, though valuable, occupied but a very small space in the stowage of the vessel. I took with me Mr. B. as passenger, my cousin Mr. Freegift Coggeshall as chief mate, my brother Francis Coggeshall as second mate, and a crew of nine men and boys, including the cook and steward.

Thus loaded and manned, we sailed from New-York, on the 15th of November, 1821, for Lima. For the first and second days out we had fine weather and fair winds from the westward. On the third day, November 17th, we met with strong gales from the eastward and a high head sea running, so that we were compelled to lay to ten or twelve hours. Our decks were filled with water and the schooner began to leak, which was a bad sign at the commencement of a long voyage. The next day the wind shifted to the westward, when we again made sail and stood on our course to the eastward. We continued to have strong gales from the westward and very bad weather until the 4th of December, when we made the Island of St. Mary's, bearing E. S. E. five leagues distant. This is one of the Azores or Western Islands, and lies in lat. 36° 59' North, long. 25° 10' West.

We lost here two days, by reason of strong gales from the S. S. W., with a high head sea, and very squally weather. After getting into lat. 24° N., we took the regular trade winds, and generally had pleasant weather; but whenever we encountered a strong breeze, we found the schooner leaked considerably, and being deeply laden, she was extremely wet and uncomfortable.

On the night of the 17th of December, 1821, when in lat. 16°, long. about 25° W., we caught fifty-eight flying-fish on deck. The schooner was so deep and low in the water, that large numbers of these fish came on board. The next day, December 18th, a great number of flying-fish were washed on board, and others flew on board in such numbers, that we had, during these two days, enough to serve all hands in abundance. The schooner continued to leak more and more, and we now kept one pump employed almost constantly.

From this time to the 25th, nothing remarkable occurred. Christmas being an idle day, we killed the only remaining pig, all the others, eight in number, having been drowned by the salt water, which almost always flooded the decks when there was a high sea.

On the 27th, saw a sail, standing to the northward; and this day we crossed the equinoctial line, in long. 26° W.; light winds and variable, with dark, rainy weather; thermometer stood at 84° at two P.M. We continued to experience light winds and variable, with dark, rainy weather, for forty-eight hours, when we struck the S. E. trades in lat. 4° S. We had for many days fine breezes from the S. E., and very pleasant weather. I have almost always found this region of the South Atlantic—say from 5° to 20° S.

latitude—a delightful part of the ocean to navigate, the weather fine and mild, and the skies very beautiful, with a temperature generally not so hot as to be uncomfortable.

We sailed through these pleastant latitudes without any incident worth remarking until we reached lat. 22° 41' S., on the 6th of January, 1822, when we again had bad, rainy weather, with the wind from the westward. This continued for 24 hours, when we again had a return of the S. E. trades, and pleasant weather.

January 8th, lat. 24° 20' S.—Last night, the weather being very fine and clear, we saw for the first time what are called the Magellan clouds. They are three in number, and were not far above the horizon. They bore from us about S. S. E., and are evidently clusters of stars; two of them appeared white like the milky-way, the other was dark and indistinctly seen.

January 9th.—At 8 o'clock in the morning, the weather being hazy, with a light breeze from the S. E., the man on the lookout at the mast-head cried out "Land ho!" and told the officer of the deck that he saw something ahead that looked like a small island, and that there were thousands of birds on and around it. In a few minutes every eye was eagerly gazing at the supposed island.

I knew there was no land laid down on any of my charts near where we were, and therefore concluded that it must be the wreck of a ship. As the wind was very light we drew slowly up with the newly discovered object. It soon, however, became visible from the deck, when I took a spy-glass and examined it with close attention, but owing to the constant changes it assumed I was at loss to decide what it was, from its undulating appearance, alternately rising above the water and then again disappearing beneath, until within half a mile's distance, when all doubt was solved, and we found it to be an enormous dead whale floating on its back. It was very much swollen, and at times was apparently some six or eight feet above the water. There were innumerable flocks of wild fowl hovering over and alighting upon it. Many of them appeared to be devouring it, and making loud and wild screams, as if exulting over this grand but accidental feast.

In order to ascertain with more precision its length and size, I hove the schooner to, a short distance to windward, and went in my boat to examine it, which I did to my entire satisfaction.

When approaching near, it became so offensive that I was obliged to keep at a respectful distance to windward, and there watch the numerous flocks of sea-birds that were revelling upon it. In the midst of their din of discordant screams, it was strange to witness with what delight they tore off portions of the fish, and how at each moment their number seemed to augment.

After leaving this scene, I came to the conclusion that dead whales like this are one great cause of so many "dangers" and "small islands," being laid down on all the old charts, which dangers are found not to exist. Such objects as these were probably discovered in dark, windy weather, when it would have been dangerous to have approached near enough to the supposed islands to ascertain what they really were. Thus we have, even at the present time, laid down all over the Atlantic ocean, rocks, shoals, and dangers, the greater part of which do not in reality exist.

January 10th lat. 26° 10' S.—During the early part of the last two nights we have seen the four bright stars called the Southern Cross. They are very brilliant, and with a little help of the imagination form a pretty good representation of the Christian cross; and I have no doubt that many of the early Roman Catholic navigators believed they were placed in the heavens to substantiate the truth of the Christian religion.

January 15th.—This day, at noon, we fell in with and boarded the ship *Hannibal,* of Sag Harbor, seven months out on a whaling voyage. They informed me that they had on board 3000 barrels of oil.

At 9 o'clock, P.M., spoke the whaling ship *Fame,* of New London. We were now in lat. 37° 20' S., long. 49° W.

On the 17th Jan. we had clear, pleasant weather, with light and variable winds. At 10 o'clock A.M. our long., by a good lunar observation, was 50° 38' West, lat. at noon 41°1' South. At 6 o'clock of this day we fell in with the ships *Herald* and *Amazon.* They were cruising in company for whale, and both belonged to Fair Haven, Mass. The captain of the *Herald* came on board to ascertain his longitude; he said they had seen no land for the last two months, and had been too busy to pay much attention to the course or position of the ship; that he knew nothing of lunar observations, and had no chronometer; he was therefore desirous to ascertain the present position of his ship. I had an excellent chronometer on board, and, as the lunar observation taken that day agreed with the chronometer, I told him there was no doubt that I could give him the exact latitude and longitude. He said he had only been eight months at sea, and had then on board 1400 barrels of oil; that the *Amazon* had taken 1100 barrels, and that he should soon steer to the northward on his way home.

When the whale-boat belonging to the *Herald* was alongside the *Sea-Serpent,* the boat was higher than the deep-loaded pilot-boat. The captain of the *Herald* said to me:—"Well, captain, you say you are from New-York, bound for Lima, but seriously, are you going round Cape Horn in this little whistle-diver?" "I shall certainly try it, captain," said I, "and hope I shall succeed." "Well, then, captain," he replied, "but tell me, did you get your life insured before you left home?" "No," said I, "but I left my family in comfortable circumstances, so that if I should be taken away they will have enough to live upon; besides, I am a good schooner sailor, and am accustomed to these whistle-divers, as you call them."—"Well, captain," said the whaler, "I must say you have good courage, and I hope you may succeed; but for my part, I had rather kill a hundred whales than go round the Horn in this little craft." After this dialogue we parted with mutual good wishes for future prosperity and happiness, and each resumed our course upon the great trackless deep. The next day, Jan. 18th, we had strong breezes from the S. E., and though the winds were fresh and strong, and considerable sea, we were able to steer on our S. W. course under reefed sails.

I must not omit to mention the singular fact, of a flock of seabirds which followed my schooner for the last ten days, namely from lat. 26° S., and were now still hovering near the vessel, sometimes a little ahead, and then again about thirty or forty yards astern. They were generally a little astern and frequently alighted on the water, and appeared to watch every small particle of food or grease that was thrown overboard. They were fifteen in number, and about the size of a common tame pigeon. They are called by seamen, cape pigeons.

From this time to the 22nd of January, nothing remarkable occurred until on that day, when we met with a severe gale from the southward, attended with a high head sea, so that at midnight we were obliged to lay to under a close reefed foresail. We were now in lat. 46° 50' S., long. 58° 26' W. At noon I caught three large albatross, with a hook and line buoyed up by several corks and baited with fat pork. One of the largest measured across his wings, from tip to tip, eight feet four inches. They were covered with white feathers three or four inches thick. They appear to be thus kindly protected by Providence from the cold in these inclement latitudes. In low latitudes, where the weather is hot and sultry, the birds are thinly covered with feathers, which are mostly of high and brilliant colors. The fish also, in hot climates, partake of the same gay and bright colors; such for instance as the parrot fish, the red snapper, and many others. After passing these hot regions and approaching the latitude of 50°, and so on to the latitude of Cape Horn, the birds are generally all white and clothed with an immense mat of down and feathers. Among the fish, likewise, I saw no gay-colored ones, in these cold regions; on the contrary, I frequently saw large schools of porpoises pied, and sometimes quite white.

While sailing and travelling about the world, I have often been struck with the wisdom and goodness of God, not only to man but to all His creatures, in adapting their condition to the different climates of the earth. We find the colored man adapted to the sultry, burning climates, and the white man constituted to endure the cold. So it is with beasts, birds, and fish.

I first began to notice the kindness of Providence, when only a boy trading to the islands in the West Indies. I observed that the sheep we used to take there from Connecticut, though thickly covered with wool, would shortly lose their fleeces, and eventually become hairy like goats. On the other hand, the higher the latitude, and where the cold is most intense, the thicker and finer is the fur on the animals, for example, where the bear, seal, and musk ox are found.

As we increased our latitude, the weather became daily more and more rough and boisterous; we encountered storm after storm, and the weather was more cloudy, cold and disagreeable, which kept us reefing and changing almost hourly. On the 26th of January, at 5 A.M., daylight, we made the Falkland Islands, bearing from S. to S. E., distant five leagues; the winds being light and the weather moderate, we stood in shore. The wind being at this time at W. S. W., we were unable to fetch to westward of the islands, and therefore commenced beating up along-shore to weather the westernmost island. These islands appear of a moderate height, and generally rocky and barren. Lat. by obs. this day 51° 18' S., long. about 61° 6' W. We continued to beat to the westward all this day and the day following; standing off and on the land with open, cloudy weather, and moderate gales from the S. W. Saw a high rock appearing like a lofty sail; marked on the charts Eddystone Rock.

On Monday, January 28th, the land still in sight; at meridian the wind shifted to the N. W., which enabled us to weather the land, and thus we passed to the westward of this group of islands and steered on our course to the southward, and westward towards Cape Horn; lat. by obs. at noon 50° 58' S., long. 61° 50' W. In the afternoon of this day the weather became thick and rainy; passed several tide rips, and saw a number of penguin. The little flock of cape pigeons before alluded to still followed the schooner, our constant companions by day and by night, in sunshine and in tempest. The variation of the compass here is from one and three-quarters to two points easterly. The weather was now cold and disagreeable, temperature by Fahrenheit's therm. 50° above zero.

Tuesday, January 29th.—Light winds and variable. This day the weather appeared to change every hour or two; at times the sun would shine out, and then suddenly disappear and become obscured by a thick fog. This would continue but for a short time, when a strong breeze from the northward would blow all the fog away and the sky remain pretty clear for a few hours, then the sun would again break out and shine for an hour or two, and perhaps another hour would bring a flight of snow. Sometimes, even when the sun was shining, the decks would be covered for a few minutes with snow, which would soon melt away and be followed by a violent shower of rain and hail. In fine, I find it very difficult to describe the weather in this dreary region; though we were in the midst of summer, we had all the seasons of the year in the course of a day. These continual changes kept us constantly making and taking in sail throughout these twenty-four hours. Lat. by obs. 53° 1' S., long. 64° 0' W.

Jan. 30th.—These twenty-four hours commenced with a strong gale from the westward, with a high head sea running. At 1 P.M., hove to under a two-reefed foresail; dark, cloudy, cold weather, with violent squalls of hail and rain. At midnight the gale moderated, when we again made sail, the schooner laboring violently and making much water. Lat., by observation, 53° 30' S., long. 64° W.

Jan. 31st.—This day commenced with strong gales from the westward, with a high head sea running; weather dark and gloomy. The wind throughout these twenty-four hours continued to blow strong from the westward, and being directly ahead, we found it impossible to gain to the westward, and were glad to hold our own without losing ground. During the day we had much thunder and lightning. Lat., by observation, 54° 1' S., long. 64° 00' W.

Feb. 1st.—Last night the sky was clear for a little while in the zenith, when we saw the Magellan clouds nearly over our heads. This day we had a continuation of strong gales from the westward, and very bad, stormy weather; we, however, continued to ply to the windward under close-reefed sails, but having a strong westerly gale and a lee current against us, we made but little progress. At 6 A.M. made Staten Land; this land, like the Falklands, appeared cold and dreary, and only a fit habitation for seal and wild fowl, which are here very abundant. The sea in this vicinity also abounds in whales of monstrous bulk. At noon the body of Staten Land bore N. by W., twelve leagues distant. At meridian the sun shone out, when we found our latitude to be 55° 31' S., long. 64° 8' W.

Feb. 2nd.—This day, like the last, was dark and gloomy, with a continuation of westerly winds, but not so strong as to prevent our plying to windward, under close-reefed sails. The thermometer fell down to 45° above zero. In consequence of contrary winds and a lee current we gained but little on our course during these twenty-four hours. Lat., by observation, 56° 20' S., long. 65° 27' W.

Feb. 3rd.—On this day, when within about 50 miles of Cape Horn, a terrible gale commenced blowing from the westward. It continued to increase until it blew a perfect hurricane, and soon created a mountainous sea. We got our foreyard on deck, and hove the schooner to, under the head of a new foresail. I then ordered all the bulwarks and waist-boards to be knocked away, that nothing might impede the water from passing over the decks without obstruction, otherwise so great a quantity would have lodged in the lee-waist that our little schooner would have been water-logged and swamped with the weight of it. With crowbars and axes the waist-boards were all demolished, and the sea broke over the decks and passed off without injury to our little bark, and she rose like a stormy petrel on the top of the sea, which threatened every moment to swallow us in its abyss. The ocean was lashed into a white foam by the fury of the tempest. The same weather continued with but little intermission for a space of five days. During a great part of this time it was almost impossible to look to windward, so violent were the hail and snow squalls. In the midst of this tempest, my officers and men behaved nobly: the most perfect order prevailed; not a whisper of fear or contention was heard during the whole of our perilous situation. To render the men more comfortable, I removed them all from the forecastle to the cabin, where they continued to live until we had fairly doubled the Cape and found better weather.

My Italian passenger was terribly alarmed during the tempest, and entreated me, in piteous tones, to put away for Rio Janeiro. He said if I would do so, he would instantly sign an agreement to give me all his interest in the vessel and cargo. I resolutely declined his offer, and told him that while we had masts and sails, and the vessel would float under us, I would never put back.

This Cape is rendered more dreadful from the fact of its inhospitable position, and being so far removed from any civilized port. It is a cold, cheerless, barbarous coast, where no provision, or supplies of any kind, can be had in case of shipwreck or disaster, so that the greatest vigilance and perseverance are necessary to bear the many obstacles that present themselves.

Feb. 8th.—The gale abated, and we were again enabled to make sail and ply to the westward. Our faithful little pigeons had hovered about us during the long tempest, and now resumed the journey with us. We got an observation of the sun this day at noon, and found ourselves in lat. 57° 33' S., long. 66° 12' W.

Feb. 9th.—We had, throughout these twenty-four hours, favorable gales from the N. E., and open, cloudy weather. Made all sail and steered to the westward, and gained 160 miles distance on a direct course, and every thing began to wear a better appearance. We made better progress this day than we had done since our arrival in these high southern latitudes. Lat., by observation at noon, 57° 16' S., long., by chronometer 71° 4' W.

Feb. 10th.—This day commenced with strong gales from the southward, with dark, squally weather; under reefed sails, standing to the northward and westward; made a distance of 155 miles per log. Towards noon the sun shone out, when we found ourselves, at meridian, in lat. 55° 44' S., long. 74° 48' W. We had now fairly doubled Cape Horn; and I hoped in a few days to descend to lower latitudes, and find warmer and better weather. It was how fifteen days since we made the Falkland Islands, so that we were from thirteen to fifteen days weathering Cape Horn, which is not an unusual length of time, and had our vessel been a good ship of three or four hundred tons, we should have suffered nothing in comparison with what we did undergo, in a deep loaded, pilot-boat schooner, of one hundred and forty tons, leaking badly. From the 10th of February to the 16th, we generally had light and variable winds from the northward and westward, so that we made but slow progress during the week, and nothing worth recording occurred.

Feb. 17th.—This day commenced with light breezes from the S. W., and fine weather. During the night, in a squall, a small fish was washed on board. It weighed before it was dressed about half a pound, and in appearance was not unlike a brook trout, except that it had a greenish color. I directed the cook to prepare it for my breakfast, and told him to fry it with a few slices of salt pork. At breakfast, I divided the fish between my passenger, the chief mate and myself. We all ate the fish with a good relish, and returned on deck; but very soon after, we were all taken sick: the mate was seized with violent vomiting, and became death-like pale and languid.— The passenger was also sick, but not so much so as the mate. I was not very ill, but felt a burning sensation in my mouth and throat for several hours afterwards. Upon examining the scales and intestines of the fish, and the knife with which it was cleaned, we found them all of a deep greenish color, indicating that the fish must have been very poisonous. What it was I know not. It is remarkable that one of so small a size could poison three persons.

During the remainder of this day we had light breezes from the W. and fine weather. We only made about 100 miles on our course through these twenty-four hours; at noon our lat. by obs. was 47° 56' S., long. 78° 17' W.

From the 17th of February, to the 22nd of the same month, we had light winds from the southward and westward, and generally good weather; we steered to the northward. We were daily getting the weather more mild and pleasant, as we approached the lower latitudes. We met with nothing worth remarking during the last five days. We were now in lat. 38° 45' S., long. 79° 29' W.

Feb. 23rd.—We had fresh breezes from the S. W. and fine weather throughout these twenty-four hours, and made 166 miles distance to the northward. Lat. by obs. at noon 36° 0' S., long. per chron. 79° 34' West.

Feb. 24th.—This day commenced with fine fresh breezes from the southward, and very pleasant weather, which we sensibly enjoyed after getting through those tempestuous regions into the bright and gentle Pacific Ocean, which daily became more and more mild and tranquil. At 8 o'clock in the morning we made the island of Mas Afuera bearing N. N. W., about eight leagues distant. At 11 o'clock A.M. it bore west, three leagues distant. This island lies in lat. 33°45' S., long. 80° 38' W. It is a high, abrupt, rugged looking place about fifteen or twenty miles long and perhaps five or six broad. The shores are very steep, and I believe it is only accessible on the N. W. side in a little bay, where boats can land in good weather. It has no harbor, notwithstanding it was formerly a famous island for taking seal. Some twenty-five or thirty years ago, several good voyages were made by ships from New England, which took seal skins from this island to Canton in China, where they disposed of them, and returned to the United States, richly laden with teas and other China goods. One of these voyages was made by a ship called the *Neptune,* commanded by Captain Daniel T. Green (in which were two young men belonging to my native town, from whom I obtained this information). This ship was owned in New Haven, Connecticut, and took from this island fifty thousand seal skins and sold them in Canton for $2 each, and thence returned to New-York in the year 1799, with a cargo of teas silk goods, nankeens, &c. The owners and crew cleared by the voyage about $100,000.

This trade was carried on for several years very advantageously, until at length all the seal were killed or driven away from the island. The sealing ships were then compelled to search for a new field, in distant seas and on lonely desert islands, where the seal had never been disturbed by man. When they first commenced killing seal at Mas Afuero, the animals were so tame and gentle that thousands were killed with clubs. These poor animals, unconscious of the danger, made no attempt to escape; but in a few years after they became so knowing and shy, that it was difficult to kill them, except by stratagem. I have subsequently seen them in different places along the coast of Peru, and found them so extremely wild and timid that they would plunge into the water when approached, and at this time it is very difficult to kill them, even with spears and muskets.

This day we also saw and passed by Juan Fernandez. This island is not so high as Mas Afuero, but is more fertile and productive. It lies in latitude 33° 46′ S., longitude 79° 6′ W. It belongs to Chili, and is about 400 miles west of Valparaiso. It has a tolerable harbor on the south side, and has been used lately by the Chilian Government as a sort of Botany Bay for state prisoners. It has become a place of general interest to the world from its having been made the locality of Robinson Crusoe's adventures, by Defoe.

It was now one hundred days since we left New York, and we had still more than 1000 miles to sail before we could reach Lima, but as we expected to get into the S. E. trade winds in a day or two from this time, I anticipated the remainder of the passage with pleasure.

February 25th.—Throughout these twenty-four hours, we had fine breezes from the southward, and very pleasant weather. We were now sailing with a fair wind, with all our light sails set. Our little schooner was well adapted to these smooth seas and gentle breezes; we made 190 miles during the last twenty-four hours, and were at noon in latitude 30° 23′ S., longitude 80° 28′ W.

February 26th.—Fresh breezes from the S. E., and clear, pleasant weather throughout these twenty-four hours. We had now taken the regular S. E. trades. It was delightful to sail before the wind in this mild climate and smooth sea (which is so appropriately called the *Pacific* Ocean), after having been buffeted and tossed about off Cape Horn so long in so small a vessel. During the last twenty-four hours our little vessel made 200 miles with perfect ease, and almost without shifting a single sail. Lat. by obs. at noon 27° 4′ S., long. 80° 28′ W.

From the 26th of February to the 5th of March, we had a continuation of the S. E. trade winds, and fine pleasant weather, running constantly on our direct course, and daily making from 150 to 200 miles.

Our friendly birds, which had constantly followed us for the last fifty-six days, from the coast of Brazil and round Cape Horn, still kept about us. They were not so constantly near our vessel as before we came down into these mild latitudes, but they made little excursions and then returned. I sometimes missed them for an hour or two, and feared, in two or three instances, that they had entirely left us and would no more return to cheer us, but to my agreeable surprise they always came, and were at this time within a few yards of our stern, and appeared attached to our little bark and to the hands that occasionally fed them. They were indeed a great source of entertainment, and their fidelity was a constant theme of conversation and interest to us.

March 5th, 1822.—This day commenced with light winds from the S. E., and, as usual, fine, clear weather. At 4 o'clock in the afternoon we made the Island of Lorenzo, bearing about N. E., 25 miles distant. At 8 in the evening we got near the island. It being too late to run into port, I concluded to stand off and on under its lee, and wait until daylight to run in an anchor.

March 6th.—We came to anchor near the forts at Callao—the seaport of Lima—all well, after a passage of 110 days from New-York.

It was not until we came to anchor that our little guardian birds left us and flew out of the harbor.

We found Callao and Lima in the hands of the patriots (as the natives of the country were called), and that the Spanish army had retreated to the interior; of course, the blockade was raised, and the object of my voyage in a great measure defeated.

I have before stated, that we purchased this little, fast-sailing vessel, in order to evade the blockade by superior sailing, otherwise it would have been more advantageous to the owners to have bought a more burthensome vessel at a less cost, and far more comfortable for me to perform a voyage round Cape Horn in such an one, than it was in a small pilot-boat schooner.

After entering my vessel and going through the necessary forms at Callao, I forthwith proceeded up to Lima, and presented my letters of introduction to several gentlemen, who were merchants residing in that city, and was not long in making an arrangement with Don Francisco X. Iscue, a respectable merchant, to take charge of my business, and act as my general agent and consignee. Señor Iscue was a native of Old Spain, but was married to a lady born in Lima. He had an interesting family, and was an honest, worthy man, and a very correct merchant. Through this gentleman I disposed of most of that part of my cargo which was at all adapted to the market, such as provisions, and a part of my manufactured goods. All the butter sold at $1 per lb. Flour was at this time selling at $30 per barrel. Some articles of my cargo sold at an enormous profit, while many others would not bring prime cost.

Soon after my arrival at Callao, the ship *America,* Captain De Koven, of New-York, arrived with a full cargo of flour. I believe he brought about 3500 barrels, which were sold at a very great profit. To Capt. De Koven I sold my quicksilver at invoice price, which amounted to about $3500.

As all communication was cut off between Lima and the interior, I was unable to dispose of the quicksilver at any price, except to Capt. De Koven. He was bound to Canton, and took the article at invoice price to dispose of it in China. I subsequently lent him $11,500 in dollars (which, together with the quicksilver, amounted to $15,000), and took his bill on the owners of the *America,* in New York, for the amount at sixty days sight. The owners of the ship were Messrs. Hoyt and Tom, Elisha Tibbets, and Stephen Whitney.

I soon had all my cargo transported to Lima, and in about twenty days after my arrival sold the schooner *Sea-Serpent,* for ten thousand five hundred dollars. Such goods as I could not dispose of at private sale, I sold at public auction; and on the 6th of June, 1822, closed the accounts of the voyage, and I am sorry to add, made little or nothing for my owners. My own private adventure sold tolerably well; and what, with my wages, commissions, etc., I made for myself what is called a saving voyage.

I waited about a fortnight for a passage to Panama, but was unable to obtain one. On the 15th of June, I was offered the command of the fine Baltimore-built brig "*Dick*," burthen 207 tons, and only two years old. This vessel belonged to the Italian gentleman who came out as a passenger with me in the *Sea-Serpent.* He was desirous of employing the *Dick* in the coasting trade, on the western coast of Chili and Peru. I was also glad of employment for a few months, until the sickly season had passed away in Panama and Chagrés, (having decided to return to the United States by the way of Panama and across the Isthmus of Darien to Chagrés). The Italian was an honest man, but, not having been bred a merchant, relied on me to manage the voyage of his brig.

After I had disposed of the *Sea-Serpent,* I paid off the mates and seamen, and allowed each of them two months' extra pay, according to law, and then procured nearly all of them situations on board of other vessels. Both mates, when I left Callao, were pleasantly situated as officers, on board of English vessels, coasting between Chili and Peru; and the seamen got good berths and generous wages; so that none of my crew were left in distress, or unprovided with employment.

As Mr. B. the owner of the brig had decided to proceed with her down the coast of Peru, to Truxillo and Pagusmayo, and there purchase a cargo of sugar, rice, and such other articles of provision as were then much wanted in Lima, I lost no time in shipping officers and seamen, and getting ready for the voyage, which under ordinary circumstances would require about two months to perform. On the 28th of July we were ready for sea.

Callao is the seaport of Lima, and lies in lat. 12° 2' S., long. 77° 4' W., seven or eight miles west of Lima. Callao is strongly protected by forts, castles and walls, with broad and wide exterior ditches. To a stranger the castles at first view appear like a small walled city. Outside of these vast and expensive fortifications, there is a considerable number of houses, magazines and shops, generally lying along the bay, and in some places extending back, perhaps, a short quarter of a mile.

This village is called Callao, and the fortifications are called the Castles of Callao. The road between Lima and the port is level and good. The port of Callao is formed by a bay which is sheltered by its own points and the Island of St. Lorenzo, which lies at the south entrance, about eight or ten miles distant from the Castles at Callao. As I have no map or book before me, and write entirely from memory, I may perhaps make some little error in the distance, but not in the main facts. Callao Bay is a fine, broad, clear expanse of water, and deep enough for a line-of-battle ship in almost any part of it, and on the whole, I should pronounce it a very safe and good harbor, particularly in this mild and gentle climate, where there are no violent gales or tempests. In this respect the inhabitants of this coast are favored beyond any part of the world I have ever visited. The oldest men in this country know nothing of a storm or a violent gale of wind; so uniform is the weather, that the Fahr. thermometer in Lima rarely varies more than six or eight degrees. It generally ranges between 75° and 80°. Although it is sometimes hot at noonday, the nights are cool and comfortable, owing to the snow and ice in the mountains not very far distant in the interior. When Peru was a colony of Spain, Lima was a populous and comparatively rich city; but in consequence of continued wars and revolutions it has become poor. For the last eight years there had been a constant demand for young men to join the armies, which has rendered the population less than it was previously. The city of Lima, the capital of Peru, lies about seven miles from the sea, and is pleasantly situated at the foot of the

Cordilleras. The little river Rimac takes its rise in the mountains and runs through the city, and supplies the inhabitants with an abundance of excellent water. Over this stream there is a fine stone bridge with six arches. On this bridge and in recesses are placed seats for the citizens, which renders it a favorite resort for the *elite* of the city. It is said that before the revolution, Lima contained about eighty thousand inhabitants; at the time of which I write it numbers only about sixty thousand, exclusive of the military, who I should judge were about eight or ten thousand. There are several large churches and public buildings, which have rather an imposing appearance.

The Cathedral in the centre of the city, which forms the east side of the Plaza Maza, is the grand resort of all the better classes of people, and is a pleasant place. In consequence of the earthquakes to which Lima is subject, the houses are generally built low, not often more than one or two stories high, and of very slight materials, namely, dried clay and reeds, with a light coat of plaster, and then whitewashed or painted. I believe that if it should blow and rain a few hours as it does sometimes in the Bay of Honduras, that the whole city would be washed away; but fortunately for the inhabitants, it never rains in the city. The high and long chain of Cordilleras in the interior, acts as a perfect conductor for the clouds and storms. There only the clouds break and the rain falls in torrents. It therefore becomes necessary, notwithstanding the heavy dews, to irrigate the fields and gardens in the neighborhood of Lima.

I think the city is about two miles long, and one and a half broad. Through the principal streets water is conducted from the Rimac. This tends very much to cool and cleanse the town, which, if blessed with peace and a good government, would be a very delightful city, bating an occasional alarm of earthquakes.

A few weeks before my arrival, the Castles at Callao and the city of Lima, were vacated by the Spanish army and taken possession of by General San Martin and Lord Cochrane; the former at the head of 8,000 or 10,000 Chilian and Peruvian troops, and the latter, the Admiral, commanding the Chilian squadron of two or three frigates and several smaller vessels. I believe there was very little fighting but a kind of capitulation was agreed upon between the parties. The Spanish army marched out and retreated into the interior, when the patriot army took possession with little or no bloodshed. Still the inhabitants of Lima were, during the time I remained there, in constant dread of a return of the Spanish army. The city and its dependencies were daily agitated and unsettled, and the whole country was convulsed with war. The Government was almost daily making forced loans and contributions upon the inhabitants, which caused them to secrete their money for fear of its being taken from them. Every fine horse belonging to private individuals was seized for the use of the army; even the horses of foreigners were sometimes taken, but they were generally returned after a suitable remonstrance to the commanding officer.

This has been rather a long digression, and I will again return to my narrative.

The brig *Dick*, under my command, was ready for sea on the 28th of July. Before sailing, I wrote the particulars of the voyage to my owners, and also to my family up to this date, and the next day sailed for Truxillo, with the owner of the brig on board.

It was 6 o'clock in the evening when we got under way; we had light winds from the S. E., and foggy weather during the night, and ran to the leeward under easy sail until daylight.

July 30th.—During the first and middle part of these twenty-four hours we had a continuation of light winds and thick weather. After running about fifty-six miles log distance, it lighted up, when we found ourselves in mid channel between the Islands of Mazorque and Pelada, which are about two leagues asunder.

No observation of the sun, it being obscured by fog.

31st.—First and middle part of twenty-four hours light breezes from the S. E. with a continuation of cloudy weather. At 11 o'clock in the forenoon, we passed a schooner beating up the coast. We set our ensign, and indicated our wish to speak him, but the unsocial fellow would not shorten sail, and appeared to avoid us. At noon saw a ship running down to the westward. We continued to run along shore to the northward, and made about 100 miles by the log. At noon our lat. by obs. was 10° 29' S., long. about 77° 50' W.

Aug. 1st.—At 1 o'clock in the afternoon we saw the land, bearing E. S. E. eight or ten leagues distant. We had light breezes and calm weather all the twenty-four hours, and only made ninety-six miles, running down along the land, generally at a distance of ten leagues. Lat. by obs. at noon 9° 14' S.

Aug. 2nd.—First and middle part of these twenty-four hours, light airs from the S. E. and clear, pleasant weather. At 12, midnight, hove to and lay by until 3 A.M., daylight, when we made sail. At 5 in the morning, saw the island of Guanap, bearing S. E. about four miles distant. We then hauled in shore. Brisk breezes at S. E. and fine, clear, pleasant weather. At 10 o'clock in the forenoon, the city of Truxillo bore east, and in half an hour afterwards we came to anchor at Guanchaco, in seven fathoms water; the church at that place bearing E. by N. about a league distant. This is an Indian village situated on the beach of the sea, and is the seaport of Truxillo. It lies in lat. 8° 8' S., and long. about 79° 0' west of London.

I should perhaps rather have called Guanchaco the roadstead or anchoring ground of Truxillo, for it certainly cannot properly be called a harbor. It is open to the broad ocean, and has nothing to shelter ships that touch or trade on this part of the coast. The Indians who live in the village of Guanchaco are expert boatmen, and with their own boats transport all the goods and merchandise landed at that port for Truxillo, or exported therefrom. They are perhaps 500 to 800 in number, are governed by their own alcalde and under officers, and live almost entirely by boating and fishing. The ships that touch here cannot with any safety use their own boats, and always employ the boats or canoes of the Indians, the surf being too high to venture off and on without the aid of these men, who are almost amphibious. They are trained to swimming from their infancy, and commence with a small "Balsa," in the surf within the reefs, and by degrees, as they grow older and larger, venture through the surf, and out upon the broad ocean. These "Balsas," are made of reeds bound firmly together, with a hole near the after end, for one person; the forward end is tapered, and turned up like a skate or a Turkish shoe. Those for children are perhaps from five to eight feet long, and those used by the men are generally about ten or twelve feet long, and about as large in circumference as a small sized barrel. An Indian placed in one of these Balsas with a paddle bids defiance to the roaring billows and breaking surf. I have seen the men go off through it in one of these reedy boats, when it seemed impossible that a human being could live in the surf, and have with, great anxiety observed them at times when a high rolling sea threatened to overwhelm them, watch the approaching roller and duck their heads down close to the reed boat, and let the billow pass over them, like a seal or a wild duck, and force their way with perfect confidence through the surf, where no white man would for a moment dare to venture. One of these men would, for half a dollar, convey a letter from the shore through the surf, to a ship laying at anchor in the Roads, when no boat dare attempt it. I was told that for a small sum of money, one of these Indians would take a valuable piece of silk goods (secured in oiled cloth and fastened round his body) on shore, and deliver it to the owner perfectly dry, even in a dark night. The moment they land they take up the Balsa and place it in an upright position in the sun to drain and dry, and thus it is kept ready at a moment's warning for any employment that may offer.

While here, I used sometimes to amuse myself with throwing small pieces of copper coin into the water, to see the Indian boys dive to the bottom and pick them up. I never could learn that any of these Indians were drowned, though the people of Truxillo told us of many accidents, when white men were drowned, in attempting to land in a high surf.

The morning we arrived at Guanchaco, there came in also an English ship from Lima, and anchored near our brig.—Very soon after, a large launch, manned with nine Indians, came alongside of us, to take the captains, supercargoes, and passengers of both vessels on shore. As there was considerable surf on, great anxiety was expressed by the supercargoes and passengers, respecting the safety of landing. I had a conversation with the patroon of the boat, on the subject of landing. He said that if we would commit ourselves entirely into his hands, there was no danger; and that he supposed the gentlemen would be willing to pay half a dollar each, if landed dry and in perfect safety. This we all readily agreed to, and soon started for the shore. I think we were five in number; and as we approached the shore, a few yards outside the surf, the sea was terrific, and breaking "feather white." Some of the gentlemen were in favor of returning, but were soon overruled by the majority. I attentively watched the eye of the patroon, who appeared cool and collected, and, by his manner, inspired me with confidence in his ability to perform what he had undertaken. He requested the gentlemen who feared the result, not to survey the scene, but to lie down in the stern-sheets of the boat, and thus give him room to manage the boat according to his own judgment. At this moment, I saw a man on the beach, on the watch for a favorable instant for us to pull for the shore. The man on the shore and our patroon made signals with a handkerchief on a cane. The boat's head was kept off shore until the signal was given and answered, to dash through the surf. In an instant the boat was wheeled round with her head towards the land, when every man pulled to the utmost of his strength, and in a few minutes we were safe within the breakers. These strong, brave fellows, then took each a passenger on his back, and carried him ashore in great triumph. We were all so sensibly touched with the conduct of these men, that many dollars were voluntarily thrown into their hats and caps; and a thrill of gratitude passed over my mind, that will remain with me till the hour of my death. We call these people savages, and say that they are incapable of great actions. I defy the white man to contend with them in the management of a boat in the surf, on the sea-shore.

The alcalde furnished us with horses, and we were soon on the road to the city of Truxillo, which is pleasantly situated on level ground, about eight or ten miles from the landing at Guanchaco. I think it contained, at this time, about eight or ten thousand inhabitants. There are two or three considerable churches; many of the houses are well built, and have a comfortable appearance. The ground and gardens around the city are well cultivated, and produce abundance of excellent fruit; and the whole aspect of the town and its vicinity is extremely pleasant. Although this place is located so near the equator, the climate is not uncomfortably warm. There is, however, a great drawback to a residence in this place, in the frequency of earthquakes. I was told by some of the most respectable citizens of Truxillo, that the town had been two or three times nearly destroyed by earthquakes, and that the great earthquakes were generally periodical,—say at intervals of forty years—that some thirty years had now passed away without a very destructive one, and that they had serious fears that they should experience another terrible convulsion before many years should elapse.

We found here no sugars or other produce to purchase, nor could we hear of any of consequence in the neighboring towns to leeward. Two vessels from Lima had lately been here, and to the adjacent towns, and bought up all the inhabitants had to dispose of.

After remaining here a few days, my owner and myself returned to Guanchaco, without making any purchases, except some poultry and fruit for sea-stores.

On our way back to the landing, we passed over very extensive ruins, which appeared at least two miles in length: they were the remains of clay walls, and various fragments of what had once been an extensive city of the Incas. We saw also a large mound near Guanchaco. It was 50 to 80 feet high, and, perhaps, from 150 to 200 feet long. These mounds were no doubt made by the ancient Peruvians, and are found all along this coast. Some of them are very high and large, others quite small. I have seen a great variety of Indian relics, that were dug out from this mound, such as earthen drinking vessels, made to resemble cats, dogs, monkeys, and other animals; others, again, were made exactly to resemble a fish, with a handle on its back, and its mouth open to drink from. These articles were well executed, and of very fine clay. The present race of Peruvians are altogether incapable of manufacturing any thing of the kind equal to these ancient Indian relics. I have no doubt, if these mounds were fairly excavated, that a great variety of valuable Indian relics could be found, which are now hidden from the world.

We arrived at the landing on Thursday, August 8th, in the afternoon, and found too much surf on the beach to attempt going on board until the next morning, and as there was no hotel or tavern in Guanchaco, we took up our abode for the night with the alcalde or chief magistrate of the village. This person was an intelligent Indian, who had in his early life made several voyages to Manilla, and appeared familiar with all parts of the western coast of Peru. He seemed to be a sensible, judicious person, and managed and governed the people of Guanchaco in a quiet, paternal manner. During the evening he entertained us with a narration of his voyages from Peru to the Philippine Islands, when Peru was a colony of Spain. He also related to us many anecdotes of his race, the ancient and rightful owners of this bloodstained soil.

The high mounds all along this part of the coast appear to be monuments of their wrongs and sufferings, and call to mind the days when Pizarro, with his band of merciless adventurers, sacrificed thousands and tens of thousands of these innocent worshippers of the sun, robbed them of their gold, and finally despoiled them of home and country. Even to the present day, these poor people are not exempt from severe persecutions in the way of taxation and oppression. They are now forcibly taken from their quiet homes to fill the ranks led by military chiefs, and thus compelled to mingle in the deadly strife of contending parties. Whether the one or the other governs, it is to them only a change of masters, for they cannot be supposed to feel any interest for, or sympathy with, either of them. And thus it has ever been in this wicked and unjust world, the strong triumph over and oppress the weak.

The good alcalde had supper prepared for us, and placed mattresses and blankets on the tables for Mr. B. and myself. Previous to retiring to rest I took a stroll round the house, and saw, beneath a shed or back piazza, three of the alcalde's children, little boys, I should judge between ten years old and three, lying asleep on a raw dry bullock's hide, covered only with another. The air was chilly, and it struck me at the moment as inhuman treatment to expose children thus to the open air without other covering than a raw hide. I immediately inquired of our friendly host why he thus exposed his children. His answer was, that it was their general custom to harden them and give them good constitutions; that he himself was brought up in the same manner; and being thus inured to the cold while young, they felt no inconvenience from it in after life.

In the morning the sea was smooth, and the surf not bad. After taking leave of the polite and friendly alcalde, we left Guanchaco in the Indian launch, got safe on board, and at 3 o'clock on the 9th of August, weighed anchor and made sail for Payta.

After getting our anchor on board, we found the stock broken in two pieces, and thus rendered unfit for use. We steered to the westward along shore with a good S. E. trade wind, and pleasant weather. Through the night we had moderate breezes and a continuation of fine weather. At 5 o'clock in the morning, daylight, saw the Islands of Lobos de Mer and Lobos de Terra, bearing S. W., three leagues distant. They are of moderate height, and without trees or cultivation. Towards noon the winds became light, inclining to a calm. Lat. by obs. 6° 32' S., long. about 81° W.

On the 10th of August, we had light winds and fine weather, and made but little progress on our course during the day, still steering down along shore with the land in sight.

Aug. 11th.—This day, like the last, commenced with light airs and calm, warm weather. At 8 P.M., Point de Ajuga bore E., two leagues distant. During the night, light airs and fine weather. At daylight, saw Point de Payta, bearing N. E., eight leagues distant; at 8, got near the Point, and steered up the Bay of Payta. At 11, a breeze sprung up from the S. E., when we ran up the bay and came to anchor at noon, in nine fathoms water, directly opposite the town. We had little or no cargo to dispose of, and there was no freight to be obtained, consequently we remained here only twenty-four hours, and got ready for sea.

Payta is situated on a fine bay of the same name, and is the principal seaport of Puira, a very considerable town in the interior, some ten or fifteen leagues distant from this place.

The town of Payta is located very near the beach, and the whole surrounding country for some miles distant is a barren, sandy desert, not even affording fresh water. The inhabitants are supplied with this article, brought from a little river running into the head of the bay, at a distance of six or eight miles. The town probably contains about 1,500 to 2,000 inhabitants of all colors; a great portion, however, are Indians, and a mixture of the Spanish and Indian races.

The houses are generally built of cane and straw, with thatched roofs. It is a very healthy place, and the people, who are generally poor, live to a great age. It lies in lat. 5° 3' S., long. 81° W. of London, and is one of the best harbors on the western coast of Peru. It is a great resort for American and English whale ships. The bay of Payta is large and clean, and I believe the whalers send their boats to the little river at its head, and soon get a bountiful supply of pure, wholesome water; at the same time the ships are safe and quiet while they remain in this capacious bay.

At 2 o'clock in the afternoon of the 12th, with a fine fresh S. E. trade wind, we sailed out of this bay, bound for Guayaquil. At 6 P.M., got abreast of Point de Parina, about a league off shore; at the same time saw Cape Blanco bearing N., half E., twenty-four miles distant. During the night we had fresh breezes, with a little rain. At 6 A.M. saw the land, bearing from S. W. to N. E., five or six leagues distant. Lat. by obs. at noon, 3° 37' S. At this time Point Los Picos bore S. E., distant about four leagues.

Aug. 13th.—This day commenced with light airs from the S., with very warm weather. At 4 P.M., passed near the American whale-ship *Rosalie*, of Warren, R.I., which was lying at anchor, near Tumbes. This ship had been thirteen months absent from the United States, and had only taken 200 barrels of oil.

At 8 P.M., we came to anchor in five fathoms' water, near the mouth of the Tumbes river, the small Island of Santa Clara bearing N. by W., distant about four leagues. Light wind at N. E. Here we lay at anchor all night.

Aug. 14th.—This day commenced with light breezes from the N. E., and fine weather. At 8 A.M., got under way with a light wind from the N. W. by N. The tide now commenced making up the river, which enabled us to gain ground, beating up with its assistance until noon, when the wind became more favorable, from the W. S. W. At 3 P.M., got abreast of the west end of the Island of Puna; pleasant breezes and fine weather.

At 7 P.M., we came to anchor in four and a half fathoms of water, the east end of Puna then bearing N. N. W., four leagues distant. It being dark, and having no pilot on board, I judged it imprudent to make sail, and therefore remained at anchor during the night.

Aug. 15th.—This day commenced with clear, pleasant weather, with light winds and variable. At 6 A.M., received a pilot on board, and at 8 got under way with the flood tide and stood up the river, which had now become more narrow, but was still deep and not difficult to ascend. The banks along the river on both sides are low, but the land rises as you recede from the river into the interior to immense mountains, many of which are volcanic. We continued to beat up the stream, and at 6 P.M., just before dark, came to anchor in the river opposite the city of Guayaquil in six fathoms of water, a short quarter of a mile off the town.

It is about forty miles from Guayaquil to the Island of Puna, where the river pilots reside, and it is at this place that the river fairly commences;

for below Puna, it may more properly be called a wide bay or gulf opening into the sea.

We found lying at Guayaquil some fifteen or twenty sail of vessels of different nations, four or five of which were American ships and brigs, among them the ship *Canton,* of New-York, and the brig *Canton,* of Boston. The names of the others I do not now recollect.

After lying here a few days, undecided what to do with, or how to employ, the brig, my owner, on the 22d of August, sold his vessel for $14,000 to John O'Sullivan, Esq., captain and supercargo of the ship *Canton.* Captain O'Sullivan gave the command of the brig to Lieutenant Hudson, now Captain Hudson, of the U.S. Navy.

He loaded her in this port for a voyage to Upper Peru. At this time there were lying at Guayaquil two large Calcutta ships loaded with Indian goods. From these ships Captain O'Sullivan, purchased the greater part of a cargo for the *Dick.* The balance was made up of cocoa, and a few other articles. Myself, officers and crew were now paid off, and left the vessel in charge of the new owners.

I was anxious to return home to New-York, and of course did not regret being sold out of employment. I had long been acquainted with Capt. O'Sullivan, and was glad to meet him here. I also met with another acquaintance in the person of Francis Coffin, Esq., supercargo of the brig *Canton.*

Mr. Coffin got a fine freight of cocoa for Cadiz. I think it amounted to $17,500. I was glad to have good fortune attend him, as he was and is, if alive, an honorable gentlemanly man, of sterling worth and high integrity.

I was now living on shore, anxiously waiting a passage for Panama, to return home across the Isthmus. Capt. O'Sullivan had with him three or four young gentlemen, belonging to New-York. These young men joined the ship *Canton,* in New-York, as ordinary seamen, but not liking a sea-life were anxious to return home. Capt. O'Sullivan gave two of them liberty to leave the ship, but would not supply them with money. He told me, however, that if I thought proper to take them along with me, that he had no doubt their friends in New-York would refund the money I should expend in paying their passages back to the U.S.; and as they were here destitute, I consented to take them, pay their passages and other necessary expenses to New-York, and rely upon the honor of their families to refund me the amount when we should arrive there.

After waiting a few days, we heard of a small coasting vessel which was to leave this place for Panama in a few days. She was a full-rigged brig, of about twenty-five tons burthen, with a captain, boatswain, and eight men before the mast. A vessel of the same size in the U.S. would have been sloop-rigged, and provided with a captain, one man, and a boy. In this vessel I agreed for a passage to Panama for myself and my two young American friends. This brig was called "*Los dos Hermanos.*" There were two other (Guayaquil gentlemen) passengers, besides myself and the before-named young men, who agreed to sleep on deck; as I paid one hundred dollars for my passage, I was supplied with a berth in the cabin, if it deserved the name, for in fact it was more like a dog's kennel than a cabin. It had no windows or sky-light, and was nearly filled with bags and boxes, and had only two berths, and no table. The two passengers belonging to Guayaquil, occupied one of the berths, and I the other.

Guayaquil lies in lat. 2° 12' S., long. 79° 42' W., and is about 150 miles to the southward of Quito. The city of Guayaquil lies on the right bank of the river, and contains about 20,000 inhabitants, and although built of wood, a great portion of the houses are large and comfortable, and well adapted to the climate. Several of the public buildings are spacious and firmly built with tiled roofs, among which are the customhouse, college, and hospital. The city is located on low, level ground, and of course difficult to drain, which at certain seasons of the year renders it very unhealthy. The educated classes of society are polite and hospitable. The ladies dress in good taste, and are decidedly the handsomest women on the western coast of this continent; in fact, the beauty of the Guayaquil ladies is proverbial. The lower classes are a desperate looking race. They are a mixture of the Spaniard, Indian, and Negro, and appear ripe for any kind of villainy or disorder.

The principal wealth of Guayaquil proceeds from the cultivation of cocoa, which is their staple article. They also export timber, boards, hides, and some tobacco. The cocoa plantations lie on both sides of the river for several miles above the city. It is brought to Guayaquil upon floating rafts of light buoyant wood called, in this country, Balzas. These rafts are in general use for all kinds of transportation. Many of the poorer classes live upon them. They float up and down the river with perfect ease and safety. In them the cocoa is taken on board of the ships that load here. On these Balzas they erect tents and awnings, and thus protect themselves and their cargoes from the sun and rain. Along the river and thence down to the seacoast, the land is very flat, and in the rainy seasons a great portion of the low grounds are inundated; consequently the inhabitants in such places build their houses on large timbers, or posts, some eight or ten feet above the ground, and find it necessary to have ladders to get into them. When flooded in the rainy seasons, they pass from house to house in boats.

In this warm latitude, where the sun is nearly vertical, the weather is generally very hot, and the vegetation extremely luxuriant and rank; consequently none but those born and reared in this climate can reside in these low lands on the banks of the rivers and creeks, with any degree of safety.

To the eastward, some ten or fifteen leagues in the interior, I beheld lofty mountains rising one above another, until at last the eye rested on the majestic Chimborazo. There it stands, a mountain on the top of other mountains, terminating in a lofty sugar-loaf, snowcapped peak, alone, in its own grand and unrivalled sublimity; and although some seventy-five or eighty miles from Guayaquil, it appears as though it were within a very short distance. This grand sight, however, is not an every-day occurrence. On the contrary, one may remain at Guayaquil for several days, and even weeks, without getting a good view of the peak. When the clouds are dispelled, you behold the whole mountain from the base to the top in all its beauty and grandeur. The sight of this sublime object richly rewards the traveller for the expense and privation of coming to this country.

While I remained here the weather was extremely warm, and one can easily imagine that to be supplied with ice and ice-cream must have been a most acceptable luxury, and so we found it. As often as once or twice a week I saw a flag hoisted at a favorite cafe as a signal for ice and ice-cream for sale, announcing at the same time that some one had arrived from the mountains in the interior with a supply of this article, which was soon converted into excellent cream.

Guayaquil is supplied with great quantities of excellent fruit, common to tropical regions. Pine-apples are very abundant and cheap, as are oranges, bananas and plantains. Water and musk melons are also cheap and plenty. The beef and mutton, as in most other hot climates, is indifferent, and the beef appears even worse than it otherwise would do, in consequence of the slovenly manner of cutting it up. They do not dress it as in other countries, but tear and cut the flesh from off the bone of the animal in strings, and sell it by the yard or "vara." As this is the first and only place in which I ever bought beef by the yard, I thought it worthy of notice in my narrative.

About noon, on the *31st of August,* the captain of the brig *"Los dos Hermanos"* sent me word that he was ready for sea, and wished all his passengers to repair on board forthwith. Not having much baggage to look after, I took leave of the few friends I had in Guayaquil, and hurried on board. On our way to the brig, we passed through the market and purchased a large quantity of fruit for sea-stores. Among other things, I purchased some twenty or thirty large water-melons, which I found preferable to every kind of fruit. I never shall forget how gratefully refreshing we found them on a hot, calm morning, under a vertical sun, with the ther. at 85° above zero.

We did not leave the town until 3 o'clock in the afternoon; and, as the wind was light and variable, we drifted slowly down the river with the ebb tide, until about 10 o'clock, when it became quite dark, and we anchored for the night. Here again I was pleased with what to me was a novel occurrence. Far away to the eastward, in the interior, I saw a great light and innumerable sparks of fire, which illuminated the sky, so as to render the scene vivid and beautiful. Upon inquiry, I found it was a burning volcano, at a great distance in the interior. It appeared to be some thirty or forty miles distant, while it was, in fact, perhaps fifty leagues off.

The next morning, at daylight, September 1st, we got under way, and made a short cut to the sea, through a passage to the northward of the island of Puna. Our brig drew very little water, and we were therefore able to pass through small rivers and creeks where larger vessels dare not venture.

I soon discovered that our captain was a vain, ignorant, superstitious man, and knew nothing of navigation. He had neither chart nor quadrant on board. Fortunately for us, however, our contramaéstre, or boatswain, was a good seaman and an excellent pilot. He was a native of Old Spain, and although deficient in education, was a discreet, respectable man. He disciplined and managed the crew, and left little or nothing for the captain to do, but eat, drink, smoke, and sleep. The man was only an apology for a captain, and was in the habit of following the land along shore on his voyages between Guayaquil and Panama; whereby, in lieu of making a straight course, he prolonged his passage to double the number of days necessary. I had with me a quadrant and many charts of the western coast, from Guayaquil to Panama, on a large scale, and politely pointed out to him the true and straight course. I say politely, for I have ever found, that with the ignorant and superstitious of all nations, the greatest possible caution and delicacy must be observed when advising them, otherwise their self-love and jealousy take fire, and they become your enemies.

This vulgar captain at first inclined to adhere to his own opinion,—said he had navigated this part of the coast for many years, and always with success, and was afraid of sudden changes. His countrymen, the two passengers, however, fell in with me and persuaded him to follow my advice, and endeavor to shorten the distance of the passage. The two passengers alluded to were merchants, or shopkeepers, who visited Panama occasionally to purchase and sell goods, and on their way up and down, used to touch at a small place called Monte Christi, to trade, and to this place we were now bound on our way to Panama.

There were five passengers,—making, with officers and crew, a total of fifteen souls on board the "*Dos Hermanos*"—all of whom lived on deck, night and day, except the two Guayaquil traders and myself. The contramaéstre had the entire management of the vessel, and appeared to be always on the watch, both by night and day. The sailors were not divided into watches, as is the custom on board of vessels of other nations, but all slept in the long-boat on deck, on a dry ox hide, with another spread over them. Whenever it was necessary to make or take in sail, they were all called; and when the work was done all lay down to sleep again. They appeared to work with alacrity, and were always ready to obey the boatswain without grumbling. We had been out but a few days before we encountered much hot, rainy weather. At these times our situation, in the little hole of a cabin, was deplorable. When it rained violently, a large tarpaulin was spread over the companion-way to keep the cabin dry.—On such occasions, particularly in the night, the captain and the deck passengers would crawl in for shelter, and I was often obliged to leave my berth, and struggle through the crowd to get a little air at the door to prevent suffocation.

We were provided with only two meals a day; the first, called breakfast, about 11 o'clock in the forenoon, was taken always on deck. This meal was either a fricassee or puchero, with bread and a little common, low Catalonia wine. The other meal we generally had at four or five o'clock in the afternoon, and it was composed of about the same in quality, served up in one large dish placed in the centre of the quarter-deck. Our polite captain always helped himself first, and then advised every body to do the like. The food of the sailors on the main-deck consisted of plantain and charque or dried beef. Thus situated, we passed some days, creeping along at a slow pace, and making but little progress on our course, with variable winds, and very hot, calm weather.

On Sunday morning, Sept. 5th, at daylight in the morning, we ran into the little bay of Monte Christi, and came to anchor very near the shore, in three fathoms of water.

This is a clean little bay, with a fine sand beach, and a few small houses, called ranchos and shops, at the landing. The town of Monte Christi is located three or four miles inland from the port, in an easterly direction. This lonely little harbor lies in lat. 1° 1' S., long. 80° 32' W. of London. It was quite destitute of shipping, there being no vessel there except our little brig. We procured horses from the rancheros at the landing, and soon galloped over a pleasant road, to the town. It being Sunday morning, the whole town, or as the French say, "tout le monde," were decked out in their holiday dresses. Our captain and the two Guayaquil traders had planned a great deal of business for the day, and were very impatient to attend mass, that they might proceed to its execution afterwards. Accordingly, we left our horses at a poor little posada, and then hurried to the church. I went with them near the door, and after having excused myself for leaving them, took a stroll about the town. Every body appeared to be on the move towards the church, arrayed in gaudy dresses, of bright red and yellow colors. These simple people seemed as fond of displaying their gay attire as children decked out in their holiday suits.

After a little survey of the town, I entered a house for some water, when the following dialogue occurred between the master of the house and myself. After presenting me with a chair and giving me a welcome reception, he said, "I suppose you landed this morning from the brigantine, on your way to Panama?" "Yes, I did so," I replied. "The captain and the passengers have all gone to mass, how is it that you did not go also—are you not a Christian?" I answered I was, but having a very imperfect knowledge of the Spanish language, I preferred walking about the town. I then took the same liberty with him, and inquired why he did not go. He replied that he attended early mass, and was always very attentive to his religious duties. He then questioned me on the religious faith and belief of my countrymen in England. I told him I was not from that country, but from North America. He then called me an Anglo-Americano, and seemed to have a confused idea that we were the descendants of the English, and lived in a distant region of which very little was known, and inquired whether our belief and faith was the same as that of the English; that he had always been told that the English were all heretics and unbelievers. I told him that the religion of the two countries was about the same, that neither of them were heretics or unbelievers. He expressed great surprise and then asked me if we believed in "el Padre et Hijo y el Espiritu Santo." On my answering him in the affirmative, he appeared still more astonished, and said, then he had always been greatly deceived, that he had from his childhood been told by the priests and friars that the English were all infidels, and did not believe in the Trinity, nor yet in the "Holy Mother of God, the pure and holy Virgin Mary." I then told him there was certainly a great difference between the belief of his countrymen and mine, on the subject of worship due to the Virgin Mary, and holy reverence to a great many saints, but that the greater part of the churches, both in England and North America, professed to believe in the Trinity. He appeared very well satisfied with my explanation,—and said he had no doubt we had been misrepresented and slandered; and that he would inquire further into the subject from the first intelligent Englishman he should meet.

While I am on this subject, I will relate an anecdote that occurred one evening at the lodging of Captain O'Sullivan, while I was at Guayaquil. Among other questions, the mistress of the house, a middle-aged, good looking lady, asked me whether there were any Jews in my country. I told her there were many. She then asked me what they looked like, and whether they had tails. I was for a moment surprised, and thought she was jesting, and hardly knew how to answer,—when she observed, that she had always been told that Jews were strange-looking creatures, and had long tails like cows hanging down behind them. She said she came to Guayaquil about two years before, from a village in the interior of Colombia; and that from her infancy she had been always told by the priests, that Jews had tails, and were odious, frightful-looking creatures. I was astonished at her simple ignorance, for she was not one of the lower order, but a woman of polite manners, and spoke the Spanish language with ease and grace.

I have related these two incidents from a thousand other similar ones, that have come under my observation while travelling about South America, not with a view of exposing the ignorance of these honest, simple-hearted people, as objects of ridicule, but to hold up to the world the wickedness of these vile priests and friars, who delude and darken the minds of unfortunate beings, who are the subjects of their cunning priestcraft. In the United States we abhor the military despot who enslaves and chains the body; but is not the man who darkens and enslaves the mind, ten times more guilty than the military despot? I can overlook with some degree of patience a great many defaults and superstitious prejudices in the uneducated and ignorant, but have very little patience or charity for these vile leaders of the blind, who know better than to prey upon the ignorance and credulity of their fellow-men, either in matters of church or state. The wicked policy of keeping mankind in ignorance, in order to profit by their want of knowledge, cannot but excite the indignation of him who loves his fellow-man.

Monte Christi is situated on an undulating surface, moderately high, with one considerable church located on rising ground, in the centre of the town, which probably contains about 1500 inhabitants. The houses are generally one story high, and are built of sun-dried brick; some, however, are two stories, and have tile roofs.

The weather here is so hot that the inhabitants keep within doors during the middle of the day. In the evening it becomes cool and pleasant. This town and its vicinity, like most other places near the equator, are subject to periodical wet and dry seasons. During the heavy rains, many of the people remove to the hills, taking their cattle and other domestic animals along with them; and at the commencement of the dry season, return to their former habitations. I understood that the dry seasons last from December to April, and the wet during the rest of the year.

My stay here was so short that I could collect little reliable information on the subject of the general state of this country. I found the people generally a mixed breed of Spaniard, Indian, and Mulatto.

Our captain and the two Guayaquil traders, after mass on the day of our arrival here, arranged their commercial affairs with the principal shop-keepers of the town, and when we had partaken of a tolerable dinner at the little posada, we all mounted our horses about 4 o'clock in the afternoon, and returned again to the port. Here we landed several bags of cocoa, and a quantity of boxes of merchandise; and took on board some dry hides, and eight or ten bags of dollars; and after renewing our sea-stores of plantain and live-stock, got under way just before dark, and steered out of the bay on our course for Panama.

I learned from the two Guayaquil traders, that they were in the habit of leaving goods with the shop-keepers at Monte Christi, to dispose of for their account, and always stopped on their way up and down from Panama to Guayaquil, to receive the amount of what they had sold, either in money or in the produce of the country. I was surprised at the amount of the cargo and money transported in this trifling little craft. I think one of these gentlemen told me there was about $30,000 on board of our little brig, besides other valuable articles, which we were now taking to Panama, with which to pay debts and purchase merchandise for Guayaquil and the western coast of Colombia.

I am thus minute on the subject of this small trading vessel, to show that although a craft of this description would not be considered capable or safe to make a sea voyage along the coast of the States, here the mild winds and smooth seas do not endanger almost any kind of vessel that will float, whilst trading along the coast between Guayaquil and Panama.

During the night there was a pleasant little breeze from off the land, and the next day, we had light and variable winds, with fine weather. At noon, I amused myself, while sailing along shore, by taking a meridian observation; and it so happened that the sun at noon was vertical, or directly over head, and I could therefore sweep his image with the quadrant all round the horizon, and fully realize that we were on the equator, and consequently in no latitude. Our longitude at this time was about 80° 00' W. from London.

We continued to have light and variable winds, with occasional showers, for several days after crossing the equator. The weather during the daytime was generally very warm, and we had little or nothing to screen us from the rays of the sun, in this small and very uncomfortable vessel. Our captain, as I have before said, was an ignorant, ill-bred man, and took no pains to secure the comfort or convenience of his passengers;— these evils rendered the time extremely tedious. We had, however, got about three degrees to the northward of the line, and were now making a pretty straight course for Panama. By the persuasion of the passengers and myself, our captain consented to steer boldly on our course to the northward, and not to follow the land along the whole length of Chuco bay, as he was inclined to do. He had neither chart nor quadrant on board,—and upon reflection, I was not surprised that he should not venture far out of sight of terra firma. The contramaéstre was a good seaman and an excellent fellow; and frankly acknowledged that he knew nothing of navigation, though he was well acquainted with the land, and could navigate up and down the coast almost by instinct. As we increased our latitude to the northward, the winds gradually freshened, and we got on without any material accident.

On the morning of the 16th of Sept., 1822, we made Point St. Francisco Solano, and the land to the eastward of the entrance of the bay of Panama. Point St. Francisco Solano is a prominent headland, and lies in lat. 6° 49' N., long. 77° 47' W. We steered up to the northward, keeping in sight of the land on the eastern side of the bay, and found the coast clear and easy to navigate. During the night the wind was light. The next day, Sept. 17th, we made several islands lying in this beautiful bay,—and as the weather was fine and the sea smooth, it was very pleasant sailing among the islands. We steered to the northward, and now had land on both sides of the bay. On passing the islands, we saw several men in boats employed in catching pearl oysters. The shells, I believe, are here not of much value, though considerable quantities are occasionally shipped from Panama to England.

The next day, Sept. 18th, we came to anchor off the town of Panama; and in a few minutes after went on shore, and forever bade adieu to our captain and the brig *Los Dos Hermanos.*

I was, of course, delighted to get on shore at Panama; but I was not a little disappointed to find the city so badly supplied with hotels. Although there were two or three tolerable cafés, where one could get something to eat and drink, still, I believe, there was not a good hotel in the place. I was told that the best way of living there, was to hire a room or two, and and then get a black woman to cook. I accordingly hired a few rooms for myself and my two young friends, and engaged a black woman to dress our food and keep the rooms in order. In this way we got along tolerably well, and without any great expense.

To my satisfaction, I met here Captain John Brown, of the schooner *Freemason,* of Baltimore. This schooner was lying at Chagres, and Captain Brown expected to sail for the Havana in about a fortnight. I engaged a passage with him for myself and the two young gentlemen who came with me from Guayaquil.

The *Freemason* was the only American vessel lying at Chagres; and we deemed ourselves fortunate in meeting with so good an opportunity to return to the United States, by way of the Havana.

Captain Brown soon introduced me to his consignee, J. B. Ferand, Esq., the American consul at this place. I found Mr. Ferand to be a polite, obliging, gentlemanly man, and he was to me always a kind friend.

As it was quite healthy at Panama, and very sickly at Chagres, I concluded to remain in the former city until the *Freemason* was ready for sea; and not having any business to do, I had sufficient leisure to walk about the town and its vicinity, and view the Key of the Isthmus, as Panama is sometimes called.

The city of Panama lies at the head of a fine broad bay, of the same name, sprinkled with islands sheltering the harbor, and beautifying the surrounding scenery. It lies in lat. 8° 59' N., and long. 79° 22' W.; and like most other towns built by the Spaniards, is strongly walled and tolerably well fortified. It belongs to the republic of Colombia, and contains about ten or twelve thousand inhabitants. The streets are generally regular—and many of the houses are commodious and well built. Some of the public buildings are large and substantial, particularly the cathedral and several convents, and also the college. The college of the Jesuits, however, is now but a ruin. The environs of the town are pleasant, and the grounds in the neighborhood tolerably well cultivated. It was once a great place for trade, but had, during the last twenty or thirty years, gradually declined in its commerce. There was, however, some little trade still carried on; and should a canal or a railroad be constructed across the Isthmus, Panama will revive again. The natural position of the city is excellent,—and it will, in my opinion, at some future day, become a place of considerable importance.

The tide rises here to a great height—(I do not recollect precisely how many feet)—at the full and change of the moon, but as near as I can remember, some eighteen or twenty feet. Large vessels anchor at a considerable distance from the town, and lie afloat at low water; the small coasting vessels anchor close in near the walls of the city, and consequently lie on the mud at low water. The inner harbor is quite dry; the sand and mud flats extend off to a great distance, which at low tide give to the harbor an unpleasant aspect; but at the flood, the tide rises rapidly; the mud and sand banks are soon covered, and the whole scene agreeably changed from dreary banks to a living sheet of healthful salt-water.

It often struck me while strolling about this town, how admirably it was situated for a great commercial city; with a wide and extensive coast,—one may even say, from Cape Horn to Behring's Straits—with innumerable islands in the vast Pacific Ocean—with an open and easy navigation to China, over a sea so mild and gentle, that it might almost be traversed in an open boat. All these facilities are open to this town on the Pacific; and when we add to these its capacities of a general commerce on the Atlantic Ocean to Europe, the United States, and the West Indies, its location surpasses every other on the face of the globe. And now, what is necessary to bring about this great result? I answer—a just and good government, with a few enterprising capitalists, and five hundred young men from New England to give the impetus. Whaling ships—merchant ships trading to China—coasting brigs, schooners, sloops, and steamboats, would spring up like mushrooms; and in a few years this place would become one of the greatest commercial emporiums in the world. A practical, intelligent merchant, acquainted with the commerce of the world, will see by a glance at the map, that I have stated nothing respecting it either unreal or extravagant.

A few days before we left Panama, Captain Brown made an arrangement with the municipal government of this place, or perhaps with an agent of the republic of Colombia, to take as passengers about eighty Spanish prisoners and their colonel, from Chagres to the Havana, and also a Colombian officer, by the name of Barientes (I think he was a major), to take charge of the business as commissioner.

These Spanish prisoners, I understood, capitulated at Quito, on the conditions that they should leave the country and be sent to the Havana in a neutral vessel, at the expense of the Spanish government. The Colombian government agreed to furnish them with provisions, and pay Captain Brown a certain sum to land them at the Havana; I think it was about $1800 or $2000. This money was paid in advance at Chagres.

Captain Brown had now so far accomplished his business, that I began to make my arrangements to leave Panama; and for that purpose, hired a guide and five mules to transport Messrs. B.C. and A.D., my two young American friends, myself and our baggage to Cruces. For the guide and the five mules, I paid forty-two dollars;—and thus, after remaining at Panama fourteen days, on the 2nd of October, at 4 o'clock in the afternoon, we left the city for Cruces. We travelled slowly along—myself and the two young men mounted on the riding mules (the other two were loaded with our baggage), the guide generally walking, in order to pick the best of the road and take care of the mules. He, however, rode occasionally on one of the baggage mules. The road for three or four miles after leaving the city was tolerably good, or rather the different foot-paths, for I saw nothing like a road on the whole route from Panama to Cruces. From Panama to the foot of the hills—a distance of about five or six miles—there is a gradual elevation, and nothing to prevent making a good road at a small expense.

We passed over this part of the way rather pleasantly, and just before dark took up our abode for the night in a miserable posada, where neither a bed nor any thing eatable could be obtained. I got liberty to spread my mattress on the floor,—my young friends had each a blanket with them, and we all lay down in the same room; and though thus badly accommodated, were glad to get shelter for the night.

At daylight, our guide called us to mount the mules and make the best of our way. Our bedding was soon rolled up and packed on one of the animals; and we resumed our journey over one of the worst roads I ever travelled—up and down hill, through mud-holes, and over stony ground. Sometimes we met with large stones lying in the mud and sand, that had been washed out of the earth and not removed. Over these stones, many of which were the size of a barrel, we were obliged to pass. At other times the mules would mire above their knees, in passing through a deep slough.

After getting through a low spot of mud and water, the next turn would bring us to a cut in the rocks, just wide enough for a loaded mule to pass. These passes are frequently made through the solid rocks; and as they have probably been used a century and a half, the mules' feet have worn large holes, and these are generally filled with water, so that the poor animals, whether going through the mud, slough, or rocky pass, have a difficult task to perform.

On the way, we frequently met with men carrying valuable goods on their backs, to and from Panama to Cruces. Almost all fragile and valuable goods are conveyed across the Isthmus by porters on their backs: such as China and glassware, clocks, and other merchandise. Coarser and heavier goods are transported by mules. During the day, we occasionally saw huts and small ranchos along the roadside, mostly inhabited by a miserable, sickly-looking set of creatures, a mixed breed of the Spaniard, Indian, and Negro.

There is very little cultivation of the soil. The hills and valleys are generally well wooded and watered, but in a wild, savage state; and the people that vegetate here, live by raising cattle, pigs and poultry, and are extremely filthy and ignorant. The porters that convey goods on their backs from Cruces to Panama, are paid, I was told, from five to six dollars each way. The labor, however, is extremely severe, and none but the most hardy can long endure the fatigue.

We could scarcely get any thing to eat on the road, and did not arrive at Cruces until late in the afternoon, and then very much worn down with fatigue. Although the distance from Panama to Cruces is only 21 miles, the journey is tedious from the badness of the roads.

Cruces is a small town,—consisting of some eighty or a hundred little houses, lying on the west bank of the river Chagres, about 50 miles above its mouth, at the head of navigation. The houses are one story high, and generally built of wood with thatched roofs. The ground on which the town is situated is pretty level, and about twenty feet above the river. We found here comfortable accommodations, and had a good night's rest, after the fatigue of a long day's ride.

The next morning, the weather being fine, I walked about the town. The inhabitants are generally shop-keepers and boatmen, with a small proportion of mechanics. As Captain Brown was still in Panama, I was in no hurry to push on, being told that this place was more healthy and pleasant than Chagres. His clerk, a young Spanish gentleman, whose name was Francisco, joined us here, and was a friendly, polite young man, and very companionable. During the day I hired a boat, or rather a large canoe, and four men to take us down to Chagres;—we were to furnish our own stores. The canoes on this river are very large and long. They are made by hollowing out a solid tree of Spanish cedar. Some of them carry over one hundred half barrels of flour. Whole barrels of flour are rarely brought to Chagres, owing to the difficulty of transporting them from Cruces to Panama. The canoe I hired for myself, and the three other passengers was of middle size, and the price agreed upon to take us down was thirteen dollars. After having purchased stores for the passage, we got a good dinner and remained at Cruces until near sunset, when we embarked.

The canoes have hoops of bamboo bent over the after part of the craft, which is covered with a water-tight awning, so that the passengers are sheltered from the sun by day, and the dews and rain by night. With our mattresses and blankets spread in the stern sheets, we managed to sleep pretty well during the night. The river is not very wide, but generally deep and extremely crooked, and runs down very rapidly. I should think it from a quarter to half a mile wide. Its banks are generally abrupt, and from thirty to fifty feet high. Near the river, the wood is frequently cleared off, with now and then a little village, or a few small plantations; but receding a mile or two from the river, it appears like a vast wild forest, and a suitable habitation for wild beasts. In these jungles one would imagine they could remain undisturbed by the slothful race of men who inhabit the Isthmus. The trees here grow to an enormous size, and vegetation is rank and green all the year round.

Our lazy boatmen knew that we were not in a hurry, and therefore let the canoe drift down the stream pretty much all night, without rowing. Early in the morning we stopped at a small village, and bought some eggs and milk for breakfast; after remaining here about an hour, we pulled slowly down with the current. Soon after mid-day we brought up again at a small landing place, purchased a few trifling articles, and took our dinner under the shade of a fine large old tree on the bank of the river. This was on the 5th of October, and at 2 o'clock in the afternoon we re-embarked and pulled down for our port of destination. At night-fall it became dark and foggy, and we did not reach Chagres until 9 o'clock in the evening. As there was no hotel on shore, we went directly to the vessel, and had scarcely got on board and taken out our baggage, before it commenced raining, and continued to pour in torrents during the whole night. From 10 o'clock till midnight we had loud peals of thunder, and vivid lightning. At daylight it ceased raining, but there was a dense vapor like fog until about nine o'clock in the morning, when the sun shone out, and as there was not a breath of wind, it was extremely hot and uncomfortable, and the exhalations were so dense and bad that we found it difficult to breathe the foul atmosphere. This was on the 6th of October. Chagres is a small insignificant village, lying on low wet ground, along the eastern bank of the river's mouth, in lat. 9° 21'N., long. 80° 4'W., of London. To the windward, or eastern entrance of the river, there is a point of land of moderate height, projecting some-what into the sea, and forming a shelter for vessels lying at anchor in the mouth of the river, which here widens so as to form a sort of harbor; this, together with the bar at the entrance, renders it a safe port from all gales of wind. To the leeward, and along the western bank of the river, the land is low, and overgrown with rank grass, and high mangrove bushes.

At 10 o'clock, notwithstanding the sun was shining with intense heat, I went on shore to take a look at the village, or town. We soon brought up in a "pulperia" or grog-shop, which appeared to be the only resort for strangers, there being no hotel or tavern in this miserable place.

On the eastern point before mentioned, there is a small fort, at which, and about the town, there is a military garrison of perhaps thirty or forty sickly-looking soldiers. They are mostly mulattoes and negroes, badly clothed, and worse fed. The commanding officer of this little garrison, and the great man of the place, was a middle-sized mulatto, about thirty or thirty-five years old. Captain Brown's clerk, Mr. Francisco, told me we had better call on the commandant or captain of the garrison; that he no doubt expected all strangers to pay their respects to him on their arrival. This I was quite willing to do, and by all means to treat the public authori-ties with all proper respect and attention. We therefore forthwith repaired to the house of the commandant; we found him comfortably lodged in good quarters, and we were received with much ceremony. The com-mandant was dressed in full uniform, with two immense epaulettes, and assumed an air of consequential dignity; he offered us wine, and made a great flourish of male and female attendants. This visit of ceremony lasted about half an hour, when we took leave, the commandant politely bowing us out of his premises.

The Schooner *Freemason* was the only American vessel lying in port; there were two or three others, and these small coasting vessels which are employed trading up and down the coast.

Both of the mates and two of the seamen of our vessel were ill with the yellow fever, and hardly able to keep the deck; and here we were to remain for several days, to wait for our passengers and their stores, which were to be furnished by the Colombian government, and also to be brought from Panama. The stores for the eighty Spanish prisoners consisted of charque, plantain, and a small portion of hard biscuit. The colonel and commissioner were better provided, and were to mess with Captain Brown and myself in the cabin. Captain B. had agreed to furnish water, and the poor sick mates, who were hardly able to crawl about the deck, were endeavoring, with a few sailors, to get all the water casks filled up from the river before the captain should arrive.

Previous to leaving Guayaquil, I became acquainted with an elderly intelligent Spaniard, who had been for many years at Porto Bello and Chagres; he told me by all means to wear woollen stockings or socks during the time I remained at Chagres, and to bathe my feet two or three times a day with brandy or some other kind of alcohol, and by no means expose myself to the night air or noonday sun. I strictly followed the old man's advice while I remained here, and have to thank him, with God's blessing, that I escaped taking the fever. I enjoyed excellent health during my stay at Chagres, which is, perhaps, the most sickly place on the face of the globe.

During the day, I observed the clouds were driven by the N. E. trade-winds, and were collecting and hanging above and about the hills and mountains in the neighborhood, and I may also add all along the northern coast of the Isthmus; towards night they lay in immense masses, and appeared, as it were, to rest on the tops of the lofty forest trees, which crown these high hills and mountains. Soon after sunset we began to see the lightning, and hear the thunder above the mountains, and it was kept up with increasing fury until about 9 or 10 o'clock in the evening, when the rains began to fall in perfect sheets of water.

I have witnessed copious showers in other countries, but nothing to compare with the torrents that fell here during the night; I have also seen it lighten and heard it thunder in other parts of the world, but never saw or heard anything to equal what I nightly witnessed in this place. Peal after peal rends the air, and, to a stranger, throws an appalling gloom over this doomed portion of the earth. In the morning about ten o'clock the sun broke out as on the previous day, and I found it difficult and dangerous to go on shore without an umbrella to protect me from the rays of the burning sun.

As the history of one day is exactly that of another, I deem it unnecessary to say much more on the monotonous life I led. With respect to the weather, it continued about the same during my stay, a bright burning sun during the day, with torrents of rain during the night, accompanied with vivid lightning and thunder.

Although it is very easy to descend the river Chagres in a large canoe, well protected from the sun by day, and the dews and rain by night, it is not so easy to ascend it against a very rapid current running from three to six miles an hour, according to the high or low stage of the water. Loaded canoes are often a week getting from Chagres to Cruces; the men are obliged to track up the stream, and with boat-hooks haul up along shore by the trees and bushes.

To convey passengers, the light canoes are taken, and they generally make the passage in two days. If asked whether there is sufficient water in the river for a steamboat, I would answer that I believe there is, and no obstruction but want of sufficient employment to support the expense of a boat. At this time there were very few passengers crossing the Isthmus, and too little trade to give any encouragement to establishing a steamboat on the river.

On the 8th of October Captain Brown arrived, with the Spanish colonel and the commissioner, Major Barientes, with all the sea-stores, both for the Spanish soldiers and the officers, and now all was hurry and bustle getting ready for sea. The next day, Oct. 9th, I called with Captain Brown to pay our respects to the mulatto commandant, and to take a memorandum of this man in authority to purchase whatever he should please to order from Baltimore. Captain B. had already made two or three voyages from Baltimore to this place; and as he expected to return there again in a few months, he of course had a great many little commissions to execute for the élite of Panama and Chagres. On our arrival at the quarters of the commandant, we found him decked off in a new suit of gaudy uniform,—and here I witnessed a ludicrous farce between Captain Brown and the mulatto major. The latter was a vain and conceited coxcomb, evidently bent on showing off and playing the great man. Captain Brown was a plain, blunt Scotchman, and understood not a word of Spanish, but was endowed with a good understanding, and was by nature kind and benevolent. Independent of these qualities, it was his interest to keep smooth weather, and be upon good terms with the major;—he therefore waited with patience to receive the orders of the gallant commandant. I lament that I possess not the graphic powers of Dr. Smollett to describe the ludicrous.

Captain Brown's secretary, Mr. F., was seated at a table with pen, ink and paper, to note down the orders of the mulatto gentleman, who, to show his learning, endeavored to give his directions in phrases of bad French, interlarded with a few words of English. He would now and then walk about the room for a few moments, and admire himself, from head to foot, in a large mirror suspended at the head of the room. Mr. F. modestly requested him to give his orders in the Castilian language; but this plain dealing did not suit the taste of the major, who reproved him for his presumption, and then would reverse the order and direct him to commence anew, and strictly follow the orders given in his own way. The animated gesticulations and pomposity of the yellow major, and the unmoved indifference of the captain, formed so striking a contrast, that it was with the greatest difficulty I could command my risible faculties. This farce lasted about an hour, when we took our leave of "señor commandant," and left him to admire himself without interruption.

I can only imagine one reason why the Colombian government should place such a vain fool in the command of so important a post, and that is, that the place is so unhealthy that no white man could live there.

Oct. 11th.—At 9 o'clock in the morning we weighed anchor, and with the boat ahead to tow, and a light air off the land, sailed out of the harbor bound to the Havana. After getting a mile or two from the river's mouth, it became quite calm. There we lay exposed to the hot sun for two hours, waiting for the sea breeze, to beat up to windward far enough to stand to the northward, and thus clear the land to the westward, and make good our course out of the bay.

The schooner *Freemason* was a good vessel, of about 100 tons burthen, and a pretty fair sailer. In the cabin were the captain, the Spanish colonel, Major Barientes, and myself. In the steerage were the two sick mates, and the two young men that came with me from Guayaquil. The main-hold was left for the Spanish soldiers. Two of the crew in the forecastle were ill with the yellow fever, and the mates unfit for duty, and, notwithstanding all these evils, we were delighted to leave Chagres for the broad ocean, and once more to breathe the pure sea air, and thus fly from pestilence and death.

At 11 o'clock, after lying becalmed two hours, a breeze sprung up from the E. N. E., when we commenced beating up to windward; and just at sunset, after having made fifteen or twenty miles up along shore, we steered to the N. N. E. all night with a stiff trade-wind from the east, and the next day, Oct. 11th, at 4 P.M., made the island of St. Andrew. This island lies off the Mosquito shore, in lat. 12° 30' N., long. 81° W. After passing this island we kept the trade-wind, and as it was light, we made but little progress during the night. At 6 A.M., soon after daylight, we made the island of Providence. This island is of a moderate height, and lies in lat. 13° 27' N., long. 80° 39' W. of London; distant about sixty miles to the northward of St. Andrew. We ran within a mile or two of Providence, namely, to the westward, or in seamen's phrase, under the lee of the island. Thus we continued on our course to the northward, and passed to the windward of the numerous small islands, reefs, and shoals, lying off the coast of the Mosquito shore.

Just at night on this day, Oct. 13th (sea account), Captain Brown was taken very ill, and unable to come on deck; the second mate sick below, and the chief mate, poor fellow, so reduced from the effect of the fever contracted in Chagres that he was with difficulty able to keep the deck during the day. We were now in a dangerous and very difficult situation, surrounded with reefs and shoals, and no one to take the command of the vessel. The old Spanish colonel and Major Barientes saw our situation, and begged me for God's sake to take the command of the schooner. I was placed in a very delicate position; but under all the circumstances of the case, consented to do so. I mustered all the men in the forecastle, well enough to keep watch, and they numbered two. With these, and my two New-York friends, and the cook, I took command of the schooner; and as the weather was dark and squally, I kept the deck all night, beating about in the passage until daylight, when we again got a strong trade-wind from E. N. E., and fine, clear, pleasant weather. We were now clear of all the reefs and shoals, and made a fair wind for Cape Antonio, on the west end of Cuba. At 10 o'clock in the morning, Captain Brown was better, and able to come on deck and resume the command of the schooner.

The Spanish colonel was a gentlemanly man of about sixty. He had been in the armies in South America seven or eight years, and in many severe engagements, and always fought with honor to himself and to his country; but was beaten at last at the battle of Quito, where he and many of his countrymen laid down their arms and capitulated to be sent out of the country. He was indeed a war-worn soldier, and I fear had been poorly remunerated for his hard and severe sufferings. He was a kind, amiable man, with very modest and unassuming manners, and won the respect and esteem of all those about him.

Major Barientes, the commissioner, was a fine, healthy looking young man, about thirty or thirty-five years of age; he had been several years in the Colombian service, and I have no doubt was a gallant fellow, and was now on his way to a colony of Spain, to deliver the colonel and the

Spanish soldiers up to the government of Cuba, and claim from it the money and the fulfilment of the capitulation made at the battle of Quito.

I was often amused with the conversation of these two gentlemen on the subject of the different battles fought in South America between their respective countrymen, each, of course, endeavoring to make his own countrymen superior and victorious. Generally, their conversations and recitals were carried on in a good spirit; sometimes, however, they would wax a little warm in these little disputes. I good-naturedly reminded them that here we were all friends together, and had no fighting to do; this always brought them to a just sense of their relative situations, when their arguments would take a gentle tone, and end in mutual good wishes that the war between Spain and her colonies might soon terminate. I found them both well-bred and agreeable fellow-passengers.

The mates and seamen were now convalescent, and every thing went on smoothly, and in a few days we made Cape St. Antonio, and proceeded on our course without any incident worth remarking, until off Mariel, the day before we arrived at Havana. Here we fell in with a Spanish sloop of war, ship-rigged, and mounting eighteen guns. She ranged up near us, and seeing so many men on our decks, either took us for a privateer or a pirate. Her guns were pointed, and every thing ready to give us a broadside, although so near that she could, no doubt, see we had no guns. Our captain expected every moment to receive her fire. We were lying to when she hailed and ordered us to send our boat on board instantly, or she would sink us. We had but one boat, and it was dried up with the sun, so that the moment it touched the water it leaked like a sieve. Still the order was imperative and must be obeyed. Captain B. requested the colonel and myself to go on board, and show him the schooner's papers. We got into the boat, and, with constant bailing, made out to get on board of the ship, though not in a very good condition, being wet up to our knees. We showed our papers to the captain, who was a very young man, and, after a little delay, we were requested to take seats on the quarterdeck.

The colonel explained the substance of the capitulation, his misfortunes, &c. &c. The captain appeared rather to upbraid than sympathize with the good colonel, who was old enough to be his father. I felt vexed with the upstart. Our visit was of short duration. The captain of the ship neither invited the veteran to take a glass of wine, nor any other refreshment, nor was he at all polite. I sincerely regret I do not recollect the name of this worthy old warrior, who bore such treatment with so much patience.

While in the boat, I observed to the colonel that his countryman, the captain of the ship, did not treat him with the consideration and courtesy due to his rank and misfortunes. He mildly replied that he was a very young man, and was probably promoted by family interest, and had little sympathy for the unfortunate.

The ship soon made sail, and we steered on our course, and the next day, Oct. 28th, came to anchor at Havana, eighteen days from Chagres. The health-boat soon came along-side, and we were allowed to go on shore.

Major Barientes went on shore in full Colombian uniform, and, I was told, was well received by the governor, but whether he ever recovered the money due to his government, I have never been able to learn. I took a kind farewell of these two worthy gentlemen, and we never again met.

I was very anxious to get home, and as there was no vessel to sail soon for New-York, engaged a passage to Philadelphia, on board the hermaphrodite brig *James Coulter*, to sail the next day. I advanced a small sum of money to my young protégés, taking their orders on their friends in New York for the money I had already paid for their passages and other expenses, and left them under the protection of the American Consul at this place.

The next day we got under way, and sailed out of the harbor, bound for Philadelphia. I regret I do not recollect the name of the young man who commanded the *J.C.*, he was an active, capable ship-master, and a worthy man. I had the good fortune to meet on board the *James Coulter*, an old friend, Captain Frazer, of Baltimore, and as we were the only passengers on board, we were very happy to meet each other, and renew our former acquaintance. We had formerly met in Europe, and now, after many years separation, it was delightful to make a passage together. I do not recollect any thing remarkable during our passage home. Every thing went on in perfect good order, and we had a very pleasant passage of only fifteen days to the city of Philadelphia.

I think I paid $50 for my passage, and was well satisfied with both the vessel and the captain. We landed in the afternoon of the 14th of November, 1822, and the next day I took the steamboat for New-York, and arrived in that city at noon, the next day following, after an absence of just twelve months.

I had not received a syllable from home during my long and tedious absence, and was extremely anxious to hear from my family and friends, and therefore with precipitation I hurried to the counting-office of my friend. I met my friend B., and not a word was spoken, but I saw in his face that I was doomed to be a miserable man, and that I was bereft of the dearest object for me that earth contained. I conjured him to speak out and let me know the worst. I told him I was a man, and could bear grief. He then told me that my wife died in Brooklyn, on the 3rd of October, and was interred on the 5th, and that she had left me a fine little daughter, about seven months old.

I forthwith proceeded to my melancholy abode, and although I was stricken and cut to the soul, and bereft of her my soul held the dearest of earth's treasures, still, what could I say, but repeat the words of a man more afflicted than myself, "The Lord gave, and the Lord hath taken away, and for ever blessed be his holy name."

A few weeks after my return home, my worthy friend Richard M. Lawrence, Esq., who at this period was President of the Union Marine Insurance Company in New-York, called at my house, and generously offered me a situation as inspector of ships in that company. The situation had lately been vacated, and was now offered to me with a very handsome salary. I, however, declined the kind offer of my excellent friend, with many thanks; not wishing at this time to remain long on shore.

Had my wife been spared me, I should have thankfully accepted the offer, but being bereft and disappointed in my anticipations in life, I was again cast adrift and almost alone in this world of change and disappointment.

THE CAPTAIN OF THE ONION BOAT

WILLIAM HOPE HODGSON

Big John Carlos, captain of the *Santa*, stood looking up at the long tapered window in the otherwise great, grey blank of the convent wall, a dozen yards away.

The wall formed the background of the quay, and between it and the side of the vessel was a litter of unloaded gear and cargo. The Captain's face, as he stared upward at that one lonesome window, had an extraordinarily set expression; and his Mate, a little lop-shouldered man, very brown and lean, watched him over the coaming of the main hatchway, with a curious grimace of half-sympathy and half-curiosity.

"Old Man's got it bad as ever," he muttered, in an accent and language that spoke of the larger English. He transferred his gaze from the silent form of the skipper, standing, in the stern, to the long taper of the one window that broke the towering side of the convent.

Presently, the thing for which the two men watched, came into view, as it did twice daily, at morning and evening—a long line of half-veiled nuns, who were obviously ascending some stairway within the convent, on to which this solitary window threw light.

Most of the women went by the window quietly, with faces composed, and looking before them; but here and there a young nun would take this opportunity to glance out into the Carnal World which they had renounced for ever. Young, beautiful faces there were, that looked out momentarily, showing doubly human, because of the cold ascetic garb of renunciation which framed them; then were gone on from sight, in the long, steadily moving procession of silent figures.

It was about the middle of the procession, after a weary line of seeming mutes had gone past, that the Mate saw that for which he waited. For, suddenly, the great body of the Captain stiffened and became rigid, as the head of one of the moving figures turned and stared out on to the quay. The Mate saw her face clearly. It was still young and lovely, but seemed very white and hopeless. He noted the eager, hungry look in the eyes; and then the wonderful way in which they lit up, as with a strange inward fire, at sight of the big man standing there; and the whole face seemed to quiver into living emotion. Immediately afterwards, she was gone past, and more mutes were making the grey, ascending line.

"Gord! that's 'er!" said the Mate, and glanced towards his master. The face of the big skipper was still upturned and set with a fixed, intense stare, as though even now he saw her face at the long window. His body was yet rigid with intensity, and his great hands gripped tightly the front of his slack jumper, straining it, unconsciously, down upon his hips. For some moments longer, he stood like this, lost to all knowledge except the tellings of his memory, and stunned with his emotions. Then he relaxed abruptly, as if some string within him had been loosed, and turned towards the open hatchway, where the Mate bent once more to his work.

"W'y don't 'e get 'er out," the Mate remarked to himself. "They've bin doin' that years 'n years, from wot I can see an"ear, an' breakin' their blessed 'earts. W'y the 'ell don't 'e get 'er out! It's easy ter see she's a woman, a sight more'n a bloomin' nun!" In all of which the little crooked shouldered Mate showed a fund of common sense; but likewise an insufficient ability to realise how thoroughly a religious belief may sometimes prove a stumbling-block in the pathway to mere human happiness.

How a man of the stamp of Big John Carlos came to be running an onion boat, must be conjectured. His name is explained by his father having been a Spaniard and his mother an Englishwoman. Originally, Big John had been a merchant, of a kind, going to sea in his own ship, and trading abroad.

As a youth, he had become engaged to Marvonna Della, whose father had owned much property, farther up the coast. Her father had died, and she had been an heiress, sought by all the youths about; but he—Big John Carlos—had won her.

They were to have been married on his return from his next trading voyage; but the report went home to his sweetheart that he had been drowned at sea; and indeed he had truly fallen overboard; but had been picked up by a China-bound sailing-ship, and had been a little over a year lost to his friends, before he had managed to reach home, to carry the news that he still lived. For this was before the days of the telegraph, and his one letter had gone astray.

When at last, he reached home, it was to find sad changes. His sweetheart, broken-hearted, had become a nun at the great convent of St. Sebastian's, and had endowed it with all her wealth and lands. What attempts he made to have speech with her, I do not know; but if his religious scruples had allowed him to beg her to renounce her vows and retirement, and return to the world to be his wife, they had certainly been unsuccessful; though it is quite conceivable that no word had ever passed between them, since she had put the world behind her.

From then onward, through nine long years, Big John Carlos had traded along the coast. His former business, he had dropped, and now he wandered from port to port in his small craft. And twice in every year, he would come alongside of the little wharf opposite to the great, grey wall of the convent, and there lie for a week, watching year by year that long narrow window for the two brief glimpses daily of his lost sweetheart.

After a week, he would go. It was always a week that he stayed there by the old wharf. Then, as if that had exhausted his strength—as if the pain of the thing had grown in that time to be too dreadful to continue, he would haul out, and away, whatever the weather or the state of trade. All of this the little twisted Mate knew, more or less clearly in detail, having learned it in the previous visit, which he had made with Big John Carlos to the insignificant port where the convent stood.

And she—what can the young nun have thought and felt? How she must have fought to endure the grey weary months between the far-apart visits; and day by day glanced out of the tall stair-window, as she passed in the long, mute procession, for a sight of the little onion boat and the big man standing in the stern, watching—tense and silent—for that one brief glimpse of her, as she passed in the remorseless line of figures. And something of this also, the little crooked-shouldered Mate had realised, vaguely, and had achieved an instant though angry sympathy. But his point of view was limited and definite:—"W'y the 'ell don't 'e get 'er out!" was his brief formula. And that marked the limit of his imagination, and therefore of his understanding.

His own religious beliefs were of the kind that are bred in the docks (London docks, in his case), and fostered in dirty fo'cas'les; and now he was "come down to this onion shuntin'," as he would have worded it. Yet, whatever his religious lack, or even his carelessness on a point of ethics, he was thoroughly and masculinely human.

"W'y the 'ell——" he began again, in his continual grumble to himself; and had no power to conceive that the woman, having taken a certain step, might believe that step to be unretraceable—that usage, belief, and finally (bred of these two) Conscience might forbid even the thought, stamping it as a crime that would shut her out from the Joy of the Everlasting.

The Joy of the Everlasting! The little twisted man would have grinned at you, had you mentioned it. "W'y the 'ell don't 'e get 'er out!" would have been his reply, accompanied by a profuseness of tobacco-juice.

And yet, it is conceivable that the heart of the woman was, even this long while, grown strong to do battle for dear Happiness—her heart that had known, silently and secretly and dumbly, all along, the unnatural wickedness of her outrage of her Womanhood. Visit by visit, through the long years, her heart must have grown fiercely strong to end this torture which her brain (darkened with the Clouds of Belief) had put upon her, to endure through all her life.

And so, all unknowingly, because of the loyal brain *that would not be aware* of the growing victory of her heart, she was come to a condition in which her beliefs held her no more than if they had been cords that had rotted upon her, as indeed they might be said to have done. That she was free to come, the little Mate had seen, using his eyes and his heart and his wit. To him, it was merely a matter of ways and means—physical. "W'y the 'ell——!" that was his puzzle.

Why? With an angry impatience, that came near to verging upon the borderland of scorn, the little Mate would question inwardly. Was Big

John Carlos bit wiv them religious notions, same as the other dagoes! He did not understand the complaint, or how it was achieved; but he knew, as an outside fact, that there was something of that kind which infected the peoples along the coasts he travelled. If Big John were not troubled in this way, "why the 'ell——" And so he would return to his accustomed formula, working furiously, in sheer irritation of mind:—"If 'e ain't religious, *wot* is it? Carn't 'e see the way 'er eyes blessed well looks at 'im! Carn't 'e see she's mad an' double mad to be out wiv 'im!"

Why did not John Carlos attempt to win back for himself the one thing that he desired in all the world? Maybe (and I think that it is very possible) in the early years of his return, he had so striven; but the young nun, shaken with the enormousness of the thought, hopelessly weighted with her vows, had not dared to think upon it—had retreated with horror from the suggestion; had turned with an intention of double ardour to seek in her religious duties, the calm and sweetness, the peace and joy, which she felt to be lost to her forever in any more earthly way.

And then had followed the long years, with her heart fighting silently and secretly—*secretly almost from herself*—unto victory. And the man (having lost the force of that first fierce unpenting of his intention to win her—and mayhap having been repulsed, as it would seem to his masculine mind, *hopelessly*) had fallen back under the sway of the religious beliefs, which ruled him in his more normal hours; and so, year by year, had withheld from any further attempt to win her; striving to content his soul with those two brief visits each year to the old wharf; each time to endure a mad week of those futile watchings for his beloved.

Yet, in him, as in the woman, there had been going forward, without his knowledge, that steady disruption of religious belief—the rotting and decaying of all arbitrary things, before the primal need of the human heart; so that the olden barriers of "Impossibility," were now but as shadows, that would be gone in a moment, when next the Force of his Need should urge him to take his heart's desire.

His first attempt—if there had ever been such—had been the outcome of his natural want—his Love—; but lacking the foundations of Sureness of Himself and of his Power to withstand the Future. Indeed, it is conceivable that had he succeeded at the first, and gained his desire, the two of them would have wilted in the afterblast of thought and fear-of-the-hereafter, and in the Fires of Scruples which would have burned in their path through all the years.

But now, whatever they might do, they would do—if it ever came to pass—with a calm and determined Intention; having done their thinking first, and weighed all known costs, and proved their strength, and learned the utterness of their need to be truly greater than all else that might be set as balance against it. And because of this, they were ripe—wanting only the final stimulus to set into action the ready Force that had concentrated through the years.

Yet, strangely, neither the man nor the woman *knew*, as I have shown, that they had developed to this. Their brains refused to know; their Consciences looked, each with its blind eye, at their hearts, and saw nothing to give cause of offence to the ethical in them; or, did Conscience catch an odd glimpse, with its seeing eye, of impossible wickedness, there followed hours of imagined repentance, deep and painful, resulting in a double assuredness, within the brain (and "Manufactured" Parts) of a conquered and chastened heart, and of fiercer resolutions for the future Torture of Salvation. But always, deep within, the unconquerable heart fought for the victory that was each year more assured.

And so, as you have already seen, these two, the man and the woman, were but waiting—the man for some outward stimulus, to put into action all the long-pent force in him, revealing to him his actual nature, developed and changed in the course of the long years of pain, until he should be scarcely likely to recognise himself in the first moments of his awakening to this reality. And the woman, waiting, subconsciously, for the action of the man to bring her to a knowledge of the realities—to an awareness of the woman she had become, of the woman into which she had developed, unable any more to endure the bondage of aught save her heart that leaped to the ordering of Mother Nature. Nay, more, fiercely and steadfastly eager to take with both hands the forbidden joy of her Natural Birthright, and calm and resolute and unblinking to face the future, with its unsolvable problem of the Joy of the Everlasting.

And thus were these two standing, as it might be said, on the brink of their destinies; waiting, with blinded eyes, and as that they listened unknowingly for the coming of the unknown one who should give the little push forward, and so cause them to step over the borderland into all natural and long craved for happiness.

Who would be That One?

"W'y the 'ell don't 'e get 'er out?" the Mate had asked the First Hand, who knew all the story, having sailed years with Big John Carlos. But the First Hand had raised his arms in horror, and made plain in broken English his opinion of the sacrilege, though that was not how he had pronounced it.

"Sacrilege be jiggered!" the Mate had replied, humping his twisted shoulders. "I s'pose though there'd be a 'oly rumpus, hey?"

The First Hand had intimated very definitely that there would be a "rumpus," which, the Mate ferreted out, might involve some very unpleasant issues both for the man and the woman guilty of such a thing. The First Hand spoke (in broken English) as if he were the Religious Conscience of his nation. Such things could not be tolerated. His phraseology did not include such words; but he was sufficiently definite.

"Nice 'ealthy lot o' savages, *you!*" the Mate had explained, after listening to much intolerant jabbering. "Strike me! If you ain't canniballs!" And straightway saddled on to the unfortunate Catholic Faith the sins peculiar to a hot-blooded and emotional People, whose enthusiasms and prejudices would have been just as apparent, had they been called forth by some other force than their Faith, or by a Faith differently shaped and Denominated.

It was the little crooked Mate who was speaking to Big John Carlos, in the evening of the sixth day of their stay beside the old wharf. And the big man was listening, in a stunned kind of silence. Through those six days the little man had watched the morning and evening tragedy, and the sanity of his free thoughts had been as a yeast in him. Now he was speaking, unlading all the things that he *had* to say.

"W'y the 'ell don't you take 'er out?" he had asked in so many words. And to him it had seemed, that very evening, that the woman's eyes had been saying the same thing to the Captain, as she looked her brief, dumb agony of longing across the little space that had lain between; yet which, as it were, was in verity the whole width of Eternity. And now the little Mate was putting it all into definite words—standing there, an implement of Fate or Providence or the Devil, according to the way that you may look at it, his twisted shoulder heaving with the vehemence of his speech:—

"You didn't orter do it, Capting," he said. "You're breakin' 'er up, an' you're breakin' *you* up; an' no good to it. W'y the 'ell don't you do somefink! Rescue 'er, or keep away. If it's 'ell for you, it's just 's much 'ell for 'er! She'll come like a little bloomin' bird. See 'ow she looks at you. She's fair askin' you to come an' take 'er out of it all—an' you just standin' there! My Gord!"

"What can I do," said the Captain, hoarsely; and put his hands suddenly to his head. He did not ask a question, or voice any hopelessness; but just gave out the words, as so many sounds, mechanically; for he was choked, suffocating during those first few moments, with the vast surge of hope that rose and beat upward in him, as the little twisted Mate's words crashed ruthlessly through the shrouding films of Belief.

And suddenly he *knew.* He knew that he could do this thing; that all scruples, all bonds of belief, of usage, of blind fears for the future, and *of* the Hereafter, were all fallen from him, as so much futile dust. Until that moment, as I have shown to you before, he had *not* known that he could do it—had not known of his steady and silent development. But now, suddenly, all his soul and being, lighted with Hope, he looked inward, and saw himself, as the man he was—the man to which he had grown and come to be. He knew. *He knew.*

"Would she. . . would she?" The question came unconsciously from his lips; but the little twisted man took it up.

"Arsk 'er! Arsk 'er!" he said, vehemently. "I knows she'll come. I seen it in 'er eyes to-night w'en she looked out at you. She was sayin' as plain as your 'at, 'W'y the 'ell don't you take me out? W'y the 'ell don't you?' You arsk 'er, an' she'll come like a bird."

The little Mate spoke with the eagerness of conviction, and indulged in no depressing knowledge of incongruities. "Arsk 'er!" was his refrain. "You arsk 'er!"

"How?" said the Captain, coming suddenly to realities.

The little man halted, and stumbled over his unreadiness. He had no plan; nothing but his feelings. He sought around in his mind, and grasped at an idea.

"Write it on an 'atch cover, wiv chalk," he said, triumphant. "Lean the 'atch cover by you. W'en 'she comes, point to it, 'n she'll read it."

"Ha!" said the Captain, in a strange voice, as if he both approved, and, at the same time, had remembered something.

"Then she'll nod," continued the little man. "No one else ever looks outer that winder, scarcely, not to think to read writin', anyway. An' you can cover it, till she's due to show. Then we'll plan 'ow to get 'er out."

All that night, Big John Carlos paced the deck of his little craft, alone, thinking, and thrilling with great surges of hope and maddened determination.

In the morning, he put the plan to the test; only that he wrote the question on the hatch-cover in peculiar words, that he had not used all those long grey years; for he made use of a quaint but simple transposition of letters, which had been a kind of love-language between them, in the olden days. This was why he had called "Ha!" so strangely, being minded suddenly of it, and to have the sweetness of using it to that one particular purpose.

Slowly, the line of grey moving figures came into view, descending. Big John Carlos kept the hatch-cover turned to him, and counted; for well he knew just when she would appear. The one hundred and ninth mute would pass, and the one hundred and tenth would show the face of his Beloved. The order never changed through the years, in that changeless world within.

As the hundred and seventh figure passed the narrow window, he turned the hatch-cover, so that the writing was exposed, and pointed down to it, so that his whole attitude should direct her glance instantly to his question, that she might have some small chance to read it, in the brief moment that was hers as she went slowly past the narrow panes. The hundred and ninth figure passed down from sight, and then he was looking dumbly into her face, as she moved into view, her eyes already strained to meet his. His heart was beating with a dull, sickening thudding, and there seemed just the faintest of mists before his vision; but he knew that her glance had flown eagerly to the message, and that her white face had flashed suddenly to a greater whiteness, disturbed by the battle of scores of emotions loosed in one second of time. Then she was gone downward out of his sight, and he let the hatch-cover fall, gripping the shrouds with his left hand.

The little twisted man stole up to him.

"She *saw*, Capting! She 'adn't time to answer. Not to know if she was on 'er 'ead or 'er 'eels. Look out to-night. She'll nod then." He brought it all out in little whispered jerks, and the big man, wiping his forehead, nodded.

Within the convent, a woman (outwardly a nun) was even then descending the stairs, with shaking knees, and a brain that had become in a few brief instants a raging gulf of hope. Before she had descended three steps below the level of the window, even whilst her sight-memory still held the message out for her brain to read and comprehend, she had realised that spiritually she was clothed only with the ashes of Belief and Fear and Faith. The original garment had become charred to nothing in the Fire of Love and Pain, with which the years had enveloped her. No bond held her; no fear held her; nothing in all the world mattered, except to be his for all the rest of her life. She took and realised the change in her character, in a moment of time. Eight long years had the yeast of love been working in her, which had bred the chemistry of pain; but only in that instant did she *know* and comprehend that she was developed so extensively, as to be changed utterly from the maid of eight years gone. Yet, in the next few steps she took, she had adapted herself to the new standpoint of her fresh knowledge of herself. She had no pause or doubt; but acknowledged with an utter startled joyfulness that she would go—that all was as nothing to her, now, except that she go to him. Willing, beyond all words that might express her willingness, to risk (aye, even to *exchange*) the unknown Joy of the Everlasting for this *certain* "mess of pottage" that was so desired of her hungry heart. And having acknowledged to *herself* that she was utterly *willing*, she had no thought of anything but to pass on the knowledge of her altered state to the man who would be waiting there in the little onion boat at sunset.

That evening, just before the dusk, Big John Carlos saw the hundred and tenth grey figure nod swiftly to him, in passing; and he held tightly to the shroud, until the suffocation of his emotion passed from him.

After all, the Rescue—if it can be named by a term so heroic—proved a ridiculously easy matter. It was the spiritual prison that had held the woman so long—the Physical expression of the same, was easily made to give up its occupant.

In the morning, expectant, she read in her fleeting glance at the onion boat, a message written on the hatch-cover. She was to be at the window at midnight. That evening, as she ascended in the long grey line of mutes for the last weary time, she nodded her utter agreement and assent.

After night had fallen thickly on the small, deserted wharf, the little twisted Mate and the Captain reared a ladder against the convent side. By midnight, they had cut out entirely the lead framing of all the lower part of the window.

A few minutes later, the woman came. The Captain held out his big hands, in an absolute silence, and lifted the trembling figure gently down on to the ladder. He steadied her firmly, and they climbed down to the wharf, and were presently aboard the vessel, with no word yet between them to break the ten years of loneliness and silence; for it was ten years, as you will remember, since Big John Carlos had sailed on that voyage of dismay.

And now, full grown man and woman, they stood near to each other, in a dream-quietness, who had lived on the two sides of Eternity so long. And still they had no word. Youth and Maiden they had parted with tears; Man and Woman they met in a great silence—too grown and developed to have words over-easily at such a moment-of-life. Yet their very quiet, held a speech too full and subtle, aye and subtile, for made-words of sound. It came from them, almost as it were a soul-fragrance, diffused around them, and made visible only in the quiet trembling of hands——that reached unknowing unto the hands of the other. For the two were full-grown, as I have said, and had come nigh to the complete *awaredness* of life, and the taste of the brine of sorrow was yet in them. They had been ripened in the strange twin Suns of Love and Pain—that ripen the unseen fruit of the soul. Their hands met, trembling, and gripped a long, long while, till the little twisted Mate came stumbling aft, uneasy to be gone. Then the big man and the fragile woman stood apart, the woman dreaming, while the big man went to give the little Mate a hand.

Together, the two men worked to get the sail upon the small vessel, and the ropes cast off. They left the First and Second Hands sleeping. Presently, with light airs from the land, they moved outward to the sea.

There was no pursuit. All the remainder of that night, the small onion boat went outward into the mystery of the dark, the big man steering, and the woman close beside him; and for a long while the constant silence of communion.

As I have said, there was no pursuit, and at dawn the little twisted man wondered. He searched the empty sea, and found only their own shadow upon the almost calm waters. Perhaps the First Hand had held a wrong impression. The Peoples of the Coast may have been shocked, when they learned. Maybe they never learned. Convents, like other institutions, can keep their secrets, odd whiles. Possibly this was one of those times. Perhaps they remembered, with something of worldly wisdom, that they held the Substance; wherefore trouble overmuch concerning the shadow—of a lost nun. Certainly, not to the bringing of an ill-name upon their long holiness. Surely, Satan can be trusted, etc. We can all finish the well-hackneyed thought. Or, maybe, there were natural human hearts in diverse places, that—knowing something of the history of this love-tale—held sympathy in silence, and silence in sympathy. Is this too much to hope?

That evening, the man and the woman stood in the stern, looking into the wake, whilst the Second-Hand steered. Forrard, in the growing dusk, there was a noise of scuffling. The little humped Mate was having a slight difference of opinion with the First Hand, who had incautiously made use of a parallel word for "Sacrilege," for the second time. The scuffling continued; for the little twisted man was emphatic:—

"Sacrilege be jiggered! Wot the 'ell——"

The physical sounds of his opinion, drowned the monotonous accompaniment of his speech. The small craft sailed on into the sunset, and the two in the stern stared blindly into distances, holding hands like two little children.

NEW SHIP AND SHIPMATES— MY WATCHMATE

RICHARD HENRY DANA, JR.

Tuesday, Sept. 8th. This was my first day's duty on board the ship; and though a sailor's life is a sailor's life wherever it may be, yet I found everything very different here from the customs of the brig Pilgrim. After all hands were called, at daybreak, three minutes and a half were allowed for every man to dress and come on deck, and if any were longer than that, they were sure to be overhauled by the mate, who was always on deck, and making himself heard all over the ship. The head-pump was then rigged, and the decks washed down by the second and third mates; the chief mate walking the quarter-deck and keeping a general supervision, but not deigning to touch a bucket or a brush. Inside and out, fore and aft, upper deck and between decks, steerage and forecastle, rail, bulwarks, and water-ways, were washed, scrubbed and scraped with brooms and canvas, and the decks were wet and sanded all over, and then holystoned. The holystone is a large, soft stone, smooth on the bottom, with long ropes attached to each end, by which the crew keep it sliding fore and aft, over the wet, sanded decks. Smaller hand-stones, which the sailors call "prayer-books," are used to scrub in among the crevices and narrow places, where the large holystone will not go. An hour or two, we were kept at this work, when the head-pump was manned, and all the sand washed off the decks and sides. Then came swabs and squilgees; and after the decks were dry, each one went to his particular morning job. There were five boats belonging to the ship,—launch, pinnace, jolly-boat, larboard quarter-boat, and gig,—each of which had a coxswain, who had charge of it, and was answerable for the order and cleanness of it. The rest of the cleaning was divided among the crew; one having the brass and composition work about the capstan; another the bell, which was of brass, and kept as bright as a gilt button; a third, the harness-cask; another, the man-rope stanchions; others, the steps of the forecastle and hatchways, which were hauled up and holystoned. Each of these jobs must be finished before breakfast; and, in the meantime, the rest of the crew filled the scuttle-butt, and the cook scraped his kids (wooden tubs out of which the sailors eat) and polished the hoops, and placed them before the galley, to await inspection. When the decks were dry, the lord paramount made his appearance on the quarter-deck, and took a few turns, when eight bells were struck, and all hands went to breakfast. Half an hour was allowed for breakfast, when all hands were called again; the kids, pots, bread-bags, etc., stowed away; and, this morning, preparations were made for getting under weigh. We paid out on the chain by which we swung; hove in on the other; catted the anchor; and hove short on the first. This work was done in shorter time than was usual on board the brig; for though everything was more than twice as large and heavy, the cat-block being as much as a man could lift, and the chain as large as three of the Pilgrim's, yet there was a plenty of room to move about in, more discipline and system, more men, and more good will. Every one seemed ambitious to do his best: officers and men knew their duty, and all went well. As soon as she was hove short, the mate, on the forecastle, gave the order to loose the sails, and, in an instant, every one sprung into the rigging, up the shrouds, and out on the yards, scrambling by one another,—the first up the best fellow,—cast off the yard-arm gaskets and bunt gaskets, and one man remained on each yard, holding the bunt jigger with a turn round the tye, all ready to let go, while the rest laid down to man the sheets and halyards. The mate then hailed the yards—"All ready forward?"—"All ready the cross-jack yards?" etc., etc., and "Aye, aye, sir!" being returned from each, the word was given to let go; and in the twinkling of an eye, the ship, which had shown nothing but her bare yards, was covered with her loose canvas, from the royal-mast-heads to the decks. Every one then laid down, except one man in each top, to overhaul the rigging, and the topsails were hoisted and sheeted home; all three yards going to the mast-head at once, the larboard watch hoisting the fore, the starboard watch the main, and five light hands, (of whom I was one,) picked from the two watches, the mizen. The yards were then trimmed, the anchor weighed, the cat-block hooked on, the fall stretched out, manned by "all hands and the cook," and the anchor brought to the head with "cheerily men!" in full chorus. The ship being now under weigh, the light sails were set, one after another, and she was under full sail, before she had passed the sandy point. The fore royal, which fell to my lot, (being in the mate's watch,) was more than twice as large as that of the Pilgrim, and, though I could handle the brig's easily, I found my hands full, with this, especially as there were no jacks to the ship; everything being for neatness, and nothing left for Jack to hold on by, but his eyelids.

As soon as we were beyond the point, and all sail out, the order was given, "Go below the watch!" and the crew said that, ever since they had been on the coast, they had had "watch and watch," while going from port to port; and, in fact, everything showed that, though strict discipline was kept, and the utmost was required of every man, in the way of his duty, yet, on the whole, there was very good usage on board. Each one knew that he must be a man, and show himself smart when at his duty, yet every one was satisfied with the usage; and a contented crew, agreeing with one another, and finding no fault, was a contrast indeed with the small, hard-used, dissatisfied, grumbling, desponding crew of the Pilgrim.

It being the turn of our watch to go below, the men went to work, mending their clothes, and doing other little things for themselves; and I, having got my wardrobe in complete order at San Diego, had nothing to do but to read. I accordingly overhauled the chests of the crew, but found nothing that suited me exactly, until one of the men said he had a book which "told all about a great highwayman," at the bottom of his chest, and producing it, I found, to my surprise and joy, that it was nothing else than Bulwer's Paul Clifford. This, I seized immediately, and going to my hammock, lay there, swinging and reading, until the watch was out. The between-decks were clear, the hatchways open, and a cool breeze blowing through them, the ship under easy way, and everything comfortable. I had just got well into the story, when eight bells were struck, and we were all ordered to dinner. After dinner came our watch on deck for four hours, and, at four o'clock, I went below again, turned into my hammock, and read until the dog watch. As no lights were allowed after eight o'clock, there was no reading in the night watch. Having light winds and calms, we were three days on the passage, and each watch below, during the daytime, I spent in the same manner, until I had finished my book. I shall never forget the enjoyment I derived from it. To come across anything with the slightest claims to literary merit, was so unusual, that this was a perfect feast to me. The brilliancy of the book, the succession of capital hits, lively and characteristic sketches, kept me in a constant state of pleasing sensations. It was far too good for a sailor. I could not expect such fine times to last long.

While on deck, the regular work of the ship went on. The sailmaker and carpenter worked between decks, and the crew had their work to do upon the rigging, drawing yarns, making spun-yarn, etc., as usual in merchantmen. The night watches were much more pleasant than on board the Pilgrim. There, there were so few in a watch, that, one being at the wheel, and another on the look-out, there was no one left to talk with; but here, we had seven in a watch, so that we had long yarns, in abundance. After two or three night watches, I became quite well acquainted with all the larboard watch. The sailmaker was the head man of the watch, and was generally considered the most experienced seaman on board. He was a thoroughbred old man-of-war-man, had been to sea twenty-two years, in all kinds of vessels—men-of-war, privateers, slavers, and merchantmen;—everything except whalers, which a thorough sailor despises, and will always steer clear of, if he can. He had, of course, been in all parts of the world, and was remarkable for drawing a long bow. His yarns frequently stretched through a watch, and kept all hands awake. They were always amusing from their improbability, and, indeed, he never expected to be believed, but spun them merely for amusement; and as he had some humor and a good supply of man-of-war slang and sailor's salt phrases, he always made fun. Next to him in age and experience, and, of course, in standing in the watch, was an Englishman, named Harris, of whom I shall have more to say hereafter. Then, came two or three Americans, who had been the common run of European and South American voyages, and one who had been in a "spouter," and, of course, had all the whaling stories to himself. Last of all, was a broad-backed, thick-headed boy from Cape Cod, who had been in mackerel schooners, and was making his first voyage in a square-rigged vessel. He was born in Hingham, and of course was called "Bucket-maker." The other watch was composed of about the same number. A tall, fine-looking Frenchman, with coal-black whiskers and curly hair, a first-rate seaman, and named John, (one name is enough for a sailor,) was the head man of the watch. Then came two Americans (one of whom had been a dissipated young man of property and family, and was reduced to duck trowsers and monthly wages,) a German, an English lad, named Ben, who belonged on the mizen topsail yard with me, and was a good sailor for his years, and two Boston boys just from the public schools. The carpenter sometimes mustered in the starboard watch, and was an old sea-dog, a Swede by birth, and accounted the best helmsman in the ship. This was our ship's company, beside cook and steward, who were blacks, three mates, and the captain.

The second day out, the wind drew ahead, and we had to beat up the coast; so that, in tacking ship, I could see the regulations of the vessel. Instead of going wherever was most convenient, and running from place to place, wherever work was to be done, each man had his station. A regular tacking and wearing bill was made out. The chief mate commanded on the forecastle, and had charge of the head sails and the forward part of the ship. Two of the best men in the ship—the sailmaker from our watch, and John, the Frenchman, from the other, worked the forecastle. The third mate commanded in the waist, and, with the carpenter and one man, worked the main tack and bowline; the cook, *ex-officio*, the fore sheet, and the steward the main. The second mate had charge of the after yards, and let go the lee fore and main braces. I was stationed at the weather cross-jack braces; three other light hands at the lee; one boy at the spanker-sheet and guy; a man and a boy at the main topsail, top-gallant, and royal braces; and all the rest of the crew—men and boys—tallied on to the main brace. Every one here knew his station, must be there when all hands were called to put the ship about, and was answerable for every rope committed to him. Each man's rope must be let go and hauled in at the order, properly made fast, and neatly coiled away when the ship was about. As soon as all hands are at their stations, the captain, who stands on the weather side of the quarter-deck, makes a sign to the man at the wheel to put it down, and calls out "Helm's a lee'!" "Helm's a lee'!" answers the mate on the forecastle, and the head sheets are let go. "Raise tacks and sheets!" says the captain; "tacks and sheets!" is passed forward, and the fore tack and main sheet are let go. The next thing is to haul taught for a swing. The weather cross-jack braces and the lee main braces are each belayed together upon two pins, and ready to be let go; and the opposite braces hauled taught. "Main topsail haul!" shouts the captain; the braces are let go; and if he has taken his time well, the yards swing round like a top; but if he is too late, or too soon, it is like drawing teeth. The after yards are then braced up and belayed, the main sheet hauled aft, the spanker eased over to leeward, and the men from the braces stand by the head yards. "Let go and haul!" says the captain; the second mate lets go the weather fore braces, and the men haul in to leeward. The mate, on the forecastle, looks out for the head yards. "Well, the fore topsail yard!" "Topgallant yard's well!" "Royal yard too much! Haul into windward! So! well *that!*" "Well *all!*" Then the starboard watch board the main tack, and the larboard watch lay forward and board the fore tack and haul down the jib sheet, clapping a tackle upon it, if it blows very fresh. The after yards are then trimmed, the captain generally looking out for them himself. "Well the cross-jack yard!" "Small pull the main top-gallant yard!" "Well *that!*" "Well the mizen topsail yard!" "Cross-jack yards all *well!*" "Well all aft!" "Haul taught to windward!" Everything being now trimmed and in order, each man coils up the rigging at his own station, and the order is given—"Go below the watch!"

During the last twenty-four hours of the passage, we beat off and on the land, making a tack about once in four hours, so that I had a sufficient opportunity to observe the working of the ship; and certainly, it took no more men to brace about this ship's lower yards, which were more than fifty feet square, than it did those of the Pilgrim, which were not much more than half the size; so much depends upon the manner in which the braces run, and the state of the blocks; and Captain Wilson, of the Ayacucho, who was afterwards a passenger with us, upon a trip to windward, said he had no doubt that our ship worked two men lighter than his brig.

FRIDAY, SEPT. 11. This morning, at four o'clock, went below, San Pedro point being about two leagues ahead, and the ship going on under studding-sails. In about an hour we were waked up by the hauling of the chain about decks, and in a few minutes "All hands ahoy!" was called; and we were all at work, hauling in and making up the studding-sails, overhauling the chain forward, and getting the anchors ready. "The Pilgrim is there at anchor," said some one, as we were running about decks; and taking a moment's look over the rail, I saw my old friend, deeply laden, lying at anchor inside of the kelp. In coming to anchor, as well as in tacking, each one had his station and duty. The light sails were clewed up and furled, the courses hauled up, and the jibs down; then came the topsails in the bunt-lines, and the anchor let go. As soon as she was well at anchor, all hands lay aloft to furl the topsails; and this, I soon found, was a great matter on board this ship; for every sailor knows that a vessel is judged of, a good deal, by the furl of her sails. The third mate, sailmaker, and the larboard watch went upon the fore topsail yard; the second mate, carpenter, and the starboard watch upon the main; and myself and the English lad, and the two Boston boys, and the young Cape-Cod man, furled the mizen topsail. This sail belonged to us altogether, to reef and to furl, and not a man was allowed to come upon our yard. The mate took us under his special care, frequently making us furl the sail over, three or four times, until we got the bunt up to a perfect cone, and the whole sail without a wrinkle. As soon as each sail was hauled up and the bunt made, the jigger was bent on to the slack of the buntlines, and the bunt triced up, on deck. The mate then took his place between the knight-heads to "twig" the fore, on the windlass to twig the main, and at the foot of the mainmast, for the mizen; and if anything was wrong,—too much bunt on one side, clues too taught or too slack, or any sail abaft the yard,—the whole must be dropped again. When all was right, the bunts were triced well up, the yard-arm gaskets passed, so as not to leave a wrinkle forward of the yard—short gaskets with turns close together.

From the moment of letting go the anchor, when the captain ceases his care of things, the chief mate is the great man. With a voice like a young lion, he was hallooing and bawling, in all directions, making everything fly, and, at the same time, doing everything well. He was quite a contrast to the worthy, quiet, unobtrusive mate of the Pilgrim: not so estimable a man, perhaps, but a far better mate of a vessel; and the entire change in Captain T—'s conduct, since he took command of the ship, was owing, no doubt, in a great measure, to this fact. If the chief officer wants force, discipline slackens, everything gets out of joint, the captain interferes continually; that makes a difficulty between them, which encourages the crew, and the whole ends in a three-sided quarrel. But Mr. Brown (the mate of the Alert) wanted no help from anybody; took everything into his own hands; and was more likely to encroach upon the authority of the master, than to need any spurring. Captain T—gave his directions to the mate in private, and, except in coming to anchor, getting under weigh, tacking, reefing topsails, and other "all-hands-work," seldom appeared in person. This is the proper state of things, and while this lasts, and there is a good understanding aft, everything will go on well.

Having furled all the sails, the royal yards were next to be sent down. The English lad and myself sent down the main, which was larger than the Pilgrim's main top-gallant yard; two more light hands, the fore; and one boy, the mizen. This order, we always kept while on the coast; sending them up and down every time we came in and went out of port. They were all tripped and lowered together, the main on the starboard side, and the fore and mizen, to port. No sooner was she all snug, than tackles were got up on the yards and stays, and the long-boat and pinnace hove out. The swinging booms were then guyed out, and the boats made fast by geswarps, and everything in harbor style. After breakfast, the hatches were taken off, and all got ready to receive hides from the Pilgrim. All day, boats were passing and repassing, until we had taken her hides from her, and left her in ballast trim. These hides made but little show in our hold, though they had loaded the Pilgrim down to the water's edge. This changing of the hides settled the question of the destination of the two vessels, which had been one of some speculation to us. We were to remain in the leeward ports, while the Pilgrim was to sail, the next morning, for San Francisco. After we had knocked off work, and cleared up decks for the night, my friend S—came on board, and spent an hour with me in our berth between decks. The Pilgrim's crew envied me my place on board the ship, and seemed to think that I had got a little to windward of them; especially in the matter of going home first. S—was determined to go home in the Alert, by begging or buying; if Captain T—would not let him come on other terms, he would purchase an exchange with some one of the crew. The prospect of another year after the Alert should sail, was rather "too much of the monkey." About seven o'clock, the mate came down into the steerage, in fine trim for fun, roused the boys out of the berth, turned up the carpenter with his fiddle, sent the steward with lights to put in the between-decks, and set all hands to dancing. The between-decks were high enough to allow of jumping; and being clear, and white, from holystoning, made a fine dancing-hall. Some of the Pilgrim's crew were in the forecastle, and we all turned-to and had a regular sailor's shuffle, till eight bells. The Cape-Cod boy could dance the true fisherman's jig, barefooted, knocking with his heels, and slapping the decks with his bare feet, in time with the music. This was a favorite amusement of the mate's, who always stood at the steerage door, looking on, and if the boys would not dance, he hazed them round with a rope's end, much to the amusement of the men.

The next morning, according to the orders of the agent, the Pilgrim set sail for the windward, to be gone three or four months. She got under weigh with very little fuss, and came so near us as to throw a letter on board, Captain Faucon standing at the tiller himself, and steering her as he would a mackerel smack. When Captain T—was in command of the Pilgrim, there was as much preparation and ceremony as there would be in getting a seventy-four under weigh. Captain Faucon was a sailor, every inch of him; he knew what a ship was, and was as much at home in one, as a cobbler in his stall. I wanted no better proof of this than the opinion of the ship's crew, for they had been six months under his command, and knew what he was; and if sailors allow their captain to be a good seaman, you may be sure he is one, for that is a thing they are not always ready to say.

After the Pilgrim left us, we lay three weeks at San Pedro, from the 11th of September until the 2nd of October, engaged in the usual port duties of landing cargo, taking off hides, etc., etc. These duties were much easier, and went on much more agreeably, than on board the Pilgrim. "The more, the merrier," is the sailor's maxim; and a boat's crew of a dozen could take off all the hides brought down in a day, without much trouble, by division of labor; and on shore, as well as on board, a good will, and no discontent or grumbling, make everything go well. The officer, too, who usually went with us, the third mate, was a fine young fellow, and made no unnecessary trouble; so that we generally had quite a sociable time, and were glad to be relieved from the restraint of the ship. While here, I often thought of the miserable, gloomy weeks we had spent in this dull place, in the brig; discontent and hard usage on board, and four hands to do all the work on shore. Give me a big ship. There is more room, more hands, better outfit, better regulation, more life, and more company. Another thing was better arranged here: we had a regular gig's crew. A light whale-boat, handsomely painted, and fitted out with stern seats, yoke, tiller-ropes, etc., hung on the starboard quarter, and was used as the gig. The youngest lad in the ship, a Boston boy about thirteen years old, was coxswain of this boat, and had the entire charge of her, to keep her clean, and have her in readiness to go and come at any hour. Four light hands, of about the same size and age, of whom I was one, formed the crew. Each had his oar and seat numbered, and we were obliged to be in our places, have our oars scraped white, our tholepins in, and the fenders over the side. The bow-man had charge of the boat-hook and painter, and the coxswain of the rudder, yoke, and stern-sheets. Our duty was to carry the captain and agent about, and passengers off and on; which last was no trifling duty, as the people on shore have no boats, and every purchaser, from the boy who buys his pair of shoes, to the trader who buys his casks and bales, were to be taken off and on, in our boat. Some days, when people were coming and going fast, we were in the boat, pulling off and on, all day long, with hardly time for our meals; making, as we lay nearly three miles from shore, from forty to fifty miles' rowing in a day. Still, we thought it the best berth in the ship; for when the gig was employed, we had nothing to do with the cargo, except small bundles which the passengers carried with them, and no hides to carry, besides the opportunity of seeing everybody, making acquaintances, hearing the news, etc. Unless the captain or agent were in the boat, we had no officer with us, and often had fine times with the passengers, who were always willing to talk and joke with us. Frequently, too, we were obliged to wait several hours on shore; when we would haul the boat up on the beach, and leaving one to watch her, go up to the nearest house, or spend the time in strolling about the beach, picking up shells, or playing hop-scotch, and other games, on the hard sand. The rest of the crew never left the ship, except for bringing heavy goods and taking off hides; and though we were always in the water, the surf hardly leaving us a dry thread from morning till night, yet we were young, and the climate was good, and we thought it much better than the quiet, hum-drum drag and pull on board ship. We made the acquaintance of nearly half of California; for, besides carrying everybody in our boat,—men, women, and children,—all the messages, letters, and light packages went by us, and being known by our dress, we found a ready reception everywhere.

At San Pedro, we had none of this amusement, for, there being but one house in the place, we, of course, had but little company. All the variety that I had, was riding, once a week, to the nearest rancho, to order a bullock down for the ship.

The brig Catalina came in from San Diego, and being bound up to windward, we both got under weigh at the same time, for a trial of speed up to Santa Barbara, a distance of about eighty miles. We hove up and got under sail about eleven o'clock at night, with a light land-breeze, which died away toward morning, leaving us becalmed only a few miles from our anchoring-place. The Catalina, being a small vessel, of less than half our size, put out sweeps and got a boat ahead, and pulled out to sea, during the night, so that she had the sea-breeze earlier and stronger than we did, and we had the mortification of seeing her standing up the coast, with a fine breeze, the sea all ruffled about her, while we were becalmed, in-shore. When the sea-breeze died away, she was nearly out of sight; and, toward the latter part of the afternoon, the regular northwest wind set in fresh, we braced sharp upon it, took a pull at every sheet, tack, and halyard, and stood after her, in fine style, our ship being very good upon a taughtened bowline. We had nearly five hours of fine sailing, beating up to windward, by long stretches in and off shore, and evidently gaining upon the Catalina, at every tack. When this breeze left us, we were so near as to count the painted ports on her side. Fortunately, the wind died away when we were on our inward tack, and she on her outward, so we were in-shore, and caught the land-breeze first, which came off upon our quarter, about the middle of the first watch. All hands were turned up, and we set all sail, to the skysails and the royal studding-sails; and with these, we glided quietly through the water, leaving the Catalina, which could not spread so much canvas as we, gradually astern, and, by daylight, were off St. Buenaventura, and our antagonist nearly out of sight. The sea-breeze, however, favored her again, while we were becalmed under the headland, and laboring slowly along, she was abreast of us by noon. Thus we continued, ahead, astern, and abreast of one another, alternately; now, far out at sea, and again, close in under the shore. On the third morning, we came into the great bay of Santa Barbara, two hours behind the brig, and thus lost the bet; though, if the race had been to the point, we should have beaten her by five or six hours. This, however, settled the relative sailing of the vessels, for it was admitted that although she, being small and light, could gain upon us in very light winds, yet whenever there was breeze enough to set us agoing, we walked away from her like hauling in a line; and in beating to windward, which is the best trial of a vessel, we had much the advantage of her.

SUNDAY, OCT. 4th. This was the day of our arrival; and somehow or other, our captain always managed not only to sail, but to come into port, on a Sunday. The main reason for sailing on the Sabbath is not, as many people suppose, because Sunday is thought a lucky day, but because it is a leisure day. During the six days, the crew are employed upon the cargo and other ship's works, and the Sabbath, being their only day of rest, whatever additional work can be thrown into Sunday, is so much gain to the owners. This is the reason of our coasters, packets, etc., sailing on the Sabbath. They get six good days' work out of the crew, and then throw all the labor of sailing into the Sabbath. Thus it was with us, nearly all the time we were on the coast, and many of our Sabbaths were lost entirely to us. The Catholics on shore have no trading and make no journeys on Sunday, but the American has no national religion, and likes to show his independence of priest-craft by doing as he chooses on the Lord's day.

Santa Barbara looked very much as it did when I left it five months before: the long sand beach, with the heavy rollers, breaking upon it in a continual roar, and the little town, imbedded on the plain, girt by its amphitheatre of mountains. Day after day, the sun shone clear and bright upon the wide bay and the red roofs of the houses; everything being as still as death, the people really hardly seeming to earn their sunlight. Daylight actually seemed thrown away upon them. We had a few visitors, and collected about a hundred hides, and every night, at sundown, the gig was sent ashore, to wait for the captain, who spent his evenings in the town. We always took our monkey-jackets with us, and flint and steel, and made a fire on the beach with the driftwood and the bushes we pulled from the neighboring thickets, and lay down by it, on the sand. Sometimes we would stray up to the town, if the captain was likely to stay late, and pass the time at some of the houses, in which we were almost always well received by the inhabitants. Sometimes earlier and sometimes later, the captain came down; when, after good drenching in the surf, we went aboard, changed our clothes, and turned in for the night—yet not for all the night, for there was the anchor watch to stand.

This leads me to speak of my watchmate for nine months—and, taking him all in all, the most remarkable man I have ever seen—Tom Harris. An hour, every night, while lying in port, Harris and myself had the deck to ourselves, and walking fore and aft, night after night, for months, I learned his whole character and history, and more about foreign nations, the habits of different people, and especially the secrets of sailors' lives and hardships, and also of practical seamanship, (in which he was abundantly capable of instructing me,) than I could ever have learned elsewhere. But the most remarkable thing about him, was the power of his mind. His memory was perfect; seeming to form a regular chain, reaching from his earliest childhood up to the time I knew him, without one link wanting. His power of calculation, too, was remarkable. I called myself pretty quick at figures, and had been through a course of mathematical studies; but, working by my head, I was unable to keep within sight of this man, who had never been beyond his arithmetic: so rapid was his calculation. He carried in his head not only a log-book of the whole voyage, in which everything was complete and accurate, and from which no one ever thought of appealing, but also an accurate registry of all the cargo; knowing, precisely, where each thing was, and how many hides we took in at every port.

One night, he made a rough calculation of the number of hides that could be stowed in the lower hold, between the fore and main mast, taking the depth of hold and breadth of beam, (for he always knew the dimension of every part of the ship, before he had been a month on board,) and the average area and thickness of a hide; he came surprisingly near the number, as it afterwards turned out. The mate frequently came to him to know the capacity of different tell the sailmaker very nearly the amount of canvas he would want for each sail in the ship; for he knew the hoist of every mast, and spread of every sail, on the head and foot, in feet and inches. When we were at sea, he kept a running account, in his head, of the ship's way—the number of knots and the courses; and if the courses did not vary much during the twenty-four hours, by taking the whole progress, and allowing so many eighths southing or northing, to so many easting or westing; he would make up his reckoning just before the captain took the sun at noon, and often came wonderfully near the mark. Calculation of all kinds was his delight. He had, in his chest, several volumes giving accounts of inventions in mechanics, which he read with great pleasure, and made himself master of. I doubt if he ever forgot anything that he read. The only thing in the way of poetry that he ever read was Falconer's Shipwreck, which he was delighted with, and whole pages of which he could repeat. He knew the name of every sailor that had ever been his shipmate, and also, of every vessel, captain, and officer, and the principal dates of each voyage; and a sailor whom we afterwards fell in with, who had been in a ship with Harris nearly twelve years before, was very much surprised at having Harris tell him things about himself which he had entirely forgotten. His facts, whether dates or events, no one thought of disputing; and his opinions, few of the sailors dared to oppose; for, right or wrong, he always had the best of the argument with them. His reasoning powers were remarkable. I have had harder work maintaining an argument with him in a watch, even when I knew myself to be right, and he was only doubting, than I ever had before; not from his obstinacy, but from his acuteness. Give him only a little knowledge of his subject, and, certainly among all the young men of my acquaintance and standing at college, there was not one whom I had not rather meet, than this man. I never answered a question from him, or advanced an opinion to him, without thinking more than once. With an iron memory, he seemed to have your whole past conversation at command, and if you said a thing now which ill agreed with something said months before, he was sure to have you on the hip. In fact, I always felt, when with him, that I was with no common man. I had a positive respect for his powers of mind, and felt often that if half the pains had been spent upon his education which are thrown away, yearly, in our colleges, he would have been a man of great weight in society. Like most self-taught men, he over-estimated the value of an education; and this, I often told him, though I profited by it myself; for he always treated me with respect, and often unnecessarily gave way to me, from an over-estimate of my knowledge. For the capacities of all the rest of the crew, captain and all, he had the most sovereign contempt. He was a far better sailor, and probably a better navigator, than the captain, and had more brains than all the after part of the ship put together. The sailors said, "Tom's got a head as long as the bowsprit," and if any one got into an argument with him, they would call out—"Ah, Jack! you'd better drop that, as you would a hot potato, for Tom will turn you inside out before you know it."

I recollect his posing me once on the subject of the Corn Laws. I was called to stand my watch, and, coming on deck, found him there before me; and we began, as usual, to walk fore and aft, in the waist. He talked about the corn laws; asked me my opinion about them, which I gave him; and my reasons; my small stock of which I set forth to the best advantage, supposing his knowledge on the subject must be less than mine, if, indeed, he had any at all. When I had got through, he took the liberty of differing from me, and, to my surprise, brought arguments and facts connected with the subject which were new to me, and to which I was entirely unable to reply. I confessed that I knew almost nothing of the subject, and expressed my surprise at the extent of his information. He said that, a number of years before, while at a boardinghouse in Liverpool, he had fallen in with a pamphlet on the subject, and, as it contained calculations, had read it very carefully, and had ever since wished to find some one who could add to his stock of knowledge on the question. Although it was many years since he had seen the book, and it was a subject with which he had no previous acquaintance, yet he had the chain of reasoning, founded upon principles of political economy, perfect in his memory; and his facts, so far as I could judge, were correct; at least, he stated them with great precision. The principles of the steam engine, too, he was very familiar with, having been several months on board of a steamboat, and made himself master of its secrets. He knew every lunar star in both hemispheres, and was a perfect master of his quadrant and sextant. Such was the man, who, at forty, was still a dog before the mast, at twelve dollars a month. The reason of this was to be found in his whole past life, as I had it, at different times, from himself.

He was an Englishman, by birth, a native of Ilfracomb, in Cornwall. His father was skipper of a small coaster, from Bristol, and dying, left him, when quite young, to the care of his mother, by whose exertions he received a common-school education, passing his winters at school and his summers in the coasting trade, until his seventeenth year, when he left home to go upon foreign voyages. Of this mother, he often spoke with the greatest respect, and said that she was a strong-minded woman, and had the best system of education he had ever known; a system which had made respectable men of his three brothers, and failed only in him, from his own indomitable obstinacy. One thing he often mentioned, in which he said his mother differed from all other mothers that he had ever seen disciplining their children; that was, that when he was out of humor and refused to eat, instead of putting his plate away, as most mothers would, and saying that his hunger would bring him to it, in time, she would stand over him and oblige him to eat it—every mouthful of it. It was no fault of her's that he was what I saw him; and so great was his sense of gratitude for her efforts, though unsuccessful, that he determined, at the close of the voyage, to embark for home with all the wages he should get, to spend with and for his mother, if perchance he should find her alive.

After leaving home, he had spent nearly twenty years, sailing upon all sorts of voyages, generally out of the ports of New York and Boston. Twenty years of vice! Every sin that a sailor knows, he had gone to the bottom of. Several times he had been hauled up in the hospitals, and as often, the great strength of his constitution had brought him out again in health. Several times, too, from his known capacity, he had been promoted to the office of chief mate, and as often, his conduct when in port, especially his drunkenness, which neither fear nor ambition could induce him to abandon, put him back into the forecastle. One night, when giving me an account of his life, and lamenting the years of manhood he had thrown away, he said that there, in the forecastle, at the foot of the steps—a chest of old clothes—was the result of twenty-two years of hard labor and exposure—worked like a horse, and treated like a dog. As he grew older, he began to feel the necessity of some provision for his later years, and came gradually to the conviction that rum had been his worst enemy. One night, in Havana, a young shipmate of his was brought aboard drunk, with a dangerous gash in his head, and his money and new clothes stripped from him. Harris had seen and been in hundreds of such scenes as these, but in his then state of mind, it fixed his determination, and he resolved never to taste another drop of strong drink, of any kind. He signed no pledge, and made no vow, but relied on his own strength of purpose. The first thing with him was a reason, and then a resolution, and the thing was done. The date of his resolution he knew, of course, to the very hour. It was three years before I knew him, and during all that time, nothing stronger than cider or coffee had passed his lips. The sailors never thought of enticing Tom to take a glass, any more than they would of talking to the ship's compass. He was now a temperate man for life, and capable of filling any berth in a ship, and many a high station there is on shore which is held by a meaner man.

He understood the management of a ship upon scientific principles, and could give the reason for hauling every rope; and a long experience, added to careful observation at the time, and a perfect memory, gave him a knowledge of the expedients and resorts in times of hazard, which was remarkable, and for which I became much indebted to him, as he took the greatest pleasure in opening his stores of information to me, in return for what I was enabled to do for him. Stories of tyranny and hardship which had driven men to piracy;—of the incredible ignorance of masters and mates, and of horrid brutality to the sick, dead, and dying; as well as of the secret knavery and impositions practised upon seamen by connivance of the owners, landlords, and officers; all these he had, and I could not but believe them; for men who had known him for fifteen years had never taken him even in an exaggeration, and, as I have said, his statements were never disputed. I remember, among other things, his speaking of, a captain whom I had known by report, who never handed a thing to a sailor, but put it on deck and kicked it to him; and of another, who was of the best connections in Boston, who absolutely murdered a lad from Boston that went out with him before the mast to Sumatra, by keeping him hard at work while ill of the coast fever, and obliging him to sleep in the close steerage. (The same captain has since died of the same fever on the same coast.)

In fact, taking together all that I learned from him of seamanship, of the history of sailors' lives, of practical wisdom, and of human nature under new circumstances,—a great history from which many are shut out,—I would not part with the hours I spent in the watch with that man for any given hours of my life past in study and social intercourse.